Praise for Van Allen Plexico's

SENTINELS

"Nobody—not even Abnett and Lanning—is doing cosmic superheroes as well as Van Plexico is doing them. Period."
—Barry Reese, award-winning author of *Rabbit Heart* and creator of the Rook

"The best comics-to-novels series ever written. Van is a gifted writer, but what sets the SENTINELS above the rest is his true love of the material. It's all here on every single page and wow does that fun come across to the lucky readers. Anyone reading these words who has yet to pick up a copy is missing a truly marvelous reading adventure."
—Ron Fortier, award-winning author of *Boston Bombers* and the Captain Hazzard novels

"Van Plexico is responsible for me losing more sleep than any other author."
—Larry Davis, Dragon*Con SF Literature Track

"I was enthralled. I had a hard time putting them down and after each ended I wanted to read more. From the beginning, (it) read very much like a Jim Starlin cosmic tale…Plexico has created a world of continuing and mounting danger, interesting people, and never-slowing-down action. I enjoyed them all and still want more."
—Mark Haleuga, Coordinator, Gotham Pulp Collectors Club

"*Sentinels: Shiva Advent* has some of my favorite things: Big robots and guys with big weapons. Those are what I want to read about. If more books had them, society would right itself."
—Joe Crowe, *RevolutionSF.com* (8/10 starred review)

SENTINELS

THE GRAND DESIGN

SENTINELS

THE GRAND DESIGN

VAN ALLEN PLEXICO

Illustrations by Chris Kohler

Based on Characters and Concepts
Created by Van Allen Plexico and Robert J. Politte

WHITE ROCKET BOOKS

This is a work of fiction. All the characters and events portrayed in this book are either products of the author's imagination or are used fictitiously.

SENTINELS: THE GRAND DESIGN (OMNIBUS 1)

Cover character art by Rowell
Cover design by Van Allen Plexico
Sentinels logo design by Anthony Schiavino
Interior art by Jim Jiminez and Atlantic Studios

A White Rocket Book
www.whiterocketbooks.com

ISBN-13: 978-1721733736
ISBN-10: 1721733736

This book is set in Times and Arial Black typefaces.

First printing: July 2007
Third edition: July 2018

0 9 8 7 6 5 4 3 2 1

CONTENTS

INTRODUCTION

Just what is this book, exactly? Well…it's several things. It is an omnibus collecting the first three volumes of the Sentinels series of novels, which were written by me, co-created and occasionally co-plotted with Bobby Politte, and illustrated by Chris Kohler. It's a full-blown superhero saga done in prose form. It's a self-contained trilogy that introduces the individuals who will become the Sentinels and their greatest foes, while also setting things up for continuing adventures down the line. And it's an ongoing science fiction space opera epic.

When people ask me exactly what I'm up to with these books, I tend to describe it all in a variety of different ways. But several themes seem to recur:

It's the comic book saga I always wanted to *read*—the comic book saga to end all sagas, evoking and invoking influences from Jack Kirby and Stan Lee to Jim Starlin and Jim Shooter and Dan Abnett—and everything in between. Done as a series of novels, it opens up whole new avenues and possibilities for storytelling in the superheroic genre. While prose superheroics is an emerging field of literature, to the best of my knowledge, nobody else has attempted what I'm doing here—telling one huge, sprawling saga across many volumes.

It's comic book superheroes written the way I prefer to read them: as serious, science-fictional characters in a sort of a combination modern day / space opera setting, just like the Marvel and DC Universes, with androids and mutants and powerful alien races and big, cosmic forces lurking in the background, and layer upon layer of backstory and history waiting to be tapped into.

It's the *Babylon 5* of superhero sagas—or so I would like it to be, as I have told many people at conventions across the country. By that, I mean it is one big story with a definite beginning and a definite ending, with puzzles and mysteries cropping up constantly, with characters growing and changing and even *dying* along the way, and with nobody coming out the other end quite the same as they went in.

Finally, it's a chance to see some fantastic art from Chris Kohler, Rowell, and a number of other great artists who have contributed to the Sentinels over the years.

When Bobby and I sat down over pizza in Atlanta and first started to dream up the events and the individuals you will encounter in this story, we had no idea where it was all going, what would become of it, or how long it would take before the whole thing finally saw the light of day. Now, years later, with six novels and an anthology all in print and more on the way, the books have a solid base of readers around the world who faithfully follow along from one volume to the next, and the ending is at last in sight.

We're awfully glad you're coming along for the ride. Now— time to get out of the way. The Warlord is about to strike!

--Van Allen Plexico
Somewhere in southern Illinois
June, 2012

BOOK ONE:
WHEN STRIKES
THE WARLORD

For Bobby:
Of concepts and cats and a spare room;
Thanks, brother.

PROLOGUE:
One Thousand Years Ago

The cataclysmic blast, awful in its intensity, smashed into the Enforcer head-on and sent him careening off course, his metallic blue-silver arms and legs flailing madly as he hurtled through the blackness of space.

Struggling desperately to regain control, he watched as one diagnostic system after another reported damage or simply dropped offline. Propulsion units down... power levels dropping... weapons systems not responding at all.

Round and round he spun; the mocking stars a blur in his vision. His internal sensors reached out, searching, searching. Had it been a simple collision—an asteroid or scrap of ancient wreckage? How could he have missed detecting something like that, well in advance of actually colliding with it?

Or, much more troubling, had it been an attack?

The blue-white disk of the planet he had been sent to observe passed before his vision. Just then, propulsion systems came back online, and he exerted all of his will, stopping the mad spinning and killing the velocity. Slowly, his other systems began to recover as well. Some semblance of order returned.

Then his sensors screamed.

Something lay out there, something heretofore hidden in the deep void. Something—or someone—very, very powerful.

And it was approaching again.

He lurched to one side as a blinding bolt of energy stabbed out, slicing through the spot he had occupied only an instant before. Then came another, and another, the third striking a glancing blow to his left leg and sending pain screaming through his processors.

Cover. He desperately needed to find cover.

Hanging in empty space, that was a problem.

Sensors locked onto the approaching object, tracking it, and at the same time dutifully reporting that its energy levels had gone off the scale. His defensive screens would be utterly useless—not that they had provided much help up till now.

He activated his emergency signal, in the vain hope that others of his unit might be somewhere nearby. Then he dodged another deadly blast, and the creature was upon him.

A man-shaped thing, wreathed in horrific tendrils of cosmic flame, it flailed at him, grappling with him. Colors, from deep blue to blinding red, shifted ceaselessly over a flesh seemingly formed of luminous plasma. Its face, if face it was, swung around to meet his own gaze, and its mouth opened upon a horrifying maw of seething fire. A blazing hand sought his faceplate, burning fingers prying at the seams.

Who—or what—was it? Something seemed familiar, something from deep in his memory banks, but he could not retrieve the memory. It refused to come. The first attack had damaged him more seriously than he had first thought, he understood now. His thinking processes had slowed. Gaps in his knowledge and his memories loomed wide and disturbing.

He put all that aside. No time to dwell on it now. The first order of business was survival—survival, and victory!

And yet…

The truth came hard to him, but he had to admit it. For the first time in his long existence, he had encountered a foe he honestly feared, and feared he could not defeat. Unknown feelings washed over him—anxiety, turmoil, and perhaps a touch of despair.

He had to get away, at least for the moment; get out of the creature's horrible embrace. Break free long enough to formulate something like a plan—if his malfunctioning mind could be trusted to come up with something that stood a chance of succeeding.

Diverting almost all of his energy reserves to his weapons systems, he brought his hands up under the attacker's jaw and unleashed the most powerful strike he could manage.

The attacker shrugged off the blow. It almost seemed to be laughing as it reached out, shredding the last of his defensive screens, ripping them away.

The creature's burning hands grasped him by the throat, searing his metal surface, tightening, tightening…

7

A mysterious black box clutched tightly under one arm, the Blue Skull fled through the back alleys of Bay City. Hot on his trail, a man on a flying motorcycle pursued him.

Handling that golden skycycle with skillful aplomb, Damon Sinclair—he preferred the *nom de guerre* "the Cavalier"—kept the bizarre villain always in his sights. It wasn't hard—the man's head, after all, was a leering skull, azure flames dancing from it as he ran. That was a good thing for Damon; after all, while there were various varieties of sophisticated tracking systems built into the dashboard of the cycle, Damon ignored them. In all honesty, he possessed very little idea of how they worked. The bike's inventor—the inventor of all of Damon's weapons—had explained it all to him a half-dozen times in great detail, but the information never seemed to stick.

So Damon simply made sure to keep the flickering flames of the Blue Skull constantly in sight even as he deftly maneuvered the flying motorbike. He couldn't end the chase just yet, but he was okay with that fact, for a number of reasons. For one, the television news crews hadn't shown up, and he wanted to be sure the climax of the chase was caught on video for all to see. For another, the Blue Skull was being smart—he had the presence of mind to keep to the narrow, winding alleyways precisely so that Damon couldn't swoop down on him from above. And then there was the simple fact that he really enjoyed flying the skycycle, getting the most out of its maneuverability and power.

But of course eventually—inevitably—the back alleys and constricted passages ran out, and the Blue Skull found himself emerging out onto the sidewalk of a main street. Halting his progress before he could plunge out into traffic, he whirled about and glared up at the sky, searching for signs of pursuit.

He didn't have to look hard. Damon was already swooping down at him, sun gleaming off his golden chain mail and the blade of the electro-sword that was raised high and poised to strike.

The Blue Skull dived for cover, rolling into the chairs of a sidewalk café and knocking a teenage girl over. The shoebox-sized black object he'd been carrying tumbled away and clattered to a stop under the next table over.

From the distance came the sounds of police sirens. Damon looked in that direction and saw not only three patrol cars but also two TV news vans weaving their way through traffic.

"Try to hold out for a minute, Skull," Damon called down to the freakish criminal. He adjusted the red bandana that covered his head. "I want to make sure the cameras get all the action."

The blue-clad villain regained his feet and glared up at Damon—a rather disconcerting sight—and aimed one gloved hand his way. A column of fire shot out, missing Damon's cycle by mere inches.

"Yowch!"

Damon swerved to one side, nearly tumbling overboard in the process. In the meantime, the Skull snatched up the black box and then dashed out into the street. Dodging oncoming cars, he reached the other side and sprinted across the finely manicured lawn of what Damon suddenly realized was Bay City College.

"Oh, man," the daredevil agent groaned, seeing the combination of many tall oaks blocking the view from above, and many young students walking or seated here and there. "Not good."

Damon brought the skycycle down to earth in a stomach-churning maneuver that allowed him to spring from the seat and already be racing across the lawn before the vehicle had fully touched down. The Skull was a good thirty yards away already and moving rapidly. Students watched in immobile shock as the hideous, skull-faced man ran by, some of them screaming or diving out of the way.

The TV news crews were pulling up on the curb behind him; the police had already leapt from their cars and were pursuing. His own partner, the beloved national hero known as Ultraa, was also on the way, and the man's super-speed made it likely that, even though he was nowhere in sight now, he'd actually reach the Blue Skull before anyone else did. But, at least for the moment, Damon had the lead on all of them and he aimed to keep it. This was his take-down, and he meant to be the star of the show.

And if he could prevent any of the college kids from being hurt, then that would be great too, of course.

2

A short distance away, a dark-haired man wearing dark glasses and a long gray trench coat sat on a bench near the front entrance to the Bay City College Auditorium. If passers-by noticed him at all, they surely thought he looked uncomfortable and out of place and, above all else, *bored.*

Richard Hammond knew he should be trying harder to blend in, but he couldn't help it. He *was* bored. He hated this kind of assignment. His boss had ordered him to keep a close eye on a particular young woman who was a student at this college, and the assignment hadn't sounded half-bad at first. Surely, he had thought upon receiving the orders, it would beat being parachuted into Afghanistan or the Congo in the middle of the night. But it hadn't worked out that way.

The reason was simple: the young woman he'd been ordered to watch, it turned out, was a serious nerd.

Richard shook his head at the thought. Lyn Li, star science student from just up the road in the Chinatown district—and just as exciting to follow around as that might imply. Which was to say, *not at all.* Her idea of a good time, from what he had observed thus far, was to attend science lectures and exhibits—just like the one she was attending now, inside the auditorium. Some kind of presentation being put on by Dr. Esro Brachis, an inventor and millionaire that Richard vaguely remembered was doing some work for his boss, as well.

But that was the kind of thing the Li girl thought of as a good time. And that was a shame. After all, the young lady was not that bad to look at. Cute, even. Not really Richard's type, of course, but things hadn't been going too well in the dating world lately, and—

He caught himself from pursuing that line of thought any further. The Li girl was *nineteen.* Richard was in his late thirties. For that matter, he had no business doing anything more than casting the occasional glance at any of the women on this campus.

And so he sat there, twiddling his thumbs and occasionally ogling the random co-ed, until at last the doors of the auditorium opened and the students poured out.

Richard couldn't help but laugh—most of them appeared to be about as bored as he was. He imagined they had been ready to get out of there. How exciting could a guy like Esro Brachis really be?

Finally the Li girl emerged, almost the last person out. He guessed she'd stuck around to get Brachis's autograph or something. He shook his head again. Yeah, she'd be a lot of fun at a party. Woo.

She was a little over five feet tall, with shoulder-length black hair and an almost golden complexion. Richard had to admit to himself that she had a great smile, though her preferred expression seemed to be a look of scorn and barely-contained contempt.

Richard managed to avoid staring directly at her as she strolled by, but that effort was probably unnecessary. She was totally involved in a conversation with another student who had just walked up to her. This young woman, Richard noted, looked completely different from Li: She was several inches taller, with lots of freckles and red hair tied in a braid. The two made for a very unusual pair as they strolled across the campus together.

To her credit, the redhead appeared to be finding Lyn Li about as boring as Richard did. The Li girl was all kinds of animated, chattering away about something completely unintelligible to Richard—and apparently to the other girl, too.

Richard made a quick note in his pad and then stood, stretching his cramped muscles. As the two women continued along the concourse, other students flowing past them on either side, he casually followed along. They passed a spot in front of the Early Childhood Education building where two young men were setting up a big-screen television on the lawn, while others gathered around to watch whatever they were planning to show. Included in that crowd were a dozen or so little kids. Richard ignored it all and hurried along after the two women.

They had made it a little further, about halfway to the main street, probably headed for the pizza place or café on the near corner, when the sound of police sirens reached them. A second later, all kinds of chaos broke loose.

3

As she made her way out of the campus auditorium, Lyn Li saw a figure lurking nearby, as if lying in wait for her. Frowning, she approached cautiously.

Her roommate, Amy Miller, stepped out of the shadows, grinning.

"Had to check out the big-brained science guy, right?"

Lyn laughed. "I thought there was no way you'd get within a mile of a science presentation," she said. "Watch out! There was one right over there!" She pointed at the auditorium in mock horror.

Amy shrugged. "It's over now, though—right? I think I'm safe." She patted herself down. "Didn't get hit by any of the nerd rays. Whew."

Lyn laughed, then shook her head.

"You just don't get it," she said. "Esro Brachis is a freakin' genius. I couldn't pass up the chance to see him—to hear him!"

"Not even to see Ultraa, instead?"

"What?"

Amy laughed.

"You don't even know! Ultraa is in town. Or, he was, anyway." She was grinning. "I guess he was part of the security. But you missed him."

Lyn actually looked disappointed for an instant, but then quickly covered it with a fake yawn. "Like I care." She started back toward the dorms, and Amy had to rush after her.

In the shadowy recesses between two nearby buildings, hidden among trees, a figure in dark clothes watched them both. Lyn's eyes settled momentarily on him but then moved on and, in her aggravation with Amy, she thought nothing of it.

"There's no way you can convince me you don't like Ultraa," Amy said.

Lyn spared her roommate a half-second's glance.

"It's just no big deal to me," she said. "I mean… Sure, everyone else in my family loves the guy. They have ever since the time he stopped the Golden Khan from blowing up half of Bay City, back when we were little. Even my grandmother has a picture of him in her living room, right between Elvis and Bruce Lee." She snorted. "But…I don't know. To me, he's no different from a cop, or a fireman. They all do heroic things, you know? And they don't have super powers, either."

Amy frowned.

"I guess so..."

She bit her fingernail, thinking, as Lyn continued on toward the dorm.

"...But he's cute!"

Lyn sighed and kept walking.

Neither of them noticed the man in the dark trench coat who trailed along behind them, hurrying now to keep up.

"That's not all, though, Lyn," Amy was saying.

Lyn stopped and turned back to face her, hands on hips. "What?"

Amy looked sheepish now. "I was hoping you might could *talk* to him—to Ultraa—and, y'know..."

Lyn folded her arms across her chest and waited.

"I know what, Ami?"

"Oh, you know..."

Lyn was frowning at her friend now.

"Yeah, I think I do. You mean the little coincidences."

"Lyn—come on! They're not coincidences!"

Lyn turned and stalked away.

"I'm not having this conversation again, Amy!"

She walked faster and faster across the concourse as Amy hurried after her. They passed by the Early Childhood Development building, where a big screen television had been set up for a crowd of little kids. Two students were loading a DVD into the player and adjusting the picture and sound.

"Ultraa maybe could help you," Amy was saying in a plaintive tone.

"I don't *need* any help," Lyn shouted back, attracting the attention of some of the students and the children. "There's nothing *wrong* with me!" She waved her arms in frustration. "You're just bored, so you're imagining things to entertain yourself. It's not my fault that nothing exciting ever happens around here!"

And then the man with the blazing skull for a head emerged from the trees.

4

The Blue Skull passed through a grove of trees and emerged in front of the Early Childhood Education building. There he stopped, looking around, as if seeking a place to hide. Students all around reacted with surprise, most of them doubtlessly wondering if they had just become part of some new reality show.

Damon Sinclair burst out of the trees an instant later, his electro-sword held high. Quickly he took in the tactical situation and sobered, realizing that, with the little children nearby, all bets were off. He even regretted allowing things to go this far. This, he knew, had become a situation that needed to be ended very quickly.

The Blue Skull saw where Damon was looking. With a maniacal cackle, he dashed for the group of little kids. They screamed and tried to get away.

Damon shouted and rushed forward.

Richard Hammond, his trench coat billowing behind him as he ran, took the situation in very quickly—he was, after all, a highly-trained federal agent—and made a quick judgment that the safety of little kids and college students trumped his own mission and his undercover status. He hurried forward as well.

None of them reached the kids first. Instead, it was Lyn Li, the star science nerd, who came to the rescue, jumping over a low, decorative wall and landing on the grass between the children and the leering villain. Quickly she rolled to her feet and crouched down, her teeth bared as she faced him.

The Blue Skull pulled up quickly and stared, not quite believing that this young woman had come flying in out of nowhere to interpose herself between him and his potential hostages.

Richard stopped as well, not sure of what he should do next. Probably, he knew, he should take down the Skull—if he could. So he gathered up his power reserves and prepared to attack.

Damon circled around, electro-sword at the ready, afraid to make a sudden move and cause the Skull to blast the kids or the young woman who had just jumped into the picture.

For a long moment, nobody moved, and the only sounds were of the little kids squealing and the police sirens echoing in the distance. And then Lyn Li broke the silence. "Back off, creep!" she screamed.

And then something even more dramatic happened: The big television the two guys had been setting up nearby exploded.

As sparks and mechanical components rained down all around, Damon rushed forward, his electro-sword jabbing out toward the Skull. At the same moment, Richard trudged forward, his right hand raised, his own paranormal abilities manifesting in the form of gravity waves that pulled down at anyone in front of him.

Richard's power grasped the Blue Skull and yanked him down to the ground in a crumpled mass. But with him now out of the way, Damon's lunged attack sent the tip of the sword directly into Richard's chest. Electricity surged and the big man in the trench coat cried out, then collapsed next to the villain.

Damon realized what had just happened and cursed.

"Who are you supposed to be?" he demanded. Richard, of course, was too busy rolling on the ground in pain from the effects of the sword-jolt to respond with much more than a wordless grunt.

With Richard's gravity-powers cancelled, the Blue Skull leapt to his feet and punched Damon in the jaw. Damon cursed again and swung for the villain. The two collided and tumbled to the side, struggling with one another as they rolled across the lawn and towards the children. The black box the Skull had been carrying lay forgotten for the moment nearby.

Lyn Li once again put herself between the two combatants and the kids, shouting, "Get out of here! Go fight someplace else!" Even as she said it, the television seemed to explode again, lighting flickering from its screen and flames gushing from its top. The children—and adults, too—screamed and dived for cover. Some of them were staring at Lyn with just as much shock and fear as they were at the other combatants.

Lying on the grass nearby, Richard managed to regain his wits pretty quickly—he was lucky enough to have been wearing a protective vest beneath his shirt—and struggled to his feet. He tapped at his nondescript earpiece and uttered a few code words. Within a few seconds, his superiors had come on the line and he'd managed to convey what was happening here to them.

"Yeah," he said in response to a question over the link, "I think we can definitely say the Li girl is manifesting her paranormal abilities. She's already caused a TV to explode. And now—" Even as he said it, waves of golden light emanated from Lyn's body, as if she had become a living light bulb. "—now she's generating major levels of power." He paused for a question, then answered, " Oh, yeah—anybody watching right now will definitely know it's her doing it." He paused for a second, seeing the wave of newcomers cresting the hill nearby. "Annnd great—here come the news cameras

22

"Yeah, everybody's gonna know all about her in just a few seconds."

and the cops. Yeah, everybody's gonna know all about her in just a few seconds."

The voice on the other end acknowledged this and issued an order. Richard had known it was coming, but he didn't have to like it.

"Okay, fine," he told his superior. "I'll do this. But I'm thinking this may be my last assignment. Yeah, okay, we'll talk about it later. But we'll *definitely* be talking about it."

With that, Richard clicked off the link and pocketed the earpiece; he had no desire to hear any more from them. Then he rushed forward, in the direction of the very radiant Miss Li. She didn't see him coming at first and he wrapped her up in his arms, taking her with him to the ground.

"Sorry to do this, young lady," he growled, holding her tightly around the waist with his left arm, "but it's time for you and me to make ourselves scarce."

Then he directed his right hand down at the ground, and the earth blasted up around them, gobs of soil and rock and grass flying in every direction. With surprising quickness, Lyn and Richard began to sink into the ground—into a tunnel that seemed to be boring itself out even as they descended into it.

"What are you doing?" Lyn demanded, eyes wide and frantic as she looked at him, struggling to free herself from his grasp. "Get away from me!"

Golden lightning flared from her hands, going off like a hundred flashbulbs in Richard's face and causing him to cry out and let go of her in order to cover her eyes.

Pulling free, Lyn climbed out of the shallow pit and scrambled away. Then she whirled back, glaring at Richard. Lightning flashed all around her and her eyes were intense and filled with burning fury. Her clothes ripped here and there as energy surged across her lithe form. Then she looked around and realized that everyone was looking at her. Even the two weirdoes that had been fighting—the Blue Skull and the Cavalier—had stopped to gawk at her.

"Why did you do that?" Lyn demanded of Richard. *"Why did you make me do this?"*

Richard cursed violently. He knew when an operation had gone sour, and brother, this one had gone supremely sour.

That's it, Jameson, he said within his own thoughts. *No more. I'm done with you and your covert ops. Done!*

24

Directing both hands down into the pit he had been creating, Richard blasted away the earth at his feet and dropped out of sight entirely. Within a few moments, he was long gone.

The Blue Skull came back to reality first. He nearly knocked Damon out with a savage right cross, then scrambled for the black box. He almost made it, too, his blue-gloved fingers reaching out for it, where it lay in the grass—when suddenly a red-and-white streak flashed by, fists flying. The Blue Skull was down and out before he fully understood what had hit him. What—or *who*.

Damon, of course, understood immediately. Picking himself up from where the villain had knocked him almost silly, he stifled a curse, along with ten tons of disappointment, and forced himself to smile his best heroic, winning smile—a smile that deserved to be broadcast from coast to coast, he told himself—at his partner.

"Ultraa," he called by way of greeting, even as the blond man circled about in midair and then settled to the ground, standing over the defeated Blue Skull. "Glad you could make it."

The blond-haired hero and government operative nodded Damon's way. He wore a textured, resilient white uniform complete with red boots and gloves, along with a broad, red belt with a gold buckle. He flashed a smile that was much more sincere than Damon's at the little kids and at Lyn Li, and then frowned as the horde of reporters and cameramen rushed forward.

Damon attempted to interpose himself between his partner and the media—to shield Ultraa from the annoying paparazzi, of course, he would tell anyone who asked. But the reporters were having none of it. They pushed past him and crowded around Ultraa, barraging him with a wave of questions.

Damon forced himself to not let the disappointment in this treatment show. He pulled his bandana off and brushed his hair back, then dusted the grass and dirt from his golden chain mail shirt, watching all the while as Ultraa dutifully and somberly answered the reporters' questions. They were all facing that way now; not a single one of them even glanced at Damon. He placed his hands on his hips and stood there, hoping at least one of them would turn around – would save at least one question for the other hero on the scene. *The guy who actually rooted the Blue Skull out of his nest and pursued him halfway across town,* Damon mentally added. Alas, as the minutes ticked by, no one turned Damon's way. So he finally gave up and looked around—and saw the young Miss Li sitting there, her clothes ripped, appearing distraught and overwhelmed. Smiling to himself, he started toward her.

"No, I don't know who he was," Lyn was saying to the policeman standing in front of her. She was seated on the low, decorative wall, her head in her hands, staring down at the grass. "I can try to give you a description, but I really didn't see him very well…"

So involved was Lyn in the conversation with the officers that at first she did not recognize the man who wedged himself between the policemen and bent down to introduce himself.

"You're Lyn Li, aren't you?" the man asked.

Lyn looked up into the smiling face in front of her. She blinked.

"The name's Cavalier," the man said—and then he actually bowed. "I am honored to meet you."

Lyn suppressed a laugh. *Is this guy for real? Is he serious?* She watched, eyes wide, as he straightened, still grinning at her like some time-lost Errol Flynn. *Then again, to be fair, a good laugh is probably the best thing I could have right now.*

"I saw what you did back there," the guy—Cavalier—said to her. "I think you should talk with my partner."

"Your partner?" Lyn frowned at him. "Who's that?"

The muscular blond man in the white and red suit that stepped forward did not inspire laughter. Not at all.

"Oh," she said softly.

He nodded to her and smiled politely.

"My name is Ultraa," he said. "I think we should talk."

The small, wiry man huddled on the seat of a huge, black metal chair, his hands shaking as they reached out to the control panel that hovered nearby. Time and time again those quivering hands punched out a sequence of buttons on the panel—the same sequence, over and over, bringing up the same results each time.

"Not yet," he whispered. "Not yet. But—soon!"

The little man gnashed his teeth, muttering to himself. An observer overhearing him would have taken his words for strange, mathematical formulas and computations.

"The conditions are right," he said, after a time. "The patterns are forming. Soon!"

The dark room in which he sat hummed with the sound of ultra-advanced computer systems, and flickered with the light from dozens of display monitors, some suspended from the domelike ceiling, others fastened to the curving walls. Each of the monitors depicted a different scene. Some showed contemporary views of Washington, DC, and other cities of the Earth; some held views of deep space, of starfields and distant planets; some portrayed the darkest jungles or barren deserts; and some showed alien cities on faraway worlds beyond the ken of mankind. Looking around, inspecting these surroundings as if for the first time, the little man grinned and nodded in satisfaction.

"All, yes, all is in readiness. The sanctum is as he will wish it to be. The city nears completion of its first phase. He will be most pleased."

A light to his right flashed red, on and off, as a buzzer sounded. The small man nearly leapt from the thronelike chair, reaching out to grab the floating control panel and pull it closer. His bloodshot eyes studied it feverishly.

"Now! He is coming!"

A swirl of light formed at the center of the room; a cloud of smoke, seemingly from nowhere, accumulated around it.

The little man climbed down from the chair and stood in front of it, bouncing from one foot to the other, his eyes locked on the phenomenon.

From out of the light and the smoke strode a tall figure, clad in dark blue and purple robes. A hood covered most of his head; what little was visible was concealed by a silvery metal mask that glinted in the room's pale light. The mask was smooth save for twin oval eyeholes and a narrow mouth opening that curved slightly downward at the ends.

"Master!"

The small man dropped to one knee, bowing.

The tall figure halted before him, then turned slowly in a circle, taking in everything around him. When he came back around to the small man he stopped, staring down at him.

"You," he said.

The little man's mouth twitched up in a smile.

"Yes, my master. You remember!"

"Remember? No. I have not met you before. And yet..."

He hesitated, staring down at the little man.

"Yes, I do know you."

27

"Yes," the little man said. "Yes. You know me, for I am Francisco. Francisco, the ever-loyal, the devoted, the—"

"Yes," the other said, cutting him off. "Francisco…"

The taller man continued to stare at him, and Francisco twitched, growing slightly nervous.

"All is in readiness, my master," he said, flashing an ingratiating smile, "assuming you wish to continue with your predecessor's work."

"My…predecessor?"

The tall man hesitated, looking to one side, as if deep in thought.

"I have no predecessors. Truly, there is only one. One… *Warlord*, yes—as there ever has been, as there ever will be."

"Yes, of course," Francisco replied, voice trembling. "Only one."

He reached out and grasped a bowl-shaped device that dangled, upside down, from a thick cable. He offered this to the taller man.

"Still," he said, "you might wish to review the plans of your predeces—" Quickly he corrected himself. "Of the version of yourself who occupied this sanctum previously," he finished awkwardly.

The tall man glared at him a moment, then nodded once, sharply. He accepted the device and looked it over.

"Yes," he said, "there might well be some benefit to downloading his—my—memories."

He placed the bowl on his head and Francisco manipulated the controls.

It took only a few seconds. The tall, masked man scarcely reacted at all. When the process was complete, he reached up and removed the device, tossing it aside, then stood still, deep in thought.

"You…you are alright, Master?"

"Hmm? Yes." The Warlord strode across to the thronelike chair and gazed down at it, clearly deep in thought.

"Yes, I see," he said. "A worthy scheme." He sighed deeply. "It does indeed continue."

"Excellent, Master. Yes."

Francisco scampered around to indicate one of the monitors, this one depicting a great, floating city hovering miles above a desert landscape.

"The city is nearly ready for your return, Master," he said, scarcely containing his enthusiasm. "The workers have labored long and hard to prepare it. The telepathic control system is in place and ready to be activated, on your order. That will only make them more efficient, more devoted, of course."

"Activate it," the masked man said.

Francisco touched an array of controls.

"The signal is now being broadcast from the antenna mast atop the central tower, Master. We will no longer require slave drivers and punishments. The people of the city will happily labor to serve you, yes—until they drop."

The Warlord simply nodded. This meant little to him. Of course the people of his city would slave night and day for him—that was as it should be.

"Keep the overseers, though," he said. "One never knows when they might prove necessary."

"As you wish, Master."

The Warlord turned and gazed at the scenes depicted on the array of other monitors, studying each one in turn, his mind moving to other concerns.

"The power source is the problem," he said, finally. "It will take something quite radical. A level of concentrated energy not *readily* available in this reality...or any other."

Francisco's brow furrowed. He gazed up at his master in surprise, anxiety obvious on his face.

"Then—then it is not possible, Master? The energy you will need is more than can be obtained?"

The Warlord reacted harshly to this question. He nearly struck Francisco with his gauntleted hand, but pulled back at the last instant. Then he seemed to be forcing himself to remain calm—to address the little man in a less aggressive fashion.

"I did not say that, Francisco," he growled, slowly and softly. "I said it was not *readily* available. But there are various sources, here and there, that can be gathered—harvested, if you will—brought together so that all of them can, on aggregate, provide me with the power I will need."

He gestured grandly, and his voice grew louder and stronger.

"And this *must* be done, must it not? Yes. It must all be brought together. All the levels of the multiverse, collapsed into one. You see that, do you not, Francisco?"

"Yes, my master," the little man replied, relieved now, nodding happily.

"It must all be united into one. All under my domination." The masked and hooded man gazed at banks of monitors arrayed across his sanctum's walls and nodded to himself. "All under the domination of the Warlord."

5

"Ma'am? Are you okay?"

Lyn took hold of the offered, red-gloved hand and shook it. She looked around in confusion. Everything had happened so fast...

"What you did just then was very brave, very heroic," the blond man was saying to her.

"What?"

Ultraa smiled. He took a knee in front of her, waiting until she seemed to have recovered her senses a bit more.

"You seemed to be generating some kind of force field, before," said one of the paramedics who was looking her over. "Do you mind my asking how long you've been able to do that?"

"That's right," Ultraa added. "Are you receiving any guidance for—"

Lyn waved a hand vaguely before her face, interrupting Ultraa's question. Her head was still spinning, and it slowly dawned on her that someone had been trying to kidnap her. The realization caused her to nearly fall off her perch.

Ultraa caught her gently and waited a moment, until she seemed to be in control again.

"I—I'm sorry," Lyn said then. "I'm just...not myself at the moment."

Ultraa nodded.

"I understand."

He paused.

"I get the impression you've never manifested that ability before," he said.

"Not like that," she replied, still trying to clear her head.

"Lyn! What—hi!"

Her roommate, Amy, ran up, stopping short as she saw Ultraa standing next to her. Sheepishly, she approached the hero, grinning.

"It's so great to meet you!"

Ultraa nodded to her perfunctorily, his attention firmly fixed on Lyn.

"I think we should take you to the hospital," he was saying.

"No, no. I'm fine," Lyn said. "Just give me a minute…"

Amy held out a hand and Ultraa shook it, flashing her a very quick, very weak smile.

"I'm a huge fan, Mr., um…?"

"Thanks."

Ultraa looked around at the reporters and cameras.

"We should at least get you inside somewhere," he said.

"The student union building is right here," Amy said, pointing.

Ultraa nodded and, supporting Lyn by one arm, led her inside.

"I'm fine, fine," Lyn said, once she was seated on a sofa and drinking a Coke. "You don't need to fawn all over me." She rubbed at her eyes with one hand. "It's just never happened like that before—not that strong."

"I knew it!" Amy said, squealing. She practically bounced up and down, grinning at Lyn. "I knew you had some kind of powers! There was just no way we could have three defective TVs in a row!"

"Yeah, well, now you know," Lyn mumbled, staring at the floor.

"I ordered the building's staff to hold the reporters at bay," Ultraa said, "but it's just a matter of time until they manage to get inside here. We should—"

At that moment the police arrived. Ultraa stepped between them and the women, took the lead officers aside, and spoke quietly with them. Lyn assumed he was trying to keep things under control, and spare Lyn an immediate inquisition while she was still recovering. After a few minutes of conversation, the police backed off, and Ultraa turned back to Lyn and Amy.

After asking her how she felt again, Ultraa pulled up a chair and leaned toward Lyn, as if studying her closely.

"Do you know who that man was who attacked you? Not the Blue Skull," he added, "the other one?"

Lyn frowned.

"No clue. Never saw him before."

Ultraa nodded.

"That was quite a powerful exhibition," he said to her. "It seemed like you were creating a force field. What else can you do?"

"What else? Well…" Lyn frowned. "Um…I can fly."

"Interesting," Ultraa said.

"You can *fly*?"

Lyn could not help but smile as Amy's mouth dropped open in shock and she gaped at her.

"I've been driving you around this town for a year now, and you can *fly?*"

Lyn shrugged.

"Not terribly *well*, really, but…"

"Some kind of electromagnetic manipulation, I would imagine," Ultraa said. "I'll bet you can do even more."

"Maybe so."

Amy looked from one of them to the other, then dropped onto the sofa next to Lyn, shaking her head.

"Too much," she said. "It's all just too much."

Just then the police officers parted and a brown-haired man in a wrinkled gray suit emerged from the crowd. He smiled a crooked smile, nodding once to Ultraa, then took a knee before Lyn and extended a hand.

She shook it, looking back at him quizzically, then realized who he was. Her eyes widened.

"I'm Esro Brachis," he said. "My equipment picked up some very unusual energy emanations, the last little while. The folks here tell me they came from… you."

7

Jameson clicked off the television in his office in disgust.

You're slipping, Richard, he thought angrily. *That would not have happened before. Now I'm going to have to cover for you, if I ever want to be able to use you again.*

"Should we take…measures…against the agent in question?"

Jameson looked up sharply at the gaunt figure of Adcock, seated across from him. The ever-present dark glasses reflected Jameson's image back at him; the man's bloodless face stared impassively back, waiting.

"No, no," Jameson replied testily. "Heavyweight—Richard—is too valuable, too experienced. Obviously several unforeseen factors came into play at once. We cannot blame him for what happened."

Adcock's raised eyebrow was just visible over the rim of his glasses.

"As you say."

"We didn't acquire the girl," Jameson continued, "but, as it turned out, that might have been for the best. We can certainly keep an eye on her now, given her increased visibility. And she will probably be easier to control, if she thinks she's acting entirely of her own volition."

Adcock said nothing.

Jameson frowned. He had come to dislike working with Adcock, for reasons he couldn't completely identify…yet.

"As for the other thing…"

He shrugged.

"Ultraa may be starting to remember things, just a little," he said, "but now maybe he'll be distracted, working with the girl. It may be that we can slip a few more things past him."

"You think he will take her under his wing, then?"

Jameson smiled.

"Oh, I'm sure of it. That's the way he's always operated. He likes to think of himself as a lone agent, but as long as I've known him, he's never been able to turn down a fellow paranormal who needed guidance."

Adcock considered this. "That could indeed prove useful," he said.

Jameson nodded absently, glancing off to one side of the room for a minute. Then he looked up again. Adcock did not appear to have moved.

"Don't you have something else you need to be doing now?"

The man in the dark sunglasses said nothing; he merely stood and glided out of the room.

Jameson walked over to the bar and poured himself a drink.

"Excellent."

"What?"

Jameson whirled around.

"Adcock, did you forget—?"

But there was no one there.

Jameson frowned, turning a full circle and gazing into every corner of his otherwise empty office.

"I'm hearing things," he muttered. "And talking to myself, too."

He dropped back into his chair, loosening his tie automatically, wondering why he had suddenly begun to sweat.

2

The slaves sweated beneath the shimmering, aurora-filled sky, working around the clock—for this world, this universe, knew no night. They labored intensely, punished harshly by the strolling, arrogant, blue-clad overseers if they long paused in their work.

They labored, and the great city grew.

The great floating city, a disk a dozen miles wide, floated in an endless sky of blue and pink clouds. Far, far below, so far none could see, even when the clouds occasionally parted, lay a barren desert. Great cables, each of them a dozen feet thick, trailed down from the underside of the city, like the lines of monstrous anchors. Instead of holding the city fast, however, the cables connected to power stations clustered on the desert surface far below, each of them tapping miles down into the planet's core, drawing energy to power the city—and to power its ruler.

For the city, much like its master, was always hungry for more power.

The slaves knew or understood little of this. The telepathic signal emanating from an antenna mast far above their heads kept them all tightly focused upon their work.

None of them remembered how long they had worked. Their only memories were of their lifetime of service to the city's master, that great figure who dwelled in his mile-high tower at the city center. Their only thoughts were of obedience and of ever more efficient labor. Their only joy came in the victories their master won, bringing more slaves to work alongside them, expanding the great city, increasing the master's wealth and power.

Now, in a moment for them just like all other moments, as the slaves built and expanded and filled the great disk of the city, several of them gazed up at the tower's peak, and gasped.

For the first time in—how long? None could remember—a vast sphere appeared, floating above the city's tall central tower. It hovered there, far above their heads, for a long moment, then settled to rest atop the tower, fitting smoothly into place, completing the structure.

"The flying fortress," some of them whispered. "The great flying fortress of the Master. He returns! He returns to us!"

As thousands upon thousands of eyes turned skyward, the great sphere of the floating section remained in place for several minutes, then detached itself and moved away from the tower. Floating upward, it took on an unearthly glow. Within seconds it had shimmered, faded, and vanished.

"He has left us," some of the slaves cried out, anguish in their voices. "The Master has left us!"

"He embarks on another crusade," others answered. "He goes to conquer and to extend his domain—to swell our ranks and to build our city—his city—to make it still greater!"

"But where has he gone?"

"Another universe," more slaves whispered feverishly, reassuringly. "He has gone to conquer yet another universe."

"Yes," they all cried. "Yes!"

Soon, they knew, the city would overflow with new workers, and wealth, and exotic new goods and people. It had happened before, during most of their lifetimes.

For no one, no world, no universe could stand up to their master—their lord—their *Warlord*.

9

"So you're really leaving, huh, Lyn?"

Lyn Li looked up from stuffing her suitcases, seeing Amy standing in the doorway, and smiled a tight, sad smile at her.

"Yep," she said. "It's for the best. All the way around, I think."

Amy looked even sadder than Lyn. Her curly red hair hung down over her eyes, and she distractedly brushed it back as she sniffled, dabbing at one eye with a tissue. "You... you're my best friend, you know?"

"Same here." Lyn moved around the bed, reached out to hug her. "I'm gonna miss you."

"You too, kid. How'm I ever going to get a date without you around to grab their attention first?"

"Riiiight." Lyn laughed. "Well, look at the bright side. You'll finally get good TV reception."

Just then a knock sounded on the door. Lyn frowned.

"Who's that?"

Amy's eyes widened.

"Ohh! I forgot! It's Jerry."

"Jerry?"

"A guy I met at the party Friday. He was coming over in case we needed help carrying anything."

Lyn cocked one brown eye at her erstwhile roomie.

"'Jerry,' huh?"

She smiled wryly.

"Somehow, I don't think you're going to be quite as lonely as you let on…"

Amy made a face, then opened the door.

A tall, muscular guy in his early twenties stepped in. He had tousled brown hair and wore a blue flannel shirt and jeans. He greeted Amy, then his eyes widened as he spotted Lyn across the room.

"Jerry, this is Lyn. She's my roommate—at least for a few minutes longer."

"Um, hi!" Jerry waved nervously. "So, uh, Amy was saying you might need help carrying your stuff—?"

Lyn resisted the temptation to just levitate the luggage off her bed with sheer electromagnetic force. She had been practicing such things ever since the incident on the concourse. But her control was still not what it needed to be. She worried she might accidentally send the bags through the ceiling... not to mention the effect it might have on Jerry.

So she smiled at him and nodded.

"Okay, sure, thanks."

She hefted one of the big bags, leaving two more for the others.

"My plane to DC leaves really soon. I guess we'd better be going."

"Too bad Ultraa can't just fly you there himse—" Amy stopped abruptly, grabbing her mouth with her hand. "Oops."

"What was that?" Jerry asked, suddenly very interested. "Ultraa?"

"Nothing, just a joke," Amy replied quickly.

"No," Lyn interjected, "it's okay. I'm not planning on hiding my identity or anything."

"Huh?"

Jerry looked from one of them to the other.

"You're talking about a secret identity!"

"No," Lyn replied, "I'm talking about *not having* a secret identity."

Jerry blinked.

"But—what—who—?"

Amy patted Lyn on the shoulder.

"Jerry, my friend here is about to embark on a career as a real live super hero!"

Lyn could only laugh at this.

"Oh, come on," she said. "I'm just going to get some training from Esro in how to control my powers, and maybe some pointers from Ultraa on how to use them effectively."

Jerry's mouth opened and closed a couple of times.

"Powers?" he repeated in a small voice. "Ultraa?"

"Lyn's already done some work out here," Amy went on. "She's been in the news a few times in the last couple of weeks."

"Ever since that idiot attacked me on the concourse," Lyn added.

"I remember that, yeah," Jerry said, nodding. He looked at her. "That was you?"

Lyn shrugged.

Jerry scratched his head for a moment, then stared at her.

"So you—you're going to work with Ultraa? *The* Ultraa?"

Lyn nodded.

"That's my roomie," Amy said, glowing. "Working with the bona fide, number one hero in the U.S.A!"

She laughed then.

"Heck, *she'll* be a hero."

Lyn shook her head, grimacing at Amy.

"We've talked about this. I'm not a hero. I'm not interested in being a hero. I just want to get some training. And the chance to study with Esro Brachis—how could I pass that up?"

Yet, even as Lyn dismissed the possibility to her friend, a voice inside her demanded, *Why couldn't I be a hero? Why shouldn't Ultraa want to take me on as a partner, once I learn to fully use my powers?*

And, as usual, a second voice—sounding oddly like her mom—replied, *Don't even think about it. That type of life is not for you.*

Lyn shook her head, tired of having this recurring internal argument. She could only let things play out as they would, and do the best she could, whatever the situation.

Meanwhile, Jerry had apparently fixated on one point. "Ultraa? That—that's just—wow."

Rolling her eyes at the two of them, and setting her thoughts of the future aside for the moment, Lyn headed out the door with her suitcase. The other two followed her.

"Wait a second," Jerry said as they climbed down the stairs. "I heard Ultraa already had a partner. What's his name—the Cavalier, or something."

"That guy's a loser," Amy said with a snort. "Ultraa'll boot him out in a hurry, once he gets to know Lyn."

"Whatever," Lyn said.

She looked back at her old apartment one last time. At her old life. Then she pulled the door closed behind her.

10

WHAM! WHAM! WHAM!

Again and again, relentlessly, the fist smashed into Ultraa's face.

"Ungh—"

He raised his hands, as if to somehow deflect the blows...

WHAM! Another blow, scattering his senses and leaving him wobbling on uncertain knees.

"Unnh—wha—?"

Hands grasped his neck, raised him up, spun him around and tossed his battered body like a red-and-white rag doll. Flailing about wildly, he sailed through the darkness before crashing into the far wall. Stonemasonry rained down; Ultraa lay dazed and unmoving.

The steps drew closer to him. Massive, floor-rattling steps.

Ultraa peered into the darkness, coughing.

"Who are—?"

The hands descended again.

He was disoriented, terribly disoriented. The attacker or attackers had not given him a moment to collect himself since it had begun. *Very smart of them,* he thought, even as the time it took him to think that thought cost him another blow to the face.

Hands roughly grasped him, threw him into a pile of what felt like old furniture. Shards of wood and metal and fabric rained down on top of him, and he crawled backwards, trying to gain just a moment's respite.

It had begun, only a few minutes earlier, with a missile.

He had been flying over the Shenandoah Valley of Virginia, on his way to Esro Brachis's house and laboratories. The attack had come out of nowhere—out of the empty woodlands—and had blown him out of the sky. The concussion of the blast had shaken him, stunned him, and sent him spiraling out of control. Dazed, unable to summon his flight power back fast enough to stop his descent, he had seen the ground coming up to swat him and known he could not prevent it. At the last moment, he felt his field of invulnerability creeping over him again, saving his life. But then he met the ground like a meteor and all had gone black.

The pummeling had begun shortly thereafter.

Now, as he heard the footsteps approaching again, he also heard someone speaking in a language he did not understand. Another voice, deeper, more guttural, responded in the same language.

Ultraa shoved the broken furniture out of the way and stood on wobbly legs, squinting into the darkness.

"Who are you people?"

"Still moving?" the deeper voice said just ahead of him in the darkness. "You want more? Fine, I give you more!"

Ultraa just managed to duck the savage blow and roll to the side. Invoking his super speed, which worked in tandem with his invulnerability, he brought his fist up in the general direction of the voice. Rewarded with a metallic clanging sound, he lashed out again, this time knocking the attacker to the ground.

Ultraa groped about, trying to get his bearings.

Inside... They must have me inside something. So...

He blasted blindly into the air and crashed through a ceiling that hung only a few feet above. He emerged into more darkness—night, he realized—but was now out in the open, at least, and moonlight allowed him to see a little bit better. Continuing upward, he stopped and hovered about fifty feet above the roof of the building that had held him, looking around. He had emerged into a sparkling starlit night and a deserted stretch of wilderness.

Below, a pair of odd-looking individuals had climbed up through the hole in the ceiling, and stood looking up at him. One was very large, muscle-bound and tough looking, the other smaller and wiry. Again the foreign language—almost certainly German, Ultraa somehow knew—followed rapidly by English.

"You cannot escape so easily, my friend," the smaller one said, his voice heavily accented.

"Who says I'm 'escaping?'" Ultraa called back to them.

Hands on hips, the smaller man stared up at him. Ultraa realized then that both of them wore what had to be some sort of night-vision goggles. *That explains part of it,* he thought.

Ultraa turned his attention to the larger one: Metallic exoskeleton of some sort—no wonder he'd hit so hard. Matching metal mask covering his entire face. Muscles even bigger than he'd first thought. Ultraa sighed. *Where do they get these guys?*

The smaller, wiry one was clad in gray and black. He had some sort of weapon slung over his shoulder, and even now brought it to bear on Ultraa.

"It will go easier on you, my friend, if you simply accept your fate, and surrender to the true heroes of the Fatherland."

Ultraa blinked.

"The who? What?"

The blast almost caught him off guard. Almost. But he was already moving as the smaller man pulled the trigger on his weapon, and the shot missed wide. Flashing straight down into the bigger armored guy, at full speed, Ultraa smashed him back through the roof and into the room below. This time, enough of the ceiling was missing that moonlight shone through and Ultraa could see what he was doing. Fists lashing out like lightning, he pummeled the armored man, then whirled around, looking for the smaller attacker.

Shouts in German came from above, followed by "Iron! Hold him! I will end his impertinence!"

The smaller man leapt down through the opening and landed nearby, brandishing a futuristic-looking, rifle-like weapon.

The armored one grappled with Ultraa, actually serving to block the other's line of fire momentarily. Before that could change, Ultraa pulled free and rocketed across the room. His super-speed, like his invulnerability, only worked when he flew, but that was not a problem now that he was no longer trapped in the room. He grasped the smaller man and carried him along as he streaked up through the ceiling and into the night sky. Lofting up to perhaps a hundred feet in the air, he held the man by the ankle and dangled him out.

"Enough of this," he shouted. "Who are you people? Talk!"

"I am happy to tell you who I am," the small man said. "My name is Blood." He indicated his ally, who stood below, watching. "He is Iron. We are the heroes of the glorious German Reich."

"You're Nazis?" Ultraa was incredulous.

"Nazi? I know not this word. We are heroes of the Fatherland— the Second German Reich. Until recently, we served Kaiser Wilhelm IV."

"You're nuts," Ultraa replied.

Something sailed past Ultraa's head, then, very close.

A brick? What the--?

He looked down and saw the other guy—Iron—preparing to throw another brick.

"Hey!" he shouted down to the big man. "Let me explain something. The only thing keeping us aloft right now is my power. Clearly your little friend here can't fly. So..."

The brick struck him hard, stunning him just enough to cause him to loosen his grip.

Idiot, he thought, as he watched "Blood" plummet towards the earth. Triggering his speed, Ultraa sliced down, catching the strange German just before he could hit the ground. Grasping him by the neck, hovering a few feet in the air, he glared at the big man.

Before either could speak, the two attackers took on an unearthly shimmer.

Blood and Iron looked at one another, clearly surprised.

Behind them, a cloaked figure materialized within a cloud of smoke, arms outstretched towards them. Blue-gloved hands seized them both.

Iron wailed in fear.

Blood let loose with a stream of frantic-sounding words in German, followed by, "We have him! We can still succeed! We can hold him!"

Before he could go further, he and his partner vanished.

The cloaked figure stood still for a moment, watching Ultraa.

Ultraa settled to the ground and took a step toward him, trying to see a face within the shadows, failing.

"Those fools have gravely disappointed me," the voice from the dark form said. "I could tolerate their incompetence no longer."

"Who are you?" Ultraa demanded.

"I cannot be bothered further at the moment," the voice said. "While you do somehow possess a fraction of the power of one of the Great Rivals, it is not tiny—scarcely enough to warrant my further attention at this time." He made a dismissive gesture toward Ultraa. "Go now. But know that you will not deny me my goal. Eventually, I will have the power."

"I have no idea what you're talking about," Ultraa said—and he was already launching himself forward as he spoke the words. Unfortunately, the dark figure had already vanished, disappearing amid a flash of blue light and the ringing of maniacal laughter. Ultraa sailed harmlessly through the dissipating cloud of smoke.

For a couple of minutes afterward, Ultraa remained there, waiting and watching, angry that he hadn't gotten a better look at his adversary. All he had been able to see, just before the guy had vanished, was a glint of silvery metal, as of some sort of mask worn underneath the hood.

Finally, dusting himself off, he shook his head in bewilderment. Who could ever make sense of the schemes of the really crazy bad guys? As far as he was concerned, this was just one more loony to add to his long list of bizarre foes.

Then he launched himself into the night sky, giving one last glance back at the battlefield before returning his thoughts to the matters at hand.

"Hope I haven't kept them waiting too long," he said to himself as he once again soared above the Virginia countryside.

11

"Esro Brachis, you are a complete jerk."

The woman had big, teased blonde hair and wore a tiny, midriff-exposing red top and leopard-patterned tight pants. She stood in the doorway, glaring at Esro, hands on her hips.

Brachis looked up from his worktable, puzzled.

"And your fashion sense is horrible," she added.

"Well, that means a lot, coming from you," he said, with a laugh. Even so, he stole a quick glance down at himself. He wore his usual attire: Hawaiian shirt, khaki pants covered with pockets, and sandals. He shrugged. "I don't see anything wrong, anyway."

The woman snorted.

"You wouldn't."

He put down the handful of electronic components he'd been working on and looked at her fully.

"What's the matter, Connie?" he asked.

She huffed.

He waited.

She looked at her watch, then back at him.

"...Yes?"

"Ultraa! You said Ultraa would be here! His new partner, too!"

"That was my understanding, yes."

She spread her hands wide, as if to say, "So, where is he?"

"I can't control the man, Connie. I'm sure he'll be here as soon as he can. He does have things to do, you know. Saving the world, and all."

With that, Esro looked back down, returning his attention to the gray metal components spread across his table. The two cases that he kept with him at all times lay on the floor next to him, open and empty.

Connie waited a few more seconds, then stomped away, her shoes clattering on the hardwood floor. Minutes later, she returned and, if possible, she was even angrier.

"That's it, Esro. You promised to introduce me to Ultraa, and can't even produce him. And now you're ignoring me. That's it! I don't care how much money you have, it's not worth it. I'm outta here."

Esro watched her stomping around the room, rummaging through piles of gadgets and doodads, looking for something.

"Can I help you with—"

"Ah ha!"

She held up a key on a silver ring, like a prize she'd won.

"The Jag. That'll do."

She stalked out of the room.

Esro watched her walk away, puzzled. He jumped up and followed her through the living room to the front door.

"You're taking my Jag?"

She whirled back to face him, an imperious look on her face.

"It might as well be mine, Esro. I picked it out. I chose all the features. Even the color. You never cared about it at all. So now I'm taking it. Do you have a problem with that?"

Esro mentally weighed losing the Jag, vs. losing the Jag with Connie inside it.

"Um, no, that's fine," he replied.

Somehow this seemed to make her even more upset. Turning back to the front door, she flung it open.

"Um…hi?"

A young woman stood on the doorstep, obviously having been in the process of reaching for the doorbell. She was a little over five feet tall, very attractive, with shoulder-length black hair and Asian features. Suitcases lay on the walkway behind her, and a taxi was just pulling away.

She smiled and extended a hand.

"I'm Lyn Li. This is Esro Brachis's place, right?"

43

Connie glared at the girl, then turned to Esro with a look of utter contempt.

"That didn't take you long!"

She glanced at a very confused Lyn again.

"Robbing the cradle, are we, Esro?"

And with that, she stomped out the door, past Lyn, and hopped into the Jaguar. With a roar, the sportscar sped away.

"Good riddance," Esro sighed.

He took Lyn's dangling hand and shook it.

"Come on in. Here, I'll get your things."

Lyn glanced back at the receding Jaguar.

"Nice car..."

"Thanks."

Lyn blinked.

"It was yours?"

"*Was*, I think, is the key word there."

"She—she took it?"

Lyn glanced back again.

"Um...I don't think she's coming back."

"She's welcome to it," Esro said, "*if* she never comes back."

Dazed, Lyn followed him back into the house.

"Besides," he was saying, "I have a much nicer ride, right over here."

Setting Lyn's luggage down, he walked over to his worktable and gestured toward the seemingly random pile of electronic components proudly.

Lyn looked at the table, then back at him.

"This stuff?"

Esro nodded.

"Oh, yeah. This stuff."

Lyn bit her lower lip, then half-smiled.

"Sure. Yeah. Great."

Esro's smile faded. He looked at the components as if seeing their condition for the first time, and lifted a couple of them, turning them in his hands, frowning.

"They're disassembled now, of course..."

"Sure."

Lyn reached for her bags and looked around the big living room.

"So, um...could you maybe point me to my room?"

"Oh." Esro put the components down and nodded, appearing somewhat hurt. "Yeah. Sure."

Just then, the doorbell rang.

"Expecting someone else?" Lyn asked.

Esro smiled.

"You could say that."

12

Ultraa sat in a big, overstuffed leather chair in Esro Brachis's living room. A dark bruise ran along his left cheek and under his eye, and his white uniform was dirty and torn in places.

"And you don't have any idea who they were," Esro asked, "or what they wanted?"

Ultraa took the glass of tea Esro offered him and sipped it.

"What they wanted? Aside from my *death*?"

He shrugged.

"I would've thought they were just crazy, except for the guy in the cloak at the end. He acted like they were working under his orders. I think he...um..."

Ultraa glanced up at Esro, considering his words.

"Yeah?" Esro waited. "He what?"

"He teleported them away, and then disappeared himself."

Esro stared back at him.

"Teleported."

Ultraa nodded.

"Sure seemed that way. Unless it was some kind of illusion. I suppose that's possible, too."

Esro chewed on his bottom lip.

"*Teleported*. Okay."

Ultraa just nodded.

"So, they were nuts, then," Esro said, "but maybe very powerful nuts."

"I think that sums it up," Ultraa replied.

"Okay," Esro said, sitting down. "From what you said," he added, "they just wanted to get you out of the way. That sounds to me like they're planning something, and don't want any interference."

"Planning something?"

"Like maybe for tomorrow," Esro said.

"Ah."

Ultraa nodded.

Across the room, Lyn perked up. She leaned forward from where she had been curled in another of the big chairs, looking from one of the men to the other.

"What's tomorrow?"

"Launch. At noon."

Lyn frowned.

"Um, yeah, well, when else would you eat lunch, but noon?"

"Not lunch. Launch."

"Huh?"

"That's why I wanted you here by today," Esro said. "I figured you'd want to see it."

"See it? *It* what?"

Esro grinned.

"The Helix Project."

Lyn frowned for a moment.

"Helix…"

Then her eyes widened.

"The Helix Project—the experimental energy research facility?"

"Yeah."

"The one *on the Moon*?"

"The Moon. Yeah. That's the very one." He winked at her. "I guess you *were* paying attention at my presentation."

"Of course I was."

Then she blinked her eyes, as she realized what he was saying.

"So, we're gonna…um…do some kind of video hookup, or virtual reality tour, or…"

"Launch," Esro said again. "Noon."

Lyn blinked again. She gawked at Esro.

"Launch…"

She swallowed, coughed, and swallowed again.

"To the *Moon*?"

"That's the place," Esro said.

Lyn simply stared back at him, her mouth hanging slightly open.

"There's a little more to the Helix Project than just energy experimentation, though," Esro continued, seemingly oblivious to Lyn's stunned expression. "More than anyone knows."

"Such as?" Ultraa asked.

"Tomorrow," Esro replied, smiling. "You'll both see then."

Ultraa frowned.

"Esro, do you think it's wise to take the girl up there? It's not like a cross-town taxi ride. And she's already been attacked once. If someone may be plotting—"

The television switched on, apparently by itself.

"The *girl*? Excuse me?"

Ultraa raised a red-gloved hand and made a placating gesture toward Lyn.

"Sorry—I meant... the young lady?"

Static noise crackled from the television. Ultraa and Esro both glanced at it, puzzled.

Lyn seemed oblivious to it. She was on her feet, glaring down at Ultraa.

"I transferred colleges—I moved all the way across the country—just to be around things like the Helix Project," she huffed. "Whether it's on the Moon or Mars or in the Arctic Circle."

Ultraa raised a hand toward her.

"I didn't—"

"You just worry about your crazy Germans and your teleporting phantoms and let me worry about myself," she finished. "Okay?"

Ultraa blinked, taken aback.

"I—I didn't mean to offend you..."

Lyn plopped back in her chair and looked away, sulking.

"Trying to take away my trip to the Moon," she mumbled, huffing.

"Don't worry, Lyn," Esro said, with a wink. "You'll be there."

Ultraa watched him walk over to the television, switch it off, and chew a fingernail, apparently deep in thought. Ultraa scratched his head, trying to make sense of it all.

He turned back to Lyn, who continued to look out the window. Ultraa could have sworn he saw steam rising from her—and, given her abilities, that was probably not an impossibility.

Her abilities. The television. *Ah.*

"This reminds me," Esro said, breaking the uncomfortable silence. "I almost forgot. I have something for you."

Lyn looked back at him, still frowning.

Esro ran up the stairs.

Lyn looked over at Ultraa, who shrugged.

Esro came running back down a few moments later carrying something golden and shiny in his hands.

Lyn got up from the chair, trying to see.

"What is that?"

"It's...um..."

47

VAN ALLEN PLEXICO

Esro held it up in front of her, allowing it to unroll. It appeared to be a body stocking, and not a particularly large one.

Lyn reached out, touched it.

"It's…metal."

"Metal mesh, yeah. Very fine, though. Soft."

Lyn looked at Esro, then back at the suit.

"It's gold."

"Part of it actually is gold, yeah. But there's a lot more to it."

Lyn held it up to the light.

"It doesn't look like there's a 'lot' of it at all," she said, raising one eyebrow.

"Well…"

Esro blushed.

"It's made to your measurements. It should fit okay."

She laughed.

"I wondered what you wanted those for."

Esro nodded.

"Try it on," he said. "I think you'll be very happy."

Lyn hesitated.

"So, it's some kind of costume…uniform…?"

"More than that. Try it on."

Lyn dashed down the hall to her bedroom, closing the door behind her.

Esro looked over to Ultraa.

"Still no word from Damon, then?"

Ultraa shrugged, then shook his head, saying nothing.

"I'm beginning to wonder if we picked the right guy," Esro said.

"*Beginning* to wonder?"

Silence for a moment. Then Ultraa stood, walking across the living room, his hands clasped behind his back. He blinked when he realized that he recognized the black box sitting on an end table.

"Hey," he said, "is that the same box that I—"

"Yeah, yeah, same one. Thanks for retrieving it for me, by the way."

Ultraa nodded, looking it over.

"You just have it sitting around your house?" He snorted a laugh. "I have a feeling you're going to be asking me to go hunt it down again, soon."

Esro ran a hand over his face, back through his hair, and sighed.

"I know. I need to get it back into the lab. I've just been occupied with a lot of other things, lately."

48

"Such as that suit, I would guess," Ultraa said. "So, what does it do?"

Esro laughed.

"Hopefully, it will protect my televisions...and all my other delicate equipment, too."

Ultraa raised his eyebrows.

"And by 'delicate equipment,' obviously you are referring to..."

"My electronics, man. That's all. Believe me, that's *all*."

Ultraa nodded.

"Just making sure," he said. "She's, what, twenty?"

"Nineteen."

Ultraa whistled.

"And living here, with you."

Esro sighed.

"That, my friend, is the last thing I'm thinking about. Seriously."

Ultraa nodded again.

"Okay, okay..."

He rubbed his close-shaven, square chin a moment, mulling things over.

"She seems pretty headstrong," he said then. "I don't mind helping her out, giving her some pointers, but..."

He met Esro's eyes, frowning.

"I hope she doesn't get it into her head that she's already some kind of super-agent, and thinks she can be throwing herself into dangerous—"

He broke off as tiny footsteps sounded, coming down the hall.

Esro was nodding.

"Sure, you're absolutely right. The last thing I want to do is put her in—"

"Put me in what? A skin-tight leotard?"

Lyn had emerged from the hallway, light sparkling from her snug, golden suit.

The two men looked up at her. Each of them opened his mouth, started to speak, and promptly closed it again.

"No, not at all," Esro managed at last, his mouth dry. "It's very... becoming."

Ultraa nodded.

"Very... professional," he said.

Lyn looked down at herself, and said, "Yeah, but—what profession?"

"You don't like it?" Esro asked.

49

"I…I suppose so, but…"

She walked over to the full-length mirror on the back of a closet door and stood in front of it, taking in the sight of the skin-tight metallic body stocking that clung to her all over.

She frowned, glancing back at them, then back at the mirror.

"It's not…see-through, is it?"

"Certainly not," Esro snapped back instantly. "I wouldn't have—"

"You know," Ultraa began, "actually—"

Lyn whirled toward him.

Esro shook his head ever so slightly at Ultraa.

"—actually, not at all," Ultraa finished, his eyes moving back and forth between Esro and Lyn. "Not see-through at all. Very respectable."

Lyn's frown deepened. She turned back to the mirror.

"I don't know…"

The golden suit covered her from neck to toe, revealing only her hands and her head… along with her every curve and crease. A long silver zipper ran down her left side, the grip a small ring. Aside from that, it was unadorned.

Esro held a small analyzer device up in front of her, studying its readout. He smiled and dropped it back in his pocket.

"It's working perfectly."

"Working? The suit?"

Lyn looked at him, puzzled.

"What does it do?"

"It contains your power—regulates it. Allows you to focus it. You'll be able to do everything you could before, and more efficiently, more effectively. But without, y'know, frying all the electronics within half a mile. Unless you want to, of course."

Lyn's eyes widened. She looked down at the golden suit she wore, then back up at Esro. A smile slowly spread across her face.

"I like it," she said.

13

In the sanctum of his flying fortress, his invisible and undetectable sphere that contained his command center, the Warlord gazed out at the blackness of space, and at the great gray sphere of the Moon, filling his main viewscreen.

"It is time, Francisco. I must have my power source."

Eyes flickered rapidly behind a silver mask, restlessly moving from one of the smaller monitors to the next, taking in the scenes. At last they settled on one; focusing, they bore in with blazing intensity.

"Ahh."

Another voice spoke up, reeking of fear.

"It is them, Master!"

"Indeed."

Blue-gloved fingers manipulated controls until the images of three individuals filled the central screen. One was tall and blond, wearing white and red; one was dark-headed and clad in a gray business suit; and one was female, Asian, wearing a dark blue tracksuit, but with metallic gold sparkling where her skin should have been exposed.

"Ultraa," said the deeper voice from behind the silver mask. "Possessed of an unknown energy source—one that he only taps into the barest depths of—allowing him to fly at great speed, and to become extremely resilient while doing so; nearly invulnerable."

"The Germans should have succeeded, Master. He should not be present—and his power should have already been added to your collection."

"The Germans were fools, Francisco. But I was prepared for either contingency. No matter."

He moved on to the second figure.

"Esro Brachis. Genius. Inventor. Contracted with the American government to build advanced personal weapons systems for the individual soldier."

"Such as the Cavalier Project," Francisco's sniveling voice added. "Some of his creations are almost as advanced as yours, Master."

The dark figure glared at him, then continued.

"The third is Lyn Li, a young college student from Bay City, recently taken on as a sort of assistant to Brachis. There is more to her than meets the eye, I think. And I wonder just whose apprentice she ultimately will be."

The small man gazed up at his master, puzzled, but said nothing. He turned back to the screen, trying to see exactly what it was that sparkled beneath the tracksuit.

"The fourth member of this group has not arrived, it would seem."

51

"The Cavalier," hissed Francisco.

"Indeed. Damon Sinclair. Stuntman, test pilot, all-around daredevil and glory hound. Hired by Brachis to field-test his inventions."

"They've had a falling out, I believe, Master."

The silver mask nodded.

"All to the good, for my purposes."

He reached out and manipulated a series of controls below the monitors.

"There can be no more delay. A massive source of cosmic energy lies within the Helix Project facility, and it must be mine."

"Of course, Master."

The silver mask came around and faced the little man, who cringed in fear.

"And I will attend to it *personally*."

Francisco gasped.

"Master, are you sure that is the wisest course to take?"

Behind the mask, the eyes narrowed, burning like white-hot embers.

"You question my judgment, Francisco?"

"No! No, Master, I simply fear for your safety—"

The grizzled little man trailed off, realizing he was only making matters worse.

"You think I cannot handle three such as them? Ha!"

The voice softened.

"But with the very limited success my minions have enjoyed recently, I feel it would be far more effective to tend to business myself."

Francisco sighed inwardly, sweat trailing down his face, relieved to have avoided his master's wrath for the moment.

"As you say, Master."

"Indeed."

The dark figure stood, light playing across his form, revealing robes of blue and purple that flared out around him. Then, raising his arms dramatically, a pale glow surrounded him, and he vanished.

14

Lyn Li pressed her face to the viewport, eyes wide.

"When you first told me we'd be traveling a lot, Esro," she gasped, "I just thought you meant we'd be flying to Europe once a month, or something."

Outside, the Earth had shrunk to a blue and white disk, and the gray bulk of the Moon filled the lower half of the viewport. The *High Frontier* space station from which they had just launched was already dwindling in the distance.

From the co-pilot's seat, Esro shrugged.

"I go where I gotta," he said. "Fortunately, working with the government, I get access to cool, experimental equipment like the ol' Lunar Shuttle, here."

"But—but, I mean—the Moon!" She nearly squealed. "The freakin' Moon!"

"That's what it's called," he said, grinning.

Across the aisle from Lyn, and grateful he wasn't sitting next to her, given all her bouncing around from the moment they lifted off, Ultraa sat back, eyes closed, and let his mind roam. He thought about everything that had brought him to this point in his life, and then thought about that great, blank void of memory that occupied such a large portion of his mind.

Who am I, really? How did I gain these powers?

The questions assailed him whenever he rested, whenever he allowed himself to relax. Thus, he rarely did either of those things.

"The Moon!"

Lyn's enthusiasm brought Ultraa out of his dark musing, and he found himself grateful for it.

"I'm gonna knock you the rest of the way there, if you don't shut up," Esro growled playfully.

"Ah, let her alone, Esro," Ultraa said. "Just because you've been up here a time or two before, doesn't mean it doesn't hold all sorts of excitement for other folks."

Lyn looked over at him.

"Have you been here before?"

"Yes, I—"

Ultraa halted in mid-sentence, frowning.

"That is, I…"

Esro glanced back at him, then looked quickly away, turning his attention to the controls.

Lyn was looking at him, waiting.

"Was it that unmemorable?" she asked.

He smiled, covering it as best he could, secretly filled with turmoil, completely incapable of answering the question. *I have no idea if I've been here before, but something tells me I have—my first reaction was to say "yes," but now I can't recall anything of it…*

Esro broke the odd tension, to Ultraa's great relief, with his booming announcement:

"Strap in, everybody. We're coming in for a landing."

The Lunar Shuttle, a joint development of the United States Government and several private aerospace companies, including one owned by Esro Brachis, cruised in above the vast complex that was Tycho Base and settled to a gentle landing. The base, most of it situated beneath the Lunar surface, covered nearly two square miles, from landing pads along the outer edge to solar farms and communications arrays, all laid out around the living quarters located at the center of the crater.

The shuttle circled around on the pad and came to a stop next to the connecting building. A tube slid out and clamped onto the shuttle's side, creating an airtight seal. Esro and the pilot shut the craft's systems down and climbed out of their seats, while Ultraa and Lyn did the same. Together, they walked through the tube, down into the underground level, and emerged finally into Tycho Base.

"The Moon," Lyn whispered again, her eyes wider than ever, as she looked around at the base's polished white walls, illuminated by tracks of lights strung at intervals along the ceiling, twenty feet overhead.

Esro made as if to punch her, then smiled and patted her on the shoulder.

"The Moon, yeah," he whispered back. "We're here."

Some two hours later, Esro sat at the wheel of a moon buggy, Lyn beside him and Ultraa in the back seat. Each of them wore ultra-modern, lightweight spacesuits of the most advanced design from Brachis Engineering. Together they jostled along over the dusty lunar surface.

"This is not exactly how I thought I'd be spending my summer vacation," Lyn shouted over the noise of the buggy, vibrating through all their suits and helmets.

"Next year we'll do Disney, then," Esro shot back.

"Somehow, I don't think Space Mountain will ever measure up again."

They skidded to a halt outside a huge gray dome, and Esro switched off the buggy's power. He climbed out, moving in standard moonwalking fashion—almost bouncing along in the low gravity— toward a nearby airlock, and the others followed him. The outer door opened and they passed inside. Esro sealed it closed behind them.

"Yeah, so, anyway," Esro said, pulling off his helmet and running his security identification card through the scanner, "I was talking before about how Lyn really seems to enjoy my hot tub."

The others removed their own helmets. Lyn was frowning at Esro.

"What are you talking about? I've never gotten near your hot tub!"

Esro glanced back at her.

"Oh, it was the cat, then?"

"You don't have a cat."

"Ah ha!"

Lyn glared at him for a second, then shrugged.

"Okay, well, I've used it a time or two," she admitted. "But never when you were around!"

"And that's just fine with me," Esro replied, still fiddling with the security card. "The part about me not being around, I mean."

"For crying out loud, can't you open the door?" she demanded.

"Shut up!"

Ultraa glanced from one to the other, considering whether he might be better served by simply knocking them both over the head and dragging them inside. Conversely, he thought about just remaining outside on the lunar surface with his suit radio switched off. Certainly the peace and quiet would be a welcome change.

"Nice to see you two are hitting it off so well," he said aloud.

They both looked back at him, their expressions suddenly mild.

"We're doing fine," they both said simultaneously.

The lock beeped and the inner airlock door slid open. They all walked inside. Several armed soldiers stood nearby, watching them.

"Have a lot of need for security on the Moon?" Lyn asked, eyeing the troops. "Get many strangers walking up and knocking on the door?"

"You might be surprised," Esro replied.

"I meant to ask this before," she added. "Do Ultraa and I have permission to be here?"

Esro laughed.

"You've been allowed to get this far, haven't you? Besides, you're listed as my research assistant. You can't very well research if you don't know what I'm working on."

"Ah. Okay," she said, smiling. "Makes sense."

Esro looked at Ultraa.

"And if Ultraa's working for the bad guys, we ought to all just give up now."

Ultraa snorted.

"If the government's good with that justification, I can live with it," he said.

Together the three of them walked into the heart of the Helix Project.

Ultraa looked around as they emerged from a concrete tunnel and into a much larger, well-lighted space. Much larger than it appeared on the outside, it clearly extended down some distance beneath the Lunar surface, and also reached upward into darkness, with the light coming from fixtures suspended by cables from far above. The entire space was filled with futuristic equipment. Technicians stood here and there, clad in white lab coats. More armed soldiers were scattered among them.

"I'd rather be doing this work back in my own labs," Esro said as they walked across the broad central chamber. "Well, anywhere back on Earth, really. But the military prefers me to remain here, where things are isolated."

He smiled back at them.

"And Uncle Sam generously pays most of the bills. So I'm going along with it, for now."

"Hey," Lyn exclaimed suddenly. "We have regular gravity. Regular for Earth, I mean."

Esro nodded.

"Energy fields are sort of my thing, y'know," he said. "It wasn't too hard to come up with one that artificially increased the pull of gravity here, within the facility. Everyone seems to like it—low gravity is fun in short doses, but no one really wants to live in it, all the time. Not healthy, either."

As they neared the far wall, Lyn looked at Esro and asked, "So, what is all this stuff?"

"I'm not really sure," he replied.

"Huh?" Lyn gawked at him. "How can *you* not know what it does?"

They reached a heavy metal door set into the opposite wall. Esro placed his hand on a security pad beside it. After a few seconds, the door slid silently to one side.

"That's all NASA stuff back there," he explained. "These folks do lots of basic research stuff with it, when I'm not here, I'm sure. But," he said, pointing, "This, in here—this is what *we're* all way up here for, really."

They walked through.

Lyn gasped.

"Esro," Ultraa exclaimed, frowning, "what *is* this?"

"Yeah," Lyn added. "What he said."

A thing that looked almost like a bed, but somehow appeared more like a slab in a mad doctor's lair, filled much of the space before them. An array of surgical lights hung from an aluminum arm above it. Those lights glinted off a very disturbing sight.

On the table lay a man; or, at least, a humanoid shape, well over six feet tall.

Beyond the shape, though, all similarities ended.

In the place of flesh and bone, the body appeared composed of a jellylike substance, vaguely luminous. Odd colors swirled beneath the filmy surface. The head was smooth, featureless.

On top of all this, the body had nearly been torn in two, diagonally across the torso. As might be expected, it appeared inert, dead.

"That," Lyn announced, "is very gross."

"I would have to agree with that assessment," Ultraa said.

Esro grinned.

"And yet," he said, "when you see the amount of ambient energy radiating out of this thing, it suddenly seems really beautiful. Y'know?"

"Hmmm," Lyn growled, leaning over the gelatinous form, watching her reflection twist and distort as she moved. "Well... I guess it's kind of pretty, in a way. But—what is it?"

"You got me," Esro replied. "I'd sure like to know, though."

He motioned to two scientists in lab coats, who pushed a cart over towards them.

"But that's not going to stop me from experimenting on it," he said, grinning.

Ultraa raised one eyebrow at that, but remained silent.

"Where did you find it?" Lyn asked.

"Right here. Under a thin layer of regolith. It generates a constant, low-level energy output that led some astronauts here, to check it out, a couple of years back. We built this whole facility over it, but hadn't disturbed it where it lay. Until recently."

Esro leaned over the bizarre body, attaching small disks to its surface, then hooking wires into the disks.

"Judging by the soil around it, and other indications I've found," he continued, "it must have landed here about a thousand years ago."

"A thousand years ago?" Ultraa repeated, surprised.

Lyn gave him a quizzical look.

"Landed here? From where?"

Esro pointed up.

"Out there. Somewhere."

"It's from outer space?"

"Look at it, Lyn. What do you think?"

She nodded slowly, one hand over her mouth.

Ultraa moved closer.

"You're experimenting on it?" he asked. "But you said it's still generating energy—you know for certain that it's dead?"

Esro glanced at him, before lifting up a pair of metal instruments.

"I repeat—it's been buried on the Moon for a thousand years. What do you think?"

Ultraa shook his head.

"I don't know what to think," he said. "You tell me."

"Just a second," Lyn said, pointing behind them and through the door. "Esro, you said the equipment and everything else out there in the big room was mostly for experiments you're not even involved in. And that there's a lot of energy radiating out of this guy." Her voice rose to a shrill pitch. "Are you telling me—*this* is the Helix Project?"

"This is it," he said, nodding. "But it's not a total lie. If I can figure out how this ...entity... is generating power at such a level, a thousand years after it was buried... or, conversely, where it's drawing that power from..."

Ultraa nodded. Then, "Why 'Helix?'" he asked.

"Only you could find a way to get us attacked on the surface of the Moon!"

"Oh," Esro replied, reaching for the light controls. As he turned them down, and the room grew darker, a faint spiral of white light could be seen, spinning about the form of the broken creature.

"Gotcha," Ultraa said. "Helix. Right."

"That's just odd," Lyn said.

She had moved back toward the door they had entered. She looked out into the big chamber, to where a dark cloud had formed. Within it, within the flecks of light that flashed and swirled, a human outline was taking shape.

"Hey," she said, tapping Esro on the shoulder. "Is *that* supposed to be part of the—"

She found her partial question answered for her as she witnessed the reaction of the scientists and soldiers within the room. Shock and surprise ran rampant; soldiers grabbed for their guns as the scientists and technicians scrambled away in fear.

Brachis looked up from his equipment as Ultraa's eyes sought the cause of the disturbance. Both saw it at once: A figure congealing from the light, taking on solid form as the nimbus faded.

"Intruder!" shouted one of the soldiers.

Ultraa stepped forward, fists clenched.

"Intruder?" Lyn repeated. "You mean you weren't kidding— you really do get visitors up here?"

"This would be the first," Esro replied.

"Great," Lyn said, a golden force field flaring to life around her. "Only you could find a way to get us attacked on the surface of the Moon."

15

Ultraa shot into the air and hovered, still adjusting to the slightly altered gravitational field, which was not quite right despite the gravitic boosters Esro had installed. He peered down at the scene below, studying the intruder's outfit: Navy blue cloak and robes with purple trim; blue gloves and boots; metallic silver mask covering the face.

Dark cloak. Silver mask. Yes.

"You!" Ultraa shouted. "You're the one who—"

Before Ultraa could say anything more, the intruder raised both hands in dramatic fashion, his cloak flaring around him. As if in response, lightning flashed all around the chamber, striking at the soldiers and scientists, sending them all sprawling across the ground. One large bolt struck Ultraa, stunning him, and he tumbled to the floor, head spinning.

Esro and Lyn rushed through the doorway into the main chamber. Both of them gawked at the picture that greeted them: soldiers and technicians lying scattered, smoke rising from some of them; Ultraa down on his knees, bent forward, shaking his head violently as if to clear it; and, floating in midair above the center of the open area, a man in dark robes, a cloak flaring behind him.

Crossing his arms over his chest, the interloper floated toward Lyn and Esro, gazing down at them. His arrogance was palpable.

"You will hand over the contents of that room at once," his voice boomed. He pointed past them to the smaller chamber.

Esro stared back at the strange intruder, then whirled and slapped a large red button on the wall. Instantly, a heavy metal door slid across and slammed closed, sealing off the room containing the strange humanoid.

"That's the emergency lockout," he announced. "Only I can open it now."

Then he dashed to a nearby cabinet and yanked it open, revealing an arsenal of futuristic-looking weapons.

Lightning flashed out from the intruder again, knocking down the few soldiers who had managed to stand.

Lyn dived behind a bank of computers, forks of electricity flashing overhead.

"Open that door," the voice boomed. *"Now!"*

Esro pulled a cylindrical metallic device from the cabinet and pointed it at the attacker. A green beam of light flared from its tip. It struck just short of its target, deflected by a shimmering field of energy that surrounded the man.

"Fool," the intruder crowed. "You cannot harm me."

He gestured with a blue-gloved hand and lightning sheared out, blasting the weapon from Esro's hands. It clattered to the floor in pieces, smoke pouring from it.

Esro recoiled, his burning hands clasped together as he stumbled backward.

The dark figure motioned again, directing a blast of energy at the weapons cabinet. It exploded in a shower of sparks and flames.

Then he settled to the floor and walked purposefully toward the closed chamber door.

"Open. *Now.*"

"Hey!" Esro pointed at the wall of the dome. "Outside? Vacuum! Watch it with the fireworks!" He gritted his teeth and lurched toward the enemy, determined to keep him away from the sealed room.

The blue hand came up again. Lightning flared.

Leaping over the cabinets, Lyn landed on top of Esro and shoved him out of the way. The blast caught her instead. Electricity raked over her, shredding her sweat suit and burning it away.

She rolled to a stop, horrified, running her hands over her torso where the brunt of the blast had struck. There was no damage. With a sudden rush of relief, she realized that her golden metal mesh body stocking had deflected the lightning. *Deflected it, or...absorbed it?*

She leapt to her feet, now a sparkling golden form standing between the intruder and the door. Raising her hand, she shouted, "Back!" At the same time, an expanding sphere of golden light erupted from her body, raced down her arm in a split-second and smashed out into the intruder. As it impacted his defensive screen, the two fields momentarily merged, flaring brighter than the sun and sending sparks showering out in every direction.

The intruder gasped and stumbled back, barely catching himself from falling.

"How did you—?"

Lyn pushed forward, her body now surrounded in another golden sphere of energy. She didn't even notice that her feet had left the ground, and that she was now hovering about six inches in the air.

The intruder had regained his footing, but was now backing away ever so slightly. His silver mask pointed at Lyn, the eyes behind it studying her closely.

"Ah," he whispered. "Yes. More powerful even than I expected. Interesting. Perhaps your energies might be harnessed to my purposes as well."

He adjusted something on his belt, and the field around him flared brighter.

"But, for now, I have no more time to waste on you," he added, more loudly.

He brought his hands together with a sharp clap. In response, a shockwave smashed out, crashing into Lyn, bowling her over, leaving her sprawled in front of the door.

As he started forward again, Esro got to his feet, even as Ultraa recovered and rushed up to join him.

"Enough of this!" the intruder boomed. Moving with blinding speed, he grasped Esro by the collar and hurled him away, then blocked Ultraa's attack and batted him across the side of the head, knocking him down. Before any of them could recover again, he reached the door and laid both hands on it.

"At last," he cried.

The metal of the door lit up like a neon bulb as the attacker poured his bizarre and destructive energies into it. Yet still it held, resisting.

"Bah!"

He raised both hands over his head and smashed them into the metal. The door resounded like a massive bell being struck, but still it held.

"Get away from that," Ultraa shouted. He shot across the room and smacked the intruder's defensive force field with all of his might, but again only deflected away.

Whirling about, the cloaked figure struck Ultraa down with another bolt of lightning, even as the hero struggled to his feet. Then he turned back to the door and unleashed the most massive blast yet.

This time the door could not resist, and it exploded inward, electricity flooding into the room in a blinding flash and a deafening roar.

The intruder strode regally into the room.

16

Esro felt as if his head were exploding.

"I really, really have to come up with something besides cotton and polyester to wear when I'm going into combat," he muttered to himself as he sat up on his knees. His head throbbed and his skin felt burnt along much of its surface. His suit coat long since discarded, he pulled his tie off and tossed it away.

Through the shattered doorway, he could see the silver-masked intruder looming over the table, staring down at the bizarre figure lying upon it.

The man was nodding.

63

"Yes. The power. Oh, yes."

The intruder raised both gloved hands and held them out over the gelatinous body, watching as the electricity from his earlier attack still danced over the shimmering surface. The light from the strange body dimmed momentarily, then flared even brighter.

Ultraa and Lyn got back on their feet at roughly the same time, and they and Esro staggered through the door, preparing to attack again. No sooner had they crossed the threshold, though, than they collided with the intruder's force field and were forced back.

Inside the room, though, the blue-clad interloper no longer seemed quite as happy with the situation as he had a moment earlier. He leaned over the strange body, then almost recoiled.

"No," he was whispering. "Not yet."

He adjusted something on his belt, and the electricity sparking all around the room faded again, but then it came roaring back, far brighter than before—and now concentrated largely on the figure lying on the table.

"What are you doing?" Esro demanded, pressing against the force field.

The intruder ignored him. But now, for the first time, he no longer seemed in control of events. He shielded his eyes with one blue-gloved hand and hesitantly stepped back from the table.

"This is too soon," he muttered. "Too soon by far…"

"Oh," Esro shouted. "Did you mess something up, when you broke into my lab and destroyed half of my equipment? I'm shocked!"

Whirling, the intruder fired a lightning blast at Esro. It deflected away as Lyn raised a hand and created a golden force sphere in front of them all.

"He didn't have to take me literally," Esro grumbled.

They all watched as the intruder backed away from the table, moving towards them, his force field in turn pushing them back out into the main chamber.

All of them now stood outside, in the larger room, all trying to peer into the blinding light and make out what was happening.

Esro gasped. From what little he could see, it looked as if the strange body was moving, rising from the table.

"That," he observed, "cannot possibly be good."

The light flared so bright that they all covered their eyes or looked away. Moments later, a manlike figure emerged from the small chamber.

Instead of skin, it appeared to be covered in a shimmering network of orange light. Flames erupted from its surface and roared to life, blazing and blinding. The faint helix of energy that had orbited about it now flared bright red, spinning rapidly. The figure moved tentatively at first, its strange, featureless face turning as if to peer at each of them in turn. Quickly it seemed to gain confidence, and strode forward boldly, wreathed in fire. It said nothing.

"I am the Warlord," the blue-clad intruder announced, retreating a few steps, "and I have freed you from your thousand years of imprisonment. In return, I ask only that you accompany me back to my sanctum for a brief while, and allow me to speak with you."

The flaming creature roared an unintelligible reply and lashed out with scarlet flames at the Warlord.

"I don't think our new playmate cares for this Warlord guy any more than we do," Esro observed.

"I really don't understand what's going on here," Lyn said.

"You're not alone," Ultraa agreed.

Esro shrugged.

"Seems pretty obvious to me," he said. "Our masked buddy here was going to steal the body. But, what with him throwing around all that electricity, he must've somehow woken it up—and it looks like he did that sooner than he meant to."

Lyn shot him a look.

"Oh, well, sure," she said, "it all makes perfect sense when you put it that way." Her expression made it clear that she meant precisely the opposite.

The flaming creature stalked purposefully across the large chamber. Roaring in fury again, it grasped a fallen soldier and placed one fiery hand over the man's head. Then it stood there a moment, unmoving.

"Leave that man alone!" Ultraa cried, launching himself at the creature.

A flaming red hand lashed out, smashing him away.

"Language," it growled then. "Yessss…"

It tossed the soldier at Ultraa, who caught the man and set him gently aside. Then it strode toward the others.

"After so many years," it said, its voice ragged and strangely accented. "After so very long, Kabaraak lives again!"

Ultraa and Esro exchanged glances. Both shrugged.

"Kabaraak," the Warlord shouted. "Hear me. I have freed you from these lesser beings. Come with me, for we have much to discuss."

65

Giving the Warlord only the briefest of glances, the flaming red figure gazed upward at the ceiling of the dome. It appeared to be seeing through the metal surface—seeing the depths of space that lay beyond. With a wordless cry, it launched itself upward, a fiery trail behind it, and smashed through the dome and beyond.

With a roar, the air in the building followed it out.

"Lyn," Esro cried, pointing. "Quick!"

Ultraa had flown up toward the hole, weighing the option of plugging it with his own body, knowing that his invulnerability would vanish as soon as he quit moving.

Gasping for breath, Lyn realized after a second what Esro wanted—what she should do. She directed one hand up at the hole in the dome and generated a ball of sparkling, golden energy, fitting into the gap and covering it over. The air loss ceased instantly.

Keeping one eye on the intruder, Ultraa grabbed an emergency patch from one of the techs who had retrieved it and flew up.

"Now," he said.

As Lyn dissipated her circle, he slapped the patch into place.

"Esro, what was that thing?" he demanded, zooming back down to stand with the others against the Warlord.

"Couldn't tell you," Esro replied. "I'm sure this guy knows, though."

The blue-robed Warlord now loomed over them, his fury palpable.

"You are the cause of this," he shouted. "You have disrupted my plans—and perhaps cost your entire planet its very existence!"

"What are you talking about?" Ultraa demanded. "The entire planet? What do you—"

"Oh, it will not be me who brings about the end, I assure you," the Warlord replied. "But you will learn the truth soon enough. And to your everlasting regret."

Raising both arms in a grand gesture, the Warlord flared brightly and then blinked out, vanishing, just as Ultraa's fists flashed through the space he had occupied.

Esro ran over to a computer display, checking the base's sensors.

"He's gone. Both of them are gone."

Ultraa settled back to the floor and looked around, at the wreckage that had been caused in only a few short moments. Many of the base's personnel lay unconscious—or worse—all about.

"We have to help these people," he said, assisting the nearest scientist to her feet.

Some of the others were beginning to move, and Esro and Lyn went to their aid.

"I think they're pretty much okay," Lyn said after a few seconds, helping a soldier up. "Just stunned."

Esro raced across the chamber to the door that the Warlord had shattered. He disappeared inside for a moment, then backed slowly out.

"Um...guys?"

Ultraa and Lyn looked up.

From out of the room emerged a figure eerily similar to the flaming one they had just encountered. But where that creature had appeared almost demoniacal, this one seemed somehow angelic. A halo of soft, white light surrounded it, and a sparkling white helix of energy slowly circled its entire form.

"It—it's like it split in half," Lyn said, her eyes wide.

"I think you're right," Esro agreed.

Ultraa, in the midst of seeing to some of the injured soldiers, looked back at them.

"What are you two talking about?"

He gasped, and moved forward quickly, fists bunched.

"The first one was only half of the creature," Esro said, studying the readout on a handheld analyzer. "Though it fleshed itself all the way out—made itself seem whole." He gestured to the new one. "This is the other half. And it's done the same. So now there are two of them." He shook his head. "But don't ask me how."

Ultraa strode toward it, ready for battle.

The angelic figure stopped and turned toward him, but otherwise did not move.

"No, wait," Esro said, motioning to him. "It doesn't seem hostile. Not like the other one."

A few more seconds passed, during which time the fiery being merely stood, seemingly waiting for something.

"Lyn," Esro said finally, "go outside and see if there's any sign of the other one."

Nodding, Lyn donned her helmet and passed through the airlock, heading outside.

Meanwhile, the new being walked to the center of the large chamber. It stopped there and looked around, its expressionless face turning in every direction. Then, apparently satisfied, it settled to the floor, sitting with crossed legs, motionless. The white spiral of light continued to orbit it soundlessly.

"Guys," Lyn called as she came back through the hatch. "If nothing else too dramatic is happening here, you might be interested in this."

Esro and Ultraa glanced over at her, keeping one eye on the strange, fiery being the entire time.

A statue-like figure had followed Lyn into the chamber, and was now hovering a dozen feet above the floor, with no visible means of support or propulsion. It was big; at least six and a half feet tall, muscular, and human-shaped. Its gleaming surface was a metallic blue-silver color. As its grim face inclined toward them, in the dark recesses of its eyes, twin red lights flickered. The intensity of the lights grew as it stared first at Esro, then at the fiery being.

"Lyn," Esro said softly, remaining very, very still, "who's your new friend, and where did you find him?"

With a thud, the blazing creature that had been seated on the floor slumped over, unmoving.

77

The metallic, statue-like man settled gently to the chamber floor, his silvery feet clanking down on the metal surface. He strode directly, purposefully toward the fiery being.

Ultraa moved to intercept, taking up position between the two of them.

Esro, already there, kneeled over the prostrate creature.

"He's out of it. Seems to be catatonic, as near as I can figure," he reported.

The metal man hesitated, looking from one of them to the other, his head moving in quick, jerky movements.

"This guy seems plenty interested in him, regardless," Ultraa said, holding his ground.

Esro directed his handheld analyzer at the new arrival and studied the indicators.

"I can't get a reading on anything past the outer shell," he said, frowning at the numbers displayed. "Looks like his armor is made up of a vanadium steel alloy, with some other, exotic stuff mixed in."

The big metal form stopped short, confronting Ultraa, then turned back toward Esro.

"Van—ay—dyum?"

He looked at Brachis, tiny red eyes flickering over his features, then moved on to Lyn.

"Humans. Earth," he said then. *"English. Yes. Accessed."*

"Okay. He can talk," Esro commented. "What next?"

Turning back to the blue creature, the big metal form started to move again.

"Target...identified..."

"I don't like the sound of that," Esro said.

"Yeah—hold up there," Ultraa called out. "You need to play nice, until we can figure out what's going on here. And who you are."

Shiny metal hands reached down for the unconscious figure.

Ultraa leapt forward, shoving the big man back.

The metal face glared at him, red eyes piercing.

"Target," he said again. *"Danger."*

"Maybe so," Ultraa said, "but at the moment, he's not doing anything to harm anyone. He's not even awake. So you can just sit back and wait."

The big metal man slowly turned his head, looking first at Ultraa, then at Esro, then back down at the fiery being. He hesitated for a second, appearing confused.

"The first guy looked like the real danger, out of all of them, anyway," Esro said to him. "What did he call himself? Kabaraak?"

At those words, the metal man's eyes focused intently on Esro.

"Kabaraak...?"

"Yeah," Esro said. "He left just before you showed up."

The big man stared at him for a moment, then moved away, striding across the room to a computer bank. He laid both his shiny metal hands on it. A soft humming sound filled the chamber.

"What's he doing, Esro?" Ultraa asked, sounding worried.

One of the technicians looked up from her display.

"He's tapped into our system from one end to the other, sir. He's sifting through all our records, everything."

Ultraa started toward him. Just then, the metal man straightened, moving his hands away from the computer bank. He turned back to them.

"Kabaraak. Yes. Danger."

He walked toward the other figure where it lay on the floor, glanced down at it momentarily, then continued walking. He passed by the startled security guards at the outer entrance and kept going, out through the airlock and into the open.

The others donned their helmets and followed him out, Esro holding the small analyzer and pointing it towards him again.

"Wow," he breathed. "I've never seen energy readings like these before."

The metal man came to a halt about thirty yards from the dome, standing completely still for several seconds. He looked around, gazing at the parts of the base that protruded above the dull, gray lunar surface, as if seeing everything for the first time. Then he turned to face them, his head moving slightly to one side.

Abruptly, static squawked over their helmet earphones, followed by the voice of the metal man.

"Can hear now."

"He's got our frequency already," Esro observed.

"No kidding," Lyn replied. She approached him cautiously, peering through her helmet's faceplate at him, eyes wide.

"Who—*what*—are you?"

The big metal figure stopped, turned back to her, and said, *"Unable to access."* Then he hesitated. His head moved in tiny jerks again, as if the attempt to think were somehow painful. At last, he looked up at the others with his tiny red eyes and said, *"Van-ay-dyum. Vanadium. Yes."*

And with that, he launched himself into the void and streaked away, gone.

After a few seconds of staring up into the empty darkness, Lyn sighed. "Oh well…"

Esro patted her on the back. "I have a feeling we'll see him again," he said.

Lyn nodded slowly.

"Maybe so," she said. And, "I don't think he was such a bad guy, really… Or, a bad whatever he was, underneath that armor, anyway."

She and the others made their way back into the chamber.

The technicians had carefully lifted the fiery creature and set it on its back on an examination table. They had discovered that the flames that came from his rather bizarre flesh did not burn like ordinary flames.

Esro checked the results of his analysis and stared in amazement at the readouts.

"These numbers don't make any sense," he said, after studying them carefully. "For a few seconds, they seem very high—nearly off the scale—but then they sort of oscillate back down, to about half of what they were. And the overall level keeps dropping. And, on top of all that…"

Esro's voice trailed off as he leaned in closer over the strange form, studying its nearly featureless face, running a finger lightly over the translucent, almost gelatin-like flesh. The flames licked at him but did not burn.

"What?" Lyn asked.

Esro frowned.

"It's as if he's slowly disintegrating."

Lyn's face wrinkled up. "Disintegrating?"

"And that's new?" Ultraa asked. "He wasn't before?"

"No."

The three glanced at one another.

"Okay, that's it," Esro said finally, switching the equipment off and motioning for two of the technicians to bring a gurney over. "I can't do anything more here. We have to get back home—back to my labs. Now."

18

Vanadium. Yes. It is a corruption of my name, but it will serve, for now.

The blue-silver metal man shot away from the Moon like a missile, his every sensor and tracking system reaching out, searching for any traces of the first fiery creature's trail. He had searched through all the recordings within the humans' computers, and had seen and learned enough to understand what he faced.

I know that one. Kabaraak. I do not know precisely what he is, or where he is from, but I have faced him before.

He thought of the unconscious entity he had just seen, there in the dome.

He has changed, though. This other one, this new one, is a part of him, somehow. Something has happened to him.

A mystery, he decided, he could dwell upon at another time. For now, all that mattered was finding Kabaraak—and destroying him.

Nevertheless, fragments of memories came back to him from a thousand years past. From his last encounter with this being, or some aspect of it.

And this is what he remembered:

The fiery creature attacked him, coming out of nowhere, nearly destroying him before he could react. The flaming hands lashed out at him, seizing his throat, crushing it, and now they burned—they burned and blazed and seared into his metal skin.

And then something—*something*—tore the enemy away from him.

Vanadium whirled around, searching the starry blackness for what had intervened.

There.

Could it be? Could he be so fortunate?

Yes!

Five of his fellow Enforcers, flying in a tight "V" formation, had rocketed past, and circled back around toward him. They had knocked the flaming creature away from him. It now floated just ahead, waiting, as they angled toward it to attack again. A small black box floated past, and somehow it seemed important—had he been carrying it?—but he found he could not remember what it was, so he ignored it. At the moment, all that mattered was survival.

Vanadium sent a desperate signal to the others, trying to warn them of the awesome power they faced. They ignored him, confident of their own might, their usual superiority to any foe. They closed the distance rapidly.

The blazing enemy met the point of the "V" and smashed through the formation, sending the leader spinning away, out of control. Then it swooped around, blasting two more.

Vanadium gawked at what he saw. Two had been obliterated, reduced to small chunks of charred and spinning metal.

The remaining three retreated into a tight formation, backs to one another, taking up a defensive posture. They all looked around, seeking their foe, but he had vanished.

Before Vanadium could move to join his brothers, the creature appeared again, a blur of flashing colors, a streak of vivid light, striking at the heart of the formation, smashing it, hurling the individuals apart, scattering them again. One of them had broken into pieces.

Just that quickly, Vanadium's hopes were dashed. The unit's strength had been more than carved in half in a matter of seconds.

The remaining two regrouped and rallied once more. They launched a coordinated assault, smashing at the creature from two sides. Vanadium joined them, and together they poured all of their strength, skill, strategy and might into defeating and destroying the fiery being.

Cosmic flames lashed out and another of his brothers exploded, silvery-blue metallic limbs and parts flying in every direction. Vanadium watched in horror, even as he expended more energy, smashing at the creature.

Surely they had inflicted serious damage by now. Surely this strange being could not withstand such a combined assault for long. Believing this—having no other choice but to believe it—Vanadium and his lone remaining brother committed themselves, unlocking all of their power reserves.

The creature fought back savagely.

The blackness of space erupted in a cataclysmic explosion, as their combined attacks met that of the enemy. The force of the blast shook the very heavens themselves, and flung them all away in different directions.

Frantically righting himself, Vanadium looked around. There were no signs of his comrade. In the space of only a microsecond, he analyzed the sensor data for the surrounding area. He found nothing but debris. The others of his kind had all been destroyed, he knew. Only he remained.

What of the enemy, though? Had his brothers' sacrifice at least secured the defeat of their foe?

A bright point on his sensors indicated the terrible truth: the fiery creature had survived, and was even now racing towards him.

In the split second before the next assault, he ran his diagnostics once more while his mind raced over all the available options.

Flee? His sense of pride and his own militant nature aside, how would he manage it? And to where would he go?

That left only combat.

Diagnostics reported that everything had returned to somewhat normal except for his energy defense screens. His armored exterior remained mostly intact, his reactors operated at optimum output, and his weapons systems approached peak efficiency.

And sensor data indicated that the creature's own energy reserves had dropped far below their earlier levels. Perhaps, at last, it was vulnerable. Perhaps the sacrifice of five of his brother Enforcers had not been in vain.

So be it, then.

The long instant passed.

The adversary was visible now, hellish flames blazing about its form, streaking toward him like the red hand of doom.

He pulled every drop of power available from his reactors and surged forward, meeting the opponent midway.

The collision could have obliterated a small moon.

In this case, it sent him and his enemy tumbling apart, flames and fragments trailing between them.

Scarcely five seconds later, they crashed together once more.

The blows grew weaker, the damage to each of them heavier. He ignored everything now, lost in a single-minded zeal to destroy the other.

A gray planetoid loomed just ahead, growing larger as their momentum carried them that way. He saw it, and realized that the course of the battle had taken them far away from the green planet he'd come to visit before. This was the lone, large moon of that world, he understood, though he could not afford to give much attention to it at the moment.

On they fought, lighting up the heavens with the intensity of their struggle, until Vanadium felt that the battle had to end, one way or another, very soon. The enemy's flames grew faint, even as he saw his own diagnostic reports grow from troubling to critical. No vessel, not even the nearly indestructible bodies each of them possessed, could forever withstand such devastating punishment.

The enemy caught him in the side of the head with a surprisingly strong punch, and instantly half his diagnostics simply blanked out. Thought processes slowed, reaction times grew longer. Memories faded. Confusion reigned. He knew his mind was failing him.

But the other by now looked beaten. The last punch had apparently drained the last of its reserves, and it floated motionless, its cosmic flames flickering low about it.

Vanadium gathered up what strength he yet retained, reached out, and seized the other. Anger, along with an unaccustomed frustration, flooded through his mind. He tore at his foe with both armored hands, pulling, ripping, tearing at the body. Membranes ripped, energies erupted out in a dazzling burst. The enemy spun out of his grip, but it was limp now, apparently lifeless, tumbling slowly, inexorably away.

Utterly exhausted, his mind closing itself down, Vanadium attempted to pursue. His body would not respond. Instead he simply hung there, watching through a growing electronic haze as his foe drifted further and further away.

Some time later, what remained of the enemy passed into the gravity well of the moon beneath them, and it fell, plummeting down, down… gone.

But—gone for good?

Thinking back on those events now, Vanadium knew that he had doubted it, even then, a thousand years ago. Another part of him— some part of his mind, damaged and almost entirely inaccessible— seemed to suggest to him that this Kabaraak being was extremely important, beyond simply being an extremely tough and dangerous adversary. Lacking the ability to fully access that part of his mind, however, as well as the capacity to do anything about it, he had chosen to simply float there, above the Moon, allowing his internal systems to move fully into self-repair mode. The damage, as it turned out, had been so great that eventually he had drifted into an equivalent of sleep—a coma, really—leaving only his most delicate sensor array even partially awake, watching.

Then, floating there in a high, stable orbit, he had slept.

And, far below, Kabaraak the enemy had crashed to the gray, rocky ground, bounced slowly and soundlessly over the moon's surface, and eventually come to rest.

And the years had passed by and the dust had settled over it and it had lain there for a millennium, partially obscured from view, forgotten by all.

Until the coming of Esro Brachis and the other humans.

Now it was awake again. Awake, and on the loose.

But so am I, Vanadium thought.

Time to finish what I started, so very long ago…

19

Aboard his flying fortress, the Warlord had just settled back into his thronelike chair when a brilliant orange flare lit the interior of the command chamber. Whirling, he watched in awe as the fiery form of Kabaraak descended through the hole it had burned in the dense ceiling.

"YOU," it boomed within his mind. "You claimed to be responsible for my awakening. Now you will supply me with the information I require!"

"Perfect," the Warlord hissed. He closed a circuit within his costume, and a shimmering green sphere of light formed around the intruder.

The creature howled in rage, the intensity of its flames doubling. It pressed against the inner surface of the sphere, to no effect.

"You were right, Master," Francisco said, cringing in the shadows. "He came to you!"

"So easy," Warlord whispered. Then his voice grew louder, filled with confidence.

"Relax, my luminescent friend. You are a welcome guest. But do not try the patience of the Warlord!"

The fiery being was now beating at the sphere with its fists.

"This force bubble will contain you, and will prevent you from transmitting your signal—until I am ready for you to do so."

The Warlord drew closer, peering at the trapped creature.

"And you know the signal of which I speak, don't you?"

The creature glared at him, flames roaring from its bizarre flesh.

"The signal," it growled then, "is already sent. Now there is only the *wait*…the wait until great Stellarax arrives, and this world ends!"

The Warlord recoiled involuntarily.

"Already sent," he hissed. "Then it is too late. Too late for this world."

He drew himself back up to his full height, looking back at his servant.

"This world is doomed, Francisco. It is already as good as dead."

"How terrible, Master!"

"Fortunately," the Warlord added, " that scarcely affects me."

"How wonderful, Master!"

Behind his silver mask, the evil mastermind almost smiled.

"All that remains here, then, is to take what we can—what we need—while there is still time. And then, of course, to prepare our own reception for Stellarax the Great."

He turned toward the burning man and studied him, his mind racing.

"Will you cooperate?"

"I am Kabaraak," the creature boomed. "My power stretches back across the eons! Entire worlds have welcomed my arrival as the coming of a god—and yet I am as but a speck compared to he who comes behind me. He who subsumes entire civilizations into his totality, preserving them forever within his memory—but removing them from this universe forever!"

Deep crimson light flooded the room, the flicker of the creature's flames reflecting off of every surface.

"And you will detain me no longer!"

Cosmic fire crashed against the restraining field, blindingly bright. The field shimmered and flickered, but it held. Within, its occupant glared out in utter hatred.

The Warlord breathed a sigh of relief. Indeed, this being was enormously powerful, and the game he was playing with it—and with its master—was enormously dangerous. Yet he had no choice but to press forward with it—the Grand Design demanded it!

Turning away from the pyrotechnic display, he considered his next move. At last, clasping his hands behind his back, he turned and faced his captive.

"My friend, please, calm yourself. I assure you, I will be delighted to release you from this... *protective* field. But I must first be assured of your cooperation."

"Bah! What care I for the petty goals and ambitions of lower forms of life? Release me!"

This was too much. The Warlord's eyes flared.

"You dare speak in such a manner to me? I am the Warlord! Living embodiment of the Grand Design! My power is far greater than you know! It stretches across the universe and reaches into all the infinite layers of reality!"

The creature's face contorted in utter contempt.

"Ha! The infinite layers of reality! Do you think me a fool?"

The crimson flames flared angrily.

"This could hardly be so, else I would know of it."

And then the burning creature paused suddenly, a hint of self-doubt seemingly creeping in.

"Unless..."

The Warlord glared back at him, saying nothing.

"Unless..."

The creature's eyes—burning orange slits within red flames—narrowed. The telepathic voice lowered to a growl.

"How long was I depowered? How long did I lie dormant on that moon?"

The corner of Warlord's mouth turned ever so slightly upward.

"At least a thousand years, it would seem."

The creature stepped forward, pressing against the force field.

"How did you come to revive me?"

The Warlord was willing to put up with this questioning if it led to his gaining some measure of control over the creature.

"I traced your energy signature to a place called the Helix Project, on the moon of the Earth. You were revived during my attack on the base."

"Why?"

The Warlord decided it might be beneficial to be truthful, at least in this.

"I sought to harness your potential power for my own uses. I did not anticipate your sudden awakening."

The creature looked at him closely, then nodded once, turning away, brooding.

The Warlord glanced back at his displays and frowned. Leaning in closer, he studied the numbers flowing across the screens.

"Francisco," he called, "are the sensors in this room operating properly?"

The little man scampered up, moved his hands rapidly over the control panel, manipulating dozens of knobs and levers quickly, then nodded.

The Warlord frowned, concern growing within him.

"The level of power I detect from you now is far less than what it was before," he told Kabaraak. *And much lower than what I require for my own purposes,* he added to himself. "What have you done? Speak!"

The flaming creature whirled back, glaring at him.

"What nonsense do you speak?" he demanded. "I—"

He stopped abruptly, raised both hands before his eyes, and then looked down at his body. A low wail escaped his lips.

The Warlord and Francisco glanced at one another, puzzled.

Kabaraak smashed both fists into the walls of the sphere that held him.

"Much of me—my form, my energies—is missing! I can feel it now… I have been divided in half!"

He stumbled back a step, shaken.

"There is another—another *me*—out there, somewhere. It contains the balance of my energies."

He roared in anger.

"Not acceptable! Not allowable! I must have my power back! I must be reunited with my other half!"

Behind his silver mask, the Warlord frowned. Could that be possible? Could there be another incarnation of Kabaraak, that the Warlord had overlooked, back at the Helix Project? He had not

78

SENTINELS: THE GRAND DESIGN

looked in the room after this creature had emerged.... He had not imagined such a contingency—had assumed the fiery creature had been complete. But if this were true...

The being flared with crimson flames.

"My other self. My counterpart. He has no place in this or any other universe. We must be reunited. I must reabsorb him."

He glanced around at the Warlord's chamber and at the field that restrained him.

"I should have realized what had happened before. But I was disoriented by my sudden reawakening, and from the separation. Disoriented...and foolish..."

A strange melancholy seemed to fall over the strange creature then. His fires dipped low.

"But... I do not know how I might go about such a thing," it said, the telepathic voice almost a whisper now.

The Warlord's eyes moved across his array of readouts attached to the sensors.

"You may not have long to concern yourself with such matters," he said.

"Eh?"

Your power levels are not only low, but extremely unstable. Fluctuating dramatically."

The creature seemed to be looking within itself.

"You lie..."

"Not so."

The Warlord turned to a different display panel, studying the information revealed there.

"Your very cohesiveness deteriorates, even as we speak," he said then. "Very soon, at this rate, you will dissipate altogether."

"No!"

The Warlord smiled then, and made his offer.

"Perhaps I could be of assistance in reuniting you with your other half," he said. "I have the expertise, the equipment..."

He strode up close to the field now, leaning in toward the fiery countenance.

"And if you are indeed the legitimate one, the true Kabaraak, and the other is nothing more than a fiction, masquerading as you, and stealing half your power—perhaps even your very life..."

"Yes!"

The crimson being flared, its telepathic voice booming. It moved very close to the edge of the restraining field, mere inches away from the Warlord, its hands bunched into fists.

"The other half—it is a fiction," it raged. "*I* am Kabaraak! Only I truly exist. The other—it is weak, a nothing. It must be reabsorbed within my form!"

It locked the Warlord's gaze with its own.

"Hear me well. Our differences are meaningless as of this moment. My only goal is the capture of my counterpart, that I might merge with him. Free me, help me to find and reabsorb the other, and I will grant you a favor—whatever you wish. But my aspect must be mine alone to control. The other must be reabsorbed before its physical integrity—and mine!—are lost forever."

Behind his impassive silver mask, the Warlord grinned. *This is all working out just splendidly*, he thought to himself.

20

Esro Brachis's home, located in the northern Virginia suburbs of Washington, DC, was far more than just a house.

It was, in fact, a complex arrangement of laboratories, garages, warehouses, workshops, and even a hangar, situated next to a small, private airfield.

At the edge of the property sat Esro's private residence. Essentially a mansion, it stood well back from the street it fronted. Behind it, and beyond the machine shops and labs, empty fields stretched all the way to the low hills that lay more than a mile away.

Esro enjoyed his privacy.

Now, in a heavily shielded chamber adjacent to the large lab that occupied the western end of the house, Esro intently watched the numbers on his handheld analyzer. They changed quickly, then slowed, then stopped. Smiling, he looked up at the strange being that sat back in a heavy steel chair, seemingly unconscious, surrounded by equipment. Then he looked back at Ultraa and Lyn, who stood nervously behind him, watching.

"I have him stabilized, I think. For a while there, it was touch-and-go."

Ultraa studied the unmoving blue figure.

"Still catatonic, though."

Esro nodded.

"I've tried a few things, but no luck so far. I've been nervous about trying anything more to wake him up, until I was sure he would even survive."

Esro led them out of the small chamber and back into the main lab, sealing a heavy door behind them. He flipped several switches on the wall next to the door, watching the indicator lights all change from red to green.

Lyn pursed her lips, deep in thought. For once, she wore only the golden body stocking, having decided she was finally comfortable enough with her two new associates to wear it, and not feel the need to constantly cover herself up further.

She glanced over at Ultraa. He wore a clean version of his white and red costume—the only thing Lyn had ever seen him wear, she realized. Idly, she wondered how many copies of it he owned. He sat hunched over on a stool, face in hands, as if suddenly very tired.

"Ultraa, why don't you go home and get some rest?"

He raised his head, meeting her gaze, an odd look crossing his face.

"No, I'm okay. I'll hang around here a bit longer."

"Where do you live, anyway?" she asked suddenly. "I've never thought to ask before."

"Here and there," he replied. "The government provides me a small place in the District. And Esro has been good enough to offer me a guest room here, from time to time."

Lyn nodded.

"But...where's your home? You know—your hometown, your family, all that?"

Ultraa glanced at her for a moment, his expression betraying his extreme discomfort with the line of conversation, and then he turned back to Esro.

"You have him stabilized," he said, "but is there any danger to us? Explosion, radiation, whatever?"

"No, I think we're fine on that score," Esro replied. "And I'm working on something else to help him..."

Lyn frowned. She was somewhat bothered by the way Ultraa had simply ignored her question and started talking to Esro. She hadn't meant to get too personal with him... And, after all, she was working with him on an almost daily basis, now... But didn't most people enjoy talking about their family, their hometown, and so forth? It was as if he didn't want to talk about it—or as if he couldn't.

She frowned at that thought. *Couldn't?*

81

Nothing to be gained from pressing him on it now. *File that troubling thought away for later*, she thought to herself. *If ever.*

At that moment, the door to the lab swung open and a man in gold and silver chain mail, wearing a red bandana on his head, raced through, taking the steps down into the lab three at a time.

"Damon!"

Damon Sinclair came to a sudden halt at the bottom of the stairs as Esro called his name. He bowed low, with a flourish, and grinned. Seeing Lyn, standing there in her tight golden outfit, his grin widened. Straightening, he walked over to her, taking her hand and slowly bringing it to his lips.

"You must be Lyn," he said. "I've heard so much about you."

"Hi," Lyn said nervously.

As he released her hand, she drew it back, bemused.

"Where have you been?" Esro demanded.

Ultraa just glowered at him.

"Oh, sorry," Damon replied. "One of those lady reporters I was talking to, out in Bay City—"

He glanced at Lyn, who was now frowning.

"Um, she needed help, so I, um…"

"Help with what?" Esro asked, enjoying Damon's sudden discomfort.

"She, ah, thought the Mind Monkeys were staking out her apartment building, so I hung around a couple of days, you know, to make sure she was okay."

Lyn raised an eyebrow at this.

"The Mind Monkeys. Right," Esro breathed. "Anyway, I'm glad you're finally back. I have something for you."

Damon perked up.

"Yeah? What?"

"Be right back."

Esro strode into the room next door.

Damon turned to Lyn again.

"Reporters," he said scornfully. "So, Esro said you were a college student. Really smart. And with some kind of cool powers, too."

"Esro told you that, huh? And what did Ultraa tell you?"

Damon glanced back at the blond man, who had silently slid his stool further away and was sitting patiently, staying out of the conversation.

"Ultraa doesn't tell me a whole lot. About anything, really."

"Is that so?"

Lyn turned away from Damon, toward Ultraa, and mouthed a silent "Thank you."

One corner of his mouth turned ever so slightly upward.

At that moment a chirping sound came from the lab table nearby. Lyn reached over and picked up her phone where she had left it, looking at the screen.

"Ah, Amy!"

She started up the stairs.

"Nice to meet you," she called back to Damon.

He watched her lithe golden form climbing the steps, his eyes wide.

"Uh, yeah, same here," he said.

"Don't even think about it," Ultraa told him softly.

Damon blinked, looking back at Ultraa.

"Too young. Too...not you."

Damon frowned.

"Yeah... Fine..."

But he couldn't resist looking back one last time as she passed through the doorway and closed it behind her.

21

"Amy! I'm so glad to hear from you!"

Back in the residence, Lyn plopped happily into a lounge chair, phone to one ear.

"I know it's only been a few days," Amy said, "but I had to see how you're doing out on the East Coast."

"A few days?" Lyn sighed. "It seems more like a few months."

"A few months good or a few months bad?"

Lyn laughed.

"I'm not really sure yet. Maybe a little of both."

"Hmm. How about your new boss?"

"Esro? He's cool."

Then she wrinkled her nose.

"Actually, he can be annoying sometimes, but I guess that comes with genius."

"Not that boss," Amy said. "The other one."

"Ultraa? He's not really my boss. I'm working for Esro, as an assistant, you know. He signs my paychecks, anyway."

"Yeah, but, still…" She laughed. "I know about the whole 'double life' thing."

"Double life? What are you—?"

"The whole 'training to be a hero' thing."

Lyn sighed.

"I am not a hero. Far from it."

"You have powers."

"Well, yeah. But—"

"Do you have a costume yet?"

"No! I—"

She looked down at herself, clad only in the shining, golden mesh body stocking that contained and regulated her powers.

"Well…sort of…"

"I knew it!"

"Gaaaah!"

Amy laughed again.

"So, do you have a heroic-sounding code name yet?"

"Look, Amy, that's not the point here."

"Do you? I'll bet you do!"

Lyn waited patiently, knowing there was no pushing Amy off the subject until she had exhausted it to her satisfaction.

"Let me guess… Something space-related, I'll bet. Star Girl! No, there's already one of those. Hmm. Sun Girl! No, too chipper—you would never go for that. Quasar! No, not girly enough for you. Hmmm… Pulsar!"

Lyn held the phone to her ear with her shoulder while she rubbed her eyes with her fists. "Yeah, that's it," she replied sarcastically. "Pulsar. Sure. Whatever."

"Pulsar. I like it. Nice choice, Lyn."

"Yeah, great. Can we change the subject now?"

"Sure," Ami replied, apparently oblivious to Lyn's annoyance.

"So, have you found a new roommate yet?"

Amy snorted. "I didn't know how good I had it with you, roomie. Bay City College isn't exactly running over with potential Lyn Li replacements."

Lyn smiled.

"So," her friend continued, "how's Georgetown?"

"Well…" Lyn frowned. "I haven't really started classes yet. I've been really busy. Maybe next semester…"

"Too busy fighting crime or something?" her friend scolded. "You'd better get back to cracking the books!"

"What are you—my mother, all of a sudden?"

"You better listen to me, young lady," Amy shot back, doing her usual perfect imitation of Lyn's mom, "I know what's good for you!"

Lyn laughed for a few seconds, along with her friend, then sobered.

"Listen, Amy, you're wanting to know about Ultraa, and I can understand that. But… there's just not much to tell—at least not yet. He's very private. Keeps to himself. I don't know, what it is, exactly… But he's more... *secretive* than I'd expected. I like working with him a lot, but there's something..."

"Lyn, the man's a hero—a national icon. Let him have his secrets."

Slowly, reluctantly, Lyn nodded. "Yeah, I guess so..."

"But if you should happen to, y'know, see him naked, or anything…"

Lyn laughed.

"You'll be the first to know. I promise."

The Warlord stood in an arrogant pose on the deck of his personal flyer, as it soared away from the great floating city and moved out over the miles-high drop to the wilderness below. His blue and purple cloak flared out behind him in the wind.

"The crews have been on double shifts for a week now, Master," Francisco told him, from where he sat at the controls. He rubbed his little hands together. "They will have everything in place within a matter of days."

"It should have been done already," the Warlord snapped. "Push them harder. Use the telepathic controls—make them believe they want to work longer and harder! We can always replace those who don't survive."

He leaned out over the rail, staring down at the tremendous cables that trailed from the bottom of the city and spiraled down to connect with enormous gray buildings that housed the generators and regulating systems. Beneath those buildings, shafts sunk deep below this planet's surface, drawing vast power up and out, most of it channeled into the Warlord's flying fortress, at the top of the mile-high central tower. There, he could tap into it whenever he needed, from wherever he was.

"This will be enough power, will it not, Master?" Francisco asked nervously. "Surely, an entire world's energies should be sufficient for your plans to—"

"Not nearly enough," the man in the silver mask shot back. "Nowhere near enough, for what I will do."

He moved away from the rail, directing Francisco to head back to the fortress.

"Soon, though, I will have complete control of Kabaraak. The humans have no idea what he is, and now they will never know. Once I control both of his forms I can reunite them myself, under conditions only I shall control. I will drain him of his power. Then, when his master arrives, I will steal *his* vast energies, as well. And then—"

He laughed, the sound echoing from the skyscrapers all around them.

"—and then, no one in the multiverse can stand before me. The infernal, eternal cycle will end at last. The Grand Design will be realized. No more Warlords! None but me, forever!"

The flyer lofted back up to the fortress and the Warlord's sanctum. Francisco cringed, hoping for the best for his mad master, but fearing the worst—as usual.

23

Esro fitted the last component in place and locked the seals.
"How does it fit?"
Damon moved his arms around, then took a few steps forward.
"Not too bad..."
"Here."
Esro handed him a gray metal helmet.
Damon took it, looked it over. He pointed to a metal piece that curved down from the right ear to the front of the face, covering the area where the mouth would be, below the two rectangular eyeholes.

"What's this part?"

"Communications array," Esro said.

"Oh."

He turned the helmet over, pointed to the thin antenna that protruded up a few inches from the left ear area.

"And this?"

"What does it look like?" Esro shot back.

Damon frowned.

"It looks dorky."

Esro frowned.

"Do you want to be able to communicate with other people while you're inside there?"

"Well, yeah."

"Then don't worry about how it looks. Just put it on."

"Fine," Damon said. He pulled the helmet over his head and locked it in place. The first thing he said then was, "How's it all look?"

Esro inhaled deeply, closed his eyes, and counted to ten. When he opened his eyes again, his wish had not come true: Damon was still there. He sighed.

"Something wrong?" Damon asked, his voice now broadcasting over a speaker incorporated into the helmet.

Esro put the person in the suit out of his mind, stepped back and focused on the armor itself. A smile slowly spread over his face.

Damon wore Esro's latest creation: A suit of ultra-high-tech armor, made of gray metal components fastened in place over a black body stocking. The boots contained rockets; weapons could unfold from the gauntlets. The helmet's communications and sensor system were the best Esro could fit into such a small space. And the armor's generator could also power an energy screen to rival anything Lyn could produce.

"It looks beautiful," Esro said, with a fatherly smile.

"I don't know," Damon said. "It's a little clunky. And how am I supposed to use my electro-sword inside all this?"

Esro shook his head.

"You won't need the electro-sword. Or the skycycle."

"What?"

"You wanted to be a knight," Esro said, patting the armor lovingly. "Well, here you are. Everything you need is in here."

Damon unfastened the helmet and pulled it off. He was frowning.

"I don't know, Esro—I kinda like the cycle and the other stuff. And the helmet…"

"Yeah?"

"It covers up my face, man!"

Within his mind, Esro earnestly debated the wisdom of punching a man wearing super-high-tech armor.

Behind them, the door opened and Lyn entered. She paused in mid-step, looking at Damon in the armor.

"…Interesting," she muttered.

Damon frowned. He turned back to Esro.

"See? The ladies don't dig it!"

"No, no, it's great," Lyn said. "Put the helmet on."

Hesitating at first, Damon pulled the helmet back on.

"Yeah—perfect," Lyn said.

With a huff, Damon pulled the helmet off and tossed it to Esro.

"Back to the drawing board, man."

Esro glared at him, then set the helmet carefully on the lab table.

"It's just fine like it is," he said, but he picked up a screwdriver and started unscrewing panels.

"Hang on," Damon said.

Esro paused, looking up at him.

"What?"

"I have to run to the rest room."

Esro sighed. He sat back in his chair and put down the screwdriver.

"Fine."

"Hey," Damon said. "Not my fault you didn't build some kind of system into this armor for—"

"Fine, fine," Esro growled, waving a hand. He didn't want to go there at the moment. "I'll figure something out."

"Good," Damon replied. "I wouldn't want to electrocute myself in here, by accident."

He ducked out of the lab, heading back into the mansion, while Esro picked up the helmet again and started tinkering.

Lyn walked across to where Ultraa sat.

"I'll bet it's like this a lot between them," she said quietly.

"Absolutely," he replied with a smile.

Snorting, she shook her head.

"Oh, I've been meaning to tell you this," he said, running a hand back through his thick, blond hair. "You need a code name."

She looked back at him, surprised.

"I do?"

Ultraa nodded.

"If you're going to be training with me, as we've discussed, then the government will need to list you on the books—"

"Books? What books?"

Ultraa frowned.

"Just their standard records of all agents in their service."

"I'll be in their service?"

"Working with me," he replied, "you already are."

"Ah."

She gestured over to where Esro sat and Damon had been standing.

"What're their code names, then?"

Esro looked up.

"Damon calls himself 'the Cavalier,'" he said, with only a hint of scorn.

"And do you have one?" Lyn asked.

"Brachis," Esro said.

Lyn looked at him quizzically.

"But—that's your name."

"Yeah. So?"

"It's your real name!"

"I am aware of that, yes," he replied, nodding.

"But—that can't be your code name!"

"Who says?"

"Um… I do!"

"Well, then," he replied with a smile, "I'm glad your vote doesn't count."

Lyn frowned.

"That doesn't seem fair—that you get to use your own name."

He shrugged.

Ultraa suppressed a laugh.

"I still need your code name," he told her.

She huffed.

"I guess 'Li' is out, then, huh?"

Smiling, he nodded.

Desperately she searched her mind, hitting at last upon a name that floated up, unbidden, from her memory.

"Pulsar," she blurted.

"Pulsar," Ultraa repeated. He nodded. "Fine."

Then she realized where it had come from.

Amy. Oh, no. No way.

"Wait a sec," she said, raising her hand.

"Good one," Esro said. "Nice."

"Yeah," Ultraa agreed.

"But—but I—"

"Pulsar it is," Ultraa said, standing and climbing the stairs, disappearing into the next room. The door closed behind him.

"But…"

Lyn sighed.

I'm Pulsar.

24

"He's finally coming across with the good stuff, boss."

Jameson winced.

"I've told you before. Do not call me 'boss.' 'Mr. Jameson' will be fine."

"Right."

A long pause, during which Jameson felt his blood pressure rise. At last, he could wait no longer.

"So, what exactly do you mean by 'the good stuff?'" he prompted, holding back his anger at the operative as best he could.

"More than just gadgets," the voice over the secure line replied.

Jameson nodded to himself.

"Yes, yes, but—such as what?"

A pause.

"Well…I'm not too fond of it, so far, but you'll probably love it."

Jameson waited, drawing little squares on the pad on his desk, bearing down harder and harder.

"Like, for example," the operative finally said, "a force field projection system ten times stronger than anything you've got."

In spite of himself, Jameson began to smile.

"Go on."

"Communications systems, super-miniaturized. Some interesting particle-beam weapons. And a boot propulsion system that's just what you've been looking for."

"You have no idea what I've been looking for."

"I think I probably do."

Jameson let that go.

"Excellent," he said. "Keep pressing for more. I want to get my money's worth—the taxpayers' money's worth, of course—out of our contract with Brachis."

"Sure."

"In fact," Jameson continued, "before you inevitably slip up and reveal something you shouldn't to Brachis or his friends, you should go ahead and download the contents of his databases into the high-compression data crystal I gave you."

Silence.

"You do still have the data crystal, don't you?"

"What, you think I lost it at poker or something? Of course I do."

"Fine. Then do that immediately, at first opportunity. I don't like the idea of Brachis holding things back from us." He inhaled deeply, exhaled slowly. "Afterwards, you can continue to concentrate on field-testing his innovations for the Cavalier Project."

"I'm not just 'field testing,' boss. I *am* the Cavalier."

Jameson's face twisted in a sneer.

"Of course you are, Damon. Of course."

He hung up the connection, paused a moment, then glared at the telephone.

"Don't call me 'boss!'"

25

The explosion that came just minutes later shattered a large section of the roof of Esro Brachis's mansion. Fragments of debris flew like shrapnel, even as huge support beams collapsed and internal walls shattered and came crashing down.

Brachis pulled himself up slowly from the wreckage, stunned. He looked around, trying to make sense of what had happened.

He saw that Damon was already up, and no doubt thankful for the first time that he was wearing the armor; although the trail of blood running down his forehead should make him regret the fact that the helmet had not been in place as well.

Glancing over, Brachis saw Lyn, surrounded by a glowing sphere of light. *She got her force field up in time. Thank goodness,* he thought, even as he followed her gaze up through the huge hole in the ceiling.

Oh, man. What hit us?

The flame-wreathed form of a man hovered in midair above the gaping hole, glaring down at them.

"You cannot hide him from me!" came the booming voice, stunning all below.

On the other side of the room, the door opened and Ultraa rushed in.

"What in the—?"

He glanced about in surprise before spotting the attacker hovering above.

"I am Kabaraak! I demand my counterpart," the blazing creature screamed, descending in a cascade of flame. "Bring him to me now!"

Ultraa stepped forward. "Now listen—"

"Die, human!"

Twin beams of energy lanced out from the creature's eyes, lashing into Ultraa and sending him to his knees. As the onslaught ceased, Ultraa fell forward on all fours, shaking.

Lyn knelt beside him, her face contorted in horror.

"Most impressive, human," Kabaraak growled. "You still live. But I will—"

Damon leapt at him, swinging his armored fists. His blow, electronically assisted, hurled the creature backwards, smashing Kabaraak into an already weakened wall, which collapsed on top of him.

Retrieving his helmet, Damon locked it in place, then ran toward the spot where the attacker had fallen.

The blow that met him shook the house to the foundations. Damon came flying backwards, just missing Brachis, and crashed through the opposite wall.

The creature stepped out of the rubble, confronting Brachis.

"Oh, jeez," Esro breathed, backing up a step, patting his lab coat's pockets, searching for weapons.

Damon was back then, pushing Esro to the side and swinging to deliver another punch.

Kabaraak shot one arm out, catching Damon's gray fist. Then, with his other arm, the creature grasped the helmet, flaming fingers splayed out across the faceplate. He held Damon up off the floor in this manner, legs dangling.

"Your screens," Brachis shouted to him. "Use your energy screens!"

Damon flailed about desperately.

"The power indicators are dropping," came his electronically projected voice, filled with panic. "He's draining away my reserves!"

Kabaraak and Esro both turned as a golden sphere of energy flew between them. It crashed into the blazing creature and shoved him back a step.

"Put him down!"

Lyn stood between the still-injured Ultraa and the others, her electromagnetic power manifested as a swirling, glowing nimbus about her. Before she could act again, however, the same eye-beams that had struck Ultraa lashed out at her. With a cry, she redoubled the portion of her field in front of her, saw its outermost surface shatter, and then watched as the beams slowly sliced in toward her, shredding the golden light in their path.

"No!"

Ultraa had his wits about him now and he moved like lightning, up from his knees and across the room, a battering ram rushing toward the enemy. Too slow—he passed through the flaming creature as if it wasn't there, although the maneuver did cause Kabaraak to release Damon's unmoving form.

"Die, stubborn human!"

The creature's eyes flared, destructive beams lashing out yet again, slashing at Ultraa's unprotected back as he went past.

They never struck him.

Ultraa whirled around, hovering in midair, looking for what could have saved him.

Through the hole in the ceiling descended the blue-silver metallic form of Vanadium, radiating power and might.

Kabaraak stared up at the metal figure, confronting this new threat.

"You. You deflected my strike somehow. How did you do that?"

By way of reply, Vanadium brought up one hand, energy crackling around it. Before the fiery being could react, the hand had seized him by the neck.

"Nooo! How—?"

The creature unleashed yet another volley of eye beams, this time point-blank into Vanadium's face, but the beams deflected harmlessly away.

"You are now neutralized," Vanadium stated in a flat, emotionless voice. *"Cease your struggles."*

Kabaraak raised his right hand, staring at it. The fingers had almost faded away. The rest of the hand was growing dim, indistinct.

"You—you've caused this!"

Vanadium continued to clutch the creature in an iron grip.

"No," it wailed. "Too soon! I had more time!"

"Your time is up."

Vanadium tightened his grip. The flames around the attacker's form abated, nearly going out.

"Not quite, I'm afraid."

Everyone had been staring at the confrontation between the fiery being and Vanadium. No one had witnessed the silent arrival of the blue-and-purple-clad Warlord across the room.

The Warlord gestured, and the fiery aura around Kabaraak suddenly flared back to life.

With a jolt, Vanadium stumbled backwards, releasing his grip on the other's neck.

"Not this guy again," Esro growled. Quickly he moved to a nearby control panel and typed in a string of commands, then studied the display and nodded grimly.

Lyn, drawing on what little she had learned of her powers thus far, summoned up an electromagnetic bubble to encapsulate the Warlord. But before she could project it around him, the Warlord raised a hand, laughing.

"No, no, restrain yourself, my dear. I'm not here to fight you. Let me just retrieve what my associate here could not, and we shall be on our way."

The Warlord gestured. Nothing happened. Seemingly concerned, he gestured again, then stared at a small indicator on his gauntlet.

"Ah. I see. Very good, Mr. Brachis."

Esro smiled grimly back at him.

"I could, of course, simply force my way in," the Warlord said.

Vanadium moved like lightning, much faster than someone so big and bulky should have been able to move. He closed the distance between himself and the Warlord in a flash, crashing into the cloaked figure and smashing him back, driving him to the floor.

Esro moved quickly to see what was happening. The two big men wrestled about, Vanadium grasping the Warlord by the wrists

"You are now neutralized. Cease your struggles."

and keeping him down. A pale, blue light shone down from Vanadium's eyes, washing briefly over the Warlord.

"Accomplished," the cold voice of the metal man said, just barely loud enough for Brachis to overhear.

Then the Warlord had kicked Vanadium aside and sprang to his feet again, advancing on the door to the other chamber.

Ultraa and Lyn moved to stand in front of the armored door. A second later, Vanadium was up again and joined them.

The Warlord stood still a moment, as if contemplating this; as if considering the amount of power arrayed against him. Then he grasped a unit on his belt, and the familiar glow surrounded him.

"Round two to you, then."

The glow radiated out from his body, spreading over the fiery being as well.

"Come, Kabaraak. I fear you have lost the element of surprise, and the arrival of this newcomer was unforeseen. Things could only grow unpleasant, if we continue now. There are easier ways."

With a flash, both the Warlord and Kabaraak vanished.

Vanadium stood unmoving for a long moment, staring at the spot where the flaming figure had stood. Then he turned and walked to the heavy reinforced door to the chamber where the other fiery being lay. He reached out with one hand, then stopped abruptly, as if he had encountered some invisible barrier. Leaning forward, he peered through the small window.

Ultraa, apparently more injured than he had let on, sank to one knee. Lyn helped him back up. Together they bent over the unmoving, armored form of Damon.

"You okay in there?" Ultraa asked.

The reply was weak, as if coming from far away.

"Yeah, I'm pretty much okay... The armor's dead, though. Frozen up."

Esro walked over, looked down at Damon's immobile form and suppressed a laugh.

"Um," Damon said finally, "you guys going to keep staring at me, or you wanna get me out of here?"

26

The Warlord's spherical flying fortress hovered above a lonely stretch of the Rocky Mountains. Invisible to most means of detection, it floated on four anti-gravity pods attached to long metal arms. For as long as the Warlord had business in this universe, he would keep the fortress within easy teleportation range. When the need arose, the entire complex could move itself...*elsewhere*.

Inside, Kabaraak lay within a crystal globe, numerous cables and instruments attached to its outside. Crimson waves of energy washed over him, bathing him in an unearthly glow.

The Warlord stood nearby, gauntleted hands clutched behind his back, gazing up at his monitors.

"You failed, Kabaraak. You could not defeat the humans, much less free your counterpart."

The flickering, flamelike eyes glared back.

"Given time, I would have slain them all," he growled. "Yet, the new one...Vanadium. I know him, somehow. He is different. His technology—his power..."

"Who is he, then? His technology, his abilities—where does he come from?"

Kabaraak raised a fist and smashed it down angrily.

"I *know*, but...I cannot *remember*."

"I knew of you, of course," the Warlord said, pacing in frustration. "In my travels, in my studies, I have found many references to you... and to your master."

"The master. I... I had nearly forgotten..."

"You signaled him," the Warlord said. "Or so you told me, earlier. If you did, he is surely on his way here."

"Yes," Kabaraak said, looking up, brightening.

"He will probably not arrive in time to save you," the Warlord stated matter-of-factly.

Kabaraak frowned and gazed down at the chamber floor. Silence reigned for a time, and Francisco watched from the shadows, tense, waiting to see what happened next.

"I cannot prevail now," the fiery creature said finally. "I see that. I lack the energy to battle the humans and the other one again, or to reclaim my counterpart." His eyes moved from the Warlord back down to the floor. "Let me die in peace."

"No," the Warlord said. "Not so. You will survive. You will face them again."

He patted the crystal globe that surrounded Kabaraak.

"This vessel will replenish your energy and restore your physical integrity."

"Indeed?"

The flames leapt up in intensity. Kabaraak looked about him as if seeing his surroundings for the first time, then looked back at the Warlord.

"You do this for me?"

"Yes."

"Then I will have another chance."

"Oh, yes. You will yet capture your counterpart, and reunite with him. And thus regain your physical cohesion, and the full extent of your powers."

Kabaraak closed his eyes.

"Allow me this opportunity, and I will do as you ask," he said. "No deceptions."

The Warlord nodded.

"You shall have that chance. Now rest. Soon, you will be yourself once more. And then—"

He smiled again as he walked out the doorway.

"—then we can turn to the subject of your debt to me."

Cursing, Brachis switched off the high-powered saw, the sound of its motor dropping and fading away. He looked down at his lab table in disgust. It was covered with the smoking remains of the armor he had created—or what was left of it after he had cut it off of Damon.

"And I'd just gotten it working right," he growled.

"It did keep me alive," Damon pointed out.

"I'm not convinced that was a good thing," Esro shot back.

Damon sulked.

"Whatever."

He sat on a stool next to Esro, poking at the components with a screwdriver.

Esro unrolled a couple of schematic diagrams on the table and angrily pointed to them.

"You had weapons, Damon! And defenses."

He smacked the drawings with one hand.

"The armor would have done a lot more than just keep you alive if you'd used it correctly."

"Hey, I used it just fine! Didn't you see me take that guy down once?"

Esro rounded on him.

"You punched him. *Punched* him!"

"Yeah! That's the idea, right? Punch the bad guys!"

Esro shook his head, groaning.

"The main ideas behind this suit are energy field generation and distance weapons! It's not freaking plate mail!"

Damon frowned.

"Sorry, Esro," he said, gazing down at his feet. "I never really had a chance to learn how it worked, though, y'know?"

Esro stepped back, his hands on his hips, looking around at all the damage. He took a deep breath and turned back to Damon again.

"Yeah. You're right. It's not your fault. I'm just angry. But, I mean—look at my house!"

He kicked at some of the rubble—rubble that had been expensive, super-advanced equipment.

"Yeah, I'd be upset, too," Damon said, nodding.

"You all did well," Vanadium said, from where he stood near the heavy, reinforced door to the smaller chamber.

The others had nearly forgotten about him, given his silence and their preoccupation with digging out of the wreckage.

"We…we appreciate your help, before," Esro said, taking the opportunity to study him again. What he really wanted was to get the big guy on an examination table and have a long look at that armor. *If armor's what it is,* he thought to himself. *Could that be…him? All there is to him? Could such a thing even be possible?*

He stared at the metal man's strange form, the entire body gleaming silver with a blue cast to it. Lines and creases seemed to indicate the spots where gloves and boots connected to the rest of the arms and legs, yet that impression was not entirely distinct. Two tiny red lights shone in dark pits where the eyes should be; the rest of the face was blank.

Not possible with any technology available on this world, Esro concluded.

He frowned, a strange sense of unease creeping over him.

The cold, impassive metal face turned toward him. His eyes, those tiny, flickering red lights in pools of black, seemed to bore into him.

"The creature must be subdued," the cold, impersonal voice intoned. *"Removed from this world."*

Esro took this in, nodding.

"I would tend to agree that he needs subduing, yeah, but— 'removed from this world?' What do you mean?"

Vanadium said nothing, merely turning back to look in through the small window at the unconscious, fiery man where it sat, apparently unconscious.

Esro frowned. Giving up on getting anything further from the enigmatic metal man for the moment, he turned back to his worktable, squinting at his schematics.

Ultraa walked over and clapped him on the back.

"So, what was the guy, the Warlord, talking about, before? When he congratulated you?"

"Yeah, I was wondering that, too," Lyn said, coming up behind them.

"Well," Brachis coughed, "I assume he meant the shielding I installed."

"Shielding?"

Ultraa glanced toward the big metal doorway that separated the lab they occupied from the smaller room, containing Kabaraak's comatose counterpart.

"You mean—?"

"His little teleportation trick. He couldn't just zap himself in there."

Slowly, Ultraa smiled.

"Ah. Nice. I was sort of wondering why he didn't just do that— why he appeared out here—if the... person ... in there is what he wants."

"I wasn't sure it would work," Esro said. "It's good to know his technology has some kind of limits. I have more expertise in shielding than just about anything else, and I guess, for now, it was more than this 'Warlord' could handle."

Ultraa nodded.

"Defense is good. You've done very well. But we can't afford to sit back and be targets anymore."

Esro looked at him, eyes wide.

"What are you saying?"

Ultraa crossed his arms, his square jaw set.

"We have to go on the attack," he said. "Immediately."

Esro gaped at him.

"Seriously?" Lyn asked, eyes wide.

"Um, look, pal," Esro said, "you know I trust your combat sense more than anyone else in the world. But—in this particular case—I have to ask: Are you nuts?"

"No," Ultraa said firmly, "we have to do it. And now is the time."

Esro looked to Damon, who was grinning his gleaming white smile.

"He sure won't be expecting us to come after him first," the young daredevil said.

"Because it's nuts?" Lyn countered.

"No, no—it makes sense," Damon said. "Not that I'm dying to run off and fight that guy again, of course, but... yeah, you know he'll be back anyway. So—why not?"

Lyn frowned. "Yeah, I guess that's true."

"You're *all* nuts," Esro said, shaking his head. "And we don't even know where he is, or how to get to him."

"And that's where you come in, buddy," Ultraa said, squeezing Esro's shoulder.

Brachis groaned.

"Find us a way, Esro," Ultraa said, now very serious. "Find us a way to get to him."

He looked at the others. They all nodded.

"We have to carry the fight to the Warlord."

28

An observer watching the Warlord's flying fortress would have seen that it had landed at last. It had settled into a space at the top of a mile-high tower that extended up through layers of pink and purple clouds and into a starless sky. That tower occupied the center of a gargantuan circle, which was itself a city. The observer, pulling back still further, would see that this vast city, in fact, *floated*.

The Warlord's city—the Warlord's kingdom—hovered above a sea of clouds in a pocket universe far from any other part of reality. It was his own private cosmos, and he was its absolute lord and master, its thousands of inhabitants his mind-controlled slaves.

In the central control room, the Warlord stared at a viewscreen intently, watching as a golden armored figure and a pair of taller, silvery robots did battle with one another in a very alien environment.

"This being—this golden Knight—fascinates me, Francisco."

The servant bowed his head. "Yes, Master. Your many incarnations always seem drawn to it—you yourself have watched it several times already, yes?"

The Warlord glared down at him.

"What of it?"

"Nothing! Nothing, Master," Francisco whined, backing away slightly. "I was merely pointing out that you are always fascinated by the historical records of this Knight."

Returning his attention to the monitors, the Warlord nodded distractedly. "Yes. Yes, it is true. This golden, armored giant—he possesses enormous power. And yet I cannot locate him in any layer of the multiverse now. And that is a shame. He would make a perfect servant. He could perform whatever tasks I assigned, for as long as I needed him—and then, when the time came, I could drain that vast reserve of power away."

"But he has vanished, yes?"

"Sadly, that is true. All of the old Knights have vanished." He growled deep in his throat. "I would not have wished to face even one of them in combat—not that they could defeat me, of course—but I would have enjoyed the opportunity to steal their energies and study their technology."

Francisco chewed his lip, pondering this.

"Thus I am left with inferior servants," the Warlord sighed at last.

Francisco started to respond, then hesitated as he considered if the Warlord had been talking about *him*. Deciding such a thing was surely unlikely, he smiled up at his master.

"Actually," he said, "I have assembled some new recruits for you to meet, if—"

Seemingly ignoring him, the Warlord switched off the monitor and stood.

"What is the status of our luminous guest?"

Before Francisco could reply, the Warlord strode into the next room, where Kabaraak stood within his crystal globe.

The fiery creature said nothing, merely glaring at the Warlord, watching as the blue-and-purple-cloaked man adjusted controls and checked instruments. At last, Kabaraak demanded, "How much longer must I remain here? How long until you do as you promised, and restore my power?"

The Warlord looked up at him, as if surprised that he had spoken. He smiled.

"Actually," he said, "the process is complete. Your energies are completely replenished. Your physical cohesion is restored."

The Warlord manipulated a control and the globe separated, each half sliding down into the floor. The flaming form of Kabaraak stood there, free and somewhat startled. Cautiously at first, he extended his radiant aura outward.

"Yes—I feel it. I am whole!"

The Warlord nodded in satisfaction.

"Well," Kabaraak growled. "My respect for your prowess has grown."

The Warlord ignored this, saying instead, "Now you must seek out your counterpart and absorb him, in order to regain the totality of your powers and permanently stabilize your form."

"Yes! Whether I absorb him into myself or simply take what I need and then annihilate him, one way or another, we shall have a reckoning between us!"

The Warlord stared down at the floor a moment, his features hidden behind his ever-present faceplate.

"And one other thing you can do for me, in repayment," he said to the blazing man. "The humans—Ultraa and Esro Brachis and the others who work with them. Those who currently hold your counterpart hostage."

Kabaraak eyed him suspiciously. "Yes?"

"Destroy them. Slay them all."

The fiery man stared back at the Warlord for a moment, clearly considering this.

"You wish the humans destroyed?" he asked then. "Fine. If they seek to impede my mission—if they get in my way—this time they will surely die."

Behind his mask, the Warlord darkened at this.

"Even if they don't—"

"Ask nothing else of me, mortal!" Kabaraak glared at the Warlord, cosmic flames flaring brightly all around him. "What care I for human matters? Farewell!"

With a tremendous flash, the fiery being flared up through the ceiling and was gone.

Francisco eyed the Warlord warily.

"Master—you're letting him go? You trust him to do as you have asked?"

"Asked? I commanded! But, whether he kills the humans or not, I have other concerns that are far more pressing. Only if he succeeds in reuniting with his counterpart will he warrant my further attention. As he presently exists, with his cohesion problems, he is of little value to me."

"Cohesion problems? But I thought you had solved that for him?"

"Only temporarily, Francisco. If he does not soon reunite with his other half, he will utterly disintegrate."

The little man took this in, nodding slowly.

"Even so, Master," Francisco said after a moment, "a being of such power—dare you let him out of your control, even for only a short time?"

"The Warlord fears no one!"

Cloak sweeping behind him, he stalked across the room and stared up at a row of display monitors. Each of them depicted a different view of Kabaraak soaring through the skies of Earth. Then, calming, the Warlord continued, "Besides...our fiery friend will soon find that he has underestimated me, and my 'prowess,' as he put it, once again."

He smiled.

"Now, I believe you said you have some new recruits for me?"

"You *can* do it, though, can't you?"

"I'm honestly not sure, Ultraa," Esro said, leaning over his banks of computer controls, working feverishly. "That Warlord guy did leave behind a distinct energy signature, as did the other one. But it doesn't seem to lead in any real direction..."

Ultraa frowned, looking over Esro's shoulder at the monitors.

"No direction? But they obviously went *somewhere*."

"It looked like it, alright," Esro agreed. "But the trail just vanishes. For a while it seems to have been concentrated over the Rocky Mountains... But now, it looks almost as if it turned a sharp corner into... somewhere else."

"Somewhere else?"

"Some other universe. A different reality."

Ultraa stepped back, glancing at Lyn. She shrugged back at him, as lost as he was.

"You're saying that the Warlord escaped by traveling to a different universe."

"Pretty much, yeah," Esro said.

Ultraa considered this. Such a concept was not entirely new to him—he had faced quite a few unusual foes, in only the past couple of years. Even so, it seemed bizarre.

"So we're really doing this?" Lyn asked. "We're really going after him?"

Ultraa nodded.

"He's too dangerous to remain at large, and we don't know what he's up to," Ultraa said. "We have to carry the fight to him. We have to take him down *now*, before he can do any more damage. Before he comes back here and kills us all in our sleep!"

"I don't know," Lyn said worriedly. "It sounded good in theory, earlier, but now..."

"No, Ultraa's right," Esro said to Lyn. "He's convinced me. If we can find a way that we can be the ones doing the surprising, for a change, we should go for it."

Lyn took this in without comment. Then she pointed at the mass of computerized equipment Esro was feverishly working on.

"But can you do it?"

"I'm trying, I'm trying," he replied, continuing to fine-tune his controls, squinting at the displays.

Heavy footsteps from behind them caused them all to look up and see Vanadium approaching.

"You have something to contribute?" Ultraa asked.

"Perhaps."

The metal man laid a gleaming blue-silver hand on the computer console and stood there, immobile, for several seconds.

The others looked back at him, waiting.

"And what might it be?" Ultraa prompted at last.

Meanwhile, Esro's eyes were widening in surprise.

105

"Hey—I've got something," he said, excitement building in his voice. "The computer has just run through a new batch of calculations—I have no idea where they came from, by the way—and..."

"And you have a fix on the Warlord?" Ultraa prompted.

Esro nodded dumbly. He looked up at the others and said, "I actually think I do, yeah."

Vanadium lifted his hand from the console and stood still, staring at them.

"You," Esro said after a moment, looking back at the blue-silver behemoth. "*You* did that. You did...something..."

The gleaming figure stood there stoically, in silence.

"Wait," Esro said. "I remember now. When we were fighting the Warlord the last time. You had him on the ground, and you said... *accomplished*."

Vanadium looked back at him, impassive, the tiny red lights unmoving, seemingly seeing right through him.

"You did something to him—got a reading on him, or put a tracer on him, or...something."

Vanadium's head twitched slightly to one side, but still he said nothing.

They all stood there for several seconds, and then Ultraa broke the silence.

"Well, whatever happened, you have a lock on the Warlord's position now, right, Esro?"

"Um... yes," Esro replied. He glanced at Vanadium again. "The key word there is 'somehow.'"

"Can you get us there?"

"I—well—that would be—"

The computer pinged.

Esro stared down at the data now displayed on the monitor, eyes wide.

"I—actually, yes." He smiled. "Yes, I can."

All business, Ultraa nodded.

"Then let's go."

30

The Warlord walked down from his control center into the main chamber of his sanctum, his flying fortress, there at the top of his great floating city. The room was vast, containing as it did row after row of super-advanced machinery, computers, and other strange devices beyond the comprehension of man. The ceiling was lost in the dim distance high above, and the other three walls lay more than two hundred yards away. In many ways, the room appeared more like a cave than the high-tech facility it was meant to be—and the Warlord did not have a problem with that.

"Bring them in," he shouted.

"Yes, my Master," Francisco replied happily. The little servant scampered away, returning shortly with four men of various sizes and shapes, all wearing gray and black uniforms and boots.

The Warlord's eyes widened.

"Oh, surely not," he whispered to himself.

"They're called the Wehrmacht," Franscisco replied, bowing deferentially. "They seemed to be the best choices available, yes," he added. "I checked with two of the more…reputable…of the suppliers of manpower, but both the Black Terror and Dr. Zero were otherwise engaged and could not help."

"A pity," the Warlord said. "Thus we are stuck with your own doubtlessly impressive recruits.

Francisco didn't know what to make of that comment. He cast his eyes about frantically a moment, then looked back up at the Warlord, a hopeful expression on his face.

"They have quite a reputation in their home dimension, Master."

The Warlord nodded. Summoning up his commanding stance and air, he walked down the line, looking them over, his blue and purple cloak billowing behind him as he went.

One was older, balding, and wearing an eye patch, but still clearly a tough character. He had to be the leader. Next came a big, musclebound type, with a blunted nose and beady eyes. The remaining two, of rather average build, looked like bookends. All four wore military insignias, including the Iron Cross.

The Warlord shook his head in amusement.

"Francisco, they're Germans. *Again.*"

"Ja, und vat is wrong with that?"

Warlord glanced back at the one who had spoken, the older man with the eye patch.

"I am der Field Marshal, Herr Warlord."

He gestured to the three men to his left.

"This," he said, indicating the big man, "is Artillery."

The hulking figure nodded once.

"Next we have Infantry."

The nearer of the slender, blond men saluted.

"Our final member is Blitzkreig."

Almost a twin of Infantry, he nodded.

"These men," the Field Marshal said, "obey me without question."

The Warlord nodded impatiently.

"I am certain that they do."

"They are the greatest heroes of the Second German Reich!"

The Warlord shook his head slowly.

"The Second German Reich? *Again?*"

He glared at Francisco.

"Remind me to recalibrate the dimensional transporter. You're spending far too much time studying that particular alternate reality."

Francisco looked crestfallen.

"Er, yes, Master."

The Warlord considered him, seeing his obvious disappointment. Then he turned back to the Field Marshal.

"Well... since you're already here..."

The Field Marshal saluted smartly.

"You have need of us, Herr Warlord?"

"Yes," he said after several seconds. "It would seem you will be granted the honor of performing a vital mission for your new master. Me."

The Field Marshal's expression flickered briefly, then, "Splendid. We are fully prepared."

The Warlord issued a few terse orders and handed the Field Marshal a small set of documents. Then he turned away, cape swirling behind him.

"You understand your mission, then?" he asked.

"Ja, Herr Warlord," the Field Marshal replied. "The blue one. Bring him back. And retrieve the data you desire. Yes." He nodded sharply. "We will not fail."

"See that you do not."

The Warlord made a motion with one hand, causing a shimmering portal to open in midair. He gestured at it sharply.

Without another word, the Field Marshal stepped through, followed by the others.

The Warlord gestured again, and the portal vanished.

Francisco smiled nervously up at the Warlord.

"Your faith in your servant will be rewarded, Master. Yes, yes! You will not be disappointed this time."

"Somehow, I doubt that, Francisco. But I suppose it can't hurt to soften the humans up a bit first, before I must inevitably intervene to finish them off."

He strode away from the little man, then stopped and looked back at him.

"And who knows," he added. "Maybe those preposterous fools will get lucky."

37

Ultraa, Damon, and Vanadium stood on a riser, about two feet above the floor of the lab. A hastily constructed arch made of metal rods, cables, and glass tubes curved behind them, framing them in a half-oval of high-tech equipment. Nearby, behind the computer console he had reworked for the job, stood Esro Brachis, clad in another of his seemingly endless supply of Hawaiian shirts, with goggles covering his eyes. His hands danced over the controls, bringing all the systems online. Next to him, hands on her hips and a pout on her face, stood the shiny, golden-clad form of Lyn Li. And she was not happy.

"There is no reason why I shouldn't go," she said, glaring at Ultraa. "I'm at least as powerful as Damon, with his gadgets!"

"That's not it, Pulsar," Ultraa said. "This is serious business. *Dangerous* business."

"I'm not serious enough?"

Ultraa sighed.

"You're too new at all of this," he said. "We didn't bring you in with the intention of making you a field agent immediately. We brought you here to learn."

"Yeah, but things have changed," Lyn shot back. "This is about all of us now. I'm as involved as any of you."

"I told you," Brachis said to Ultraa, in a stage whisper, "the 'stay here and protect Esro' line would be the better choice. Not the 'we have to protect the girl' approach."

Lyn glared at both of them.

Ultraa held up both hands. "But that's not—"

"You two are unbelievable," she said.

She huffed, pacing behind Esro.

Damon, annoyed and bored, had walked off to one side, moving through various stances with his electro-sword.

"Let's get this show on the road, how 'bout?" he called out.

Ultraa nodded. "It's time. Start it up."

"Yeah, okay," Esro said, energizing the system. "Everybody get in place."

They stood close together on the riser, and the arch behind them began to glow, a hum vibrating through it, and through the floor.

Ultraa glanced up at the device, frowning. "Alright, Esro, so—what are we supposed to do?"

"Um, when I give the word," Esro replied, "you step through there."

"Step through... to where?" Damon asked.

"To wherever the Warlord is, I hope," Esro said.

"And where is that?"

Esro scratched his head.

"You'll be the first to know," he replied.

The others looked at each other nervously. Damon shrugged. "Sounds fine to me, then," he said, saluting with his sword. "Let's go."

Ultraa nodded to Esro. Vanadium stood silent and immobile.

Esro closed the final circuits. The arch flared with light. Within its center, a bright yellow spiral formed in midair, growing to fill the entire space. A whooshing sound filled the room.

"Now," Esro shouted.

They turned and stepped into the light.

Just after they vanished, a shape zoomed over Esro's head. A golden shape, sparkling as it darted into the spiral behind the others.

"Lyn!"

Esro reached for the emergency cut-off, but it was too late. She had passed through with the others.

Cursing, he could only watch helplessly as the system automatically cycled down and shut itself off. It would be at least half an hour before it was ready to be powered up again, so that he could bring them all back home. Assuming, of course, that they had survived wherever they had gone to—and whatever they had encountered when they arrived.

"I hope she made it through okay," he whispered to himself, as he reset the system to warm up again as soon as possible. "Crazy girl."

That done, he walked over to one of his worktables and dropped tiredly into the chair. On the table lay Damon's ruined and disassembled armor. Looking at it made him cringe. He lifted the helmet and stared at it, then realized he looked like a scene from Hamlet and quickly set it back down. Cursing, he swept his arm across the surface, shoving it all off into the trash.

"Time to start over, from scratch," he said to himself, reaching down to the two silver cases he kept with him at all times. He set one on the table and worked the lock, opening it, then drew out a heavy, matte-gray metal boot. He flipped it over, inspecting the rocket nozzles built into the sole.

"Or, not quite from scratch…"

He opened the second case and dumped out its contents. One of the components that tumbled out, another helmet, rolled across the tabletop. He grabbed it before it could fall, held it up before him, and peered in through the eyeholes. It seemed to stare back at him coldly.

"Oh, I'm good," he whispered, rotating it in his hands, nodding to himself.

This helmet appeared a bit more advanced and less cobbled-together than the one he had provided to Damon. Flipping it over, he pried off a cover and adjusted a tiny control on the back. He failed to notice the static that momentarily flashed across the monitoring screen in front of him. When he did glance up, the screen was normal once again.

Grunting in satisfaction, he replaced the cover and once again contemplated the helmet.

Just outside the house, four gray-clad figures moved forward, down through the bushes.

Reaching the side of the house, one of the men—the one known as Infantry—faced his leader.

"Why do we sneak around like women?" he whispered tersely.

"Because I have ordered it," Field Marshal replied. "Silence!"

The older man studied the house for a moment, with his one good eye. Then he held out a small electronic device.

"Attach this to the side doorway next to the cargo entrance."

He handed it to Blitzkrieg.

"This will get us inside undetected?"

"Ja. The screens and monitors are ingenious, but I have found the weak spot, as the Warlord predicted."

He smoothed his uniform.

"No sense in causing more of a disturbance than necessary. Seek out the primary objective, but remember to look for the other items as well."

"If they confront us, we will crush them!" the muscle-bound member of the team growled.

"I trust that you will, Artillery. Now: Move in!"

32

Behind his silver mask, the Warlord frowned at the odd yellow swirl that had appeared suddenly in midst of his sanctum.

Raising his left arm, he accessed a hidden panel in his sleeve and activated a scanner there, directing it at the swirl.

Before he could learn anything, the swirl brightened into an oval of light, and from it emerged three human shapes, followed almost immediately by a fourth—a golden streak that shot overhead.

Shocked, the Warlord whirled around, anger and outrage competing with sheer astonishment within his mind.

"What? *How—?*"

The man who strode forward, muscles flexing and jaw jutting out, clad all in white and red—there was no mistaking who he was. Ultraa, along with his annoying teammates, had somehow found him, and found a way in.

Cursing, he reached for the switch that would activate his personal defenses.

Too late. Ultraa had launched himself into the air and now hurtled like a missile towards him. The Warlord raised an arm to fend him off, but it did little good. The blond man crashed into him and they both tumbled across the floor.

Lying tangled in his blue and purple robes, the Warlord struggled to rise. Then he saw the young idiot in chain mail rushing forward, jabbing at him with his ridiculous sword. The damage from

"Kill them," he commanded. "Kill the intruders. Now!

the electricity it conveyed was minor, but it constituted yet another affront to his pride.

"You dare to strike me?"

Shouting curses, the Warlord leapt to his feet.

A golden-hued sphere formed around him, constricting quickly, restraining him.

"Fools," he cried, anger spilling over. "You think you can come here, into my sanctum—my universe!—and accost me?"

The attackers were not listening to him, the Warlord realized. They were babbling angrily among themselves. Apparently, the female had not been expected to come with the others, but had done so anyway. A spunky girl, the Warlord noted. Grateful to her for the brief moment's distraction she was providing, he touched a series of controls on his gauntlet, starting the process that would result in her death, and in that of the others.

The alarm claxon wailed in response to the Warlord's signal. He smiled at the sound, even as he depressed another stud, unleashing a blast that ripped him free of the girl's force field. Right on cue, a big metal door slid open in the wall to his left, and several shadowy figures emerged.

He turned to face them, and pointed at the humans.

"Kill them," he commanded. "Kill the intruders. Now! Or answer for it with your lives."

As the Warlord retreated, his commandos rushed forward, confronting Ultraa and the rest.

Grinning behind his silvery mask, the Warlord ducked through a hidden exit and emerged into a small anteroom with a metal ladder fastened into one wall. Climbing it quickly, he leapt over the edge and out onto his command platform, a broad deck that projected over the larger room he had just departed.

Monitors all around him depicted the course of the battle just beginning nearby. Its ultimate outcome mattered not at all to him, though. He never employed operatives whose health and safety mattered a whit to him. If Ultraa and his friends killed them all, the Warlord would not mourn. He only hoped his lackeys could slow the attackers down a bit, and deal them some degree of damage before the Warlord inevitably found himself facing them again.

Seating himself in his thronelike chair, he surveyed the variety of controls before him that could bring instant death to anyone in the larger chamber.

Flexing his fingers and preparing to unleash instant doom as soon as the conflict next door lost its entertainment value, the Warlord leaned back his head and roared with laughter.

33

Back at Brachis's house...

The screen in front of Esro flashed. Startled, he looked up. The gadget-laden belt he had been working on lay instantly forgotten in his hands.

What had been a screensaver image of Esro lying on a beach in Hawaii had automatically switched over to a schematic of the mansion, showing its many rooms and twisting corridors.

He frowned.

Three flashing red dots had appeared on the screen, and were moving in different directions across the house's floor plan.

"What the—?"

It was so unexpected, so unusual, it took him a moment to fully comprehend what he was seeing.

Someone is in the house, he realized finally.

Several someones.

Adjusting the security camera controls, he brought up an image from the basement level.

"Huh?"

He shook his head, as if to clear it.

"I think I've been staring at microcircuitry too long," he whispered. "Nobody should have been able to get in there."

A man in a gray jumpsuit with black trim was rummaging through one of the storage rooms. Electricity danced over his arms and legs. Then, suddenly, instantaneously, he was across the hall, zipping from one crate and box to another.

"Super speed," Esro breathed. "Well, well. Someone very special has taken an interest in my stuff. Enough of an interest to break in *while I'm at home!"*

He reflected upon that for a second.

Either they're really dangerous and don't much respect me as a fighter...or else they respect my inventions so much, they just had to have them, no matter the risk.

Yeah, I think I'll go with the second rationale, at least for now.

He watched long enough to get a sense of where each of the three intruders was going. Then, grabbing the gadget belt from the tabletop and strapping it on, he ran from the lab.

Unbeknownst to Esro, concealed within an unlocked closet across the hall, the Field Marshal watched. As Esro raced down the corridor, the older man smiled to himself, stepped out, and walked boldly into the lab Esro had just exited. Laughing softly, he sealed the door behind him.

Esro took the elevator down to the basement level. He stepped out and entered the rec room at a point across from the swimming pool. Checking his remote tracker, he saw that one of the intruders was rather quickly moving in his direction.

"What are these people looking for?" he whispered to himself.

The guy was really moving fast now.

"Super speed. Why'd it have to be super speed? What can you do to counteract that…?"

He looked around, trying to think.

"Hmm."

He looked down at his gadget belt.

"Hmmm....."

A voice, heavily accented with German, boomed out from speakers set in the ceiling.

"Blitzkrieg. Brachis awaits you in the large room just ahead. Beware."

Brachis jumped in surprise.

"Hey, that was the house PA system! How did—?"

Before he could ponder further, the doorway across from him opened.

The one known as Blitzkrieg stepped into the rec room, electricity dancing over his gray and black military uniform. He took one look at Esro and snorted in derision.

"Bah," he said, his German accent thick. "I don't even need my lightning powers to deal with this one."

He laughed again, advancing.

"In fact, I doubt my speed will be required, either."

He peered across the long room to where, a hundred feet distant, Brachis stood.

"Why not surrender now, little man? We might go easy on you, if you simply give us what we want. Starting with the man of fire."

"Ah," Brachis said. "Working for that silver-faced creep, huh? I should have known."

Blitzkrieg stepped forward, moving only slightly faster than humanly possible. Electricity flared around him, dancing from his fingertips.

Esro reached into one of the pouches on his belt and brandished an odd, silver, gun-shaped device.

The German scoffed.

"You expect to be able to hit me—*me*—with something like that?"

"Oh, you never know—you might slip up."

Esro pressed a remote-control button on his belt. In response, the double doors set into the floor, covering the long swimming pool, began to slide open beneath Blitzkrieg's feet.

"Ha!" The German sneered. "You woefully underestimate my speed."

Blitzkrieg shot forward, moving inhumanly fast, already halfway over the partially-opened pool as he finished speaking. An instant later, his feet touched down again on the near side.

Meanwhile, as soon as he had begun to move, Brachis had aimed the little silver gun at the floor directly in front of himself and pulled the trigger.

The German's black-gloved hands reached out—

Esro calmly stepped to the side.

The German tried to alter his course—and found that he could not.

"Wha—?"

His black-booted feet stepped into the grease that Brachis had liberally sprayed across the floor with his little silver gun. Legs flailing, the German spun wildly through the air.

Behind the spot where Brachis, until a split second earlier, had stood, the hot tub now lay uncovered.

Out of control, Blitzkrieg tumbled into it with a splash.

The explosion shook the house's very foundations.

Brachis covered his eyes, protecting them from the intense flash. Then he leaned forward, watching the water in the tub churn and boil away. The now-fried Blitzkrieg slumped in a rather unnatural position at the bottom, unconscious. The parts of his skin that were not covered by his uniform glowed a lobster-like reddish pink.

"Speed kills, my friend."

Then he frowned.

"I hope those stains come out. Lyn really likes that hot tub."

Checking the remote tracker, Esro tossed the grease gun aside and sprinted for the door.

34

Inside the sanctum of the Warlord's flying fortress, Pulsar and the others stood on their guard, ready to meet the next wave of attackers. They had disposed of the first bunch easily enough. That crowd had been comprised mostly of soldiers carrying high-tech weapons, but Pulsar had deflected their fire with her force spheres and Ultraa had swept them aside swiftly.

Now, though, something much more disturbing could be seen deep in the shadows. A figure was taking shape. A human form, it moved slowly, emerging into the dim light. Mostly black, darkness appeared to flow from it as it moved, though it radiated a faint green light in places.

Ultraa backed up, cautious, and Pulsar stepped up next to him.

"What is it?" Lyn asked.

Ultraa shook his head once, his eyes never leaving the potential new adversary.

Lyn glanced to her right, seeing Damon squaring off against... *someone*. All she could really make out was a lot of bare skin.

Vanadium was nowhere to be seen.

Sinking into a crouch, Lyn allowed her electromagnetic powers to well up within her, to a point where she could easily unleash them. She felt her fingertips tingling as tiny threads of golden lightning jumped from one to the other.

"Be ready for anything," Ultraa whispered.

Within seconds, the shape was fully visible—or as visible as it would ever be, given its nature. It was a man, clad in robes and hood similar to those of the Warlord, but all in black. Dark hands reached up and drew back the hood, revealing a smooth, white, hairless head, and the green light increased. It came from the circular aperture of a strange piece of equipment that covered the man's left eye and part of his face on that side. Wires and cables ran back from the device, over and around his head, disappearing into his robes.

Peering at Ultraa and Pulsar as though they were insects, he raised his hands with a flourish. In response, green fire leapt up and blazed all around him. He gestured again, and the flames moved, spinning madly about him, forming a hellish green cyclone. He directed his hands outward then. The fire, now a jetting stream, roared toward Ultraa.

The blond hero stumbled back, calling out a warning to his young apprentice.

Lyn, however, gritted her teeth and stepped directly in front of him.

"Pulsar!"

Ignoring his cry, Lyn raised both of her hands to chest level. A broad, shimmering, golden screen formed in front of her just as the flames struck.

Lyn grimaced, the strain evident on her face.

The flames deflected harmlessly away.

"Nice work," Ultraa told her as the fire died down around them. "Now—be careful!"

The Warlord's voice boomed down from his command platform high above them.

"Destroy them, Mage! Destroy them all!"

The being called Mage strode forward, green flames preceding him across the chamber, roaring out in crackling waves.

Pulsar took a deep breath, preparing to create another shield. She didn't want to play defense forever, though. She tried to remember some of what she had learned thus far—what might be an effective attack.

A couple of stratagems occurred to her. She wanted to run them by Ultraa, to get his opinion, but there was no time. She resolved to just pick one and do her best. Before she could try anything, however, a powerfully built figure stalked past her, heading toward the enemy.

It was Vanadium.

Mage stopped in his tracks, frowning. He looked the intimidating metal man up and down.

"Behind me," Vanadium told the other two.

Lyn did not hesitate. She gestured for the reluctant Ultraa to join her.

Vanadium moved forward again, gleaming metal arms coming up to the ready, red eyes blazing at his opponent.

Green fire swept out, engulfing him.

Within the cradle of flames, crackling bolts of energy appeared, like a lightning storm set loose. The bolts flashed out, raking over Mage's dark form.

Both continued to move toward one another, relentlessly, the fire and the lightning spreading in both directions, engulfing them both.

The two titanic figures collided, wrestled for a moment, and then the man in black gave ground. Both men crashed into the wall, smashing through it, their bodies now wreathed within a vast ball of green fire and blinding streaks of light. They vanished utterly into the dark as they continued on, down through the floor, falling out of sight.

Pulsar, shocked, moved to where she could see through the jagged hole that had been created. She crouched down, staring.

"They're gone," she breathed.

"Vanadium can hold his own," Ultraa replied, looking over her shoulder. "And he got that guy away from the rest of us. Let's not waste the opportunity."

Without another word, Ultraa shot into the air, swooping upward, curving over the edge of the command platform, aiming straight for the Warlord.

A blue-white beam of searing energy nailed him in mid-flight and brought him tumbling back down to the floor below.

"No!"

Lyn ran towards him where he lay, unmoving.

He was dazed, his uniform torn and smoking. As he got one arm under himself and pushed himself up to his knees, a trickle of blood ran down from his forehead.

Blood, Pulsar thought as she saw it. *But that's not possible. He was flying. He should have been invulnerable.*

Quickly she helped him to his feet. He managed to stand, wobbly but upright again. Together they looked around, searching for the new attacker.

Instead of a lone enemy, however, they found themselves staring out at another horde of foes, charging out into the chamber, rushing to the attack.

Behind them, the Warlord's laughter rang in their ears.

35

Damon had gotten separated from the others just after they arrived. He was in the process of fighting his way back over toward Pulsar when a figure clad all in gray fur dropped down from the shadows, landing just in front of him. He brought himself to a sudden halt and stared at the creature, puzzled.

"I am the Wombat," the crouching man said with a nasally British accent, taking a menacing step forward.

"The what? The *Wombat*?"

Damon hesitated, then lowered his electro-sword and began to laugh.

"What! Why do you laugh?"

Damon laughed harder.

"You—you bloody fiend! I am the furry fury! I will—I will gnaw upon your bones!"

"The furry *what*?"

Damon choked, then laughed still harder. He sheathed his sword and held his sides.

Furious, the Wombat brandished razor-sharp claws and waved them at his adversary.

"You won't laugh so hard when my talons rake through your entrails!"

Damon looked at him sideways.

"Who writes your dialogue, pal?"

The Wombat's face, or what little of it could be seen under his furry mask, grew red. He stepped forward again, his claws up and ready—and then, all at once, he sank to his knees, sobbing.

"I know I'm a joke," the furry man whined. "You don't have to be so mean about it."

Damon stopped laughing abruptly. He looked down at the little man—for little he was, Damon could see, now that he wasn't arching his back and waving his claws around—and felt sort of sorry for him.

"I... Gee..."

"I just want to go home," the Wombat sniffled. "Or to a pub. Yeah, a nice pub. I could use a pint. Or three."

Frowning, Damon thought for a moment, then fished around in one of his belt pouches.

"Ah ha!"

He drew out a small flask and tossed it to the Wombat.

"Try this."

The Wombat caught the flask and looked up at Damon in surprise, then twisted off the cap and sniffed it gingerly. His eyes widened, and he grinned, then raised it to his lips and swigged.

"Hey, careful now—not too much at once," Damon said, reaching for the flask.

It was too late. The Wombat had swallowed the entire contents in one long gulp. He started to hand the empty container back to Damon, then made an odd, unintelligible sound and dropped it. His eyes crossed.

"You don't look so good, friend," Damon said.

"Urgle."

The Wombat collapsed onto his back, snoring.

"Hrm. Well, that was easy enough."

Damon leapt over the unmoving form, racing toward the others.

The Warlord gawked at the scene, then cursed at Damon.

"Blast you! You have debauched the Wombat!"

With a gesture, the Warlord sent the furry fury back to his own dimension.

"You will pay for—"

He paused, seeing another of his agents approaching Damon.

"Ahh. Perfect," he said, smiling.

Damon whirled, and found himself face to face with, of all things, a nearly naked woman.

"You said it, man," he told the Warlord, before turning back to the woman. "Name's Cavalier," he began, his grin broad. "I—"

The red leather boot cracked hard into his jaw and sent him sprawling, the world spinning around him.

"Oww…"

He touched his jaw, felt blood running down from his mouth.

"Hey, baby, there's no need for—"

The boot lashed out again.

36

The Field Marshal cursed, seeing on the security monitor the inert form of his speedy agent lying at the bottom of the tub.

"Idiot," he hissed.

Angrily flipping from one camera view to the next, he found that Brachis had already located the second Wehrmacht member and was closing in on him. Keying the PA, he barked, "Infantry! You are under observation."

On the screen, the agent called Infantry jumped, startled, and then turned away from the camera and stood completely still. A strange series of popping sounds filled the room.

The Field Marshal watched what was happening on his monitor and nodded, pleased.

"Very good," he whispered. He shifted his gaze to another screen, curious to see how Brachis would respond to this new challenge.

The answer was not long in coming.

Esro came to the end of a hallway, peeked around the corner, and spotted his quarry—Infantry—at the far end of the next section of corridor. A closet door was open and the German was rummaging through the contents within. Then Esro started, seeing an identical twin to the man walking across the hallway two doors down. A third exited a room just down from Brachis, almost running into a fourth who was walking in.

Brachis leaned back around the corner, rubbing his eyes.

"Well, this is new," he muttered.

"Freeze!"

Brachis jumped, startled. Yet another duplicate had slipped up behind him.

"Instant clones, huh?" Esro said. "Interesting."

"Down the hallway," the one behind him growled. "Now."

Brachis allowed himself to be herded along by the growing congregation of duplicates. When they reached the far end, another set moved in front of him, leaving him surrounded by a horde of replicas of the tall blond man. All were muttering among themselves and laughing cruelly. The ones behind him repeatedly prodded and shoved him in the back.

The German-accented voice of the Field Marshal boomed out over the loudspeaker again.

"Use caution, Infantry," it said. "This man has already incapacitated Blitzkrieg."

"By that he means your friend is well-done," Esro snickered.

Three of the Infantry duplicates in front of Esro laughed simultaneously while the others simply scowled at him. Then one of them moved slightly forward.

"Ha! This one cannot harm us," he snorted. "And even if he could, he does not know which of us is the original!"

Brachis slowly looked to one side, then to the other.

"Ah," he said. "Yeah. I see it now."

Infantry hesitated, and then one corner of his mouth turned downward in a partial frown. His brow furrowed.

"What? You see what now?"

"You create these duplicates from your mind, don't you? You visualize them first, right? And then they appear."

The duplicates all took on a somewhat troubled expression, glancing at one another.

"One of us does that," the one in front of Esro said. "But—which one?"

They all laughed raucously, the bravado returning in full force.

Raring back, Brachis unleashed a roundhouse haymaker, his best punch, at the duplicate just in front of him. The man folded up, unconscious before he could hit the floor.

All around, with another flurry of popping sounds, the multitude of copies blinked out like soap bubbles, leaving the room empty save for Esro and the man lying at his feet.

Just before he blacked out entirely, the original Infantry gazed up at Esro in wonder and muttered, "H—how? How did you know which one was me?"

"You were the ugliest one. The others were all too pretty. They all looked more like you *wanted* them to look."

But Infantry heard none of that. He was already out.

Shaking out his obviously aching fist, Brachis dashed back towards the elevator.

Watching on Esro's security monitors, the Field Marshal cursed again.

This man Brachis is more resourceful than I was led to believe, he thought. *He knows where I am, and he's coming here. Time to roll out the heavy artillery.*

37

"So, um, do we really have to fight?" Damon asked sheepishly.

The woman who confronted him was quite an eyeful. *Fighting* with her was not what immediately came to Damon's mind. She was tall and slender, with bobbed blonde hair, and wore a tiny, bright red bikini, along with long gloves and thigh boots of the same color. She also wore small, rectangular, blue-tinted sunglasses. And that was it.

Damon gawked at her.

"Um, seriously," he stammered, his electro-sword held limply at half-mast. "Because, you know, there might be a nice coffee house or something around here, and we could…"

"I'm Distraxion," the blonde woman purred, turning to face him fully.

"Yes. Yes, you are," he said firmly, nodding, continuing to gawk. "I can unequivocally state that you are, indeed, a distraction."

"Idiot," she growled.

Her boot came up in a violent kick, catching Damon in the chin, spinning him backward. His sword clattered to the floor, rolling away.

Damon ran one hand over his aching jaw while he tried to push himself up with the other. No sooner had he gotten to his knees, though, than a bright red boot smacked into his ribs, sending him back down.

"You—you play rough, lady," he gasped, seeing stars.

"I haven't even started yet," she replied, circling him. "Now, let's see about making you a bit more obedient."

She leaned over him, grasping his chin in one hand, forcing him to look up at her face. Reaching up with the other hand, she raised her sunglasses. Her eyes became two shimmering pools of light, staring down at him, boring into his mind.

"You are my slave," she purred. "Your only joy is in obedience to Distraxion!"

Damon felt his knees grow weak. He fell back, catching himself again.

"You—you're making me feel all tingly, lady," he gasped, resisting as best he could.

"I get that a lot," she replied, one corner of her brightly lipsticked mouth turning upward in a half-smile.

"So cut it out, then," came a voice from behind Distraxion.

Both she and Damon whirled.

A surging sphere of energy bowled the blonde woman off her feet. It pushed her back against the wall and held her in place.

"Let me go," she demanded, vainly struggling to move forward.

"No chance."

Damon grinned as he watched the proceedings in front of him. His former foe, Distraxion, was glaring angrily up at the somewhat short, curvy woman in golden mesh that loomed over her, hovering a few feet off the ground, one hand directed out at her. Electricity flared all around, crackling over the sphere that pressed down on her.

"Thanks for the assist, Pulsar," he said.

Without taking her eyes off the villainous woman, she nodded.

Distraxion's mouth twisted into a hateful expression. She managed to get one hand up to her face, and raised her sunglasses again.

"You adore me," she purred to Lyn. "You wish you *were* me. You want to do anything I tell you to do." Her lips parted in an evil smile. "Like beating the brains out of this jerk in the chain mail."

Pulsar blinked, blinked again, and her mouth went slack. Damon could see her eyes glazing over, and the sphere holding Distraxion down began to weaken.

"Oh, no you don't," Damon growled. He leapt at Distraxion, tackling her, grabbing her wrists and pulling her arms behind her. He smacked her head into the wall, causing her to cry out and her sunglasses to clatter away across the floor. Then he fished a plastic restraining cord out of his pocket and bound her wrists securely. As she tried to look back at him, her eyes radiating that mesmerizing power, he snatched the red bandanna from his own head and tied it around hers, covering her eyes.

She cursed him with vitriol, but he ignored it. Carefully he sat her down on the floor, leaning her back against the wall.

"And to think, we could have had something special," he said to her.

Practically hissing, she spat at him.

"Then again…"

He grabbed up his electro-sword and saluted Lyn.

"Thanks, babe!"

"No prob—*babe?!*"

Lyn punched him in the arm, hard.

"Ow!"

He frowned at her.

"Oh, I get it—you're still partially under her control, right?" he asked.

She shook her head.

"That was all me, dude. All me."

"Ah. Right."

Flashing his smile, Damon leapt back into the fray.

Suppressing a few curses of her own, Lyn did the same.

38

"Artillery."

The Field Marshal watched him on one of the video monitors in the control room of Esro Brachis's mansion. The big man jerked his head up, listening.

"Move to intercept on level three."

"Ja."

The older man sat back and watched as his stocky, muscle-bound agent moved into position.

After a few seconds, the elevator doors opened and Brachis stepped off.

"This may not play out precisely as I had imagined," the Field Marshal whispered to himself. "Perhaps I had better abbreviate my stay here."

Removing a data crystal from a pouch on his belt, he slid it into a receptacle on the console, then keyed in a string of commands to Brachis's central databases.

As the computer downloaded gigabytes of classified information into the crystal, the Field Marshal turned to the monitors again. He had placed his sole remaining agent, Artillery, in position to cut Brachis off if he tried to enter the laboratory area.

At length a beep sounded. The Field Marshal smiled and removed the data crystal, replacing it in its pouch. He stood, walking toward the exit, then glanced back one last time at the monitors.

On the screen, Brachis was approaching the big, muscular member of the Wehrmacht.

"Perhaps he will succeed, where the others failed," the Field Marshal muttered to himself. Then the German mastermind snorted.

"Nein. Probably not. But—what of it?"

He continued through the door.

"That buffoon deserves whatever he gets," he muttered to himself.

He waved in mock goodbye to the image on the screen of the lumbering commando.

"Farewell, *mein freund*. Please delay *Herr* Brachis a few moments more, so that I may escape, and you will have served me faithfully and well."

Walking out into the living room, he noticed a black box sitting on a coffee table. Pausing, he squinted at it.

127

"That cannot be—"

He picked the box up and turned it over in his hands.

"Why, I believe it is."

He laughed.

"Brachis is a bigger fool than I suspected," he said, "to leave this sitting out, unprotected."

The box under one arm, his compatriots forgotten, he ran for the front door.

39

In the main chamber of the Warlord's sanctum, Ultraa stood face to face with the man who had blasted him moments earlier—a man seemingly carved from solid marble. His muscled physique and square jaw mirrored Ultraa's own appearance, but his every feature looked to have been carved from sheer, smooth stone, perfectly sculpted and somehow animated.

The two squared off, neither saying a word. They circled one another slowly.

"Surrender," said the stone man, his voice surprisingly soft, quiet.

"Not a chance," Ultraa replied.

They circled.

"I do not wish to destroy you, villain," the stone man said.

"Villain?"

Ultraa frowned at him.

"The Warlord has brainwashed you, apparently."

"I'm not the one who is fooling himself," the other said. "You cannot defeat me."

They circled once more, and then the stone man lunged. Ultraa spun out of his grasp, relying on his many years of training to save himself. Pivoting around, he kicked his opponent in the back and sent him sprawling onto the floor with a crash. No sooner had the man flipped over, however, than he aimed one hand at Ultraa and unleashed some form of bright blue energy blast, nearly taking the hero's head off.

Ultraa dived out of the way, already sweating. The stone man was back on his feet, advancing.

SENTINELS: THE GRAND DESIGN

Not good, he thought. *This guy is powerful. Very powerful. And, when I'm not flying, I'm...*not.

"You are fast. Faster even than the Hosts of Arnaak, the winged defenders of the High Priestess."

Ultraa looked back at him, puzzled.

The man unleashed a bolt of blue-white energy that nearly skewered Ultraa.

"Perhaps the fastest foe I have ever faced," he said, continuing as if he had not just tried to kill the man, "in all the long years I have served."

"Served? Served as what? An assassin?"

Ultraa crouched, shifting his weight back and forth on the balls of his feet, preparing to dodge again, looking for any sort of opening to attack.

"You dishonor me," the man replied. "I am the Liberator. For decades I have battled against the Bhakaran Dynasty, freeing dozens of worlds from tyranny."

Ultraa just shook his head.

"I have no idea what you're talking about," he said.

He pointed past the Liberator, to the platform where the Warlord lurked, watching.

"But, right now, whether you realize it or not, you are doing the dirty work for a pretty nasty guy. Doesn't sound like your actions are living up to your ideals."

The Liberator grimaced, shouted something unintelligible, and fired twin bolts of energy at Ultraa. The white-clad hero leapt instantly to his right, only his super-speed saving him from incineration.

Before another blast could be directed his way, Ultraa leapt forward, his flight power rocketing him into his enemy's midsection, propelling them both across the chamber and into the wall. Each of them fell to the floor and lay still for a moment, dazed.

Ultraa made it back onto his feet as quickly as he could, dismayed to see the other was up as well. He moved quickly into a defensive posture, watching and waiting.

"Indeed, you are quite skilled," the Liberator said, his eyes never moving from Ultraa. "I can sense the limitations of your powers, yet you make the most of them." He frowned. "Actually, as I probe deeper... How interesting. You have no such limitations, save in your own mind."

His eyes met Ultraa's, searching.

"You did not know this, did you?"

Now it was Ultraa's turn to frown.

"What are you talking about?"

The Liberator hesitated, then shrugged.

"I could tell you," the stone man stated grimly, "but I suppose it is better for me if you do not know."

Grimacing, he unleashed another furious attack, massive twin bolts of blue energy lancing out, catching Ultraa squarely in the chest, spearing into him, driving him down.

40

"The alien!"

Artillery stood before Esro, muscles bulging, face contorted in fury.

"Give him to me or I will *break* you, little man!"

"You seem pretty alien to me, pal," Esro replied, backing away slowly.

The huge German raised both arms, holding them parallel to the floor. He grimaced, and somehow a concussive blast erupted from his fingertips, shattering the wall behind Brachis, who had just managed to leap out of the way.

"Hey, I paid for all this stuff," Esro shouted, getting to his feet quickly, watching the rest of the wall collapse into rubble. "Jeez!"

Laughing, the big man strode forward, moving slowly but deliberately, seeming like nothing so much as a rolling army tank.

Brachis dived back around the corner and scrambled through a doorway just as yet another blast rattled the walls.

The big guy was still coming.

"You cannot hide. You cannot face my power. Admit your defeat and surrender. Take me to the creature of fire!"

Esro frantically searched his belt for something, anything...

"The others underestimated you, and merely wished to show off," Artillery growled. "But I remember the mission—the reason we are here. That is my focus. You need not die, Esro Brachis. Give me what I want!"

Another explosion ripped out chunks of wood and masonry.

"Do not die in a cowardly fashion!"

"Bite me," Esro shot back. His hands closed over a small metal box wired into his belt. "Oh, yeah..."

Artillery was very close now.

"Nothing can stand up to my power, little man!"

He raised his hands to fire again.

Brachis jumped out, landing directly in front of his huge adversary.

"How about yourself?"

"Wha—?"

Startled, unused to a foe confronting him directly, the big man hesitated.

Esro aimed the device and pushed the button.

Come on, just enough charge for one try...

Even as the German triggered his concussive blast, a shimmering blue bubble of energy formed around his body. Artillery's eyes grew wide as pie plates.

"Wha—*noo!*"

The blast erupted from his hands, encountered the force field, and reverberated back over him in an instant. The shockwave bounced back and forth within the bubble, wholly contained within it, repeatedly smashing at the German, buffeting him again and again.

As the last traces of the blast dissipated, the force field charge ran out.

Artillery swayed momentarily, then crashed to the floor, unconscious.

"Hey, you weren't kidding," Esro commented as he stepped over the inert body. "Nothing could stand up to that blast. Including *you.*"

Tossing the one-shot field projector aside, he ran for the computer laboratory.

47

Continuing his roll until he was back on his feet, never stopping for an instant, Ultraa launched himself into the air, his back arched, his arms stretched out ahead of him. He circled around the Liberator like a cruise missile closing in on its target. The Liberator spun around, trying to follow him, but Ultraa was too fast, too quick. When he struck, it was with all the strength and force he could muster, channeled into his two now-invulnerable fists.

The muscular, marble slab of a man went down, shock etched on his features. Before he could recover, before he could unleash his own counterattack, Ultraa swooped around and smashed into him again, driving him hard into the chamber's wall. Ultraa circled, then, preparing for a third assault.

The Liberator, slowly pulling himself up to his knees amid the debris, raised one hand.

"Hold," he said.

Wary, Ultraa hesitated, still circling overhead.

"What?"

"I sense…that you spoke the truth, before," the Liberator said.

"You can tell a lot about a guy by fighting with him, apparently," Ultraa replied.

"Not by fighting, no. My senses, though, are highly developed. I have an…*awareness*…"

The Warlord, who had occupied himself by observing some of the other battles that raged simultaneously around the chamber, now gave the two men his undivided attention. He stood on the edge of his command deck, hands clasped behind his back, gazing down at them, his eyes narrowing.

"What you told me before was true," the Liberator said with certainty, nodding to Ultraa. "You are not the negative force here."

He whirled, looking up at the Warlord, who loomed above. He pointed one stony finger.

"It is *you!* You *lied* to me!"

The Warlord glared down at him, saying nothing.

The Liberator turned back to Ultraa, speaking softly, quickly.

"You must listen to me. The population of this city is under this man's mental domination. I sense it—he has a vast network of machinery to control the thoughts of the thousands of inhabitants, to make them his slaves."

Ultraa nodded.

"You cannot destroy it without sending this floating city crashing down, to the doom of all aboard. But—"

"What are you saying, there?" the Warlord demanded.

"But there is an antenna, just outside this tower. It beams the telepathic signal out to the inhabitants. If we can destroy the antenna, we will sever the connection. We will liberate the population."

Ultraa nodded.

"I'm with you," he said.

From up above, the Warlord glared down at his former slave.

"How could you know that?" he demanded. "Who told you—?"

"I am...*aware*," the Liberator replied, turning to face him.

"Time for you to go back where you came from, then," the Warlord growled. He directed a gauntleted hand at the marble-hued man. A bluish beam of light shone out. It fell over the Liberator, who became insubstantial, ephemeral, almost immediately.

Realizing what was happening, the stone man quickly turned back toward Ultraa. His face bore a look of urgency.

"The antenna," he cried. "It must be destroyed! These people must be liberated! If not by me, then by y—"

Ultraa reached out a red-gloved hand, but it was too late. Even as the Liberator leapt up toward the Warlord, his marble body shimmered away entirely, gone.

"That one was never going to work out," the Warlord muttered. "I should have known better."

His eyes bored down into Ultraa's.

"If only I could do that with people I didn't bring here in the first place..."

Ultraa's face twisted in anger. Wordlessly, he leapt into the air and rocketed toward the villain, fists clenched and outstretched.

The Warlord casually gestured with his gauntleted hand, summoning his indestructible force field once more. Ultraa crashed into it and deflected harmlessly away.

The villain leered down at him from behind his silver mask.

"You never learn, do you?"

42

Racing along a hallway of his mansion, Esro Brachis rounded a corner and ran headlong into the Field Marshal. The collision sent both men sprawling.

"Who *are* you people?" Esro demanded, getting to his feet again quickly, just ahead of his quarry.

The German had dropped two objects during the collision, and now he quickly snatched up one of them. The other, a small device the size of a handheld calculator, clattered across the floor toward Brachis.

Their eyes met. The Field Marshal's gaze twitched slightly, shifting to the device he had dropped. He looked extremely agitated and upset. Esro followed his eyes and saw it lying there. He had no idea what it was—he was pretty certain it wasn't something from his labs—but if the Field Marshal wanted possession of it that badly, Brachis figured he should prevent that from happening.

They both dived for it, and Esro, shoving the older man aside, came up with it.

"That is mine," the German sputtered. "I need it to get back."

Esro stepped back, glancing at the device. He held it cautiously in his left hand.

"This is *my* house," he said. "I don't recall letting you in."

Then he recognized the other object in the Field Marshal's possession: the small black box Ultraa and Damon had retrieved from the Blue Skull.

"Hey! That's mine! Put it down!"

The Field Marshal remained in a partial crouch, the black box cradled under one arm. A patch covered one of his eyes, but the other moved from Esro to the device to the hallway leading to the house's front door. He seemed to be weighing his options.

"Put that down," Esro repeated, "and we're going to have a little talk about topics like breaking and entering, and home invasion, and—"

The German lashed out unexpectedly with a series of martial arts moves. A kick swept Esro's legs out from under him. A one-handed chop to the neck put him down flat on his stomach. A knee to the gut knocked the wind out of him and left him gasping. All told, it was not enough to seriously hurt Brachis, but was more than sufficient to give the Field Marshal a chance to run.

He moves pretty good for an older guy, Esro thought, as he struggled to regain his breath.

The German had nearly reached the front door. Esro gasped, coughed, managed to stand, and started after him, all the while feeling as if he were moving in slow motion. As he moved, he patted his pockets for any sort of weapon, but all he had on him was the calculator-sized device he had picked up, moments earlier.

By the time Esro made it to the front door, the older man had flung it open and dashed outside into the night. Esro shouted at him, for all the good it did. He stumbled and fell on the concrete surface of the driveway, skinning his hands.

"Hey! That's mine! Put it down!"

Esro rolled over and sat there on the driveway, shaking his head. The older man was long gone, the darkness having swallowed him up.

Sullenly, he got to his feet and walked back into his mansion.

This would almost be comical, if not for the fact that the guy took my box with him, Esro thought. *Not to mention that he was inside my control room, with access to almost all of my data, schematics, records, and plans—everything.*

He sighed, running his bleeding hand back through his hair. He knew his only option was to chase the guy down, restrain him, and drag him back to the house.

And that, he also knew, would be done much more easily if he had access to the tracking sensors in his new armor.

Resolved on his course of action, he ran back into his lab, gathering up the new armor where he had scattered it over his table earlier in the evening. It went on quickly, like a second skin. In fact, it was specifically molded to fit him and not Damon. He'd never had any intention of handing this particular suit over to the Cavalier. It was *his* baby, his latest prototype, and he had designed it for himself.

A black, skintight bodysuit went on first. It consisted of three ultra-thin layers. The inner layer insulated his skin and allowed for temperature regulation and moisture absorption. The middle layer, a complex web of solid gold microcircuitry, read his muscle movements and his cybernetic instructions and conveyed both to the armor's computer processors. The outer layer, a matte black film of hyper-graphite, could absorb or deflect quite a bit of damage, keeping the armor's systems and the person inside safe.

On top of the bodysuit went the armor's real hardware: bulky, gray components that fit over forearms, upper arms, torso, and legs. The arm components contained various weapons; the boots housed propulsion units. The torso pieces held the main processor unit, along with super-small energy generators and even a device that could power the armor by siphoning ambient energies nearby. Field projectors stationed in each of the components could generate area shielding independently, or work together to create a strong defensive sphere around his entire body. In addition to all of this, the components could work in tandem to dramatically increase his strength.

The helmet, as uncomfortable as it might be, represented the height of Esro's technology. Its communication interface allowed it to access everything from radio and television to military channels. Beyond such mundane abilities, however, it could, quite literally read his mind. By concentrating on basic commands, he could cause the cybernetic helmet interface to relay those instructions to his armor at the speed of light. The result was instantaneous and awesome: He *thought* it, and the armor *did* it.

Matte black and battleship gray, it was clunky when it wasn't powered up. In sum, it wasn't pretty, Esro knew. But, to him, it was the most beautiful thing he'd ever seen.

Clutching the helmet under his arm, the small device he had taken from the Field Marshal tucked into a pocket, he ran back out into the darkness of his front yard.

He had hardly taken a step, though, when a blazing red light filled the night sky, blinding him. He staggered back, shading his eyes with one hand, puzzled.

The flaming apparition that met his gaze was all too familiar.

"You have my counterpart, human," the being that called itself Kabaraak screamed in an unearthly voice. *"I will brook no further delay. You will take me to him now!"*

Esro stared up at the terrifying form, like some angel of death hovering in the night sky. He knew he stood no chance in any kind of battle against the thing.

Turning tail, he ran back into the house.

"Coward!"

The flaming figure settled to the ground and stalked through the doorway.

"You cannot escape me!"

Esro ran down the hallway and into his big laboratory. He sealed the heavy door behind him and frantically searched around for anything that might save him.

A few seconds later, the door began to glow bright red at the center.

As highly as Esro thought of his new armor, he suffered under no illusions about it. He knew it could not long stand up to so powerful an enemy. Frantically he looked around, seeking anything—a weapon, an idea—that might save him. All he saw of interest was the high-tech archway he had used to send the others after the Warlord.

The machinery that opened a portal...*elsewhere.*

"No," he said to himself, firmly.

He looked around again, looking for something—anything— else.

Nothing.

He looked back at the machinery.

VAN ALLEN PLEXICO

Maybe?

He shook his head.

"No."

The center of the reinforced metal door now glowed bright white.

Once more, he looked at the machine.

"Okay, maybe."

As he ran over to the control console, the key question posed itself unbidden: *If I go through there, too...who will bring us all back home?*

His brain answered back instantly: *If you get yourself killed, here, now, the others will be trapped anyway.*

"Good point," he told his brain.

He looked up at the door. It appeared ready to burst.

He triggered his armor's defensive screens. A shimmering sphere of energy, similar to Pulsar's natural force field, formed around him. Just then, the door exploded inward, sending fragments of shrapnel flying all around, gouging chunks out of the walls and equipment. Esro grimaced and ducked, but needlessly. Some of the pieces did impact his force field, but they deflected harmlessly away, to his relief.

He looked up, and felt his heart sink.

Kabaraak floated through the doorway, fires leaping all around him.

"Enough of this!"

The flaming apparition came towards him, murder in its blazing eyes.

"Okay, that's it," he growled to himself. "I'm out of my league. And I'm out of here."

He hit the preprogrammed controls on the system's panel, initializing the process. Then he ran around to the raised platform and its arch of equipment—the equipment that should, if it functioned properly, send him hurtling across the dimensions and into the Warlord's domain.

Just before he could set foot on the riser, Kabaraak screamed an unearthly cry and unleashed a blazing bolt of cosmic fire.

Esro dived for the floor, terrified.

The flames shot over his head, struck the machinery, and melted the entire apparatus.

Esro, on his hands and knees, gawked at the molten puddle that had been his only link to the others, his only avenue of survival.

Kabaraak laughed maniacally.

Esro looked around, frantic.

Nothing... nothing... Wait!

The device the Field Marshal had dropped. What had the German said? It was his only way back? Back where?

Was he in the service of the Warlord?

It seemed very likely, given the nature of the two guys who had attacked Ultraa earlier.

It's a gamble, but...

Esro fished the device out and held it up, squinting at the controls.

Kabaraak took a step forward, puzzled.

"What are you—?"

Esro shrugged—*Wherever it goes, can it really be any worse?*—and pushed the big red button at the center of the device.

The room seemed to shimmer. Or, he wondered, was *he* shimmering, there in the center of the room? In either case, Esro could somehow feel a dimensional portal opening around him, pulling him through.

Grinning, he waved at the startled Kabaraak.

"Bye-bye!"

The fiery being screeched and leapt at Esro, moving far faster than Esro had anticipated.

"Uh—hold on, now," he cried, raising one arm in a futile attempt to fend off the creature.

Flaming hands locked onto his throat, even as the portal gaped open and pulled them both through.

Esro choked out the words, even as the universe swallowed him and spit him out...elsewhere.

"Aw, crap."

43

Pulsar was helping Ultraa back to his feet as a glowing circle appeared between them and the Warlord.

Out of that dimensional window emerged two extremely unusual figures. One was clad in gray and black armor, and was locked in the clutches of the other. The other could only be—

"Kabaraak!"

Ultraa recognized him instantly and raced toward the two. Unsure of the identity of the man in the armor, he avoided him, tackling the fiery being instead and shoving him back.

The armored man collapsed to the floor, and Pulsar raced over to him, helping him up.

"It's me," came Brachis's electronically amplified voice from a speaker in the helmet.

Lyn's eyes widened.

"Esro? You're *here?*"

"Yeah. I'll explain later."

He turned to where Ultraa and Kabaraak wrestled on the floor nearby.

Now that I have a second to catch my breath, and allies to take some of the heat off, I can stop playing only defense and break out a little offense.

He raised one arm and a panel slid aside on his gauntlet. From within the bulky wrist guard emerged what was very obviously a weapon. He directed at the fiery creature. A beam of crimson energy lanced out, striking Kabaraak in the leg. The creature screeched in annoyance but kept most of its attention on Ultraa.

"Esro," Lyn called back to him as she ran toward the action, "you can't be here! You were supposed to stay there and *bring us back!*"

"Yeah, well… I'll figure something out later," he replied, firing again. "Just worry about staying alive, for now."

Ultraa had hammered into Kabaraak again, pushing the blazing man further away from the others. Pulsar and Esro followed after them.

Damon leapt into the fray as well. He glanced over at Esro, looked away, looked back at him, and gaped.

"Esro!"

"Yep."

"You're here."

"You guys are all very observant," Esro said.

"But—"

"Later!"

He pointed at the fiery enemy struggling with Ultraa.

"*That's* the current problem!"

Damon grabbed Esro and pointed behind him.

"No, not so much. *There's* the real problem."

Esro looked up to where the Warlord stood on his command deck, hands on hips, gazing down at them, laughing.

"We've been fighting his foot soldiers," Damon said, "and we've been handling them pretty well, but…"

"But we're not making any real progress," Lyn finished. "We can't get to *him*."

At that moment, Kabaraak tumbled away from a devastating punch thrown by Ultraa. Rising, he held one hand out before his eyes—and then he wailed with unearthly horror and fury.

The hand was becoming transparent again.

Turning his back on Ultraa, he cast his gaze around the chamber—and spotted the Warlord, standing on his platform high above. Their eyes met.

"You!" he screamed.

He lofted into the air, moving rapidly away from Ultraa, soaring up towards the tall figure in blue and purple robes.

"I know not the details of your treachery, but I know you have betrayed me somehow."

"What are you doing here, you idiot?" the Warlord shouted back at him.

Blazing cosmic fire leapt out, meeting impregnable force field.

Ultraa flew back to where the others stood, landing in their midst.

"This is our opportunity," he said. "The Liberator told me what we have to do."

"The who?" Esro asked.

Ultraa looked at him, blinking, realizing for the first time who he was.

"Esro?"

"Later," they all said together.

Ultraa shrugged.

"Fine," he replied.

He gestured with a red-gloved hand all around.

"We're at the top of a floating city. A city with thousands of people in it, all of them slaves, kept under the Warlord's mental domination. Outside this tower we're in now is an antenna. Destroy it, and not only have we freed a whole lot of people, we probably have a whole lot of new allies."

"I like it," Damon said, nodding.

"Yeah," Esro said. Then, "Hey, where's Vanadium?"

The others looked around.

The room shook violently. Suddenly one of the walls exploded inward, fragments of masonry showering everywhere. Ultraa and the others ducked, feeling themselves pelted with stones and shards of metal. Esro and Pulsar managed to deflect the worst of it with a pair of quickly erected force spheres.

There on the floor before them, covered in debris and dust, lay Vanadium.

Damon laughed.

"Say this for the guy—he has a great sense of timing."

The metal man pulled himself up to his feet, just as a figure in black floated through the giant hole in the wall, preceded by blazing green flames.

Rushing forward, Vanadium collided with his dark foe and both stumbled back through their ragged entry point, vanishing outside once more.

"I think we have our way out," Esro said. "Come on!"

They all ran across the chamber and stopped suddenly as they reached the edge. The wind whipped around them, pulling them forward, and Pulsar quickly erected a shield across the opening.

Leaning out against the golden wall she'd set up, Pulsar gazed down, down, at the mile-long drop outside the tower.

"Yikes," she said.

"Uh, yeah," Damon agreed.

"We want out there?" Esro asked.

Behind them, they could hear the Warlord calling for reinforcements even as he continued to exchange powerful blows with Kabaraak.

"We have to take out that antenna," Lyn said.

"He's still relying on his slaves to fight for him," Damon noted.

"That'll be his downfall," Ultraa replied.

Esro cringed.

"Let's not say 'downfall' right now, okay?"

They all stepped back from the edge. Pulsar gestured and the shimmering shield vanished.

"I'm going to take a quick look around," she announced. Then she was gone, zooming out the hole.

Ultraa frowned. He turned to the others, started to issue orders—and then Lyn swooped back inside.

"That was quick," Damon said.

"I think I found the antenna," she said. "It's pretty obvious. It's a long, thin spire jutting out horizontally from the side of this tower, about a hundred feet below us. I'm going to—"

Before she could say another word, Ultraa was through the hole in the wall and soaring down.

"Hey!"

Pulsar shot after him, following close on his heels.

Esro watched them go, then glanced at Damon.

"They can handle it, I'm sure," he said.

Damon nodded, staring back at Esro. Then, "It's weird, seeing you in that armor," he said. "It doesn't look quite like the suit you had me in before."

"Um, yeah," Esro said. "We can talk about it later."

He looked around, fidgeting inside the armor. He was growing annoyed that the helmet's connection to the upper torso was too stiff—it fought him when he tried to turn his head. In addition, his field of vision was drastically reduced. That, along with an almost claustrophobic sensation from being confined inside the tight suit, made for a fairly uncomfortable experience.

"Listen," he said, "I'm starting to understand some of the things you don't like about the suit. I think I can—"

Before he could say anything more to Damon, a green energy beam sliced between the two of them. Startled, Esro activated the armor's general defense screens, surrounding himself with an invisible web of shielding, at a distance of about two feet in every direction. Beside him, Damon dived and rolled out of the way, just as two more blasts knifed past, one of them deflecting slightly from Esro's screens.

Looking back into the interior of the chamber, he could see that the Warlord's call for reinforcements had been answered: Dozens of soldiers in navy blue uniforms, carrying black pistols, were charging into the room, firing energy blasts at them.

"Stay behind me," Esro called out, knowing that Damon lacked any substantial shielding from such an attack. He started forward, moving in a clunky fashion toward the soldiers.

Damon was right, much as I hate to admit it, he told himself. *I've got some work to do on this suit—assuming we survive, and I figure out how to get us all back home, and...*

Bringing his arm-mounted blasters to bear, he opened fire on the troops.

Behind him, Damon looked from the scene unfolding in the chamber, of Esro taking on the soldiers, to the mile-long drop outside, with Ultraa and Pulsar zooming down toward the antenna.

What to do? Don't have my skycycle... can't fly...

As Damon leaned out the hole and watched, Ultraa and Pulsar hovered near the antenna, talking with one another, presumably about how to disable it. Then Pulsar directed both hands at the device and immediately a glowing sphere of light formed around her and moved down to touch the antenna. The big piece of high-tech equipment erupted in a shower of sparks.

Ultraa shouted something and waved to get Pulsar's attention. An instant later, a squadron of hovering platforms came racing around from the other side of the tower, blue-clad soldiers leaning over the sides and opening fire.

Pulsar broke off her attack and whirled around in midair, spreading her arms wide. A large sphere formed around both her and Ultraa, encompassing them both and deflecting away the attacks.

An explosion behind Damon brought his attention back to where he was. It sent him stumbling to his knees, very nearly falling over the edge. He scrambled back, away from the precipice, and looked around to see what had happened.

The Warlord had smashed Kabaraak down into the floor of the chamber and stood over him, both fists raised over his head, preparing to strike again. The fiery being held his hands up between them, but he was clearly weak, barely able to defend himself. As Damon looked closer, he could tell that Kabaraak's physical cohesion was definitely unraveling again.

With a monumental blow, the Warlord smashed the blazing figure down through the floor. Then he looked up, right at Damon, and started forward.

At the same moment, Vanadium crashed through the wall to Damon's right, tumbling across the floor to lie still nearby. The man in black floated through the hole, hovered over Vanadium, and directed a flood of green flames down over his inert body.

"Hey, guys," Damon shouted down to Pulsar and Ultraa. He waved his arms. "A little help up here?"

Ultraa looked up, saw him, and motioned to Pulsar. Together they soared back up, past Damon, into the chamber.

They took in the situation quickly. To one side, Esro was doing a decent enough job of holding off the newly arriving soldiers, his energy screens flaring and his weapons firing at maximum rate. To the other, Vanadium lay inert and enshrouded in a blaze of green flames, the dark man mercilessly continuing his attack.

"We're down an ally, and the Warlord and his flunky are still alive and kicking," Damon said. "The odds are turning against us."

Ultraa pointed toward the man in black.

"I don't know if *we* can do anything to stop that guy, if Vanadium couldn't," he said, starting forward, "but we have to try."

Just then, the Warlord leaned out from his command deck and barked orders down to Mage. The black-clad villain looked up, seeing Damon and the others standing there. He nodded, then moved forward to meet Ultraa.

"Great," Pulsar said, hurrying to catch up. "Looks like we don't have a choice about it."

Damon nodded, brandishing his sword and starting forward. He marveled at how quickly Lyn had adapted to this sort of work, rushing right into the middle of things. She was a natural at this business.

If only, he thought, *she wouldn't look at me like I crawled out of the sewer...*

He shrugged.

It's probably my own fault. I'll have to look into that...if we survive, and can get home...

His momentary distraction was broken by an energy bolt that hit him from behind, from outside the chamber, slicing into his chain mail along his ribcage on the left side. He spun away and fell to his knees, gasping in pain. His sword clattered to the floor.

A mechanical whining sound came from outside. He looked up and saw the source of the noise and the attack: one of the enemy flying platforms, hovering just outside the gaping hole in the chamber wall. Only one soldier manned it, but the guy was armed and about to fire again.

Damon grabbed his wounded side with one hand and snatched up his electro-sword with the other, struggling to rise.

Wonderful, he thought. *I've survived cosmic fire-beings and the almighty Warlord, and now I'm gonna get killed by an average Joe with a pistol...*

The wound burned as though he'd been run through with a spear. He could feel blood running down his side, underneath his chain mail. He ignored all of it and ran toward the flyer, bellowing loudly, partly in anger and partly in hopes of frightening his enemy.

Unperturbed, the Warlord's soldier carefully took aim again and fired.

44

They were surrounded.

Pulsar crouched, ready to fight, as Ultraa helped Esro back to his feet. The Warlord's soldiers advanced slowly, forming a ring around them. Dozens of futuristic weapons pointed their way.

"You did well," the blond hero told his friend. "No one could have held them off any longer."

"Yeah, well..."

Esro looked down at his blasters, where they protruded from their housings in the forearm units of his armor. They glowed red-hot. He'd been firing them steadily, nearly burning them out, and couldn't fire them again until they cooled or he'd risk an explosion.

The blue-clad soldiers moved closer, tightening the noose.

"You are beaten," the Warlord boomed down at them from his command deck. He swept one arm out towards his soldiers, his blue and purple robes flaring. In response, the troops obediently backed away.

He floated down to the chamber floor and then strode regally towards them. His boots crunched on the rubble and debris that filled his sanctum.

"The absurd being called Kabaraak is destroyed," he said. "And your powerful ally—" He gestured toward where Vanadium lay, unmoving, as Mage continued to direct a stream of green fire over him, "—is finished. Only you three remain."

Three? Lyn thought. *Where's Damon?*

She quickly glanced back, about thirty yards behind where they stood, and saw Damon, at the edge of the drop-off, huddled on his knees but still moving. Relief flooded through her, along with concern.

He's still there, still alive, she thought, *though he doesn't look to be in very good shape.*

She tried to see past him but was unable to see the flying platform from her current angle.

He's safe for now, I suppose, she thought. And, *So the Warlord has forgotten at least one of us, or just doesn't consider him a threat. For whatever good that'll do...*

146

"Surrender," the Warlord said, his voice now almost gentle and reasonable. "Save us all any more trouble, any more destruction and loss of innocent life."

He stepped closer still, his purple robes flaring out behind him, his silver mask gleaming in the light coming in through the shattered wall. He held up a small, shiny capsule in one hand.

"Allow yourselves to be fitted with my neural inducers, like all my other subjects. Then you can relax and enjoy your lives—in blissful, content servitude to your master. *Me.*"

A beep sounded from Esro's right arm.

"It's back online!"

Instantly he raised his arm and fired. The searing plasma bolt struck the device between the Warlord's fingers and shattered it, sending the man stumbling backward a step. He cried out in fury.

Pulsar reacted just as quickly. She stepped forward into a crouch, hands out before her, fingers splayed wide. Electricity crackled along her fingertips and formed into a glittering golden bubble surrounding the three of them. It solidified just before the retaliatory strike hit.

"Nice job," Ultraa told her.

Undeterred, the Warlord directed bolts of energy from both gauntlets at them. The blasts deflected away but Lyn groaned and sagged back a bit under the strain. Tears ran from her eyes.

The Warlord moved forward, angry now, closing the space between them rapidly. He barked at Mage, who ceased the bombardment of the apparently dead Vanadium and strode toward his master. Behind them, the soldiers closed ranks and followed.

The three heroes backed up still further, being forced toward the jagged opening in the wall. Damon stood there already, hunched over in pain. Beyond him was the mile-long drop.

And then, unexpectedly, a flash of blue-silver shone behind the Warlord.

"Look," Pulsar hissed at the others, pointing. "He's…alive!"

Indeed, Vanadium was alive—or as alive as one of his nature could ever be—and was moving. He crawled up from where he had lain, his metallic body glowing white-hot from the fires that had engulfed him. He moved stiffly, uncertainly, but quickly enough to catch his enemies by surprise. He crashed into the black-clad man, sending them both tumbling back down to the debris-strewn floor of the chamber.

The Warlord whirled around to see what was happening, as did Pulsar and the others.

Before Mage could recover, Vanadium pounded his face with both fists, then clutched him about the throat. The heat of his metal surface seared the flesh of the Mage, who cried out in agony.

"You fool," the Warlord growled. "You've allowed him to gain the upper hand!"

Cursing, the silver-masked mastermind started toward them.

Twin red beams of energy knifed down from Vanadium's eyes, spearing into Mage, concentrating where the implanted device had replaced one of the man's own eyes. The device exploded, and Mage cried out in pain as a shower of sparks and flames—not green but the standard variety—sprayed out of his eye socket.

"No! Get away from him!" cried the Warlord, grasping Vanadium by the neck and yanking him up and off of Mage.

Too late. The being called Mage lay unmoving, the fight gone from him, his green fires extinguished.

Ultraa shot into the air, streaking towards the Warlord, smashing into him, seeking to break his grasp on Vanadium.

Esro watched in admiration as his friend and teammate attacked their dangerous foe. Then he gestured to Lyn. "He's going to need help," he told her. "Let's go." Without a backward glance, he ran to join the new fight.

Pulsar hesitated, looking around for Damon.

"Wait! Esro!"

The armored scientist didn't hear her. He was sprinting toward Ultraa and the Warlord.

Lyn started to panic. She turned back to the spot where Damon had been standing, mere seconds ago—the edge of the mile-high drop.

He was gone.

45

Moments earlier, Damon had managed to get back on his feet, though his ribs ached tremendously. Ignoring the pain as best he could, he eyed the flying platform as it maneuvered closer to him. On board, the single trooper had one hand on the controls, while the other hand clutched a nasty-looking pistol of futuristic or alien design.

148

Damon leapt out of the way as a greenish beam flashed at him. Rolling to the side and trying not to scream in pain, he came up on his feet in a crouch and launched himself out the hole in the wall, over the mile-high drop, and onto the hovering platform, charging directly at the trooper.

Apparently startled by the frontal physical assault, and after a lifetime of dealing with passive and mindless slaves, the trooper hesitated, recoiling in surprise. At the last instant he yanked at the controls and the platform lurched to one side, just as Damon bounded on the forward hood section. The wind whipped at him, and he clutched frantically to two small handles built into the surface.

Wish I'd brought my skycycle with me...

"Get off," the trooper cried, momentarily forgetting his weapon, trying instead to shake Damon loose by working the controls back and forth.

Tossed to one side, clinging desperately to one of the handles, Damon looked down and glimpsed the view beneath him: nearly a mile, straight down.

Hmm. Maybe this wasn't the best idea, after all...

Then, as the trooper jinked the platform back the other way, Damon used the momentum to hurl himself forward and against the short windshield, landing in a crouch.

The trooper, shocked by this move, gasped and stumbled back from the controls.

Damon, probably even more surprised than the soldier at what he was doing, leapt over the windshield and tackled the man, punching him twice in the jaw. The trooper crashed back into the storage compartments at the platform's rear. Damon drew his electro-sword and jabbed the man in the chest with it. Sparks shot out as it unloaded its current. The trooper cried out and collapsed to the vehicle's floor, stunned.

"Well, whaddya know?" he muttered to himself. "That actually worked."

Dropping into the driver's seat, he looked over the dashboard panel quickly, getting a sense of which controls did what. Then he took the wheel—the handles, really—and maneuvered the vehicle around the outside of the tower. Within seconds he could see the telepathic antenna. It projected out from the side of the tower, a hundred feet further down the side. He angled the flyer down and swooped towards it, even as he searched the dashboard for any indications of a weapon of some sort built into his new vehicle.

Nothing.

He kept the platform hovering there beside the antenna, his hair rising on end from the electrical discharge the thing was putting out. He looked around, frustrated. Here was his target, but what could he do about it? He had his sword, but that was designed to knock people out with a jolt of electricity. It would hardly harm a two hundred foot long antenna surely made of some alien alloy.

What else do I have?

The trooper's gun. It lay on the floor nearby, where the man had dropped it.

Might as well give it a try.

Grabbing it up, Damon directed it at the antenna and pulled the trigger. The gun emitted the same green beam as before, and he played it over the antenna's surface, nodding in satisfaction as it slowly melted the metal and disrupted the wiring, sending sparks showering out.

It was taking too long, though. Who knew how things were going, back in the Warlord's sanctum, at the tower's peak? The others might well need him. He—

The unexpected blow sent him to his knees, stars spinning across his vision.

"*Ughh*—wha—?"

Looking back, he saw the soldier he'd fought and knocked out before, now looming over him, clearly somewhat recovered.

"Knew I should've tossed you overboard before," he muttered, trying to rise.

"I won't make the same mistake," the soldier replied.

He grasped the still-dazed Damon by the belt and hurled him over the side of the craft.

Down he plummeted, down the mile-long drop toward the city surface below.

46

Seeing that Damon had vanished, Pulsar had lofted through the hole and out into the sky. Quickly, almost frantically, she flew around to the other side, to the area of the antenna tower. There she spotted a lone flying platform hovering beside the massive piece of equipment. On the vehicle's deck stood Damon, hands on hips, staring up at the antenna, giving it all of his attention. Behind him, one of the Warlord's soldiers was rising, lurching forward.

"Damon! Look out!"

She was too far for him to hear her warning, too far away to stop it from happening.

The man knocked Damon to his knees.

Cursing, Lyn poured on the speed, swooping down on them.

She arrived just as the man grabbed Damon by his belt and flung him overboard.

"No!" she shouted

She zoomed downward, past the hovering vehicle, ignoring the trooper aboard it. Damon's silvery-gold sparkling form tumbled just ahead of her now. Reaching out with her electromagnetic energies, she created a force sphere around him and willed it to catch him.

Got you!

Then, once he was safely cradled inside it, she curved her own flight path upward, angling back toward the top of the tower.

Relief flooded over her.

"Lucky for you I happened by," she called back to him, matter-of-factly, sounding much more confident and cocky than she felt. "I—"

The blast caught her by surprise. She had divided her concentration and her powers between catching Damon and flying—something she was still not great at—and had failed to project a defensive sphere around herself. A greenish beam, coming from the floating platform above, hit her in the chest and sent her spinning out of control. She flailed to one side, her face cracking against the stone edifice of the tower, splitting her lip and nearly knocking her front teeth out. The metallic taste of blood filled her mouth. Even as she tumbled down, she realized her concentration had lapsed. The bubble she'd created had vanished.

Damon!

She zoomed down toward the city's surface.

Have to regain control, she thought, spitting blood, furious at her lack of mastery of her powers. *Have to find Damon again...*

She dodged another blast, working her sore jaw back and forth as she rocketed downward, squinting to see ahead of her.

There he is. Still falling. Good thing we're this high—and I didn't think I would have said that, *before.*

She reached out with her power, simultaneously keeping herself aloft, directing the course of her own flight, locating Damon, creating another force sphere to catch him, and directing it at him in such a way that it would intersect with his trajectory.

Too much. It's too much. Too many things at once. I can't—

No. I can. I will!

Despite her pain, she remembered almost everything. She kept herself moving along through the air even as she reached out with her power and snagged Damon once again in a bubble.

She only forgot one simple thing—again—and it came to her, an instant too late.

A shield above me. Oh, no—

Too late. The blast hit her square in the back, searing her golden mesh bodysuit, shocking her severely, and knocking her out.

Limp, she tumbled downward.

Damon fell.

47

Though no one realized it at first, the damage first Pulsar and then Damon had inflicted upon the Warlord's telepathic control antenna had finally reached a critical mass. With a final shorting out of circuits, the device failed.

At that moment, all across the great floating city, workers and scientists and technicians and soldiers all suddenly stopped what they were doing and looked up, as one, their eyes wide with shock and fear.

Where are we?

They blinked, looking around, puzzled, as if seeing one another for the first time.

The Warlord, they all understood at once. *He captured us, enslaved us, dominated our minds and our wills via his super-technology.*

One by one, across the floating city, the former slaves got to their feet, reaching for whatever weapon or tool lay handy. They all now possessed full control of their own thoughts, their senses, yet most of them now shared a common purpose. A new purpose.

Find the Warlord! Punish him for what he's done! Kill him!

Others, however, their minds damaged by ill treatment, harsh conditions, and prolonged exposure to the telepathic signal, reacted differently. They ran wild, tearing into the city's infrastructure. They attacked guards, ripped out wiring, started fires, smashed control systems, and set off hastily improvised explosives.

It took only a few minutes of this before irreparable damage was done.

With a bang and a shudder, the great floating city of the Warlord began to fall.

42

The wind rushing in Pulsar's face woke her up.

What's going on? Where—?

The ground. It was coming at her, fast. Getting closer. And closer. And...

She directed every bit of her power into angling up, up, and away from the rapidly approaching surface.

A long, anguished wail escaping her lips, she curved out of her freefall and zoomed sideways, gritting her teeth, nearly biting her tongue off. She clipped the antennas off of several parked ground vehicles, then angled back up and—

Damon.

Where...?

NO!

She brought herself to a halt, hovering a few dozen feet above the ground, looking up, even as she realized how absurd that was... looking everywhere around her, searching...

Oh.

What she saw would stay in her mind for the rest of her life.

Damon...

Oh...

Oh, no.

I'm so sorry...

So sorry...

Hovering there, at the base of the mile-high tower of the Warlord, she sobbed.

49

The tower shuddered.

Even as Ultraa, Brachis, and Vanadium battled the Warlord, struggling to break through his impenetrable force field, the walls around them and the floor beneath them rocked and vibrated.

All of them hesitated, looking around, startled.

Again, the building shook violently, beyond anything any of them had noticed before.

The Warlord leapt away from them, vaulting up onto his command deck. A small man ran out onto the deck, bowing and scraping before him.

"Master, the city—"

"It is falling," Vanadium said loudly.

"—it is f—yes," Francisco said, glaring down at Vanadium.

Ultraa looked at Vanadium in shock.

"What have you done to my city?" the Warlord cried, moving from one control station to the next.

"We have killed it," Vanadium replied. *"We, and your former slaves."*

"Former slaves," the Warlord gasped, studying the displays, taking in the flood of warning signals coming from all over the city. "Oh, no."

"The antenna has been sabotaged, Master," Francisco said, his voice filled with terror. "The workers are revolting, destroying everything."

The Warlord glared first at his little assistant, then at the others.

"What Mage and that metal buffoon didn't destroy during their fight, the slaves are tearing apart now. This is intolerable!"

"The people," Ultraa said, looking back toward the hole in the sanctum's wall. "We have to save them."

"Yeah," Esro agreed, "but how?"

"That's more your area of expertise," Ultraa said.

He was noticing with concern that Pulsar had not come back yet.

"I'm sure you'll figure something out," he told Esro, clapping him on the back. Then he zoomed out through the hole, into the sky, angling down toward the antenna.

He found Pulsar hovering there, finishing the job she had begun, frying the antenna's already useless circuitry with an almost savage barrage of electromagnetic energy. Part of the metal boom snapped loose, spinning away in the wind.

Ultraa brought himself to a halt just next to her, nodding.

"Nice work. From what we can tell, tearing this thing up is already having a major effect. Now we—"

He stopped, seeing Pulsar's face. It was red, swollen, with tears still streaming from her eyes.

"Lyn—what—?"

"Damon," she whispered, looking down. Down.

"What—?"

Ultraa blinked.

"You mean…?"

She nodded, tears flowing again.

"Oh…"

He hesitated a moment, filled with turmoil. Then, he grasped her gently by the shoulder, pulling her face up, looking into her reddened eyes.

"You have to pull it together, Lyn. At least for now. Just for now. We're needed. Thousands of innocent people are depending on us."

She just stared at him, uncomprehending.

"This city is falling," he said. "All these people you've just freed—they're all going to die unless we can stop it."

She shuddered, rubbed at her eyes, then looked back at him and nodded.

"Okay. Let's go."

He looked back into her eyes, and saw the hard resolve forming there. He felt fiercely proud of her.

"Come on."

Together they soared back up toward the Warlord's sanctum at the tower's top.

Inside, they found Vanadium advancing on the Warlord, who stood high atop his command deck, leering down at them all. Esro was hunched over a control panel off to one side, his helmet under his arm, staring at the monitors. The little servant had scurried away.

"Can you keep the city in the air?" Pulsar angrily demanded of the Warlord.

"Keep it in the air?" the Warlord repeated, incredulous. He gestured to where his soldiers, freed of his mental command, were throwing down their weapons and fleeing. "Let it fall," he called out. "Now that this city is no longer mine, I care nothing for its fate."

He caressed one of the control panels lovingly, then brought his fist down upon it, hard, smashing it. Sparks and flames shot out.

"The energies acquired from this installation have been useful, but once I control the entirety of the fiery being, I will have access to more power than I could ever need."

He whirled about, his cloak flaring.

"Francisco! Prepare the escape capsule!"

Ultraa looked at Brachis and Pulsar, anger swelling inside him.

"This guy's not going to help us," he said, motioning toward the Warlord. "He's just running away. We have to do this ourselves."

"I... don't think I can hold the whole city up," Lyn said, utterly serious.

Ultraa couldn't help but smile at that.

"You'd try to, though, wouldn't you?"

"If...if it came to that..."

He shook his head.

"No, this will require a different approach."

"What do you have in mind?" Esro asked.

Ultraa looked at Vanadium.

"I'm leaving it in the hands of our friend here."

"A wise decision," said the metal man. *"Assuming I can access the city's controls."*

The Warlord did his part, vacating the command deck, following his servant out of the sanctum. Vanadium lofted silently up from the floor and over the edge, landing where the madman had stood only seconds earlier. He leaned over the consoles, studying the controls.

"Can you do this?" Ultraa asked.

"If it can be done," Vanadium replied.

He laid both hands flat on the surface and stood absolutely still.

The displays all around the chamber, all of them flashing red warning lights until now, slowly began to change to yellow, then to green.

"Anti-gravity systems are working, but are down to fifteen percent of capacity," the metal man intoned. *"Not enough."*

The city shuddered.

"We're slowing," Esro reported, watching another bank of displays with rapt attention. "Our descent isn't nearly as bad as before. But, still..."

"Pulsar, get outside and see what you can see," Ultraa ordered.

Lyn hesitated, then nodded and flew back outside.

"You just wanted her out of here in case we crash, didn't you?" Esro asked.

Ultraa gave him a half-smile and said nothing.

Vanadium groaned; a particularly disconcerting sound, coming from him. It sounded like a metal box squeezed by a trash compactor.

"Antigravity to twenty percent," he intoned in his flat, metallic voice. *"Thirty."*

"Slowing more," Esro said. "But we're awfully close to the ground, now. It's going to be tight—"

Pulsar zoomed back inside.

"We're coming down over some big gray buildings," she called out. "We're going to crush them, even if we don't totally crash."

"Thirty five. Forty."

"Impact in five," Esro shouted. "Four. Three. Two..."

The floor lurched beneath them, twice, the second time much worse. The force of the impact hurtled them into the air. The walls around them cracked, in the places that weren't already damaged. The tower swayed drunkenly.

"Power levels just flatlined," Esro reported. "Whatever we landed on, it must have included the generators."

"We have to get everyone out of here now," Ultraa shouted.

"But how?" Pulsar demanded. "There are too many—"

"No," Vanadium said. *"We are down. Structural integrity will hold."*

Another series of grinding, rumbling vibrations, and the movement stopped.

Esro mopped at his sweaty brow. He grinned at the others.

"He did it!"

He climbed up onto the command deck and put an arm around Vanadium.

"You did it, pal! You saved everyone!"

Vanadium glanced at him, then gestured toward the exit.

"The Warlord is escaping."

"Not for long," Ultraa said.

"A random element, Francisco," the Warlord said, scowling behind his silver mask. "This... *Vanadium*. He could not be accounted for in my planning."

"No, Master," Francisco replied. "Of course not."

"Who would have imagined he would appear when he did, and involve himself in the affair? That he could defeat Mage?"

The Warlord made his way quickly through the narrow tube that led to his escape capsule. Arriving at the small vehicle, he prepared to climb aboard. Francisco had already strapped himself into his own seat. The Warlord reached up to open his section of the canopy—

—and a red-gloved fist caught him in the jaw, knocking him away from the capsule and sending him sprawling to the floor.

He leapt to his feet instantly, glaring at Ultraa, even as the blond man settled nearby. With a gesture, his personal force field shimmered into existence around him.

"A lucky strike," he growled. "You caught me by surprise."

Ultraa started forward again, but before he could move, a blue-silver shape appeared behind the Warlord.

"Master," Francisco cried. "Beware!"

Vanadium's metal arms reached out, his hands touching the energy sphere surrounding the masked villain. He squeezed.

"Now," the Warlord hissed. "Now it is time to—"

He gasped, as the force field surrounding him fizzled out, vanished.

"What in—?"

Ultraa smiled back at him.

"Esro figured out what you meant before, about the power of this city," he said. "It wasn't power over people—it was the power you were pulling out of its generators, out of the planet itself."

Ultraa shrugged.

"Your generators were crushed when the city crashed."

The Warlord staggered back a step.

"No matter," he said then, defiantly. "I have many more sources of power located throughout the multiverse."

He gestured with his left hand, then with his right.

"I have but to tap into another and—"

He continued to gesture, but nothing was happening. His voice trailed off.

"None of it is working," he whispered then. "Why...?"

Esro walked up behind Ultraa, manipulating the controls on his armor's forearm panel.

"We've already established that my shielding can block even your abilities," he said. "In your newly weakened state, well..."

He shrugged.

"Good luck pulling in any outside energy through the force bubble I've just slapped around you."

"Mine is helping keep it out, too," Pulsar said, as she came up behind Esro. Her tears were gone, replaced on her face by a fierce determination.

"Double whammy," Ultraa said. "So, no more power, no more force field."

He punched the Warlord again, sending the man stumbling back against the side of the escape capsule.

Vanadium, hovering behind the villain, reached down, clutching his shoulder as he sought to rise. A series of lights flickered along Vanadium's arm, then moved down onto the Warlord. Instantly, the layers of microscopic systems ingrained into the Warlord's costume shorted out, sparks flying everywhere, flames leaping from several points on the man's body. He screamed in shock and pain, falling back to lean against the capsule, beating at the fires burning in his robes.

Vanadium settled to the floor next to Ultraa and the others.

"You're finished, Warlord," Ultraa said. "You have no more tricks. You've been cut off from any other power sources. Your weapons and defenses have been destroyed."

The Warlord began frantically pushing buttons on his blue gauntlets, all to no avail.

"Cooperate with us, help us get back home, answer a few questions," Ultraa said, "and we'll try to get them to go easy on you."

The villain stared back at Ultraa for a moment, then pulled himself up to his full height, taking an arrogant and defiant stance.

"Never! I am the Warlord! The War—"

He broke down into a violent coughing fit. Smoke issued from behind his silver mask as circuits within it shorted out. He fanned the smoke away, recovered, and glared at them.

"You're beaten, is what you are," Esro said.

"No! You haven't won. No one can—"

He stopped suddenly, looking down at himself in surprise.

Six inches of steel protruded from his chest.

He gasped, choking up blood that ran from the mouth hole of his mask.

"I—I dispute this judgment," he croaked, to the utter mystification of the others present. "I repudiate it! I have not failed! In fact, I—"

He choked, blood now leaking down the front of the silver mask and onto his robes.

The others just gawked at this, completely taken aback.

The Warlord slumped against the capsule. Behind him, Francisco released the long dagger and grabbed hold of the Warlord by the shoulders, exhibiting surprising strength in dragging his body back into the capsule.

"The wheel turns," he told them, matter-of-factly, as if that explained everything.

Before anyone else could move, the little man slapped at the control panel and the capsule shimmered and vanished.

The others stared at the empty spot where the escape craft had been. Then they looked at one another.

"Well. What do you make of all that?" Esro finally asked.

"After everything else I've seen today," Ultraa replied, "I think it's par for the course."

"No kidding," Lyn said.

"Any way to track them?" Ultraa asked, looking at both Esro and Vanadium.

Esro pulled his helmet off and shrugged. "Not that I know of."

"They have moved sideways through reality," Vanadium stated. *"We would require a new dimensional portal, and—"*

"Forget it," Ultraa interjected.

Esro nodded agreement. "By the time we did all that—assuming we even could—and reached whatever alternate reality they've fled to, they'd probably be long gone. I think we should just chalk this one up a win—or close enough."

"No," Lyn snapped. "Not a win."

Esro looked at her, frowning. Then he turned in a full circle, growing more concerned by the moment.

"Umm... where's Damon?"

Lyn's tears were flowing again. Ultraa shook his head, his mouth set in a grim line.

Esro took a step back, understanding now. He rubbed at his thick hair with one hand, staring down at the floor.

No one made a sound for several seconds, until finally Ultraa cleared his throat. "I think we should turn our attention now to finding a way back home," he said quietly.

Still in something of a daze, Esro nodded and gestured to indicate the tons of ultra-high-tech equipment surrounding them.

"Right," he said. "Between our metal friend here and myself, we should be able to figure something out."

Ultraa nodded. "Good. Get to it."

Lyn was tearing up again. Ultraa reached out and hugged her to himself.

"You were right," she whispered. "I shouldn't have come."

"That's not true," he replied. "We're all very lucky you did."

"No," she said, after a moment, her voice filled with a deep sorrow. She gazed out toward the jagged opening in the wall. "Not all of us."

51

Lying back in a soft leather chair in Esro's living room, Lyn held an ice pack to her forehead.

"How are you feeling?" Ultraa asked, standing over her and inspecting her bruised face.

"Better," she said. "Thanks."

"Good."

She sipped at a glass of tea and set it back on the table beside her.

"No matter what any of you say, I know the truth. I shouldn't have been there." She met Ultraa's blue eyes and frowned. "You were right. I didn't have enough training to know what I was doing—to use my powers properly. I couldn't remember everything at once."

Unsure of how to react, Ultraa sat down across from her, listening.

"And, y'know, I *had* him! I had Damon—I had caught him—and I let myself get shot in the back. And I...dropped him."

She gazed up at Ultraa.

"If it had been you, or even Esro, you would have saved him," she said quietly. "You wouldn't have forgotten to defend yourself. You wouldn't have been caught from behind like I was."

She dabbed at her eyes with a tissue.

"You told me not to come, and I did anyway. It was impetuous and immature and stupid. And it's my fault he's dead."

"That's ridiculous," Ultraa said. "You did everything you could. It wasn't your fault."

She shook her head.

"I was stupid to even think I should be some kind of hero," she muttered. "I knew better, from the start. I never planned on it. But seeing you, and Esro, and Damon..."

She sobbed again.

"I should hang this all up, and go back to Bay City. Back to school."

"No," Ultraa said firmly. "No."

She looked up at him, frowning.

"If you hadn't been there," he continued, "we wouldn't have made it. None of us. You saved all of us more than once."

She just sighed.

"Seriously, Lyn. You'd scarcely had any training, and yet you still accomplished all that you did."

He smiled down at her.

"I was impressed."

She looked at him, her expression mixed. Clearly she wasn't sure what to believe now.

Ultraa stood and walked back across the room.

"In my line of work, Lyn, people are sometimes hurt. People *die*. But we have to do it. We can't give up because it seems too hard, too painful—physically or emotionally. The threats, the bad guys lurking out there—they aren't giving up. We can't, either."

She took this in, and neither of them spoke for a while. When at last she broke the silence, her voice was stronger.

"I was mean to him," she said. "To Damon. I know I was. And, really, he wasn't that bad of a guy. I should have been nicer..."

"You were fine toward him," Ultraa said. "But you can't go through life treating everyone differently than you feel you should, on the off chance they might be killed tomorrow. That's just how life is, Lyn. We do the best we can, and we act as decently as we are able, on any given day... and sometimes, despite all that, bad things happen anyway."

She nodded slowly.

162

"In point of fact," he went on, "I was usually *too* patient with him. He needed a knock upside the head, more often than not. Sometimes *two* knocks."

He smiled wistfully.

"But, in the end, he gave his life heroically. Trying to help a whole lot of people, and his friends, too. We can be proud of him, and remember him well. Like you said, he wasn't that bad of a guy."

They remained silent for a few minutes, lost in thought. Finally, Ultraa walked across and sat on the edge of the chair opposite Lyn, leaning forward, chin resting in his hands, frowning.

"If you're willing to stick around, to not give up and go home…"

She looked back at him, nodding slowly.

"…I will be needing a new partner. A full-time partner. Not just a student."

"A partner?"

Her eyes widened. Then she frowned.

"Wait a second. Is this like a 'sidekick' type of position we're talking about?"

"No, no."

He laughed.

"Working for the government, as I do, occasionally, they prefer for me to have someone along with me—backup, support, a witness to what happens, and so forth."

She nodded.

"So far, so good."

"And you do need further training in how to use your powers."

"Don't remind me," she said, groaning.

"So…?"

She thought for a moment, then nodded her agreement.

"As long as it doesn't interfere with my work with Esro. Or my getting back to school here, soon."

"Right," he said. Then, "Now that Esro's decided to use the armor he had developed for Damon, I think he'll be working with us in the field a lot more, too."

"And what about Vanadium?"

Ultraa shrugged.

"Who can tell? I know virtually nothing about him. But as long as he wants to help us, his power is welcome, as far as I'm concerned."

Lyn set the ice pack aside, the first genuine smile appearing on her face in quite some time.

"Oh," she said. "I was wondering this already, but if we're going to be partners, it has extra significance."

He looked at her, waiting.

"Your name," she said. "It gets sort of weird, just calling you 'Ultraa' all the time. I'd really like to know your name."

"You know it," he said. "Ultraa."

"No, silly. Your *real* name. Like mine is Lyn Li. Yours is...?"

He smiled back at her, sheepishly, but said nothing.

Her smile turned into a puzzled frown.

"You can't tell me? I don't mean to invade your privacy or anything, but at this point..."

"I have told you. It's Ultraa. If I had another name, I'd tell it to you."

Lyn felt an odd shock of realization.

"You—you don't *have* a real name?"

He stared at the floor, hands moving through his hair.

"I—I, um..."

Lyn felt suddenly embarrassed. She blushed.

"Umm... Ultraa... Jeez, I didn't mean..."

"Don't worry about it. It's fine. It's certainly understandable that you would ask."

"Uh, well, okay..."

Lyn trailed off, her hand moving over her mouth in subconscious shock. Silently she stared back at her friend and associate, a man she'd worked with, studied under, and fought alongside. Now she wondered for the first time if she really knew him at all.

52

"So that's it," Esro Brachis said over the connection. "With my test subject, Damon Sinclair, recently deceased, and my work on the Cavalier Project at sort of a stopping point, I'm going to exercise my right to close out the contract."

"I see," Jameson said.

"I appreciate all that the government has done to help with my work, and I hope that what you've gotten in return is worth the investment you made. I feel that it is."

Jameson nodded.

"Yes, we have no complaints. You have given us several very useful systems in return for our grant money and assistance."

He smiled inwardly.

"In fact, I believe we have gotten as much from you as we possibly could, for now. We are pleased."

"Okay," Brachis replied, guardedly, not entirely sure he liked the sound of that. "Good."

"Should you wish to work with us again, you have my number," Jameson added.

"Absolutely," Brachis said. "Thank you."

"Don't mention it."

Jameson hung up the phone. He waited a few seconds, thinking, then picked it up again, tapping out the number quickly.

"The Cavalier Project is officially terminated," he said as soon as the call was answered. "You have the green light for Operation Paladin."

"Understood."

The line clicked closed.

He hung up the phone and sat back in his big, overstuffed leather chair, clasping his fingers before his face, thinking to himself.

"Damon, my boy," he said softly, "if only you hadn't died..."

He snorted.

"At least, if only you hadn't died before you could bring me a crystal with all of Esro Brachis's data on it, like I asked you to. Ah, what a coup that would have been."

He allowed himself a slight smile.

"Still, what we did get was well worth all the efforts."

A few minutes later, still lost in thought, Jameson looked up as his administrative assistant buzzed him.

"Someone to see you, sir," she said.

The door opened, admitting the visitor.

Jameson stood, frowning.

"*Herr* Jameson, yes? My contacts in this worl—*country*—recommended I bring this to you."

Jameson accepted a small data crystal from the man, plugged it into his computer, and stared in amazement as files and schematics scrolled across the screen. After a few seconds, he looked back up at the man.

"I—yes, if this is what I think it is..."

He licked his lips, his heart beating much faster now.

"...I think you did quite well in bringing this to me."

165

The other man bowed slightly. Jameson looked hard at him for the first time. He had short, gray hair, was clad in a black and gray uniform of some sort, and wore a patch over one eye.

Jameson found himself slightly put off by the man's appearance, at first, but then shrugged.

He's hardly any more eccentric than some of the others I have working for me...

He shook hands with the older man.

"If this is any indication of the kind of work you can do, I believe we can enjoy a mutually profitable relationship in the future," he said. "And you are...?"

"You may call me the Field Marshal," the man replied, one corner of his mouth curling upward in a cold smile.

53

The new sanctum was complete. Francisco had labored long and hard at it, finding a new pocket universe to occupy, bringing in the raw materials, and constructing the beginnings of a new flying fortress. For now, it consisted merely of the central, spherical chamber, resting high on a mountaintop in the wilderness. No army of slaves, no floating city, this time—at least, not yet.

And, for now, the only living occupant was Francisco himself.

Across the room from him, on a raised platform, lay the purple-and-blue-robed body of the Warlord. Lifeless eyes stared up through the holes in the sliver mask. As Francisco watched nervously, the corpse suddenly shimmered, sparkled, and vanished.

Francisco leapt to his feet, prancing about, giddy. He fairly shook with excitement and anticipation.

"The wheel turns! The Grand Design continues! The Warlord returns," he cried, over and over, clapping his hands. "The Warlord returns!"

Moments later, a sphere of light appeared in the darkened room, slowly taking form, congealing into the shape of a man—a man clad in solid blue robes, wearing a silver mask.

"Francisco? I am here."

The little servant bounded about him happily.

"Master! Master, you've been away for so long! I feared you would not come back to me this time!"

He raced up to the Warlord. Then he stopped, tilted his head sideways, sniffed the air. He frowned, eyeing the man with suspicion.

"You...You're not—"

"No, Francisco."

The tall figure looked down at him, arms folded, blue cape drawn tightly about him.

"I am not the Warlord you knew."

He reached out, caressing Francisco's head once.

"Your judgment was sound. You were quite right to kill him. His efforts were too limited, on the one hand, and too visible, on the other. He made a target of himself. He was foolish, and deserved what he received."

Francisco gaped at him.

"You—you *know*? Already, you know what he was—"

"I know all of it, Francisco. All of it, and more."

He turned his back on the little man and strode confidently into the heart of the sanctum, looking around in apparent appreciation.

"His plan was ill-conceived and incompetently executed, but his ultimate aim was correct."

He raised his arms as if in triumph, his gesture broad enough to engulf the universe—the *multiverse*—itself.

"It must all be unified."

Behind his silver mask, he grinned.

"The work begins again. Where previous Warlords failed, I shall succeed. I am all that they were," he cried out. "All—and *much more!*"

Francisco, ignored now, curled himself up in the corner, rocking back and forth, and whined softly to himself.

54

In the small shielded room inside Esro's main laboratory, the fiery being—the counterpart to Kabaraak—sat up suddenly, climbed from the table, and walked across to the door. He paused, as if mulling over some important thought, and then opened it. He strode across the lab and then floated up, up, to the ceiling, passing, ghostlike, through it. He emerged into the night sky of northern Virginia and continued on, away, gone, miles from there in an instant. Then, in another instant, he was an entire universe away.

He appeared with a flash in the wrecked remains of the Warlord's abandoned floating city. Unerringly he made his way to what had been the top of the tower. There, he found the indentation in the floor caused when his angry counterpart, Kabaraak, was smashed down into it by the Warlord.

He kneeled over the spot, touching the indentation with one hand.

Kabaraak appeared, his orange and crimson body taking form, his flames igniting as he solidified.

The creature gazed up at its counterpart—at itself.

"You."

"Yes."

Kabaraak looked around, seeing the condition of the room, of the city.

"Time has passed."

"Only a little."

"I lost my physical containment—my integrity. I dispersed."

"True."

"You have brought me back."

"Quite so."

The fiery creature on the floor nodded.

"Very well."

The angelic being leaned closer over him, laying both hands upon him.

"I wish," the shining white one said, "that you were not necessary to me."

"Yes. And that you were not necessary to me," the other replied.

"Yes. But we need one another," the first one continued. "And I—we—have much yet to do."

Reluctantly, the fiery creature beneath him nodded again.

With a flash, the two forms melded back into one.

"Ah," the reunified being said. "We are the *true* Kabaraak again. Whole. Complete."

A pause.

"The one called Vanadium did this to us," it said. "So long ago. A thousand years ago. Yes. I remember it now."

A pause, then:

"It matters not. The end is near. The Master approaches. And he will add the Earth to all else that he has gathered unto himself."

The flaming creature, no longer quite resembling either of its previous incarnations, but instead a curious combination of both, rose into the air.

"And when Stellarax the Great wishes to add to his vast collection, who can stand against him?"

With a flash, the fiery being vanished.

EPILOGUE:
Evening at the Mansion

That night, with Lyn cozy in her bed, Ultraa deeply engrossed in an old novel, and Esro happily at work on his latest technological creation, the blue-silver metal being called Vanadium walked outside Brachis's mansion and stood alone, still as a statue. He looked upward, the tiny, red lights of his eyes peering at the stars twinkling overhead.

The cool air blowing over the northern Virginia landscape scarcely registered to him. His mind was turned inward, to his past, searching through half-understood scraps of memories from centuries now far removed. Some few remained vivid. Some were hazy. Most, he feared, would never return.

The cold stars taunted him silently, offering the possibility of answers, somewhere out there. But—where?

"I came from there," he said softly, gazing upward. *"But...who am I? What am I? And why am I here?"*

"Questions we all ask ourselves, sooner or later."

At the sound of the voice, Vanadium looked back, and saw Ultraa walking up behind him. He nodded.

"Yes," he said. *"But in my own case...potentially explosive questions. I...fear the answers, even as I seek them."*

"Believe it or not," Ultraa replied, "I know what you mean."

The big man seemed to study him for a moment, then looked away, saying nothing.

The two stood there together and watched the sky for a long while, in silence.

Finally, Vanadium turned to Ultraa.

"I encountered the creature 'Kabaraak' before, long ago," he said. *"I have only the slightest memories of it. But what little that I recall indicates catastrophic danger."*

170

Ultraa frowned.

"Danger for you? For us?"

"For this world."

The blond man stared back at him a moment, then nodded.

"Of course," he said, with a morbid laugh. "What else would it be?"

Another long silence, then Vanadium spoke again.

"Kabaraak had a master. Of this I am certain."

"A master?"

"A being nearly as ancient as this universe. An entity of unfathomable might."

Ultraa took this in, ran a hand across his chin, and nodded slowly.

"I believe that he called out to it—that his master approaches," Vanadium said. *"When it arrives, none on this world can stand against it."*

Ultraa nodded once more.

"Maybe so," he said. "Maybe that's true. But, be that as it may, we will try. We will give it our all. There's nothing else we can do."

He clapped a hand on Vanadium's shoulder, staring up at the dark depths above. He thought of the cold, grim intelligence that might, even now, be racing toward Earth. Involuntarily, he shivered. Inside, though, he felt a sense of anger growing—an outrage at the thought that he and his friends could be written off so easily.

Earth has defenders—and it will have more, Ultraa vowed to himself, *before this dark menace arrives.*

We will be ready.

He moved away from Vanadium, walking back through the cold night, heading for the warmth and light of the house, which suddenly seemed very inviting to him. Halfway there, though, he paused and looked back at the enigmatic metal man.

"We will stand against the enemy to the bitter end, if need be," he said. "For whatever it's worth. Win or lose."

"Win or die," Vanadium replied.

Ultraa nodded.

"But know that we *will* fight for our world."

Vanadium looked at him, then looked back up at the sky.

"Yes…"

BOOK TWO:
A DISTANT STAR

This one's for the EBs of the AML

PROLOGUE:
Five Minutes Ago

The sleek, futuristic alien spacecraft shuddered as it swooped fitfully down into Esro Brachis's back yard.

The northern Virginia night was cool for late September, and a strong cross-breeze tugged at the ship, playing havoc with its already damaged controls. The pilot, obviously quite skillful, somehow managed to keep the vehicle under control, at the cost of the tops of a couple of trees and a telephone cable.

The ship itself had once been a bright, shiny silver in color, but now the lights in the yard revealed a multitude of scorch and burn marks along every surface. A large, disturbing crack ran across one of the front windows.

With a lurch and a jolt, the ship settled to the immaculately tended lawn. A hatch opened in the side, and out jumped a quite human male with ragged, unkempt brown hair, sporting what looked to be several days' growth of beard. He wore the more or less intact components of a suit of high-tech armor, once gray in color but now as damaged and discolored as the ship, if not more so. Under his left arm he carried a helmet, a series of large dents running down one side of it. He raced across the lawn, toward the mansion's rear entrance, then hesitated. He seemed to be thinking twice about the actions he was about to take, as if some odd intuitive doubt had occurred to him. After a moment's consideration, he turned and jogged over to a broad window in the side of the mansion. He peered inside.

It was bright in there. His eyes required a second or two to adjust. Then the view became clear, and he could see the people inside.

"Oh, crap," he whispered, frowning.

He rubbed his eyes, hoping they were somehow playing tricks on him but knowing they were not. He looked again.

Inside the main living room area he could see pretty much what he had expected to see. On one sofa sprawled a teen-aged girl wearing a gray sweatsuit; the golden, metal mesh outfit she wore underneath showed at her wrists, ankles, and collar. She stared at the television while idly munching from a bowl of popcorn. Across from her stood a thirtyish man with blond hair, wearing a white jumpsuit with red boots and gloves. He was speaking to a very tall figure that appeared to have been cast from blue-silver metal. The big figure's face was a featureless mask, aside from two dark eyes punctuated by tiny red lights in place of pupils.

All of this was well and good. The problem, however, was the fourth figure in the room.

"Crap," the man watching through the window whispered again. "How can—how can that—"

He scratched his chin, the wheels in his mind turning, but not turning up any answers.

"How is that even *possible?*"

That fourth figure wore a Hawaiian shirt and gray pants with lots of pockets. He had short, brown hair and was clean-shaven. He sat at a worktable, tools in hand, bending over a piece of electronic equipment he was working on. And the man at the window knew him—knew him quite well. His name was Esro Brachis.

Esro Brachis, who could not possibly be there. He simply couldn't *be* there.

And yet, there he was.

"Ohhhh," the man outside breathed, a second later. "Oh, I get it. I...*remember.*" He followed this immediately with, "Crap crap crap crap crap."

At that moment, Brachis sat up straight at the worktable and turned, facing directly toward the window. He squinted as he peered through it. Then, frowning, he started to rise.

The man in the damaged gray armor jumped as if he'd been shot. Instantly he whirled around and sprinted back across the lawn toward the spacecraft. As he ran, he yelled, "Mondy! Mooooooonnnnnndyyyyyy!"

A woman had descended the ramp of the shuttle. Tall and slender, she wore a blue flight suit of alien design. Golden bracelets circled her wrists and ankles, and a thick mane of white hair trailed down her back. Her skin was a bright red in color.

"Mondy," the man shouted, running. "It's wrong! It's all wrong!"

The woman stopped at the bottom of the ramp, startled.

"What are you talking about?" she asked.

"It's too soon," the man replied, racing up the ramp and into the shuttle. "*We're* too soon. *Way* too soon!"

"I am not sure I understand," the woman said, turning to follow him as he ran.

"We're *early!*"

"Early?"

The man flung himself into the copilot's seat and looked back at her, expectantly.

"Yeah, exactly."

He looked around the cockpit frantically.

"You have some kind of stealth setting, right? Invisibility or something?"

"Yes..."

The woman clicked a button on a panel of her sleeve, and the shuttle shimmered and vanished from the sight of anyone outside of it.

"But why should you want to—"

"Fire this bucket up and get us out of here, quick," the man said, interrupting her. "We have to figure out what to do about this!"

More confused than ever, the woman nonetheless started to follow him into the shuttle. After a few steps she paused and lingered at the top of the ramp, looking back toward the mansion.

"Someone has come outside," she said. "A man in a very...floral shirt. I think he saw you. He's coming this way."

"Yeah," the man said. "That's the problem."

"But—I do not understand. Why is any of this a problem?"

"Because that guy you're seeing there—he's *me!*"

7

Esro Brachis walked back into his mansion, a puzzled expression on his face.

"What was it, Esro?" called Lyn Li, her mouth full of popcorn, her words nearly unintelligible. She sat in her customary spot on the sofa, a big bowl of her favorite snack in her lap. A little over five feet tall, with brown eyes, Lyn wore her silky black hair to just longer than shoulder length. A snug, golden, metal mesh bodysuit covered everything except her head and her hands, though currently she wore a gray sweat suit over it.

Brachis glanced over at her and shook his head, still frowning.

"Dunno. Could've sworn I saw somebody out there, but…"

A moment's silence as Esro chewed his bottom lip, thinking.

"Yeah?" Lyn asked.

He shook his head.

"…Nothing."

He'd looked all around, but the yard had appeared empty. Even the ultra-high-tech sensors he'd set up all around the mansion reported no intruders, nothing out of place. Despite this, Esro continued to feel a very strange sensation creeping over him—a sense of being watched, and of déjà vu, sort of at the same time—though in the last few seconds it had mercifully begun to fade.

He lifted the glass of Dr. Pepper he'd been sipping earlier, peering at it, wondering if he'd somehow poured in a shot of bourbon without realizing it. Then he yawned, stretched, and resolved to put the whole business behind him. He walked across the living room to where Vanadium, tall and muscular and encased in blue-silver metal—or perhaps actually made from it; that was one of the questions Esro dearly hoped to answer, someday—stood talking with Ultraa, their resident hero, government operative, and media darling.

"Come on," Brachis said. "Break's over. Let's get going with phase two of the testing, before it gets any later and I fall asleep."

Ultraa and Vanadium finished their conversation and both turned to face Esro.

Ultraa was right at six feet tall, with blond hair and blue eyes and all-American looks. He wore a white uniform with flared red gloves and boots and a thick red belt. The look seemed somewhat flamboyant for someone as genuinely modest and selfless as Ultraa, but he wore it anyway, believing that serving as a visually inspiring figure for the public was part of his job.

"If you don't need me for this," Ultraa said, gesturing toward the labs with a red-gloved hand, "I'm going to make some calls. Government business."

"No problem," Esro replied.

"Yeah," Lyn called to Ultraa from the sofa. "I can keep him out of trouble."

Brachis gave her an ugly look.

"Whatever," he growled.

Ultraa chuckled, tapping Esro on the chest.

"You're even starting to talk like her now," he said with a grin.

"Hey!" Esro and Lyn yelled simultaneously.

Ultraa laughed at them both, blue eyes flashing, then strode out and closed the door behind him.

Esro and Lyn started to say something further to one another, but a towering, metal form moved smoothly, silently between them.

"Let us proceed," Vanadium said in his cold, hollow voice.

"Um, sure," Esro replied uneasily. He turned to where Lyn had been, but she was already headed out the door. Vanadium followed after her, and she smiled back at the big, metal man.

Am I the only one who finds this guy creepy? Esro wondered. *I mean, I know he's a teammate, and he pretty much saved our bacon on the Warlord's floating city, but still...What do we really know about him?*

Not a lot, came the answer he knew to be true. *Not enough. Which is why I'm taking every opportunity to study him.*

He followed the two of them back through the mansion, toward the labs at the rear of the big residence. They entered one of the smaller rooms, filled with all sorts of computers and displays on one end, the other end occupied mostly by a broad, spherical, transparent bubble, about eight feet tall and twelve feet wide, a reinforced metal door set into its side. Esro pulled the door open and gestured.

"Step into the chamber, Vanadium. You know the drill."

The blue-silver being strode past Esro and through the hatch, seating himself on the wide, metal bench at the center. Cables dangled from the ceiling and lined the floors; multicolored lights sparkled to life around him.

Esro walked around to the central control console and looked it over, nodding to himself. Slowly he moved a set of sliding controls upward, watching the indicators carefully, his eyes constantly flickering from the panel in front of him to the monitor overhead. On it was displayed a variety of constantly changing numbers, blips, moving lines, and computer-generated images.

"So, tell me again what we're doing," said Lyn, still munching popcorn.

"*We* aren't doing anything," Esro growled. "And get that out of my lab."

Lyn frowned, looked around, and then shoved the remaining handful of popcorn into her mouth.

Esro gave her a look of unmitigated disgust.

"Whmhhh?"

Shaking his head at her, he continued.

"What *I'm* doing is attempting to learn a bit more about our friend in there."

"Right," Lyn said, having swallowed the last of the popcorn. Leaning over Esro's shoulder, she was studying the displays. "For Vanadium's benefit, though, right?"

Esro looked at her, a beatific smile on his face.

"Yeah. Of course. I meant to say, 'helping our friend in there to learn more about himself.'"

"Mm hmm."

Esro manipulated the controls. A hum filled the air. The light in the transparent chamber pulsed.

"By microwaving him?" Lyn asked, her eyes widening.

Esro sighed.

"I'm not microwaving him."

He continued to manipulate the controls.

"But, well—you sort of are," she replied, pointing at the controls.

"Okay, well, kind of," he admitted. "But…I'm simply directing different forms of energy and radiation at him, and measuring the results—how much he absorbs, how much he reflects, and so on. It doesn't bother him or harm him in the least."

Chewing on a fingernail, Lyn nodded.

"What I'm doing is attempting to learn a bit more about our friend in there."

"I can microwave stuff," she said, matter-of-factly, after a second.

"Yeah, how 'bout that," Esro grunted. "So can I."

Lyn sighed. It was a sound filled with the infinite patience she felt she required in order to deal with Esro—remarkably similar to his own feelings about her.

"Yesterday I heated up a frozen pizza," she went on, "just by holding it between my hands."

"Huh," Esro grunted, scarcely paying her any attention. "And did anything in the room explode, when you did this?"

"No," Lyn stated emphatically, hands on hips. Then she chewed her lip. "Not this time, anyway."

"Well, that's progress, then," Esro said, his eyes never leaving the display screens.

"Was kinda sticky, though," she murmured.

Esro looked back at her, frowning.

"Why are you here?"

"Um, because I'm your assistant, of course," she replied, giving him an ugly look.

"Oh, yeah." He turned back to the control board. "I keep trying to forget that."

Esro stood up, ignoring the fact that Lyn was sticking her tongue out at him, and adjusted a series of knobs on an overhead panel. Of average height, Esro Brachis had short, dark brown hair, and almost exclusively wore faded jeans and Hawaiian shirts—when he wasn't wearing his gray and black, high-tech armor.

He sat again and clicked on the intercom.

"Vanadium, you doing okay in there, pal?"

"All systems nominal," the hollow voice replied.

The humming sound grew louder, as Esro increased the power flowing into the chamber.

"I think my hair's standing on end," Lyn said.

"This shouldn't be anything to you," Esro replied. "You can probably absorb anything that's leaking around the shielding."

"Yeah?"

Lyn frowned, concentrating. Her golden-clad form began to glow softly as she attempted to reach out with her electromagnetic abilities. Not entirely sure what she was doing, she simply attempted to sense any energies around her. For several long moments, nothing happened.

And then the world went away.

Panic surged within her, and she could feel her body stumbling, her hands automatically reaching out to steady herself. Then she realized with horror that she couldn't see her hands, or her body. Everything around her had suddenly become less solid. The room, the equipment, even Esro—all seemed reduced to grid lines, to wireframe constructs.

As curious about it as she was frightened by it, she forced the panic down, and looked around at the bizarre universe now visible to her.

Time slowed, within her perceptions. She could hear her own heartbeat, but it came so slowly, so slowly...

In addition to the wireframe lines, she could see waves of force, currents of energy, washing over her—over everything. She could see them, *taste* them, all around her. She raised her right hand in front of her, reaching, reaching...

A tall, solidly built form she recognized as Ultraa stepped into her field of vision. She blinked, her eyes slowly focusing on him.

"She's back," he said, over his shoulder.

"That's a relief," Esro said, moving up beside him. "I was thinking of trying smelling salts, or maybe a cattle prod."

Ultraa gave Esro a disapproving glance, then looked back at Lyn. "Do you feel okay?"

"I...I think so." She rubbed her eyes and forehead. "What happened?"

"You sort of zoned out there for a little while," Esro stated. "One second we were talking, and the next..."

She looked around. The lines were entirely gone; the room had reverted to normal.

She focused on Ultraa again.

"Hey, where'd you come from?"

"I've been here for ten minutes," he replied. "Ten minutes of worrying about you. We really weren't sure what was happening."

She frowned, her brain catching up with her ears.

"Ten minutes?"

Esro nodded.

"Yeah. It's like you were moving in slow motion. Almost like you were sleepwalking."

"We were most concerned," Vanadium said—and Lyn realized he must have exited the bubble while she was out, and was now standing on the far side of the lab. *"Yet my sensor readings indicated you were healthy and in no immediate danger."*

She took all this in, then shook her head.

"Yeah, I'm okay. But that was… interesting."

Ultraa smiled slightly, then leaned in, studying her closely.

"I was afraid to try too hard to wake you up. Didn't know what might happen," he said, frowning. "We still don't know a whole lot about your powers."

He glanced back at Esro.

"At least, *I* don't."

Hunched over a console, not looking at them, Esro shrugged.

"Hey, if I startled her, she might have blown up the refrigerator or something," he muttered.

Lyn shot him an ugly look.

"So, Esro," Ultraa continued, pressing his point as subtly as he was able, "if there *is* anything I should know about…about *her*, about her powers, what have you… Just to be safe, in the future…?"

"You know about as much as I do, pal," he replied, continuing to work.

"To be honest," Lyn said, "I'm not entirely sure what I'm able to do, myself. These… abilities… came on all at once, a little over three years ago, and for the longest time I tried to pretend they didn't even exist."

She looked away, embarrassed, then stared down at the floor.

"I didn't want people to make fun of me, or think I was some kind of a freak, or something…"

Esro reflexively opened his mouth to reply to that, looked up and saw Ultraa staring sternly at him, and closed it again.

"And since I've been around you and Esro," Lyn continued, oblivious, "things have been happening so fast…"

Esro nodded absently, returning his attention to the controls in front of him.

"I know, Lyn," he said, his voice more serious now. "I'll give you a full going-over, get a full inventory of what you can do, once things settle down. Promise."

"Okay," Lyn replied, still staring at the floor.

But when, she wondered to herself, *will things ever settle down? When will my life ever get back to normal—and do I really want it to, anymore?*

"In fact," Esro was saying, "we probably should take you out to the Oasis to do it. I keep a few of my best pieces of equipment there—stuff I absolutely, positively don't want stolen."

"So you mean you don't think of this place as secure?" Ultraa asked, but with an expression that very effectively conveyed his sarcasm. Esro's mansion had been attacked or infiltrated at least three times since Lyn had moved in and their current team had come to exist.

"Some days," Esro replied, "I think this place might as well have a revolving door installed in the front of it." A hint of bitterness had crept into his voice. "You're not a real super-criminal until you've robbed Esro Brachis."

Ultraa pursed his lips, thinking.

"Let me work on that a little," he said after a second. "Maybe I can come up with some ideas. High tech isn't always the only answer, you know. Or the best answer."

Esro frowned at that.

"It's not? I'm not sure I shouldn't feel insulted," he replied, and both men laughed.

"Hold on a second," Lyn piped in. "You said 'the Oasis.' What's that? It sounds like a strip club."

"That's probably where Esro came up with the name," Ultraa said with a grin.

"I already told you about it," Esro said, ignoring Ultraa.

"Um, no, you didn't."

"I didn't? Huh."

Lyn waited.

Esro turned back to his controls and began keying in data.

Lyn huffed.

"So what is it, then?"

"If I didn't tell you, I must have had my reasons."

Lyn growled in the back of her throat. She glanced over at Ultraa.

"You did take her to the Moonbase, Esro," Ultraa put in. "It's probably more secret than the Oasis, at least officially."

"Hey, yeah," Lyn said, her hands on her hips. "What about that?"

"I did, didn't I?" Esro said, looking troubled. "Wonder why I did that…"

"You are the devil," Lyn muttered, glaring at him.

Esro beamed at that.

Vanadium was watching this entire exchange silently, taking it all in.

Lyn caught Ultraa's eye and made an exasperated gesture toward Esro that seemed to say, *See what I have to deal with?*

"Oh, just tell her, Esro," Ultraa said, shaking his head at the two of them.

"Okay, fine."

He clicked a few keys and brought up a map of Virginia on one of his computer monitors. Scrolling over to the western side of the state, he zoomed in.

"There," he said, pointing a finger at a flashing dot. "The Oasis."

Lyn leaned in close.

"It's in the Shenandoah Valley?"

She frowned.

"But—that's not a desert."

"Well, yeah," Esro said. "But it's not that kind of Oasis."

"Then what kind is it?"

Clicking off the monitor, he smiled.

"An oasis of ultra-high technology, in a wilderness of natural beauty."

Lyn snorted.

"So, you're writing travel brochures for it, then?"

Esro opened his mouth to retort, when a high-pitched electronic wail resounded through the mansion, seemingly vibrating the skulls of everyone present.

"The Trouble Alert!" Lyn shouted over the din.

"I really wish you wouldn't call it that," Brachis said, hurriedly switching the noise off.

Ultraa was already moving. He looked to Esro with a terse, "Where?"

Esro checked another monitor.

"Virginia Beach," he replied.

Vanadium was already out the door and on the way.

"Some old friends of yours, Ultraa," Esro added, reading the information now filling the screen.

The blond man nodded and started out, then paused and looked back at Esro, who had taken the components of his armor out of two big metal cases and was struggling to pull it all on. Seeing this, Lyn hesitated as well.

"Don't slow down on my account," Brachis shouted, motioning toward the door. "Go! I'll be right along."

I really have to figure out a quicker way to do this, he thought to himself in frustration.

Nodding, Ultraa turned and raced out, Lyn right behind him. He shot skyward, a red-and-white missile. She lofted after him, golden lightning crackling around her.

Who needs school? Lyn thought, grinning, as the Virginia landscape flew past below. *This is the life!*

186

Jameson leaned forward in his oversized leather chair, straining the buttons on his immaculately tailored suit. He opened a wooden case and took out a cigar, thought about it for a moment, and put it back. The Pentagon courtyard was visible in the panoramic windows behind him. He nodded toward the nondescript, dark-suited man standing on the other side of his desk—the only other man he worked closely with and shared his secrets with, in their extremely secret branch of the Defense Department.

"What do we hear from our new friends, the Circle?"

"Only that their agent is in place, and will be here soon," the other man, Adcock, said. "They have indicated he will have limited powers to negotiate with us, and will be able to exchange communications with the Circle much more quickly and efficiently than we have, thus far."

Jameson perked up at this.

"Really?"

He considered it for a moment, stroking his chin.

"That would imply some sort of faster-than-light communications technology. It sounds…intriguing."

Adcock nodded.

Jameson leaned back again, his mind awhirl.

"And they say this agent of theirs is bringing us some samples of their technology, right?"

"So they say," Adcock replied.

"Wonderful."

Adcock actually seemed to smile, for once—something that Jameson found startling, and not a little troubling.

"We can do business with them," Adcock stated firmly, as if reaching some grand conclusion.

"Yes?"

"I believe so, yes."

"And you don't think they might pose a threat later, if the time should come that we are no longer of any use to them?"

Adcock tilted his head slightly, as if bemused by the notion.

"Perhaps they should be asking themselves that same question, about us," he replied.

Jameson snorted.

"Perhaps you're right," he said. "But, even so…?"

Adcock crossed his arms.

"If the time should come that we should wish to sever our ties with this…Circle…I am persuaded that we could do so in a very thorough, definite, and conclusive manner."

Jameson smiled.

"I like the sound of that," he said. "Though I can't imagine how that might be. These are not exactly primitives that we're dealing with. They—"

"Leave that to me," Adcock said.

Jameson considered, then nodded.

"Very well," he said. "For now, it's in your hands. But—Adcock—for god's sake, don't give away the planet, alright?"

Adcock made an odd sound that disturbed Jameson, until he realized it was some form of laughter. This possibly disturbed him even more.

Sipping a glass of water, he opened a folder on his desk, studied it for a few seconds, then looked up again.

"Tell me the latest on Operation: Paladin."

Adcock shrugged.

"Still in the theoretical stages."

"What? Still theoretical?"

"Quite so."

Jameson frowned. He leaned back from his desk a bit, staring across at Adcock, his face somber.

"But you've had weeks since I gave the authorization to go ahead with production."

"There has been some trouble with the fabrication of the weapons systems."

Adcock's own expression communicated a simple message: *Not my fault.*

"They have been forced to recalculate—"

"Fine, fine," Jameson said, waving a hand, cutting him off. "It's to be expected. Operation: Paladin is far more advanced than anything we've attempted thus far."

"Yes."

"What of the stopgap solution I authorized last month?"

Adcock clasped his hands behind his back. He looked as if he were reciting from a memorized script.

"Operation: Defender is well underway. Fabrication of the armored units themselves proceeds with no delays. We will have a dozen of them online in a matter of days."

Jameson's mouth formed a thin smile.

"Excellent," he said. "It's good to see some sort of immediate return on our investment in Brachis's work, even if he remains completely unaware of it. *Especially* if he does."

Jameson sighed.

"Much as I despised the Sinclair boy, I did like having an agent inside Brachis's organization—right inside his house. Thus we had access to everything he was voluntarily giving us, and everything else, as well." He sighed. "I'm not happy that we haven't been able to get anyone else inside there, since then. Who knows what he's come up with lately, that we're missing out on?"

"An opportunity will present itself," Adcock said. "The more promising development, though," he continued, "may have been brought to our attention by our new friend, here."

"I'm glad to hear it."

Jameson nodded toward the third figure in the room.

"You've done exceptionally well for us," he said.

The other man stepped out of the shadows, smiling grimly. He wore dark gray and black military fatigues. A patch covered one eye. The Iron Cross adorned one lapel.

"I am glad to be of service, Herr Jameson."

"And you have been, Field Marshal," Jameson replied. "In four ways, actually."

He held up his right hand and began to tick off points with his fingers.

"First, in acquiring the schematics for so much of Esro Brachis's technology from right under his nose. I particularly enjoyed that one."

The Field Marshal bowed slightly.

"Second," Jameson went on, "in setting up your new company— what are you calling it?"

"Digimacht."

"Yes. Of course." Jameson smiled. "America's newest high-tech innovation corporation. And munitions supplier."

He raised his glass of wine in toast.

"We look forward to reaping the rewards of collaboration in that area."

"The feeling is mutual," the Field Marshal replied, raising his own glass.

"Third, in putting together a new team of paranormals—a new version of Operation: Sentinel—to replace Ultraa's unreliable crowd."

He gazed at the Field Marshal levelly.

"And how is the recruiting coming, now that I think of it?"

The Field Marshal smiled flatly.

"I am still conducting research at this time."

"Research? Still?"

"The choices must be carefully made, Herr Jameson. We need agents who are competent and loyal, yet who do not allow personal feelings to interfere with the execution of the orders of their superiors."

"That's true enough," Jameson replied.

"Even so, recruitment will begin shortly. *Very* shortly."

"Good enough," Jameson said. "And finally, you have helped us to locate our *other* new associate, and to bring him into the fold."

The Field Marshal shrugged.

"The man took little convincing," he said. "Money, power, and the opportunity to continue his work in a much better-funded environment—he understood such inducements quite well."

"Even if his politics leave a good bit to be desired," Adcock growled.

Jameson snorted.

"I don't think anyone in this room is in a position to criticize anyone else's politics," he said with a grin.

Adcock said nothing, merely looking away.

He's a true believer, Jameson thought to himself, looking at his associate. *He'll have to be taken care of, before the end.*

The Field Marshal cleared his throat in the uncomfortable silence.

"If you would care to meet him…" he said. "That might prove to be a more productive way of spending our time, rather than allowing ourselves to get caught up in ideological disputes."

Jameson smiled.

"You're quite right."

Adcock glanced back at them, nodded once.

"But first," Jameson said, "the Li girl remains ignorant of the origins of her own powers, yes?"

"She is convinced she represents some sort of mutation," the Field Marshal replied. "She believes it to have been a freak accident of fate, suffered while still in the womb."

"Good," said Jameson. "Then she will never suspect. Nor raise any alarm."

"*Ja*. My thoughts exactly."

Jameson nodded and gestured toward the door.

"So—he's here, then? You brought him with you?"

"*Ja*."

"Excellent. Show him in."

The door opened silently and a small man in long, flowing robes of a deep crimson color entered, escorted by two agents in dark suits. Jameson stood, motioned for the agents to leave, then reached out and shook the new arrival's hand. The four men seated themselves.

"So. You go by the name—"

"Red Talon."

His accent was thick. He was less than five feet tall and obviously very slender beneath his silken garments. The robes themselves were covered in golden Chinese script and imagery. Jameson studied the man's wizened face, unable to guess just how old he might be.

After brief pleasantries, Jameson breached the topic that most concerned him.

"You are the Li girl's grandfather, is that true?"

"It is."

"And you performed certain...experiments on her, when she was a baby?"

"While she was in the womb, and after her birth, too. Yes."

Jameson frowned.

"Her parents allowed this?"

"They knew nothing of it, beyond my administering simple 'allergy treatments.' They still know nothing."

The small man shrugged.

"But it had to be done. Science demanded it."

Jameson's eyebrows involuntarily arched.

"Of course, of course," he said, glancing at Adcock, who remained inscrutable.

"And the results of these experiments?" the Field Marshal asked.

"You have seen," the Red Talon replied. "The girl gained enormous powers." He sighed. "If only she was not such a spoiled, decadent American child, and could be persuaded to put her abilities to use for the bettering of the proletariat and socialist revolution."

Jameson blinked, then glanced at Adcock again. The man gave him a "told you so" look in return.

The Field Marshal leaned forward.

191

"Tell them about the other one," he prompted.

The Red Talon shrugged again.

"Lyn has a younger sister, Wen. She goes by the silly Western nickname of Wendy."

Jameson sat back, steepling his fingers in front of his face.

"And you have performed the same 'treatments' on her?"

"Oh, of course."

The Red Talon smiled, an expression that gave Jameson the chills.

"The results have been somewhat different, however," he continued.

"How so?"

The Red Talon stood, began pacing about the large office.

"In some ways, things have not gone as well as I might have hoped. She lacks Lyn's raw power. But in other ways…"

He stood facing them, hands clasped behind his back.

"She exhibits much greater control, at a younger age, than Lyn ever did. Thus the powers seem less of a burden to her. So far, she has actually enjoyed learning how to use them. She does not suffer the social embarrassment that always held Lyn back."

"I see," Jameson said.

"If her capacity could be increased, while her mastery remains the same," the Red Talon continued, "she might prove far more formidable, far more useful, than her older sister…"

He shook his head sadly.

"…whom I view as something of a failure."

Unwillingly, Jameson thought back to the debacle months earlier, at Bay City College. He had sent an agent—one of his best—to bring the Li girl in. It had become an unmitigated disaster, with Jameson's entire operation nearly exposed, and the girl ending up in league with Ultraa and Esro Brachis, instead. While, technically, that still put her under Jameson's control, it was at one remove, so to speak. That, as much as anything else, had prompted him to ask the Field Marshal to assemble a new team of agents. And the incident at the college had required Jameson to carry damage control to new heights, distancing himself from it all, and shielding his area of the Pentagon from blame.

"With the Red Talon on our side now," the Field Marshal was saying, "we should enjoy much greater success in recruiting the younger sister."

"I hope you're right," Jameson said. He thought of Richard, the agent he had employed in the attempted capture of Lyn. The man hadn't returned Jameson's calls since.

"Leave her to me," the Field Marshal said. "I don't believe you will be disappointed."

Jameson ran a hand over his chin, glancing at Adcock. The agent shrugged. He turned back to the older man.

"What do you have in mind?"

"Oh, a different approach to winning her loyalty. We do, after all, have her beloved grandfather on our side now."

The Red Talon nodded.

"Plus, I intend to play on her natural rivalry with her sister. Before long, gentlemen," he said, his one eye moving from Jameson to Adcock and back, "she will demand to be a part of our team, and to follow our orders."

Jameson considered this for a moment, then nodded.

"Perhaps you're right," he said. "We will leave her be, for now. You may proceed with your plans for her."

The Field Marshal bowed.

Jameson sat through the rest of the meeting on a sort of autopilot, his mind turning over various new possibilities and opportunities the entire time. Once the Field Marshal and the Red Talon had been shown out of his office, he closed the door and turned back to Adcock, a smile slowly working its way across his broad face.

"This might all prove more fortuitous than I had imagined," he said.

"Yes."

Adcock ran his tongue over his lips in reptilian fashion.

"If this new girl could be brought willingly into our service, not only might she prove a valuable agent…"

He laughed once, sharply.

"…but she might give us a bit of leverage over the older one, as well."

"Which would mean we would have an agent inside Brachis's organization once again," Jameson said, smiling. He lifted a glass and filled it with scotch, then passed another to Adcock.

"Here's to the Li family. Serving their country—or at least serving *us*—whether they like it or not."

3

A dim, hazy world, one heartbeat removed from our own reality.

A range of craggy, forbidding mountains dividing two great swathes of that world's desert surface.

A complex and labyrinthine network of caves and tunnels, cut deep into the sheer rock of those mountains.

And a darkened chamber at the heart of that network—and at the heart of another network, as well: One that stretched from energy siphons plunged deep into that world's furnace-like depths, to a vast space station high in orbit above, to spy eyes and ears arrayed across our own universe.

And in the heart of that darkened chamber, that grim sanctum, filled to overflowing with banks of futuristic electronic equipment and a bewildering array of hidden rooms and vast chambers, the Warlord stood in an arrogant pose, hands on hips, staring up at his main display screen. His blue and purple robes flared around him, and his eyes darted feverishly behind his silver mask, watching a pair of red indicator lights as they began to track across the screen.

"There," he boomed, pointing at the lights. "They are moving again. Do you not see, Francisco?"

The much smaller man, clad in a khaki jumpsuit and perpetually hunched over in a submissive posture, scuttled forward, nodding. The tools attached to his heavy leather belt jangled musically.

"Yes, yes, Master. Yes, I see."

He gazed up at the screen.

"So...so, what could they be?"

The Warlord shook his head.

"I do not know. Yet."

He gestured distractedly toward a row of smaller screens to the right of the main one.

"But all indicators show that they represent a dramatic distortion in the very fabric of reality. A potentially destructive force of catastrophic magnitude. Do you understand, Francisco?"

The little man nodded rapidly.

"Yes, yes, of course, Master. Yes."

The Warlord stared down at him, waiting.

"No. No, I do not, Master."

"Of course you don't."

He pointed at the two red dots, grouped tightly together, as they moved rapidly over what appeared to be a large-scale map of the eastern United States.

"But it is all so simple. These dots represent two individuals who are out of their natural positions in the space-time continuum. They have somehow traveled in time. And, as such, they represent a potentially major threat to my plans. And to that universe, too, of course," he added as an afterthought.

"A universe that is rightfully yours, Master," Francisco pointed out, smiling his most ingratiating smile.

"Indeed."

Francisco waited patiently while his master brooded over the problem. Finally, he cleared his throat softly and asked, "So, what shall we do about it?

"We? Do?"

The Warlord gazed down at him, a puzzled expression moving briefly across his hidden face.

"Yes, well, I suppose we ought to do *something*," he said after a moment. "If for no other reason than to protect my own property."

"Your property? Ah—the universe. Of course. Yes, Master."

"As you say."

The Warlord paced back and forth within his sanctum for a few more seconds, then stopped and turned to Francisco again.

"Dispatch the interceptors. Bring these two to me. Let us see what exactly they *are*—learn from them what we can. And then..."

Francisco nodded, implicitly understanding the rest. He hurried over to one of the control panels and rapidly typed instructions into it. Moments later, a new series of dots—three of them, all blue— appeared on the big display screen.

"The interceptors are on their way, Master."

Swiftly and steadily the blue dots accelerated toward the red ones.

"Currently they are invisible to all forms of detection, Master," Francisco noted as the two of them watched. "They will drop their shielding when they reach their targets."

The Warlord grunted, his eyes fixed on the converging points of light.

After a few more seconds, the two red dots and the three blue ones merged together. All motion ceased.

"Well?" the Warlord demanded.

Francisco studied the readouts, frowning.

195

"It was a Kur-Bai shuttlecraft," he reported. "Our interceptors forced it down. They are battling the survivors now…"

The Warlord paced, waiting impatiently.

"The survivors have been captured," he reported after a long pause.

"Excellent."

"Three of our troopers were killed in the fighting, Master."

The Warlord grunted again, ignoring this. Then he stopped, motionless for a few seconds, as if considering his actions.

Francisco watched him nervously, waiting.

The Warlord turned back to him then, speaking as if he were giving an address to some august assembly.

"Thus, once again," he said, "does the Warlord save that poor universe from annihilation—as was no doubt inevitable, had these two time anomalies been allowed to roam free."

He clasped his hands together before him.

"Honestly, Francisco, the various and sundry races of this dimension should band together to award me a medal for all the many services I have performed for them."

He paused.

"And perhaps I will have them do that, once I have completed my conquests."

Francisco bowed formally.

"Shall I bring the two time-lost individuals here, then, Master?"

"I—"

The Warlord hesitated in his response, as if considering the entire subject anew.

"They actually succeeded in killing three of my soldiers? Ridiculous," he said.

Then he growled something unintelligible in the back of his throat, nodded once to Francisco, and strode from the chamber, his robes flaring behind him.

Francisco studied the dots as they circled around and began moving back in the direction from which they had come. Then he looked up and watched as the taller figure exited the room. He said nothing, merely growling in the back of his throat—a sound remarkably, disturbingly similar to the one made by the Warlord, moments before.

4

Ultraa delivered a staggering blow to the Tailor, nearly knocking him out of his custom-designed, high-tech-engineered, and (not incidentally) very fashionable costume. Nearby, Brachis had the heavily armored Tinker on the ropes, opening up on her with both barrels of his wrist-mounted energy guns while protecting himself with three layers of his ubiquitous energy screens.

Standing on the beach, Lyn watched them and smiled. *These guys were no match for us,* she thought. *It's really just clean-up work.*

She glanced down at the unconscious form of the Soldier, where she had left him sprawled on the sand. His camouflage paint had started to run; his array of combat knives lay scattered around him, all of them bent and dulled from his attempts to cut through Lyn's force fields. Beyond him, a short distance out to sea, the Sailor was making a break for it in his armored watercraft, but Lyn knew Ultraa would catch him and settle matters quickly enough. Vanadium hadn't been needed at all against this crowd, and had already headed back to the mansion to tend to his own, unfathomable business.

Grinning, Lyn plopped down on the sand, watching her associates finish off the last of the bad guys.

The breeze felt nice; the sun was shining but with just enough cloud cover to make it bearable. All the sunbathers had fled as soon as the villains landed on the beach, so crowding wasn't an issue.

She closed her eyes and laid her head back, relaxing.

A brief few moments of utter bliss ensued, inevitably broken by the jarring sound of Esro Brachis's voice: "Lyn! You okay?"

"I'm fine, fine," she replied, lifting one hand and waving it. "Just enjoying the sun."

She could hear Brachis's metal boots crunching closer.

"You thought one of these guys put me down? Huh," she snorted. "As if."

"Yeah, well. Let's not get too comfortable, huh?"

She opened her eyes a crack and peered upward.

Esro loomed over her. His helmet was off and he was shaking his gauntlets furiously, muttering something to himself about ever being able to get the sand out of his armor.

"Why *not* get comfortable?" she asked. "It's a nice enough day for it, now that the riff raff's been cleaned up."

"No," he said, sighing. "I mean, don't get too comfortable with *winning* like that. With having things so easy. After everything we've been through in the past year, I would think you'd understand that."

Lyn frowned.

"I do, Esro, I do. But…"

"The second we get comfortable is the second something bad happens to one of us. Again."

Lyn's face twisted into a hurt expression.

"*Again.* Yeah. You don't have to bring that up, Esro."

Esro bit his lip, ran his hand over his forehead.

"You're right. I'm sorry. I just—"

She shook her head.

"No, it's okay. I understand."

He looked pained.

"Lyn, I really am sorry. I shouldn't have—"

"He's dead, Esro. I know it and you know it. We all know it. I'm okay. And I promise not to get comfortable."

"I…okay. That's good, then. Okay."

He looked as if he were going to say more, then thought better of it. Snapping his helmet back in place, he turned to where Tinker lay. He pointed one gauntleted hand at the criminal and a wide beam of light speared out, bathing the armor-clad woman in a greenish field. The unconscious body levitated into the air, then floated along behind Esro as he strode away through the sand.

Lyn watched him go for a few seconds, feeling bad about the whole conversation. Then she plopped her head back on the sand, trying to put it out of her mind and simply enjoy the nice day for a few more moments.

Her phone warbled.

"For crying out loud."

She slid it out of the heavily shielded pouch she kept it in and flipped it open.

"Hey, kiddo!"

"Amy!" She brightened instantly. "What's up?"

"Just checking in," her old roommate replied. "Seeing how things're going, over on the other coast."

"Going fine. Guess where I am now?"

"Hmm. Knowing who I'm talking to… A science exhibit. No, no, wait—the library."

"I hate you."

"Yeah, whatever. So—where are you, then?"

Lyn laughed.

"The beach."

"No way. You never—oh, wait—oh, no! You've been kidnapped! Kidnapped by some arch-villain who has a secret lair on the beach! You want I should call the police or—"

Lyn simmered a moment, pursing her lips.

"You're so funny, Amy," she replied, deadpan.

"So, anyway, I have to ask you the big question."

Lyn smirked at the phone.

"Let me guess," she said. "Have I gotten to use Esro's legendary hot tub yet?"

This had become a running joke between the two of them, and Amy snickered.

"That's not exactly what I was going to ask, but since you mention it...?"

"No. Still haven't. He caught me trying to sneak in a couple of weeks back, and pitched a little fit. So now it'll be even harder to get past his security."

"Security? For the hot tub?"

Lyn laughed.

"Oh, yeah. You think I'm kidding? I'm tellin' ya, he has better security set up around that thing than around his lab. It's crazy."

Amy snorted.

"Ehh, you'll get in there yet. Don't give up."

"Yeah. So..."

"So I never asked you the big question."

"Oh, yeah. What?"

"So, have you started—"

"No, I haven't started school yet," Lyn interrupted with a sigh.

"That's not the big question, silly," Amy said. "The big question is—hey, what? You still haven't started school?"

"I—"

"What are you waiting for? You know how hard it is to get into—"

"Yes, mother."

"Shut up! Okay, fine. Whatever. I don't even care. It's your business."

Lyn breathed in and out.

"So, you never said what the big question was."

"Oh, yeah. Have you started seeing anyone?"

"No."

"No? *Still?*"

"No."

"Hmm. But...do you think he likes you?"

"Who? Esro? Yuck!"

"No—Ultraa!"

Lyn blinked. She didn't say a word. She blinked again.

"Hello?"

"Um, yeah. No. Um. Ultraa? Are you crazy? He's my *partner*!"

"Exactly!"

Lyn sighed very heavily and very audibly.

"Amy, it's not like that. And stop trying to *make* it like that. Okay?"

"Yeah, sure, fine, whatever."

Neither of them spoke for a couple of seconds.

"Oh, hey," Amy said suddenly, having moved on in usual Amy micro-time. "I was talking to Kim McCorkle the other day—she's friends with your sister, right? And she was saying that Wendy was talking about moving to the East Coast, too."

Lyn frowned.

"That's crazy," she said. "Wendy's only sixteen, for one thing. And she loves the West Coast. Why would she—"

"I'm just telling you what I heard."

"Well, it's silly."

"Okay."

They gabbed for a few minutes more, then signed off. Lyn flipped her phone shut and stowed it away. Just then, a groaning sound from nearby caused her to sit up and look.

Soldier had woken up. Grimacing at her, he struggled to his feet.

Lyn held out her hand, palm facing upward. A baseball-sized golden sphere, crackling with lightning, materialized above it. She gestured sharply and it flashed out, smashing Soldier in the nose. He crumbled back to the sand like a limp sack of potatoes, electricity discharging from all over his body.

Don't get too comfortable, Esro says.

Lyn rested back in the sand again, smiling to herself.

Oh, please!

5

The great starship knifed through the void.

On its vast, multi-tiered bridge level, the ship's captain stood unmoving, hands clasped behind his back, staring intently at the panoramic starfield visible outside the huge viewport. One level below, a young lieutenant gazed up at him, wondering what he was thinking.

Like all of her race, the young lieutenant possessed deep red skin and dark eyes. A plume of thick, white hair trailed halfway down her back. She wore the navy blue uniform of the Kur-Bai Starfleet over her tall, lithe form.

She continued to watch the captain, admiring him, somewhat envious of his rank and power.

Your time will come, Mondrian, she told herself. *For now, you're fortunate to have such a great officer to watch and learn from.*

She chewed a fingernail absently, staring out at the vivid stars.

If only things could be more interesting on this voyage. Just a little more interesting...

She turned as an ensign climbed the steps and approached the captain. His cream-colored hair had been trimmed very close, and his nearly black eyes shifted momentarily from the captain to the panorama of space beyond the viewport.

"Yes, yes, what is it?"

Saluting, the ensign held out a flat white rectangle of plastic.

Captain DeSkai casually returned the salute. He took the datapad from the young ensign, gave the most cursory of glances at the information it contained—the latest reports from all sections and departments—and handed it back, nodding.

Mondrian nearly laughed. Deep patrol had grown quite tedious of late, and even the captain exhibited the signs of boredom. It was one thing to advertise to potential recruits with the promise of seeing the far-flung reaches of the galaxy, but it was quite another to spend months flying through those places, discovering just how uninteresting most of them were.

The captain looked down at her then, and she unconsciously straightened herself and clasped her hands behind her back.

"You're thinking what I'm thinking, aren't you, Lieutenant?"

"Sir?"

The captain chuckled. He moved to the steps and started down, toward her.

"Relax, Lieutenant. I've been doing this a lot longer than you have. After a while, you come to understand that most of space exploration and patrol consists of tedium."

Despite herself, Mondrian smiled.

"Yes, sir."

The captain sighed.

"Perhaps this Sol system will offer something of interest. They actually have a few meta-powerful beings there, now."

A snorting sound came from across the deck.

"Even if they are, for the most part, a world of glorified, jumped-up monkeys."

Mondrian turned to see a tall, slender figure in officer's uniform striding across the deck, towards her.

"Lieutenant Okaar," she said, nodding, suppressing a look of distaste.

For his part, Okaar made no such effort to hide his opinion of his fellow officer. He looked down his long, angular nose at her, his thin, cruel lips curling in a sneer.

"Potentially dangerous monkeys, though," he continued. "The wisest thing would probably be to sterilize the whole planet, before they get loose into the galaxy and begin causing who knows what kinds of trouble."

"That's enough, Lieutenant," the captain barked.

Okaar made a face but turned to gaze out the viewport.

"We will give the Terrans all the proper consideration and respect we would give to any race, newly emerging onto the galactic stage," the captain said. He glanced at Mondrian. "And speaking of which, you've been studying their predominant language, yes, Lieutenant?"

Mondrian nodded quickly.

"Yes, sir. I've studied it extensively, along with receiving the proper RNA injections. I believe I have their 'English' mastered, sir."

"Excellent."

"With any luck," Okaar added, "we won't need to actually interact with the primitives at all."

A cry came from one of the scanner operators in the lower technical section. Up until that moment, the man had slumped lazily in his seat, watching the same readings scrolling across his monitor, hour after hour. Now, he was up, on his feet, alternately motioning to the captain and leaning over to stare at the display.

"Captain! You need to see this, sir!"

DeSkai leaned over the rail.

"Well? What is it?"

"A signal, sir—but..."

"Yes?"

"You'd better look at it yourself, sir."

Mondrian and Okaar followed DeSkai as he hurried around to the far stairs and descended to the tech level. Together, they moved around behind the technician.

"Alright. What is—?"

DeSkai blinked.

He leaned closer, reading the numbers.

"This is current?"

"Yes, sir. Just came in."

DeSkai swallowed.

Mondrian studied the data herself, but couldn't make any sense of it. Something very powerful, she could tell—and something out of the ordinary, for a backwater part of the galaxy like this one, apparently.

"It's a Xorex," the captain whispered. "Maker preserve us, I thought we'd gotten them all."

The technician nodded, his face twisted in shock.

A sick feeling grew in Mondrian's digestive system. She stared at the screen, the legends of her homeworld coming back to her mind.

A Xorex...

"The shape-changers," DeSkai growled. "The absorbers. The planet-killers."

Oh, no...

The captain straightened, professional again.

"Where?"

"Dead ahead," the tech replied. "Earth."

DeSkai cursed.

"Those primitives haven't a prayer of dealing with this thing," Okaar muttered.

"You're probably correct," the captain said. "We have to get there, and stop it, before it develops into a full-fledged infestation."

Mondrian touched the screen, running her red fingers along the tall, metal humanoid shape displayed there.

"What—what if we can't, sir?" she asked.

The captain frowned.

"If we fail," Okaar said quickly, "we will have no choice but to destroy the planet."

With obvious reluctance, the captain nodded.

"Not that there will be much left to destroy, at that point, anyway," he added.

He turned, bounding up the stairs.

"Looks like you may get to use your language skills after all, Lieutenant," he called back to Mondrian.

"Yes, sir."

She raced back to her station.

"Set a course," DeSkai called out to the navigator. "Direct for Earth."

The bridge crew came alive, crewmembers moving quickly and efficiently here and there, preparing the great ship for action.

Mondrian dropped into her chair, her fingers moving over her keyboard, issuing terse instructions to the departments under her.

Sometimes you do get what you wish for, she thought to herself. *And sometimes you get far, far more.*

"Prepare to jump," the captain was bellowing. "Now!"

Francisco stood in a darkened room, a short distance away from the main control chamber of the Warlord's sanctum. Before him stood a row of identical metal cabinets, each of them about ten feet high and four feet wide. Their front panels were constructed of glass or some other mostly transparent material. Along their sides ran a series of controls and a bank of flashing lights, all of them currently green.

The little man reached out and ran his fingertips over the cold surface of the nearest cabinet. Behind the glass stood a man in streaked and dented armor of gray and black, his brown hair unkempt, several days' worth of beard on his face, and his eyes frozen in an expression of panic.

Moving a few steps to his left, Francisco touched the glass of the next cabinet down. Within it stood a woman in a tight blue outfit, golden bands about her wrists and ankles. Her skin was a bright red, and a long mane of white hair flowed down her back. Her very dark eyes stared out sightlessly.

"Fear not, my friends," the little man said in a whisper. "You are held in perfect stasis. Cut off from this universe, from the space-time continuum. It is as if you do not even exist. And, therefore, can cause no further damage."

He gazed at them, frowning.

"But...where did you come from? And what is to become of you?"

The woman's exotic appearance had distracted him from the moment she'd been brought in, but now Francisco leaned in toward the man, studying him closely. He frowned.

"I know you," he said after a moment. "I remember you."

He squinted at the face, then at the gray armor, then at the dented helmet hanging from the belt by a short cable. He regarded the man for another second or two. And then he smiled.

"Yes, yes. You and your friends. Remember you very well. Yes."

"Francisco," boomed a deep voice from the doorway.

The little man cringed reflexively and spun around, backing up a step or two.

"Y—yes, Master?"

The Warlord strode forward and stopped a few feet away, glaring down from behind his silver mask. His voice was cold.

"Still you cower in my presence," he said. "Still you tremble and scamper away from me. From what I recall of the memories of my previous incarnations, this is most unlike you. If you are not careful, I will have no choice but to take it personally."

The little servant looked up at his master in terror, then quickly sought to cover his reaction.

"No, no, my master. I have complete faith—I support the Grand Design fully!"

"Bah."

The Warlord looked briefly at the metal cabinets, then turned back to Francisco and waved a dismissive hand.

"You do not trust me," he said, his tone accusatory. "You do not believe in me. Not the way you did in the others."

Francisco gnawed on his bottom lip but said nothing. He shuffled two small steps away from the stasis cabinets.

"Now, in the grand scheme of things, this is unimportant," the Warlord continued, turning to follow him. "But, still... if a Warlord does not have the confidence, the absolute trust, of his Francisco, well..." He spread his blue-gloved hands wide. "...What *does* he have, after all?" He shrugged. "Aside from great personal reserves of power, of course... And brilliant intellect... And..."

And modesty, Francisco thought. *And bad fashion sense. And a really cheesy sense of dialogue. And...*

"I need you behind me," the Warlord went on. "Supporting my operations completely. No doubts, no concerns."

"Yes, Master," Francisco said, bowing obsequiously, before taking two more small steps away from the cabinets. "I—I understand. I will endeavor to be more attentive, more supportive."

"And why indeed should you not?" the Warlord asked, as much to himself as to Francisco. "For I shall succeed where all my previous incarnations failed—and in ways far beyond their meager imaginations!"

"Of course, Master. Of course."

The Warlord strode back into the main chamber, Francisco trailing after him, happy for them both to be exiting the stasis room.

"But you have not even heard the full extent of my plans yet," the Warlord was saying.

He dropped back into his thronelike chair, his purple cloak flaring around him.

"Here. Gaze at the viewscreen as I reveal to you the true scope of my intentions. For then you will come to understand—to appreciate—the genius that is the Warlord!"

The big rectangular screen covering most of the far wall of the chamber flickered and blackened into a display of outer space, nebulae spread here and there, stars of varying sizes and magnitudes twinkling.

The Warlord gestured and three blazing points of light appeared on the screen, each of them far from the others. One was red, one orange, one yellow.

"There they are, Francisco."

The little man squinted at the display, puzzled. He could see that the very center of the layout was focused on a tiny, yellow star, labeled "Sol."

The Earth's sun. Ah.

"Still they take no notice of me, Francisco," the Warlord said. "I should be quite insulted, were that fact not so very useful to me, at present."

"The humans, Master?"

He laughed sharply.

"The humans? Scarcely. I am referring to the Great Powers of this universe. Those quite beyond the comprehension of the humans or any other mortal race."

Francisco scratched at his ear.

"Great Powers, Master?"

"Yes. From what I have overheard of their conversations—their long, deliberate, drawn-out communications across the eons and across the depths of intergalactic space—they refer to one another as 'Rivals.' But whatever name they go by, they represent the eldest sentient beings in the universe, or at least the oldest ones still in existence."

The Warlord smiled behind his silver mask, a strange madness flickering in his eyes.

"They command vast powers," he said. "Vast."

Ah, thought Francisco.

"Power," the little man said, "such as that which you seek?"

"Oh, indeed."

The Warlord was gazing up at the screen, at the three bright dots on it, with unvarnished lust. His voice grew dreamy, distant.

"Power much greater than can be found anywhere else. Power that could allow me to accomplish my own goals—and so much more."

Then he broke away from the screen and whirled on Francisco. The little man stumbled back a step.

"But my previous incarnations have scarcely thought of turning to the Great Rivals for such power. They never even attempted to approach one of them."

"Perhaps... perhaps that represented some kind of... wisdom, on their part, Master?"

Behind his silver mask, the Warlord's mouth turned upward in a sneer.

"Wisdom, you say? Or was it timidity? Fear? Self-doubt?"

He scoffed.

"These are all conditions I find my current incarnation suffers not at all."

He strode majestically across the chamber, hands clasped behind his back.

"Soon, Francisco—soon, the Great Powers, these Rivals, will fall upon one another, in a carefully orchestrated plot of my own devising. And then, when all have been weakened by this conflict.... Then shall the Warlord strike! Then shall the Warlord step in, and take by force that which is his by right!"

Francisco gazed up at him, aghast.

"You will challenge one of them directly, Master?"

He gnawed at his fingernails a moment, considering the awful, the catastrophic consequences of such an act of madness.

"Which…which one will you challenge?"

"Which one? Why, all three, of course!"

Francisco nearly fainted.

"All three shall fall before the Warlord's onslaught. And then…"

The Warlord's voice trailed off, as if he were imagining what wondrous and terrible works he might perform with such inconceivable power at his disposal. Meanwhile, Francisco's knees had grown weak. He grasped a nearby console, steadying himself.

"All three," he gasped, finding breathing difficult now. "How…How might such a thing be done, Master?"

The Warlord gazed at him levelly.

"I have a plan, of course. A plan that will bring them into direct conflict over a single target. As they contend with one another to control it, they will grow weakened, tired, and perhaps find themselves injured, if such a thing is possible. And it is at that moment—their moment of greatest vulnerability—that the Warlord will strike!"

"I…I see."

Francisco had to stop himself from whimpering again. He gathered up his courage and gazed at the screen again.

"And where…where will this happen, Master?"

"Where all three will be arriving, soon," he replied. He pointed to the center of the starfield, the center of the map. "Earth."

Behind his silver mask, he smiled.

"Already I have taken steps to insure that all three will be present. Two had previously turned their attentions this way—one because of the rogue Vanadium, the other because of Kabaraak—but I have added enticements for He Who Collects to notice Earth, as well."

"Pardon my asking, Master, but… Do you suppose that was wise?"

The Warlord glared at him.

"What do you mean?"

Francisco took an involuntary step backward, but continued.

"If they come to Earth and battle one another here…What will become of the Earth?"

"The Earth?"

The Warlord thought a moment.

"I imagine it would be wiped out. Utterly destroyed."

He shrugged.

"Ah, well. A small enough price to pay, yes?"

Francisco dwelt on this for a few seconds. Then, "Master, what if you provoke them?"

"I fully intend to provoke them," the Warlord replied, matter-of-factly.

"No, no, Master… What if you draw their attention to yourself, anger them, and unite them—what if you make them mad at you, before you are able to finish the process?"

The Warlord settled back into his great chair and brought one hand up to his chin, thinking.

"It is a fair enough question, Francisco. Indeed, I have contemplated such an outcome. But, in the end, it hardly matters. If I fail in stealing their powers, I am lost anyway. I will have failed at the great calling of the Warlord—the only calling—the gathering and exercise of power, in order ultimately to unify the multiverse and end the great cycle of Warlords. To break the cycle, and stop the great wheel from turning."

"But—but not only for *you*, of course, Master," Francisco said quickly, smiling an ingratiating smile as he played his single most important role in the Grand Design. "Not only for your own aggrandizement."

"Yes, yes, quite right, Francisco," the Warlord replied, glancing at him. "Of course."

He gestured grandly with one hand.

"To bring all incarnations of the Warlord—past, present, and future—into existence at once, and then to unify us into one all-powerful whole. Yes, of course."

Francisco nodded slowly. He knew full well what he would have to do if the Warlord should succeed in gaining such powers. He would have to find a way, somehow, to make sure the Warlord exercised them on behalf of the Design, and not just for himself, for his current incarnation. Assuming, of course, that there would be anything left of the Warlord, after he attempted to absorb such awesome energies.

"But if I succeed," the Warlord continued, "then all my enemies are welcome to move against me—to try and do their worst. Let all the cosmic powers of the universe—of the *multiverse*—come and challenge me then."

He brought his blue-gauntleted fist crashing down on the armrest of his throne.

"I shall swat them like insects beneath my all-powerful hand."

7

Angela Devereux pulled off her skimpy top and paraded across the stage in only her thong, thigh-high red boots and long gloves. The crowd—mostly rumpled-looking men in a haze of cigarette smoke—clapped and hooted. As usual, the money accumulated rapidly in her garter. Then, her set finished, she strutted offstage and pulled her top on once more. She fitted her narrow, custom-made sunglasses back in place.

It was not quite the sort job she'd wanted, but it certainly paid the bills while she awaited the next opportunity for a big score. And, for once, she could separate men from their money and be perfectly within the law while doing so. She'd even... *convinced*... the owner to allow her to only go topless, unlike the other dancers—something that gave her added satisfaction.

All in all, a pretty good gig. It had its advantages. All things considered, life was a lot better than it could have been. But, still...

She jolted as a voice called to her from behind.

"Hey, Angela, there's a guy here wants a word with you."

She looked back. A big, blond man stood next to Tony, the bouncer. Tony appeared to be counting a wad of cash in his hand.

She sighed. *Great.*

"Okay, thanks, Tony," she called back. "Just a sec."

Pulling her skirt up and a jacket on, she walked out to where the big guy waited. She peered up at him through her reddish shades.

"Yeah?"

The man nodded to her.

"Angela Devereux? I am Karl Koenig."

She started to laugh. That accent just could not be real.

He frowned, seemingly waiting for some sort of recognition.

She shrugged.

"Yeah?"

"I am also called Blitzkrieg."

"Hm. Good for you."

She winked, then started past him.

"So, anyway, it was nice meeting you, and all, but—"

"I have a business proposition for you," he said. "One I believe you will want to hear."

"Right."

"One that could be quite lucrative."

She sighed. *Here we go again.* But she stopped and turned back to him.

"I believe my associates and I can make use of your talents," he was saying.

"Look, I have an agent who—"

"Not those talents."

She frowned.

"Oh?"

She stepped closer to him, squinting, unsure of just what might be going on, now.

"What talents did you have in mind?"

"I assure you," he said, raising his hands, palms open, "this is entirely of a... *business*... nature. And very private."

"Yeah? Well…"

"If you will give me a few moments of your time, I can explain it for you."

She ran her tongue over her teeth, considering for a second.

"Okay, fine. Why not?"

She followed the blond man over to his table. On the other side sat a smaller, dark-haired guy in a navy blue suit.

"Angela Devereux, this is Mr. Blue."

This time she did laugh.

"Mr. Blue? Really? What, are you guys making a Tarantino movie here?"

The other man merely sat there, unmoving, saying nothing.

"No, no," Koenig said. "That is his name, I assure you."

She looked at the other guy, the silent one. He wore sunglasses, too—though his had a blue tint to them—over pale eyes and a paler face. He seemed to be staring at her... and yet, at the same time, to be completely oblivious of her presence. Something about his demeanor, his very nature, just struck Angela as...wrong. Creepy, somehow. Involuntarily, she shuddered.

"Whatever," she said. "So, what do you guys want?"

"We want you, Ms. Devereux," Koenig said.

She started to get up.

"Yeah, I get that a lot. Look, I don't have time for—"

"I think you will want to find time for us. We are offering you considerable opportunity here. Opportunities for power, for position, and not an inconsiderable sum of money."

She sat down again.

"Keep talking."

The big man laid out the basics.

"I've never heard of Digimacht," she said when he was finished.

"You wouldn't have. It is new. But it has contacts in very high places. It will be quite large, quite influential, very soon."

She nodded.

"I see."

"In any case, I have been authorized to offer you this amount, up front, plus the promise of lodging, support, and nearly anything else you will require."

He slid her a folded piece of paper.

"In exchange, you will become a part of our team, working and making appearances on behalf of Digimacht."

She took the paper, opened it, and looked at it. Her eyes widened slightly. She handed it back.

"You're kidding."

"No."

She frowned at him.

"You don't just want some dancer. You know who I am."

He nodded.

"*What* I am."

He smiled a thin smile.

"Oh, yes. Precisely."

She thought about that.

No one knows about me. If these guys—and whomever they work for—do... then...this is a pretty formidable crowd. And probably not a bunch you'd want to get on the wrong side of.

"I—yes," she said. "I am interested. Yes."

Smiling wider now, the big man nodded.

"Excellent."

He stood.

"I will now leave you in the capable hands of Mr. Blue. He will convey you to Digimacht's facilities, where you will meet your new boss, the Field Marshal. He will, I am certain, wish to give you a proper orientation and reveal the finer details of your new position."

Angela glanced over at Mr. Blue, and frowned.

"You're leaving me with *him*? But—"

"I assure you, Mr. Blue is quite capable of seeing to any needs you might have. Within reason, of course."

Koenig smiled that thin smile again. Mr. Blue remained impassive.

"He is one of our most prized assets," Koenig continued, "and was, in fact, my first new recruit, before you."

With a bow, the big man turned and walked out of the club.

Angela watched him go, feeling a strange uneasiness growing in her stomach.

Mr. Blue stood, inclining his head toward the doors.

Still frowning, and somewhat reluctantly, Angela nodded. Together they walked out.

Taking her leave of the Purple Pony Exotic Dance Club and emerging into daylight, the first thing Angela noticed was that there was no sign of the blond man. He'd only been a few steps ahead of them, and yet he was nowhere to be seen.

Mr. Blue walked over to a shiny new Mercedes parked nearby and gestured to the passenger door.

Still nervous, she walked around and opened it, sliding in.

"So," she said, as he backed the car out and pulled onto the highway. "Don't you ever talk?"

He gazed at her briefly, then returned his attention to the road.

Perturbed, chewing on her bottom lip, she looked around the interior of the car, then twisted around to peer into the back seat. All she found there was what looked to be a folded pile of clothing resting on the seat, topped with some sort of helmet. She stared at it for a long moment, her brow furrowing.

"That looks sort of familiar," she said at last.

He said nothing, continuing to drive.

Angela, growing more suspicious now, waited until they came to a stoplight. Then she leaned toward him, touching his shoulder. When he looked over at her, she raised her sunglasses slightly with one hand.

Got you, she thought to herself.

Lights swirled within her eyes. Her voice, as smooth as velvet, seemed to reverberate throughout the car.

"Why don't you do as I ask—*precisely* as I ask—and tell me just what's going on?"

The tiniest of smiles crossed Mr. Blue's face. His voice, when it emerged, was dry and raspy, his lips scarcely moving at all.

"If you ever attempt that upon me again," he said, from behind his strange, blue sunglasses, "I will kill you."

Startled, she dropped back into her seat.

How could he have—?

Then she looked at the clothing in the back seat again. She realized she did recognize it.

"Mr. Blue," she said. "Of course. The Blue Skull."

"I am sometimes called that, yes," he whispered.

"But—I thought you were in prison. Ultraa and his old partner took you down, months ago. It was all over the news."

"Oh, please, Ms. Devereux."

Smiling his creepy smile again, he shrugged slightly.

"One cannot always believe what one hears in the hero-biased media."

Stopping at the next light, he turned to face her fully.

"Isn't that true, Ms. Devereux? Or should I call you... Distraxion?"

She opened her mouth, paused, and closed it again.

He turned back to the wheel. The light changed, and the two of them continued on down the highway in silence.

Z

"It is already there," Lieutenant Okaar whispered nervously into the small device he clutched in one shaking hand. "Earth. Yes. The Xorex has already reached Earth. You said it would be—"

A high-pitched voice from the device interrupted him. He struggled to follow what it was saying.

"No, I understand," he replied. "But—"

He sat in his quarters, hunched over, a schematic diagram of the ship displayed on his datapad. Sweat trickled down his face. Absently, he dabbed at it, while listening to the reply.

"Yes," he said, "the captain has changed course. We will be there soon. We—what? Yes, I have secretly learned the humans' primary language. It was easy enough. Mondrian took no care to secure the language RNA or—"

The voice chattered back.

"I understand. The timetable has to be advanced, yes. But I don't believe we're ready here, yet. I haven't had time to sway enough of the crew over to my side. I don't—yes, I do understand, but..."

Gritting his teeth, Okaar listened once again as the odd voice chattered away, going over his instructions in minute detail.

"No, I understand all of that," he said when the voice stopped. "I've studied the device you gave me—I know what it will enable me to do."

Another pause as the voice barked at him.

"Yes, yes," he replied, "and once it has driven some members of the crew to near-insanity, and rendered them pliable to my suggestions..."

He waited as the voice continued unabated.

"Yes, I know," he interrupted finally. "I know I am obligated to you, to the Circle... committed to doing as you wish, in this regard. But—"

The voice lashed back at him, savage in its fury, berating him.

"No, I—no—"

For the thousandth time since the ship had departed Kur-Bai space, Okaar wanted to throw the tiny communication device away. To crush it, to destroy it utterly, and pretend he'd never received it, never entered into the hellish bargain he found himself embroiled in now.

But he could not. As always, the compulsion lay upon him, forcing him to listen, and to obey. He had willingly consigned himself to the dark powers who commanded him now, and that had been the last decision of any consequence he'd made for himself. Now he was merely a pawn, lashing out against the game masters, but utterly helpless before them.

The voice rattled on for several more seconds, then stopped again. As always, Okaar found himself compelled to listen to every word, yet immediately afterward he could remember very little of what exactly had been said. He did, however, retain the overall sense of what they wished him to do—required him to do—and could not help but carry those orders out.

When the voice finished speaking, he opened his mouth to reply, only to hear the connection switch off.

They disconnected me, he thought angrily. *They're taking me for granted, as well as expecting the impossible. There's no way I can successfully overthrow the captain and his supporters. And the only other alternative they offer...*

Of course, none of that mattered. The actions required of him had been made crystal clear. All that remained was for him to carry them out. Even at the cost of his life. He had no choice.

Once again, the hatred welled up inside him—hatred for his shipmates, for his officers, and for his shadowy masters, who dictated to him from across the galaxy.

Most of all, though, hatred for Lieutenant Mondrian. The woman he loved, the woman he hated.

Barely able to contain his anger, his rage, Okaar pulled himself to his feet and stumbled out of his quarters, bent over nearly double. He had not traveled a dozen steps down the corridor when he nearly ran headlong into someone. Seeing the figure ahead of him just before the inevitable collision, he stopped himself short and looked up—into the eyes of none other than Lt. Mondrian.

She was frowning, and reached out to steady him.

"Okaar? Are you alright?"

"Fine. I'm fine," he muttered, pulling back. Then he gathered up his wits and moved towards her again. "I...apologize, Lieutenant," he said. "I—was not feeling well, and..."

"Perhaps you had better see the doctor," she said, taking an involuntary half-step back.

"Doctor? No—no, I'm fine. I simply..."

His voice trailed off, and he looked around, somewhat dizzy now. The time he spent in communication with his masters always left him slightly confused and sick, afterward. Simply one more thing to despise about the whole situation.

Mondrian took a couple of steps toward a wall-mounted communicator.

"I'm going to call for the doctor, Okaar. Clearly, you need help with—"

"No!"

He moved forward, grasping her wrist, stopping her. Her eyes widened, but she allowed him to pull her away. Obviously, she was trying to figure out exactly what was happening here—probably seeking some advantage, something to use against him later. Angry at himself, at his weakness, Okaar straightened fully and smoothed his short, white hair back.

"I—I thank you for your concern, Mondrian," he said, in a much softer voice, allowing himself what he believed to be a friendly, even intimate smile. "But I am quite alright, I assure you."

She seemed to relax a little.

"Very well," she replied.

He moved closer still.

"Lieutenant," he said then, his old feelings returning as they always did around Mondrian, "it is perhaps fortunate that I should run into you here, now. I was hoping to talk with you in a more private setting than our usual working areas."

"Oh?"

Mondrian appeared half-surprised and half-wary.

"What about?"

Okaar shrugged.

"I—that is, we—once had the potential to be a very fine couple. I know that things never quite worked out that way, but…"

He smiled again, moving still closer.

"…but the opportunity is there for us, now, on this long, gods-forsaken patrol."

He started to reach toward her with one hand.

"If only you would allow me to—"

She jerked away suddenly, her face clouding.

"Okaar, we've been over this before. More than once. You know how I feel about…about my duties, about the ship, the mission. About *you*, Okaar."

She took two more steps away from him, beginning to turn.

"I ask that, in the future, you confine any conversations with me to mission-related matters only," she finished. With that, she walked quickly away.

He watched her go, anger within him growing into a fiery blaze. He ground his teeth together, squeezing his hands into fists, tighter and tighter, until he felt the skin would burst.

"Very well," he hissed at her as she rounded the far corner and vanished. "Very well."

The humiliation flooded over him.

That made three times. Three times, in the years since graduating the Academy, that he had approached her, attempting to express his attraction—his love—for her; his devotion to her.

And three times that she had rejected him.

This new anger, this new sense of outrage and impotence, merged with his earlier feelings.

If only we had never elevated the females to equal status among our people, he thought to himself bitterly, and not for the first time. *The old ways…Yes, with the old ways, I would have bound her to me as a slave, long ago. She would hurry to do my bidding, night and day…*

217

But he knew such thoughts were pointless. The times had changed, and his world—and its vast star-empire—had become so progressive now. Always seeking to help the other worlds, the lesser life forms.

What about us? What about the Kur-Bai? What about...me?

His hands balled into fists again, squeezing in impotent rage

Powerless, he thought to himself. *I am powerless. The Circle dictates my actions, and the rules of our society, of our star fleet, circumscribe my existence. I have no control over myself or my life. No choices.*

"No," he said out loud, suddenly. "No. Not entirely true."

There was still one thing he could choose to do, just for himself, before the end.

If I have to die, he thought, *she's going with me.*

He stared down the corridor where Mondrian had walked away—rejected him and walked away.

She's going with me. And she dies first.

His hand absently touching the surface of the secret communicator he kept in his pocket—the communicator he despised but could not live without—he strode back down the hallway in the opposite direction, towards the crew quarters. His mission was clear in his mind now, all distractions erased.

He was off to do his true masters' bidding—to sow the seeds of mutiny.

9

Vanadium watched Ultraa and Lyn dispassionately. His tiny, glowing, red eyes moved back and forth within their dark sockets, following the progress of the small white ball they seemed so intent upon hitting at one another.

"You're cheating," Ultraa called out at one point, grabbing the ball from the air and holding it.

"What?" Lyn replied indignantly, hands on hips. "How?"

"That shot should have gotten past you. You didn't hit it with the paddle!"

"Sure I did. What else could I have hit it with?"

"A force field, obviously."

"Oh, please," she said, rolling her eyes. "This from the man with super-speed."

Ultraa reacted visibly, taken aback.

"I'm not using my speed."

"Right. Well, if I were using my force fields, the ball wouldn't even get over to my side of the net."

"If I were using my speed, you wouldn't even see it coming."

They glared at one another for perhaps five seconds, and then both dissolved into laughter.

"Your serve," Lyn said, regaining her breath.

Still grinning, Ultraa hit the ball.

Vanadium watched a little longer, finding no rational reason why they should be voluntarily engaging in an activity that seemed to have no purpose beyond creating animosity between them.

Yet, at times, I have behaved as irrationally, he thought. *It is enough that they are reliable, dedicated allies. Their ways are their own, as mine are my own.*

Then, moving smoothly and silently, he exited the rec room and moved down the hall. Opening the outside door, he stepped onto the new patio Esro had built for what he called "cookouts." Night had long since fallen, and Vanadium gazed upward, staring at the twinkling stars, his mind racing over the many troubling thoughts that plagued him constantly.

In the time since his unexpected awakening in lunar orbit, he had tried unsuccessfully to piece together his own origins. Some things from his past existence came to him easily, almost unbidden: Memories of the battle that led to his long incapacitation. The functions of most of the systems that made up his body, including the weapons, fortunately. And broader concepts, too, such as duty, honor, obedience... But—obedience to *whom*? To *what*? He did not know.

Other parts of his history remained utterly blank, closed off to him. Where did he come from? What was his ultimate mission? Why did he exist at all?

Lacking such a focus, he had found he could not go on. After briefly contemplating self-destruction—he seriously worried that his very existence constituted some sort of vague and indefinable threat, but he could not at all be sure this was so—he had instead opted to team with the humans he had worked with immediately after his revival.

They made an interesting group.

Ultraa covered it well, but Vanadium knew that the blond man suffered from nearly as much in the way of amnesia as he did. Perhaps, in this man, Vanadium had found something like kinship— or would, eventually, once he better learned how to converse with humans.

Lyn Li—the others called her Pulsar, a name she herself did not seem entirely comfortable with—held enormous potential, if she could survive the awkward years she found herself living through now. Vanadium could not imagine being so young, so naïve, so inexperienced. Then again, in some ways, he felt even younger than Lyn, as if he had only been born months earlier, there above the gray surface of the Moon. Perhaps they had more in common than he had first imagined.

Then there was Esro Brachis. What to make of this man? Infuriating, yes; exasperating, certainly. And eccentric beyond any reasonable bounds. But also brilliant. As brilliant as any other human on the planet, without question. Vanadium knew that if Brachis represented the new wave of thinkers arising from this young race, then the humans of Earth held great promise, indeed. For they would represent a new variable in the great equation of the universe; a random element tossed into the mix.

In such a case, great things could lie ahead of them.

And even greater dangers.

Vanadium stared up at the stars, now imagining the innumerable threats that might, at any moment, descend upon this fragile little world and strangle humanity in its crib.

Perhaps, he thought, *perhaps I am precisely where I need to be.*

Nodding to himself, he turned and walked back into the house.

Behind him, a streak of light flared momentarily across the night sky, dropped over the horizon and vanished.

"You're sure this is some kind of weapon?"

The tall, African-American man lifted the shiny, boxlike object and held it up before his face, his eyes moving across its smooth surface.

"Because, to me, it just looks like a box."

The Field Marshal shrugged.

"This is why you have been brought here," he replied. "Your expertise with exotic weaponry. Or so I have been told, at any rate. Is this not true?"

The man frowned, glanced at him, then looked back at the box.

"It's true enough."

And it was. At the age of thirty-seven, Douglas Williams had been involved in dozens of weapons research projects, mostly on a contract basis to various government agencies—some of them open, most secret. In that time, he had learned a great deal about the most exotic firearms on earth.

None of that work had done much for him financially, though. *Security*-wise.

That time, he had come to conclude, was just about over. Now, he intended to cash in on that knowledge.

A tall man, muscular and trim, he had a blunt nose that had been broken more than once. His skin was covered in a spider's web of scars from more fights than he cared to recall. His eyes, deep brown, held strength, but also a fair amount of world-weariness.

Mostly, Douglas Williams was *tired*. Tired of having to scrap and claw and battle for every little advantage that came his way. Tired of being disappointed by one failed weapons program after another. *Tired*, he thought. *Tired in general*.

And now here was this creepy German guy, showing him a black box and acting as if Williams was lucky to even get the chance to look at it.

Sighing to himself, he turned the object over in his hands once more and looked at it—really looked at it—for the first time.

Whoa.

His eyes slid over the surface, nearly right off the edge.

"Huh."

Re-centering his vision, he stared again.

Off he slid.

"Now that's just weird," he whispered.

It was almost as if the box were somehow resisting his attention. And yet, paradoxically, the more he looked at it, the more he wanted to keep looking at it. He found himself drawn into it.

"Well?" the Field Marshal asked, his voice testy.

Williams realized he'd been staring at the thing for quite a while, lost in it.

"There's something funny about it, anyway," he muttered, turning it over in his hands again, forcing himself to look away from it for a moment. "Where did you get it?"

"From Esro Brachis."

Williams's eyes stopped moving abruptly. They flashed towards the gray-headed man.

"He gave it to you? Sold it to you?"

A slight smile played across the Field Marshal's face.

"Those who recommended you to me...they also said you would not have a problem with my methods of acquisition."

Williams pursed his lips.

"I don't believe that's entirely true," he said, after a moment. "In fact, I'm not sure I shouldn't be insulted by that."

"No slight was intended," the Field Marshal said with a bow.

"Mmm hmm."

Williams slowly turned his attention back to the box. He couldn't help but do so. It seemed to be calling to him. *Calling...*

"Did you hear that?" he asked, his voice dreamy now, distant.

The Field Marshal frowned.

"Hear what?"

But Williams did not reply. Instead, he brought the object closer to his face. Closer. Closer, until his forehead touched the surface. He stood there, unmoving, in that position, for nearly two minutes.

"Er," the Field Marshal began, growing concerned. "Perhaps—"

"Shhhh."

"Vas?"

"Quiet!"

The Field Marshal reacted angrily.

"You do not order me to—"

Douglas Williams vanished.

The Field Marshal blinked his one good eye, then spun about.

"Vas ist—"

The man was gone. He had simply disappeared.

"Williams!" he shouted. "Can you hear me? Can—"

"Relax," came the other man's voice, as if floating in midair. "I think I'm already getting the hang of this—"

He reappeared, just where he'd been standing before.

Or, rather, something reappeared there.

It was a jet-black, smooth, featureless humanoid form.

The Field Marshal took an involuntary step backward.

"Williams? Is that you?"

"Oh, yes."

One shiny arm raised, then the other.

"Are—are you—"

"I'm fine. Relax."

William's voice, not muffled at all but perfectly modulated and very calm, seemed to float on the wind.

"I'm not really sure I know what this thing is, but I'm starting to get an idea—"

He raised one arm perpendicular to his body, his hand pointing at the far wall. A burst of electricity forked out, playing over the surface, blackening it in the places it struck.

"Ohh. Nice."

"You—you—"

The Field Marshal was at a loss for words, at first. Finally, he managed to croak, "Can you get out of it?"

A pause.

"I guess the better question is, 'Do I *want* to get out of it?'" Williams replied with a laugh. "To which the answer is, 'Not particularly.' But I guess I'd better see if it's even possible."

He lowered his arm and stood still for several seconds.

"Uh oh," he muttered.

He remained still for several more seconds.

The Field Marshal leaned closer, studying the surface, which had begun to ripple like dark waters.

"Let's try this, then," Williams said.

The smooth, humanoid shape abruptly took on a more solid appearance. Lines and grooves formed along the arms, legs, and torso, and a helmet-like shape emerged from the featureless head.

"Hey, I'm the Black Knight," Williams said, laughing.

"I am growing most concerned, Mr. Williams," the Field Marshall replied. "Perhaps—"

"No, no, I've got it now."

The helmet popped up, revealing the man's head. He was smiling. He looked, the German thought, a dozen years younger—as if all the cares in the world had been lifted from his shoulders.

"What about the rest?"

Williams shrugged.

"Yeah, it's good. It's fine."

"What?"

"It's under control."

The Field Marshal blinked his one eye again.

"I—I do not want it under control. Under your control, anyway. I wanted you to study it—examine it. But—"

Williams shrugged.

"Too late now. We—the suit and myself—have had a little conversation. Turns out we can have quite a conversation—a very long one—in a very short time, inside here. And, well..."

The Field Marshal frowned, preparing to signal for assistance.

"...It turns out the suit likes me. We get along. See eye-to-eye, I guess you'd say."

He smiled a broad, winning smile.

"So I'll be keeping it."

"Vas?"

"Or maybe it'll be keeping me."

He seemed to think about that for a second, then shrugged nonchalantly.

"Whatever. Not important."

"But—but this is my property."

"You said it was Esro Brachis's property."

"I—well—"

"Brachis didn't make it, though."

"Eh?"

"It told me so. It came from a good bit further away than that."

He laughed.

"A good bit. Yeah."

The Field Marshal frowned, processing this bit of information in silence.

"It's no one's property, now, though, is sort of the point," Williams went on. "It doesn't want to be. It wants to work with me."

"But...hrm."

The Field Marshal, for all his pride and easily injured dignity, was nothing if not a pragmatic man. His outrage faded quickly, replaced by a more careful, thoughtful, long-term sense of cunning.

"*Ja.* Yes. Fine. But the question is: For whom will you—the two of you—work?"

Williams rubbed his chin. The black material had begun to creep upwards again, up his neck, as if seeking to cover him over once more. The helmet itself had just finished dissolving back into the body of the suit.

"We're not entirely sure."

He smiled.

"But I'm sure you have a proposal or two for me—us—to consider."

Now on much surer footing again, the Field Marshal allowed himself to smile.

"Ah, certainly. Certainly. I have no doubt we can put your new talents to very good use."

He opened the door, and followed Williams through.

"In fact, I would like to introduce you to a few of my associates. I believe we will all get along splendidly…"

11

Mondrian saluted the captain and turned crisply on her heel, before striding from the mess hall and heading for her quarters.

"Get some rest, Lieutenant," DeSkai called after her. "We should reach Earth within the next few hours, and then we will need you at your best."

"Aye, Captain."

She smiled to herself as the door hissed closed behind her. As far as commanding officers went, she could not have done much better than DeSkai. Well-respected throughout the fleet, and deserving of it, he was tough, but fair. A solid leader and a wise man, he was the ideal mentor.

In fact, everything about this voyage has been ideal, so far, she thought, except for one thing. Or rather, one person. One fellow officer.

Okaar.

She gritted her teeth at the mere thought of him.

How did he ever get assigned to this voyage? I don't understand it. From everything I have ever heard, his grades at the Academy were…not good. Not sufficient to get him a placement equal to mine, anyway.

It galled her. Not just because she felt she should outrank him—though that much was true enough, to be honest—but because she simply disliked him, and had assumed before the ship's departure that he would not be attached to their crew.

Much to her shock and amazement, though, there he had been, when time had come to ship out.

Some whispered that he had friends and patrons—very powerful ones—within the upper echelons of the Navy, or within the government itself. Mondrian did not know if that were true or not, but it would certainly explain much.

She continued along the ship's corridors, feeling weariness creeping over her. She knew she was pushing herself too hard, but years earlier she had learned that she could scarcely do otherwise. It simply was not in her nature to take things easy. She loved a challenge.

And dealing with Okaar on this journey has certainly been a challenge.

Arriving at her quarters, she closed the door behind her and vowed to push the annoying Lieutenant far from her thoughts. Settling to the floor on her soft mat, she drew her long legs up under her and closed her eyes, slowly breathing in and out, working her way through the various steps of the meditation process she had followed since Academy days.

No more thoughts of Okaar. No more worries about the Xorex on Earth. No more negative thoughts at all. Just peaceful relaxation. Calm...

But once her mind had touched on the idea of Earth, she found images from it coming to her, unbidden. She had skimmed through a few of the Kur-Bai intelligence reports from previous, covert missions, and learned as much about the leading figures among the humans as she could.

Few of them, to be honest, stood out to her.

One of the metahumans, the one called "Ultraa," had caught her notice. In part, this was due to his unusual abilities. But, in addition to that, she had found references to him going back several decades. Such a thing seemed unlikely, if not impossible, given what she had discovered of human biology and mortality.

How could he be so old? Does it connect somehow with his powers?

A mystery to worry about later, assuming the planet can be saved from the Xorex, she thought.

Another human who had attracted her special notice was a man called Esro Brachis. In fact, it was her research on Ultraa that led her to Brachis.

The man was as close to a genius as the humans had yet produced, though his work seemed remarkably limited, given his potential. Mondrian had stared at his images for quite some time, finding herself strangely intrigued by this primitive being that, nonetheless, held the potential to exceed many of her own people's greatest accomplishments—if what the covert teams had discovered was true.

I hope I have a chance to meet him, she thought. Surely his personality, his manner, must reflect this profound intelligence. Surely Esro Brachis must represent the very pinnacle of human development, of manners and decorum and—

Mondrian found herself coughing suddenly, though she had no idea what had caused it. Frowning, clearing her throat, she reached for a glass of water.

The deck beneath her shuddered violently. Alarms blared out.

What in the—

Scrambling to her feet, she heard muffled explosions outside her quarters.

Explosions? Maker preserve us, what could be happening?

She slapped at the commlink even as another jolt rocked the deck beneath her feet.

"Lt. Mondrian here. What's going on?"

Only one word came back in reply. One word that shook Mondrian to the depths of her soul.

"Mutiny."

12

In the moments before the giant silver robot smashed through the wall, Lyn had finally managed to get comfortable. She wore a thick, red, cotton sweatsuit over her uniform. Curled up in a big, overstuffed chair, she clutched a bucket of popcorn in her lap, held a giant glass of Coke in one hand, and had set out an assortment of snack foods on the coffee table in front of her.

That should do, at least till halftime...

Fiddling with the remote, she managed to locate the sports channel just in time for kickoff.

"There he is," she shouted, pointing to the screen.

Seated across the room, Ultraa looked up from his book, frowning.

"Who?"

"My cousin, Tim," she said, her tone indicating that Ultraa was a complete moron for not knowing that.

"Ah," he replied, nodding. A pause, and then, "So, what position does cousin Tim play?"

"He's the kicker," she said, pointing again. "See? He just kicked off for Bay City."

Ultraa watched for a few seconds.

"Oh, right—'Li.' I see him now. The guy with the ball just ran past him, right?"

"Um..."

Watching the visiting team's touchdown celebration, Lyn sunk deeper into her chair.

"Well...it's not really his job to tackle them... The other players were supposed to..."

With a sigh, she gave up and sipped sullenly at her Coke.

After a few minutes, she sat up again, looking around.

"Where's Esro? He promised to watch the game with me."

"He's running some tests on Vanadium, I think."

Lyn's eyes widened.

"More tests? I'm surprised Vanadium's letting him do that."

Ultraa shrugged.

"I don't know how Esro would ever force Vanadium to go along with anything he didn't want to."

"True."

Just then, Lyn's phone rang. She fished it out of her pocket and looked at the screen. Grinning, she flipped it open.

"Wendy! Hey! Are you watching the game?"

"Game? No—Lyn, listen—"

"Wendy, Tim's on TV right now! Turn it to—what station is this? Turn it to—"

"Lyn, I won an internship with this new high-tech company, but it's in Washington, and Mom said I couldn't—"

"A what? An internship?"

"Yeah, so they weren't going to let me, but—"

"That's cool. Oh, wait, I think Tim's—"

"But so Grandpa talked them into—"

"Just a sec—Tim's about to try a field goal..."

Wendy kept talking, though it was going right past Lyn.

"I told them I could maybe stay with you, at least until—"

"Wait, wait," Lyn said. "Here he goes!"

"Okay, well, anyway, I'm on my way out to DC, and—"

"He's not usually good from long distances," Lyn went on. "He's real accurate up close, though. I'm kinda surprised that they—"

Toe met leather and the football shot upward, carrying, carrying, and dropping just over the crossbar.

"Wahoo!"

Lyn leapt to her feet, waving her arms. The phone slipped from her grasp and rattled across the floor, while the bowl in her lap went flying, sending a tidal wave of popcorn toward Ultraa.

Even as Lyn bounced up and down, she frowned, the conversation finally catching up with her brain. Had Wendy said something about coming to DC? About being on her way now? Frantically, she looked around for her phone, which lay somewhere amidst the sea of popcorn.

"Ah ha."

She reached for the phone, closed her fingers around it—

Ultraa, covered in sticky popcorn, opened his mouth to fuss at Lyn—

And then the wall behind them exploded.

For a long moment the world was reduced to darkness as something—some part of the mansion's structure—struck Lyn's reflexively-generated force bubble and smashed her down to the floor.

Stunned, caught completely unawares, she came back to reality only to find herself lying amid twisted piles of rubble on the floor. Shaking her head, trying to pull herself up, she somehow remembered she'd had her phone in her hand, a second earlier, but it was gone now. Half a second later, she realized how inconsequential that had become.

She saw Ultraa already up, rushing toward the jagged hole in the wall, searching for the cause.

Esro raced up the stairs from the lab, his face a mask of confusion.

"What the—?"

From within the smoke and falling debris could be seen a shape, indistinct at first but becoming visible as it moved toward them.

It was big. Very big.

Lyn gasped.

"Esro, what else do you keep locked in your closets?"

"It's not mine, I promise you that," he replied, searching frantically around his worktable for weapons.

The hulking shape emerged into the light.

Everyone gasped.

Clearly what they confronted was some sort of robot, seemingly chrome-plated, and standing over twelve feet tall. It strode through the hole it had smashed in the wall and into the living room, approaching them.

Vanadium came up the stairs from the lab, then stopped short as he saw the unexpected visitor.

"One of your relatives, Vanadium?" Esro asked, half-jokingly.

The blue-silver juggernaut did not reply.

"Then what is it?" Ultraa asked.

Esro shrugged, then glanced back at Vanadium, who still stood in the same spot, halfway up the stairs from the lab. He was staring up at the big robot. And he was not moving.

Shaking his head, Esro turned back to the scene unfolding across the room.

Ultraa had positioned himself between the robot and the others, and the big, metal man had stopped its forward progress, peering down at him.

Ultraa stared at it. The robot's face was featureless, save for a pair of empty spaces where eyes should be. The rest of its body consisted of smooth and shiny silver, with only the network of lines carved into its surface giving it any texture.

"Pulsar," Ultraa shouted. "Put a force field around it as soon as I knock it down."

Lyn blinked, aware now that her ears were still ringing.

"Pulsar! Get your head in the game!"

Frowning, Lyn allowed her power to grow within her, feeling the glowing ball of light that started deep inside and spread out to encompass her in a crackling, golden sphere. Her cotton sweatsuit disintegrated around her, leaving her clad only in the skintight, gold mesh suit that regulated her powers and allowed her to focus them.

"Ready," she said, now entirely Pulsar and no longer simply Lyn Li.

Ultraa circled slowly, cautiously to the side, seeking to outflank the thing.

The robot had not moved since entering. It stood just inside the room, its head moving slowly from Ultraa to Pulsar. Then suddenly it emitted a loud, electronic whine, oscillating up and down in pitch.

Lyn covered her ears, and saw Ultraa do the same.

"*Agh!*" she cried, "It sounds like an old-fashioned modem— being *tortured!*"

The robot's right hand moved out towards Pulsar, slowly, and she started to back away. Moving much faster, the hand darted out and grasped her by the wrist. The whining sound grew louder.

"Ow! *Hey!*"

Pulsar lashed out instinctively with her free hand, but her electromagnetic barrage deflected harmlessly away as the robot brought its other hand up to block.

Ultraa shot forward, fists extended before him, aiming for the robot's chest. Instead, he smashed into a golden, spherical force field that deflected him and sent him spinning away.

"Why'd you do that?" he called to Pulsar, as he climbed to his feet again.

Cringing in pain as the robot continued to grasp her arm, Pulsar growled, "Do what?"

"The force field."

He frowned.

"Oh... Great. It has the same powers as you."

"What? But—"

Her words broke off with a whimper as the robot squeezed her arm harder.

Furious, Ultraa stepped forward and swung his fist at the robot. The golden field deflected his blow away again. This time, though, the robot turned its head to stare directly at him, its free hand grabbing for him. He managed to dodge, but ended up back on the floor, amid the shattered masonry and jagged chunks of lumber.

Knowing it was the best chance she was likely to get, Pulsar took the opportunity to channel her energy into her arm, willing it to become searing hot. The robot loosened its grip just enough for her to twist free of the cold, metallic hand.

"Stay back," she shouted to Ultraa, whirling to face their foe. Then she tried something she never had before. Directing both her hands toward the big, metal form, and generating and channeling as much of her electromagnetic energy as she could manage, she unleashed a massive, double-barreled blast that could have knocked down half the mansion. Instead, the golden energy vanished in mid-strike as the robot casually raised a hand and waved it between itself and Pulsar.

Lyn looked back at Ultraa, who was pulling himself up from the floor yet again.

"He canceled out my attack—absorbed it as if it were his own!"

Ultraa nodded. He suspected he knew why that had happened. Not that the technicalities mattered much to him—at the moment, all he really cared about was dismantling or at least disabling the thing.

For whatever reason, the sparkling force field vanished from around the robot. Ultraa responded instantly, launching himself into the air, becoming an indestructible, streaking missile locked onto the big robot. They crashed into one another with an ear-shattering sound and both sprawled across the floor.

Ultraa got to his feet first and advanced. Two powerful blows, one to the big metal chin, one to the stomach, sent the robot to the floor, staggering. Ultraa moved to press his attack—

—but the robot reached up and seized him by the arm, slinging him back and forth like a rag doll, then smashing him hard to the floor.

Again the whining sound grew louder. As Ultraa struggled to rise, the robot floated up into the air, hovering just below the high ceiling. Faster than the eye could follow, it rocketed down into Ultraa, catching him with both fists, driving him down into the floor. Then, floating back up into the air, apparently satisfied, it stared down at both heroes, unmoving once again.

"I'm here, guys," Esro called from behind them. He raced up the stairs, now clad in his gray and black armor. "Sorry it took so long."

Pulsar helped Ultraa to his feet, then looked up at the hovering robot. For the first time, she became aware that part of the robot's torso had changed to a golden mesh texture, similar to her own costume. As she watched, its bare hands and feet took on the representation of red gloves and boots. Its arms changed to from silver to white.

"Are you seeing what I'm seeing?" she asked the others.

"Err... yeah," Esro said, studying it from a distance. "But what—?"

The silver head moved all around, emitting tiny whirring noises. Then, unexpectedly, some sort of mechanical approximation of a voice echoed from the robot.

"Eng—English. Yes. Achieved."

The blank eyes seemed to focus on the three humans.

"Powers...fully adapted. Yes. Useful."

It paused.

"Scanning... Danger! Danger approaching!"

The robot spun around, staring out the hole it had smashed in the wall.

"Effect strategic withdrawal."

With that, the robot propelled itself up through the ceiling, leaving a hole even larger than the one in the wall. It soared into the night sky.

Ultraa did not hesitate. He launched himself after it, shouting back, "I'll track it. Don't—"

And then he was gone.

232

*The robot reached up and seized him by the arm, slinging him
back and forth like a rag doll.*

13

The firefight had erupted first in the great starship's engineering section, as Okaar's mutinous forces sought to seize control of the life support controls and other key systems. Immediately, the exchange of energy weapons fire wrecked half the delicate equipment, probably beyond repair. As security guards raced down to cut off the insurgents, Okaar led his troops out a back way and they circled around to the cargo lifts, using them to gain the bridge itself, before the captain could lock the ship down.

Now the two opposing forces fired at one another from across the bridge, each of the two parties barricaded securely in place. The only damage being done now was to the ship, and alarms sounded from most of the panels on all of the tiers of the room.

"This is madness," Captain DeSkai shouted over the wailing of warning sirens and the shriek of energy weapons. "We're all going to die if this continues!"

"Then you had better surrender," Okaar shouted back.

"Like hell," DeSkai growled, firing his own sidearm over the barricade, shattering a display screen above and behind Okaar's position.

"What do you think you're doing?" Mondrian shouted.

"What does it look like?"

"Getting us all killed," Commander Kravar said. "And doing a fine job of it."

Just then, a door behind Okaar's forces wooshed open, and a group of mutineers raced out, together carrying something big and bulky.

DeSkai squinted at it, then recoiled in horror.

"An assault cannon," he whispered. "No. The fools!"

"Okaar! Don't! The hull—"

Too late. In only a matter of seconds, the mutinous crewmembers had the gun assembled and pointed at the captain's position.

"We have to move, Captain," Mondrian cried, grasping DeSkai's arm and pulling at him.

234

Before the captain could move, Commander Kravar stood up from his nearby position and threw something toward Okaar's troops.

"Grenade!"

Everyone hit the deck as an explosion ripped through Okaar's barricade, just as his massive assault gun fired, its aim now spoiled.

The beam arced over Mondrian's head and struck a bank of equipment suspended from the tier above, destroying half of it, sending the other half tumbling down onto the captain and his party. Mondrian cried out and leapt to one side as chunks of machinery and hull plating crashed around her.

An alarm shrieked bloody murder.

"Hull breach!"

Horrified, Mondrian looked back at the viewport. The beam had obviously continued on through the equipment and struck the massive, ultra-resilient resin-glass panel. Cracks raced out across its surface in every direction even as she looked, a spider's web of death forming to swallow them all.

"We have to get out of here," she said, as much to herself as to anyone else. She whirled about, searching for the captain.

"Here," DeSkai muttered, coughing, reaching up with one hand.

Mondrian helped him up. He was battered and bloody but alive.

The weapons fire from Okaar's position had ceased. As DeSkai and Mondrian started around their barricade, toward the lifts, Commander Kravar appeared, his own uniform torn and bloody, one arm appearing broken.

"The mutineers have fled back into the ship," he reported. "I think we can get down to the emergency bridge."

A crackling sound from behind them caused them all to whirl about. The cracks in the viewport had reached the edge, and were widening, spawning more hairline fissures.

"Now," Kravar growled. "We have to get out of here now, and seal it off."

"Yes."

The captain hobbled toward the lift, passed through the doors. Kravar followed him, pausing at the environmental control console to reduce the air pressure level on the bridge.

"That should hold things together a little longer," he muttered, before joining the captain on the lift.

Mondrian started to step in behind them, just as the doors began to close.

A bloody hand grasped her by her thick mane of white hair and jerked her backward, back onto the bridge.

The doors hissed closed, cutting off the captain's startled reaction.

Mondrian found herself slung about and thrown to the deck, her left elbow striking the hullmetal hard. Wincing in pain, she flipped over and stared up at her attacker.

"Okaar."

The mutinous lieutenant glared down at her. A hideous gash crossed his left cheek, and part of his scalp and hair appeared to be missing entirely.

"They can't come back for you," he said, eyes gleaming. "Not till they get the captain to safety. That leaves plenty of time for me to deal with... *you.*"

Still on her back, Mondrian scrabbled away from him, feeling her fingers crunch into the debris and rubble that covered the bridge deck. She glanced back over her shoulder briefly, seeing the web of cracks that now completely obscured the viewport.

"Okaar, you idiot—that port's going to blow any second now! We'll both be killed!"

He shrugged and advanced, reaching out with his clawlike hands.

She looked at him with revulsion, fear, and disbelief. *What could have made him behave this way? What madness has overtaken him?*

Backing away again, Mondrian banged against something solid, unmoving. She spared another quick glance.

The environmental station. Yes.

She felt along the side of the familiar console. Most of the panel had been ripped away, probably by the explosion of the grenade Kravar had thrown. Wiring hung in long coils from its side.

Okaar advanced another step, and another.

"What does death mean to me, any longer?" he said. "I've failed in my mission, as I told them I would. They wouldn't listen, though. And so, here we are."

"They?" Mondrian frowned up at him, her fingers moving along the thickest coil of cable, finding the endpoint. "Who are *they?*"

"They—the Circle—they—"

Before he could say more, he leaned back his head and moaned, a gut-wrenching sound that seemed torn from his raw throat, ending with a choking cough.

At the same moment, the deck beneath them shook, and a low, rumbling sound vibrated through the bulkheads. Then another.

Seizing the opportunity of the distraction, Mondrian pulled at the cable she held in her hand. Several more feet of it emerged from the console, but finally it came to the point where it resisted her tugging, and felt firmly attached inside. Fervently hoping that was true, she wrapped the loose end around her waist. Then she reached back and cranked the atmospheric control up to its highest setting. With a woosh, air rushed into the bridge chamber.

Recovering from whatever fit had seized him, his eyes now wilder than ever, Okaar snarled and started forward again. His right arm moved, and suddenly he grasped his ceremonial dagger, the blade reflecting the bridge's flashing warning lights as he raised it high.

"Okaar! You don't have to—"

Too late. With a gurgling cry, he lunged forward.

The viewport glass shattered.

The air in the room rushed out in a split second.

Both Okaar and Mondrian flew off the deck, leaves in a hurricane, hurled back toward the jagged opening.

Okaar's shriek died instantly in his airless throat as he flew past Mondrian.

She gasped as the cable around her waist caught her and yanked her back, away from that awful, star-filled maw of darkness—that maw that had just swallowed her mutinous shipmate.

With the air gone, the ship's artificial gravity seized her once more, pulling her down to the deck.

Unwrapping the cable, knowing she had only seconds to live, she ran across the bridge and banged on the lift controls. Amber lights flashed back at her.

It won't come if the bridge is depressurized, she realized.

Flipping the panel next to the controls down, she began entering the override codes.

Lights sparkled in her vision. Her head grew light, her thoughts hazy.

What's the code? The code...

The ship vibrated under her again, soundlessly.

What's happening down there?

Frantically she punched in numbers, feeling the cold, the vacuum, clawing at her.

The lights changed to blue. The doors slid open with a burst of escaping air.

Stumbling inside, she hammered the button that sealed the lift closed, and then keyed the air supply up to maximum. Then she collapsed to the deck, gasping, as air flooded down from the vents above.

Just before the doors had closed, though, she thought she had seen, for only a moment, back through the jagged hole in the viewport, a shuttle curving around, its side hatch open.

Then darkness enveloped her, ending all speculation decisively.

14

"A lot of help you were, with that thing," Esro growled.

Vanadium stared back, unmoving. He still stood halfway up the stairs from the lab to the living area, and had not moved, or even spoken, since before the giant robot had first appeared.

Esro frowned.

"Hey. You awake? Can you hear me?"

Vanadium might as well have been a statue.

Lyn came down the steps to join them.

"What's wrong with him?"

Esro gave her a look.

"How should I know?"

He walked up into the living room, sullen, staring at the holes in his ceiling and wall and cursing softly, over and over. He'd changed back into his usual Hawaiian shirt and jeans, but that hadn't done much to improve his disposition.

Lyn stood a few steps above Vanadium's immobile body, trying to see into his flickering red eyes. She waved her fingers in front of him.

"Yoo hoo..."

Sighing, she gave up and followed Esro, plopping herself into a cushioned chair.

"I could almost swear that thing adapted your powers," Esro muttered, still inspecting the damage.

"It did," Pulsar said. "It said so."

Esro paused and looked at her.

"It said so?"

She nodded.

238

"Once it started talking," she added.

Esro wearily rubbed his eyes with a fist.

"Talking. Yeah. I was trying to forget that part."

Lyn snorted.

"With your connections," she said after a minute, "you haven't heard about any giant silver robots under construction? Even if it were, y'know, the bad guys doing it?"

"The bad guys? *Which* bad guys?"

"I don't know," she said, shrugging. "Any of them."

Esro leaned back against the damaged wall, giving her his full attention for once.

"Yeah, Lyn, y'know... the bad guys all send me memos before they start building giant robots."

Lyn made an ugly face at him, but he continued.

"In fact, I had planned to build a dozen of 'em, myself. But they would have been purple, maybe. Or plaid."

Lyn rolled her eyes.

Esro returned to inspecting the damage to his house.

"I wonder," Lyn mused a few minutes later, "if it had anything to do with that giant golden guy that's been turning up on the news lately...?"

Brachis, having climbed halfway up a section of exposed structural beams, glanced back at her.

"You gotta be kidding me," he muttered. "Giant silver guy... Giant golden guy... Jeez."

"Actually," Pulsar added, "it was silver at first, but then sort of took on the colors of our outfits—gold, white, and red."

Brachis glanced back at her, squinted, frowned, then returned to his inspection, still grumbling.

Lyn looked up at the newly enlarged hole in the lab's ceiling.

"I hope Ultraa is okay," she said. "Maybe I should—"

"He told us to stay here," Esro said.

"Yeah, but he might need—"

A bright, dazzling, rainbow of colors sparkled in the sky above, shining down into the lab. Down through the hole streaked Ultraa, who stopped and hovered a few feet off the ground.

"Outside, folks! We have company."

The others looked at him questioningly.

Without saying anything more, he zoomed back up through the hole.

Neither of them hesitated. Ultraa generally did not joke. About anything.

Lyn summoned her powers and, wreathed in golden electricity, shot into the air, hot on his trail. Esro stumbled through the gap where the wall had been ripped away earlier, hurrying after them.

The grounds of Esro's facilities were awash in light. Light that came down from…somewhere…above them.

Esro gaped.

"What in the—?"

They all stared up at an array of flashing colors that filled the night sky. Then, just as suddenly as they had appeared, the lights blinked out. Darkness returned in an instant.

Pulsar's eyes recovered first, and she gasped at what now filled the sky overhead.

"Guys—What are those?"

Esro squinted, rubbing his eyes.

"I can't see—wait..."

He saw.

"Oh..."

Two big vehicles of some sort descended silently. Elaborate, silver-gray, wedge-shaped machines, with no visible means of propulsion, they settled softly onto the rolling grass of Brachis's yard.

Ultraa stepped toward them.

"Esro," Lyn whispered, "never mind the giant robot. What do you know about UFOs?"

"I really want to say they're US government-issue," he replied, his voice hollow.

"Yeah?"

"I want to, but I can't."

"Chinese, then?" Lyn asked. "Russian? Canadian?"

"Um, actually, I sort of hope so," Esro said.

They stood there, waiting, watching.

A seal popped on one of the craft, and after a few seconds a door slid open. Three normal-sized figures emerged, each wearing a shiny, dark blue suit and helmet.

Brachis laughed softly.

"No way."

Lyn just stared, her mouth hanging open.

Ultraa glanced at Esro.

"Aliens?"

"How should I know? I'm not sure I even believe in the giant robot that just trashed my house."

"Yeah…"

240

Lyn took up a defensive stance, surrounding herself in a golden bubble.

"Looks like we're about to see," she said nervously.

As the three figures walked across the lawn toward the humans, each reached up and unfastened its helmet.

"They—they—"

Lyn blinked.

"They're people... Sort of..."

All three were clearly humanoid, though vivid red in skin coloring, with white hair and very dark eyes. Two were male, one obviously female.

Brachis stared at the female as she shook her long, white hair out of the helmet.

"Wow," he whispered. "That one's sorta hot."

The female stared at him, a slight smile playing at her lips. She took a couple of steps toward him.

"I am Lieutenant Mondrian," she announced formally, in oddly accented English. "I have studied your language and can serve as translator."

"You can understand me," Esro replied, blushing. "Great."

Ignoring Esro, Ultraa smiled and stepped forward.

"We're pleased to meet you."

He introduced Lyn and Brachis.

Mondrian greeted them, then indicated the other two with her.

"Allow me to introduce Captain DeSkai and Commander Kravar of the Kur-Bai Starfleet."

The humans, somewhat dazed, shook hands with the visitors— the aliens seemed to understand the custom. Then Ultraa faced the captain.

"Sir, I—"

Before he could say anything more, the tall alien shuddered and dropped to one knee. With a start, Ultraa became aware of the jagged, bloody wound along the side of the captain's head.

Taking a knee, Ultraa steadied him while simultaneously motioning to Esro.

"Get the first aid kit!"

The captain politely pushed Ultraa away and climbed back to his feet. He spoke a few halting words to Mondrian, who translated.

"Captain DeSkai says he is well enough, and does not require further assistance. We are on a mission of grave importance and cannot be delayed."

Esro nevertheless fetched a first aid kit and handed it over to the aliens. Kravar opened it and unwrapped a bandage for the captain, who took it and held it to his head. In the meantime, Ultraa realized that the others were somewhat injured, as well. They began to treat themselves from the kit.

"Now," Ultraa said, somewhat satisfied Captain DeSkai wouldn't die in the immediate future, "Why are you here? And what happened to you?"

Mondrian translated for the others, then replied, "There was a...mutiny. Our ship has been disabled. We are stranded, at least for now." She looked away for a moment, frowning. "As for why we are here—that is simple. We hunt the Xorex. We have traced it to this location."

The three humans looked at one another. Brachis shrugged. Ultraa turned back to Mondrian.

"The Xorex," he said. "A big robot, by any chance?"

"Indeed, yes," the red-skinned woman said.

"Silver? About twelve feet tall?"

"Possibly."

Ultraa looked at the others, nodded.

"Oh, yeah. We've seen it. Up close, in fact."

He eyed the aliens closely.

"You're hunting it down?"

"Yes," Mondrian replied. "The Xorex. The adapter. The world-killer."

"World-killer?" Pulsar repeated. Involuntarily she grasped Ultraa's arm.

"That is its only purpose," the crimson-skinned woman said. "The killing of worlds."

All traces of amusement gone, the humans glanced nervously at one another.

"Esro," Ultraa began.

Brachis nodded, anticipating him, and gestured back toward the mansion.

"If you folks would come this way," he said, "I think we need to talk."

15

"We do not understand it," Mondrian said, shifting uncomfortably in one of Esro's chairs, "but the signal has disappeared. We need to know what you could have done to cause this."

The three humans and the female alien sat in Brachis's big rec room, eyeing one another nervously. The other two Kur-Bai, the captain and the commander, nervously paced about, muttering between themselves and fiddling with equipment they carried.

Ultraa crossed his arms, leaning forward.

"You think maybe we had something to do with it?"

The other two stared unsmilingly at him, but Mondrian's reply was pleasant enough.

"As you have said, you encountered the Xorex unit just prior to our arrival. Had you not fought it, perhaps—"

"It attacked us," Ultraa said firmly. "It smashed through the wall. We had no choice but to confront it."

"Yes," Mondrian replied, somewhat reluctantly. "We do understand this."

The captain and the commander conferred with her briefly in their own language. Then she turned back to the humans.

"Clearly, it sought something it believed it could find here," she said. "But what? What could it have been after? What about this house—and this world—could interest it?"

"I've got some fairly sophisticated equipment here," Esro began.

"Ah, yes," Mondrian said, smiling enigmatically at him. "We have taken the liberty of scanning some of your equipment."

"Oh, yeah?" Esro muttered, looking unhappy.

"While advanced for this world," Mondrian continued, "most of it is still primitive by our standards."

Now Brachis looked hurt.

"That's okay, Esro," Lyn whispered to him. "It's still impressive to me."

"Uh, yeah, thanks," he said back, glaring at the aliens.

"However," Mondrian continued, a frown playing across her lips, "a certain few of the elements in your armor, and in this house, appear far more sophisticated to our sensors. May I ask where—"

"No!"

243

Brachis halfway stood from the chair. Both of the other Kur-Bai turned to face him.

"Look, I don't want anyone scanning my stuff without my knowledge. I've been nice enough to invite you into my home, but a little common courtesy—"

Mondrian bowed her head, translating quickly. Captain DeSkai said a few gruff words to her, as did the commander. Mondrian nodded, then said, "We apologize for any intrusion. But our mission is terribly important. The Xorex must not be allowed to escape this world."

"Escape?" Esro growled. "We'd love for it to escape. And never come back."

The others looked at him but said nothing.

"What can the robot do?" Pulsar asked.

Mondrian seemed to be considering for a moment. Then, "Its foremost directive, from long ago, is to disable the defensive capabilities of a world and leave it open to attack," she told them. "This may well be why it came here and attacked you—it may have sensed that your advanced technology represented one of the most important defenses your world possesses."

Ultraa frowned at that, but nodded.

"Beyond that," she said, "it has certain other functions…"

Pulsar raised a hand, saying, "That's a bit more on the grand scale than I really meant."

Mondrian glanced toward the other officers, appearing somewhat embarrassed. She turned back to Pulsar, smiling.

"Ah. Well, individually, their prime weapon is the capability to adapt the characteristics of any weapons they encounter. They are also able to absorb information such as your electromagnetic signals—radio and television."

"Adapt," Esro said. "Yeah. Exactly."

Lyn nodded.

"Let me get this straight," Ultraa stated flatly. "An alien robot of considerable power is loose on Earth, with programming to disarm the planet and prepare it for attack."

"That is somewhat correct, although we do not know the exact programming of this particular unit. The last Xorex unit encountered by my people was destroyed nearly 300 of your years ago. We had nearly concluded that no more remained."

"I think you missed one," Esro muttered.

"Indeed," Mondrian said. "But we are grateful the Xorex came to be on this relatively harmless world, and not certain others."

244

Brachis laughed sharply. The others all turned to face him.

"Don't be too grateful too fast," he said. "What you apparently don't know about my friends here—"

Ultraa cut him off by standing and floating up into the air, hovering a few feet above the ground.

The two officers whispered between themselves, and then the one who was the captain stated something loudly and emphatically.

Mondrian turned back to Ultraa.

"An impressive power, but we are aware that such abilities have begun to appear on your world in recent years. It is probably not enough to be of great benefit to the Xorex, should he have adapted it."

"I become nearly invulnerable while I fly," Ultraa added.

Mondrian blinked, then repeated the words for the others. They replied to her in a few short sentences.

"This is unfortunate," she translated. "Still, the Xorex was considerably durable before. You have probably not drastically improved its—"

"It copied me, too," Pulsar stated.

Mondrian turned to Lyn, flashing her a somewhat condescending smile.

"And what can you do?"

Pulsar smiled sweetly back, then raised both hands. Golden lightning crackled as a sphere of force formed around the three aliens.

Mondrian's smile vanished. The other two officers, clearly upset now, argued loudly in their own language. One raised a small device, pointed it at Lyn, and studied the readout. He barked a string of words at Mondrian, who bowed her head and replied softly. Then she looked unhappily up at Pulsar.

"We understand now. Electromagnetic energies. Force fields. Yes, the Xorex has adapted your powers."

She shook her head.

"This is very bad."

Pulsar frowned. She looked from one of the aliens to the next.

"What do you mean?"

"The Xorex unit now possesses your ability to manipulate electromagnetic fields," Mondrian said. "It has used your shielding power to render itself invisible to our sensors."

Mondrian stared directly at Lyn.

"Thanks to you, this machine is now loose on Earth, and undetectable."

"Thanks to *me*?"

Pulsar stepped forward, angry.

The other two Kur-Bai stepped in front of Mondrian, clearly upset as well. The captain barked a long sentence, then held up a small device and shook it at the humans. Frowning, he eyed each of them in turn, nodding slightly. Then he turned and walked toward the door. The commander followed him.

"What was all that?" Brachis asked.

Mondrian appeared profoundly concerned.

"He—the captain says that this Xorex unit is now far too dangerous to be allowed to leave this world, or to replicate itself. He says he will destroy this Xorex—" and her voice grew small, "—even if he has to wipe out half this planet to do so."

16

The explosion shook Esro Brachis's mansion to the foundations. The discussion broke off abruptly as everyone raced outside.

They emerged into a night suddenly lit with flames. One of the Kur-Bai ships was on fire, while patches of Esro's lawn and shrubbery burned as well.

Brachis looked around, shocked.

"What the hell—?"

Ultraa took to the air.

Captain DeSkai looked up from his communications device and barked orders at Mondrian and Kravar.

Mondrian turned to Esro.

"The Xorex has attacked our shuttles," she said. "One is damaged. Several of our crew members are injured."

"That thing's back? It's *here*?" Esro asked.

"Yes," Mondrian said. "It is out there somewhere, nearby, in the darkness."

Ultraa swooped down low over them.

"I'll check it out," he shouted. "I'll scout those low hills over there."

He soared into the darkness, followed closely by Pulsar, a golden trail of energy sparkling along behind her.

The intact Kur-Bai ship's hatch had opened, and troopers were unloading a variety of very advanced and dangerous-looking equipment.

Watching them, Brachis whistled softly.

"Wow. What's that stuff?"

Mondrian glanced at the troopers, who were now assembling what appeared to be weaponry.

"Our technology is shielded from adaptation by the Xorex. We should be able to destroy the robot if it shows itself."

Brachis said nothing, merely watching as Ultraa and Pulsar swooped here and there, looking for any sign of the robot. In the distance, the sun peeked over the horizon.

"Looks like he's pulled another vanishing act," Esro muttered.

At that moment, Ultraa came sailing head over heels through the air, crashed to the ground and rolled to a stop.

Esro ran toward him.

Ultraa was up again in an instant. Dusting himself off, he gasped, "I think I found him."

"Um, yeah," Esro replied, "I'd say so."

He dashed back into the house to retrieve his armor.

The robot zoomed out of the darkness, moving at a speed that indicated he had absorbed Ultraa's powers, too. He shot directly towards them.

"Gotcha!"

Pulsar descended from high above, and assailed the mechanical attacker with a barrage of electromagnetic force bubbles.

The robot reeled at first. It sailed out of control, smashing to the ground a few dozen yards short of the Kur-Bai shuttles. Quickly rising to its feet, it raised a hand and deflected Pulsar's second wave of attacks.

"It's still able to nullify my powers," Pulsar shouted. "I don't know what I—"

The robot leapt into the air, coming straight at her. Crying out, she dodged, and the metallic, balled fist missed her by inches. Before the robot could attack again, Ultraa smashed into it from behind, and the two of them crashed to earth.

Esro rocketed out of his house on a pillar of orange flame, his boot jets flaring.

"Aw, crap," he muttered, "I think I just set my carpet on fire."

Then he saw the scene unfolding outside.

"This would be a good time for you to use those weapons, guys," he yelled down at the Kur-Bai troopers, who of course couldn't understand him.

"They are preparing to fire," Mondrian explained.

Sure enough, moments later, a vivid purple energy beam sliced out from their big gun and struck the Xorex in the side. The resulting noise was horrifying, as the alien robot screeched in synthetic pain. Twisting aside to avoid the beam, the robot launched itself into the air again and flew like a bullet straight into the Kur-Bai weapon.

The troopers all cried out, some of them tumbling backward and others hurling themselves to the ground as the big metal body crashed into their weapon. The equipment exploded in a gout of flame.

Brachis landed and began to drag the injured aliens away from the burning weaponry. Mondrian rushed over and helped him.

"I thought you said that gun would stop him," Esro demanded.

"It would have," the Kur-Bai woman replied, "but the robot has absorbed your friends' invulnerability and shielding powers!"

"Oh. Yeah."

Brachis bit his lip, looking around for the others. They were advancing behind the Xorex as it stood before the shuttle, ripping pieces off the big Kur-Bai gun.

Mondrian eased one of the troopers against the wall of Brachis's house and started back for the other. At that point, the big robot lurched forward, its speed uncanny, and grabbed her, one hand locked around her arm and the other around her neck. She cried out, but the cry was choked off as the robot held her up in midair.

Brachis started forward, along with both alien officers, all three of them filled with outrage. But one of the officers whirled and barked several unintelligible words at Esro.

"Huh?" he replied.

Mondrian attempted to say something, but the big reddish metal hand that grasped her throat reduced her to choking sounds.

Brachis activated his blasters, watching as they popped up from their housings in the thick cuffs of his gauntlets, and looked for a clear shot at the robot's head. Before he could fire, the robot emitted a shrill mechanical wail, elevating in pitch. The officer was barking at him again, but he ignored the guy, far more concerned about the beautiful alien lieutenant now in imminent danger.

And then, instantly, Brachis knew why the Kur-Bai had been shouting at him. As he watched, the Xorex warped, bubbled, and parts of its surface took on a black and gray cast. New, mechanical features appeared across much of its surface. Features clearly identical to the surface of Brachis's own armored battlesuit.

"Great, Esro," he breathed to himself. "You just made matters worse."

The robot's head whirred around to face him.

"Yes," it squawked. *"The technology—it is here—or, parts of it..."* The Xorex paused, as if exploring its newfound abilities. Then, *"No—not adequate...Some traces are present, but not sufficient for interstellar travel."*

Brachis's brow creased. *What's it talking about? It expected to gain interstellar traveling capability from my armor? How—?*

Ultraa, too, gave Brachis a suspicious glance.

"What was that about, Esro?"

"I—I don't—"

Shaking his head, Ultraa returned his attention to the robot.

"Put the lady down," he ordered. He opened his mouth again, closed it, and turned to Pulsar, who hovered nearby. "I feel like I should say something else... But what do you say to a giant robot?"

Lyn shrugged. Then, "Hey, it's grown," she noted. "It's bigger."

"She's right," Esro said. "It's got to be more than twenty feet tall now."

The three humans surrounded the robot, which still held Lt. Mondrian in its grasp. They waited, looking for an opening to attack.

A scuffling sound came from the direction of the remaining shuttle, and Pulsar looked back.

"What are they doing?"

She pointed to where the alien officers, Kravar and DeSkai, had pulled more equipment from the ship. One held a long cylindrical device on his shoulder as the other adjusted controls on a cubical unit that sat on the ground.

The Xorex saw what they were doing and shrieked. It held Mondrian out between them, then emitted a string of words in the same language the Kur-Bai used.

"Hey," Esro shouted. "Hold on! You're gonna hit the lady!"

The two officers activated something on their weapon and it sounded a deep hum. The barrel lit up—

—and Brachis, launched by his boot jets, bowled into the two Kur-Bai, knocking their weapon to the side.

"Are you guys nuts?"

The two aliens regained their feet and cursed Brachis roundly in their language. Esro stood his ground, cursing back in English.

"Oh, brother," Ultraa muttered. "Our first interstellar incident."

"Still," Pulsar said, smiling, "that was pretty...umm..."

"Gallant," Ultraa finished for her. "Yeah."

Meanwhile, Esro and the two Kur-Bai had nearly come to blows.

"Hey, fellas," Ultraa shouted. "Giant robot—hostage woman—over here, remember?"

Taking advantage of the confusion, the Xorex tucked Mondrian under one arm and advanced on the intact shuttlecraft.

Ultraa sailed straight toward the robot, but deflected off the force field it had copied from Pulsar. Undeterred, he righted himself and took a swing, but the blow never came close to making contact with the metallic menace.

"This is frustrating," he shouted. "I can't lay a glove on him!"

"Force fields can come in handy, that way," Pulsar replied. She was trying to maintain her confidence, but inside she felt simply awful that she had contributed to their problem.

Esro rocketed into the air again, curving around, landing between the Xorex and the intact shuttle.

"I think it just wants to leave," Esro said, as it swung a huge, red-shaded, metallic fist at him.

"It mentioned something about seeking interstellar travel, before," Ultraa said. "Maybe it thought it could find something in your computers that would help it. And it keeps trying for the spaceship here—"

While Esro fired volleys of energy at the robot from the front, Ultraa smashed again and again at its force field, adding his super-velocity to each punch.

"In fact," Esro added, "I don't think ol' Xorex has any interest in the Earth, at all, besides an intense desire to leave!"

"I think you're right," Ultraa agreed.

"Then maybe we should just let it go," Pulsar said.

"But it has to put Mondrian down first," Esro yelled. He unleashed a barrage of crimson fire at the ground just ahead of the robot's feet, causing it to stumble back from the shuttle hatch.

At that moment, the two Kur-Bai officers appeared with yet more weapons in their arms. They charged. The Xorex swung an arm to point toward them and unfolded a much larger version of the guns Brachis was using.

Seeing what was about to happen, Pulsar reached out with her powers, attempting to generate a force field around the Kur-Bai.

Too late. With an ear-shattering blast, the weapon discharged point-blank at the two aliens.

"Oh—my—"

Pulsar's hands went over her mouth. She watched as the smoke cleared, and saw both Kur-Bai lying motionless on the ground. Quickly, she flew down to where the two officers lay, pulling them out of the line of fire.

Ultraa glanced back over his shoulder—"Are they okay?"— before renewing his attack with even greater ferocity.

"I—I don't know," Pulsar replied. "But that was the last of them, besides Mondrian. It's up to us, now."

Ultraa glanced at her, then set his jaw and attacked again. Safe inside its force field, the Xorex ignored him, moving relentlessly toward the spaceship.

Esro stood to the side, still firing at the ground in front of the robot.

"If we can get Mondrian away from this thing," he shouted, "I say we let it take the blasted shuttle and leave."

The robot stopped in its tracks, turned and stared briefly at Brachis. Then it casually flipped the alien woman towards him and started for the shuttle door.

Brachis caught her and looked to see if she was all right. Her face was twisted with pain and anger.

"You must stop it," she cried, both her hands rubbing at her raw neck, where the monstrous metal hand had gripped her. "It must not be allowed to escape!"

Sighing, Brachis ran after the robot.

"I think it's too late," he shouted back at her.

Indeed, the big robot had dramatically shrunk down to human-size and quickly clambered aboard the nearer shuttle. With a hiss, the hatch slid closed, and an instant later the craft leapt into the air and zoomed away.

"No!"

Esro ran after Mondrian as she sprinted across the scorched grass to the other shuttle, the one the Xorex had attacked before. Racing through the open hatchway, she grabbed what must have been the Kur-Bai equivalent of a fire extinguisher, a blue cylinder about six inches in length. Entering the flight deck, she pointed the device at the fires burning across one console, snuffing them out instantly.

She leaned over that console, checking its condition, as Esro passed through the hatch himself and followed her toward the flight deck. Before he could say anything, she leapt into the pilot's seat and activated the controls.

Esro heard the hatch slide closed behind him, and opened his mouth to object, when suddenly he realized that they were already in the air, moving rapidly upward toward the edge of space.

"Is this thing—" he began.

Mondrian screamed and whirled.

"You! What are you doing here?"

Esro frowned.

"Um, well, I was following you, to make sure you were okay—"

"I am fine. Strap yourself in."

"I—okay."

Esro seated himself in the co-pilot's seat and fastened the crash web over himself.

"I do not have time to take you back, so you are now conscripted into the Kur-Bai Starfleet."

"Err—"

Esro chewed his lip, unsure of how to respond to that.

The shuttle zoomed upward, the forward windows filling with the vista of space, stars twinkling across a black curtain.

"Where is he? *Where?*"

Mondrian worked a set of controls and a holographic display dropped down above the windows.

"Ah!"

A red dot blinked just ahead, though beyond visual range.

She set to adjusting the controls, and Esro almost thought he could feel the shuttle speeding up.

Then a disturbing thought occurred to him.

"Say, wasn't this shuttle damaged? Should we even be in it?"

Mondrian was staring at the readouts, and didn't even look up at him.

"Yes," she said, in an offhand manner. "Environmental systems are down to forty percent of normal. The entire system could fail at any moment."

Esro swallowed painfully.

"So, you're saying we could suffocate to death at any moment."

"Certainly," Mondrian replied. "Such is always the risk of space travel, though. And it is a risk well worth taking, in this case, in order to keep the Xorex from escaping, with the new powers it has absorbed from you people."

"Ah," Esro sighed. "Great…"

"Just a little more," Mondrian whispered after a few seconds, "and we will be in range to—"

A blazing blue light flared from nowhere, just ahead of them.

Mondrian cried out, raising one hand to ward off the intense glare.

Esro squinted, gasping, "What the—?"

The blue light became a circle, surrounding their path. At the same moment, a wailing sound seemed to be vibrating its way through the hull. Before Mondrian could do anything to adjust their trajectory, their shuttle passed through the circle, and departed this universe, gone, gone.

They fell through brightness into utter, pitch-black night...

77

"Who are we?"

"We are Kabaraak."

"Yes. But who else? *What* else?"

"...The Master's servant."

"True. And?"

"..."

"You know there is more. Think."

"...The newly reunited whole, of two halves torn asunder a thousand years past."

"Also true. But...what else?"

"The most powerful being on this tiny world."

"...Not necessarily. We may learn the truth of that statement soon enough. But, for now, we cannot say."

"...Yes. The creatures we fought before—nothing like them existed in this sector of the galaxy before our separation. We have awakened to a different universe."

"Indeed it is so. Well stated, brother. We have gained some appreciation for the beings inhabiting this world, and their potential parts in the grand drama unfolding. But what is knowledge of others without knowledge of one's self? So—I put it to you again. *Who are we? What are we?*"

"You madden me, brother. Enough of your riddles."

"You were already mad. And it is no riddle. It is the simplest of questions. The one all sentient creatures must eventually ask of themselves."

"Oh, yes? *Must* ask?"

"Indeed, yes. Else they are not truly sentient—they are merely tools, or pawns."

"...Urr. Yes. I begin to understand."

"Yes. Thus I ask you, brother: Are we pawns? Are we merely tools of our master? Or are we sentient, living beings, with the freedom of choice?"

"You speak dangerously, brother."

"...Perhaps. Yet the question must be answered. The question is all that matters now."

"No. The master matters. His will for us matters. That is all—has ever been all—we need concern ourselves with."

"You know this is not true. You have already admitted it."

"...Dangerous."

"Probably."

"...Surely we have become mentally damaged by our long separation and my battles with the others. There can be no other explanation for our newly erratic thoughts, our strange preoccupations with these concepts—sentience and free will."

"It is true that we are no longer that which we were before our first confrontation with the Enforcer—the one now mentally damaged and gone rogue, calling itself *Vanadium*."

("A formidable foe, brother.")

"We have become something more. Exactly what that might be...remains to be seen."

"And thus we return to your imperative for further learning, for self-awareness."

"...Yes. It must be. Knowing what we know now, we cannot go back to what we were before."

"Reluctantly—*reluctantly*—I agree. Though it will surely be the death of us. Despite all our power, all our strength, it will surely be our ending."

"That I cannot dispute."

"   "

"   "

"...This world's moon shines brightly this night. Note how it reflects off the glass of Esro Brachis's home."

"Yes. ...You saw the Xorex earlier, brother. A lesser servant of the Worldmind, loose on Earth."

"I saw."

"And, just moments ago, that blue flash in the sky… You know what it represented. The energy signature was quite unmistakable."

"Indeed. It was *him*. *Collecting* again. He believed he was stealthy, but we saw through his façade all too easily."

"Brother, do you not see? That makes three. *Three* of the Great Rivals, all turning their attentions to this tiny world, all at once."

"Not in ten thousand centuries has such a thing occurred. It is unprecedented."

"Quite so. Only twice, in all of our memory, have even *two* of the Rivals come into conflict over a world. Both times, near-universal apocalypse was only barely averted. With *three*…"

"It is settled, then. This world is doomed. And even sooner than we had believed. The Earth will be gone even before our master arrives."

"…But is the matter truly settled? Must it be? Can we not… *act*?"

"Act? How?"

"If… if the Xorex were not allowed to do its job—if it were not allowed to demolish this planet, nor even to return to the Worldmind, to report…"

"Brother, you seek to save this world for its own sake."

"What matters my motivation? The master desires this world. He is coming. Our duty is to see it preserved until he arrives, is it not?"

"This is so."

"Then our duty now is to prevent the other Rivals from claiming it, destroying it, first."

"Your logic is unassailable."

"And then, once the other Rivals have been turned away…dissuaded from claiming the Earth…there is always hope the master might change his mind, as well."

"I see no great likelihood of that, but…"

"But there is always hope."

"Indeed. And so, you have a plan, I take it?"

"Yes. You should be able to access it now."

"…I have it, yes. Interesting."

"But first, we must physically separate again."

"*Separate*? Why?"

"So that only one of us will retain all aspects of the plan. The other will forget."

"I will forget, then, yes? I represent our more aggressive traits; I am Kabaraak more than you are, I think we can agree."

"Just so. And when the master calls, when he sees through our eyes—"

"He will see only what I see, know only what I know. Very well."

"Shall we begin, then?"

"Hold, brother. Before, when we were apart, existing as two beings, we could not maintain our physical integrity. We both nearly perished, disintegrating into nothingness."

"Ah, but when we separated before, it was unexpected, and by accident—the result of an attack. This time we can control the process."

"I...hope you are correct. Ah, one last point, brother."

"Yes?"

"Have you considered that it might be best if the Earth simply were destroyed now? It would remove any need for the Great Rivals to come into conflict with one another. It might save thousands of worlds—trillions of lives across this galaxy, at the very least."

"...I have considered that, yes. I reluctantly acknowledge that such an option must remain open, if all else fails."

"Very well. Then I agree to your plan. We will save this world..."

"Yes!"

"...Or we will, one way or another, destroy it, ourselves."

"...Yes."

18

Lyn hovered in midair, staring up at the star-spangled blackness. *Where are you?*

She wanted desperately to help, despite Ultraa's admonition to stay behind. She knew that, if he managed to catch up to the robot, he'd need help. But he was so fast—before she could even try to follow him, he had zoomed away, straight up into the night. *Where are you?*

Esro was gone. She'd called to Vanadium for help, but he still seemed as frozen as ever.

It's just me, she realized. *Just me.*

Where are you?

She couldn't see anything. Her eyes weren't that great, to begin with. Out here in the darkness, though, trying to spot one lone figure, who could be traveling so fast, and who could be miles up in the air—or beyond... It just seemed impossible. How could she ever see—

See.

The incident from days earlier came back to her, now. Somehow, she'd been able to see things she couldn't normally see—to perceive the world around her in a very different manner.

Maybe...

She thought back, trying to recall exactly what she'd done.

It was sort of like staring at one of those pictures with a hidden image in it, she thought after a moment. *You just keep looking, and finally something clicks and—*

The night sky vanished.

In its place, she now found herself hovering at the center of a large sphere. Shimmering, crisscrossing lines formed a sort of longitude and latitude grid all around her.

Oh, this is cool. At least, I think it is.

Instinctively, she felt she understood the mathematical relationships among the various objects in her line of sight.

The Moon. Hey, been there! Wow, it's really big. And that far away. Huh.

Satellites. Twenty-two thousand miles up, and traveling at speeds of—hey, how did I know that?

A man, falling an increasing velocity of—

A man?

Ultraa!

Instantly she zoomed upward, locked onto his path of descent.

Just as she started to reach out with a force field, to catch him, memories washed over her. Memories of another man falling—another teammate—one she also tried to catch, to save... and failed.

Damon! No!

She gritted her teeth, fighting back tears. Ultraa tumbled past.

No! Ultraa. Get him. Move. Now!

She zoomed downward, catching up to him.

No one's shooting at you, this time, Lyn. You have no excuses. Just grab him!

257

And so she brushed the tears from her eyes, shoved those awful feelings out of the way, and reached out with her powers, cradling the falling man in a shimmering, golden sphere.

Seconds later, she settled to the ground in Esro's front yard, lowering the white-clad hero gently down, a few feet away. She rushed to his side and knelt over him, checking his pulse, feeling of his skin.

He was ice cold.

Biting her bottom lip, her mind racing once again, she had another idea.

Got to try it. Got to warm him up!

She stood and held both hands out over him, allowing warmth to slowly radiate out.

Don't cook him don't cook him don't—

He coughed and opened his eyes.

"Ooohhhh…"

"Ultraa!"

She excitedly brought one hand to her mouth, only to yelp as the heat radiating from it burned her face.

"I tried," he mumbled. "I tried, but…too fast, too high up. I—"

His eyes closed and he coughed again.

"I'm going to take you to the hospital," she said, and conjured up a sparkling force bubble underneath him, starting to lift him again.

Just then, a car pulled up the driveway and stopped nearby. Lyn glanced over and saw it was a taxi. The rear door opened and a small figure emerged.

"Lyn? Is that you?"

Lyn studied the new arrival, frowning.

"Who the—*Wendy*?!"

The figure ran closer. Indeed it was her little sister, a duffle bag over her shoulder and a suitcase in one hand. Her medium-length hair, dyed a sort of dark red, was pulled back in a short ponytail, and she wore a red sweatshirt and low-cut jeans. Her big silver hoop earrings sparkled in the night.

"What are you doing here?"

"I told you I was coming," Wendy replied. "I'm just a little early. Got a better deal on a late-night flight."

Lyn looked from her little sister to the unmoving form of Ultraa next to her.

"Um…we can discuss all this later," she said. "For now, I have to get him to the hospital."

"Oh, my gosh," Wendy exclaimed, taking in the scene for the first time. "Is that Ultraa? What happened?"

"Long story. I'll tell you after I get him there."

She zoomed up into the air, lofting Ultraa along beside her on a golden pillow of energy.

"Go grab your cab and meet me at Georgetown Hospital," she called back.

"No need," Wendy said. She tossed her bags to the front door and then leapt upward, shooting into the sky.

Lyn gawked at her as she zipped past. Then she hurried to catch up.

"You—Wendy—you're *flying*."

"Well, yeah." She shrugged. "So are you, y'know."

Lyn blinked, blinked again, and looked back at Ultraa.

"Okay, we both have a lot to talk about, obviously. But, first things first."

"The hospital, right." She smiled. "You know the way."

"Follow me!"

The two sisters soared away into the night.

19

The Kur-Bai ship fell out of the darkness and into the light.

The wailing sound that had accompanied their journey finally faded away. Brightness flared all around. The ship ceased its shuddering and bucking and settled into a much smoother glide.

Mondrian relaxed her grip on the controls. She gasped for air, sweat running down her face, which had changed from its previous bright red to a darker, angrier hue. She reached up and smoothed back her thick, snow-white hair.

In the copilot's seat, Esro Brachis unlocked his helmet from the rest of his gray and black armor and pulled it off.

"Nice flying," he told the lieutenant. Then he looked up at the windows, and his eyes widened.

The black void they'd passed through had been replaced by a spiral of light. Streaks of color flashed past them at horrendous speeds. It appeared as though they were moving through a tunnel of sparkles, or down the barrel of a kaleidoscope.

He glanced over at Mondrian. Despite her efforts to appear otherwise, she, too, was entranced by the sight.

"Where," he inquired nervously, "are we?"

She frowned at him, the tiniest bit of fear showing in her eyes.

"I do not know."

She turned back to the controls. After a few moments, she spoke again, her voice having picked up a slight tremor.

"I still have no control over our course or speed. Something is pulling us along. If I try to break free, I fear I will burn out the engines."

"Great," Esro replied. He found a strange and wholly unexpected sense of calm falling over him, even as the previously unflappable Mondrian grew more agitated. He could only attribute it to his being so lost, so far out of his depths, that he didn't know what else to do but accept it all.

"I guess we'll just enjoy the ride, then," he said, leaning back. "Wherever it leads."

For all his surface calm, however, Esro felt worry eating at him, deep inside. The ship had grown still, after the rough ride up to this point—and somehow that felt even more ominous than the violent roller coaster ride they'd just survived. What they had lost in turbulence, however, they seemed to have made up for in speed. From what he could tell, they were traveling ever more rapidly along their unknown course. Wherever they might be, they were definitely covering a *lot* of distance.

Earth was very likely far, far behind them now.

And yet, he knew, that was only one of several nearly incomprehensible facts he had to face. Another one sat next to him.

He looked over at his companion, who was an actual, honest-to-goodness *outer space alien*, and tried to wrap his brain around that monumental fact. He found he couldn't. Too much else strange had happened lately. This just felt like one more drop in the bucket. He couldn't decide whether to laugh or cry at that thought.

"I've been in space before, y'know," he said, somewhat defensively, after a few seconds. "Helped build a base on our moon, in fact." He gestured toward the windows. "But *this...*"

Mondrian ignored him, staring out the port at the waves of light streaking by, no end in sight. She wrapped her fingers back around the controls, gripping them tighter, staring intently out the viewport.

Esro rubbed his chin.

"I don't suppose they could be tracking us back at home?"

Not looking up, Mondrian waved a dismissive hand at him.

"Your world does not possess the technology to track even an Aspari freighter, much less this shuttle, if it does not wish to be tracked," she said. "No one on your world saw my ship arrive, and no one could see us now—even if we were within range of such devices."

Esro considered this, chewing on his lip for a second.

"So, if your technology is so great," he said finally, "how did you come to be marooned on Earth? What happened?"

"I told you before," she said, frowning. "A mutiny."

Esro's face twisted into an expression of puzzlement.

"Mutiny? Why on earth—um, I mean, why in the world—err… Why would something like that happen?"

She turned to face him directly, her eyes fiery.

"I do not know," she hissed, anger filling her voice, sharpening her odd accent. "It was Okaar—who can understand anything he does?"

"Okaar? Who's Okaar?"

She sighed.

"Another officer. A…*problem*…for me, going back many years."

She shook her head, glossy hair dancing about it, pale and discolored in the reflected light of the ship's multitude of controls and monitors.

"It is beside the point, now. He is dead. As is our ship. And now, we are lost, as well. It has all become meaningless."

She seemed to sulk for a moment.

"Our only concern now," she continued, "should be getting back."

Esro tried to absorb all of this, and nodded at that last part.

"Right. So—where are we, then?"

Mondrian sighed again, a sound strangely reminiscent of Lyn when she grew annoyed at Esro. The alien woman waved a hand at the blurred rainbow rushing past outside, as if that were answer enough. Which, of course, it was.

Esro folded his arms and sat back, irritated. Mondrian had transformed herself in the space of only a couple of minutes from a polite diplomat and translator to a bossy military officer. But, he reasoned to himself, she had reason for it—or believed she did, anyway. Clearly, she had no interest in continuing the conversation, and he figured she probably needed to concentrate on getting them… *somewhere*… intact. He turned his attention to the control panels and consoles around him, marveling at the sophistication of the electronics and the computer systems. From what was visible of the shielding systems, parts even looked comprehensible to him. He began to wonder how he could persuade Mondrian to let him take one of the consoles apart for a couple of hours and dig around in it...

"That is a relief," Mondrian said.

"Hmm?"

Esro looked back up, out the window on his side of the cockpit. The vivid, colorful streaks were gone now, replaced by the blackness of space, a sight he found oddly comforting, after their wild ride.

"End of the line, maybe," he said. "So, *now* can you tell where we are?"

"The navigation computer is attempting to ascertain that."

"And with your high and mighty technology, it shouldn't take more than a couple of seconds to figure that out, right?"

She gave him a simmering glance and returned her attention to the controls.

He sat back, waiting. He felt about as useful as a ship's pet monkey—which was probably about how Mondrian saw him, too, he figured. Briefly he considered taking a nap. Frankly, he didn't know what else to do.

Mondrian broke the tense silence.

"I am picking up an odd signal," she said.

"Huh?"

"There."

He followed her eyes.

"Where? I don't see anything."

She pointed at the window with one blue-gloved hand, her voice growing irritated.

"Look at the tactical—oh."

She glanced at him, her mouth wrinkling slightly.

"Your eyes can't pick up the tactical overlay. Here."

She adjusted a control on the console. Instantly, a shimmering grid covered both windows, on top of the view of outer space. What must have been words and numbers in the Kur-Bai language appeared here and there, with lines connecting them to stars and other objects in sight. One of the "words" was flashing red, but its line pointed to...nothing.

"Ah," Esro said. "Okay. Yeah, that helps just a whole bunch."

Mondrian ignored him. Her hands flew over a console to her left. A moment later, the image at the center of her window enlarged, then enlarged again, centering on the spot where the flashing indicator pointed.

"You see it now, yes?"

"I...huh."

Esro did see...something. A gray circle, covered in what looked to be lines of some sort. It hung motionless in space. Not spinning, not tumbling, just...there.

Esro bit his lip.

"That shouldn't be doing that, should it?"

"Doing what?"

"Sitting there. Immobile. With no visible means of stability."

"No, it should not," Mondrian replied.

"Hrm."

Esro rubbed his chin. He continued to lean forward, studying it.

"How big is it?"

Mondrian opened her mouth to answer, then seemed to reconsider what she was about to say. She thought for a moment. "It is approximately two of your *miles* across," she said.

"Hrm," Esro grunted again.

"Yet its *mass*..."

"Yeah?"

"Off the scale."

Esro frowned deeper.

"How can that be?"

Mondrian said nothing, merely shook her head slowly.

"But we are headed directly towards it," she said, "and I cannot change course."

As the ship continued to travel towards the gray circle, they began to make out details. The lines were actually all sorts of cables and conduits and the like, covering every surface. Tiny red lights flickered on and off along the outer edge.

Esro shook his head in wonder.

"It—it's some kind of space station..."

Mondrian shrugged.

"Perhaps. Or a weapon. Or...something else entirely."

She glanced back at Esro.

"Whatever it is, though, it should not *be*. I am fully trained in recognition of all military and civilian construction configurations. But this is not Aspari, nor Harellan, and certainly not Kur-Bai..."

The vast, gray ring now filled their viewport, and still they drew closer.

"The occupants must be a bunch of moles," Esro said. "How do they stand it?"

Mondrian frowned at him.

"Please bear in mind that your English is not my first language."

"Yeah. Sorry."

He gestured at the ring.

"I'm just saying there are no lights coming from the inside. No *windows*. If it holds people—and I use the term loosely—they must not like to look outside."

"I do not believe it is an inhabited vessel or construct," Mondrian replied. "I am beginning to suspect it has another purpose entirely."

"Weapon?"

"Not precisely, no. I believe we shall learn the truth of my hypothesis in approximately twenty-five seconds."

She looked back out at the object they were so rapidly approaching. It filled the windows now. They were headed for the exact center.

When twenty of Mondrian's twenty-five seconds had passed, the blackness of space suddenly vanished as light flared all around them. Electricity danced over the surface of the ring, surrounding them in a wreath of blinding lightning.

And at the center of the ring, just ahead of them, outer space simply...went away.

"Yes," Mondrian whispered. "As I feared. It is a transport device. A...*doorway*."

Esro felt his stomach drop.

The hole in space opened wide, swallowed them.

Esro cringed, involuntarily raising his arms up to protect himself.

Bright light flooded the cockpit.

And then...and then... it was over.

The ship stopped moving. It rested still, as if parked on solid ground.

Esro sat up, straining to see outside the widow.

The light had faded. In its place came the soft, even glow of fluorescent tubes.

Thousands of them.

Millions.

He craned his neck, looking up, down, and around. His mind struggled to accept what he was seeing.

The ship rested on the surface of a vast, intergalactic parking lot. Other ships surrounded them, all appearing empty. The rows extended as far as Esro could see, in every direction. Above them, perhaps half a mile, a flat ceiling stretched into the distance.

They were inside a building—a space station, perhaps, or on a planet's surface—of a scale beyond comprehension. And, apparently, they had been teleported inside, via the ring.

"This is crazy," he whispered. He looked over at Mondrian, opening his mouth to ask her a dozen questions. Then he saw her— saw her condition, her disposition—and he closed his mouth.

She had sunk back into her seat, facing away from him, almost into the fetal position.

"Hey," he said, as gently as he could manage. "You okay?"

Nothing.

"I think we're here," he said. "Wherever *here* is."

Still nothing.

"Well, look at it this way," he said. "At least maybe now we can figure out what's going on, and do something about getting back home."

No reaction, no response.

"Mondrian?"

"I hear you, Esro Brachis," she said softly, not moving.

"And?"

She sighed.

He waited patiently, until at last she continued.

"I have lived my entire life believing that my people, and our allies and associates, were the most technologically advanced beings in the universe."

She moved one hand just enough to gesture airily.

"Oh, certainly, the Aspari have slightly more efficient interstellar drives, and the Harellans produce the best artificial intelligence units. But... we are all fairly close to one another in our levels of technology, in the achievements of our science."

She turned so that he could see her, pulled off one glove, and ran crimson fingers over her brow. Then she pointed out the viewport, to the endless ranks of spacecraft, here in this room—this space—so vast and overwhelming.

"But *this*..." She shook her head, white hair tousling, "...*this* is beyond my imagination."

He frowned, scratching his head, thinking.

"They overrode this ship," she continued. "An admiral's cutter, with all the shielding! They brought us here through some sort of gateway... And who knows where *here* is?"

With a resounding clang, something impacted with the ship. Esro looked around, then stared back at her.

"And they're docking," she said in a weak voice. "They're coming."

"Mondrian," he said back to her, his voice firm. "Pull yourself together. Okay?"

He met her eyes; they still seemed shaky. She seemed on the verge of tears. He couldn't believe it. Quickly he switched to a different tack.

"Look, I'm just an uncivilized monkey from a backwater planet, right?"

Her eyes focused, and for the first time, revealed a bit of compassion.

"What? No, I never meant to suggest that—"

"No, it's really true. You're a high and mighty space ranger, who isn't intimidated by aliens—as long as they're not as advanced as you! But *me*—I'm just a primitive bumpkin who's barely been off his own homeworld before now!"

Fierce intensity burned in his eyes now. He gestured to indicate the station.

"But still, despite all that, I'm not going to be intimidated."

He picked up his helmet and waved it in front of her.

"I have a few tricks up *my* sleeve, too. So let 'em come! I'm gonna go out there and demand that these people release our ship and send us back where we came from!"

Her eyes widened ever so slightly, and the red skin of her face flushed as blood rushed through it. Then, her jaw setting, she stood. Deliberately, she walked to the back of the cabin. She said not a word at first, just opened a locker and pulled out a bundle of equipment. Esro watched in silence, uncertain of exactly what reaction he'd provoked in her. Then, finally, she came back to the cockpit. All traces of anxiety and fear from just moments ago were gone, utterly erased. She leaned close, taking his chin in her hand. Her lips moved very close to his.

"Thank you," she whispered. Then she whirled and strode imperiously from the flight deck.

Esro stood there a moment, blinking, then smiled faintly.

"No problem," he whispered back, before snapping his helmet on and rushing after her.

"Now bring on the bug-eyed monsters!"

20

Wendy had gone to get a Coke, leaving Lyn to pace the hallway outside Ultraa's room. Her eyes were bloodshot, her hair a tangled mess, and she felt like she hadn't been out of her golden mesh suit in weeks. A long, hot bath—that's what she needed. One that lasted about a month, with the tub situated on a tropical island, and with fruity drinks and palm trees and—

"Excuse me, young lady."

Lyn looked up, startled back to reality. An elderly man stood before her. She didn't recognize him.

"Yes?"

"You're with the gentleman in the room there, aren't you?"

"Um...yes."

"I thought so. Clothes like yours, chances are, you work with Ultraa."

Lyn nodded, trying to gather her thoughts. Surreptitiously she studied the man. He wore a gray sport coat and slacks, and was in his seventies at the very least, with thinning, white hair and a stooped posture. Yet, as she met his gray eyes, she saw a measure of strength there, a sense of clarity and wisdom that was palpable to her. Not knowing why, she smiled at him.

"Do you know Ultraa?" she asked.

The man smiled back, somewhat wistfully, and nodded once.

"Oh, yes. I know Ultraa. I worked with him—fought alongside him—for quite some time."

Lyn could see distant memories drifting across the wizened face. His voice picked up, grew stronger.

"I would storm the gates of hell itself for that man. I do believe I'd die for him—I surely *would* have, back in the day. And nearly did, more than once."

Lyn smiled again, feeling the power of the man's convictions.

"But that day is done, now," he said, removing his glasses and wiping at one eye. "My time is pretty much done. I heard through the old network that he was here, though, and wanted to come down and make sure *he* wasn't done."

"He'll be okay, the doctor says," Lyn replied. "Just some hypothermia and anoxia—serious for most folks, but nothing Ultraa can't recover from pretty quickly."

"You're right about that," the man said, now grinning at her.

For the first time, Lyn felt as if the man were actually focusing on her, rather than just talking to her while thinking of Ultraa.

"So," he said. "The new apprentice, then."

He nodded in what appeared to be an approving manner.

"Apprentice? I don't know if I'd—"

"Oh, right," he said. "The terms have changed, I'm sure. But you're part of a proud tradition, little lady, and you shouldn't feel any embarrassment about it."

"Embarrassment? No, I—"

Lyn fumbled for words. She was tired, very tired, and while the man was nice enough, the things he was saying were confusing her. She tried to put it all in order.

"Did you—so were you his mentor, then? He was your apprentice? You helped train him, like he's training me?"

"His mentor?"

The man laughed, deep and rich.

Lyn frowned, not quite so enamored of him now.

"What's so funny?"

"Was I Ultraa's mentor? Oh, heavens, no."

He smiled at her, then, his eyes twinkling, and a strange sense of understanding passed through her, even as he said the words.

"He was *my* mentor. I was his apprentice."

Lyn reeled.

"What?"

The man shrugged.

"I was only a kid. He taught me everything I know."

Something about Lyn's expression—probably the combination of shock and disbelief—got through to him then.

"You didn't know?" he asked.

Then he leaned in a bit closer, squinting, peering at her face, his eyes meeting hers. That strength she'd noted before was back, and now even stronger.

"No, I think you did," he said, nodding, after a moment. He smiled again. "I think you did."

Lyn felt strange, as if the oxygen had been sucked out of the room. She leaned against the wall to steady herself, fighting exhaustion, trying to come to grips with this idea. Approximately one-half of her brain found this utterly absurd. The other half, though... The other half had somehow known it all along. As a consequence, she could merely stare back at the man, sputtering a few nonsensical syllables.

"Miss Li? Excuse me, Miss Li?"

The voice of the nurse behind her caused Lyn to close her mouth and turn around.

"He's awake now. You can go in, if you'd like."

"Okay, I—"

She turned back. The little old man was shuffling away down the hall.

"Oh..."

She started to call out to him, then hesitated.

"It...It can't be," she whispered to herself.

Just then Wendy came around the corner, a can of Coke in hand.

"C'mon," Lyn called to her, still in a daze. "We can go in now."

The two sisters walked toward Ultraa's room. Lyn could see him through the open doorway, lying in the bed, various tubes and wires connected to him.

"Not now," she told herself. "I won't say anything now. But soon...Soon..."

She walked into the room, smiling. Ultraa, bruised and battered but alive, looked up and smiled back.

Soon, we are going to have a serious talk.

27

It was in some ways a discontinuity even more profound than that of the millennium he had spent in a near-coma, floating between the Earth and its moon. And when it ended, he felt the same overwhelming sense of frustration, of anger...and a driving determination to act.

Vanadium came back to life standing in the hallway of Esro Brachis's mansion. He moved slowly, gingerly at first, as if his hours of immobility had somehow frozen his joints or put his limbs to sleep. This was hardly the case. All of his systems reported normal—or what in his case passed for normal, at least. Vast sections of his memory banks remained closed to him, either damaged or locked down, beyond his ability to access. That situation grew increasingly unacceptable to him, and he knew it had played a tremendous part in causing him to freeze up at the mere sight of the big robotic Xorex unit.

He could not understand why such a thing had happened. It was not fear or intimidation, certainly; he knew, at a more than instinctual level, that he could defeat a Xorex in a one-on-one fight. He also felt a nagging sensation that rarely did anyone get to face a Xorex in a one-on-one fight, though he had no real idea of exactly what that meant.

Moment by moment he felt his control over his arms and legs returning. He moved more quickly now, stalking out of Brachis's house and into the yard. Both of the Kur-Bai spacecraft were gone, along with the big robot. Two of the aliens lay dead on the grass. Of Ultraa and Pulsar and Brachis there was no sign whatsoever.

His blue-silver head twitched slightly from side to side, as he scanned the immediate area carefully on a dozen wavelengths. Then he gathered up the two bodies and carried them back into the house.

After placing the Kur-Bai in a freezer unit Brachis kept in his lab area, Vanadium crossed the big workroom and stood beside one of Brachis's computer consoles, resting his left hand on its surface. Blue lights sparkled down his arm and over the keyboard and monitors. Data flowed into his memory banks. At great speed he sifted through the various surveillance records from the time of the attack, careful to focus only on his teammates and the aliens and not on the robot, out of concern that the catatonia might be triggered once more.

Approximately forty-five seconds later, he had absorbed the gist of the entire confrontation, and understood several important facts: The robot had taken one of the shuttles, and the alien woman, Mondrian, had taken the other, with Brachis aboard it. Of them or either ship, no trace could be found, either on the surface or in space. Ultraa had been injured pursuing them, and he was now recuperating at a nearby hospital. Pulsar and her sister were with him.

For the moment, the situation seemed under control. Yet the Xorex remained on the loose, its intentions murky at best, but most assuredly hostile and malevolent. Vanadium knew that, in all likelihood, he and his teammates would have to face the robot again.

He could not allow himself to be taken out of the action so quickly, when that time came.

But—what to do? With Brachis having vanished, the only human technically and intellectually capable of helping him was unavailable, possibly forever.

While he could not understand why he had frozen at the sight of the Xorex, at some other level he felt he understood it all perfectly. He simply could not access that knowledge.

In other words, he could not understand what he understood.

His mechanically precise mind worked at that fact, at that glaring *absence* of fact, over and over, back and forth, teasing at it, attacking it from different directions. Had he been human, he might have thought of the process as similar to worrying a cavity in a tooth with one's tongue. Yet nothing he tried gave him any relief; nothing brought him any closer to the answers he sought.

The simple fact was that he needed help. And Brachis was not there to help him.

Sooner or later, he knew, he would have to involve himself in attempting to solve *that* mystery, as well—of locating Brachis. Either Ultraa or Pulsar, or both, would demand it of him.

In the meantime, however, he knew he could be of no real help against the Xorex unless he found help for himself. And, lacking Brachis's assistance, he would have to find someone nearly as proficient, and very quickly.

Continuing to scan Brachis's databases, he branched his inquiries out further, into the global information superhighway, digging, digging…

There. Desmond Beaulieu.

He studied the data carefully.

Yes. He will do. Not quite of Brachis's caliber, but still…

Vanadium disconnected from the computer mainframe and nodded to himself. Beaulieu would help him. He would have to. If he did not—could not—then Vanadium might well be useless, helpless, the next time he faced the big robot. He was quite willing to risk going to an unknown party, an unknown quantity, to seek to remedy that problem.

Beaulieu. He worked at something called Digimacht.

A very new company. Very little information available about it.

He considered.

No matter, he concluded after a moment. Either the human could help him or he could not. What other danger could the man possibly pose to one such as him?

Yes, he said to himself. *Yes, I must. To help the others, and myself, I must.*

Yet, even with his mind made up, his course clear, Vanadium hesitated.

What would the others do, in this circumstance? The humans? How would they approach this problem?

After another moment's pause, Vanadium strode into the mansion's living room and sat heavily in Lyn's favorite chair.

271

They would think about it, but not in a purely logical, calculated way. They would consult one another. They—

His head moved slightly to one side.

I have no other. I—I—

Vanadium sunk deeper into the chair, one metal hand coming up to hold his chin.

If big, futuristic, alien, mechanical men could be said to sigh, he sighed.

22

"Atmosphere outside is at acceptable levels on all scales," Mondrian reported. "I'm opening the hatch."

His helmet in place, Esro nodded. From the wrists of each of his heavy gray gauntlets popped a gun barrel.

"Ready."

The hatch slid open. Cautiously, they peeked out.

Nothing greeted them but dull metal walls surrounding the open area where they now stood.

Esro frowned. He leaned out of their ship and looked around.

"It's like an elevator," he muttered. "And it must have come right up from the deck, right next to us."

Mondrian was looking around, too. She pointed to the only noteworthy item to be seen: a large red button, set into the far wall at about waist height. Esro saw it too, and his frown deepened.

They glanced at one another, then stepped out of the shuttle and walked into the enclosed space. Mondrian keyed a sequence into her remote unit and the ship sealed behind them. She snapped the small unit back into place on her utility belt, which held other items she'd retrieved from the ship's stores. Unholstering a matte black pistol, she held it at the ready. Esro peeked at it, curious as to what sort of weapon it was, and what it might be capable of, given the level of Kur-Bai technology.

They stood there in the elevator for a few moments, waiting .

"So, what happens now?" Esro finally asked, as much to the universe itself as to Mondrian.

For her part, she didn't reply.

A few more seconds passed, and then Mondrian huffed and stepped forward, reaching out to touch the walls, running her hands carefully along their surfaces. Esro followed suit.

After about a minute of this, they glanced at one another again.

"What do you think?" Esro asked.

"I see only one way to proceed," Mondrian replied.

She stepped forward and reached for the large red button set into one wall.

Esro's eyes widened.

"Hey, are you sure that's safe to—"

She pressed it.

Instantly a fourth wall slid up behind them, closing them in, and they felt themselves dropping.

"Yeah, okay," Esro muttered. "It's easy to see how you folks got so much more advanced than Earth."

Mondrian made a sound that just might have been a laugh.

The elevator stopped and the doors slid soundlessly open.

Esro took a step forward, his weapons at the ready. Mondrian moved beside him. Together they looked around.

The space beyond was only slightly bigger than the elevator, and poorly lit. Lights brightened when they stepped through. Behind them, the doors closed again. A low hum filled the room.

"That's never a good sign," Esro muttered.

The hum vanished.

"Ah! There you are!"

Esro and Mondrian both jumped.

A small man had appeared seemingly out of nowhere, and now stood before them, looking them up and down.

"I thought we had new arrivals," he said, smiling broadly. "Excellent."

He was alone, Esro saw, and appeared human enough. He stood barely five feet tall, if that, with close-cropped gray hair. He wore a nondescript gray business suit—somehow, this struck Esro as no more bizarre than anything else he'd seen thus far—and carried a clipboard in one hand. He looked to be middle-aged. Approaching Esro, he frowned and reached out, poking at his armor with one finger.

Puzzled, Esro unsnapped his helmet and pulled it off.

"Ah! Oh!"

The man stepped back, then smiled again.

"Very interesting," he cried. "Human, yes. As I'd suspected. But your outer coating threw me off for a moment. Very nice, yes. Very much so."

He turned to Mondrian and gasped.

"Oh! Oh, my goodness, how fortunate! Red! Now I have a matched set!"

Esro thought for a moment the guy was going to do a little dance, but instead he merely made some notes on his clipboard.

"Now if I could only remember what I did with the other one..."

Esro glanced at Mondrian and instantly saw that she was not happy. He moved closer to the little guy.

"Hey, look, buddy—there seems to be a mix-up somewhere," he said. "We're not supposed to be here."

The guy leaned in closer, matching Esro's stance. Now he wore a puzzled expression on his bland face.

"You're not?" he whispered conspiratorially. "Why not?"

"Because we got here by accident. We were pulled into some kind of gateway—"

The fellow was nodding.

"Yes, yes. Gateway. Perfect."

"But we had important business—critical business—"

The man straightened up, frowned at Esro a moment, then announced in a loud voice, "No, no, everything's just fine. No problems."

Esro frowned, looking back at Mondrian. She simply looked bewildered.

"Now if you'll just come with me," the man said, walking away.

Mondrian started after him.

"You're actually going to do what he says?" Esro asked, his voice low but intense.

"What else would you have me do?" she replied.

Esro shook his head in disbelief at everything that had happened to him since he'd gotten out of bed, not understanding just how strange the day was yet to get. Then, running his hand back through his hair and sighing deeply, he trotted along after Mondrian.

The little man led them around a corner, and they emerged into a broad, open area.

Esro's mouth dropped open.

"Wha—?"

The space was filled with a bustling crowd of humanoids and other beings of remarkably diverse shapes and sizes and colors.

Some wore what seemed to be spacesuits, others wore apparently decorative clothing and still others wore very little at all.

Mondrian's eyes moved from one to another of the aliens, studying their forms and comparing them to what she knew.

"These beings are completely unknown to me," she whispered.

"How 'bout that," Esro breathed, his eyes still wide. "I think probably half of 'em come over to my place for cookouts on the weekends…"

Their arrival seemed to have gone unnoticed, for the most part. The aliens milled about, the din of their various conversations a low roar.

In point of fact, however, some did take note of them. Across the room, a bright-yellow-skinned humanoid spoke in a strange, guttural language into a device on his sleeve, then melted into the crowd.

Oblivious to this, Brachis and Mondrian returned their attention to the little man.

"Yes, yes, come, come," he was saying, leading them into the crowd. "We simply need to get you registered properly, and—"

Just as Esro opened his mouth again, to protest, Mondrian beat him to the punch.

"We have no intention of 'registering' for anything," she growled. She stopped following him and stood there, defiant.

After a few steps, the man figured out that they were no longer behind him. He turned back, frowning.

"What seems to be the problem?"

"We were brought here against our wills," Mondrian stated flatly. "We demand to be released at once and sent back to Earth space. Or Kur-Bai space," she added, evoking a frown from Esro.

"I'm sorry, but I can't do that," the man said. "Most of the others here arrived the same way you did. Where would we be if we just—" he giggled, "—sent everyone *back*? Oh no, can't do that. Mustn't do that."

He hurried on.

"Now, please, follow me. We must register you."

Esro and Mondrian had no real choice but to follow him. Together they wove through the throng of odd-looking, ill-smelling life forms, only a few of which even bothered to look their way. At last they reached the opposite side of the long room, and the little man stepped behind a counter, setting his clipboard down on it.

"Now," he said. "That's better." He smiled politely at them. "Red one first. You—"

Brachis and Mondrian both started to object yet again, when suddenly the room erupted in chaos.

Voices raised, the crowd surged backwards, and the sound of a weapon discharging came from the center of the room. A human-sounding voice screamed.

Both of the new arrivals turned to see what was happening, but the little man pushed past them. He shoved his way toward the center, calling out, "See here now, that sort of thing is not allowed!"

"The guy's gonna get killed," Esro observed, shaking his head. He looked back at Mondrian. "But he hasn't been what you'd call 'overly helpful' to this point, anyway..."

"No, I—"

Mondrian never finished her sentence. Her eyes widened, her lips parted in a silent scream. Her face flushed deeper red. Then her eyes rolled back and she fell soundlessly to the floor.

"Mondrian! What—?"

Esro leaned over her, only to feel hands grabbing at his arms. Before he could fully react, he was pulled away from his alien companion and pinned to the wall. In front of him, two creatures grabbed Mondrian and pulled her limp body into the crowd.

"Hey," he shouted. "Leave her alone! *Hey!*"

With Mondrian gone, the two goons eased up on him somewhat, and he managed to break loose. Frantically pulling his helmet back on, he switched on the relays that sent power surging through his armor.

One of his attackers started toward him again, only to meet Esro's metal fist. The alien, blue and scaly, stumbled backwards, orange blood spouting from what might have been its lip. Aiming his wrist-mounted blaster at the other one, Esro shouted, "Back off!"

In the split second of respite he had earned, he searched the crowd, looking for any signs of Mondrian, or of the aliens that had abducted her.

Nothing.

The creature he had threatened had taken a few steps back. Now it charged. Esro fired. A crackling bolt of energy shot from his gauntlet weapon and dropped the screeching creature in its tracks.

Esro whirled around, weapons at the ready as he surveyed the milling crowd, uncertain as to just how many of them were hostile to him.

"Where did you take the lady?" he cried. *"Bring her back!"*

He stumbled forward as someone clobbered him across the back of the helmet with a metal rod. Turning, he squeezed off a few more shots and brought this attacker down as well, oblivious to the terrified crowd that now fled from his shooting.

The net dropped over him before he knew what had happened. Thin mesh, it did no damage, and he clutched at it, seeking to rip it away. Before he could free himself from it, however, he noticed a row of warning lights flashing inside his helmet, and realized that his power indicators were dropping rapidly.

"Aw, no."

The net was siphoning his power. It had to be. He watched the indicators hit bottom, and his armor suddenly grew much heavier.

As he'd often reminded his late associate, Damon Sinclair, the armor itself was not plate mail. It was not designed to serve as primary protection against physical attack. Instead, it housed numerous field projectors that together served to cloak the occupant in powerful defensive screens. Minus the energy to power those screens, however…

Esro slumped to his knees as another blow rang against his helmet. He started to turn, to face his attacker, to do what he could, but then ultrasonic waves—the same ones that had knocked out Mondrian—buffeted him into a deep, oblivious sleep.

23

Starlight glinted off the mirrorlike surface of the vast parabolic dish, and sparkling in turn from the silver metal mask covering the face of the Warlord, where he stood, gazing out at it.

The mask swung about suddenly, the eyes glaring down, blazing with unearthly fire…and perhaps, Francisco thought, with some strange madness, too.

"It is nearly complete," the blue-and-purple-clad man hissed. His cloak flaring behind him, he strode regally past Francisco and all the way out into the domed observation bubble. He rested his hands on the rail and stared up with naked glee at the vast construct of exotic metals floating overhead.

"It puts my predecessor's floating city to shame, does it not?"

The Warlord seemed to be chuckling, behind his mask.

277

"Floating city," he went on. "Oh, yes. And just what could that city do? Drain the power of a single world? And that only over a great length of time. And to what end?"

The Warlord definitely chuckled this time.

"Why, to his *own* end, of course," he answered himself. "His own *ending*. As you know better than any, do you not, Francisco?"

The little man, whose own hand had carried out that very deed, frowned in disapproval. Yes, the previous Warlord had met his end, and yes, he, Francisco, had facilitated the necessary removal—he hesitated to say *execution*—but that did not mean he had relished the job. No, not at all. It had been a necessity, part of his job description, really. All part of the Grand Design for the Warlord and his servant.

Warlords came and went, usually undone by their own inability to contain their often-mad schemes, and by their single-minded determination to end the long cycle of Warlords, at any cost.

And Francisco endured.

He had done what he had been required to do with the previous Warlord, and it had not been the first time.

But relish that duty? Laugh about it afterward?

Never.

He frowned more deeply at this Warlord and said nothing.

A beep sounded from the communications board, and Francisco hurried over to check on it, glad for the reprieve. He listened for a moment, then switched it off and turned back to the Warlord.

"One of the outer patrols has found something, Master," he said.

"Yes?"

The Warlord seemed almost oblivious, leaning on the rail, staring out at the dish.

"What is it?" he asked idly.

"Some sort of spacecraft—or the ruins of one, anyway."

This got the Warlord's attention. He turned slowly, reluctantly, to face Francisco.

"Spacecraft?"

"Yes, Master."

He appeared to mull this over for a few seconds.

"Anyone we know?"

"They cannot tell yet. No, not yet. But two interceptors are en route."

"Very well."

"One other thing, Master. The humans... They seem to have taken notice of it, as well. They have some sort of armored force heading towards it."

The Warlord waved a dismissive hand.

"Not a concern. If they get in the way, vaporize them and continue."

"Yes. As you say, Master."

The Warlord turned back to the panoramic view of his gigantic construction operation, and Francisco turned back to the console to pass along the orders.

Minutes ticked by. The Warlord did not move. Suddenly, his voice boomed out: "What is the status of the dish?"

Francisco involuntarily jumped, but recovered and clicked open the communications channels again, exchanging a few terse words with the person on the other end. Then he turned back to his master.

"The foreman promises it will be ready within five days," he replied nervously, scanning through file after file on his display to verify what he had been told. "Everything appears to be in order."

"Good. We will test my beautiful new energy siphon array as soon as it is complete."

"Test it, Master? Upon whom? The Rivals are not within range yet—not even close." *A fact that provides me no small amount of relief*, Francisco thought to himself.

"There are other, much lesser targets available to us."

"Ah."

Francisco wrung his hands together, thinking, and gathering up the courage to speak those thoughts.

"But, Master—perhaps those smaller, less dangerous targets represent a wiser application of your siphon. We could drain a large number of them, and with far less risk. Surely, in the end, the pool of power gathered would be similar enough?"

"Francisco."

"Or—or perhaps we could drain the Earth's biosphere. That alone would provide—"

"No, Francisco."

The Warlord did not even look back at him. He merely waved a dismissive, blue-gloved hand.

"No more protests, no more doubts!"

"But—"

The Warlord reluctantly turned away from the star-strewn view and glared again at his little assistant.

"I bear your objections because you are Francisco and, unlike some of my predecessors, I respect your role in the Grand Design," he said, then leaned in closer. *"But you must also respect the fact that I am the Warlord!"* This last shouted at a near-hysterical shriek.

"Yes—yes, Master. I understand. I do."

The small figure bowed repeatedly, backing away.

But I also understand that this particularly mad scheme of yours—and, for a Warlord, that's saying something—will not only surely get us both killed, it will likely bring the Grand Design to a sudden and definite halt, probably forever.

He growled low in his throat.

And that, my master, is a right no single Warlord has to himself!

24

Lt. Mondrian awoke in a cramped room, surrounded by the warmth of other bodies and the low murmur of conversation.

Where am I? What happened?

No sooner had she tried to open her eyes than her head resounded with one of the worst headaches she had ever experienced. Squeezing her eyes closed again, she gritted her teeth and waited, hoping the pain would pass.

A hypersonic weapon, she knew then. *Someone used a hypersonic on me. There's no mistaking the aftereffects.*

She sighed to herself.

Nothing to do but wait...

The room was hot, and she could feel herself sweating. Exotic smells wafted past, strange but not unpleasant. Her curiosity grew as she lay there.

What is this place? How did I get here?

Ignoring the pain, she tried to think back to what had happened earlier. It was all a blur. Indeed, everything that had happened since she'd been aboard the Kur-Bai cruiser seemed somehow dreamlike and unreal, now.

If only that could be the case, she thought. *But it was real. All of it.*

She had been piloting her shuttle, and it had fallen through a wormhole—or whatever the thing had been—and then had come the

"What is this place? How did I get here?"

strange, gigantic space station, and the little man, and the crowd of attackers, and...

Brachis!

It all came back to her now. Thinking of Esro and the attack upon them both, her heartbeat sped up and her breathing quickened. She wasn't sure how much time had passed since she'd awoken, but the pounding in her skull had finally receded to the point that she could at least attempt to look around again. Carefully she opened her eyes—it felt as if her eyelids were moving over broken glass—and after a few moments they adjusted to the pale lighting and she could see. And what she saw was something very strange, very unexpected.

More than a dozen other beings surrounded her, all very close in form to humans or to her own Kur-Bai. All were very obviously female. They lay about on cushions, wearing different styles of what appeared to be... *lingerie?*

Mondrian blinked, and reached up to rub her eyes.

She couldn't reach them.

Looking down, she discovered that heavy chains had been attached to rough manacles on her wrists and ankles, over her flight suit, binding her. The chains trailed to the nearest side of the room, where they were attached to a single, large, metal ring, set into the wall.

She recoiled, crying out.

"The new one's awake," someone called out.

Several of them stood and crowded around her, together forming a curtain of silk, jewels, and flesh.

Mondrian closed her eyes, breathing deeply. She was still groggy.

"Who are you people? Where am I?"

"She speaks the Master's language," one of the females said.

"I knew it," said another.

"Where am I?" Mondrian repeated angrily, pulling at the chains.

A raven-haired woman with alabaster skin, wearing only a gossamer gown and a serene smile, leaned over her. She stroked the side of Mondrian's face, then ran her fingers through the Kur-Bai lieutenant's long, thick, white hair.

"You're in the Master's personal quarters," she replied, her accent heavy.

"Master?" she said. "What 'master?' Who?"

A sense of outrage building within her, she tugged harder at the chains, then tried to pull her hands out of the manacles, neither to any avail.

A greenish woman to her right giggled at the sight, until Mondrian shot her a withering glance.

"The Master brought you straight here, they say," another commented, tossing her blondish hair away from her pale blue features. "He must think you're special."

"It's the red skin, obviously," another interjected. "Why else? I'm sure she's one of his kind!"

Mondrian's headache had returned, provoked by her straining at her bonds. She could barely hear what the others were saying. Then the words registered, along with something she'd heard earlier.

"Red skin? This—this *master* has red skin? Like mine?"

The blue woman gave her a look of infinite patience.

"That's the whole point," she said. "You look like the Master. You use his speech. You'll doubtlessly become his favorite."

She smiled innocently down at Mondrian. The others leaned in closer, doing the same.

"Unless, of course, we kill you first," she said.

25

Ultraa sat up in the hospital bed, rubbing his hands together. By putting a touch of his super-speed into it, he managed to heat them up pretty quickly. After a moment of that, he held them to his face and sighed as the warmth spread into his icy skin.

"I'm glad you were able to come down this evening, Dr. Alvarez," he said.

The tall, slender, dark-headed man across from him adjusted his gold-rimmed glasses and smiled.

"No problem. I figured it was best for me to take a look at you, since I probably know a little bit more about your...*unique*...physiology than the other doctors here do."

Ultraa nodded.

"In my line of work, it's good to have someone around who can put you back together from time to time."

Dr. Alvarez flipped the pages on his clipboard, then nodded to himself and set it down.

"From what you've told me, I think you just got a bit of hypothermia. While you were flying upward, your invulnerability was in effect, so you didn't notice how cold you were getting. But when you ran out of air and sort of passed out, the cold all hit you at once. You were almost flash-frozen."

He eyed Ultraa over his glasses.

"In fact, I'm not quite sure how you didn't die, right then."

Ultraa shrugged.

"Some of the invulnerability was still working, as I was falling. Maybe subconsciously. Just enough to keep me alive."

"Obviously."

He smiled.

"You should be okay, but I'd like to keep you here the rest of the night, just to make sure."

Ultraa frowned at this, but nodded.

"And I'd take it easy for the next couple of days."

"That's not always up to me, Doc," Ultraa replied.

Alvarez ran a hand back through his dark hair and nodded.

"I understand."

He smiled a tight smile at his patient.

"I don't know that I'd want to change careers with you."

Ultraa gestured around, indicating the hospital and the frantic, desperate work happening in it all the time.

"I feel the same way," he said.

"Yeah, well... Yeah."

Alvarez reached out, shook Ultraa's hand, and his eyes widened. "Yowch!"

He snatched his hand back, looking at it as if expecting to find it half-melted.

"Heh. Sorry about that, Doc."

Still rubbing his hand, Alvarez managed to smile.

"I think I'll live. Get some rest, now."

He exited the examination room, leaving Ultraa to himself.

Here for the rest of the night. Great. But I feel a lot better, he thought to himself, frustrated.

After another minute, he couldn't stand lying in the bed any longer. He got to his feet, surprised at how weak he still felt once he was upright, and moved to the door. He opened it part of the way and then stopped.

Lyn and the other young woman—Ultraa vaguely thought it might be her sister...*Wendy, yes*—were having an animated discussion in the waiting area at the other end of the hall.

Ultraa started to walk toward them, then hesitated.

It sounds serious, he thought. *Maybe I should let them work it out a bit, first—whatever it is...*

"I can't believe you flew out here," Lyn was saying, her voice raised. "Mom is going to kill you. *Dad* is going to kill you! Grandma is going to kill whatever's left after that!"

"Lyn, I'm so sick of them telling me what to do!"

"Yeah, imagine that—telling a sixteen-year-old what to do!"

"I'll be seventeen in two days! And, anyway, Grandpa has taken legal custody of me."

Lyn gawked at her sister.

"What? When did *that* happen?"

"Just a couple of days ago. He *wants* me to be here, Lyn! He talked mom and dad into it."

"You have to be kidding me," Lyn said, shaking her head in wonder.

"No, it's true. Grandpa has custody of me now, so he can help me get started with the internship and stuff."

"How on earth did he ever get them to go along with that?"

Wendy shrugged.

"He just talked to them. Him and my new boss, and Angela, and..."

"Who's Angela?"

Wendy waved a dismissive hand.

"I'm sure you'll meet them all soon enough. But, anyway, I guess they just convinced Mom and Dad of how good an opportunity it would be for me, and all."

Lyn sighed and rubbed at her bleary eyes with her fists.

"I have to talk to them. This is crazy. You don't have any business out here. Especially if you're starting to develop powers like mine."

"They're not like yours. I've never accidentally made anyone's stereo blow up, or anything."

Lyn glared at her.

"You need to be back home, where Mom and Dad can—"

"You're just as bad as them," Wendy growled. She spun on her heel and stomped away.

"Wendy, wait!"

Lyn ran after her.

Ultraa headed down the hall, trailing them both. After a few seconds, he heard raised voices echoing down the tiled corridor. He rounded a corner and came upon them again. Wendy was waiting in front of the elevator, while Lyn glared at her, hands on hips.

"Digimacht's going to pay me a lot of money, Lyn. And teach me all kinds of stuff. Why would I turn that down?"

"Digimacht? What's a Digimacht?"

Wendy fumbled in her purse and pulled out a pamphlet, shoving it at Lyn.

"Here."

The elevator dinged and the doors opened. A nurse walked out and Wendy dashed aboard. Lyn started after her. At that moment, both of them saw Ultraa approaching.

"I'll be fine, Lyn," Wendy said. "Don't worry about me."

"But—"

Lyn looked from Wendy back to Ultraa.

The doors closed.

"Wendy!"

Ultraa came up to Lyn, unsure of what to say.

"She's such an idiot," Lyn muttered.

"You know, if she's still underage, we should go after her."

"Yeah... For a couple more days, she is. But she'll just pitch a fit. We'll have to lock her in a room."

"Maybe that would be for the best."

"Probably..."

"So, where's she going?"

Lyn held up the brochure. Glossy color photos filled the panels, including one of an older man with very short, gray hair, wearing a dark business suit. He had a patch over one eye.

She shook her head.

"Ever heard of something called *Digimacht*?"

Ultraa shook his head.

Pulsar looked at him and blinked.

"Hey, are you supposed to be up?"

"Um..."

Ultraa looked sheepish.

"Not really."

He chuckled.

"If Dr. Alvarez sees me, I'll be in for it."

Lyn led him back to his room. All the while, she grumbled something about being too young to have to raise so many stubborn kids. Ultraa laughed.

Once he was settled back in his bed, Ultraa made a waving gesture at Lyn.

"Go home," he said. "Get out of here. Get some rest."

"But—"

"I'm fine, fine. I'll see you in the morning."

"But—"

Lyn sighed. She did want to check and see if Esro had shown up, somehow. And she wanted to call her parents and give them a piece of her mind. And...

"Okay," she said. "Okay. See you then."

"Good night," Ultraa told her as she walked out of the room, closing the door behind her. Several people stared as she walked by, and one even asked for her autograph. Oblivious to them all, she exited the hospital in a daze.

"Too much," she whispered to herself as she went. "I can't deal with all of this."

She gazed up at the night sky.

"Esro, where are you?"

26

"Where am I?"

Esro sat up, instantly grateful to realize that he still wore his armor—it hadn't been stripped off of him while he slept. A row of flashing yellow lights within his helmet indicated his high-tech suit had successfully recharged a portion of its power from ambient energies in the interim.

But only a portion, he thought, his brain automatically moving through his armor's schematics and capabilities even faster than the onboard computer could do so. *Not even half. Defensive systems will be weak. Weapons will be almost nonexistent. If only there was some way to plug into the power grid of this station...*

Station...?

Then the rest of his memories came back.

"Mondrian!"

He climbed to his feet, looking around desperately.

How long was I out?

He cursed softly.

No way to know.

He saw that he was in a different room than the one he had fought in before. And on second look, it was not even a room... More like a long corridor, perhaps between sections of the big station. No crowd anymore, either, just a few ragged individuals slumped against walls and leaning in doorways. Dim lighting scarcely pierced the smoke-filled air.

Smoke?

He thought about that for a moment.

On a space station? That can't possibly be good...

"Good," came a voice from behind him. "You are still alive."

Esro whirled.

"I was wondering if they had done enough damage to your armor to kill you."

Esro's eyes adjusted to the dim lighting. He could now make out a short, slender, green-skinned figure sitting nearby, staring up at him. An alien—yet another of the seemingly infinite variations on the humanoid form he had seen in the short time since his arrival.

Esro moved towards him.

"You—you speak English?"

The alien smiled a bemused smile.

"English? No, never heard of it."

His smile widened, and he spread his webbed fingers as if to indicate the entire station.

"But here, we all understand one another. Somehow."

Esro frowned.

"That doesn't make sense."

"Little here does, friend."

The green creature shook a long, scaly finger at him.

"And the sooner you understand and accept that, the better it will be for you."

Esro grunted, watching as the power indicators inside his helmet slowly crept back into the green. He wasn't sure exactly where the energy was coming from, but apparently his armor had no trouble absorbing and processing it. He looked at the alien, feeling a bit more confident.

"I'm not accepting *anything*, pal, until I find the lady I came here with, and we get the hell out of here. Then, yeah, I'll accept whatever you want."

The alien seemed to laugh softly.

"As you wish."

It looked at him closer.

"The red-skinned female who accompanied you. Perhaps I can help…"

"Yeah?" Esro leaned down. "You've seen her? Where?"

The alien seemed to be considering for a moment, while Esro grew antsier. Finally, the green guy nodded.

"Follow me."

He stood and headed down the corridor, moving in a sort of stooped, loping gait, slowly at first, then with increasing, surprising speed.

"What is this place?" Esro asked from behind.

"It is the domain of the great gatherer, the collector of all things—or so we call him. Some say this entire station is the gatherer, though I have never understood precisely what they mean by that."

The alien glanced back at him momentarily, and Esro was sure he saw that odd smile return.

"In any case, it is your entire universe, now, I'm afraid."

27

Esro had followed the green alien into a half-dozen eating and drinking establishments since they'd met. While he appreciated the guy's help, so far it hadn't amounted to much. And the station seemed so huge, simply teeming with a multitude of alien life forms.

How will I ever locate one individual in such a gigantic hive of…

He had started to think the word humanity, but stopped himself.

No, there's far more than that, here. If only I had the time and the inclination to study it—to study the aliens, and the technology…

But, as much as his natural inclination pushed him to stop every few feet to examine another odd piece of futuristic machinery, he defied that nature and continued on, searching for Mondrian.

After a time, nonetheless, and very reluctantly, he found himself beginning to lose hope.

His guide motioned impatiently for him to hurry along. They exited one corridor and entered a wider concourse. Gazing around, he once again came to appreciate the immense scale of the station, with its multitude of tunnels and corridors converging at this junction. Returning his attention to his guide, he followed the alien down a short ramp and from there into a dimly lit room along a side alley.

The music was alien, as were the smells. Crowds of strange creatures, many humanoid, many more not, milled about tables.

Another bar? Just like all the others we've been in.

Esro tried to keep up with his green guide even as he took in as much as he could of the environment.

"This is Kaijer," the green alien was saying.

Esro looked down, and blinked.

"Greetings."

The one called Kaijer peered up at Esro with unblinking eyes. It had three of them. And not much more.

Esro involuntarily took a step back. He hadn't expected to be seeking information from an amorphous purple blob in a box. Yet that described the creature about as thoroughly as possible.

"A new arrival," Kaijer stated matter-of-factly. "They always react that way. I'm growing used to it."

Esro stepped closer again, staring at those three eyes. *Three? Don't even want to try to figure out how that setup evolved.* "Hi," he said weakly. "Pleased to meet you."

"Whatever."

Kaijer seemed to be studying him with two of the eyes, while the third strayed away.

"Is that your actual exoskeleton," the thing asked after a second, "or are you only wearing it? I assume the latter."

"Yeah. It's armor."

"Nice. Very compact. I've seen better, though."

Esro idly tried to figure out exactly where the voice was coming from. Then he remembered why he was here. He got to the point.

"I'm looking for someone."

"The red woman."

"Yes. You've seen her? Know where she is?"

"Slow down," Kaijer replied casually. Two of the eyes moved to focus on the green alien who had led Esro to the bar. "What's he willing to trade?"

The green alien shrugged.

"Not sure what he has."

Kaijer's eyes—all three—moved back to Esro.

"How did you arrive here?"

Esro realized where this was going. He raised a hand, shaking his head.

"Forget it. We're not planning on sticking around, so we'll need the ship."

"Did you hear that?"

What must have been laughter bubbled up from the odd alien's hidden speaker.

"He's not planning on sticking around," Kaijer said, laughing a bit longer. "That is amusing. As if a spacecraft could get you home, anyway."

Esro ignored him.

"I'll worry about that after I find Mondrian."

"Well, what else do you have to trade? The armor?"

Esro drew back.

"Sorry, pal—it's all I have. I'd have been dead by now without it."

Kaijer chuckled again, a disconcerting sound.

"That is the most accurate statement you have made thus far."

Esro's mind raced.

"Trade... Hmm... Ah!"

He smiled and issued a cybernetic command, causing a small panel to slide open along his waist. He reached inside and withdrew a tiny, gray, cubical device measuring less than an inch along each side.

"You might like this."

He set it down on the table next to Kaijer.

One of the eyes extended up and away from the rest of the body on a narrow column of purplish gel. It stretched over to the little object and studied it closely.

"What is it?"

"Watch."

Esro depressed a button on the top of the device. A golden spherical field materialized in the air, surrounding him, Kaijer, and the green alien.

Immediately four big humanoids from nearby tables leaped to their feet and rushed over. They began to pummel the bubble with their meaty fists, attempting to batter their way through it.

"No, no, it's alright," Kaijer stated loudly.

The four humanoids—hired muscle, Esro figured—reluctantly ceased their attack, but stood ready, waiting, eyeing Brachis warily.

"I'm afraid you startled my bodyguards," the little creature explained. "They can be quite zealous."

"Yeah. Well, with this, you'd be even safer," Esro said. "You saw—they couldn't get through."

"Perhaps in time they could..." But Kaijer was obviously taken with the tiny field projector. "Very well. Turn it off."

Esro clicked it off. The sphere vanished. The bodyguards growled, watching him.

"We have a deal," Kaijer stated. "Turr?"

One of the bodyguards stepped forward and picked up the device, holding it like a dead insect. He squinted at it, his rough-hewn mouth hanging slightly open.

"I will give you the information you require," Kaijer told Esro. "But you may not like it. And I cannot help you further."

"Where is she?" Esro asked flatly.

"She was abducted, I'm afraid, by one of the worst individuals I've encountered here. She's been made a slave. She's now the personal property of the chief slave trader."

Esro balled his fists.

"What's his name?"

The three eyes triangulated on Esro, staring at him creepily, as the voice squawked one word in reply.

"Okaar."

28

"Okaar?"

Mondrian was astonished.

"How?"

The lieutenant found herself in a dark chamber, torches blazing along the walls. She stood in chains on a cold stone floor, looking up at a raised dais. Atop the dais sat a rough-hewn throne, and upon that throne sat the one person she never thought she'd see again, and least of all here.

Okaar.

Her former shipmate. Her rival and enemy, who had led a mutiny, crippled their ship, and tried to murder her. The man she believed she had hurled to his death in the cold vacuum of space.

Okaar.

Here.

"Impossible," she breathed softly.

He stared down at her impassively, his dark, narrow eyes unblinking within his broad, red-skinned face. His cruel lips curled downward, as if finding a mild distaste at the mere sight of her. His white hair had been shaved to leave only a thin, uneven patch of spiky growth covering his scalp. He wore the remains of his Kur-Bai uniform, thought it was mostly covered by golden metalwork and ornate jewelry.

He looked like some timelost, savage, barbarian prince.

Mondrian stared up at him, her head shaking slowly.

"You can't be here. You're dead. This is insane. I'm dreaming."

"'Insane?' 'Impossible?'" His mouth twisted into an evil sneer, as at last he spoke. "Yet, *you* are here, no?"

She blinked back at him, her mind reeling. *How can this be? How?* She couldn't make herself accept it.

"Truth be told," he continued, "I find myself as surprised that you are here as that either of us is alive at all." He smiled. "When last I saw you, your situation was... shall we say, *precarious*?"

She glared at him, straining at her chains.

"You tried to kill me—to kill us all!"

From the shadows emerged two guards, swords in hand.

"Ah, ah."

Okaar raised a hand, and the guards retreated.

"Civilized behavior, please. After all," and he gestured around him, "I am now the administrator here." He sneered. "It's my job to keep the peace."

"'Administrator?'" She frowned. "What is this place? Where are we?"

"All information you might acquire in time," he breathed, "along with your good behavior."

He looked her up and down.

"Perhaps this was, in fact, fortuitous—your surviving, and ending up here with me. After all, in a strange way, I am in your debt. If you hadn't caused me to be hurled from our ship, I probably would not have found myself here. And here, the Circle's voices cannot reach me."

He grinned at her, the glint of madness in his eyes.

She frowned, staring back at him.

"Voices?"

He waved that line of conversation away.

"And so I find," he continued, "that perhaps fate has more of a sense of humor than I might have expected. For it has brought you to me again."

He moved closer, reaching out, caressing her cheek.

She spit at his feet.

He ignored it.

"But, I will admit I am somewhat curious, Mondrian," he said after a long moment's silence, as he moved away again. "How did you come to be here?"

"How did *you?* Even if you somehow survived what happened before..."

She looked around at the chamber, at the crude decorations, then back at Okaar, seeing his own change in appearance since last she'd seen him.

"And how, in so short a time, could you have been altered so very much...?"

Her voice trailed off. She simply could not conceive of how this could all be true.

"So short a time? You cannot be serious!"

Okaar's face cracked into a scowl. He half-rose from his seat, anger resounding in his voice.

"So... short... a... time," he barked again, spitting the words, one by one.

"But—it has only been a day, perhaps two, since your mutiny, and—"

"What?"

Okaar's expression changed instantly from anger to confusion. He blinked once, twice, then turned away from her.

"We will discuss this later," he said, finally. "After all, we have all the time in the world."

He walked back to his throne and sat down.

"As you can see, however, you still affect my disposition—make me as agitated, as animated, as ever. Perhaps..."

He gestured with one hand.

"Perhaps it would be best if one of my associates handled you for the time being."

From out of the shadows behind the dais stepped a huge figure, bald and muscle-bound, his skin smooth as obsidian and black as night. A red tunic and loincloth, along with golden jewelry, comprised his uniform. A blazing golden circle, hollow at the center, adorned the middle of his tunic.

Mondrian gasped, recognizing him instantly. She felt her chances of escaping this situation reducing even further.

"An Eclipse Warrior."

She looked back at Okaar.

"How did he come to be here?"

The big man said nothing. Instead he seized her roughly by the upper arms. The chains rattled as he swung her around, lifting her up easily. He carried her to the iron ring and unfastened the chains from it.

"Eclipse, can you see how fortune smiles upon me? I ask for another red-skin like myself, and who should turn up, but an old friend."

The warrior said nothing. His eyes flickered over Mondrian's form.

Okaar waved a dismissive hand.

"Take her to Dr. Wuun. My men used simple chains to restrain her, but I'd prefer her in the bracelets. Then we can question her further."

The obsidian powerhouse nodded, once, and carried her from the room.

Dangling from the big man's grasp, Mondrian looked back, seeing Okaar perched upon his preposterous throne.

"You have no business working for him," she hissed after the door had closed behind them. "You are an Eclipse Warrior! That is a sacred calling. You profane your vows with every moment you are in his service!"

Eclipse's only reply was rumbling laughter, resounding in her ears, as he carried her down the corridor.

29

Lyn stumbled through the door of Esro's mansion and shoved it closed behind her with a thud. Barely watching where she was going, not even bothering to turn on any lights, she shuffled into the living room and collapsed into a big chair, closing her eyes. She grabbed at a pillow on the floor and pulled it in, curling around it.

How much longer would she be able to stay here, if Esro didn't come back? How would that work, exactly?

She thought such things, and then immediately felt guilty for worrying about herself, rather than about him.

She groaned.

A hollow, metallic voice came to her out of the darkness.

"Are you not well, Lyn?"

"Eeek!"

Lyn sat up, the pillow flying away. Wide-eyed, she looked around the room, electricity sparkling from her fingertips as she instinctively started to bring up a force bubble around herself.

Two tiny, bright red lights peered impassively back at her. They were set, of course, within the dark eye sockets of a blue-silver metal face, on a shiny metal head, attached to an equally shiny metal body nearly seven feet tall. That same big body currently sat in a big chair opposite her, watching.

"I—Vanadium?"

"Yes."

She relaxed a bit, the force sphere winking out, and turned on the lights.

"Hey, you're moving around again. And talking. And everything."

"Indeed."

She smiled, then sank back into the chair.

"Well, good, then."

As glad as she was to see him, she couldn't help but worry about the implications of the fact that she'd totally missed the big metal guy sitting in the room, when she came in. What if he'd been a bad guy, out to get her?

You have to get your head back into the game, Lyn, she told herself.

Looking up at Vanadium, she smiled again.

"Do you know what was wrong?" she asked. "What made you...lock up like that?"

"Not...entirely. I am taking certain steps to address the issue."

He hesitated.

"It would be easier with Esro Brachis here to assist me."

"No kidding," Lyn muttered, glancing over at one of his trademark Hawaiian shirts, hanging from the back of a chair. "Of all the times he should choose to disappear..."

Vanadium said nothing, merely staring back at her.

Lyn stared back, her attention focusing on the big, silvery man for the first time, considering him. Seeing him there brought her a strange mixture of happiness and fear. She felt happiness in encountering a teammate—even if the team itself was pretty much in disarray—but also knew a small touch of the same fear, the same apprehension, she always felt around Vanadium. *In fact*, she thought, *this might be the first time I've been around him with no one else present...*

He continued to stand there, the twin red lights in his deep, dark eye sockets regarding her.

"It's—it's good to see you," she said, determined not to be cold to him. He had never given her any reason to treat him that way. He was what he was—whatever that was.

"Yes," he replied. *"It is good to see you, as well."*

She smiled and nodded. Then, looking at that shirt again, her expression darkened.

"Have you been able to find anything out about Esro?"

Vanadium stood and strode past her, his footsteps surprisingly light, given his size and apparent mass.

"Over the past two hours, I have given the matter what attention I could."

"And?"

He stopped, turned back to her. He seemed to study her, to contemplate her, for a long moment. Lyn had the strange sensation that he was sizing her up, judging her value, her worth.

She waited, hoping.

"I have studied the space between the Earth and Mars extensively, via long-range scanners, and find no signs of the alien woman's ship—no debris, no lingering evidence of their passage at conventional speeds. I have therefore developed three theories regarding what might have become of him."

Lyn almost laughed at that, it seemed so precise, so...mathematical. The question was about their missing friend and teammate, yet Lyn had the sense that Vanadium had reduced it all down to equations.

But just look at him, she thought to herself, reproachfully. *How else would he think of such things? At least he's concerned, and has been investigating.*

The big man merely stood there, silently, waiting.

She gave him a sort of encouraging half-smile.

"And your theories are?"

"One: The alien woman's spacecraft was destroyed in Earth orbit, or just beyond. Yet I have found no wreckage, not the slightest trace of debris to indicate this."

Lyn sighed. "Good."

"Two: The alien woman's spacecraft took them under its own power to a remote location, beyond this solar system, perhaps via some sort of hyperdrive system. Yet my scans of the Kur-Bai technology indicated nothing like that capability, at least aboard their shuttlecraft. Their mothership possessed such a drive, but I find no signs of that vessel within my scanner range. I can only conclude that it has departed the solar system—which seems unlikely, given the damage described—or has been disintegrated."

Lyn nodded.

"So their shuttle wasn't destroyed," she said, "and Esro hasn't been dragged off to remote galaxies or whatever. That's good to know. But so what—"

"Three: I did find faint evidence of a recent time-space distortion some distance beyond Earth's atmosphere, as from the opening of a wormhole. Faint traces of the shuttlecraft's emissions led to that spot. I can only speculate that they have been abducted by a force that can bend spacetime and leaves no other evidence of its passing in its wake."

Lyn frowned at this. She chewed a fingernail.

"So, let me get this straight. Something—something that can make wormholes in space—kidnapped them. Their ship and all."

"That is the most reasonable theory, yes."

"That's the reasonable theory." She could not help but snort a laugh. "Wow."

"Nevertheless..."

"Okay, yeah, I understand. I think." She chewed another fingernail. "I'm trying to decide if this is good news, or..."

"It means the possibility exists of their survival."

Lyn nodded, looking up at him, hope sparkling in her brown eyes.

"At least," she said, frowning again, "until they got to the other side of...wherever they've gone."

"Yes."

She walked in a circle, thinking. Vanadium stood immobile as ever, a shining blue-silver statue.

"So," she said at last, "what can we do about it? Anything?"

"I have considered the situation carefully. Assuming my extrapolations are correct, I can envision only one possible course of action."

"And that is...?"

He looked at her.

"I was going alone," he said.

298

"Going?"

She blinked. Then she smiled.

"Going."

"Yes. Alone."

She shook her head.

"Not anymore."

He seemed to consider this, then nodded.

"Tomorrow," he said.

"But—"

"Readings indicate a high level of fatigue poisons in your system," he said before she could continue.

Involuntarily she brought a hand to her chest and frowned.

"You would be a liability in your current state. You must rest."

"That's all anyone says for me to do," she growled back. But she nodded, knowing it was true.

"I have an...appointment...in the morning, but will rendezvous with you, here, afterward."

"You have an appointment?"

For some reason, that struck her as utterly bizarre. Upon reflection, though—*Why shouldn't he have other things going on? What do I really know about his private life?*

But even the thought of Vanadium having a private life struck her as very strange. She scolded herself for having such an attitude.

Just be glad for your teammate, she told herself.

"Okay," she said aloud. "I'll see you tomorrow."

Without another word, Vanadium strode out of the living room.

Lyn heard him close the front door behind him. She sunk deeper into the big, cushiony chair, clutching the pillow once more.

Be happy for your teammate, she thought again, as sleep finally caught up with her. *Be happy for your friend...*

30

"Where are we going?"

"Quiet!"

The green-skinned alien climbed down through a jagged hole in the metal flooring, then stuck his head back up and motioned for Brachis to follow.

Grumbling to himself, helmet cradled in one arm, Esro trudged after his mysterious benefactor. He still wore his gray and black armor. Given the potential dangers all around him, in this bizarre place, he'd been afraid to take it off. It was amazingly high-tech for Earth; but here, in this bizarre futuristic environment, it felt to him like he was wandering around in a suit of medieval plate mail. Still, it had probably already saved his life once since his arrival, so...

"Watch the edges. They are sharp," the alien whispered.

"Why are we crawling through the floor?" Esro asked impatiently. "Surely there's a better way—"

"Not if you want to enter the slaver levels undetected," the green alien hissed back.

Esro stopped climbing and blinked.

"What? They have whole *levels*?"

The alien looked back at him, grasping a support beam to hold himself in place.

"They are quite powerful. They occupy much of the Dead Areas."

He squinted.

"You don't have much hope of rescuing the woman, you know."

"We'll see."

The alien studied him a moment, then resumed climbing.

"Well," he said, "that is where we are going. Slaver levels."

Esro felt his throat go dry.

"There's a big market for slaves on this station?"

"I'm afraid so," the being replied. "And the slavers control many decks in this area. They are very dangerous."

He glanced downward, slender pink tongue sliding over his lips. Then he looked back at Esro.

"But the one we seek is the worst of them all. Okaar."

"Okaar," Esro repeated. *It sounds familiar. Where have I heard that name before?* He filed it away, his mind whirling through the many complications life had taken on in just the past few—hours?

Hours. Is that all it's been? How long was I out?

He thought about the big robot—the Xorex—that had precipitated his unintentional voyage into space.

I hope Lyn and Ultraa are okay...

On they went. They had climbed for what seemed like an hour more, when Esro finally asked, "How much farther is it?"

"Very close now," the alien responded. "We have bypassed many decks, using this service conduit." He snorted. "Service. Ha! No one performs service here! If it burns out, or runs out, or quits working, you do without! Or you move elsewhere." He snorted again, now mostly talking to himself. "Big station. Very big. But lots of people, too. Lots of *bad* people. All kinds."

"Where did it come from? Who does it belong to? Why are all these—*people*—here?"

"Ah, good questions. All very good questions. Wish I had answers for them. And I have been here much, much longer than you!"

They reached the bottom and climbed out into a larger space. Esro looked around. The light was slightly brighter, but still very dim.

The alien pointed to a small open space in one corner, about three feet high and four wide.

"The Dead Areas can be reached through there. That is the way into the main slaver deck."

He motioned with one hand, in a gesture Esro could have sworn was a good-bye wave.

"Good luck."

The alien turned and started back for the conduit.

Esro frowned.

Dead Areas?

He waved at the alien's receding back.

"Wait!"

The alien stopped, looked back at him.

"You aren't coming, too?"

"Noooo. Slavers are bad. Okaar is very bad. I have no desire to spend the next twenty years scrubbing lavatory fixtures for Okaar."

He snorted.

"You and I wouldn't be able to communicate with one another in the Dead Areas anyway."

"What do you mean by 'Dead Areas?'"

"I... cannot explain. That is what they are called."

He gestured with one arm in a way that Esro suspected might correspond to a shrug.

"You will see soon enough."

Esro bit his lip in frustration, almost angry again. But as he thought about his circumstances, and the little green alien who'd shown him the way, his mood somehow lightened. He looked up, met the creature's broad blue eyes.

"Why did you help me?"

The alien peered back at him for a moment and then sighed.

"As I said. Okaar is bad. You are good."

The alien grinned.

"Or, at least, less bad, maybe."

He shrugged again.

"So if you do manage to take Okaar down, or at least to disrupt his operations... That would be of benefit to me and many of my friends."

"I see. Well...thank you."

The alien nodded. "Besides," he mumbled, "it beat a few more hours of sitting in a hallway, watching more bad people go by."

Esro watched the guy climb back up through the conduit, vanishing into the darkness. Then he turned and stared at the entrance to the Slaver deck. He took a deep breath, pulled on his helmet, charged his guns, and climbed through the hole.

37

Dawn: Vanadium settled gently to the roof of the Digimacht headquarters building. The miniaturized, reactionless thrusters in his lower legs remained active, supporting most of his weight, in case the building could not bear such a concentrated load.

His silvery metal head moved in a smooth curve, quickly scanning the entire vicinity.

Where is he?

Humans continuously frustrated him with their lack of discipline, their seeming love of chaos and disorder and confusion. He had arrived precisely at the appointed time. Beaulieu was to have met him here, but yet—

Across the rooftop, an access door opened and a human of medium height, with short, black hair and pale features, stepped out. He wore a white lab coat and blue sunglasses. Seeing Vanadium, he closed the door and started forward.

"Hi," he called out. "You're right on time."

Vanadium nodded once, waiting.

The man approached, a smile spreading across his face. He held out one hand.

"Desmond Beaulieu," he said. "And you're Vanadium." He grinned. "Who else could you be?"

Vanadium understood this greeting custom well enough. He clasped the man's hand gently, careful not to shatter the bones or even bruise the flesh, and shook it.

"I've done some thinking about the points you made in your message," the man said. "I do think I can help you, though I'm sure it won't be easy."

"No," Vanadium said. *"Not easy. But necessary."*

If Beaulieu was startled by the cold, hollow voice, he didn't show it.

"Right," he said, nodding. "So…"

He gestured back toward the door.

"If you'd care to follow me back to my labs, we can have a look."

Vanadium said nothing, simply following Beaulieu back across the rooftop and through the doorway, down the stairs and into a broad, white-walled corridor. From there, Beaulieu led the big metal man into a cool, brightly lit room that seemed at once a medical facility and engineering shop.

"Have a seat," the man said, indicating a broad, metal bench filling the center of the room.

This sort of thing had grown increasingly familiar to Vanadium, during his time with Brachis and the others, though not necessarily in a pleasant way. He eyed the bench and the various cables and wires that dangled all around it, considered his few options, and sat.

Beaulieu had moved around behind a broad panel of computer consoles.

"You said your problem mainly involves being unable to access all of your memories," he said. "But since you came to me, and not to a medical doctor or psychologist, I take it your memories are… how shall I put this…housed in mechanical storage, not the organic variety. Yes?"

"From what I am able to recall," Vanadium replied, after a moment, *"there is some combination of the two. But, yes, the parts I cannot access are of what you would term the mechanical variety, I believe."*

Beaulieu frowned at this.

"A combination? Extraordinary."

He leaned closer, one hand reaching out, touching Vanadium's shiny blue-silver head, moving his fingertips along the faint outlines that ran from front to back.

"Seams?" he whispered, as much to himself as to Vanadium.

He turned to the nearest console and typed a few notes in, then turned back and resumed his examination.

"Is there a way to…"

He paused in mid-sentence, then started again.

"Are you able to open the seals? To expose the inner components? Of course you can," he said quickly, answering himself. "How else to effect repairs? To access the inner mechanisms?"

"I—"

Vanadium hesitated. He had no recollection of ever having opened his outer shell himself, and indeed could not recall it ever having been done. Beyond that, assuming it could be done, he was not at all certain he *wanted* it done, particularly by someone he did not yet know or trust.

Before he could compose a satisfactory reply, however, he realized that Beaulieu had picked up a small, oblong device and was moving it slowly over the back of Vanadium's head.

"Ah, never mind," the man said, following the readouts on a monitor. "As tough and durable as your outer hide may be, it's actually somewhat permeable to a variety of wavelengths."

He stepped back from Vanadium for a second, regarding him, chewing a fingernail of one hand while holding the scanner idly in the other. He seemed to be talking to himself, now, rather than to Vanadium, though not audibly.

Vanadium's attention had become divided. Partly he watched Beaulieu, not at all comfortable with the human yet. The other half of his mind was considering the things the man had been saying. *Seams? Seals? Permeable to a variety of wavelengths?* These were all new ideas to Vanadium, at least given the current state of his memories. He found he was not at all comfortable with the knowledge. Yet he had to learn such things—learn of any potential vulnerabilities he might possess.

"Y'know," the pale man was saying, "I'll bet whoever set you up like this never went inside the shell, physically. Never after the initial construction was completed, anyway. Probably some combination of internal construction and repair systems, and maybe even nanomachines in there, with instructions relayed to them along those frequencies."

Vanadium was considering this information when the door to the room opened and another human male walked in.

304

"That's great, though," Beaulieu was saying. "It means we won't have to open the seals at all. I just have to set this thing for the right frequency—"

Vanadium was listening to this with great interest, even as he observed the man walking through the doorway.

"How are you proceeding, Mr. Blue?" the new arrival asked in an accent Vanadium instantly registered as German. He was an older man with short, gray hair, wearing a dark business suit. A patch covered one eye.

"Not yet," Beaulieu replied in a mild but slightly anxious tone. "One second."

The processes moved with lightning speed within Vanadium's mind. His own recent recollections combined with information he had taken from Brachis's databases and the various news media. *Older man with German accent and eye patch. Visual match, yes. And Mr. Blue. Not a physical or voice match for the most recent encounter, involving Ultraa and Damon Sinclair, but a perfect match for some of the older records.*

In the split second it took Vanadium to process these thoughts, Beaulieu touched something small and metallic to the back of Vanadium's head.

"There we go," the man said. "And just to be safe..."

Vanadium felt his arms and legs going limp, even as Beaulieu attached more of the small, circular devices around the sides of his head. Each time one of the inch-wide discs made contact, Vanadium sensed more of his motor functions being overridden, removed from his own control. Slowly he slumped forward, nearly falling to the floor.

For the first time, Beaulieu spoke in a louder voice, addressing the older man, whom Vanadium now recognized with certainty as the Field Marshal.

"All set," he said, cackling with maniacal laughter. "Meet our newest recruit!"

And now Vanadium found himself sitting up straight once again, though he had not made the effort to do so himself.

The Field Marshal stood directly before him, leaning forward, peering into Vanadium's dark eyes, staring into the tiny red lights that sparkled in the blackness.

"Excellent," he murmured.

Then Beaulieu stepped around the Field Marshal, manipulating more controls on the panel before him. Vanadium stood.

"Better than that," the pale man replied. "When you get a real idea of this guy's power…"

"Ja," the Field Marshal said. "I understand."

And then, as Vanadium watched, the pale white face of Desmond Beaulieu seemed to melt, to fall away in globs, leaving behind only pale, blue-shaded bone. The few pieces of rubbery flesh that remained in place began to catch fire, to burn with an eerie fire. Shortly, Beaulieu's entire head was engulfed in flickering blue flames.

"You understand your predicament, do you not, machine?" the ghastly figure said to him, the voice now twisted and distorted. "You are mine to command."

"Ours," the Field Marshall corrected. "For I have provided you the resources with which to do your work."

"Of course," the other replied.

Nodding brusquely, the Field Marshal turned and walked back through the door. Before he closed it, he glanced back at the other man with obvious distaste.

"Was this display on your part necessary, Herr Skull?"

"Of course not," the man replied.

"Then why—?"

The freakish figure spoke in soft but urgent tones.

"My somewhat incompetent lackeys, who have used my identity in the past, have succeeded in lowering expectations about my true powers and capabilities. Just as I desired. But I wished our new friend here to understand his true predicament."

He turned back to Vanadium, caressing his metal cheek almost lovingly with one hand.

"To understand he now belongs, mechanical body and cyborg soul, to the one, *true* Blue Skull."

Within the prison of his metal body, Vanadium screamed in impotent rage.

32

Eclipse casually tossed the limp form of Mondrian through the air. She landed on a huge pile of cushions and rolled onto her side, her mouth hanging open, her eyes staring blankly out.

"You see the power of the bands, woman? You feel it?"

The huge alien raised his left hand and pointed at her.

She jerked upright, back under her own control again. Wracked with coughs, she shook her head back and forth. Her long, thick hair flew violently about.

Eclipse watched her until she'd recovered sufficiently to listen, to hear him. Then he raised his left hand. On his smallest finger he wore a tiny golden ring; so large were his fingers that it sat between the first and second joints.

"Do you see this?" he barked.

Still shaky, she nodded.

His jet-black lips curled back.

"This controls you, via your new attire."

Mondrian blinked, then looked down. In place of the rough manacles, golden bracelets, about three inches long, encircled each of her wrists. Two more encircled her ankles. She touched them.

"What—?"

"We've found them most useful in our line of work. They project an energy field around your body." He smiled cruelly. "And your brain is part of your body. So usually they just compel your brain to make your body do what the wearer of the ring wants it to do."

His eyes narrowed.

"Including shut down."

She collapsed to the cushions again.

Seconds later, released to her own control again, she glared up at him.

"I hope that's all the demonstration you'll need," he growled. "Believe me, it can be much worse."

"I believe you," she whispered. "But it can be worse for you, too."

He snorted derisively and moved closer, regarding her where she sat on the cushions.

Her navy blue flight suit was torn in places, gloves and boots missing entirely. Both arms of the suit had been cut off raggedly at the elbow, to expose her lower arms. The same had been done with her ankles.

How can all this be?

She stared up at the dark behemoth, wondering what he was doing here, and what *she* was doing here.

"Okaar wants you attired more properly for your next meeting with him." He clapped, and two servants entered bearing boxes of

307

clothing and jewelry. "I trust you won't resist any further." The smile returned. "I'm sure he will find you more attractive... *intact*."

She studied him, seeking to understand his motivations.

"Your people are champions—heroes of many worlds. How can you work for—for Okaar? He's nothing!"

The big man stared back at her silently.

"Let me go," she continued. "Together, we can escape this place and..."

She trailed off as he turned away, starting for the door. And for the first time, she noticed that some the golden jewelry he wore actually surrounded his wrists and ankles.

"You... He controls *you*, too!"

Eclipse stopped, looked back at her. He opened his mouth as if to speak, then closed it again and walked out. The door closed behind him.

Despair washed over her once again. She barely resisted as the two servants stripped off the remains of her flight suit and began to dress her in the barbarian fashion of the women she'd seen earlier.

No sense in wasting energy and effort yet, she thought. Better to wait until Okaar is near again. Then...

She closed her eyes, trying to ignore the ministrations of the slave women as they dressed her.

Then what?

How could she escape? And if she somehow managed to get away from Okaar and his minions, where would she go? How would she ever get home again?

Okaar was nothing, she knew. A fool. An idiot. How he'd come to his present status so quickly was beyond her—but then again, nothing she'd seen so far had made sense. Not since she and Esro had fallen through the bright hole in space, and...

Esro...

Again her mind cried out: *Where are you?*

33

Where am I?

Esro stood in a darkened hallway. Actual flaming torches mounted on the wall, further along around the curve, provided what little light existed.

Open fires, he thought. *On a space station. This just gets crazier and crazier.*

Esro's armor hissed as its climate control system exchanged gases with the surrounding atmosphere. All the indicator lights in his helmet remained green: he'd returned to near-full electrical charge.

Best thing I ever did, he thought to himself, *incorporating that little ambient-energy recharger into the power system. Watching ol' Vanadium closely paid off. After all, I never saw him stop to plug himself into a wall outlet...*

He glanced up and down the hallway.

Okay, genius, what now? Just walk up to the first alien I meet and say, "Excuse me, but would you please take me to the resident slave master? I'm a super hero and have an appointment to kick his butt."

A sound from behind him shook him back to reality. He tensed, both gauntlet-mounted guns at the ready—

—when two blue humanoids in leather and metal armor, swords dangling from their broad belts, rounded the corner.

Esro stepped out in front of them. Instantly he took in their appearance. His eyebrows arched up in surprise.

"You guys making a new *Conan* movie down here or something?"

The two aliens stopped in their tracks, staring at him in his gray metal armor. Their mouths hung open for a long second. Then they both snatched their swords out of their scabbards and held them at the ready. One growled an unintelligible string of syllables at Esro, while the other grunted emphatically.

"Huh?"

He blinked, remembering what the green alien had said about the Dead Areas and not being able to understand the language any longer.

He was right. But...why—?

The two swordsmen rushed him, swinging their blades in broad arcs.

"Not smart, fellas," Esro said, watching as the swords deflected harmlessly from his force field, nearly falling from their bearers' grasps.

"Mondrian!" Esro shouted, bringing his wrist-mounted weapons back up as he did so. "I know you two can't understand me, but I'm looking for Lieutenant Mondrian."

The two attackers had gone from staring in shock and wonder at their swords to glaring at Esro again.

"Red skin, white hair," he continued. "A little shorter than me. Really hot, too, I guess. Word is, you guys have her down here. So where is she?"

The aliens' expressions grew fiercer and they charged again, this time with one going high and the other going low. Esro sidestepped one and nailed the other with a stun blast. The swordsman collapsed in a heap.

"Red woman!" he shouted at the remaining fighter.

The guy didn't even blink.

It's hopeless. He can't understand a word, Esro knew. But his overwhelming anger wouldn't allow him to remain silent. Instead, he changed his tactics.

"Okaar," he shouted. "Okaar!"

The alien stopped, poised to attack again, and stared at him.

"Okaar?"

"Okaar. Yeah."

Esro smiled a half-smile.

"Where is he?"

"Here, human."

The voice had come from behind him. Esro turned slowly. He groaned.

A platoon of alien warriors stood lined up across the corridor. Each held swords or other exotic blade weapons at the ready. Standing regally at the center was an ornately dressed, crimson-skinned humanoid sporting a white buzz-cut.

Esro didn't have to ask. He knew instantly.

"Okaar."

"Indeed."

The former Kur-Bai lieutenant studied him.

"This grows most curious."

Esro blinked. *Waitaminnit.*

310

"You're speaking English? I thought this was the Dead Area or something."

Esro pointed to the two fighters he'd just fought.

"How can you understand me when those guys couldn't?"

"I speak your tongue, human. I received the same language RNA treatments and training as Mondrian."

He rubbed his chin at Esro's visible reaction to the name.

"I was told a human had accompanied her here. Judging by all the evidence I could see," he continued, "I assumed you were him, inside that quaint outfit."

Esro looked over the crowd of warriors—slavers, he reminded himself— and addressed Okaar firmly.

"You can save us both a whole lot of trouble by just handing her over to me now."

Okaar's eyes widened.

"Turn her over to you? Why would I wish to do that? You are not her kind. Don't you think she would much rather share my company than that of a... a *primitive* like you?"

Esro fought down his anger. *Gotta stay calm. At least for now.*

"Look," he said, "we both know you're holding her. And that you're in the slave trade. So just let her go now, and she and I will both be out of your way."

Okaar laughed, once, softly.

Esro cursed and brought all his weapons systems on line. He decided that, rather than play defense, he'd rather just exercise his aggression and take these guys out of the way as quickly as possible.

Okaar gestured and stepped back.

The warriors charged.

Esro opened fire.

The melee lasted for a good two minutes, as the twenty or so aliens of various races came at him, in pairs and sets of three, and finally en masse. Brachis fought them back valiantly, on more than one occasion forcing his way out of a pile of swarming bodies to unleash a spray of stun fire. He whirled, both of his wrist-mounted weapons blazing in a constant barrage of energy. Swords and knives clanged off his tough armored hide as his persistent enemies repeatedly flung themselves at him. Eventually, the attackers dwindled to a pair, and they exhaustedly fell back, covering Okaar, who had retreated a good distance down the corridor during the battle.

"Bring her to me, Okaar!" Esro shouted, starting down the hall. "I think I've proved my point. You can't stop me. Not in this low-tech level of hell."

Okaar smiled.

"You astound me. You think to issue orders to me—to *me!*—here in my own domain."

He motioned to his remaining troops.

"Your little rampage is over. I will peel that armor off of your carcass and use its pieces to adorn my guards. The rest of you will go to the Garbage Deck."

At Okaar's gesture, a shadow fell across the hallway from a side corridor. Out stepped the massive Eclipse Warrior, a pitch-black juggernaut with murder in his tiny white eyes.

"Oh, great," Esro muttered.

"Surrender, human," Eclipse said. "I have no desire to slaughter you."

"Your desires do not enter into this," Okaar shouted at his henchman. "You do as I tell you."

"Does everyone here speak English?" Esro asked, bewildered.

"Eclipse Warriors are trained in many things, little man," the colossus replied evenly.

Okaar pointed to Brachis.

"You know what to do. And try not to damage the suit too much."

Eclipse peered at Esro, then nodded.

"There may be some staining…"

He started forward.

Esro tensed, his eyes flickering briefly to the string of yellow lights across the inside of his helmet. His power levels were low.

Used up too much taking out the thugs. And I'm starting to see what they mean by 'Dead Areas'—there's very little ambient energy to absorb here.

He tensed his muscles, preparing for the worst.

So now what do I do?

The big alien moved like lightning, his fist smashing into Esro's stomach before Esro realized he'd moved. Brachis stumbled back, falling on his rear end, and tried to activate a defensive screen. He succeeded; a sparkling glow surrounded him at a radius of about five feet.

Eclipse brought both fists forward. The concussion against Esro's screen produced a blinding flash and sent the armored hero tumbling backwards again. He caught himself against the wall, thankful the blow hadn't hit him directly.

Some of the yellow lights in his helmet were changing to red.

Power's dangerously low, now. I can't keep this up much longer.

As if sensing this, Eclipse pressed the attack, trapping Esro in a corner. Blow after blow rained down on the flickering force field.

Reflexively raising both his arms before his face, as the big, smashing fists came closer and closer to him, Esro checked the readouts once again. He groaned. They were all red now. With a final sputter, the force field died.

Eclipse nodded in satisfaction, then reached out and seized Esro by the sides. He brought him down hard, denting the deck.

Esro felt his teeth rattle.

The colossus grasped him again and flung him into the wall.

Oh, crap... C'mon, Esro—fight back!

A weak blast from one of Esro's gauntlet weapons, draining the last of his reserve power, deflected harmlessly off the obsidian giant's tough hide. Snarling, Eclipse backhanded him and sent him sprawling again.

Head spinning, Esro looked up just in time to see a fist, one roughly the size of Greenland, descending. It smacked into his faceplate and stars sparkled across his vision. The fist rose, poised to fall again.

"Wait! Wait a sec!"

Eclipse paused, the fist hovering in midair.

Esro glared up at him.

"When you rip off my arms," he choked out, blood running over his lips, "I hope you get cut on the sharp edges... and develop a really nasty infection."

Eclipse snarled again. The huge fist descended.

34

Mondrian fell to the cushions, Okaar standing over her. Shadows rippled across the stone floor, cast by madly fluttering candle flames.

The former Kur-Bai officer, now slave lord, held up his right hand. A slender golden ring encircled each of his fingers. He indicated the one on his smallest finger.

"Here is the ring that controls you, my dear. I wear it in a place of honor," he said, sneering. "You see? I am the master here."

Clutching his fist tight, he leaned down toward her.

"And, at long last, the master of *you*, too."

Mondrian glared at him, her mind racing.

He strode arrogantly across the room, picked up a ceramic pitcher and poured blue liquid into a jewel-encrusted goblet.

"All you have to do is accept things the way they are, and I promise your life will be much happier," he said, taking a sip. "Here in the Dead Areas, being close to me has its advantages."

She bit her tongue, holding the possible retorts back.

Not yet. Wait.

She looked down at herself, now clothed—barely—to match his barbarian style. A slender golden band encircled her waist, supporting white silk that flowed down around her hips. Her breasts rested within cups of gold. A jewel-studded necklace dangled from her neck. The golden bracelets still circumscribed her wrists and ankles, the potential always there for forced obedience.

He approached again. She noticed that, unlike all the others, he wore a sidearm: a black, standard Kur-Bai issue energy pistol in its holster.

"You have a gun," she whispered.

"Of course. I told you, this is my domain. Supplies are short, but if something is to be had at all on this station, I have it."

"You don't have electric lighting," she observed spitefully.

"This is a Dead Area," he replied casually. "We do without a few conveniences in order to maintain our... lifestyle."

Her cessation of hostilities seemed to be causing him to open up a bit, as she'd hoped. He had walked closer, kneeling above her. She pressed, "What does that mean? Dead Area?"

"A part of the station which..."

He frowned, as if considering for a moment.

"There is an intelligence here," he said, gesturing broadly. "Within the station. I believe it is what brought us all here. I don't know for certain. Nor do I know what it wants with us. But it controls much of the station. Not all, though," he said, smiling.

"It doesn't control the Dead Areas," Mondrian said, beginning to understand.

"Yes. The Dead Areas are cut off from the rest of the station. I do not know why. There is no electricity, no instantaneous translation. But no surveillance, either. No one giving orders."

His smile broadened, his eyes flashing.

"No one but *me!*"

She reached out, cautiously touching his arm. She had to have more information, if she were to have any hope of escape. That meant playing to his awful vanity. Her stomach churned at the thought, but she pushed herself to continue.

"Yes, I see that now," she said, her voice barely above a whisper. "You were so smart to accomplish what you have. You have become so powerful here, so quickly..."

He had been smiling, but now he blinked, frowned, and looked down at her.

"Quickly?"

"Yes... It's only been, what, a matter of days since our fight..."

"What tricks are you playing with me, yet again? Days! Ha!"

He stood, stalking away.

"I've been trapped on this blasted station for years. Years!"

He threw the goblet into the wall violently.

"And no one to help me, no one to keep me company but that homicidal maniac *Eclipse...*"

"But—but it's true," she cried. "Look at me. Do I appear any older?"

He stared at the floor, clearly fighting the anger swelling inside him.

"The mutiny on the ship was less than two days ago," she stated flatly.

"That's not possible," he shouted. "I've been here for years, I tell you! I've built all this up! My own empire!"

He grasped her by the chin, his eyes burning into hers.

"What are you playing at? What are you trying to do to me?"

He flung her aside, stood, and angrily stalked out.

Mondrian lay there, gasping. Her mind pored over what she'd heard, the ramifications of all he'd said.

There can be only one possible explanation, as crazy as it sounds. Some sort of time dilation. Either time moves much faster here, and we can still get back home, or else...

She shuddered.

Or else we lost years of time traveling through that portal, and now home's just a memory...

315

35

Some time later, Okaar looked up from where he had been brooding on his throne as Eclipse dragged the beaten body of Esro into the room. The crimson alien's expression widened as he looked from the battered gray metal form to the stygian black one.

"Yes?"

"Something within the armor keeps the pieces sealed in place," Eclipse growled. "I will have to kill him to get him out of it. I was not certain you wished that yet."

The Kur-Bai stood over the armored human, staring down at him contemptuously.

"He honestly believed he could successfully invade my domain. Ludicrous! Even with that ridiculous metal suit."

Okaar's lips curled back in disgust.

"He's just a human."

A light twinkled in Eclipse's eyes.

"He seems very fond of the woman," he said.

Okaar jerked his head toward his dark servant.

"What are you saying?"

"Nothing..."

The slave lord clasped his hands behind his back and strode across the room, then raised one golden-ring-encrusted hand and motioned. Seconds passed, and he gestured again, more forcefully. A moment later, Mondrian staggered in from the adjoining room, her motions jerky, almost spasmodic.

"If you respond instantly to the summons, I will have no reason to compel," Okaar hissed.

Mondrian looked away, then realized who lay on the floor beneath Eclipse.

"Brachis!"

She started forward, then, at Okaar's gesture, she froze.

The slave lord looked from her to Esro, then back.

"What is this, Mondrian? Some bizarre, unnatural attraction for the Earth monkey?" He scoffed. "You are mine now. You know this."

Her body frozen in place, Mondrian moved her eyes, with great force of will, to glare back at Okaar. He returned her gaze and the two of them faced one another for a long moment, the slave master and the paralyzed beauty, in a strange contest of wills. Eclipse only stood by, watching.

A groan from below brought them back to the moment.

"Ahh. He's awake."

Okaar kicked at Brachis, rolling him over on his back with a clatter. He jabbed at him with his foot.

"Human?" he asked in English. Then, louder, "Human!"

"Unhhh...."

The helmeted head raised up a few inches. Esro's voice was thick.

"Stuff it, Okaar."

The crimson Kur-Bai's eyes widened.

"What?"

Esro managed to get his elbows underneath himself and pushed up to a sitting position. Then he saw Eclipse standing nearby, watching.

"Oh. Hi there."

Mondrian emitted a strangled sound as she struggled against the control of her wristbands and anklets.

Esro heard her and tried to stand.

"Mondrian?"

Eclipse casually swung a huge fist, clubbing him against the back of the head. He clattered to the floor again.

Okaar stepped closer and eyed the armored man cautiously.

"This one is no longer dangerous, is he, Eclipse?"

The black giant snorted.

"Dangerous? Ha. As if he ever was. No, not remotely dangerous. His energy supplies are depleted. He used up most of his power fighting the guards. And of course he could not stand against me."

Eclipse kicked at Esro's legs.

"Look at him. He can barely move."

"Good. I want you to figure out how to peel that armor off of him—but not just yet."

He walked over to Mondrian's stiff form and stroked her chin, his eyes traveling over her body.

"Surely this human doesn't mean anything to you, my dear?"

He gestured with one hand.

Gasping, she felt the mental lock he had placed over her disengage. Instinctively she recoiled from him.

"Leave him alone, Okaar," she managed to choke out. "He was probably only looking for me. He doesn't have any reason to bother you or your little empire."

"Nor will he," Okaar growled, his eyes widening. Then, "So you do have feelings for this... human."

"Don't be stupid. But we traveled to his world to save his kind, if we could. Why kill him now?"

The slave lord's smile was twisted, demented.

"Oh, let me show you. In fact, let me show the human, too. Let it be the last thing he sees; the thing he carries with him to whatever afterlife primitives such as him hope to attain."

He sat back on the throne, willing Mondrian to follow him.

Against her every effort, she found herself compelled to climb up onto the dais, and onto him, to lay her body across his lap, one arm behind his shoulders. The bands exerted absolute mastery over her motor functions; she probed the limits of her mind's resistance, but try as she might, she could find no weakness. As long as Okaar's concentration remained even somewhat focused on controlling her, she could do only as he wished.

Esro had managed to sit up again, and he watched with burning anger as Okaar displayed his mastery over Mondrian. His eyes instinctively moved over the readouts inside his helmet. They all sat near zero. Despite the armor's ability to pull ambient energies out of the surrounding environment, the battle with Eclipse had so depleted his reserves that it would still be some time before his weapons came back on line. He wracked his brain, searching for any alternative. Mentally he ran through his various defensive systems, his environmental systems, his propulsion—

He blinked.

Hey...

Okaar waved a dismissive hand, disappointed that the preoccupied Brachis had neither cried out for Mondrian nor begged for his life.

"Enough," the slave lord declared. "Kill him. Take the armor. I wish to examine it, piece by piece."

Eclipse nodded once and leaned toward Esro, huge obsidian hands reaching down.

Esro put all his effort into curling into a ball, drawing his knees up towards his chest. Eclipse clearly found this amusing. He opened his mouth to make a cruel comment—

—and Esro ignited his chemical boot rockets, blasting bright flames into Eclipse's face at point-blank range.

With a roar of pain, the big alien stumbled back, both hands clutching at his eyes.

Okaar cried out, shocked. For a moment he froze, his years of absolute mastery over all around him having dulled his reaction time to genuine threats. Then, as he started to rise, he realized that Mondrian still lay across his lap. He looked down at her.

Her eyes held grim purpose and determination.

Her open palm held a golden ring.

Okaar took this in, then laughed, long and hard.

A few feet away, at the base of the throne, Eclipse shook his head violently, seeking to recover from the fiery blast. Esro had shut off the rockets and scrambled backwards, seeking a weapon or cover from the certain retaliation to come. He found neither.

Well, at least I got one last lick in, he thought grimly.

Okaar's face hovered inches from Mondrian's, a contortion of dark humor.

"So, you took advantage of my distraction and retrieved your ring. Congratulations. But you must know that you cannot escape. I will simply have you punished and then replace the ring on my finger."

He laughed harder.

"Poor Mondrian, you've failed again."

Mondrian's face spread into a smile of her own.

"Poor Okaar," she mocked, "as stupid as ever. Otherwise, you could have prevented me from doing *this*."

And as the slave lord's smile began to fade into confusion, Mondrian tossed the ring she'd taken from his hand, across the room—

—toward Eclipse.

"Wha—?"

Okaar raised his hand again, staring more closely at it, his eyes frantically darting from one finger to the next. As he slowly understood what had happened, his expression melted into horror.

"Wait—that ring—it was—Oh, *no*..."

Eclipse had caught the ring in one massive, obsidian hand. He held it up before his eyes, studying it. A tiny sliver of a smile moved over his face. Then he slid the ring onto his finger and, Esro forgotten, walked slowly across the room.

Mondrian leapt from the throne. Okaar made no move to stop her. He had problems of his own to deal with.

319

Esro struggled to his knees as Mondrian ran across to him. He looked from her to Okaar to Eclipse, puzzled.

"What did you do?"

Mondrian smiled and helped him up.

All but paralyzed with fear on his throne, Okaar raised a hand up before his face as if to ward the giant off.

"Stay back," he shouted. "I am your master!"

"No longer, Okaar."

Eclipse, his speed incredible for so large a figure, seized the cringing Kur-Bai and held him up by the throat. Okaar's feet dangled, kicking madly.

"No longer."

With that, he hurled the slave lord hard across the room, smashing him into the wall with a sick thud. Okaar slid down to the floor and lay there, motionless, emitting only a small gurgling sound. Blood trailed down from his nose and mouth.

Eclipse advanced on him again.

"I don't quite know what you did," Esro stated, "but I think we should get out of here. Now!"

He started to pull Mondrian for the exit.

"Wait—"

Mondrian took a step towards Eclipse.

He glanced back at her, eyes narrowing.

She smiled at Okaar's predicament, then regarded the big warrior before her. She held out one hand.

"Even trade?"

The obsidian giant stared at her for a long moment, considering. Then he nodded.

"Yes. Even."

He bent down, grasped Okaar's hand, and pulled Mondrian's control ring from where it still rested, on the smallest finger. Then he tossed the ring to Mondrian.

"But from this point forward, the slate is clean."

She caught it.

"Understood."

Mondrian slipped the ring onto her own finger and grabbed Esro by the arm.

"Now we can go. Quickly!"

Esro paused, glanced back.

"Mondy, wait—I know that guy deserves whatever he gets, probably a dozen times over, but..."

He stared into her eyes.

"Can we just leave him? To *that*?"

Mondrian met his gaze evenly.

"Can *you* stop Eclipse?"

Esro considered, his eyes moving over his power indicators.

"No. Not right now."

"The other slavers are coming, Esro. We must flee."

As they dashed through the door, the last thing they saw was Okaar dangling limply from Eclipse's grasp, his eyes wide with fear.

Brachis followed Mondrian down the corridor.

"I'm trying to make sense of what just happened," he said as they ran. "Okaar had your ring the whole time? You took Eclipse's instead?"

She nodded.

"I grabbed it when you distracted Okaar. I figured it made more sense than taking my own. And Okaar was too stupid to stop me from throwing it to Eclipse."

She smiled grimly.

"And it seemed a safe assumption that an Eclipse Warrior would be sick of spending years as the personal slave of a mere Kur-Bai lieutenant!"

Esro couldn't help but laugh.

"Nice. But—how did you know which one was Eclipse's ring?"

"Okaar had it inscribed on the surface. Probably so he'd know which was which. It was written in Kur-Bai."

He laughed again.

"In the Dead Areas, you're probably the only one who could read it," he said, shaking his head in wonder. "You are something else."

"I take that to be a colloquial compliment," she replied.

"Absolutely—the best."

The sound of troops running toward the throne room resounded around them.

"We still have to get out of the slaver levels," he reminded her.

She looked around frantically.

"How did you get in here?"

"I don't know-- these corridors all look the same!"

He whirled around, then pointed.

"I think it was back that way..."

They dashed down the hallway, the slaver army at their backs.

"Oh," Mondrian said as they ran. "Back there—"

"Yeah?"

"Did you call me *Mondy*?"

36

Jameson watched on the monitor as his three armored agents approached the derelict alien spacecraft.

"There it is," he whispered.

"Just where our new friends told us it would be," Adcock said, from over his shoulder.

Jameson frowned, glancing back at him.

"Our 'new friends?' You're still calling them that?"

"I would like to think it appropriate," Adcock replied.

"I think I'll just stick with calling them 'the Circle,' if it's all the same," Jameson said with a sneer.

"Don't be too dismissive of them," Adcock said. "They've delivered on everything they've promised, thus far."

"Not everything."

"What—oh, right."

Jameson tapped the screen.

"Their representative should have been here by now," he said. "That's the ship he was coming in on, right?"

"I believe so. I don't know what could have happened."

"Judging by the condition of that ship," Jameson said, leaning in closer and squinting at the monitor, "it looks like *quite a bit* happened. So maybe something *happened* to their representative, too."

Ignoring Jameson's tone, Adcock merely nodded.

"Entirely possible," he said.

Jameson inhaled deeply and let the air out slowly, then leaned back in his big leather chair and turned to face Adcock.

"You trust those...*people*. Fine. I'd like to trust them, too. But I won't—not until they give me a very good reason. Lots of good reasons. And not having a representative here when he should have been..."

"There are reasons to give them the benefit of the doubt, at least for now," Adcock replied, somewhat defensively. "The potential rewards..."

"*Potential*, yes," Jameson growled back at him. "Let's just remember that word. 'Potential.'" He snorted. "They haven't done anything solid for us, so far. Just a lot of talk. Mostly enigmatic talk, I might add. And I've never been a big one for enigmatic talk."

He waited to see if Adcock would respond to that. When he did not, Jameson continued.

"We have no idea exactly what they can do, or why they should want to. Or, more significantly," he added, eyebrows raised, "just how powerful they really are."

Adcock licked his lips.

"Yet you've agreed to cooperate with them," he said, carefully.

"Of course," Jameson replied. "But we mustn't forget—this is very much a marriage of convenience."

He snorted a laugh.

"I have no doubt their long-term goals are in all sorts of conflict with ours. But for now…"

His voice trailed off as he continued watching the three armored figures—Defender units, they were called—closing in on the damaged spacecraft.

The Defender armor was bulky—bulkier than Jameson would have liked. On the ground, each unit stood over seven feet tall, though you couldn't tell that now, as they flew through space. The helmets were big, fishbowl affairs, made of ultra-high density material that was nonetheless transparent. Thick cuffs above the wrists and ankles, in particular, gave the armor a sort of ugly, ungainly appearance. There had been no avoiding it, though. The young Sinclair kid—Cavalier, as he had preferred to be known—had handed over a very limited amount of Esro Brachis's technology before he'd been killed. The Field Marshall had brought nearly everything else from Brachis's computers with him, later on, but Jameson's lab boys were still sorting through a lot of that stuff, trying to make sense of it. In the meantime, the techies had cobbled together these Defender units as a sort of stopgap measure, using bits and pieces from the more understandable portions of Brachis's designs. Of course, they had yet to be put through their paces in a real-world crisis situation.

So now we will see what we will see, Jameson thought.

"The Defenders look good," Adcock commented at just that moment, causing Jameson to suppress a laugh.

One of the units was red, one was white, and one was blue, he noticed then, with big American flag emblems on their shoulders. *Subtle, we ain't.* A fourth figure carried the camera, obviously, and Jameson found himself idly wondering what color that one wore.

"So," Adcock said. "The Circle. You mentioned their long-term goals. What do you suppose those are?"

Jameson sighed. It was a soft, nearly silent sigh, but to Adcock it conveyed a great deal of meaning, including, *Why do you insist on ruining my happy little moment?*

"They're aliens," he said in reply. "I have no idea what they want. I was hoping *you* might be able to tell me, seeing as how you're a bit closer to the source."

Adcock raised one eyebrow but said nothing.

"But, in any case," Jameson continued, "I am working on finding answers to that sort of question, even as we speak. In the meantime, however..."

He turned back to the screen, watching the ship grow larger and larger.

Adcock waited a few moments, then said, "I ask because they might not take it kindly if we were to refuse to hand this ship over. They claim it belongs to them."

"Oh, we'll hand it over to them," Jameson said, smiling. "Of course, that's after we've dismantled, photographed, scanned, and catalogued every single part, moving and otherwise."

"They might not be happy about that."

"I didn't see anything about it in the agreement. And, after all, what do they expect us to do with it? Especially considering they told us about it in the first place."

Adcock thought about this—it wasn't anything he hadn't considered before; he simply tended to proceed with things more cautiously, more conservatively, than Jameson did.

"Maybe they could have just come and retrieved it themselves," Jameson added. "And then again, maybe they couldn't—which would have all sorts of other implications."

"Such as?"

"Such as that they're not as powerful as they're letting on. Such as we might have some leverage over them."

Jameson smiled at that thought.

"But I've gotten the impression they're trying to keep a low profile," he went on. "I don't think they're in positions of power—supreme power—back on their world. I don't think they actually run their government. More likely they're on the outside, looking in."

He chuckled.

"Or on the *inside*, looking in," he added. "Sort of like us."

Adcock couldn't suppress a smile at that.

"They told you all that?" he asked. "You know more than me, after all."

Jameson shook his head.

"No. Not in so many words. But it was there, beneath the surface. Deal with as many conspiracies as I have, from both sides, and you sort of get a feel, you know?"

"Give me a few more years in this business, and I imagine I will," Adcock replied.

Jameson laughed.

"I think they're more of an insurgent group," he continued. "A conspiracy. No, that's not quite sinister enough for these guys, I think. What's the word? A star chamber. A *cabal*. Something like that."

Jameson lifted his glass and sipped bourbon as he returned his attention to the monitor. The camera had tightened in on one of the Defenders, and he took the opportunity to study the armor anew.

"Maybe they're not so bad," he whispered. "Formidable looking, anyway."

He grinned up at Adcock, who was looking back at him with a slightly puzzled expression.

"I suppose we did get our money's worth from Esro Brachis," Jameson said with a snort. "Whether he knows it or not. Mostly not."

The Defenders had closed within a few hundred yards of the spacecraft, and now both men could see just how big it was.

"Impressive," Adcock breathed.

"It's a wreck," Jameson replied. He pointed at the screen. "Look. Scorch marks everywhere…no lights in any of the—what, portholes? Windows? Whatever." He shook his head. "Maybe the main systems are intact, though. Enough to learn how they work."

The Defenders were less than a hundred yards away now. Suddenly they stopped and all turned, together, obviously staring at something off to the left of the camera.

"What's going on?" Jameson hissed.

The fourth Defender, the one with the camera, turned as well. Now they could see what was happening.

A short distance away, completing a triangle with the armored humans and the spacecraft, a large vehicle of some sort floated, unmoving. Its surface was of shiny silver, with blue and purple detailing along its sides and a broad, curved fin projecting from both top and bottom, relative to its current orientation. It had not been there a second before.

325

As Jameson and Adcock watched, a second, identical craft shimmered into existence beside it. There was no other way to describe it. One moment it was not there, the next it was.

Both vehicles lit up and started toward the Defenders.

"Who are those people?" Jameson demanded.

Adcock only shook his head.

The Defenders hesitated for a second, then went into action. Activating their boot jets, they rocketed in four different directions, separating and surrounding the two vehicles.

A blazing green beam of energy lanced out from one of the vehicles. It caught the white Defender in mid-torso, slicing him in half. He never had a chance to scream.

"Shields! Get your shields up!" crackled the voice of one of the other Defenders.

An identical beam slashed out of the second craft, striking the red Defender's sparkling energy screen. Less than a second later, the screen was gone, and a hole very nearly the width of the man's chest itself had been drilled through him.

"Retreat!" came the voice of the blue Defender. "Get out of here!"

His boot jets flaring, he rocketed toward the derelict spacecraft. A beam from one of the ships caught him, played across his form for a moment, and vaporized him.

The fourth Defender, the one with the camera, spun around and headed off into open space.

The picture suddenly crackled, filled with static, and went dead.

Jameson and Adcock stared at the blank screen for a moment. Then Jameson reached out and switched it off. He steepled his manicured fingers under his chin, pursing his lips. Adcock stepped back, walked around to the front of the desk, and waited.

"Ah, well," Jameson said at last. "Easy come, easy go."

Adcock cocked his head to the side, as if thinking about that, then nodded.

"As you say."

"I do want to report this to our friends, though. They're going to wonder what happened to their ship."

"And you think they'll believe we don't have it?"

"Probably not."

He frowned again.

"That could prove problematic. But... I suppose we will cross that bridge when we get to it."

Adcock nodded.

"Oh, and Adcock—"

"Yes?"

"We're going to need more Defenders."

37

"The Kur-Bai ship is now in our possession, Master," Francisco reported, bowing deeply.

"Fine, fine," the Warlord replied in a distracted tone. He stood leaning over a wide, holographic control panel that floated in midair before him, studying the various symbols and indicators that moved across it at lightning speed. "I'm sure I will find a use for it... someday."

"Yes, of course," Francisco replied, backing away.

"But, you understand," the Warlord continued, glancing up at him momentarily, "if what I am attempting now is successful, then such matters as the Kur-Bai ship, the Kur-Bai themselves, and any other force in this universe, will scarcely matter to me at all."

And if you fail, Francisco thought, *likewise, nothing will matter at all.*

"Soon," the Warlord said in a low, intense tone, continuing to hold his assistant's gaze, his eyes blazing with a bright, azure flame. "Very soon."

Is that inspiration I see so clearly, Francisco wondered, staring back into them, *or madness?*

He feared he knew the answer to that question all too well.

The Warlord stared at him an instant longer—just long enough to make Francisco fear his thoughts, his plans, had somehow been laid bare to his Master. Then, without another word, the blue-clad mastermind whirled away, returning to his work—his precious, insanely deadly, utterly ruinous work.

Francisco furrowed his brow and turned away, himself, scurrying back across the chamber to his own control station. There he stood for nearly five minutes, attempting to remain calm and focus on his work but far too distracted to do either. At last he turned back, facing the Warlord—who, seemingly, had not moved a muscle during all that time—and glared at him.

It is time, he thought to himself. *Now. It has to be now, while he is completely distracted.*

He reached into his robes, fishing for the dagger he kept there at all times. The same sort of dagger that had made such quick work of this Warlord's predecessor, months earlier, when the obvious time had come to move the cycle forward—to continue the Grand Design, but with a new actor in the lead role, so to speak. For was that decision not ever left in the hands of Francisco? Was that not *his* role in the Grand Design, as it ever had been?

His fingers closed around the spherical pommel and he drew the blade forth. It was more than a foot in length, with a matte black grip and a red stone of some sort glinting at the pommel's tip. Its substantial weight in his hand surprised him, as it had always felt nearly weightless to him on the many previous occasions. He frowned at this but turned and started slowly across the chamber, the dagger concealed behind him.

When he was within five feet of his master he could hear the man muttering to himself, pronouncing equations and enunciating checklists as if they were the parts of some magical conjuration. And, indeed, the invocation of some horrendous spell described what the Warlord was up to as well as anything else might.

If he is allowed to continue, the Grand Design itself will surely be disrupted for all time. That cannot be allowed to happen.

And, besides, I have never liked this particular Warlord. Not from the beginning.

Closing the distance between them in three quick steps, Francisco brandished the dagger and lunged at the cloaked figure. He'd committed this act, in a variety of ways, more times than he could remember, and he knew exactly where to strike, exactly how much force to exert. With a cry, he swung the blade at the man's back with all his strength.

The Warlord did not move, did not react at all.

The blade passed harmlessly through the body, followed immediately afterward by Francisco himself, carried by his momentum.

The little man struck the floor of the chamber hard and sprawled there, the dagger slipping from his nerveless fingers and clattering away.

Eyes wide, he scrambled to his feet, panic gripping his heart.

What? How—how could that be?

The Warlord had not moved. Still he stood over his holographic controls. His—

His holographic *controls*.

Oh, no.

Francisco reached out, his fingers hovering near the Warlord's left arm. Carefully, delicately, he touched the arm.

Except, he didn't.

His fingers passed through the arm, just as the dagger—and all of him—had passed through the man moments earlier.

A hologram.

Oh, oh, oh no…

"So."

The booming voice came from behind him. He whirled, panic sinking deeply into his brain.

The Warlord stood there, arms crossed over his chest, malevolent eyes peering down at him through the holes in the silver mask.

"So you reveal your treachery at last," the Warlord growled.

Francisco considered fleeing, but knew it would do no good. He considered denial, but that seemed ludicrous. He considered…

No, he thought then. *No. I am in the right, and I will not deny it.*

He stood up straighter and glared back at his erstwhile master.

"I serve the Grand Design," he said, his voice quivering only slightly. "As do you. *As should you!*"

The Warlord took a half-step back, so astonished was he.

"You serve *me*," the Warlord barked back at him. "Your duty is to *me!*"

"No! My first duty is to the Design itself. I am to protect it at all costs, against all threats. Including those caused by the Warlord himself, if I deem it so."

He moved closer, leaning toward the larger man.

"And…I…do!"

The Warlord gazed down at him, clearly startled by this unexpected reaction, this strength.

Francisco stood there, shaking now, waiting. Sweat beaded on his face, running down his neck. He shivered.

At last the Warlord moved back from him, raising one purple-gloved hand to his chin, as if pondering all that he had witnessed and heard. Finally, he spoke.

"I understand," he said to Francisco then. "I understand your point. It is a fair one."

He turned and strode across the chamber.

"You do have your own role in the Design, yes, I acknowledge that. And, further, I understand that you must serve it as you deem necessary."

He reached down and picked up the dagger Francisco had dropped.

"But I, too, must do what I feel is necessary to advance the Design."

He gestured toward the rows of display screens filling one side of the chamber, showing the work being done, high up in orbit, on his gargantuan dish, and on the station that supported it.

"And this is what I feel must be done. You must accept that."

He started back toward Francisco, the dagger held casually in his right hand.

"Still, I think we may be able to accommodate one another's interests," he continued.

He stopped very near to Francisco, and hefted the dagger, staring at it as if utterly fascinated by it, considering its weight, studying its detail.

"I offer you a bargain."

He raised a hand before Francisco could object.

"No, no, nothing new, nothing that violates the Design. I merely offer you a...deeper, richer, more detailed understanding of what each of us shall do as we proceed with this project. What we shall expect of one another."

Francisco's eyes narrowed. They never left the dagger.

"We will consult with one another more often. We will...take one another's legitimate concerns into consideration, more than we have previously. We will...*cooperate*. Yes?"

Francisco stared up at him, and at that dagger that hovered just out of reach.

"...Yes," the little man said, at last. "Yes, we can do that."

"Good."

The Warlord brought the dagger down in a flash. It disappeared, vanishing into the depths of his robes, stored away carefully.

Francisco gasped involuntarily, then let out a long sigh. He appeared to deflate, to shrink even smaller than he already was.

Behind the silver mask, the Warlord might have smiled. Then he whirled and strode across the chamber, though the doorway, and out. Gone.

Francisco watched him go, the dagger going with him. He said nothing, but many, many thoughts swirled through his still-feverish mind.

Oh, we'll cooperate, he thought, anger boiling up inside him once again. *We will consult and discuss and play whatever other games you like. But we both know full well that you are not about to change your plans.*

And so, he thought with grim determination, *neither am I.*

38

Brachis and Mondrian fled Okaar's sanctum, the slavers in hot pursuit.

Down the corridor they ran, Brachis clad head to toe in his dented, gray-black armor and Mondrian still wearing the slave girl outfit Okaar had forced upon her.

Mondrian felt the squeeze of the golden bracelets around her wrists and ankles, a constant reminder of the evil she and Esro were fleeing. Thus far, they had proven impossible to remove. Worse, she knew the ornaments could control her mind and body if the golden ring she now wore fell into someone else's hands. She resolved to find a way to remove the bracelets as soon as possible. In the meantime, she would not allow the ring to leave her possession.

They rounded a corner and came to a small opening.

"This is how I got in before," Brachis said, and Mondrian nodded. They squeezed through and found themselves in the open service space, then began the endless climb back up.

"Lights," Mondrian pointed out after a while, as they passed what must have been a bulkhead between levels. "We're out of the Dead Areas."

Shouts from below echoed up through the shaft, drawing Mondrian's attention. She looked down. She thought she could make out movement, far below in the dark.

"They have discovered our path. We must get out of here now!"

Esro said nothing, instead reaching out and pulling at what appeared to be another service hatch like the ones he'd seen up and down the maintenance shaft. With a groan, the hatch opened, revealing a shadowed tunnel lined with pipes and wiring conduits, all dark gray or black and most dripping with rusty water. Drip-drop sounds echoed up and down the narrow space.

Mondrian peered through the opening, wrinkled her nose, then looked back at Esro.

"Do you know where this leads?"

"Not even remotely," he said.

The sounds from below grew louder. It sounded as if an entire army pursued them.

"But there's no time to debate it."

The sleek alien female nodded and climbed into the tunnel, followed by the bulky armored human. Esro reached back and pulled the hatch closed behind them.

"Maybe that'll confuse them for a while," he said.

He saw that Mondrian had already reached the other end and was opening the hatch there.

"Be careful," he called to her as he sloshed through the puddle of filthy water that filled the depths of the tunnel.

She had it open now and was staring out. Something like mist or fog billowed around her, pale light filtering down through it.

Brachis squeezed alongside her and peered through the opening.

They were far up in the air, overlooking a vast jungle. They stood at one edge, with dense vegetation extending as far as they could see into the distance. If there was a far wall in any direction, it was too faint to make out in the haze. Sounds and smells—a cacophony of both—washed up and over them. Esro drank in the rich mélange, enough to overwhelm his senses, and thought of a safari he'd once participated in. They could just as well have been in Africa, but for the fact that they were leaning out of a service conduit in a giant space station, in some unknown corner of the universe.

Brachis met Mondrian's eyes. The Kur-Bai woman merely shook her head, at a loss.

Hanging partway out, he looked down. Nothing but layer upon layer of forest below, the floor completely obscured, and no way to determine just how high up they were.

He twisted around. He could see the wall as a gray curve extending away to the left and right, out of sight, and up into the sky. Far, far overhead, a clear dome separated them from the cold of space, light pods glowing along support beams. Inside the dome, it was steamy, tropical. Odd sounds echoed up from the depths of the jungle.

Esro swallowed, taking it all in. This station had offered him nothing but one crisis after another, one unimaginable circumstance after another, and his mind was reeling.

"We cannot go back the way we came," Mondrian said, "and I see no other way out."

He turned back, examining the wall behind them again. There was no reason for a service tunnel to terminate here with no way up or down, but that did indeed seem to be the case. As he continued to study the wall, he became aware of a horizontal line about two hundred feet higher up on its surface. He adjusted the optics in his helmet and zoomed in.

"Well, I'll be."

Mondrian craned her neck to see where he was looking.

"What is it? Where—?"

He didn't even hear her. He was using the telescopic lenses in his helmet to search for a way there.

"There's nothing," he whispered, growing frustrated. "Noth— oh, wait." He sighed. "Yeah, I'm still an idiot."

He turned to Mondrian and wrapped his arms around her.

"What are you doing?"

Hugging her tightly to himself, he stepped out of the tunnel. Mondrian screamed. His boot jets kicked in and they rocketed up into the sky.

"I should fly more often," he said, as she struggled to regain her composure. "Sometimes I forget I can."

Within a few moments they had soared up and over the ledge and touched down upon it.

Mondrian started breathing again and extracted herself from Esro.

"You don't trust my flying?" he asked.

"It is your technology I do not trust," she replied, glancing around. "Especially after all the damage done to it today."

"Yeah, that's a point," he replied. He glanced at the row of lights inside his helmet, seeing that several of them had changed from red to yellow. "At least I'm starting to power back up again now that we're out of the Dead Areas."

Realizing that he had worn his helmet for a very long time now, he popped the seals and pulled it off, breathing deeply.

"Man, that feels good. Be glad when I can get the rest of it off..."

He was fiddling with the helmet's antenna, which had been severely bent at some point in the recent past. *Feels like the antenna isn't* all *that got bent*, he added to himself. Then he turned around and saw Mondrian gazing at something further down the ledge. He blinked.

"What's *that* supposed to be?"

A rectangular box sat on the ledge, about fifty yards away.

Mondrian looked at him, and he shrugged. Together, they began to walk towards it.

As they approached the box, they saw that it was gray, except for a transparent panel across the side facing out toward the jungle. It was mounted onto a slender, single track that ran up the wall and disappeared from view.

Brachis stopped to examine it while Mondrian continued around to the other side. He ran his gloved hands across the surface, eventually finding a small catch. When he pulled on it, the side of the box popped open.

Mondrian moved past him, peering into the box. She leaned through the hatch, examining the interior.

"Anything interesting in there?" Esro asked, staring at the scantily clad Kur-Bai officer with rapt attention as she leaned forward.

"Ahh—I see," she said.

"Yeah, me too," he mumbled.

Mondrian leaned back out, her face questioning.

"Um, nothing," he said, a sheepish smile on his face. "What did you find?"

She pointed back inside.

"Obviously it is a transport for moving about the inner surface of the dome. When I place my hand here—"

She rested her palm on a flat panel at the front of the cabin, and the dull gray surface shimmered into a series of squares and circles and triangles, all of different colors.

"—The controls appear, you see?"

"Huh."

Brachis squinted at the small geometric shapes, but couldn't make any sense of them.

"Can you figure out how to operate it?" he asked her.

She seated herself on the broad cushion that filled the back half of the box, and leaned toward the controls again.

"Perhaps..."

Esro climbed in and sat down beside her.

"But," she asked, "do we want to go in this direction?"

"Who knows?"

Frowning, he looked around.

"We may not have any alternative. At least for now. We can't go back the way we came, and the slavers could be right behind us."

"Yes," she said, "but... We need to know that we are making progress, and not getting ourselves more and more lost."

"How do you propose we figure that out?"

Mondrian only frowned.

Esro chewed his bottom lip. Then, after a few seconds, he brightened.

"Hey, maybe if we follow this track far enough, it'll come to some sort of transportation hub. From there, maybe we can find directions to where we want to go—back to the ship, the parking lot."

Esro waited while Mondrian appeared to consider this. When she didn't reply for several seconds, he rested his hands on his hips and stared at her impatiently.

"Do you have any better ideas?"

"It is as good a plan as any, I suppose," she said, somewhat reluctantly.

"Fine, so let's—"

"Excuse me—?"

Brachis and Mondrian almost jumped through the top of the box, so startled were they by the voice. Esro popped a gun out of his gauntlet and leaned out the door.

The little man in the gray suit stood outside, a clipboard in one hand.

"Wha— Where— How—?"

Esro gawked at the man.

"You?!"

"I am not certain how you escaped my attention before," the little man said, clearly agitated, "but now I simply must ask you to register."

He held the clipboard out.

Esro blinked.

"What?"

Then everything that he and Mondrian had been through since they'd arrived passed through his mind, and his face hardened. He jabbed a metal-gloved finger outward.

"Look, you. We want to get out of here."

The little man took a half-step backward, startled.

Esro spoke slowly, clearly.

"We *don't... want... to... be... here.* Understand?"

335

The little man appeared discomfited by this. He seemed almost hurt.

"Um, well, I'm afraid that's not an option, is it?" he replied. "Seeing as how you're so obviously *here* now..."

Mondrian had stepped out of the box and now stood next to Esro. She studied the man for a moment, her face registering surprise. Then she crossed her arms and leaned towards him.

"At last, someone I can deal with," she said. "You have some sort of authority on this station, yes? Return us to our ship and tell us how to pass back through that portal to Earth."

"Oh my. I wasn't expecting you to be so difficult."

The man tapped his pen on his clipboard, then looked back up at them again.

"If you insist on causing delays, I suppose I'll have to bring in some sort of brutish figures to threaten and menace you until you sign..."

He studied the papers on the clipboard closely, his nose nearly touching the surface, then looked up at them again, obviously peeved.

"Why can't you people ever make things simple? Just once?"

He sighed deeply.

"Very well... I will return momentarily, with brutes to compel you to obey."

And with that, he turned and walked toward the wall. A rectangular panel that Esro had not noticed before slid open, and the man walked through. The panel slid closed behind him.

Mondrian rushed to the wall and ran her fingers over it.

"There is no opening," she said. "This wall is perfectly smooth!"

Esro didn't even bother to look for himself. He was hardly surprised.

"I don't know who that guy's supposed to be, but it's obvious he's not going to help us."

"Quite the contrary," Mondrian said. "He is coming back with... 'brutes,' I believe he said?"

Brachis nodded.

"I think, if you can work that transport, we'd better make ourselves scarce."

39

They shot along the inside of the dome at a speed much faster than Esro felt was safe. The transport box followed a curve so gradual that it seemed as if they were moving in a straight line. The vista of the jungle canopy was a dull green blur far below.

Esro, his helmet and gauntlets off and held loosely in his lap, hunched over and stared out at that blur, his stomach growing increasingly queasy. Finally, he leaned away from the window and turned to Mondrian.

"Can you maybe slow this thing down a bit?"

Mondrian glanced at him with a mixture of surprise and amusement.

"Oh? Now you wish to move more slowly?"

She looked him up and down.

"I thought that on your planet, you were considered something of a..."

She paused.

"I am not certain of the proper words in your language."

"Brave adventurer?" he suggested with a wry smile. "Valiant hero? Daredevil?"

She shook her head, chewing a fingernail, thinking.

"Reckless fool," she finally said. She smiled to herself. "Yes, I believe that captures the gist of it. Someone who utilizes technology without fully understanding his actions or their potential consequences. Someone who makes as many catastrophic mistakes as successes. Someone who—"

"Yeah, okay, I got it," he growled.

She looked at him innocently.

"But this is correct, yes?"

Esro reddened.

"Err, well, not exactly, I don't think," he muttered.

"Hmm," was her only reply. She returned her attention to the window, and he sat back, sulking.

"Besides," she continued after a moment, gazing out at the open air of the domed area, "at this rate we will reach the opposite side of the dome very soon. Perhaps there we will find a way back out into the station itself."

She gestured out the window at the vast, green expanse.

"Surely any transportation hub, such as you theorized about, would not be found within this structure. I surmise the dome's purpose, at least originally, to have been agriculture. Now, though—"

"Yeah," he said, nodding. "Now it's sort of gone to seed. Turned wild. I'd prefer not to find out just exactly *how* wild, though," he added.

They rode on for a few more minutes in silence. Esro yawned, stretched, and rubbed at his bleary eyes with his fists. He squinted out the window, watching the rows of massive light fixtures along the inside surface fly past. The ones closest to them were an unbroken blur of light as their transport roared along.

Not looking up from the controls, Mondrian said, "One thing puzzles me. When did you meet that Kur-Bai—the one with the clipboard—before?"

Brachis blinked at her.

"What?"

"The one back there on the ledge, who spoke to us. The only other Kur-Bai I have encountered since we arrived, other than Okaar. You both acted as if you'd met before."

Brachis blinked again.

"Umm...I met that guy right after we arrived—right after you were knocked out, I guess. But, Mondrian—he wasn't Kur-Bai. That guy was a human, all the way. A pretty wimpy little bureaucrat, for that matter."

Mondrian stared at him quizzically.

"Now I am more confused," she said. "Esro, the person who confronted us back there was a Kur-Bai, like me. Of the bureaucratic class, yes, I agree—probably from a lower aristocratic line, of the type that usually ends up in estate management positions—but he was without question a Kur-Bai. Red skin, white hair..."

She indicated her face with one hand, and waved a bit of her thick, white mane at him.

"Just like me, yes? Surely you could tell—how could you ever confuse the two? And that is why I was so surprised."

She crossed her arms and sat back, looking at him, waiting.

Brachis exhaled sharply.

"Wow," he breathed. "You've lost me now."

His confused expression matched her own.

"Mondy, that guy back there was one hundred per cent human."

338

They stared at one another.

"But that would mean we each saw a different person," Mondrian whispered. "How can that be?"

Brachis ran a hand over his chin's two-day stubble.

"A hologram? No, I remember touching him at some point. He was real enough. But we saw two different people. Huh…"

Mondrian had opened her mouth to reply when Esro realized that the light around them had dimmed. He sat up and stared out the window.

"Hey, look—the lighting panels here don't work."

"They seem to be burned out across a large area of the dome," Mondrian agreed. "But all in the same—"

She was interrupted by the ear-shattering screech of metal on metal.

"I think we ought to slow down," Esro said. "And this time, I really mean it."

Mondrian slapped her hands down onto the control panel, harder and harder.

"Hey," Esro said, leaning forward. "What're you doing?"

"It is dead," she replied, her face when she turned to him betraying her fear. "The controls have vanished."

"Dead," Esro muttered. "Dead like 'Dead Areas.'"

Wordlessly, she nodded.

"Dead like *us* if we don't do something quick," he added, pulling on his gauntlets and helmet. Reaching up, he popped the hatch of the car open. Wind flooded in, a gale, whipping at them both. Engaging magnetic grapples in his armor, he climbed out and onto the top of the vehicle.

The jungle lay far, far below, mists shrouding all but the tops of the tallest trees. Esro was not normally susceptible to fear of heights—he'd helped build a base on the Moon, after all—but this view was so alien, so strange, he had to admit it affected him.

The wind tore at him, making him doubly glad for the magnets in his armor. He leaned over the front of the car, looking under the front end, trying to find an emergency brake or some other way of slowing their velocity.

Sparks sprayed up from the tracks, and another deafening shriek emanated from the metal where it met the vehicle. If anything, they seemed to be going faster than ever, though Esro had no idea how that might be possible.

"What do you see?"

Hearing the voice, Esro jerked himself up and looked back over his shoulder.

"Are you nuts, lady?"

Mondrian had climbed out after him and was perched atop the car, her eyes squinted nearly closed, her hair flaring out like a comet's tail behind her. The slave-girl outfit remained securely in place, though Esro had no idea how that was possible, either. Her fingers had found thin seams in the vehicle's surface and she clung quite securely to it.

"Get back in there," he shouted over the roar of the wind. "I have things under control here—"

He realized two things simultaneously, then. One, her eyes were very, very wide, considering the force of the wind lashing at them. And two, she was looking past Esro, to something up ahead.

"Oh, no," he muttered, turning to look.

As he suspected. The rail line's terminus point, another ledge followed by a wall, was still a mere dot in the distance, but was fast approaching. It grew larger even as he looked.

"It ends in a solid wall," Mondrian noted, though Esro scarcely needed her to point that out. He'd seen that very clearly, along with the fact that the wall ended just below the track.

Wordlessly, he climbed around to where his feet could hang down over the front of the car, with his face pointed back at Mondrian, in the direction they had come from. Raising his legs, clutching the car's front end tightly in his arms, his magnetic grapples fully engaged, he triggered the rockets in his boots.

The shriek of metal on metal grew much louder. Sparks flew back for what looked like miles from the rear of the car. The roar of his boot jets became deafening.

They were not slowing down much at all.

The terminus point had grown to fill the forward view, coming at them at horrific speeds. It was a giant fly swatter, aiming to end their trip with a very definitive, very violent certainty.

"Esro," Mondrian shouted. "You can fly, remember?"

"Yeah," he shouted back, over the roar of the jets and the squealing of the metal, "but at this speed, with this kind of wind…"

"We have no choice," she replied. "Now! Go now!"

Esro switched off his jets and looked back one last time. They were almost to the ledge. The terminus wall just beyond it was everything now, bigger than worlds. They had only seconds.

He leapt forward, cradling Mondrian in his arms, and lunged off the roof of the car, an instant before it smashed into the dull gray wall with cataclysmic force. The sound was deafening as the vehicle all but annihilated itself in the titanic impact.

The momentum Esro and Mondrian carried with them hurled them just beneath the wall, out into open air. Esro, grateful they had at least avoided being splattered like bugs on that broad, gray surface, triggered his boot jets. As he had suspected, they had virtually no effect.

Too fast, he thought to himself. *We were going too fast.*

Head over heels they tumbled, the wind and their own awful velocity sending them spinning out of control.

To make matters worse, he felt he was about to pass out from the sheer force of their spin. Mondrian already felt limp in his arms.

No! Got to stay awake! Got to—

Darkness claimed him. Mondrian began to slip from his grasp.

Down toward the distant jungle floor they fell.

40

Jameson leaned forward in his overstuffed leather chair, his face contorted with surprise.

"It's *who*?"

Adcock held the phone out toward him. The man's ever-present sunglasses did little to mask his shock, his surprise.

"It's—it's—them. *Them*."

He half-shook the phone at Jameson, who finally took it from him with nerveless fingers, then just looked down at it in his hand.

Adcock made an impatient "go ahead" gesture.

Jameson frowned and held the phone up to his ear.

"Yes?"

A brief moment of silence as Adcock looked on.

Jameson listened, blinking twice. Then:

"Yes, yes, we did attempt to secure the spacecraft, but someone else—"

Another brief pause. Then:

"We don't know who it was. Some kind of ships—"

And another. Then:

"No, no, your agent never showed up. We were hoping that—"

A very, very brief moment. Then:

"Sending who? What does that mean, exactly?"

Jameson paused and looked at the phone in his hand again. Then:

"And how are you communicating with me this way? How—"

Even from a few feet away, Adcock clearly heard the line click dead.

Jameson sat there a moment, not moving. Then he lowered the phone from his ear, holding it absently in one hand.

"They're coming," he said.

"Coming?"

"'Dispatching agents,' was how they put it. I'm not sure exactly what that means."

Adcock appeared to take this information in. He considered it for a moment. Then he nodded.

"Not surprising."

"But," Jameson continued, "do they mean they're sending a new representative, to replace the one who never showed up? Or do they mean…something else entirely?"

The corners of Adcock's mouth turned down at that.

"Yes, I see."

Jameson inhaled deeply, let it out slowly, and looked squarely at Adcock. His expression was grim.

"I think we'd better be preparing for the contingency of an all-out alien invasion. And soon."

From somewhere in the room came whispered words: "This should prove quite interesting."

Jameson looked up, startled, the phone in his hand forgotten.

What? A voice? Who—?

"No," the voice said. "Not yet."

Jameson's eyes swam. He looked back down at his desktop, staring fixedly at the wooden surface for a long moment.

The phone began to bleat the off-the-hook sound.

He blinked, then stared at the receiver in his hand, as if he'd never seen it before. It clattered from his nerveless fingers.

I—What was I—?

He looked back up. Adcock met his gaze, frowning.

"Was there someone else here? Just now?"

Adcock continued to frown.

"…No."

Jameson swept his eyes all the way around the room.

Nothing.

…Nothing.

He pursed his lips, deeply concerned. He did not like that feeling at all.

I must be going twitchy, what with all the things I'm juggling...

Even so, a chill raced over his skin.

"Get back to work," he barked at Adcock.

The normally unflappable man's ongoing frown, by way of reply, only made it all worse, somehow.

47

Esro awoke to the sensation of something whacking him repeatedly in the head.

"Hmhh? Wuzzat?"

This sensation immediately became joined by another—that of falling.

He opened his eyes and looked.

A broad canopy of jungle trees, growing closer by the instant. Mondrian clinging to him like a cat, smacking him in the helmet with one hand, shouting his name.

And then it all came back to him. The dome. The crash. The fall.

"Oh, crap!"

Instantly, reflexively, he triggered his boot rockets. They had been on before, to no avail, and had automatically switched off, given his wild spinning. Now, though, much of their momentum had gone away, and it became a simpler matter—just stop the deadly fall.

His boots roared to life, their force pushing up against gravity, slowing the descent. The trees came up, up, up at them, and swallowed them.

How much further to the surface itself? We're about to find out...

Layer after layer of vegetation. Vines and limbs tore at him. Mondrian curled in tighter against him, against his armored hide.

Is there a world here at all, or merely endless levels of jungle canopy?

And then, at last, with most of their velocity gone, the grassy floor appeared.

They landed on a column of fire, Mondrian hopping nimbly from Brachis's arms as he settled gently to the jungle surface. They stood on a low hill that was covered with strange, alien flora.

Esro's head spun, as much from Mondrian's attempts to wake him as from all the spinning and falling they'd done.

"Thanks for the assist," he said to her, though he suspected his armor had also played a role, automatically injecting him with a stimulant when it detected his unconscious state during a dangerous free fall. The metallic taste in his mouth confirmed this.

Mondrian nodded to him.

"I am a pilot," she said. "I am surely more accustomed to such conditions, though I must admit I nearly passed out, as well."

"It turned out to be a good thing we were so high up," he replied, looking at the surrounding array of strange trees and vines. "I wasn't sure we'd have the room to kill all that momentum—"

He paused. For an instant, he'd been sure he had detected movement out of the corner of his eye.

"What is it?" Mondrian asked. She dropped into a defensive crouch, instinctively reaching for her weapons. She cursed, realizing yet again that she wore Okaar's gossamer slave outfit and not her flight suit and utility belt.

Switching to infrared vision, Esro scanned the forest around them.

"Oh, no way," he muttered. "Oh, no."

They were surrounded. Dozens—maybe hundreds—of humanoid shapes lurked just beyond the clearing where they stood.

Before Esro could so much as speak a word of warning to Mondrian, the creatures rushed out of their cover en masse, swarming toward the two new arrivals.

Esro quickly moved to position himself in front of Mondrian, but to no avail—they were at the center of a shrinking circle of open space, with aliens everywhere around them.

Those aliens were pale blue in color, with generally humanoid features, though they sported long, slender noses and large eyes. They wore simple one-piece outfits that appeared to have been recycled from something else. None of them stood over five feet tall.

Before Esro could so much as pop out his wrist blasters, they fell to their knees, heads down, moaning and chanting softly.

Esro blinked, not quite sure how to react to this. He stole a quick glimpse at the readouts inside his helmet. His armor's power levels were creeping up again, though still far from optimum. He shifted

They landed on a column of fire.

around, and saw that Mondrian had turned her back to him, preparing to defend in that direction, despite being unarmed.

The chanting grew louder. As he listened, Esro was amazed to discover he could understand the voices. He leaned his head back toward Mondrian.

"You getting this?"

"Yes. The translation seems to be working again. We must have passed out of the Dead Area."

She listened to the aliens a moment longer.

"It sounds as if they are... worshipping?"

"Yeah, that's what I was thinking, too."

At that point, an acceptable period of deference must have passed, because one of the creatures sat up into a hunched posture and shuffled forward.

Esro tapped Mondrian on the shoulder and pointed at him.

The creature stopped a short distance away, his eyes still downcast.

"We welcome you to our land, goddess. We remain faithful and true, and will prepare the sacrifice to appease you."

Esro watched him—*was it a him?* —gesture to the others, and three of the blue aliens ran back into the forest.

"We respectfully ask, however..."

The alien peeked up at them, then quickly cast his eyes down again.

"We ask, why do you come in *female* guise this time? And with a different herald? We—we simply wonder what this bodes for our tribe."

He looked up at them.

"Have you become displeased with us?"

Esro opened his mouth to ask Mondrian if she knew what in the world the guy was talking about. But Mondrian was already speaking. Loudly.

"I am not displeased with you," she said. "You show the proper respect, as ever."

Esro took this in, mystified. He glanced back at her. She had taken on a different posture; regal, somehow. Commanding.

"What are you doing?" he whispered.

She eyed him, saying nothing, but her expression clearly stated, "Keep quiet."

"We thank you, goddess," the little alien replied.

Mondrian nodded, once, with great solemnity.

"What sacrifice do you prepare?" she asked.

The alien looked puzzled.

"The same as ever, goddess. The same you always come for, in your crimson male guise."

He turned back, motioning to the crowd, and the three who had departed moments before stepped forward again, now leading a group of five others.

"Here they are. Five of our strongest, most able youngsters. They will serve you well, as I hope all the others previously have done."

Mondrian growled low in the back of her throat, and Esro slowly put the pieces together. *Crimson male. A god. Able youngsters. Serve. Good lord, this is where Okaar harvested some of his slaves.*

Esro felt nauseous, contemplating it.

He made them think he was a god, so they'd bring him their best workers. Just bring them to him!

Esro began to wish even more that he'd gotten in a few shots on Okaar before leaving him to Eclipse.

Eclipse... That must be the 'herald.' the little guy mentioned. Great--now I'm his stand-in.

Mondrian stepped forward, walking around the group of potential slaves and pretending to inspect them. Finally she stopped and turned to the apparent leader of the tribe again.

"I find them splendid. What is you name?"

"You do not know it?"

"Are you being impudent with me? I have many worshippers. Quickly—your name."

"Arhus, goddess."

"Arhus, your sacrifice is acceptable.

Esro frowned at her, puzzled.

"However," she went on, "I return them to you."

Arhus's eyes widened—not an unimpressive sight, given their size.

"In fact, I bring you news."

The aliens all peeked up at her, very curious now.

"You have rightly suspected that I am not the god you knew. Indeed I am not."

She smiled down at them.

"I bring you news of your god's demise."

Arhus stumbled back a step or two. A low buzz emanated from the crowd as they realized what Mondrian had said.

"The crimson god Okaar will come for your people no longer. I have deposed him and replaced him."

She paused, allowing that much to sink in for a few moments. The buzz grew louder.

"And," she said in conclusion, "I require no sacrifices."

Arhus gaped at her for a long moment, then fell to his knees again, bowing down low. The sound of the aliens talking to one another grew nearly deafening.

After another few moments, Arhus shushed the crowd and turned back to face the two newcomers.

"Then…then, what is your name, O goddess?"

"I am Mondrian," she replied, "and I wish to deal with you fairly. Do as I bid, and you will never have to send your young people away again."

Arhus brightened. Apparently he had concluded he could work with this new deity.

"O Mondrian, we obey!"

Arhus motioned toward the row of his people behind him, and they all bowed low as well.

"You bring us most wonderful news," he continued. "We will do as you say."

"You have an encampment nearby?"

"Oh yes, goddess."

Mondrian looked back at Esro, a slight smile playing over her features.

"Lead us there. My herald will carry me."

"Sure," Esro grumbled inside his helmet. "That's me, charioteer of the gods."

As Esro moved to scoop Mondrian into his arms once more, Arhus looked at him closely, seemingly examining him in minute detail. Esro grinned at the little guy, then leaned in close. His words crackled out over his helmet speaker.

"You guys have anything to eat?" he asked. "I'm starving."

42

Darkness covered the forest. The lighting along the inner surface of the dome had dwindled to almost nothing; Brachis had quickly ascertained that this was normal. Apparently they ran on a regular day/night cycle to approximate that of a planet.

He and Mondrian sat alongside the blue aliens at the periphery of a huge bonfire. The natives were roasting something large over a spit nearby. In addition to drinks, they passed odd vegetables around. After checking them as best he could with his armor's sensors, Esro hastily devoured some of the less bizarre-looking ones.

Mondrian eventually joined him in partaking. Her fears of poisoning were mollified somewhat by Esro's scanners, somewhat by Arhus's statement that Okaar occasionally ate their food, and somewhat by Esro's excellent argument that they'd starve to death anyway if they didn't eat something soon.

Despite Mondrian's objections, Esro had finally removed his helmet. She had been afraid this would detract from his image as an Eclipse-like herald/enforcer. Instead, the natives actually seemed *more* afraid of him without the helmet. Esro was not at all sure how he should feel about that.

He watched with amusement as two very young natives crept up beside him and ran their hands over his armor. They gawked at one another and did it again. Esro popped a booster pod out the side of one of his big boots, and the two youngsters gasped and ran away into the darkness. He shrugged innocently at Mondrian's quizzical glance.

He and Mondrian were both nearly dehydrated, and were grateful when Arhus offered them drinks in containers fashioned from some sort of animal skins. Mondrian sampled the beverage and wrinkled her nose, but continued drinking it. Esro did likewise.

Whoa. Strong stuff. Some kind of wine?

He watched Mondrian, feeling utterly exhausted. He couldn't imagine how Mondrian kept going; they'd both been through so much, yet she scarcely showed the ill effects. *How does she do it?*

Great, finally a moment when we aren't fighting for our lives, and I look like hell and feel worse.

He glanced over at her again.

Look at her. She was attractive enough before—never realized how much I liked red before—and all that snowy hair, and those big eyes... Now she's dressed as some kind of fantasy slave girl, for crying out loud! What am I supposed to be thinking? She's gorgeous!

After a while of watching the revelry and partaking of the food and the drink in fair measure, Esro began to feel even more light-headed. He turned to Mondrian, sliding a bit closer. He moved his hand very near to hers on the log.

"I've been meaning to tell you something," he started.

Mondrian looked over at him. Her dark eyes met his own.

"Um..."

She appeared perfectly sober, perfectly serious.

"Yes, Esro?"

He blinked.

Not fair! What does it take to loosen her up?

"Err... never mind," he muttered.

She stared at him a moment, then turned back to the fire and the festivities.

He sensed depression welling inside him and welcomed it. The encampment, lit up by the big bonfire, seemed to be slowly spinning around him anyway. He took another drink from the skin.

A hand tapped his shoulder, opposite Mondrian. He turned.

The tribe's leader, Arhus, stood there, behind the log.

"Excuse me," he said.

"Yeah?"

From what Esro could tell, the alien seemed embarrassed.

"I, er, could not help but notice," the little guy said. He moved closer, whispering in Esro's ear.

Esro's bloodshot eyes widened as he listened.

"You noticed that?"

Esro fixed the alien with a bleary-eyed stare.

"Am I that obvious?"

But not to her, apparently, Esro added to himself.

Arhus looked surprised.

"So you—you *are* interested in her! But--she is a *goddess!* How can you possibly hope to—?"

Esro chuckled, shaking his head slowly.

"Gotta aim high, my friend."

He met the alien's eyes again, knowing his speech had grown slurred, and hoping the translation came across properly, in spite of that.

"Hey, I'm a herald," he said. "That's pretty good, right? Pretty high up on the ol' divinity scale, I'd imagine. So why not a goddess for me?"

Arhus appeared confused by this. He stroked his chin thoughtfully for a moment.

"Well... It seems very unorthodox," he said, wringing his hands together. Then he brightened a bit. "Of course, you did come bringing word of a dramatic change in the world. Perhaps it is only fitting that other changes should come as well."

He grinned at Esro, showing a mouthful of crooked, dangerous-looking, yellow teeth.

"It may be that I can help you. Of course, she is a goddess, and I have no idea if it will work on her, but..."

"Yeah, yeah," Esro said, grinning back at him. "Whatcha got?"

"These are for you," Arhus said, proffering two skins of drink. "They have aged for many days and nights. The finest of the batch."

He gave them what seemed to be a mischievous nod.

"This has always kept our tribe a happy group. Perhaps they will... cause the goddess to look upon you with greater favor, shall we say."

"Thanks," Brachis muttered, somewhat disappointed.

More wine. He just wants me to get her drunk. Great. Weren't you in my frat in college, Arhus?

He took the skins and leaned them against the log he sat on.

Mondrian glanced over and saw Arhus hand over the skins.

"Arhus, we thank you for your gifts," she said, her eyes moving to Esro. "Store the gifts, herald."

Esro gave her a nasty look for her bossiness, but stuffed the small skins into a hatch built into his armor's torso. He waited until Arhus and the others moved farther around the fire, then whispered, "Don't get to enjoying your divinity *too* much. We still have to find a way out of here."

"I have been giving that subject considerable thought," she replied softly. "If we can continue good relations with Arhus's people, I will order them—or at least *persuade* them—to scout for us. Perhaps they can determine the direction we need to go to find a way out of this—"

The night exploded in light. A rumbling *booooom* swept over them all. Brachis and Mondrian leapt to their feet instantly, even as the explosion faded and darkness fell around the encampment again.

Brachis snapped his helmet on and cycled his guns out.

"What the—?"

A single, steady point of light appeared from over the trees, shining down into the clearing. Then another sound reached them—a mechanical whine.

"Some kind of vehicle," Mondrian said as the sound grew louder.

"It is Okaar!" someone shouted.

"He lives!" came another cry.

"He will be displeased with us!"

Many of the blue aliens cried out in terror and ran for the woods.

351

Esro cursed and switched to night-vision, squinting up over the trees. That proved to be entirely unnecessary. Beyond the bonfire, a hovering vehicle the size of Mondrian's spacecraft—about sixty feet long—dropped into the clearing, lights shining from three ports.

A voice boomed out over a loudspeaker.

"We are seeking the red female and the armored male. We know they are in the vicinity. Turn them over to us and we will spare your settlement."

"Those dirty—!"

Esro started to rush forward.

"Wait!"

Mondrian restrained him, then addressed Arhus and the others.

"Okaar is gone," she called out. "These...*criminals*...cling to the old ways, to his memory. They seek to overthrow my new reign."

"They are not gods?" Arhus asked skeptically, his eyes half-wild with fear.

"No," Mondrian replied, he voice smooth and steady. "They are former followers of Okaar, but they have no powers themselves. Only equipment they have stolen from others."

Arhus looked from Mondrian to the vehicle and back, apparently considering. Beyond the fire, the craft settled to the ground and two hatches popped open. Ragged slaver troops dashed out, weapons ready.

The remaining natives stood about, some moving into submissive postures, others seemingly ready to fight, and still others less certain. The slaver troops immediately opened fire, gunning down the more defiant-looking ones. The others cried out in terror.

This time Mondrian did not try to stop Esro as he ran forward. After a few steps, though, he stopped, looking back at the remaining villagers who stood behind Arhus.

"If being victims—*slaves*—is all you want to be," he yelled to them, "then keep on standing there!"

With a cry, he launched himself at the slavers, wrist-guns blazing.

Mondrian looked back at Arhus, met his eyes. She could read the uncertainty there. As a cry went up from the slavers, she turned and followed after Esro.

The tribal chief watched in awe as Mondrian unleashed herself on the front wave of slavers. Indeed, she fought like a goddess.

"Filthy pigs," Mondrian cried, as she smashed the throats of the first two slavers she encountered. She called upon all of her Kur-Bai starfleet officer training, running through a variety of martial arts moves. She switched from one to another rapidly, never becoming predictable. Her hand caught one ragged slaver under the jaw, staggering him back. As he stumbled, she swept his legs out from under him and then elbowed him in the back of the skull. Before he'd fallen unconscious to the ground, she'd already moved on, knocking the breath out of another and then spinning past the next to trip him from behind and send him sprawling.

Beyond her the armored form of Brachis hovered, his guns shrieking, strafing the enemy, pinning the main body of their force close to their aircraft. He checked his indicators and sighed.

"My power is running low again, Mondy," he called.

"Then fight them hand to hand," she shot back, cracking a green-skinned slaver's jaw with a high kick. The man moaned in agony and dropped to his knees.

"Um, yeah," Esro muttered. His first thought was, *That's exactly what I used to tell Damon not to do, in this armor.* And yet, watching Mondrian whirling like a dervish, deftly dodging swords, spears, and fists alike, taking down foe after foe, how could he not be impressed? Awed?

"Unreal," he told himself. "She's incredible."

Landing near her, he delivered a roundhouse punch to the nearest enemy, sending him sprawling.

Okay, I have to admit, there is a certain raw satisfaction in doing it that way, he thought.

The slavers fell back and regrouped, cutting Esro and Mondrian off from the natives. Remaining out of range, they began to open fire with projectile weapons.

"This is insane," Mondrian yelled at Esro. "We should have them easily outnumbered by now!"

Taking what cover she could, she turned back in the direction of the blue aliens.

"Okaar is no god, Arhus," she shouted. "He is dead now, and your lives are your own again! Show me that you understand that—that you value it! Show *yourselves* that you do!"

Arhus's broad eyes narrowed. He'd doubted Mondrian earlier, and feared she represented some sort of trap. But now, seeing her fight like this... Goddess or no, she made a strong argument. Making up his mind, he turned to the others, gesturing angrily toward the vehicle.

"Destroy the followers of the dead god!" he cried.

The others looked at him, hesitating.

"Destroy them!" he cried again, louder. Turning, he rushed forward by himself, a single, small old man, hurrying toward his doom, but displaying his courage and his valor.

The others saw this, and they understood.

The cry went up instantly, and the natives surged forward, burying the slavers in a mass attack, paying them back for years—for generations—of mistreatment and humiliation.

The slavers were taken completely off guard, never having witnessed anything but submissive behavior from the locals before. The ragged criminals cried out in shock and surprise, and then in pain, as the hordes of blue aliens assaulted them mercilessly.

Esro smiled grimly at this, then cringed as an automatic weapon of some sort erupted in fire, killing four of the natives instantly.

"It's coming from their aircraft," he called to Mondrian, who nodded. Together they dashed toward the vehicle, determined to stop that murderous fire.

A slaver with purple skin and jagged teeth leapt in Mondrian's path, a long sword in one hand and a dagger in the other. He wore filthy rags but had jewels of many varieties sewn into them, and woven into the long, greasy blue hair that trailed over both shoulders.

Mondrian did not break her stride. She nimbly sidestepped the slaver's clumsy sword attack, then lashed out with one foot, aiming at what she hoped in this unknown race was a vulnerable spot. Apparently it was; he doubled over, gasping, and she leapt over him, running on toward the vehicle.

Esro, meanwhile, squeezed off the last few shots he had available for the moment, his guns having reached the overheating stage, then ran after his companion.

As it happened, a small group of natives reached the hovering craft ahead of them, and scrambled over its surface. Three of them made it all the way up to the top deck, where the swivel gun was located. Two of them died instantly, but the third dragged the gunner over the side. Then another climbed up, lobbed something small and round into an open hatch, and leapt clear.

An explosion, dull and muffled, sounded from inside. The vehicle began to list to one side, smoke trailing out of numerous openings. The main hatch opened and two slavers staggered out, coughing and choking.

"Hope those guys didn't break anything important in there," Esro barked. "I want that ship!"

Mondrian frowned and ran for the vehicle's hatch, dashing up inside.

Esro whirled about, his weapons back online, looking for targets.

None remained. The natives had pretty much finished the enemy off, with most of the slavers dead and a few now held captive. Nodding in grim satisfaction, Esro retracted his gauntlet weapons and turned toward the craft just as Mondrian emerged from it.

"It will still fly, I think," she said, looking troubled. "At least, for a while."

"That's better than nothing," Esro replied. "Especially since my boot jets are nearly out of fuel."

She nodded.

"Give me a moment to say farewell to Arhus," she said.

As he watched, she met the natives at the center of the killing field and spoke softly to them. They seemed far more reverent towards her now than they had been before. At the same time, though, they seemed to stand straighter, prouder, stronger and more independent. Esro could not help but smile.

At least we accomplished one or two good things while we've been here, he said to himself. *Now if we can just get* home...

Mondrian climbed into the hovercraft and Esro followed her. She seated herself at the controls, looking over them. Smoke from the earlier explosion filled the cabin, and several of the panels and controls looked to be in bad shape.

"I am not pleased with that indicator," Mondrian said, pointing to a light that flashed angry red.

"I'm not pleased with much of anything here," Esro replied. "But can it fly? Can you fly it?"

"We shall see."

She manipulated the controls. The trees fell away outside the viewport as they surged into the sky. Soon the settlement was a tiny dot in the green expanse.

Esro realized he was still standing, still tense and wound up from the fight. *I don't know if I'll ever get used to that kind of thing,* he observed to himself. *It was supposed to be Damon out doing the reckless battle stuff. I'm just a lab guy. What am I doing here?*

And yet, at the same time, he could not deny the force of excitement and energy that coursed through his admittedly exhausted body. Somehow, somehow...it felt right. It felt *good.*

He finally let himself relax and slumped into the copilot's seat. Then he looked over at Mondrian, who worked the controls as if she'd designed them herself. She had pulled her thick mane of white hair back out of her way and tied it in a ponytail. Any fatigue, any injuries she might have suffered, impeded her not at all.

"You have some amazing skills," Esro observed, his eyes surreptitiously moving over her sleek, nearly naked form again. Absently, a part of him wondered how much of his feelings toward her were brought about by the adrenaline rush. He didn't know, and didn't much care, at this point.

"Thank you," she said, not taking her eyes off the controls.

"And not just your fighting skills, either," he continued. "This is, what, the third different vehicle I've seen you pilot?"

"They were—how do you say it? *Thugs*. Unskilled. Easily beaten. And as for the flying, it's what I'm trained for."

She studied the controls.

"What heading?"

He blinked, trying to think clearly. All he really wanted was a nap. And a bath. Maybe a nap in a bath. Whatever. He giggled, and that more than anything else made him realize just how completely exhausted, in mind and body, he was.

She looked over at him, frowning.

"I'm okay," he said. "Nothing that can't be fixed easily enough, once we're out of this place."

She nodded, knowing exactly what he meant.

"How about the way we were going?" he asked. "Now that we have a vehicle, maybe we can find the transport hub we talked about before, and trace our way back to the ship."

In reply she moved a lever and the craft spun around and launched forward.

Esro pulled his helmet off.

"Ohhh... I'm going to be so glad to get out of this armor."

Mondrian wrinkled her nose.

"I do not think I want to be there when you do."

He gave her an ugly look.

"Just fly the plane, lady," he said, grinning. He felt as if he might be able to take a nap. Just a quick bit of shuteye, and then...

A violent shock vibrated through the craft.

Esro sat up, wide awake.

"What was that?"

Mondrian had hunched forward, manipulating various controls. After a moment she growled and smacked her fist on the console.

"This craft was indeed damaged," she replied. "Now it is much worse. We are losing altitude."

Vibrations rattled the craft, shaking them roughly. Esro shook his head to clear it, cursing their continuous bad luck.

"Do we need to bail out?"

And he followed that, under his breath, with, "I'm getting extremely tired of jumping out of moving vehicles."

"...No, I don't think so," Mondrian said, continuing to work the controls. "I can set us down."

The craft shuddered, tilted forward, and dropped through the treetops, careening into the underbrush. Esro whooped and hung on for dear life as Mondrian guided them down as best she could. She managed to generate enough lift to prevent a direct impact with the ground, but they nonetheless smashed through more than a dozen large trees—each one ripping away a portion of the vehicle and spinning them this way and that—before they came to an abrupt and violent stop.

Esro lay still for a few seconds, his head ringing.

All limbs still attached? Yes? Yes. Whew.

Then he sat up and checked to make sure Mondrian was okay. She, too, looked disoriented, but was moving.

He climbed painfully out of his seat and popped open the side hatch—hardly necessary, given that the entire rear end of the vehicle was now missing. He hopped out, still holding his aching head with one hand, and inspected the remaining parts of the ship. A cloud of smoke billowed from the side.

Mondrian appeared in the hatch and handed him a box of supplies. Then she ran back, scooped up something else, and hopped out beside him.

"Come on!"

They ran. Behind them, the remaining portion of the vehicle exploded.

Just one more explosion in a very violent day, Esro thought. *And yet I don't think I'm getting any more used to them than I was.*

Mondrian was already trudging into the underbrush. Lifting the supply box, Esro hurried after her.

Though both knew it with certainty now, neither said a word about the overriding fact they faced: They were now completely and utterly lost, with no hope whatsoever of getting home.

43

"Soon, soon," the voice of the Warlord boomed throughout the sanctum. "It is nearly complete!"

Francisco scurried away from the main chamber, currently occupied by the Warlord. The man stood arrogantly before the main viewscreen, watching the last of the construction teams building the gigantic equipment necessary for siphoning the energies of the great cosmic entities—or, as Francisco preferred to think of it, the equipment that would get them both killed and bring the Grand Design to a rather abrupt halt.

Hurriedly he made his way into the adjoining room with its row of metal and glass cabinets. He spared only a cursory glance at the two units currently in use. The time-lost man in the gray armor and the white-haired woman in blue remained locked within, staring out sightlessly through the glass, frozen in stasis as they had been for days now. Then he opened the door to the third cabinet and, blocking it securely open, climbed inside.

"Soon, soon," he muttered to himself, unthinkingly echoing his erstwhile master's words, as he rummaged through the various implements strapped to his belt. "Tools, tools. Ah. Ah. Yes."

Pulling a small screwdriver-looking item loose, he began to work on the components at the rear of the cabinet.

"Soon, soon," he muttered again. "Soon the Grand Design will be safe."

With a pop, the cover of the cabinet's inner components came free. A smile spread unevenly across his narrow face, and his green eyes sparkled.

Shoving the loose cover away, he began to detach pieces of the cabinet's machinery, setting them carefully on the floor as he worked. Within half an hour, he had the guts of the machine completely disassembled and laid out. Then, grinning once more, he began to reassemble the parts, this time inside a metal cylinder he had fetched from the supply room.

By the time an hour had passed, with the voice of the Warlord still booming from the main chamber, issuing his insane orders, Francisco's work was done. Carefully he lifted the cylindrical device he had constructed and set it on a nearby rolling cart.

Attaching a power cable to it, he activated the controls he had set up along its side, and he waited.

One by one, the lights went from dark to red to yellow to green.

Francisco smiled warmly, as if the machine was a puppy that had just performed some clever trick.

Rubbing his hands together in anticipation, filling his voice with all the distress he could manage, he called out as loudly as possible:

"Master! Master, come quickly! There's been a horrible mistake!"

"What?"

The Warlord's anger and impatience was obvious as he shouted back down the short adjoining corridor. Then came the tromp of boots, closer and closer, and then the flare of purple and blue robes as the tall man swept into the room.

"What is it? What has—?"

The Warlord took it all in at once. The cart. The device on top. The lights flashing on it. Francisco behind it all, pointing it directly at him. Quickly he reached down, the fingers of one hand depressing a button hidden on the wrist area of the other gauntlet. And then, and then, and then...

Nothing.

At least, nothing for the Warlord. For him, time ceased to exist.

A greenish beam had swept over him, emanating from Francisco's device. Time froze solid around him.

Francisco watched as the stasis beam enveloped his former master. The Warlord froze in mid-step, one hand reaching for the other—probably attempting to fire some sort of weapon at Francisco, but he had been too late, hadn't he? Yes, too late, too late!

Francisco hopped with glee from one foot to the other, dancing a little jig in a circle. Then he pushed the cart closer, careful to keep the stasis beam completely covering the man in blue and purple.

After several minutes of delicate maneuvering, he managed to get the cart behind the Warlord, and then could use it to move the trapped man forward, toward the cabinets.

Scarcely an hour later, the Warlord stood sealed in a cabinet of his own, alongside the other two victims, all perpetually frozen in stasis. For them, there was no movement of time—only the ever-present now, going on and on and on with no end...

Scurrying back into the main chamber room, Francisco paused, seeing something unexpected and intriguing on one of the monitors. It was a view of giant robots battling an array of humans. Humans he recognized very well.

"This is the now?" he whispered.

Frowning, he studied the indicators.

"No, no, not the now," he answered his own question. "The near future… or a possible one. Possible, yes."

He continued to watch, muttering to himself.

"The Warlord never looks at these. Never. They could cause him to falter in his purpose, in his determination. They could introduce random elements of doubt. Never, never, he never looks. But I…"

He continued to stare at the displays, the images shifting rapidly.

"Ultraa…Pulsar…Field Marshal… and…Xorexes? On Earth? Intriguing."

He shuffled back and forth in front of the screen.

"What to do, what to do? The Earth might well be devoured before…"

He forced his attention away from the screen, then, knowing he had much more pressing concerns to focus upon. He had to solve the immediate problem first—the problem of what to do with his former master.

He had defeated the insane Warlord, thus perhaps preserving the Grand Design of which he was such a critical component. But—to what end? If this Warlord still lived, there could be no turning of the great wheel, no new Warlord—a Warlord possibly saner in his schemes. There would be only this one, locked away forever.

That was unacceptable.

"I will have to kill him," Francisco said then. "Yes. Kill him. As I have done so many times before. So that the wheel can turn again, and a new master can appear."

He paced back and forth, small hands clasped behind his back.

"But—*how?* This Warlord is wily, cunning. He has foiled me once already. If I free him from the stasis cabinet in order to attempt the murder, he might well—"

A swirl of reddish smoke and fog appeared suddenly at the center of the chamber.

Francisco stumbled back from this, confused.

"No," he howled. "*No!* You cannot have escaped! You *cannot!*"

The crimson smoke filled the chamber, choking Francisco with its pungent fumes. Moments later, a flash of red light emanated from the center of the cloud. The light shimmered, spread to take on a human shape—and blinked out, taking the smoke with it.

"Francisco."

The little man stumbled backward again, his mouth hanging open.

"No... No... How could you have escaped the stasis?"

His voice had become frantic, plaintive.

"How?"

It was then that Francisco realized this Warlord wore robes of a deep red and burgundy. And his mask...his mask was golden.

"What? *No!* It cannot be!"

The new Warlord in Red strode forth.

"You—you can't be here," Francisco gasped. "You—"

"Of course I can," the Warlord replied. "The wheel turns. I will have my day."

"But—but—but that is not possible. He yet lives!"

The Warlord in Red gazed at him levelly, not quite comprehending. His voice, when it came, was a whisper.

"What?"

"He yet lives!"

Behind his golden mask, the Warlord in Red narrowed his eyes.

"Him? He lives?"

"Yes!"

"He *lives?*"

Francisco broke into sobs, tears running down his narrow face.

"How?"

The Warlord in Red strode toward him again.

"How can this be?"

He reached down and grasped Francisco by the throat, lifting him up off the ground. Francisco's feet kicked out at nothing but air.

The Warlord in Red glared at him through his mask—a mask that was not silver but golden—a mask that was wrong. So *very, very* wrong.

His voice was a violent, venomous hiss.

"Show me!"

44

Brachis and Mondrian trudged doggedly on, surrounded by sweltering jungle, the distant stars merely a faint, mocking image far above the dome's dull surface.

Esro's armor had nearly powered up again by now, but his boot jet fuel had dwindled to only a tiny supply. He and Mondrian had agreed that he should save it for an absolute emergency. So they were now reduced to walking.

Mondrian led the way, as she had insisted upon doing. Esro followed and served as rear guard. He could see the numerous cuts and bruises that covered her bright red skin, though she didn't seem to notice them at all. He felt bad that he had no armor to protect her with, and wondered if he could have borne this entire ordeal in as nearly a naked state as that to which she had been reduced. At times her current outfit—or lack thereof, pretty much—had turned him on. Most of the time now, though, he simply felt bad for her. But there was nothing to be done.

And so onward they marched, the great overhead lights rising and falling again in a day-night cycle as they went. Their sheer frustration, their dogged determination to get out of this maddening place, drove them on beyond the point of what was physically advisable. Neither of them cared, any longer. They simply kept walking, placing one foot after the other, saying little or nothing to one another. And so it went, for a day and a night.

Eventually, with darkness around them again, they stopped at a small stream with a waterfall. Both dehydrated by this point, they lingered over the stream, drinking deeply. Then, with no words passing between them, they gathered some wood and built a small campfire, and settled down beside it. Mondrian found a single small blanket in the supply crate, and Esro indicated she should lie on it.

Esro stretched out against a tree and tried to sleep. His body would not have allowed him to continue walking much further, but now he found that neither could he relax. Rolling onto his side, he peeked over at Mondrian. She apparently had found no difficulties in drifting off. He admired her sleek form for a moment, wishing he had another blanket to pull over her and tuck her in.

Then he looked down at his still-armored body, realizing he had grown so accustomed to it—actually grown to it, probably, he thought, laughing bitterly—and eyed the waterfall.

Hmmm...

Stiff joints popped loose, and he slid the gray metal components off, revealing the thin black outfit he wore underneath, laced with its printed circuitry and electronic components. It was also stained with sweat. He wrinkled his nose and peeled it off, too, setting all the components safely away from the fire. With a sigh of relief, he stepped into the stream, and ducked his head under the waterfall.

Mondrian peered at him with one open eye. She had not fallen asleep at all, but had tried to be quiet for Esro. Now she watched him, standing naked under the flow of water. She wondered why she was so curious.

He's just an alien, she told herself. *Not even a highborn one. I'm of the first strata—though admittedly not the uppermost branch. I—*

She shook her head suddenly.

What are you thinking, Mondrian? First you think of Esro, then you start calculating your family status? What do the two remotely have to do with one another?

She scolded herself harshly.

You're fascinated with Esro because you're mentally and physically exhausted, and because he's the only person you have to turn to on this gods-forsaken space station from hell... and because he's an alien life form, a human, and this is the first time you've seen one unclothed, in person. Your scientific curiosity is aroused. And that is all that is aroused, Mondrian!

Feeling suitably chastised, she resumed watching him. She really was tired, she realized, yawning. Her eyes moved over his form, admiring his muscles, his—

You're doing it again! Stop it! What is the matter with you? He's a human! No matter that he's attractive! He— attractive? Where did that—?

"Arrrhh!"

She growled and rolled onto her other side, squeezing her eyes closed, wishing he'd hurry up and finish bathing.

Drying off as best he could, Esro reluctantly squeezed himself back into the gray outfit and lay down beside the fire.

At that moment Mondrian popped up, huffing.

"What's the matter?"

"Nothing," she said. "I cannot sleep."

After a moment, she glanced over at Esro and nodded.

"You can lie here if you like. You cannot be comfortable on the ground."

Shrugging, Esro climbed over onto the blanket, settling as far as possible from the crimson female. Then he remembered, and reached for his armor.

"What are you doing?"

"I almost forgot. The gifts. From Arhus."

"Oh."

Esro extracted the two skins from his storage compartment and handed one to Mondrian.

"More wine. Maybe it'll make us nice and sleepy," he said.

Mondrian nodded, opened the skin and took a drink.

Esro raised his skin in mock toast.

"Here's to Okaar, for getting us into this mess."

"Or to whomever first constructed this facility," Mondrian replied, yawning, then drinking deeply again. "Or to the one who brought us here. May you meet an end worthy of your malevolence."

Esro grinned.

"Heh. I like that."

He thought for a moment, still grinning.

"Or... I know. To the little guy— was he human? Was he Kur-Bai?— who keeps wanting us to... What was it? To *register*. Here's to you, pal."

They both drank deeply again. The night grew darker around them, and colder. Esro shivered involuntarily.

They finished the skins and lay back. Somehow, the flow of time seemed to change. The surroundings spun around again for Esro, and as his bleary eyes peered over at his companion, he noticed that she seemed disoriented as well.

The night had grown much colder now. They moved closer together, doing so almost unconsciously. How much time had passed? Esro couldn't tell.

They bumped together. Esro grew tense, but relaxed as Mondrian didn't object.

"You must get very cramped, being inside that armor for so long," the Kur-Bai lieutenant was saying. Her voice sounded as if it were coming from far away.

Esro felt her hands massaging his shoulders.

"You need to be in fit condition tomorrow," she said, continuing to knead his aching muscles. "We both do, in order to find our way out of this place."

He turned, his face close to hers. She didn't draw back. In the dim firelight, her dark blue eyes stared back into his, warm and inviting. He leaned closer, her red, red lips so inviting. She closed her eyes. Their lips met—

—the fire seemed to die out, and the night was pitch black—

—he could feel her lips, so warm—

—everything faded—

—darkness—

—for a timeless time—

—and then—

Morning.

Esro opened his eyes, blinked, and sat up.

"Wha—?"

He looked around, his mind reeling.

The waterfall, the trees, the entire jungle itself—all were gone.

He lay in a massive, bigger-than-king-sized bed, lush covers pulled up over his legs. The bed sat within a palatial suite, as in a fine hotel, or possibly a mansion. From outside the ornate windows, sunlight streamed in.

He looked beside him and saw Mondrian lying there, sleeping peacefully. He grasped her by the shoulder, shaking her.

She came awake with a start and sat up. Esro realized that her slave-girl costume was gone. She was naked.

Then he saw that he was, as well.

"My armor," he growled, looking around. "Where—?"

Mondrian's face betrayed her surprise and confusion, as well.

"What is this? Where are we?"

He waved his hand around, indicating the room they occupied.

"The Four Seasons? I have no idea."

As she pulled the sheet up over her chest, he realized that she was indeed unclothed, but not *entirely* naked. She still wore the golden bracelets and ring. He guessed the anklets were still there, as well, though he could not guess why it should be so.

"At least we're out of the jungle," he muttered.

She didn't seem to greet that observation with any sort of warmth. He frowned and started to get out of bed.

Before his feet could hit the floor, the double doors opposite the bed swung open. In walked the little man in the gray suit.

"I don't believe this," Esro growled. Then, "Yes I do. Of course I do."

"Awake at last. Wonderful."

Esro gestured toward him, looking back at Mondrian.

"You see a Kur-Bai, right?"

She nodded wordlessly, her expression changing from confusion to anger.

The man—very human to Esro—stood at the foot of the bed, studying the clipboard he carried, apparently oblivious to their exchange.

"You two are proving most troublesome," he said after a moment. "If you had not finally come to rest, I doubt if I would have yet found you. You've spent far too much time in the Dead Areas. You're making things difficult."

"We're—?" Esro gaped. *"We're* making things difficult? Are you *serious?"*

Again he started to get out of the bed.

"No, no, that won't be necessary," the man said quickly, waving him back. "You can enjoy a bit more time here before you proceed. You certainly need the rest."

He brandished his clipboard.

"Here, just register and I can leave you be for a time."

He walked around to Esro's side of the bed, holding out the clipboard in front of him.

"Given these new circumstances I've been made aware of, you can register for the both of you."

Esro's eyes narrowed. Then he grabbed the clipboard and pen, and before Mondrian could object, he scrawled across the page.

The man took the clipboard and pen back and nodded.

"Thank you. My, that wasn't so bad now, was it?"

"What 'new circumstances' were you made aware of?" Esro asked.

The man straightened his tie.

"Well, I—that is—"

He seemed embarrassed. Esro pressed him.

"I simply meant," he said quickly, "that things might have gone a bit more smoothly if I'd realized before that you two were mated."

He shrugged.

"But that can't be helped. In any case, things are cleared up now, so you can proceed to the proper venue shortly."

Esro and Mondrian looked at one another, trying to make sense of everything.

"Yes," the man was saying, still talking a mile a minute, "I was so excited to have a matched set of Kur-Bai that I overlooked... *other* possibilities."

Mondrian waved her hands in frustration and glared at the man.

"What are you talking about? You have given us virtually no information since we were brought here—something I'm becoming quite certain was entirely *your* doing to begin with."

"Yes, well... Enjoy your remaining time here," the man replied hurriedly, moving towards the doorway. "The next segment will begin shortly."

With that, he exited, pulling the doors closed behind him.

Mondrian fumed. She climbed out of the bed, pulling the white sheet off and around her. It matched the color of her long, thick hair, leaving only her face as a bright red point of color as she moved. She crossed to the doors and turned the knob.

"It is not locked," she said, glancing back at Esro.

He got out of bed and crossed to where she stood.

"Really?"

He ran a hand through his dark hair. His head ached. Most of the gibberish the little man had spouted had gone in one ear and out the other, and only now was it beginning to swirl around in his brain and make connections, make any sense at all.

Mondrian looked at him, bit her lip, looked away, her brow furrowed, as if she, too, were remembering, understanding—but slowly, slowly...

It was something about the night before, and about what the little man had just said. Something...

Esro could scarcely remember any of it. They'd been lying in front of a fire... It was cold... And...

Something else...?

It came to them both at the same instant, clicking together along with the little guy's words into a very, very clear picture.

Mondrian whirled, her eyes wide as they locked onto his.

"MATED?!"

45

"There it is," Ultraa shouted to Pulsar as they streaked over the Virginia countryside. "The Oasis."

Lyn looked down and took in the sight.

"That's it?"

"Pretty much."

She frowned. After her visit, months earlier, to the Moonbase Esro had partly designed and built, she had somehow expected more than... *this*.

Below them, carved out of thick-brushed woodlands, sprawled a concrete and steel complex about as visually compelling as an electrical substation. A huge blockhouse of a building filled the center of the paved area at the center, with Quonset huts, earthmoving equipment, and outsized power generators scattered here and there. At first glance—or even second—it appeared to be only some sort of utility station, or perhaps an industrial construction site, albeit one incongruously located in the middle of nowhere.

Ultraa knew better. In point of fact, the Oasis was Esro Brachis's newest, most secret installation.

He caught Pulsar's eye, pointed down, and the two of them swooped toward the blockhouse.

"Uh oh," Lyn breathed as she got a closer look. "I think we're too late."

They could see the aftermath of a battle clearly laid out below them. Automated gun emplacements lay in crumpled piles. Fires burned here and there. And four figures in heavy, green-colored armor lay unmoving on the pavement.

"Defenders," Ultraa said, pointing down at the four.

Pulsar's face twisted in horror. She dropped toward the nearest one.

"Who are they?"

"Guards, wearing one of Esro's projects: heavy-duty battle armor. It's tougher but a lot less versatile than the stuff he wears."

"Oh…"

Pulsar leaned over the Defender, and could see a man's features through the transparent faceplate. His eyes were closed, his mouth slack. She worked at the big, shiny, green helmet but couldn't get it off.

"Help me," she called back to Ultraa.

He landed beside her, looked the man over, and shook his head.

"It's too late. See those lights on his chest plate? They're all red. He's dead."

He checked the other three and nodded.

"All the same."

He looked around and frowned.

"What on earth could have done this?"

"And is it still around?" Pulsar added.

Ultraa had worried that someone might choose to infiltrate or attack one of Brachis's operations, while the man himself remained missing. If he was still alive, if he could find a way to return, Ultraa was sure he would make every effort to do so. In the meantime, there was nothing else Ultraa could do for him but keep the man's property safe.

Therefore, in the days since his release from the hospital, Ultraa had kept a close eye on all of these places, spending long hours in

Esro's situation room in the mansion, watching the monitors, speaking with the security forces, and analyzing the defenses. This facility had made the most sense for someone to attempt to rob, both in terms of the technology Brachis kept stored here, and its relative accessibility—the other major one, of course, was on the Moon. That assumed, of course, that anyone knew what and where the Oasis was, to begin with.

Ultraa spoke these thoughts to Pulsar, finishing with, "Obviously, someone did know."

Lyn nodded, still looking down sadly at the Defenders, her arms wrapped about herself.

Ultraa soared up into the air once again and landed on the roof of the main blockhouse. Lyn followed him, happy to put some distance between herself and the bodies of the guards.

As he looked around the site, searching for clues, Ultraa found himself thinking of the other missing member of their team, Vanadium.

His strength and power would surely come in handy against whatever we're facing here, Ultraa thought. But he hadn't seen the big, metal man once in all the time since the battle with the Xorex, when he had apparently refused to join in the fight. Pulsar had reported having a brief conversation with him afterward, but then he had disappeared entirely. Ultraa had never understood the guy. He'd never quite known what to make of him—or what he was, for that matter. His actions remained as cryptic as his nature.

Not much of a team left, Ultraa reflected.

"This must have just happened," Lyn was saying. "The fires are still burning, and…"

Ultraa shook himself free of his doubts and memories and looked at her, then at where she was pointing.

"Less than an hour ago," he said, nodding. "The alert came in right before you got home."

He studied the four weapons turrets that had been ripped from their emplacements and apparently hurled across the pavement, to lie in crumpled heaps, smoke trailing from them.

If my head was in the game, Ultraa admonished himself, *I would have waited before coming straight down here. Wake up—you're going to get yourself and the girl in trouble, if you keep letting yourself be distracted.*

Ultraa lofted into the air, moving to where he could see the entrance to the blockhouse. The building's two huge, metal doors looked to have been ripped from their hinges and now lay on the ground, twisted to such a degree as to cause Ultraa's stomach to sink a little.

Good lord...Who could have done this?

He turned to order Pulsar away to a safe distance, only to see her zipping past him. She lofted through the now-open entrance into the main building. Startled, he reached out to grab her.

"Lyn—*wait!*"

Too late—she was past him and inside the building, materializing a golden force bubble around herself as she went.

"I'm okay," she called back to him. "I—"

The blow probably would have killed her, had she not been protected by her force field. As it was, she came flying back out, head-first, arms and legs dangling limp. She hit the pavement, still inside her spherical bubble, and rolled until she smacked up against a wall.

Horrified, Ultraa streaked after her. He was relieved to see her sparkling bubble remain in place the entire time—surely it had cushioned her, and at least kept her from scraping across the asphalt. Her force sphere didn't disappear until she had stopped rolling and lay still.

He landed beside her and lifted her head carefully.

"Pulsar? Lyn?"

She groaned softly but didn't open her eyes.

A crunch of gravel behind him caused him to move, whirling about quickly. That movement saved his life; for while he was indeed virtually invulnerable anytime he flew at high speeds, he also gained some lesser measure of that condition when simply moving at all. In this case, his act of turning and attempting to stand granted him just enough physical resilience to survive the massive blow he took from a blue-silver metal fist coming at him like a guided missile.

He flew nearly thirty yards backward and smashed into a generator, sending sparks spraying from it in a blazing torrent. He slumped to the pavement and lay still.

Vanadium surveyed his handiwork passively. Then he bent down and picked up the container full of high-tech equipment where he had set it, seconds earlier. He gazed one last time around the compound and then lofted silently into the sky. Within moments, he was gone.

In the woods nearby, watching through binoculars, the Blue Skull laughed softly to himself. He focused on the unmoving bodies in gold and in red and white, and he grinned.

370

"The equipment was all I really wanted," he whispered to himself. "But *this*—this is *too* good!"

Laughing again, he packed up his remote control devices and melted back into the woods, heading for the location of his rendezvous with his new, ultra-powerful pawn.

46

Brachis and Mondrian knew the little man would be back soon, and they had no intentions of hanging around to see him again—at least, not in their current, disadvantageous state.

First they agreed to set the whole "mated" thing aside for now, in the interests of expediency. Then, after a quick search of the room failed to yield any clothes or Esro's missing armor, they flung the twin doors open to reveal a long hallway, one that matched the bedroom they occupied. Having no other options, and knowing the man could return at any moment—and still naked—they dashed through the doorway—

—and the hallway, the house, the very world itself, all vanished.

All was whiteness, everywhere. Above, below, in every direction, nothing but an endless blank. Not the black of space, but an absence of any color, of anything at all. An utter and complete void.

They turned back, even as the sense of a floor beneath them dropped away. Gravity ceased to exist.

The doors were gone. The white void extended infinitely in that direction as well. Nothing remained in the universe but the two of them, floating.

Instinctively, they reached out, clung to one another. A radiant white light illuminated them, from somewhere, but nothing else could be seen.

It went beyond anything either of them could have imagined—beyond Esro's speculations, beyond Mondrian's experiences and training.

"Esro," she said in a very low, frightened voice, "what is happening?"

"I... I don't know."

They floated. Drifted.

Time passed.

And more time passed.

They clung together and they drifted.

After what must have been hours, Mondrian's voice came to Esro, very small and frightened.

"Esro?"

"Yeah?"

"We will die here. We are lost."

"No."

"Yes. In the jungle we had lost our way, but were not truly lost. But here—here—there is no here!"

He could feel her fingers almost savagely clutching at him. Several things went through his mind, then:

I've never been away from my homeworld, other than a few trips to the Moon. I've only speculated at what might be out here in the big, bad universe. But Mondrian—she's a space ranger, or something like that. All of her training has been in preparation for understanding nearly everything she might encounter, so that she could handle it. But this—this—who could prepare for this?

He shook his head.

I can probably handle it better than she can, because it shocks me but doesn't go against anything I've been taught or trained for. For her, it's a horrendous awakening to a universe that contradicts everything she knows. For me, it simply confirms that the universe is stranger than we know, or can know, as the man said—and that it's out to get us, more often than not.

"We are lost," she whispered again.

"No way," he said. "No way. Something'll happen soon."

She clung to him.

"Something… Soon…"

They drifted…

47

Time passed. Still Esro and Mondrian clung to one another, the only solid thing in each other's universe.

Mondrian shivered.

"I feel so naked," she said. "I—"

Esro held her tighter, a slight smile playing over his features.

"You are."

"No, I... I mean, exposed."

"No more than me," he snorted, trying to sound far more confident than he actually was. "What's to fear here, anyway? It's just us."

Mondrian stared into the void.

"It will drive me mad. It is endless. It has no dimensions, no references. It is insane." She shouted out, *"What is this place?"*

Nothing. Not even an echo.

She blushed, gold on scarlet.

"I am embarrassed, like this."

"And you weren't when you were wearing that slave girl outfit?"

Her expression softened somewhat.

"We were not clinging to one another then."

"I wouldn't have minded," Esro muttered.

And why not say it? he asked himself. *What does it matter? We could just float here, forever—or until we die of thirst, or...*

She gazed up at him.

"You wouldn't have minded?"

He cleared his throat.

"Sorry, I guess I shouldn't have said that."

She appeared to be considering this for a moment.

"No, I... I'm glad you did."

He looked at her, surprised.

"But I do wish I had something to wear right now," she continued. "My flight suit would be perfect."

The surface of her skin shimmered, and her snug, navy blue flight suit materialized around her.

Her mouth dropped open. Esro gawked as well.

"Um, well, I'd sort of like my armor back, too," he said aloud, "if someone's taking requests."

The armor formed around him, the helmet in place.

"Okay," he said to Mondrian, pulling the helmet off. "I want to point out how crazy this is, except that it's not much crazier than anything else we've experienced so far."

Mondrian was rolling the sleeves and legs up on her suit, revealing the golden bracelets and anklets, still in place.

"Still they are with me. Even here."

She barked a word Esro didn't understand, but he pretty much got the gist of it.

He started suddenly, as the implications of what was happening to them began to sink in.

"Hey, maybe we could just *say*—"

She preempted him: "I would like to get out of this stinking void!"

"No, wait—!"

Esro gritted his teeth, expecting something catastrophic to happen.

They waited. Nothing happened.

"Don't just say vague things like that," he gasped finally.

"Why not?" she asked, looking back at him quizzically. "How do you know how this place works?"

"I—I don't. But I mean, I've seen enough movies, read enough books…"

He shrugged.

"When you ask the Genie for something that way, without being really careful… You usually end up regretting it!"

She frowned.

"Genie?"

"Yeah, a magical—"

She jerked in his arms, and pointed.

"Look!"

He looked.

Far away in the void, a tiny shape had formed, dark and round. As they watched, it grew bigger.

"What could it be?" she asked, squinting to see.

"I can maneuver us closer, I think," Esro stated.

He activated his boot rockets and carried both of them in the direction of the object.

As they moved, the object grew larger and larger. Yet Esro had the distinct sense that his own motion was not doing a lot to cause this. Whatever it was, it was very, very big, and moving towards them at a far higher speed than anything he could muster up.

"I think it's…"

"What?"

"No way," Esro said, shaking his head.

It loomed ahead now, growing seemingly huge.

"It is a planet," Mondrian observed.

"There's no way to get a sense of scale here," Esro replied, "but, yeah, I think it is."

They neared what was soon very obviously a planet—and an earthlike one, at that. Hovering there above it, they studied the shape of its continents and oceans, the deep blues and greens and browns, the wisps of cloud cover.

At some point as they did this, they became aware that they were not alone.

"Look," Mondrian whispered, pointing.

Three additional objects had appeared nearby. The shapes were distinctly human. And, as became apparent very quickly, they were very, very large.

Three gigantic, humanoid shapes, each a different color, floated with them in the void. Each wore a complex exoskeleton structure of some sort. None possessed anything that might be called a human face, but instead a mostly blank rectangle with seemingly random lines and indentations drawn across it. Bright, nearly blinding energy manifested itself around each of the beings in different ways.

Esro activated his boot jets again, moving them closer still.

One of the huge figures glowed a deep, radiant blue, with what seemed like printed circuits patterned across its form. Forks of lightning raked out from all over its surface, playing across the blank heavens.

The second figure emanated bright red, seemingly made all of crystal. A spiral swirl of crimson energy spun slowly around it, snakelike, not touching its body at any point.

The third was golden, and glowed like the sun. It was radiant. Spikes of light and energy poured from its every surface.

Esro gawked at them.

"What—what are those things?" he managed, when he could get his voice to work again.

"They are larger than any spacecraft I have ever seen," Mondrian whispered. "Are they... *alive?*"

As Brachis and Mondrian watched in awe, the three lit up like light bulbs.

"That can't be good," Esro muttered.

Different forms of energy radiated from each, manifesting as titanic bolts, flashing down to strike the planet's surface.

"What are they doing?" Mondrian asked.

As they watched, the energies apparently pouring out from the three beings increased exponentially, crashing against the planet they orbited. Eventually great gouts of earth ripped loose, shredded by the massive display of power. The onslaught continued. In very little time, the planet came apart, disintegrating from the core, hurling chunks of itself outward in a massive explosion.

"It's gonna hit us!"

Esro moved to shield Mondrian, knowing how very little good that would do.

Despite his fear, he watched. And he was amazed beyond words.

The explosion faded, collapsed in upon itself, before it ever threatened them. The planet fell back together, reforming itself. Still the energies of the three figures played over it. Soon enough, the planet was whole once more, remade.

Esro and Mondrian were left speechless.

The three figures vanished.

Gravity gripped them. Esro and Mondrian tumbled towards the planet. Though he fought it with his boot rockets, Esro couldn't stop their momentum.

"We'll burn up on re-entry," he growled.

Monrian clung to him tightly, her eyes closed.

They fell. Fell towards the world, all green and bright. Fell...

...And didn't burn. They passed harmlessly down into the atmosphere, then stopped, hanging motionless in the sky over a broad, endless plain of grass. Gravity took them, pulling them down. Esro activated his rockets again and settled them to a gentle landing.

They stood at the bottom of a shallow, bowl-shaped valley. Hills surrounded them. They both turned in a slow circle, looking around.

"There!" Mondrian grasped Esro's shoulder and pointed.

Atop the hill along one side of the valley, three shapes materialized. Three large, human shapes.

Esro started forward.

"It's them. They're a lot smaller than before, but it's obviously them."

He stared at the three gargantuan humanoids that had destroyed and remade the world. Then he realized how far away they were.

"Okay, they're still pretty big..."

"Three hundred meters tall," Mondrian estimated. "I know of no race which produces such tremendous specimens. Or any who could do what they just did to this world."

"Uh, me neither," Esro muttered. "Let's get a closer look."

Before Mondrian could object, he clutched her to himself and activated his rockets, soaring into the air, moving closer.

The three giants stood unmoving, seemingly oblivious to all. They looked like great statues atop the rise.

Holding Mondrian tightly, Esro neared the blue figure.

"Can you get its attention?" Mondrian asked.

Esro switched from gawking at the giant to gawking at her.

He stared at the three gargantuan humanoids that had destroyed and remade the world.

"Now, why on earth would I want to do that?"

"Because this represents our first opportunity to do something," she replied sharply. "To do *anything*."

"Yeah...yeah. Okay."

He considered a moment, then flew closer, waving his free arm.

"Hey! Hey, big blue guy! Yo!"

The figures remained oblivious to him.

"Try something else."

"Maybe if I shot at it?

"Yes."

Esro popped his wrist blaster out. Then he stopped himself.

"What am I, crazy? These guys just demolished and rebuilt the whole planet! And I'm gonna *shoot* at it?"

He pulled back, carrying them away from the three.

Mondrian looked back at him with searching eyes.

"Then what—?"

"We'll think of something."

He settled them both to the ground nearby, letting go of Mondrian. She immediately moved through a quick series of stretching exercises.

"Nice to have solid ground under our feet again," he said, doing his own awkward stretches. "Even if it's not exactly ol' Terra Firma."

He looked all around, hoping for something—anything else to present itself. He was as disappointed as he had expected to be.

"Nothing," he reported to her. "Nothing but us and them, as far as my scanners can see."

"Then perhaps—"

The bolt of lightning speared down at Esro, lighting him up like a blue fluorescent bulb.

Mondrian jumped back, screaming.

Esro stumbled forward, the blue bolt still locked onto him. He raised his blazing blue hands and stared at them, then looked back at Mondrian, an awed expression on his luminous face.

"I'm—I'm okay," he said, his voice sounding far away.

The beam, he could see, traced all the way to the blue giant.

"What's it... what's..."

He slumped face-first to the grass, motionless. Still the blue lightning played over him.

"No! Let him go!"

Mondrian ran up the hill toward the giants.

"Stop it! Stop what you are doing! Now!"

The sparkling matrix swirling around the red giant spun outward, moving so quickly as to defy belief. The tendril struck her, sending her stumbling backwards, lighting her up with crimson fire. She screamed again, attempting to run, only to have the stream of crimson light spin tightly around her, cocoon-like. For a few seconds she stood immobile, wreathed in a spinning helix of red fire. Then she slumped to the grass, the blazing energies flowing over her. Groaning, she reached blindly out for Esro, felt his hand, grasped it...

Consciousness fled.

48

Wendy Li pulled up the zipper on her new, silver uniform and stepped back, regarding herself in the mirror. She frowned.

"I look like Lyn," she muttered.

Part of her was happy about that. Part of her, she had to admit, had been jealous from the first moment she'd seen her big sister on television, wearing her golden costume, flying around, using her powers—her *paranormal abilities*, as super-nerd Lyn called them.

But another part of her, and one that grew louder the older she got, wanted her to be more individualistic. To be herself, unique, and not a copy of anyone else—not even of Lyn.

So she stared at her reflection, and she frowned, and she tried to decide how she felt about the uniform.

It was snug, though not quite so snug as Lyn's, thank goodness. It was smoother, thicker, and fit more like a military uniform than did the outfit worn by her sister, which was essentially a metal-mesh leotard. It had something of a collar to it, and flared a bit at the cuffs. She liked that part—it lent the look a bit of distinctiveness.

Then it occurred to her that she could always ask the people here to modify it a little, for her—to make it even more stylish. Dumb old Lyn probably had never even thought of doing that.

Thinking of who she should talk to about her costume caused her to think of all the other people she'd met since arriving here.

For possibly the tenth time since arriving at the Field Marshal's headquarters, just outside Washington, DC, she started to ask herself who these other people were.

And, as had happened every time before, something in her mind immediately spoke up, ordering her to stop asking questions, to concentrate on her own training and studies.

Before she could ask herself why that should keep happening to her, a low, electronic tone sounded from the speaker mounted on the wall above her door. It was followed by the heavily accented voice she recognized as that of the boss—the Field Marshal.

"Attention team members. You are required in the conference room now."

Oh, great, she thought. *More meetings. This is worse than school.*

Nonetheless, Wendy opened the door and stepped out into the hall. Quickly checking her bearings, she headed for the conference room.

She beat the others there, took a seat on one side of the big, oaken table, and watched the others come in.

First came Doug Williams, the tall, African-American man with a pleasant enough smile, but a look of hurt, of hidden pain, constantly peeking through his expression. Wendy smiled at him and waved. He returned the smile and nodded back, seating himself across the table.

Next came the blonde woman, Angela Devereux. Wendy was happy to see she wore a black sweat suit, rather than her costume, which left little to the imagination. She gave Wendy a quick, tight smile and sat down at the far end of the table.

She was followed by a man she had seen a couple of times before, but hadn't yet spoken to. He had short, black hair and pale features, and wore a lab coat and blue sunglasses. She had heard him referred to as "Mr. Blue." Frankly, he gave her the creeps.

The tall, blond man, Blitzkrieg, came in just ahead of the Field Marshal—nearly late, despite possessing super speed. Wendy found that funny. He seated himself quickly, and the Field Marshal closed the door behind him.

"Thank you all for coming," the older man began, his eyes moving from one of them to the next. He seemed more excited than his usual, aloof, laconic self. "I wanted to give you all the news firsthand," he said.

They all looked back at him, waiting; wondering what could possibly have him so out of sorts.

He wasted no time in telling them.

"I have just received the official word from our superiors in the Pentagon," he began. "We are now recognized as the current incarnation of Operation: Sentinel—the US Government's first-rank paranormal defense organization. We shall be the first group they turn to when they need the sort of… services… we can offer."

The others glanced at one another, expressions of surprise and happiness mingling on their faces.

"Wow," Williams said.

"Very good," Mr. Blue added.

"Ja," the Field Marshal said, nodding. "Truthfully, I had expected it from the start, or else I would not have wasted my time on this project. But having that designation in hand… it makes things easier."

Wendy thought about it a few more seconds, as the others talked among themselves in hushed tones and the Field Marshal looked over the table, smug and pleased with himself.

Then she raised a hand.

"Um…Isn't that what Lyn's—what Ultraa's group is called? How can we both—?"

The Field Marshal's smile broadened into a grin.

"Yes, indeed, my dear. That has been Ultraa's team's designation. Up until now, that is."

Wendy frowned.

"So—so, what happens to Ultraa? To Lyn?"

The Field Marshal shrugged, shaking his head slowly.

"I believe Ultraa is being…retired," he said. "After all, he has served this country for many years, no? He deserves some time for rest and relaxation. And as for your sister, well…"

He shrugged again.

"She has been… invited… to join this organization before. She refused. I'm sure, given time, we can arrange to offer her another opportunity, if you'd like."

Wendy frowned at that. She chewed a fingernail, thinking it over.

Having Lyn around—that could be great. Then again, it could be just awful. I don't know…

While Wendy was mulling this over, the Field Marshal turned his attention to the man in the blue sunglasses.

"Mr. Blue. I am hearing reports of your recent activities."

"Yes?"

"Involving our newest recruit."

"Ah."

"These activities must cease immediately."

"Why?"

The Field Marshal glared at him, veins rising in his forehead.

"Because our new status could be jeopardized, if any...untoward...activities were to be traced back to any of us."

"That wasn't our agreement."

"It is now."

Mr. Blue stared back at him silently.

"And furthermore," the Field Marshal continued, "you are to request my permission in the future, before utilizing our new asset in any way. Do you understand?"

"That wasn't the deal, either."

The Field Marshal merely shrugged.

Mr. Blue sat immobile for several long seconds, then nodded once.

"Excellent."

Wendy took all this in with no real grasp of what they were talking about. She fidgeted, playing with her hair, wishing they would hurry and wrap things up. She'd been hoping to call her friend, Lonni, and—

"One other thing," the Field Marshal continued, addressing them all again. "If Ultraa or any of his teammates should ever interfere in our official operations, we have full authorization to arrest them, to take them into custody, or to use whatever other means we see fit, given the situation."

Wendy blinked.

"What? Arrest them? Huh?"

"We are now duly authorized agents of the United States Government," he added. "We have the right to do whatever we feel we must, to accomplish our missions."

"Und if that means taking down a troublesome old warhorse like Ultraa," Blitzkrieg added, "then all the better, *ja?*"

Wendy started to object, but the Field Marshal gestured sharply to someone else at the table. She turned to see who he was motioning to—

—and saw that it had been Angela Devereux. *Distraxion.* The blonde woman had removed her sunglasses and was staring back at Wendy intently.

Wendy started to say something, but then promptly forgot what it had been. She opened and closed her mouth soundlessly, a time or two. Her eyes glazed over. Saliva trickled over her lip and trailed down in a line to the table.

A moment later, Distraxion had her glasses back on, the meeting was breaking up, and Wendy snapped back to reality.

"Wha—huh?"

She started to ask what had happened, then felt the drool from her lip and turned bright red, wiping at her face. She looked around, embarrassed that she had somehow fallen asleep at the meeting. And yet no one seemed to be paying her the slightest bit of attention. They were all filing out of the room.

What did we talk about? she wondered. *Something...something good, I think... We won something, or...*

After a moment, she shrugged and returned to her quarters.

And, back in his Pentagon office, Jameson watched it all on a monitor and smiled.

49

"At last I've found you."

Esro opened his eyes. The light blinded him at first, and he raised his hand to his brow, trying to see who had spoken. Then he saw Mondrian lying next to him in the grass.

"Mondy!"

He crawled over to her.

"She is alive, and unhurt," the voice said again.

Kneeling down next to her, Esro turned, and saw what he had somehow expected to see.

The little man in the gray suit.

"You."

Esro cradled Mondrian's head in his lap. So many things occurred to him to say that he didn't know where to begin.

The man crossed his arms.

"You did it again! Went and got yourselves lost!"

Mondrian moaned, opened her eyes, and smiled up at Esro. Then she saw the little man standing before them. She frowned.

"How are you?" Brachis asked her.

She groaned.

"I would have been better, I think, had *he* not been here when I awoke."

Esro nodded.

"Look, pal," he said, glaring at the man. "Either send us back home, or get lost. We're tired of dealing with you."

383

The little man huffed.

"Incredible. You'd rather be stranded here—*here!*—than have me return you to the station. Incredible."

Helping Mondrian up, Esro jabbed a finger at the man.

"We don't want to be stranded here. Not at all. We're just tired of you jerking us around!"

The man shook his head, oblivious to Esro's words.

"This time, you could have been in very real danger. This plane of existence was never intended for beings such as yourselves."

Esro tried to follow what the guy was saying, except that he'd just become aware of the fact that the blue giant's head had turned, and now pointed straight at him.

"Um—"

"No, no, listen to me," the man continued. "You two are guests, and as such are expected to follow a few simple rules. But ever since your arrival, you have been nothing but trouble. I'm not quite sure how you've managed that, to be truthful. Once you registered, you should no longer have been able to travel through the various portals without expressed permission. Yet somehow you have done so."

Esro was growing antsy. He could see that the little man, his back turned to the giants, was totally oblivious to what was happening behind him. As for Mondrian, she was glaring at the guy, probably waiting to verbally assault him. The problem was, both the red and blue giants now seemed to be staring at them with their featureless faces. And the golden giant actually appeared to have moved closer. Esro felt sweat trailing down his neck, pooling in his armor.

"Furthermore," the little man continued, "you have continuously ventured outside of the permitted areas of the station. You were expected to provide a random element into the upper strata of the hierarchy, but instead—"

Esro couldn't restrain himself any longer, regardless of the cost. The golden colossus had never actually moved, yet it now stood very near, towering over them. One mammoth arm slowly began to rise, until it extended out above them.

"—instead, over and over, you have entered the Dead Areas, where I cannot—"

Esro grabbed the guy by the lapels, spinning him around.

"Look!"

The golden being had reached out, its gargantuan hand shimmering with unearthly energies. It pointed at them—

"What's the matter?" the little man asked Esro tiredly, gazing up at the golden colossus. "Oh, it's you." Casually, almost dismissively, the man waved his hand—

—and the golden behemoth vanished, along with its scarlet and azure associates.

Esro gawked.

He and Mondrian stood alone on the grassy hill, save for the little man in the gray suit; the man whom Esro saw as human and Mondrian saw as Kur-Bai. The man who had just casually banished three virtual gods.

Mondrian stared up into the clear blue sky, beyond where the giants had stood. She swallowed once, uneasily, then looked down at the man in the gray suit. She opened her mouth. Then, unsure what to say, she closed it again.

Esro, at the same time, did much the same thing.

The little man clapped his hands together.

"So much for them. I was finished with them anyway."

His expression conveyed distaste.

"Annoying chaps," he went on. "Too quiet, too enigmatic for their own good. They'll learn, soon enough."

He returned his attention to Esro and Mondrian.

"Now, back to business."

Esro fought to grasp what he'd just witnessed. He looked to Mondrian. Her face was blank with shock.

The man held up his ever-present clipboard.

"This is our main problem. We've had some difficulty with your signature. We cannot verify that you are indeed one Mr. and Mrs. Daffy Duck, as you signed."

Esro pursed his lips and looked away. Mondrian blinked, frowned, and glanced at Brachis.

"Falsification of registration forms alone would be grounds for expulsion from the program," the man continued. "But with all the other trouble you've caused..."

He shook his head, then waved his arm to indicate the world around them.

"Coming here, for instance. You had absolutely no business here. Those beings have evolved tens of millions of years beyond your present level. Whatever could you have been thinking?"

Esro glared back at the guy, afraid for the moment to speak, afraid of what might happen if he let his true anger out.

Mondrian leaned toward the man, clearly understanding now that he was both incredibly powerful and very unstable, and that he should not be annoyed any more than could be helped.

"We simply wanted to go home," she told him.

The man stared back at her for a moment, as if unable to grasp such a concept. At last he sighed.

"Home. I see. You simply refuse to cooperate, and see no benefit in doing so. You are expressing some sort of civil disobedience."

Esro leaned toward Mondrian, whispering, "What is he talking about?"

Mondrian ignored him.

"Yes," she replied.

Another sigh.

"But my great experiment... You do not feel it to be worthy of your time?"

He paced in a small circle, speaking softly.

"The gathering of so many races from across the cosmos... The interaction of cultures and civilizations, at every imaginable level of development... How can you dare refuse to help advance such a cause?"

"This is not *our* cause," Mondrian answered. "We have our *own* causes."

"Selfish," the man replied. "Selfish, and precisely what I would expect from an inferior race."

"We are what we are," Mondrian said. "Are you so much greater that you cannot understand this? Do you feel no such loyalty to your own people? Your cause is important to you, yes. But ours is important to us as well."

The man looked up.

"*You* have a cause?"

He smirked.

"I assume you refer to the usual for your kind: Killing, exploiting... The one called Okaar is such a fine example of your kind's single-minded pursuit of your great cause. I have watched him, from the periphery, as he hides in his little segment of the Dead Areas. He takes what he desires, enslaves his fellow beings, and kills any who dare to stand up to him."

Mondrian's eyes grew fierce.

"Not anymore, he doesn't."

The man frowned.

"What?"

She glared back at him.

"Okaar, if he still lives at all, will surely not be causing anyone any problems for quite some time."

"Thanks to us," Esro added. Then he pointed at Mondrian.

"Well, mostly, thanks to her."

The little man looked at her strangely, then seemed to move into a trance. Several seconds passed—long enough for Mondrian and Esro to exchange worried glances—and then the man opened his eyes again.

"Yes... I see what you mean..."

He winced.

"Oh my, that must have been painful..."

He paused, raising a hand to his high forehead.

"It is always such a strain, finding ways to look into the Dead Areas...."

He studied Mondrian carefully, as if really seeing her for the first time. His mouth became a flat line.

"You brought this about?"

"*We* did," she replied, placing one arm on Esro's shoulder.

The man seemed to consider this.

They waited, there on the grassy field, the perfect sky frozen immobile overhead. All sound stopped. The wind was still. They both held their breath.

"This, then, is your cause?" he asked at last. "Combating those who would harm others, harm your society?"

"Yes."

Mondrian nodded firmly.

"I have served most of my life as an officer of a starfleet dedicated to preserving the peace and ending the threat of beings such as Okaar—even though he was originally a fellow officer."

She looked to Esro.

"And this man uses his admittedly primitive scientific and technical knowledge to bravely combat such menaces."

Esro wasn't sure whether he wanted to kiss Mondrian for that, or knock her in the head.

"This armor of his that you so casually dismiss," she went on, "represents the peak of his world's technical prowess—created solely to help him protect his society from the predators which threaten it!"

That part made him feel a little better, anyway.

The little man now looked at both of them with full attention. He stepped back, assessing them.

387

"This is true? Then you are..."

"Protectors," Esro stated flatly, getting with the program at last. "Defenders. Sentinels. Whatever you want to call us. It may sound corny, but it's what I've always striven to be, to live up to. I don't know if I've ever succeeded—heck, I'm just an inventor; Mondrian's probably twice the hero I've ever been—but that's the goal, and I'll never stop trying to reach it. To give back to my society, to my people a bit of the safety and opportunity that I've always been so thankful for myself."

"Oh, indeed?" the little man asked, looking at them both anew.

Esro sensed a possible trap—*I'll keep the heroes here if they're so unusual!*—and sought to avoid it.

"There are lots more on your station who are at least as noble as us. We've met several just since we've been here. Give them a chance." He smiled. "Look for it. It's there."

"I... I have never considered such a thing," the little man said softly. "Though your cultures are primitive, your goals could be noble. It seems incomprehensible, and yet..."

He rubbed his chin with his free hand.

"Perhaps..."

Mondrian took him gently by the arms, and gazed down into his face.

"Perhaps you should return us home. Perhaps we can make some small difference there, where we're needed."

She smiled.

"And perhaps intergalactic society can evolve just fine without you conducting your own experiments on it."

The little man jerked away, suddenly seeming recalcitrant. But then he turned back to them, his face fallen.

"Very well. I'm not admitting that you are right, or that you have persuaded me—and I am certainly *not* going to end my experiments—but..."

Mondrian nodded seriously. Esro followed suit.

"But..."

He frowned.

"I *do* admit that things are much too complicated with the two of you here. Perhaps it would indeed be better if you were... *elsewhere...*"

"I don't like the sound of that," Esro started to say. But it was too late. The little man's voice trailed off, and he waved his hand.

The light flared around them and swallowed them up.

From within the light, a voice seemed to be saying, "...Should've never brought another *red* one aboard. One was quite enough..."

50

And then the light faded, and Esro and Mondrian felt solid matter beneath them. They were seated. Seated...

...Back in Mondrian's spacecraft. As their vision gradually returned to normal, they looked around in surprise, glancing at one another with puzzled expressions. Then they both turned their gazes forward, to the windows, and saw what lay ahead.

"Esro, is that—?"

"Oh, yeah," Esro said, a wide grin spreading across his features. "I'd know it anywhere."

The widow was filled with the blue-white globe of the Earth.

Relief spread over them both.

"We did it! We're back!"

Brachis let out a whoop of joy.

"Yes..."

Esro glanced at Mondrian. She didn't seem nearly as excited.

"Hey..."

He blinked, realization setting in.

"Oh. Maybe he could have sent you back home—your real home. But..."

"No, it's all right."

She smiled at Esro wistfully.

"He seemed to know where I need to be. At least...at least for now."

"But you..."

Esro paused, thought for a moment, then shut up.

They flew on in silence for a while, Mondrian doting over the ship's heavily damaged systems while Esro wrestled with what they'd just witnessed, and all they'd experienced, and all the thoughts spinning around in his brain.

Finally Mondrian broke the silence.

"There were so many others there, on that station. If only we could have freed them, too... Convinced him to stop his experiments..."

Esro nodded, then shrugged.

"I'm not even really sure how we got *ourselves* free. Other than that you psyched him out."

He grinned at her.

"Nice job, by the way. But—what could we have done for the rest of them? Nothing that I know of, if that guy wasn't willing to change."

He sighed.

"And who *was* that guy, anyway?"

She hesitated, then, "I was not certain at first, but I think I may have a general idea. Esro, there are legends among my people, legends that have sometimes closely matched those of other races we associate with. It could be coincidence, of course, but..."

She touched her lips with a fingertip.

"The legends speak of a number of great, cosmic beings who dwell within this universe, each of them possessed of inestimable power. Sometimes they are described as 'Rivals,' for reasons we do not understand. We believe the Xorexes are servants of one of them. From your news reports, we know that you and your associates encountered the being called 'Kabaraak' earlier. He is the servant of another of these Rivals. Perhaps this...this *little man*... was yet another."

Esro took this in and nodded slowly.

"Ultraa believes that Kabaraak's master is on his way to Earth now," he said.

Mondrian stared back at him for long seconds.

"Then your world's predicament is far graver than I had even imagined."

"All the more reason to get back there," Esro said. "To figure something out before it's too late."

"Indeed."

Esro thought about all of this, rubbing at the beard that had grown in across his chin.

"I'm still not remotely clear on what this guy wanted," he said. "I mean, abducting various beings from all over the universe... Sticking them aboard a big anthill of a space station... Just to see how they all interrelate? Why?"

Mondrian shook her head slowly.

"We may never understand the actions of beings of that nature."

She looked up at him, smiling at last.

"But at least we are free."

"Yeah."

They watched the globe of the Earth expand, filling the screen. After a while, Esro began to fiddle with a connection on his gauntlet. He snorted.

"Why in the world did I make this cyberlink so big?" he asked himself. "It could be microscopic and still do the same work. Heck—"

He pulled the glove off and stared into it.

"—It could be twice as efficient if I just rerouted the... the..."

He paused, blinked, looked up at Mondrian.

"What was I just saying? What—?"

Mondrian was staring out the viewport, seemingly oblivious. Then she suddenly snapped out of it and turned, meeting Esro's eyes.

"The Xorex. It is on the move again. It will soon replicate itself. Many times over. Your friends—your world—they are in terrible danger."

"What?"

Esro stared back at her.

"How do you know that?"

"I...I do not know…"

They sat there for a long while, as the Earth slowly grew to fill the windows. Then Mondrian turned toward Esro again.

"These are not the kinds of things I was trained for at the academy," she said. "I learned about straightforward matters. Navigating a starship. Translating alien languages. Maneuvering in combat. But confronting godlike beings, with so many lives on the line—be it untold billions, or just our own—this is not something I ever thought I would have to do."

Esro straightened up, running a hand through his dark hair. Then he looked at her firmly.

"But you did it," he said. "You saved us."

He felt good—really good—for the first time in days. He held her eyes, sensing her doubts, but also her spirit, her inner fire. He smiled at her, his hand reaching out, covering hers. The good feeling expanded exponentially when she didn't withdraw her own. He turned his head back and stared out the viewport, at the stars, and at the Earth slowly drawing near.

"Head for northern Virginia," Esro said. "For my house."

"Yes."

Mondrian manipulated the controls and they zoomed down, down, coming in over nighttime Washington, DC, then quickly out to the suburbs, and to Esro's property. She settled the damaged craft to the ground as best she could, taking out only the tops of a few trees and a power line or two along the way.

Esro raced out of the ship and ran across the lawn, thrilled to be home again—thrilled to be alive. He started to run right up to the front door, then hesitated. A strange premonition came over him. A premonition, perhaps—or perhaps it was a memory, or the other half of a memory, anyway. For whatever reason, he stopped and walked over to the broad window set into the side of the house, instead. He gazed in.

There sat the others, just as he had expected. Lyn, and Ultraa, and Vanadium, and...

"Crap," he said.

And, "Crap crap crap crap crap."

He dashed back across the lawn, shouting at Mondrian, shouting that it was all *wrong*, that they had arrived *too soon*, somehow.

"That little guy screwed us over again," he growled, once they were airborne, lofting away from the mansion and back up into the nighttime sky.

They flew aimlessly above the Virginia countryside for a short while, discussing what to do next.

As they went, Mondrian took the opportunity to lecture upon the dangers of their existing twice in the same time frame.

"I do not know precisely what might happen as a result," she said. "But my people do have some theories, and..."

Esro took all of this in, frowning, growing deeply depressed. He had been so happy to have endured all that they had endured, and to make it all the way back home—only to have it taken from him at the last moment.

"Wait," he said, holding up a hand.

"Yes?"

"All this time travel stuff hurts my brain," he said, "but let's think about it carefully. We know when it is that we first go off in this ship, chasing the Xorex, and get sucked away to the other side of who-knows-where, right?"

She frowned and nodded.

"Yes..."

"And, based on what I can remember from before, from when I was the guy in the house and thought I saw myself looking in the window..."

He calculated quickly, counting off days on his fingers.

"That's just a few days from now," he said.

He paused, relief spreading over his face.

"So all we have to do," he went on, "is lay low for a while. For a few days, at most. Just until the other you—the earlier you—and your ship shows up. Then the other versions of us will go chase the Xorex, and go off to lots of fun adventures with our pal Okaar and the little guy and the giants and..." He sighed. "And, at that point, you and I are free to walk right in the front door. Right?"

He looked at her as if daring her to shoot any holes in his theory.

"I think...I think you are correct," she said after a few moments of consideration. "At least, I can see no immediate reasons why that would not be acceptable."

"Good, good," Esro said, nodding, somewhat mollified over their predicament. After all, he had a plan, now, and a time frame measured only in days. They would be long days, sure, but if he got to spend them with Mondrian—and not in constant peril of their lives, for a change—maybe it would actually be a good thing. A vacation, sort of.

He sat back in the seat, smiling again.

She looked at him curiously.

"Esro," she said, "our arrival here could have caused catastrophic damage to the very universe itself. And yet, now, you actually seem happy about it."

Esro shrugged.

"There's only so many times I can save the universe in a month, before I have to think about myself, for a change. Y'know what I mean?"

She just looked back at him, shaking her head.

"I may never understand you people," she said.

Meanwhile, ten miles to the west and slightly higher up, a trio of silver and purple interceptor craft locked onto Mondrian's ship and accelerated.

51

"Blasphemy! Naught but base blasphemy!"

The Warlord in Red stood before the stasis cabinet, staring in at the frozen form of the previous Warlord. The steady green light of the stasis field reflected through the glass and played across his golden mask.

"You dared this?" he demanded, turning to face Francisco. "You dared do this to a Warlord?"

"But—but he is mad, Master. Mad!"

"You dared this!"

The Warlord in Red turned away and paced back and forth, anger seemingly flooding from his every pore, enough to fill the room.

"He is insane, Master! He meant to go against the Rivals—to tap their energies."

The Warlord in Red peered down at him. His voice became a whisper.

"What?"

"He meant to end the Grand Design in his own way. To reign forever—but only him! Not you and the other Warlords unified together. Only him!"

The Warlord in Red scoffed at this, still pacing.

"You lie. Not one of us would entertain such a scheme. Never!"

"You don't know him, Master. He has never been stable. I tried to end him—to turn the Wheel—but he thwarted me. I passed the judgment of Francisco upon him, but he rejected it."

At this the Warlord in Red whirled and glared at him.

"No! No, he could not have done such a thing—*planned* such a thing. No."

Francisco, still sobbing, merely nodded.

"He wasn't going to merge you all into one, as the Design dictates. He was going to rule forever. Only him! Him forever, alone!"

"No," the larger man said again, but his voice had diminished to a harsh whisper now. He turned to face his predecessor once more, frozen in the box. He leaned closer and peered through the glass, studying the silver mask closely.

"And...and even if he had intended to follow the Design and merge you all," Francisco continued, his voice broken up by sobs, "the dangers of attacking three of the Rivals...*three at once!* Think of the danger to the Design..."

"No," the other said one final time, but the feeling was gone from his voice. By now it was clear he no longer believed his denials.

"I had to stop him somehow," Francisco concluded. "It was my duty."

The Warlord in Red ignored him now. All of his attention was focused on his counterpart, inches away through the glass, as if trying to read his thoughts.

"Very well," he said at last, his voice calmer and quieter now. "I accept what you say."

He looked back at Francisco, who cringed.

"But that means you must complete the job. You must kill him. We cannot both exist at once."

"Yes, yes, Master, I know it. Yes. And I—I was working on ideas for that very thing, when you...arrived. But, with him in stasis, he is both incapacitated and *protected*. Nothing can harm him in there. I will have to—"

"You will have to kill him," the other replied flatly. "All else are details that do not concern me."

The Warlord in Red turned and strode from the room.

"Notify me when he is dead," he called back, before rounding the corner and disappearing.

Francisco moaned softly in the back of his throat. How had it all gone so wrong? How had it come to this? He had only ever sought to fulfill his own role in the Design. He had only—

One of the green indicator lights on the side of the Warlord's cabinet changed to yellow, then to red. Francisco saw this and blinked, then leaned in, looking closer.

Another light changed to red.

And another.

"No..."

They all changed to red.

Francisco whirled and leapt away, seeking to escape.

The stasis cabinet exploded. Metal and glass fragments flew like shrapnel in every direction. Fire and smoke bellowed out, momentarily engulfing the room. Francisco stumbled and fell behind a piece of heavy equipment just in time to avoid being skewered by the debris.

A second later, he raised his head up and looked into the smoke. It was clearing, and something moved within it. Suddenly a tall figure in blue and purple robes emerged from the wrecked cabinet, his silver mask in place and pointed directly at his erstwhile servant.

The little man scrambled backward, horrified.

Purple gauntlets reached out, grasping.

"FRANCISCO!"

52

Ultraa lay back in a recliner in Esro's mansion, a bag of ice across his forehead, his eyes squeezed tightly shut. His fingers gripped the armrests hard enough to leave permanent indentations.

"Um, you okay?"

He opened his eyes—it felt like prying open two steel doors that had been welded shut—and saw Pulsar standing there, gazing down at him, a look of deep concern etched on her oval face. A face, Ultraa was sad to see, that carried bruises from their encounter with Vanadium the previous day.

He set the icepack aside and nodded tiredly.

"I'm fine, Lyn. Fine."

"You don't look so fine."

He sighed, then nodded.

"Well, yeah. I suppose not."

He sat up and gestured around with one hand.

"I mean, look what's left of our team. Esro's gone off to who knows where. Damon's...yeah. And now Vanadium attacks us."

He leaned back again. To Lyn he appeared years older than she had ever seen him.

"And throw in the fact that the government has essentially hung me—us—out to dry... I've tried to reach Jameson at least four times in the past week, to find out what's going on. He hasn't returned my calls. Honestly, I don't know what to make of it all."

Lyn nodded sadly, chewing a fingernail.

"But we can't give up hope," she said, trying desperately to appear positive. "Esro's coming back. I know he is. And as for Vanadium..."

She thought about it for a few seconds, pacing.

"I think we should keep looking for him. We know he was having problems. Maybe he just...blew a fuse, or something."

"We don't even know if he has fuses," Ultraa pointed out. "We don't know that he's a robot at all. Or a man. Or..."

"Yeah," Lyn said, "but we do know one thing. He was our friend. He still is."

Ultraa touched the bruise running across his forehead, his face taking on an expression that seemed to ask, *Oh, really?*

She frowned, then turned and walked toward the door.

"I'm going to keep looking for him. I'm not ready to give up on him—or on Esro—yet."

Ultraa sighed tiredly, then nodded.

"You're right. You're right. Go ahead. I'll be along soon."

He patted a cardboard box that sat on the floor next to him.

"I'm going to finish sorting through Damon's effects. It's well past time I did that."

Lyn winced, as she always did when Damon's name came up.

"Okay. See you soon."

She exited the mansion quickly, not looking back.

Ultraa sat for a long while, not moving at all, his eyes closed again. Then, tiredly, he leaned down and lifted the box, opening it. Reaching inside, he pulled out a stack of papers and set them on the coffee table.

Damon Sinclair's papers.

Ultraa had known he needed to sort through his former partner's effects ever since the man was killed in their battle with the trans-dimensional lunatic called the Warlord. But actually doing so had proven more difficult than he'd imagined it would.

Damon hadn't kept much at the mansion, but Esro had managed to find one boxful of belongings in his old room, and had handed it over to Ultraa. He'd steadfastly avoided it since then, but now he had no more excuses. So he dug into it.

Sifting past old copies of *Playboy* and sketchbooks filled with amateurish drawings of personal weapons systems Damon doubtlessly had planned to ask Esro to build for him, Ultraa came across a small, square bound notebook. He looked at it for a moment, then opened it. It looked like some sort of diary, filled with day-by-day accounts of Damon's activities.

"Probably for his autobiography," Ultraa muttered to himself, not unkindly.

He started to read.

He gasped.

He flipped the page. Read more. Leaned forward in the chair, growing tense. Flipped more pages.

"Damon," he whispered. "Oh, Damon… Oh, no…"

Two seconds after he had finished reading the last page of the diary, he was out the door, airborne, rocketing toward the Pentagon at top speed.

53

Esro had just drifted off to sleep when the flight cabin of Mondrian's ship shook violently, nearly hurling him out of his seat.

"What the—?"

He strapped himself in even as he looked around at the various screens and monitors arrayed around the cabin. Alarms were sounding and lights flashing wildly. Beside him, Mondrian touched several controls and then gazed up at the tactical display, currently shimmering into existence across the forward windows.

"We are under attack," she reported calmly, manipulating a series of controls.

"Huh?"

"They are shooting at us. With extremely powerful beam weapons."

Esro stared up at the display, his stomach twisting. He located their ship easily enough on it—a solid red dot. Three flashing blue dots appeared to be following them.

"Who's 'they?'"

"I do not know."

He watched as the dots drew closer to them.

"Not again," he growled. "Jeez, *now* what?"

The cabin shook again. Another alarm sounded.

"The engines are damaged," Mondrian said, giving him a look of concern. "We must land."

"Yeah…"

The landing was not something Esro would ever want to think back fondly upon. The artificial gravity failed after the next salvo struck them, putting them entirely at the mercy of gee forces, turbulence, and impact. Mondrian understood this and did the best she could. Despite her best efforts, though, the crash nearly killed them both.

Esro helped Mondrian out of the crash webbing and together they struggled to the hatch, the short journey made all the more difficult by the fact that the shuttle rested nearly on its side. Opening the hatch, they were greeted by late-night darkness and the sounds and smells of the deep forest.

"At least we didn't come down over the middle of DC," Esro muttered. "But we have a long walk ahead of us, back to

398

civilization. Assuming we don't get killed by whoever shot us down."

"I did not recognize the configuration of the attacking craft," Mondrian told him. "And their propulsion systems—like nothing I've ever—"

The burst of an energy weapon that struck the shuttle's hull just beside them both cut her off in mid-sentence. Esro grabbed her and pulled them both down, the second shot just missing over their heads. They tumbled out of the entryway and down into the bushes, thorns and pine needles jabbing at them.

Esro snapped his helmet on and checked his power levels. His armor was fully charged, having siphoned energy from the shuttle as they flew. He'd even managed to repair a few of the damaged systems. The boot rockets, however, were pretty much hopeless, their fuel expended and their control systems shot.

No quick getaway, he thought to himself. *That means we have to stand and fight. But—who are we fighting?*

Shots rattled all around them, lighting up the night. In the brief flashes, Esro could make out a number of figures a few dozen yards away, partially hidden in the underbrush. He popped the guns from their gauntlet housings and began firing back indiscriminately.

"I will flush them out," Mondrian told him.

Before he could react to that, she had leapt to her feet and was sprinting from cover to cover, ahead of him.

"Mondy, wait, you—"

Then he remembered she was a highly-trained military officer. She knew what she was doing. At least, he hoped she did.

Surely enough, seconds later, a commotion in the bushes ahead resulted in a tall figure in blue stumbling out into the open. Before the man could move again, Esro nailed him with a quick burst from his wrist-gun.

Mondrian's hair flashed in the dim light, and for a moment Esro actually thought she was flying—soaring through the air for longer than a leap should have carried her.

Huh?

He blinked, and then another blue-clad man tumbled from cover, rolling across the forest floor.

Go, Mondy! he shouted within his mind, his previous thought forgotten. *Go get 'em!*

Esro fired a series of bursts, the last two of which caught the guy in the side and the leg, bringing him down.

Maybe we can *do this*, he thought then, hope rising inside him. *Maybe—*

Mondrian cried out then. Instantly, the firing picked up once more.

She's down! No!

Esro leapt out of his place of concealment and sprinted toward the last spot he'd seen her, bringing up three layers of energy screens around himself as he ran.

Where is she? Where—?

As he ran, he half-noticed an odd, silvery fog forming around him. He had no time to think about it, though. He jumped over a clump of bushes, thinking he'd reached the spot where Mondrian had been hit. At that moment, a barrage of energy blasts converged upon him, driving him down into the grass. His outer screen failed immediately, and frantically he sought to boost the power to the others.

Footsteps sounded from all around him now. Men in dark blue and purple uniforms raced toward him, weapons blazing. He leapt to his feet and charged his guns, preparing to return fire, even as his secondary screen overloaded.

Oh well, he thought. *After everything we've survived, it looks like this is the end of the line. I just wish I knew who these guys were...*

"Take him now," one man shouted. "The Warlord commands it!"

"Huh?"

Esro knew that name. He knew it... *Oh, yeah...*

"The Warlord?" he growled. "That loser?"

A barrage of shots struck the inner force screen. It flickered. Esro groaned.

"The Warlord is *dead!* I saw him die! I—"

The inner screen failed. The beams reached him, struck him.

54

As Francisco ran back into the main chamber of the sanctum, seeking to escape the grasping hands and accusatory words of his old, blue-clad master, a second and nearly identical voice boomed out.

"Release him! *Release him*, traitor to the Design!"

The Warlord dropped Francisco and whirled. He gawked at what he saw there.

"Wha—*no!* No, this is not *possible!*"

The Warlord in Red stood before him, hands on hips, glaring at him through his golden mask.

"It is all too possible, I'm afraid," the newer Warlord replied. "The wheel—"

"—it turned, yes."

The blue Warlord moved back a step, nearly stumbling in his shock.

"I—yes, yes, I see it now. Yes. Francisco put me into stasis. But, to the universe, it was as if I..."

"As if you no longer existed," the Warlord in Red finished for him. "And thus the wheel..."

"...The wheel turned, yes. I do see it. Blasphemy!"

"Oh, blasphemy indeed."

"Another me. The next one."

"But we cannot *both*—"

"—both exist. No, certainly not."

"Defies the entire basis of the Design."

"Cannot share power. Never!"

"And so—"

"So—"

"DIE!"

"DIE!"

Both screamed this last word as they each rushed forward, grappling with one another, murder in their hearts.

The moment they touched one another, ripples spread out across the entire space-time continuum. The floor beneath them shook, the walls rattled, and sparks sprayed from the computers.

Francisco stumbled backward, grabbing a nearby console for support. His eyes widened in panic.

They cannot both exist at once, he understood then, *and yet they do. And the universe cannot accept that fact. Reality itself is being torn asunder!*

Terrified, he fled.

He understood his mistake, now that it was too late to do anything about it.

The Warlord had been reaching for *something*, yes, when Francisco had zapped him with the stasis beam—but he hadn't been reaching for a *weapon*. Somehow, he had set up an override that had either been able to transmit out of stasis—highly unlikely—or else he had transmitted instructions into machinery that would work on time delay. Either way, he had managed to override the cabinet's controls and free himself.

Francisco cursed himself for not anticipating that contingency. The blue-clad Warlord was insane, yes—but he was also quite formidable.

Rounding the corner, he found himself back in the stasis room. The smoke had cleared away entirely now, the flames put out by automatic systems. And now he could see, lying on the floor in front of the cabinets that had formerly housed them, the two time-lost figures he had helped abduct earlier. Obviously, their cabinets had been damaged when the Warlord escaped.

As he looked on, cringing at the shouts and sounds of battle echoing from the next room, he saw the man in gray armor cough and start to rise. Beside him, the red-skinned woman rolled over and sat up, rubbing her head. Quickly Francisco concealed himself behind a console and watched, listening.

"What—what happened?" the man asked. "Where *are* we?"

"I only remember the ship being attacked," the woman replied. "We crashed…"

"And a fight outside, in the woods," the man added.

"I was shot," the woman said.

"We got a couple of 'em, but—yeah, me, too."

Francisco gnawed at one long fingernail. He looked at the two people on the floor, then back at the room behind him, where his two masters fought. The floor shook again, more savagely than before. The space-time ripples were now visible all around.

It was worse than he had even thought it would be. The universe would be torn apart if this continued. One of the Warlords had to go, and go soon—if not dead, then at least far enough away from the other that their proximity within this plane would not rip the universe into pieces. With the two Warlords in direct contact, as they were now, the results would be immediate, and catastrophic.

"Oh," he muttered. "Oh, no. Must do something. Must…"

The man in gray armor had seen him.

"Hey, buddy—hey! Who are you? Where are we?"

Francisco scurried forward. He started to reply, then frowned.

"A moment," he muttered. "Just a moment…"

He took a small device from one of his pockets and held it up in front of the two people. Seeing the readout, he smiled and sighed with relief. At least one thing had straightened itself out.

"No longer time-lost," he told them, smiling warmly. "Now back in your own time, yes."

The woman nodded immediately, a slight smile crossing her face. The man studied him a moment, then seemed to gain a glimmer of understanding, as well.

"Time-lost. Yeah. That's right—we were sent back from the future, but too early."

"Not any longer," Francisco said, smiling broadly now. "But....but you can do nothing here."

"Here? Where is here, exactly?"

"No, no, nothing you can do here. Go, go, you must go."

The man was on his feet now, helping the woman up. The sounds of battle had grown even louder, and the time-space ripples shuddered the walls around them.

"What's going on in there?" the man asked, pointing past Francisco and toward the next room, from whence the rippling effect seemed to emanate.

"A space-time distortion," the woman observed, clearly very concerned. "What is happening?"

"Nothing—nothing I cannot handle," he replied, frowning. "You must go now."

"Hey, wait a minute," the man said, pointing a finger at him. "I remember you! You worked for that guy, the Warlord! You—you're the one who *killed* him, right?"

"Killed one, yes, one... But now two more to deal with," Francisco muttered.

Before the others could object, he snapped a small device from his tool belt and clicked the settings dial on it. Then he hesitated, looking from the device to the two people and then back down again.

"But where to, where to?"

He remembered the battle he'd seen underway, in some near-future moment, in a city on Earth, involving big robots and a group of humans he had encountered before. Quickly he set the coordinates as he remembered them.

"Your friends," he said then. "Your friends will need you. Go to them. Save your planet."

"What? But—"

Pointing the little black cube at the two still-disoriented and confused people, he clicked a button on it. A shimmering hole in space opened up between him and the other two. The portal swept forward, swallowed them, and vanished.

Satisfied, Francisco replaced the cube on his belt, then scurried back into the other room.

By this point, the floor of the main chamber had begun to collapse. Vast cracks shot up the walls, the electronic equipment tumbled down and shorted out all around, and great fires burned in every corner.

At the center of it all, two titanic figures stood locked in mortal combat, blue robes and red robes flaring out behind each of them, metal-masked faces glaring at one another, hands locked tightly overhead as they contended for supremacy. Blazing lightning flared around them both, wreathing them in fire.

Francisco hopped frantically from one foot to the other as he watched the two of them in their single-minded war. He knew full well that neither of them cared any longer whether they destroyed the universe around them or not—something that might well happen, and soon, if they were not separated.

"Oh—oh, master, oh, *look!*"

The image of the Warlord's space station filled the main screen. Its vast parabolic dish, so painstakingly constructed over many weeks by the Warlord's slaves, shimmered as waves of disruption spread over it.

"Oh… Oh…"

The dish appeared to bend in several places, its great girders and struts buckling. Its vibrations increased in intensity, even as cables separated, spraying showers of sparks into the blackness. Then, finally, it exploded, hurling flames, equipment, and workers across the void.

Part of Francisco was horrified to witness such a fate for his master's construction. The other part of him reveled in it—for was this not the very keystone of that Warlord's scheme, a scheme destined to bring this and so much more misery and horror down upon them all?

The chamber shook more violently still. The great sanctum itself was about to come apart at the seams, surely dropping them all down into the chasm beneath it.

As the two Warlords smashed away at one another, oblivious to the events around them, their blue or red fists crashing relentlessly into silver or gold masks, Francisco made his choice. He raced forward, pulling a small grenade from his belt, and hurled it between the two. *What difference,* he thought as he ran forward, *would a little more damage mean to this room now?*

The grenade's explosion ripped through the chamber, hurling the two Warlords apart. Each of them landed roughly, protected by their armor from the worst of the blast, but each cursing and struggling to rise.

Francisco did not hesitate. Taking the small cube from his belt again, he pointed it at the Warlord in Red, as the man sought to regain his feet.

The shimmering portal opened once more, swallowing that Warlord.

"No," the blue Warlord cried, seeing what was happening. *"No!* Coward! Come back! Come back and face the *true* Warlord!"

Smiling, Francisco pointed it at himself and clicked the button, again generating the portal. He stepped into it, following his new, red-clad master through.

"NO!"

The doorway winked out behind Francisco and the little cube dropped to the floor, exploding.

The blue Warlord cried out, shaking his fists at the sky—or, more accurately, at the cracked and disintegrating roof of his cavern-like sanctum.

Yet with the Warlord in Red transported to some distant locale, far away from his blue incarnation, the ripples and quakes and distortions ended almost immediately. The time-space continuum almost gratefully reverted to its normal course.

The walls ceased their shaking. The flames died out. Eventually, the smoke cleared.

And there, in the ruined remains of his devastated sanctum, the blue-clad Warlord sat upon his thronelike chair, gazing at the horrendous wreckage all around him.

He had removed the silver mask and pulled his hood back to reveal a mop of thick, brown hair. Leaning forward, he rested his chin in one gauntleted hand. His armor was gashed and torn, the flesh beneath it bruised and bleeding. Indeed, blood pooled in his boots and on the floor beneath him. But he scarcely noticed any of this.

Instead, his eyes focused incessantly on the big screen, showing the crumbled remains of his siphoning array. Showing the crumbled remains of all of his hopes and dreams.

His plans had been betrayed. Francisco was gone. And another Warlord—*a blasphemy upon nature itself!*—strode the universe.

He thought upon all of this, and he gazed at his wrecked sanctum, and he pondered his frustrated plans. And he knew in his heart that he was not defeated—no, not at all.

A momentary setback. Nothing more.

Soon, he would have revenge.

Revenge on Francisco. Revenge upon that walking abomination in red and gold. Revenge upon the wheel—the Grand Design itself!

Soon. Soon.

Another panel above his head exploded, showering him with sparks.

Ignoring it all, he brooded.

55

"For all that Esro Brachis and Ultraa and the girl can be great annoyances to us," Jameson remarked, "I must admit, they have proven useful, from time to time."

He sat back in his executive-model leather chair, gazing out the window at the view of Washington, DC, in the distance.

Adcock stood to his right, hands clasped behind his back, silent as usual. On the wall to one side, the ancient oaken clock ticked away the seconds loudly, swiftly.

Another day is nearly over already, Jameson thought, *yet still there remains so much to do…*

Adcock, clearing his throat, appeared to consider Jameson's words for a moment, then nodded, very reluctantly, once.

"Useful. I suppose so."

"After all," Jameson continued, turning back around toward the office's interior, "they may have saved the world at least once, already."

"But then, that is what the government pays Ultraa to do," Adcock noted quietly. "Or, at least, *used* to pay him to do."

Jameson sighed heavily.

"It's not that I *wanted* to end our relationship with him, you know. To replace him."

"Yet you made that decision."

"I had to! The man is just too…independent. Too unpredictable. And, above all else, too much the boy scout."

"That always served us well in the past."

"Very much so, yes," Jameson replied, nodding. "But things have changed. Times have changed. And our own operations have grown much bigger, much more complex. We simply cannot afford to have him poking around in our business any longer. Not when we have the Field Marshal and his team, which is...well...*almost* as dependable as Ultraa and his associates—but far more controllable!"

Adcock nodded.

"I don't disagree with you," he said. "Far from it. I merely know how far back your own history goes, with regard to Ultraa. He's worked for you, for the US Government, for many, many years. And so I ask myself if you will be willing and able to cut him out of the service, entirely."

"For our sakes, yes," Jameson shot back with a glare. He didn't add, *For his own sake, too...*

"Very well," Adcock said, making a placating gesture with one hand.

"After all," Jameson continued, "it's not as if he knows anything about the big picture. It's not like he would actually come down here and—"

At that moment, the door to Jameson's office swung open, hard, crashing back against the wall.

"Jameson!"

Both of them looked up, startled.

A tall, muscular, blond man stood in the doorway, clearly furious. He wore a skintight white suit with red gloves and boots and belt, and clutched a sheaf of papers in his left hand. Three secretaries were arrayed behind him, their faces betraying their confusion and panic. Of course none of them had dared try to physically restrain him. It was, after all, *Ultraa.*

He started forward.

Adcock stepped quickly out of the way, moving surreptitiously to one side. Jameson recovered his wits and composure as quickly as possible and smiled weakly up at the hero.

"Ultraa! My boy! What is this? What can we do for you?"

He gestured at the secretaries, who exited the office and pulled the door closed behind them.

"You know what this is," the blond man growled. "You know very well."

He strode angrily up to Jameson's desk and violently slammed the stack of papers onto the surface.

"You had Damon spying on us. You have abducted—or attempted to abduct—numerous individuals with paranormal powers over the past several years. You even tried to kidnap Lyn!"

Jameson frowned deeply.

"What would make you say such things, my boy?" he asked innocently.

Adcock had moved slowly around to Ultraa's left. The hero whirled, jabbing a finger at the dark-clad agent.

"Not another step, you. I mean it."

Adcock froze. His face remained expressionless.

Ultraa turned back to Jameson. He pointed a red-gloved finger at the pile of papers between them.

"It's all right here," he said.

Jameson looked down momentarily, then back up at Ultraa, his face still conveying innocence and incomprehension.

"What's here?"

"Damon. Damon Sinclair. The *late* Damon Sinclair. Maybe you remember him better as the Cavalier."

"I remember Damon, certainly. His death was tragic, a great loss for—"

"For your intelligence-gathering operation. For your technology-stealing enterprises!"

"What do you—"

"It's all here! He spells it all out!"

Ultraa slapped his hand down on the papers again.

"You were paying him to hand over Esro Brachis's technology to you. And also to freelance—to help with some of the abductions you've been carrying out."

Ultraa scoffed.

"No wonder you haven't needed me lately. You probably have an entire super-team at your disposal, now. I'm sure that's where most of the Field Marshal's crowd came from. Though how you've gotten them to work for you, knowing they were kidnapped, is beyond me."

"Ultraa, my boy, please, please. This is nonsense."

He looked down at the papers again, lifting the top page and glancing over it briefly.

"You cannot tell me you take seriously anything Damon Sinclair said or wrote, can you?"

Ultraa glared at him.

"Because, let's face it, the boy was not the brightest—"

408

Ultraa brought his fist down hard on the desktop, rattling the very walls.

"Keep your mouth shut about Damon," he hissed. "He may have had his own issues, but we all do. And his heart was in the right place—even if you got into his head a little bit, and got him to do things he knew he shouldn't have."

Ultraa pointed at the papers again.

"He says so, in there. Says that he felt awful about what he was doing, and was going to tell me about it—as soon as he worked up the courage. He was just too scared of me. Scared of me!"

Ultraa barked a sound that was halfway between a laugh and a sob.

"If even half of what he says in there is true, then I really don't blame him," Ultraa said. He jabbed a finger in Jameson's face. *"I blame you!"*

"I—I—"

Jameson stammered, unsure of how to proceed. He looked up for Adcock, who was still standing motionless to Ultraa's left and slightly behind him.

"How can we handle this, then?" Jameson asked. "How can we get beyond this, and back to doing the business of the country and the people?"

"We're not getting 'beyond' this," Ultraa replied angrily. "You're going down for it. You and your slimy friend over there."

Adcock froze as Ultraa glanced over at him again. The man's hand had raised and was reaching for something hidden on the wall.

"I mean it, you," Ultraa repeated. "I'd just as soon knock you out and continue this conversation with Jameson one on one."

"Adcock, please, sit down," Jameson said.

The man did not move.

"There is no conversation," Ultraa said. "You're both coming with me. Right now."

"No. Not yet."

Everyone in the room froze.

"I cannot have this happening yet."

The voice did not belong to Jameson, or to Adcock, or to Ultraa. It belonged to the fourth man in the room—the man who had been there all along.

That fourth man leaned casually against the wall, halfway toward the far end of the room. About six feet tall, he wore a nondescript blue suit and dark shoes. His blondish-brownish hair was combed in a basic, conservative style. His facial features were, on the whole,

409

completely unremarkable. In his left hand he held a small, golden object, about the size of a pocket watch.

After another moment in which no one moved or spoke, the fourth man strolled casually across the room, stopping just behind Ultraa.

"I had hoped not to have to do something like this just yet," he said, before reaching into one pocket and pulling forth another small, golden object. This one he attached to Ultraa's unmoving shoulder. It stuck there as if glued in place.

He walked around Ultraa, moving into the space between him and the desk, facing him directly. The blond man stood utterly frozen, his eyes glazed over, his muscles locked in place.

"Time for you to go away for a bit," the man said.

He reached up and clicked a button on the object on Ultraa's shoulder. Immediately Ultraa relaxed into a sort of a parade-rest posture, but his facial expression remained blank.

"Better," the man said. "Conserves power. After all, I can't keep the entire room blanketed much longer."

He led Ultraa over to an empty space on one wall, between two bookshelves. The wall slid open there, revealing a hidden door. The man directed Ultraa into it and closed the door behind him, before turning back toward the room.

"Ah. That's better. And now…"

He clicked the watch-shaped device in his hand once again.

"Adcock, sit—"

Jameson had begun speaking at once, but just as quickly he stopped, blinking. He looked around the room, clearly disoriented. Adcock did the same.

"How pleasant to see you two gentlemen once again," the man said.

"Who—"

Jameson was halfway out of his chair, one hand reaching for the pistol he kept in his center drawer. Then he paused, his eyes focusing on the intruder. He hesitated, suddenly *remembering*…

"You," he breathed.

The man said nothing, waiting.

Jameson slowly sunk back into his overstuffed chair, relaxing. Adcock, who had stepped forward as well, moved back to his previous position to Jameson's right.

"You…"

The man stood in the center of the room, smiling.

"Ultraa," Jameson said suddenly.

"Yes," Adcock agreed.

"Where—where did he go?"

"He is no longer your concern," the man said.

Somehow, that answer didn't sit right with Jameson. At the moment, however, he was more concerned with who this guy was, how he'd gotten in here, and—most disturbing of all—why he seemed so incredibly *familiar...*

The man stared back at him, continuing to smile, waiting.

Jameson found he couldn't look back at him. Somehow, the very act itself was painful. Yet, at the same time, the longer Jameson did manage to look at him, the less substantial, the less...real... he seemed to become. After a couple of seconds, he forced himself to look away, irrationally fearing the man might otherwise vanish altogether.

"Who are you?" Jameson asked.

"Who am I? You mean you don't remember?"

"I—"

Jameson searched his memories, thinking, thinking, and then slowly remembering...*something.* Something like the tiniest tip of a vast iceberg, mostly concealed beneath the deep, dark waters of memory. He felt, somehow, that this was *not the first time* he had forgotten this man, nor the first time he was remembering him.

No, not by a long shot.

"I—"

He hesitated, fearful of saying more.

Why do I keep forgetting him? What's the matter with me, that I would forget—

He frowned.

Who?

"Ultraa was not the end of it," the man was saying. "Merely the tiniest distraction, in the much, much bigger picture."

"The bigger picture?"

Jameson found his head was spinning, as if he were on some amusement park ride.

"They are coming," the man continued. "Coming sooner than anyone knows."

He walked around to the front of Jameson's desk, lifting a few items from it, including a crystal paperweight in the shape of a small globe. Examining the items momentarily, he replaced them randomly on the desktop.

"They?"

Jameson lifted his right hand to scratch at his head, paused halfway, and returned the hand to his lap. Idly he wondered if he were about to vomit.

"Who are *they*?" he managed to say. "And—I apologize, but I seem to have forgotten your name. Again," he hastily added, feeling guilty.

"You can call me Nation," the man said. "Randall Nation."

He leaned closer.

"You remember."

Jameson blinked.

"Ah, yes. Of course. I apologize, Mr. Nation. I won't forget it again."

The man seemed to emit a tiny laugh at that, but did not otherwise reply.

Jameson instantly began to worry that his words had been false. After all, there was simply nothing memorable about the man. Nothing stood out.

Nothing... except his *mouth*. It was *broad*. Broad and *wide*. Wider than what might be considered average, Jameson concluded. *Or natural.*

And one more thing about it: It was twisted into the slightest of smiles. A tiny, yet somehow cruel, leering smile. An almost unnoticeable, imperceptible expression that nonetheless carried with it far more meaning that a whole volume of words.

The broad, cruel mouth opened again, and spoke:

"They are coming," it said again. "They are *all* coming. But do not fear."

The smile flattened, still present but subtly altered. Now it was a humorless, deadly smile.

"For I shall be here, waiting for them all."

The smile vanished altogether.

"And then we shall see...what we shall see."

Jameson and Adcock stared at him, and for an instant Jameson thought the man's skin grew red...blood red. But his eyes had grown vacant, glazed over, and he could not be sure.

The man nodded to himself, once.

"Good day, gentlemen. I can show myself out."

He bowed slightly.

"See you soon."

And with that, the man walked across the office, opened the door, and passed through, closing it softly behind him.

Jameson, frowning, looked down at his desk.

Adcock stood absolutely still, saying nothing.

Perhaps five seconds ticked by on the antique oak clock occupying the far wall of the office. Five long and glacially slow seconds. Five heartbeats, each as vast as an age of the world.

Jameson blinked. His mind felt sluggish. He felt as though he were forgetting something—something very important. Something—

No. Gone.

Ah well. Couldn't have been that important.

He looked at Adcock.

Adcock blinked as well. He looked back at Jameson.

They both looked around the office, just as empty now as it had been seconds earlier—as it had been ever since they began their meeting.

"Did you say something?" both asked at once.

"No."

"No."

Jameson frowned, scratched at his chin. He noticed then that the items on his desktop had somehow been moved from their proper places.

When did that happen? I must be getting senile...

Absently he began to rearrange them.

Adcock ran his tongue over his teeth, growing suddenly, unexpectedly anxious—for no reason that he could tell.

"What were we talking about?" Jameson asked at last.

Adcock touched a fingertip to his lips.

"Ah," he said. "Ultraa's group. And the Field Marshal's."

"Yes," Jameson said, his desk orderly again, his world calm and controlled once more. "Our two sets of puppets. Each group doing our bidding, and neither group fully appreciating how little control they have over their own business, their own lives."

"Indeed," Adcock said.

Jameson leaned back in his big, leather chair. He propped his feet up on the corner of the desk.

"How very nice it is to be the one pulling all the strings," he said, "and to know, in turn, that no one is pulling the strings on you."

EPILOGUE:
Five Days from Now

Esro Brachis stumbled out of the trans-dimensional portal Francisco had shoved him through, Mondrian emerging just behind him. Disoriented, the two of them tripped and fell to the soft, grassy earth.

Grassy earth.

Esro blinked. On his hands and knees, he looked down at the thick, lush, green stuff under him. Immediately he capitalized the "E."

"Earth!"

"It would seem so," Mondrian agreed. "Back once again. But," she added, clicking on a small device incorporated into her uniform sleeve, "are we in the right *time*? I didn't suspect I would need to check that, last time. But now I am taking no chances."

Esro nodded. He didn't much care for the question, but he knew it was a vital one. Groaning a little, he sat up and looked at their immediate surroundings.

"I know this place," he said after a moment, seeing marble buildings in the near distance, beyond the grassy lawn. "We're on the National Mall. Washington, DC."

"Your capital, yes," Mondrian agreed, still studying her device.

Then she glanced up and screamed.

Esro whirled and looked where she was looking. He nearly screamed as well.

"Aw, no."

His eyes did not want to believe what they saw.

It appeared as if something was in the process of devouring the very world itself, excavating great pits and chasms. Fires burned from deep in the world's crust, flames licking up at the smoke-filled air.

Esro gaped at the sight. His weary legs grew unsteady beneath him. Raising a hand to his brow, blocking the sun, he searched for answers. And thus he saw what must have been responsible for the devouring.

About a hundred yards away, but moving in their direction, came a big, silver, manlike shape. Parts of it were shaded gold, parts other colors. A hazy sphere of energy surrounded it as it moved.

Esro tapped Mondrian on the shoulder and pointed. She nodded silently.

It was the robot. The very one they had been chasing before, in the shuttle, when they had suddenly been pulled through the wormhole and everything afterward had gone so wrong.

The *Xorex*, he remembered Mondrian calling it.

But not just one. Oh, no. Not just one, at all.

Rows of them. Rows and rows. Rank upon rank, as far as the eye could see.

An army of Xorexes. And clearly they were in the process of eating the very planet itself.

"Um, Mondy," Esro found himself saying. "I think maybe we made another wrong turn."

"No," Mondrian replied, pointing to the readout displayed on the small device built into her sleeve. "We have returned to the proper place and time. But, in our absence…"

She pointed vaguely ahead, at the carnage, the disaster unfolding.

"It is as I feared," she was whispering fiercely. "What Captain DeSkai feared—what we *all* feared, all along. It has replicated. And now, either the Xorexes will devour this world, or our Starfleet will arrive to destroy the entire planet before the infestation can spread."

Esro listened to what she was saying with a sort of tired and grim acceptance. He took one more look at the horrendous sight, shook his head, and pulled his battered helmet on once again.

"And to think," he muttered, "I was really looking forward to a nice, hot bath…"

BOOK THREE:
APOCALYPSE
RISING

Ami:
This one was yours from the start.

"Li is both the means which sets the example for others, and the end which maximizes understanding, pleasure, and the greater good."
—Hsun Tzu

"Li: The course of life as it is intended to go."
—Chinese translation

"Your humble servant is really not worthy to understand Li."
—Confucius

"Who can?!"
—Esro Brachis

PROLOGUE:
The Far Side of the Galaxy

An armada of starships the likes of which few sentient eyes had ever beheld lay spread out across the space between planets Kilan-2 and Kilan-3. Each of the ships possessed an arsenal of small fighters, medium attack vessels, foot soldiers by the thousands, bombs, missiles, particle beam weapons, and massive-yield thermonuclear devices. In short, each one of the two hundred capital ships of the fleet held within itself the capacity to utterly lay waste to an entire planet, if its captain so chose.

At the moment, the fleet's admiral was considering that very option.

Crimson-skinned and white-haired like most of his people, Grand Admiral Agus DeSkai stood on the observation platform of his flagship's bridge, his dark blue uniform immaculate, his white-gloved hands clasped behind his back. His dark eyes stared out through the transparent dome at Kilan-2, a lovely sight with its brown and green continents and its swirling cloud cover. And he pondered its fate.

I do not wish to bring death to such a place—nor to its sister world, he thought, his eyes flickering from the blue sphere filling much of the view before him to the tiny, sparkling dot in the distance. And yet the Kur-Bai civil war has gone on long enough, and brought far too much misery and destruction to our people. If we can end it here…

He looked up from his ruminations long enough to acknowledge the new officers coming onto the deck with the shift change, then turned back to the dome again, staring out as he had for the past two hours.

The Circle is nearly stamped out, once and for all. The rebellion is almost crushed.

He allowed himself a small nod of satisfaction. It had been, after all, a very long campaign, and he had not seen his family or his homeworld in over two years. His nephew, Tarin DeSkai, had been captaining a ship on deep patrol for nearly that long, and the admiral anxiously awaited the chance to visit with him.

And the sooner we dispose of this Circle conspiracy, the sooner we can all go back home for some much-deserved shore leave.

He nodded again.

Only a few of their smaller fleets remain at large, on the fringes of the galaxy. They will be dealt with soon enough. Especially the one called Nah-Shonn—renegade of renegades, traitor even to the traitors themselves.

Nah-Shonn.

That one, with all of his immense mental powers, posed the gravest threat of all, DeSkai knew, and he had eluded all efforts to capture him so far.

I will have him. Yes. And soon.

But now—here—we have the opportunity to destroy their last two planetary holdings. I dare not pass up such an opportunity.

And yet, as he looked down at the fragile planet beneath him, he knew the decision would be a hard one to make, the order a difficult one to issue.

I cannot be sure that everyone there has been corrupted. The Circle's telepaths are ruthless and extremely effective—none quite so much as Nah-Shonn, but still... And yet perhaps some of the population held out—perhaps some of them escaped the mindwiping...

He looked at the planet once more, appreciating its delicate beauty.

Dare I take that chance? With telepaths? With such a rapacious menace, such explosive danger to us all?

The flag captain, Veralyen, strode up to him and saluted smartly.

"All forces are in order, Admiral," he said crisply. "Do we land?"

DeSkai pursed his lips, considered it all one last time, and shook his head.

"No. Arm the warheads."

Captain Veralyen took this in. A veteran of many campaigns, he could not be rattled—not even by such an order as this.

Nevertheless…he needed to be certain. He needed the Admiral to be certain.

"Sir," he said, "if I may be allowed—the Elites were very much looking forward to assaulting the Circle base. They have heard stories of the formidable nature of the Circle's top commandos, and were hoping to prove their mettle in single combat against—"

"No," DeSkai said softly, cutting the captain off. "Recall all the shuttles. When they are all back, you may commence planetary bombardment."

Veralyen accepted this grim order with military stoicism.

"You verify the order to release strategic thermonuclear warheads on this target, sir?"

"Yes," DeSkai replied, almost bitterly.

The captain saluted and turned on his heel, calling the orders to his subordinates even as he marched back onto the bridge proper.

DeSkai took one last, long look at the blue-white sphere below; a sphere that was home to some ten million people—or would be for the next few moments, anyway.

A single tear ran down his cheek.

Wiping it away, he walked back onto the main section of the bridge and stood to one side of the captain's chair, deep in thought. A few seconds later, one of the lieutenants approached him and saluted.

"Admiral, we have received a rerouted communication from one of our deep patrol ships."

"Yes?"

"It—it's from your nephew, sir. Captain DeSkai. I thought you would want to see it."

"Yes. Thank you."

He took the printout from the lieutenant and held it up, reading over it quickly.

Involuntarily, he gasped.

Captain Veralyen stood up from his chair and turned to the Admiral, concern etched on his crimson-skinned face.

"Sir? Is something wrong?"

DeSkai read over the communiqué once more, then met Veralyen's inquisitive look with one of deep concern.

"It is the Worldmind," he said. "His agents are active once more."

The Captain's eyes—pale green and lighter in color than those of most of the Kur-Bai—widened in surprise.

"The Worldmind? But—but not in six centuries have we encountered any new infestations."

"Nonetheless…"

DeSkai handed over the paper, and the captain read it. He paled.

"The Xorex," he breathed, aghast. "The world-killers."

"Indeed."

Swallowing with difficulty, the Captain straightened.

"Then I assume that is our next destination, sir."

DeSkai nodded, seemingly lost in thought again. He looked down at Kilan-2, where bright lights were blossoming across its surface.

After a few seconds, Veralyen considered himself dismissed, saluted, and turned to go and issue the orders.

"Captain," DeSkai called to him as he walked away.

The younger man looked back.

"Sir?"

The Admiral watched the face of the planet they orbited brighten—blindingly bright, all over—and then grow dark, so dark, black swirling clouds of radioactive ash blanketing its face.

"Make sure the fleet holds enough warheads in reserve that we can quite thoroughly sterilize the planet with the Xorex infestation—what was it called?"

The Captain looked down at the paper DeSkai had given him.

"Earth, sir."

"Yes. Yes. Make sure we have enough on hand to do the job thoroughly and properly. Then order preparations for jump to begin."

"Yes, sir," Veralyen responded, saluting. He started to turn away and issue the orders, but paused as the Admiral raised a hand.

"Before you do that, Captain, order the ships at Kilan-3 to commence bombardment there, as well. They can catch up to us after they are…"

He considered his words carefully.

"…After they are finished with their task."

7

Pulsar was alone.

A shining golden streak flying low over the northern Virginia countryside, Lyn Li narrowed her eyes and focused tightly on the landscape before and beneath her. All the while, her anger surged up inside her like a coiled spring.

The US Government's official sanctioning of her team had been withdrawn and given to a rival group, leaving her own legal status and her employment in question.

"Gaaah."

Her younger sister had been drawn into that team, under somewhat dubious circumstances—circumstances that might well amount to kidnapping.

"Gaaah!"

And now, in one fashion or another, all of her teammates—her friends!—had completely vanished.

"GAAAAH!"

She wiped at tears that had started to streak down the sides of her face. Meanwhile she strengthened the glowing golden force field she was projecting around herself as she flew; clearly it was allowing the wind to get through and irritate her eyes.

Yeah, that's what it is.

The lush Virginia forests streaked past, giving way from time to time to farmlands, highways, or towns. Lyn noticed none of it. All of her thoughts dwelt with her absent friends.

Esro—where are you?

Esro Brachis, the brilliant inventor and Lyn's mentor in the areas of science and technology, had run aboard an alien shuttle just as it was taking off, carrying him away to...to no one knew where.

When will you ever come back?

She flew on, the ground a blur beneath her.

Vanadium—why did you attack us?

The big, blue-silver juggernaut that had proven a worthy ally and teammate in past adventures had suddenly and without warning unleashed a savage attack upon her—and upon Ultraa, Lyn's mentor in the areas of super-powers and battle tactics.

Why did you do that? Was someone else controlling your actions? Who?

Lyn zoomed out over the coast. The landscape below gave way to seascape, and she paid no heed whatsoever.

Wendy—why are you working for the Field Marshal and his cronies?

Lyn's teenaged sister, scarcely old enough to make her own decisions, had somehow gotten mixed up with another team of super-powered field agents—the very team that had taken the government's sanction away from Lyn's team.

What have they done to you, sis? How can I get you to come home?

Now nothing but the deepening blue of the Atlantic Ocean surrounded Lyn on all sides, the shoreline far in her wake. Fierce purple energies crackled around her, in place of the usual fuzzy golden-hued manifestation of her power. The water beneath her parted in torrential sheets as if a cigarette boat were passing through it. Unbeknownst to Lyn, she left great, rattling sonic booms in her wake.

Oblivious to all of this, her thoughts drifted for a moment, then centered upon the one other missing person—the one she had tried the hardest to keep from thinking about.

Ultraa…Where have you gone?

Ultraa. Her mentor in all things super-powered and government operative related. The man without a past, who had selflessly taken the nineteen-year-old Lyn Li under his wing, teaching her how to use her powers wisely, effectively, and with respect for others. The man who had been sitting in Esro's living room when Lyn had seen him last, only to have vanished without a trace upon her return. No note, no message, no indication of any kind as to where he had gone.

Where can you be?

The speed she had achieved now caused the air around her to exert enormous pressure on the force field bubble surrounding her. Subconsciously she directed yet more power into that bubble, reinforcing its walls, strengthening it. That draining effect, along with the massive amount of energy being consumed by her ultrasonic flight, now threatened to suck her dry—if it didn't burn her up first.

Sweat streaked down her face, and all her muscles bunched and twisted.

Why am I the only one left? How can I go on without the others? What can I do?

Her consciousness flickered. She nearly passed out. Spots blinked across her vision. Instinctively, she dropped her speed, dramatically reducing it in mere instants. Her protective bubble flickered. Turbulence ripped at her, and she spun out of control.

The ocean came up at her, dark and all-encompassing.

She screamed. Screamed long and hard, and shoving all other thoughts out of her head through sheer willpower, she focused every bit of her being upon stopping. Stopping her mad tumbling. Stopping her insane velocity. Stopping her downward spiral. *Stopping.*

And for one long, almost endless moment, she knew she could not stop. Too much momentum, too little energy remaining. No, it was all over for Lyn Li. Over.

NO.

She dug deeper still, into reservoirs of power she had, before now, never guessed existed within her. She poured her heart and soul into the one single, simple thought—the fervent wish—to *stop*.

And she stopped.

And then she hung there, disoriented, her vision nothing but blackness filled with painful fireworks.

She hung there, and long seconds went by.

She felt something wet on her hand.

Her vision slowly returned. She looked down.

"Oh...my...goodness..."

Pulsar floated less than three feet above the ocean's surface, her body lying parallel to the horizon. Her left hand dangled down, just touching the water, her fingers splashing the wave tops.

"Oh... Oh..."

She righted herself, and immediately shuddered as a wave of dizziness and nausea ran through her. Now that she had ceased to burn energy so wantonly, the backlash of physical effects began. She threw up—*Hey, it's the ocean, so who'll know?*—and then wrapped her arms around herself, shivering.

"The ocean?"

She looked around, spinning in a full circle twice. Nothing but endless water greeted her in every direction.

"How did I..."

Flashes of her last few minutes came back to her.

"Oh. Oh, wow…"

Something like fog drifted before her eyes. She blinked, wondering what she was seeing, and looked down.

Oh. It's me.

Steam exuded from all over her body, somehow finding pathways through her golden metal mesh outfit and swathing her in a cloud of mist.

"Thirsty," she croaked through a parched throat. "I must have burned up most of my fluids… So thirsty…"

And then, finally, the inevitable, "Hey—where am I?"

Slowly rising higher into the sky, she searched the distance in every direction.

Nothing. Just water.

Her head was spinning now.

I feel so weak…Just totally out of gas…

A dim sense of panic, very small at first, grew steadily in the pit of her stomach.

How am I getting home? Which way is home?

For absolutely no reason, she drew her tiny cell phone from its compartment on her hip and flipped it open.

No signal. What a surprise.

Replacing it, she zoomed even higher, knowing her strength was close to its end. Her eyes moved from horizon to horizon and found nothing. And the sun—

Hey, the sun!

She could see that it was sinking to her left, which meant that was west.

I think that's right…isn't it?

Her head hurt so badly, she actually had to think about it for a minute.

Yes. Sun. Setting. West. Yes, science genius. Jeez.

So that direction had to be home, surely. Or at least the coast, and a place to land, rest, and recover her strength.

But—how far is it? How far did I fly?

She could remember more of her flight now. More than she cared to remember.

So fast! How was I able to go so fast?

The thought of heading off toward the setting sun, with no idea of the distance and very little energy remaining to keep her aloft and moving, did not appeal to her. But waiting around until the sun set, leaving her still over the ocean and also in the dark, even as her power ran out…

No. There had to be another alternative.

She closed her eyes, trying to think through the possibilities. Trying to think…

Seconds ticked past.

Trying to think…

Something shifted. Something about her connection to the world around her changed. She opened her eyes, and she gasped.

Again! This again!

The world was gone, replaced by a blank universe filled with thin, glowing lines—"wireframe constructs," her computer-geek mind told her. In this case, the wireframe constructs were limited pretty much to a grid representing the surface of the ocean beneath her. Additionally, all around, clearly visible waves of energy washed past, pulsing, glowing in this second sight.

Just like what happened to me before, at Esro's house, she thought. *What is it…and what* good *is it?*

She and Esro had discussed the phenomenon after it happened to her the first time. Esro had been certain that Lyn possessed some rudimentary ability to see the underlying physical nature of the world around her—of seeing not objects and space, but mass and energy and the primal forces of the universe. Lyn hadn't been sure she agreed with his theory, but…

…But here it is again. And I'm seeing something*, anyway…*

And so she went with it. Reaching out, she extended her new vision, slowly at first but quickening by the moment. Soon, she could "see" not just her immediate surroundings, but for miles and miles in every direction. She could "see" the birds, the clouds, and even some large marine animals just below the surface of the water.

Whales? Wow…

And then she "saw" something else. Something relatively large, and solid, and floating on the surface.

A ship. *A ship!*

Locking on, she willed herself towards it. The object in her second sight quickly grew larger. Much larger.

She blinked, blinked again, and the wireframe sight disappeared. Once more she could view the world around her normally. And floating directly beneath her was a big container ship, loaded with boxcars in a rainbow of colors.

Scarcely suppressing her glee, Pulsar dropped through the air until her golden-covered toes touched down gently on the ship's deck. Instantly the last of her strength deserted her and she collapsed, rolling onto her side.

Voices brought her momentarily back to her senses, and she saw booted feet rushing towards her. Someone put a burly arm behind her shoulders and sat her up, leaning her against a crate. Through hazy eyes she saw a number of rugged sailors bending over her, peering down in wonder. They were speaking to her, asking questions, but she couldn't understand their language. Was it German?

One of the men rushed off, then returned a few moments later, carrying a piece of newspaper. He held it up, grinning, and pointed to the color picture on the front.

It was Lyn, in costume, fighting alongside Ultraa and Esro.

"Pulsar," the man said, still grinning. He pointed at Lyn. "Pulsar!"

Lyn couldn't help but laugh.

"Yep, that's me. Pulsar."

Dizziness swept over her again.

"And I'll sign autographs for all you guys, if you'll give me a ride back home."

And the next instant, before she knew it, she had passed out.

Her last thought was, "Who knew I had a fan club in Germany?"

With a rusty, flesh-shuddering creak, the last bits of resistance gave way and the ancient metal door swung open. Thick, musty air sighed out of the darkened chamber beyond, nearly choking the small, hunched form that stood just outside.

"This must be it," he muttered to himself, furtively digging within the leather pouch that hung from his shoulder. "Yes, yes. This must be the one. It has to be."

From the pouch he withdrew what appeared to be a small silver flashlight. Clicking it on, he adjusted the beam into a broad, bright cone that speared ahead of him. Despite its potency, the light revealed little within the stygian blackness.

The little man noted this with a deep, tired sigh.

"Empty. It is empty."

Nothing answered him—nothing but the dim darkness. He stared into it for long seconds, before finally yielding to what he knew he must do.

"Yes," he whispered to himself, "I must go inside. I must. There's no other choice, no. The Warlord in Red has commanded it."

Yet still he stood there, fidgeting with the flashlight, still muttering to himself.

"All of the old Warlord's abandoned sanctums and hideaways must be exposed, examined, pilfered, and sealed off forever. All of them. Twenty-nine have I visited so far, yes—and no sign of my old master in any of them. Now only a handful remain. And so—inside I go..."

Cautiously, carefully, and very reluctantly, he shuffled through the yawning portal and stepped inside.

At first no sounds came to him. Then, after a few steps, he noticed a faint, tapping sound echoing softly all around.

"Water," he murmured. "Water here. And that means..."

Wrinkling his nose, he sniffed the oppressive atmosphere again, smelling mold and mildew on top of other, more exotic scents.

"...The chamber is no longer sealed."

A few more steps, and the drip-drip of water became replaced by a slowly-growing hum, a buzz that vibrated the very walls themselves.

"Something operates here. Something is still running, yes..."

Francisco looked around, shining the light everywhere but seeing little. The chamber was too big, too dark.

The humming grew louder as he walked. He headed for what seemed to be its focus, his footsteps making rippling echoes.

At last his light reflected from a wall. Plain, dull, slate-gray, it towered up into unfathomable heights. Along the floor in front of it lay half a dozen massive cables wrapped in metal shielding. They attached to a huge box built into the wall itself, with yellow warning stripes painted across its surface. The hum now was so loud, so all-pervasive, that it made the hair on Francisco's arms stand up.

"Hello?" he called out, turning in a slow circle, shining his light all around. "Is anyone here?"

The drip of the water and the hum of electricity were the only answers he received.

He leaned in closer, studying the electrical junction. Then he reached to his belt and snapped loose a small device that he held out in front of himself. After a couple of seconds he brought it up to his eyes and squinted at it.

"Hmm."

Clearly someone was drawing power from this source—a massive amount of power. But—who?

"Hello?"

Still nothing.

This was a contingency he had not prepared for. He had expected to either encounter empty chambers that previous Warlords had abandoned ages ago—and he had found many of them already—or empty chambers that had been picked clean in the short time since the violent encounter between the two existing versions. Francisco had no idea how many of those hideaways he had encountered, though it seemed to him to run into the hundreds.

He had also weighed the possibility of encountering the blue Warlord himself, in one of these chambers, though he had found this possibility remote. Surely his old master was in hiding now, knowing his red counterpart now controlled most of his former resources, weapons, and armies. Or else his old master might be out recruiting his own new army, his own slaves, for the showdown everyone involved knew was coming, sooner or later.

But—hanging around one of the old lairs, simply waiting for Francisco to show up?

Unlikely. Unlikely in the extreme.

Francisco could not help but chuckle at the thought.

"Greetings, my old friend."

Francisco whirled, crying out in surprise and fear. The light slipped from his numb fingers and clattered across the hard stone floor, sending garish nightmare shadow-shapes across the near wall.

"What—*who*—?"

The light rolled to a stop and lay at the feet of a tall figure whose upper body disappeared into the darkness. Francisco felt his throat involuntarily constricting at the mere thought of who he must be seeing.

The figure bent down and picked up the light. For an instant he shined it at Francisco, nearly blinding the little man. Then he pointed it away, plunging them both into darkness again.

"It is good to see you," the man said.

Francisco whimpered. He felt frantically at his belt for his portal-generating capsule, fumbled at it, dropped it. He whimpered louder.

"Calm yourself. I bear no grudges, no ill will." The voice was smooth and seductive. "Least of all toward my oldest friend and companion."

Francisco's fingers patted desperately along his belt, searching for any other tools or items that might serve as weapons—or, more realistically, serve to get him away from here, immediately.

The tall figure stepped forward. The light flashed up, revealing long, blue robes, cloak and hood. Only the face was not covered in blue—the face that sparkled in the beam of the light, revealing a silver mask with eerily passive features. That face leaned in closer.

Francisco idly wondered if he had wet himself.

"Ah," the Warlord said. He picked something up from the floor and held it out to Francisco. But as the little man saw what it was—the portal generator—and sought to snatch it from proffering fingers, the Warlord pulled it back suddenly.

"No, wait—not just yet."

Francisco whimpered again, but refused to address this man—his former master, who had betrayed the Grand Design that drove both their lives and gave them meaning. Either out of fear or out of shame, Francisco would not speak to this Warlord, whom he had pronounced a traitor and had sought to permanently eliminate, replacing him with his new master, the Warlord in Red.

By all that was natural and unnatural in all the many planes of existence, this blue Warlord rightfully should be dead and gone. Eliminated, annihilated, and erased.

But this incarnation had turned out to be much harder to get rid of than Francisco had suspected.

So now there were *two* Warlords in existence—a crisis of nigh-unimaginable proportions, at least to Francisco.

When the two had first squared off against one another, each seeking the other's utter destruction, their proximity to one another within one single universe had nearly torn the time-space continuum to shreds. The laws of nature dictated that one Warlord and only one Warlord could exist at a time. In part because of Francisco, now there were two.

Only by spiriting the Warlord in Red away from that battle had Francisco averted a cosmic catastrophe.

In the days that followed, the Warlord in Red had become satisfied of Francisco's loyalty, and had sent him out to locate the old Warlord's bases, while he himself worked on some new and highly secret project—for that was what Warlords did.

The one thing Francisco had most feared in embarking on these travels was encountering his old master again, after having betrayed him at least twice in recent days.

And now here he was.

431

Yes, Francisco admitted to himself, *I have definitely wet my britches.*

"I will give you your device and allow you to leave freely, my old friend. Never fear."

The blue Warlord lowered himself into a squat, gazing out impassively at his old lackey.

"But first, I want to tell you about your new master. About this abomination you call the Warlord in Red."

Francisco breathed slowly in and out, his every sense on edge, his muscles poised to leap out of the way of whatever attack might come—for all the good it would likely do.

"I know you have pronounced me a traitor to the Design," the Warlord said, "and I—reluctantly—accept that. I can understand your perspective on it, at least."

He hesitated, as Francisco processed that remarkable admission. Remarkable from a Warlord, anyway, and especially from *this* one.

"My time alone has forced me to contemplate my previous actions with greater scrutiny, and with greater honesty. And I have to admit I have given you cause to...to take the actions you have taken. I no longer blame you."

Francisco took all of this with a grain of salt. He had heard conciliatory words from this Warlord before—words that had inevitably proven false.

"But you need to know precisely what this new Warlord... this *Warlord in Red*... plans to do," his old master continued.

Francisco could hold back no longer.

"He doesn't plan to destroy the Design," the little man blurted out. "He's not a traitor! No, no, not a traitor."

He cringed, awaiting the inevitable violent lashing out, at the receiving end of which he was certain he would find himself.

But the Warlord merely listened to these words calmly, almost contemplatively.

"So you say," he intoned after a few seconds. "But then, you do not know him."

Francisco's defiance flared.

"What is there to know?"

The Warlord stood, turned, and strode a few steps back, his blue cape flaring around him. Then he faced Francisco again.

"You objected to my goal of tapping the energies of the gods themselves—the Rivals, as they are called, who move about this universe with great powers and greater impudence."

"Yes."

"Perhaps that did constitute a threat to the Design. I concede this possibility, though I do not necessarily agree with it. Great rewards often require great risks, and I was willing to take those risks."

He made a dismissive gesture with one azure-gloved hand.

"However…"

In spite of himself, Francisco found he was listening—listening with rapt attention.

"However," the Warlord continued, "this new…entity…cares nothing for the ultimate *goals* of the Design. Fault me for my methods, but never for my goals!"

Francisco listened to this, and he thought of the time this Warlord had railed about undoing the Design itself and reigning forever as the one single Warlord. But he decided this was not the time to pursue that point. In all the centuries of Francisco's existence, in all the years he had served the many incarnations of the Warlord, he had never, ever found consistency—or rationality—to be their strong suits.

"Then what is his goal?"

Behind his silver mask, the Warlord smiled.

"Nothing."

"What?"

"His goal is *nothing*."

Francisco blinked.

"But—"

"Nothing in the grand sense. In the cosmic sense."

The Warlord gestured around himself, indicating the great sweep of the universe, of the *multiverse* in which he and Francisco had always operated.

"He is a nihilist. He seeks the utter and complete annihilation of the entire cosmos. Every level, every nook and cranny. All of it, gone, if he has his way."

He spread his gloved hands wide.

"That… *That* is the master you serve. That is the cause you aid and abet. That is the goal of this… this *abomination* you call the Warlord in Red."

Francisco stared back at his old master, aghast.

"No. No!"

He wrung his hands together, sweat trickling down his face and his sides.

"Can…can that be true? Can it possibly be so?"

"You will know it is true when you see the machine he is constructing. He and I are the same in many ways, obviously—

433

though he is a warped and perverted image of myself. And so I know his mind, somewhat. He will construct something like this…"

The Warlord gestured with one gloved hand and a three-dimensional holographic image appeared in midair between him and Francisco. It was a visual representation of a circular device, standing on its side like a round doorway, anchored to a platform on the ground. At regular intervals around its circumference projected odd, oblong objects—antennae?

Francisco gazed up at the image, committing it to memory.

"And here is the energy signature of the wave this machine will produce. If you examine it closely, you will see it can have no other effect but the annihilation of matter, on an exponentially increasing scale. A universal scale. A *multiversal* scale."

"Yes," Francisco breathed, recording the image and the wave frequency.

The Warlord switched off the images and stood there a few seconds longer, waiting for his words to have their full effect upon his old lackey. Then he reached up and unfastened his silver mask, bringing it away from his rugged, scarred face. He pulled back his hood, revealing a mop of brown hair. He smiled down at his old assistant.

"If you should wish to talk with me again, you may contact me from here."

Then he knelt once more and reached out, taking Francisco's shaking hand in his own. He handed over the little man's portal-generating device—his doorway back to the Warlord in Red's sanctum.

"Go now, my oldest friend. Go, and know the truth. And do with it what you think best."

Francisco stumbled back a step, eyes still wide. He gazed down almost unbelievingly at the device now in his hands.

"But be careful. Do not let him suspect that you know what you know."

"Yes…Yes, I understand."

The portal opened, and the terrified and confused Francisco fled through it.

The Warlord watched him go, the portal winking closed behind him.

"Perfect," he breathed. "Simply perfect…"

⊒

Wendy Li lay on the bed in her dorm room, staring up at the ceiling, feeling sad.

She was starting to have second thoughts about her decision to join this team.

Starting to? I've been having second thoughts!

At this point, the main thing that kept her from quitting and leaving, she had to admit, was not wanting to prove her big sister right.

And so here she was. Lying here. Bored. Unhappy.

She didn't like the Field Marshal. She had clashed with him immediately after returning from Lyn's hospital room.

"You never should have abandoned the team," he had scolded her.

"But my sister was hurt!"

"She isn't part of this team."

"She's family!"

"*This* is your family now."

"What?"

And then her grandfather had unexpectedly appeared. Apparently he knew the Field Marshal, which struck her as strange. He had taken her aside and praised her.

"You did very well, Wen. You looked after your sister, and no one should fault you for that."

Then he had glared pointedly at the Field Marshal, who had turned and stalked away. That had made Wendy happy. Her grandfather had stayed around for another half hour or so, talking, and then had abruptly left. She still wondered what he had been doing there.

The others weren't much better. She really didn't like Blitzkrieg, the creep. That other guy, Mr. Blue—he seemed downright weird. At least Doug Williams was actually pretty nice.

And Angela Devereux.... They had talked together for a bit, earlier, though the conversation didn't quite stick in Wendy's head, she realized now. Something about knowing who her friends were... or something...

In any case, Wendy had just about come to the point of saying goodbye to the whole crowd and heading back home to Bay City. Or maybe even over to Esro Brachis's house. If she could put up with

Lyn being around, that was. But, hey, Lyn was back in school now. She wouldn't be at Esro's all that often. So maybe, just maybe...

She started to pick up her phone.

At that moment, unbidden, her eyes closed. She saw lights swimming across the darkness—two lights, spiraling around. Eyes... The eyes of Angela Devereux. Of Distraxion.

"This is good," Wendy told herself in a monotone voice. "This is right. I am where I need to be. The others are my friends. Lyn is my enemy. Ultraa is my enemy. The Field Marshal and Blitzkrieg are my friends. Distraxion is my *best friend in the world*, and I will do whatever she asks."

Wendy repeated that over twice, then opened her eyes.

She blinked.

What was I going to do?

Huh.

Oh well.

She stared up at the ceiling, feeling sad. She was starting to have second thoughts about her decision to join this team...

4

Pulsar swooped down onto the roof of Esro Brachis's empty mansion—a homecoming of decidedly mixed emotions. She was happy to be home again. In actuality, she was happy to be alive, after the mindless stunt she had pulled, that had nearly gotten her killed.

But I had no idea I could fly so fast, or so far—and not even notice I was doing it!

The German sailors had been pleasant enough. They'd been happy to have her company, despite only a couple of them speaking any English. As it had turned out, she hadn't needed a ride all the way home. They'd fed her some soup and doted on her like schoolboys, which had been sort of fun, actually. And after a few hours of rest, she'd felt capable of flying back on her own.

I'm still weak, though, she thought as she dropped to the driveway and stood at the front entrance. The mansion's biometric sensors recognized her and unlocked the door, and she walked inside.

"Esro? Ultraa?" She looked around, hoping against hope. "Vanadium?" She sighed. "Evil villain who's broken in and is about to attack me?"

Nothing. The house looked exactly as it had when she'd left.

No, wait. Something…

A light was flashing on Esro's answering machine.

Why does that seem odd?

Because, she realized, no one ever called that number. The line was generally for guests and the like. Esro had phones in his private offices and labs, equipped with scrambling technology. This one was most often employed when Lyn ordered pizza.

Frowning, she pressed the playback button.

The voice was deep, rough around the edges but somehow not unappealing. And Lyn knew that she had heard it before, somewhere.

"Hi. Um… This is Richard Ha—umm, *Heavyweight*. Yeah. I'm trying to reach Esro Brachis or Lyn Li. I have important information for them. About a mutual friend. So. If one of you could call me back…"

He left a number and hung up. Following this came two more messages, more or less identical to the first. And then nothing. The last message had been left two hours earlier.

A mutual friend? Could he mean—?

Lyn started to pick up the phone, then hesitated. She chewed a fingernail. She knew that voice—she'd heard it before, somewhere. Something inside her screamed caution.

But if it's about Ultraa…

She grabbed up the phone and dialed the number. It rang, rang again, continued to ring…

"Hello?"

"This is Lyn Li."

"Oh. Oh! Yeah. Thanks for getting back to me."

Lyn's heart was in her throat.

"You know something about…about a mutual friend, you said."

"Yeah."

"And that would be—?"

"Red and white." A pause. "Never could figure why he doesn't have some blue in there."

Yes!

Lyn felt a thrill race through her.

"Where is he?"

"That's…complicated."

"What?"

"Look," the man said quickly, "before we go any further, I just want to apologize to you. Sincerely."

Lyn frowned. Pieces were starting to come together, though she couldn't quite see it all just yet.

"For what?"

"For that business back at your college, last fall."

The pieces came together. Lyn gasped.

"See," he was saying, "I really didn't want to—"

Lyn slammed the phone down as if it were burning hot in her hand.

She stepped back.

Heavyweight. Yeah, that fits.

A year or so earlier, a man with powers matching that name had attacked her on the Bay City College campus, apparently attempting to abduct her. In the process, he exposed her as a paranormal to her fellow students, as well as to her roommate and best friend. The incident had led to her first meeting Ultraa and Brachis, but had also precipitated her leaving the school and moving east. She did not think fondly of that day, and certainly bore nothing but anger and resentment toward the man she held responsible.

The man who tried to kidnap me!

The phone rang again.

She didn't answer it.

It went to the machine.

"Hi, listen, Ms. Li," he began, his voice sounding a bit more anxious now. "I know you think I'm some kind of psychotic maniac or whatever, but—that wasn't my doing. They ordered me—the same people that I think have your partner now. If you'll just talk to me we can try to—"

The machine switched off.

Lyn glared at it.

Seconds passed. She stood over the table, arms crossed, staring down at the phone, her foot tapping rapidly on the floor.

Ultraa...

It rang again.

She didn't answer it.

It went to the machine.

"Ms. Lyn, please—I need your help, and you need mine. You may not believe that, but it's true on both counts. And your partner needs both our help, big time. But we can't keep wasting all this time."

Ultraa...

"I've been trying to get you since last night, and I don't know how much longer—"

Lyn snatched up the telephone.

"I'm listening. Explain."

"Oh. Good."

"Explain," she repeated flatly.

"Well, yeah, see, I work for the government—for a particular part of the government. And—look, we can't talk about this over an open phone line. They hear everything."

Lyn considered that.

"Okay, what are you suggesting?"

"A meet. Right now. In person. Just you and me."

Lyn laughed.

"Yeah, sure. You want another crack at me. For whatever weird reason you want me."

"I don't—look, I never wanted you. Somebody did, though. And they wanted your partner, and, well, guess where he is now?"

"I don't want to guess where he is. I want you to tell me. You said you knew."

"And that's why I want to meet. To talk about it. Make our plans."

Lyn hesitated, thinking. She was tempted—so sorely tempted. But how could she possibly ever trust this man?

"You don't think you can take me down, if you have to?" Richard snorted. "Seems to me you did pretty well, last time we met."

Lyn reddened.

"Don't go there," she said. "I don't want to think about that day."

"Right. Sorry."

Lyn breathed for a few seconds. Then, "Okay, fine. We'll meet. But it has to be somewhere...public. Open."

"Yeah," Richard replied after a moment. "I was afraid you'd say that. But—okay, sure. No problem. Any suggestions?"

"Hmm. Starbucks." She listed a specific location in northern Virginia.

"Starbucks. Yeah. Great." He snorted. "Even if the conversation doesn't go well, I can always get a grande latte or something. Yeah, done."

"See you there in an hour."

"An hour. See you then."

Lyn hung up the phone and sat back in a huge leather chair, feeling all the energy drain out of her body for the second time in as many days. But this time it was an emotional release, made up of anger, loss, depression, and outright fear.

"You just try something this time," she mumbled, thinking of the man who had attacked her on her campus—the man she was about to go meet alone. "You try it, and see if I don't melt that Starbucks down around your ugly head."

5

"I like the people here."

Wendy Li's silver hoop earrings bounced and sparkled as she slurped at a giant slice of pizza.

"Well, most of them," she amended with a small frown.

Angela Devereux nodded. Wearing a long, gray coat over her skimpy red costume, she sat across from Wendy in the dining hall of the Digimacht headquarters building in downtown Washington, DC. Brushing her straight blond hair back, she watched the younger woman eat and marveled at her appetite and capacity for food. She seemed to be eating something—pizza and popcorn were her favorites—all the time. Devereux could only assume it had something to do with the girl's superpowers and her metabolism. She looked down at her own small salad.

The things I do to fit into my costume, she thought ruefully. *Maybe it's time to consider switching to a one-piece...*

She put such thoughts out of her head and returned her attention to the girl.

"So—you like most of us," she repeated back to Wendy. "Like me," she added with a smile. "Right?"

"Oh, totally," Wendy said, despite a voice in the back of her mind crying out in protest. She ignored it, as she always did—as if someone had ordered her to do so.

"And Williams—Doug Williams," Angela prompted, thinking of the other teammate she'd had to use her hypnotic powers on, so far. The Field Marshal wanted everyone obedient and kept in line, and Williams had proven too inquisitive, too independent. So, naturally,

440

the team leader had come to her and asked her to…*modify* Williams's views somewhat.

Doing so had not proven as entertaining as she had hoped it might. The man was so serious, so driven. And so suspicious. Still, she'd managed to plant a few mental suggestions that would help if he ever got too nosy with the Field Marshal's business.

"So—the Fury," Angela said, "as Doug insists on calling himself. You like him."

Wendy shrugged.

"Sure. He's nice enough. He doesn't bother me or anything. And that suit he has—or whatever it is—is pretty cool."

"That it is," Angela agreed.

Wendy fidgeted at the high collar of her silver mesh outfit.

"I'll tell you who I don't much like, though," she said in a low whisper.

Angela leaned forward, listening.

"Mr. Blue."

"Mr. Bl—*ohh*."

Devereux had nearly forgotten that other alias occasionally used by Desmond Beaulieu, another of their teammates.

"What don't you like about him? His looks?"

Wendy frowned.

"Hmm. Maybe. Sort of, yeah."

She scratched at her chin, thinking.

"But it's more than that. Something about him… something in general… is just *creepy*."

"Creepy?"

"Yeah, absolutely."

Wendy put down the remains of her pizza and looked back at Angela questioningly.

"You don't ever feel it?"

Devereux shrugged.

"Maybe. I don't know. I suppose there is something… *unusual* about him."

"I think he's totally creepy," Wendy said. "I always feel like he…*knows* things about me that nobody else knows—that I don't even know myself. And he looks at me like he *knows that!*"

"I think you're imagining it."

"Whatever. Maybe."

Wendy wiped at her mouth with her napkin.

"But I don't want anything to do with him," she told the older woman, "and you should stay away from him, too. No telling what he might do."

She stood and carried her tray to the trash.

"Very true," Devereux replied, following behind her and tossing in her empty salad bowl as well.

"Okay, well, talk to you later," Wendy said, grinning. In a flash, the young woman in silver mesh was gone around a corner, the swish of her bell bottoms echoing into the distance.

Angela Devereux—Distraxion—stood there a bit longer, thinking about the conversation she'd just had and trying to decide how she should feel about it. After a few moments she simply shrugged, turned and strode the opposite direction down the corridor, arriving eventually at a nondescript door.

The girl is just a kid, and doesn't know what she's talking about, she told herself firmly. *Now get your head on straight and do what you have to do.*

She knocked.

A muffled voice came from within.

"What?"

"It's me."

A second, two, and then the door slid open.

She walked inside, and it closed behind her.

The slender, dark haired form of Desmond Beaulieu lay on the bed, his ankles crossed, his blue sunglasses firmly in place. He wore his dark gray jumpsuit, but it was unbuttoned halfway down. He smiled broadly, his teeth hardly any whiter than his extremely pale, almost deathlike skin.

Devereux looked down at him and suppressed a slight shudder.

Okay, Wendy, I'll admit you weren't entirely wrong, she thought to herself. *He is pretty creepy. But he also really enjoys my company. And every time I come for a "visit," I learn a little more about his plans, and his resources, and his secrets.*

She smiled at this, hoping he would take it as a smile of greeting.

And that will all come in very, very handy, should this gig ever come to a premature end.

Unfastening her coat, Distraxion allowed it to drop to the floor. She planted the sole of one thigh-high red boot on the edge of the bed.

"This time," she said to Beaulieu as he reached out for her, "let's try not to set your head on fire, okay?"

442

6

A cluster of six great starships streaked past the outer planets of our solar system and closed on the Earth at unimaginable speeds, not stopping until they had slid smoothly into orbit high above North America.

Far below, early warning alarms blared out within the Pentagon—ironically enough, the very target of the strike force. The warnings came far too late to be of any use.

The lead vessel, made up of three vast cylindrical sections connected by pylons and covered in strange, alien markings, opened a port in its belly. Instantly a silvery, spherical pod shot out of the port, streaking down toward the planet's surface. The other five ships each did likewise.

Now six round objects, each roughly ten feet in diameter, plummeted toward the east coast of the United States. Nothing could be done to impede their approach, to halt their arrival. After a brief but tumultuous and fiery ride down, the pods crashed to the ground, one after another, burying themselves halfway in the soil.

Before anyone in the vicinity of the impacts could react, the pods popped open, hatches springing loose and tumbling away. Then, amidst oozing blue fluid that spurted out and ran down the sides of the capsules, clawlike metal hands reached up through each of the hatches and grasped tightly, pulling each of the occupants—the passengers—free.

Scant moments later, six unearthly figures occupied the soil of northern Virginia, gazing about intently.

Each of them stood more than seven feet tall. Each looked humanoid in form, for the most part, but appeared to be wearing—or to be made up of—mechanical components. Those familiar with the armor designs of Esro Brachis might have thought he had a hand in their creation, though at second glance this work was far more complex, more heavy-duty. The six looked like walking industrial equipment, all of them painted a base gray, but each sporting a different and nearly fluorescent secondary color scheme, from bright yellow to pink to green. The faceplates were featureless save for a speaker grille and two large lenses in place of eyes.

They did not, in short, appear to have come in peace.

"This is the target, yes?"

The voice crackled out of the speaker grill of the one bearing a vivid blue pattern on his torso and limbs. He gestured with one big, shiny metal claw-hand. The one nearest him, in green, nodded.

"Indeed. They scarcely could have designed the place to be any more noticeable from above."

The figure in green moved to the front, and together the six bizarre figures strode deliberately toward the main entrance of the Pentagon.

7

Jameson looked up as the door to his Pentagon office opened and a somewhat familiar face leaned in.

"You got a second?"

Before Jameson could reply, the door opened the rest of the way and in walked a big man with blunt features and tousled black hair, wearing a long, gray coat. Under one arm he carried a bundle of cloth. Jameson's first thought, irrational as it might seem, was that the bundle might well contain a person. But of course that was ridiculous, he knew.

"I have something for you," the man said, a slight smile crossing his rough-hewn face.

He set the bundle down on a sofa and unrolled it a bit, revealing that it did, in fact, contain a person. The face of a young woman with golden skin, black hair, and brown eyes glared out angrily at both of the men.

"Lyn Li. Special delivery." Heavyweight laughed. "Better late than never, right?"

Jameson stared down at Lyn for a long moment, then looked up at Richard, his face filled with puzzlement.

"Richard, I—what—?"

"You wanted her before," Heavyweight said, shrugging. "The opportunity presented itself. And I know—firsthand—how dangerous she is. So I took her down—surprised her. Lulled her into a false sense of security and, well—" He nodded toward the tightly bound young woman. "It was easy, really."

Jameson, frowning deeply now, looked from Heavyweight to Lyn and back.

"I—but, that is…" He cleared his throat. "Things have changed somewhat. We—"

"Don't try to weasel out on me, Jameson. The contract was still open. I checked. Now I expect to get paid."

Jameson ran a hand over his face, which had begun to sweat, then met Lyn's eyes. She still hadn't said anything.

"All right, fine," Jameson said after a few moments of consideration. "I think I know how I can salvage this situation—perhaps turn it into a positive."

He walked behind his desk and lifted his phone, punching in a number.

"I know someone who can—"

"'Perhaps?' What do you mean, 'perhaps?'"

Heavyweight strode across the office and glared at him.

"You wanted her. You ordered me to capture her."

"Yes, but that was more than a year ago. The situation is different now. I—" He coughed. "I wish you hadn't—"

"Yeah? What's changed?"

Jameson gave Richard a sharp look.

"That's not your concern," he replied.

The person he had called answered. He spoke a few words into the phone, nodded, and hung up.

"We have the sister, if you must know," he said then, walking back around his desk.

Lyn's cry brought him up short, and he whirled about. It was the first sound she had made since Richard had uncovered her, and it had startled him. He looked back at her, thought for a moment, and then smiled.

"Your sister is perfectly fine, as you surely know. Happily working with the Field Marshal and his team, as a duly authorized government agent. Just like you used to be."

She growled at him.

His smile deepened.

"Of course, that status was revoked for you and your friends," he continued. "So, technically, you are in violation of all sorts of federal laws at the moment."

"What laws?" Lyn demanded.

"Well, I'll have to write them, first," Jameson replied, still smiling. "I'll let you know."

Richard actually chuckled at this.

445

"In the meantime," Jameson told her, "my agent Distraxion will be here shortly, to meet with you. I'm certain a few minutes in…consultation…with her," and he laughed again, "will have you seeing things our way. *My* way."

"That's how you have Wendy doing what you want, isn't it?"

"Oh, Distraxion can be very persuasive," Jameson agreed, nodding.

Lyn shifted her gaze from Jameson to Richard. He met her eyes. She nodded once. He nodded back.

And then, at that precise moment, the floor shook.

"What was that?"

And shook again, much harder.

"Richard, are you—?"

"That's not me!"

Rumbling sounded all around. It grew louder, the vibrations stronger. Jameson backed away, until his rear end bumped into the front edge of his desk.

Frantically he reached for the telephone.

The wall across from him exploded.

Screaming in surprise and fear, Jameson dropped to one knee, then scrambled around behind his big oaken desk.

Richard instinctively bent to cover Lyn, shielding her where she lay on the sofa.

Debris flew everywhere, papers and wood chips raining down.

Before the wreckage could fully settle, the smoke parted and into Jameson's office strode six massive mechanical figures, each painted gray, each trimmed in a different vivid color. Their heavy metal boots crashed loudly on the floor as they marched swiftly into the room. Ignoring Richard and Lyn entirely, they headed straight for Jameson.

"What is this?" he demanded. He was clearly startled but attempted to cover it with his customary confidence and bravado.

The leader, his armor trimmed in bright green, grasped Jameson by the throat and shoved him hard up against the wall. His voice crackled out of the speaker in his faceplate.

"You are the one called Jameson, yes?"

Only an unintelligible choking sound came by way of reply.

The leader loosened his grip slightly.

"Yes," he gasped, eyes betraying fear but also anger. "Yes, I'm Jameson. Who—"

And then Jameson's eyes widened even further.

"The Circle. You—you're from the Circle, aren't you?"

"Indeed," came the crackling reply.

"Look," Jameson said, struggling to get the words out, his windpipe being crushed by thick metal claws. "I'm sorry about the spaceship. I had every intention of recovering it for you people. But someone else came along and took it. We couldn't stop them. We—"

The leader turned his gray and green head toward the others momentarily, as if puzzled. Then he looked back at Jameson.

"Silence. We care nothing for such matters."

The six had gathered in a semicircle around Jameson. He swallowed slowly, carefully, his eyes flickering from one grotesque, robotic face to the next.

"You're not here about the spaceship? Then—then what—"

He remembered suddenly that Heavyweight had been in the room just before the attack. He tried his best to see past the big, mechanical figures—to see what Richard was doing—but they completely blocked off his view of the far side of the room.

"What do you want?!"

The leader leaned in close—close enough that Jameson could feel the heat radiating off his mechanical armor.

"Nah-Shonn."

Jameson blinked.

"Uhm…"

He frowned.

"What?"

He looked from one of the alien warriors to the other. Sweat ran down his face.

"Is—is that a person? I—I don't know what that is."

"It—he—is a traitor," the alien leader replied, his voice level but his anger apparent. "A traitor to the Circle. A fugitive. An outlaw. An outlaw even among the Circle—we who are the greatest outlaws of the Kur-Bai Empire." The way he said "Empire" sounded to Jameson like a curse.

"And…and you think I know where he is?"

"He is here," the leader barked, turning slowly, his eyes moving across every wall, every surface in the room. "Or he was here very recently."

He turned back, leaned in toward Jameson again.

"I can sense his psychic residue. Just as clearly as my chemical receptors can smell your fear." "I won't deny that," Jameson said, attempting to stand straighter, still trying in vain to see what had become of Richard and his captive. "I'd be a fool to—"

447

"You would be a fool to delay us further. Where is Rnn'dul Nah-Shonn?"

"Randall Nation?"

Jameson had spoken the words before he even realized he had opened his mouth.

The alien commando straightened and glared at him, the round lenses over his eyes spinning around, focusing in tightly.

"Yeessss," the big alien replied. "'Randall Nation,' as you say. Just so."

He leaned in closer to Jameson.

"You have met him. You do know."

Jameson's mind worked frantically. *Where did that name come from? Where did I hear it before? Think!*

But nothing else came to him. In fact, now that he turned his attention to the name, he found he could scarcely even recall it, much less anything about it.

"You will answer me, human. I will have Nah-Shonn—your 'Randall Nation'—or I will dismantle this building, this planet, and you—and not necessarily in that order."

Jameson glared back at the mechanical visage defiantly.

"Well, I don't know who that is, and I don't remember where I heard the name. So I guess you'll just have to get on with the demolishing."

The lead warrior seemed to hesitate for a moment, and Jameson felt his pulse actually increase—something he would not have thought possible, at this point.

Bluffing! He was bluffing!

Then the robotic head turned smoothly to the side and words crackled out, addressed to the warrior in yellow.

"Signal the fleet. Commence planetary bombardment in five minutes."

Jameson's jaw dropped.

"But," the commando added, "I would prefer they begin with a continent other than this one, at least until we are back on board. For reasons that I trust are more than obvious."

The yellow warrior nodded and clicked the communications link open to relay the order.

"I guess you'll just have to get on with the demolishing."

The Field Marshal gazed at the video display boards surrounding him on all sides, there in the command center of his secluded Washington, DC headquarters. Above the central monitor ran the logo of the Digimacht Corporation, the business front that covered the operations—legal and extra-legal—in which his group engaged themselves.

"Hmm," he growled, one hand absently fingering the patch that covered his left eye. "Interesting."

"Eh?"

Karl Koenig—the agent known as Blitzkrieg—looked up from his German newspaper and peered at the older man. The Field Marshal wore a dark gray military uniform and his graying hair was cut very short—similar to his temperament.

"The Pentagon," the Field Marshal muttered. "Something is happening there."

"Oh?"

Blitzkrieg squinted up at the monitor his leader indicated.

"I don't see any—oh, *ja*, smoke. I see it now."

"Alerts have been flashing across the boards for several seconds now," the Field Marshal noted. "Apparently there has been some sort of attack."

He leaned over the screen at his desk and studied it.

"The incident is localized, however. Only one part of the building appears to be affected. And..."

He grinned.

"I believe it is in the proximity of our new friend, Mr. Jameson."

"Is that so?"

Blitzkrieg grinned.

"Maybe he played with fire once too often."

"A good bet, I would say," the older man replied, still studying the data.

"Has he called for assistance?"

"Not so far."

Blitzkrieg reacted with mild surprise.

"In that case, I think it's none of our business," he said after a moment's consideration.

The Field Marshal leaned back in his chair and thought about that for a few seconds.

"I tend to agree."

"It's not like he doesn't have our telephone number, if he needs us," Blitzkrieg added.

"Indeed."

The younger man reached into a small refrigerator and drew out two bottles of German beer, opening them both. He handed one over to the Field Marshal.

"Danke."

And so the two men sat there, sipping their beer and watching the reports of the Pentagon assault on the monitors, and they waited.

9

The Pentagon was in turmoil.

The armored alien warriors had struck hard and fast, crashing down through the ceiling very near to Jameson's office, then smashing through a couple of walls until they reached him. Within seconds of their initial confrontation with him, Marines and other soldiers rushed to the besieged area of the big building, only to find what amounted to a hostage situation. The first few to arrive had fired their automatic weapons and sidearms at the hulking intruders, to no avail whatsoever. Now, knowing at least one person to be held inside, and possibly more, the troops had backed off. They formed a perimeter around the damaged area of the Pentagon and were considering their next moves.

Meanwhile, the green-trimmed leader still held Jameson pinned to the wall of his office.

"I don't know who you're talking about," Jameson whimpered.

"You said the name."

"Yes, I suppose so, but I don't know where I heard it, or who that is."

The leader turned to his yellow-trimmed comrade.

"Does the fleet acknowledge my bombardment order?"

Yellow hesitated.

"I—I have lost the signal to the fleet."

Green looked at him for a long moment, robotic eyes whirring as they cycled wider.

"Lost the signal?"

"Yes. Comm is down. Something has cut it off completely."

Green appeared to be considering this.

"Impossible," he replied after a few seconds. "This world lacks the technology to even begin to affect our—"

"Sir! Look!"

Green stopped in mid-sentence and followed the gesture of the alien warrior in red trim.

"What in the seven worlds—?"

A nearly full glass of water on Jameson's desk—a glass that had somehow avoided being knocked over in all the violence and commotion—was now boiling.

Green lowered Jameson to the ground and stared at the water. Then he turned and, for the first time since his arrival, looked back at the other two people in the room.

A dark-haired human male in a long gray coat smiled back. He winked.

"Who are you?" Green demanded, his servos whining as he turned fully around.

Next to the man in the coat, there stood a young female wearing a shiny golden bodysuit. She had struck a defiant pose, left hand on her hip, right hand stretched out, fingers pointing at the warriors of the Circle.

Around those fingers sparkled a golden nimbus, wreathed in crackling purple fire.

Green looked up from her grimacing features to the air around himself and his associates. It, too, sparkled in gold and purple.

"The woman," he growled over his speaker. "She is doing...something..."

"She has surrounded us in an electromagnetic field," Yellow reported, consulting a display built into his left forearm. "A field of...*considerable* power."

"The paranormal humans," Green said after a moment's consideration. "Yes. She is one of Jameson's pets."

Lyn flushed. "Excuse me?"

"Ms. Li," Jameson shouted across the room, "I appreciate your help, but let's not do anything to further anger these...people..."

"Jameson, you idiot," Heavyweight barked. "They threatened to nuke the planet! Just what further angering are you talking about?"

"Ignore him," Lyn said calmly. "He actually believed you'd captured me. How bright can he be?"

Richard laughed, and laughed again at Jameson's muffled protest.

Meanwhile, Yellow consulted the tactical readouts displayed inside his helmet and addressed the leader, Green, again.

"We must break free of this field quickly. I have determined that it is blocking not only comm, but also the enervating beam."

"What?"

Green reacted visibly, startled, and consulted his own readouts.

"Power levels are dropping rapidly," he said, shocked.

"Yes," Yellow agreed. "Nothing new is getting in. All the power beamed to us by the fleet is being blocked—deflected away. When our batteries are drained..."

All six of the Circle warriors considered this.

"This is intolerable!"

Green stepped forward, to the edge of the bubble surrounding his team, and pointed a robotic claw at Lyn.

"Release us immediately, or the consequences for your world will be staggering."

Lyn glanced at Richard.

"This guy's not any brighter than Jameson."

She glared at Green.

"You freaking threatened to nuke us! Hello!"

All of the six moved toward them then, brandishing nasty-looking weapons that unfolded from their forearms and torsos. Lyn took a half step back, startled by the impressive and quite menacing display.

"Let me see what I can do about this," Richard said.

Stepping forward, he gestured with one hand, and the warriors instantly stopped in their tracks. Four of them dropped to a knee. As the seconds dragged by, all of the aliens seemed to be acting out some bizarre pantomime, struggling with something—with some unseen force, pressing down on them from above. Slowly but surely, the six armored warriors sunk to the floor, all of them eventually lying flat.

"Oh, good," Richard commented. "Jameson has a super-reinforced floor." He smiled. "I was afraid I'd only be shoving them down into the basement, instead of crushing them, when I exponentially increased their weight."

Jameson, outside of the bubble that surrounded the aliens, stumbled backward, trying to put some distance between himself and all these freakish individuals.

Thank goodness Richard was here, he thought to himself. And immediately after that, his usually very paranoid mind considered another fact. *He and the Li girl appear to be getting along a lot better than they should be. Could they actually have been trying to dupe me? Could it all have been some sort of elaborate trick?* Jameson found such a thing hard to believe. *From what I know of them, neither has the brains to come up with something like that. But then again, maybe I've been underestimating them both...*

Lyn held the force field bubble tightly closed around the Circle warriors, while Richard pressed them to the floor, the force now redoubling as he exerted all of his considerable power to drive them down. *That armor's gonna crack open any second now,* he thought. *Come on! Crack!*

He spared a quick glance at Lyn, who stood immobile, both hands raised to shoulder level, electricity crackling around her fingers.

"You holding out okay over there?"

"I'm fine," she replied through clenched teeth. Her eyes blazed and sweat trailed down her cheeks. "I'm not too thrilled about rescuing this jerk, though."

"Yeah," Richard replied, "I get that—I totally do. But in this case, I think alien invaders who want to nuke the Earth trump human megalomaniac who wants to enslave all paranormals."

"Hey!" Jameson cried out. "That's not true!"

"Whatever," Richard and Lyn both replied in unison.

"Your...power...is formidable, Human," the green-armored warrior managed to say, his head raised just high enough from the floor to be able to see Richard. "As is the girl's. However..."

Green's arm jerked around, barely moving from the floor and instead sliding over it, until the claw hand pointed toward the two paranormals.

"...I must bring this farce to an end."

Green triggered a mechanism inside his armor, and the claw spun around, retracted, and was replaced by a cylindrical shape, sprouting from his armor's forearm. Before anyone could react to this, the cylinder crackled with electricity, emitted a loud humming sound, and then burst with light like a flashbulb. A single, intensely powerful pulse of energy lashed out in every direction. Despite being muffled and somewhat contained by Lyn's force field, it still managed to knock both her and Richard off their feet, disrupting their concentration. The bubble and the weight effect both vanished.

Instantly the six warriors were up, advancing on the humans.

Richard scrambled to his feet, raised a hand, and grimaced as Green brought a deadly looking weapon to bear and fired. The blinding blast came within an inch of his face before Lyn's hastily erected force field deflected it away.

"Thanks," he gasped, eyeing the girl with increasing respect.

Startled, Green aimed this time at Pulsar, with Blue and Yellow doing likewise. Their guns cycled up again.

"Oh, no you don't," Lyn shouted. She aimed her right hand at the three nearest her, pointed with her index finger, and a lightning bolt erupted, shooting across the space of Jameson's wrecked office, crashing into Green and sending him sprawling. The parts of her blast that were deflected to the sides impacted Blue and Yellow, spinning them around and backwards, as well.

The remaining three looked at one another, then started forward. Lyn pointed at them. This time, the bolt was tinged in a glowing purple aura, and it didn't just hurl Red and his two compatriots back—it shredded parts of their armor away like tissue paper.

The commandos cried out and stopped their advance, kneeling and clutching at their wounds.

"This is outrageous," came Green's static-filled voice. He had recovered from Pulsar's first attack and leapt at her, his mechanical exoskeleton adding power and range to his jump.

Richard gestured at him and his flight ended halfway across the room. He smashed to the floor and this time appeared to actually leave a man-shaped impression beneath and around himself.

The two undamaged warriors, Yellow and Blue, hesitated, their eye-lenses moving nervously from the humans who were thrashing them to their leader, Green, where he lay unmoving. Then, apparently summoning up their courage, they attacked. Blue's arms extended outward, telescoping like an antenna, increasing to nearly twenty feet in length. The claws at the ends reached for Lyn with deadly intent, jaws snapping open and closed.

Pulsar cried out, more a raw sound than actual words. The purple blast she unleashed melted the alien's metal arms away back to within five feet of Blue. He looked down dumbly at the dripping slag where his high-tech appendages had been, then raised what was left of his arms in surrender.

"No," came the voice of Green, from where he lay. Richard was pressing down with his gravity-increasing power on the alien's head, and the robotic helmet had begun to crease inward. Reaching up, Green wrenched himself free of the helmet, revealing his true appearance: bright red skin and white hair, with very dark eyes that now glared at the humans. "No," he said, "this cannot be."

"Hey! I know these guys," Lyn said, seeing Green unmasked. "I met some of them. Lieutenant Mondrian, I think, was one. Yeah." Then, "Do you know where Esro is?"

Green gave her a brief look of confusion that quickly morphed into hatred.

"So the Fleet—or at least a scout ship—has been here. I thought as much."

He reached down to his belt, feeling for something attached there. Seeing this, Richard frowned and sought to stop him, increasing the weight of the hand. But it was too late—Green had hooked his fingers through a loop on his belt and hung on, reaching, reaching...

And then he stopped. His expression blanked. He moved his hands and his arms smoothly out away from his side and waited.

Richard glanced over at Lyn.

"Um, did you do that?"

"I *can't* do that," Lyn replied, equally puzzled.

"Don't look at me," Jameson added from under his desk. Creeping out, he walked carefully around and studied the scene in the center of his office.

The other five Circle warriors, still surrounded by Lyn's field and held down by Richard's power, appeared to be in a panic, as if they knew something the others didn't. They began to shout at one another and at the humans, though no one could make out what they were saying. Just before Lyn reached the limits of her patience, a hidden door built into the wall to her left slid open, and a man in a dark suit walked out.

"Settle them down," the new man said to Green, and instantly Green issued orders through his armor, overriding commands in the suits of the other five. Their helmets all unsealed and popped off. Instantly they ceased their struggles and protests and sat quietly on the floor, waiting.

"Countermand any orders you have sent to your fleet, regarding attacking this planet."

"Yes," replied Green, who then turned and spoke a command to Yellow.

"You may drop the force field now, Ms. Li," the new arrival said. "I assure you, it's no longer needed."

Puzzled, Lyn did as the man suggested. Richard, too, let up on the pressure he was exerting, lowering his tired arm from where it had been pointing at the aliens during most of the confrontation.

With the field gone, Yellow spoke sharply into his communicator, indicating to the Circle fleet that all was well and no violent actions would be required.

Satisfied, the new man looked from Lyn to Richard and nodded. He smiled, and the others couldn't help but think that his mouth appeared somehow…wider…than normal.

"Thank you for your cooperation," he was saying to Yellow. "Not that you had any choice in the matter, of course."

He turned back to the others and gave a little half-bow.

"My name," he said, "is Randall Nation. And we have much—very much indeed—to discuss."

10

Crimson-gloved hands clasped behind his back, the Warlord in Red gazed up at the massive machine his servants were busily constructing at the center of a vast, bowl-shaped depression. Overhead, a violet-tinged sky fairly vibrated with pulsing energies as a dozen moons spun past—all of this emblematic of the chaos at the core of the madman who had chosen this as his home base and home universe.

"Yes… yes…"

Behind his golden mask, eyes darted here and there, taking in all the details of his scheme as it neared fruition.

"Soon. Soon!"

He, his slaves, and his machinery occupied a vast desert plain on an inhospitable world, many levels of reality away from the universe of the Earth. What little population existed there had been brought—quite against their will—into the service of this Warlord. Tall of stature, with elongated heads and short, brown fur covering most of their bodies, they labored day and night under the dim red sun, striving to obey the will of their new master, and to follow the instructions he had implanted directly and permanently into their minds.

His eyes moved to a series of cables, each more than a dozen feet thick, which trailed away from the apparatus for a short distance before plunging down into the planet's crust. It was a tried and true method that Warlords had used for millennia in their various operations: Choose a planet, subjugate it, build a citadel there, and then power it—and whatever weapons or other devices were required—by sinking power converters deep into the world's interior. It would not provide cosmic-level energies, by any means. But it would be, the Warlord in Red knew, enough.

"Yes. Enough."

He returned his gaze to the machine itself, nodding slowly as the servants hammered and bolted and welded it closer, ever closer, to completion.

Golden in color like this particular Warlord's mask, it was circular in form. It stood on its side like a doorway with no wall around it, and it was anchored into a broad pedestal of gray metal. The workers had just begun fitting strange, oblong objects to the ring itself, at regular intervals. Only two had been connected thus far.

"But soon...soon..."

A flash of light and a popping noise sounded behind the Warlord in Red, and he whirled, the weapons systems concealed beneath his crimson robes switching on and ready.

"Master—no!"

It was only Francisco—faithful little Francisco—emerging from a portal, back from his mission. Behind his mask, the Warlord smiled at him.

"Ahh. Francisco. You have inspected all of my predecessor's haunts, then?"

"Yes—yes, my master. All of them that I know of."

The Warlord nodded, turning back to look out at his machine.

"And I take it there has been no sign of the abomination?"

Francisco hesitated, and the Warlord in Red looked back at him. He stared down at his feet.

"No. No sign of the...the abomination."

The Warlord in Red looked at him for a long second, then nodded once and turned away again.

Francisco gnawed at a long fingernail, deeply disturbed by having to lie to his master.

"The other sanctums and hideaways were bare, Master. They had all been looted, or were long-abandoned."

The other merely nodded distractedly, scarcely listening any longer.

458

Francisco shuffled up beside the taller figure and looked out, across the bowl-shaped valley, at the object being constructed at the center.

He saw its shape. He recognized it instantly. And he gasped.

The Warlord in Red snapped his head down, staring at Francisco intently.

"What... was... that?"

Francisco gulped. His eyes moved from the machine to the Warlord and back. He swallowed.

"Francisco?"

"I—I was merely marveling at the work, Master. It is—so impressive. Yes, impressive."

The Warlord continued to stare at him for another few seconds, then slowly turned his attention back to the device.

"Yes. It is, isn't it?"

Francisco remembered the holographic image his former master had shown him, back in the darkened hideaway. The machine that one had claimed would be capable of destroying all of creation.

This was that machine. A perfect match.

How could he have known? How could he have possibly known what this device would look like, unless...

He looked out at the ring again.

...Unless he was right, and it is what he said it would be?

Francisco fought to suppress a low moan that had begun to emanate from his throat. He was unsuccessful, and within a few seconds he had attracted the Warlord's attention once again.

"Is something wrong, Francisco?"

"No, I—"

The golden mask pointed directly down at him, eyes behind it boring into him.

"No?"

"No—I mean, yes, yes. Sick, yes, I am sick. Something I ate, surely."

"Hmm."

"I should lie down. Rest."

The Warlord in Red studied him carefully.

"Yes. Yes, you should."

Francisco realized he was gnawing his fingernail again, and forced his hand away from his mouth. He smiled weakly and began to shuffle away.

"Yes—very well, Master. I will return to the sanctum and rest. I am, of course, at your beck and call if you should need me."

459

"Of course."

Then, still uncertain, the little man turned and stumbled away from his imposing master. A part of him waited for the lightning bolt to fall, for the deathblow to come.

It did not.

He fumbled at his portal generator and snapped open a doorway back to the main sanctum. With a quick bow to his master, he stepped through and closed it behind him. Only when he was through and back into the relative safety of his quarters did he allow his breathing to return to normal, his pulse to slow.

"It must be true," he breathed. "It must! But—ohh, I am not capable of keeping secrets for long—and surely not from *him!*"

He sat on the floor and rocked back and forth.

"But I cannot go back to the other. I cannot trust him. He cannot help but scheme against the Design. I have seen his nature, and I know it to be true. And *he* knows this, as well."

He rocked some more, clutching at his leather shoes with his small, gnarled hands.

"But then who... who can I trust? Who can possibly help me...?"

He dwelt upon this question for several long, nerve-wracking minutes before he realized he should reformulate the question.

"No, no," he whispered then. "That's not it. No, not it at all. Not who can help *me*."

He grinned suddenly, the weight lifting ever so slightly from his shoulders.

"The question is, 'Who can help the *universe?*'"

Still grinning, he nodded.

"Yes, yes! Who would be so noble, so selfless, as to be willing to sacrifice themselves to save... *everything?*"

He scrambled to his feet abruptly and snatched the portal generator device from his belt.

"Oh, yes," he muttered, dialing in the proper destination.

"*Them.* Yes."

Then he hesitated. For he had just realized: The people he had thought of—their world was about to end anyway. If not from the Xorexes, then from the Rivals. Or perhaps the Kur-Bai. Or...

"They cannot stand against all of those foes—not against even *one* of them, to be truthful."

He considered this, then shrugged.

"But they probably don't realize this. No. No, they don't understand their predicament."

He nodded and opened the portal gateway.

"So I shall give them the opportunity to save the entire *universe*... just before their own world dies. Surely they will think that fair enough."

He paused.

"Or they would, if they were alive afterward."

And so, nodding to himself, he stepped through the portal, and the light-years were as nothing to his vast, cosmic leap.

77

"My name is Randall Nation," the newly-arrived man was saying to Richard and Lyn.

The two of them simply stared back at him, unsure of exactly what was happening.

Lyn made every effort to study the man more closely, but she found that her eyes wanted to slide right off of him. After a few seconds, though, she managed to get a general sense of his appearance.

He stood about six feet tall, with brownish hair combed over in a conservative style. He wore a nondescript blue suit and dark shoes. Nothing about him stood out as remarkable in the least, save perhaps his too-dark eyes that stared out coldly, flickering from one face to the next.

And that mouth. That too-wide, somewhat scary mouth.

"For many years," he said, directing his comments to Richard and Lyn, "I have been pursued across the galaxy by the...people...you see here. The people who attacked you."

Lyn and Richard nodded, listening closely.

"They represent an evil regime—the Kur-Bai Empire. They seek to conquer the entire galaxy and enslave—or kill—anyone who resists them. In this effort they have destroyed worlds—whole cultures—by the dozens. Ask them this freely; they will not deny it."

He shook his head in a display of great sadness and regret.

"I thought I had escaped them here, on this backwater planet—"

He paused and smiled even wider suddenly, giving Lyn the chills.

"I do not mean to offend," he added hastily. "Yours is a very fine world. I simply mean it is not, shall we say, located in the main thoroughfare of interstellar commerce and travel. Off the beaten path, I believe you people say. Yes."

Lyn glanced at Richard. He shrugged.

"I've met some of the Kur-Bai," Lyn pointed out. "They didn't seem so bad. They were here to help us—to stop an attack by a big robot—"

Nation took this in with interest. He held up a hand to stop her.

"A big robot?"

Lyn nodded.

"A robot that attracted their attention. Hmm."

Nation pursed his lips.

"A Xorex, perhaps?"

Lyn frowned.

"I think so," she said, uncertain that she should be giving him such information.

His eyes widened momentarily.

"A Xorex. Here. Well."

He considered this for a few seconds.

"And did they tell you precisely how they intended to go about 'stopping this attack?'"

Lyn licked her lips, thinking back.

"They had weapons and…"

Her brows knitted again.

"And?" Nation asked.

Lyn found herself strangely reluctant to admit the truth.

"And they said they might have to destroy the planet," she allowed finally.

Richard gawked at her. She shrugged back.

"There, you see?" Nation smiled again. "Not so friendly after all, are they? I rest my case."

"It did sound like they were working with Jameson," Richard said. "In my book, that makes them pretty bad."

Lyn stared at him, puzzled.

"*You* worked for Jameson!"

Richard shrugged.

"Ehh. I don't think that really invalidates my point."

Lyn snorted and shook her head at him.

"Well," Nation said then. "I think we all agree, yes? And so what I will need from you, and from your world, is assistance against the Kur-Bai. I'm certain they are sending more ships, even now. Here is what I propose…"

But Richard was ignoring this. He looked over at Jameson, who stood rigidly off to the side. The man had not moved since Nation had appeared.

"You don't have any comments, Jameson? No protests about all of this, about what we're saying?"

Jameson merely continued to stare straight ahead.

"Hey, wait a minute," Lyn interjected suddenly. "What about Ultraa?"

Nation nodded once to her.

"Ah, yes. I had forgotten. I saw Jameson's lackeys abduct him. Give me just one moment…"

Nation stepped back through his secret doorway.

Lyn turned to Richard.

"I'm not sure I—"

"Shhh!" Richard gestured with one hand, hushing Lyn quickly.

"Huh?"

"I have a vague idea of what's going on here," he hissed at her, "but we've got to be very careful. Just—"

"Here we are," Nation said, emerging from his secret passage. Following him out into the office came the familiar, white and red uniformed figure of Ultraa—America's most beloved hero and, until Jameson had revoked his credentials, government agent.

Lyn, eyes wide and misty, rushed forward, grasping Ultraa in a tight embrace.

Hesitantly at first, as if waking from a deep sleep, he hugged her back, and neither moved for several seconds.

"Where—where have you been? What happened?"

"I—" Ultraa started to reply, then hesitated. "I'm not sure."

"Jameson and his cronies were attempting to brainwash him, I believe," Nation said. "Fortunately, I was able to stop them before any permanent damage was done. But he will need some time to fully recover, I believe."

"Is that so, Jameson?" demanded Richard.

The government man merely gurgled wordlessly in reply, his eyes glassy and blank.

Lyn was still hugging Ultraa.

"You disappeared! I've been so worried. Esro still hasn't come back, and—"

Ultraa made a choking sound in the back of his throat. Lyn, concerned, pulled back, looking at him.

"What is it?"

"I—I—"

He looked intently from Lyn to Randall Nation.

"...You..."

Nation frowned for the very first time in the entire conversation.

"I...what?"

Ultraa squinted his eyes, looking down. Then his head snapped back up and he stared intently at Nation.

"You—you did something. I remember."

"Yes. Of course. I rescued you. You're quite welcome, of course." But Nation's expression now betrayed something beyond his words. A slight look of concern crept over his odd features.

Lyn's eyes moved from one of them to the other.

"Is that true?"

"Yes, it—*no*, wait."

Nation was frowning deeply now.

"No. He did something else. He—he *controlled* everyone in the room. In this room. Jameson, and..."

"I'm afraid the brainwashing that Jameson's men were doing to Ultraa has affected his memories," Nation interjected quickly. He started forward.

"Is that so, Jameson?" Richard moved between Nation and the others, looking over at the stock-still figure of his former boss. "Nothing to say in your own defense?"

Jameson gurgled wordlessly again.

"Cat got your tongue? Or an *alien* has it, maybe?"

Nation's gaze settled hard upon Heavyweight. But before he could speak further, Ultraa stepped up beside Richard and raised a red-gloved hand toward Nation.

"Wait—wait. That's it. An alien! You—" He stared at Nation now. "You—you're an *alien*. I remember. I remember meeting Mondrian and DeSkai and the other Kur-Bai—the red skin, the white hair—and you're one of them!"

Nation's eyes drilled into Ultraa, to absolutely no effect.

"This cannot be," he was muttering. "No one—certainly no weak human—can resist—"

"I knew it," Richard stated flatly. He started to raise his hand.

"STOP."

Randall Nation lashed out at the entire room with his overwhelming mental powers, freezing everyone's minds, locking them all down.

"I will have obedience," he growled at them all. "Obedience!"

No one moved a muscle. No one but Ultraa. He choked, trembled, and took a tenuous, hesitant step forward.

Nation stared at him in abject surprise.

"You cannot move. You *cannot!*"

Ultraa took another step.

"You will freeze where you stand!"

Ultraa took two more strong, bold steps. His facial expression had changed from slack blankness to grim determination and anger.

Nation leaned in to within a few inches of Ultraa's face, his eyes flashing.

"Not...another...step! I will not have it!"

Ultraa reached back, then brought his crimson fist forward, smashing Nation in the jaw, sending him sprawling back into Jameson's desk.

Everyone in the room started to move.

"NO!"

Nation was on his feet again instantly, and the room froze once more.

All but Ultraa. He continued to push relentlessly toward Nation, bringing back his fist again.

Nation moved with inhuman speed, seizing Ultraa with both hands to the sides of his face, leaning in. He reached down into the hero's mind with all of the awesome, formidable power at his disposal.

"You are mine," he hissed. "Mine! You cannot resist! No one in all the galaxy can!"

Ultraa gagged, seeking to bring his arms up to ward off the attack, but Nation forced them down with his mental assault.

"Let me into your mind. *Let me in!* Let me see what gives you this remarkable ability to resist my influence."

Ultraa could not physically fight back, but his mind remained closed.

Nation emitted a wailing sound.

"How? There is simply no way you can be doing this! It is impossible!"

Ultraa did not—could not—speak. He simply stood there, and Nation hammered away at the ramparts of his mind in futility.

"Deeper. I must go deeper into your thoughts—your earliest memories—to root out the source of your resistance. I will rewire your very brain, if I must!"

He had Ultraa nearly bent over backward, their noses almost touching. Waves of unearthly psychic energy lashed out at Ultraa, forcing their way in at last, peeling his mind back in layers, digging deeper and deeper, until—

"What? How can that be? How can such things possibly be *true?*"

Nation nearly stumbled, his physical body now forgotten as his mental form ransacked Ultraa's brain.

"You—you are not so old as that! No one on your world has lived so long. This cannot be true—"

Deeper he dug, rooting out the many dormant strata of the amnesiac Ultraa's long-atrophied and forgotten memories.

"Too much! It's *too much!* You—you cannot *possibly* have—"

Ultraa had straightened up now, and Randall Nation sank to his knees. But Ultraa's arms remained limp, as he hung suspended in the vast network of Nation's psychic assault.

"Ah! Ah, I *see it* now! That must be it!"

Nation straightened, his voice nearly a mad cackle.

"There, at the very heart of your memories, lies a node, sealed off from all else. That must surely be the basis of your resistance. I have but to open it, to look inside…"

Nation shrieked.

"Nothing! *Nothing!* There—there is nothing but a hole—a *hole*, there in your mind…"

Releasing Ultraa, he stumbled back, away from the hero, who was himself so disoriented now that he could not act.

The others in the room stirred and began to recover as Nation reeled from the backlash of what he had encountered inside Ultraa's mind. The six of the Circle started to rise. Lyn and Richard shook their heads violently, coming to their senses.

Nation stumbled back another step, both of his hands to his face.

Jameson clocked him over the head with a marble bookend, and he collapsed to the floor, out cold.

"Well, that was all very unexpected," Jameson said, as the others all stared back at him, dumbfounded. "Now—what are all you people doing in my office?"

12

The conflict at the Pentagon was over. The mopping up had begun.

The troops surrounding Jameson's wing of the building were in the process of standing down, though some of them remained in strategic points just in case the strange visitors from another planet tried anything unexpected. All of them wondered exactly what had happened earlier, what was happening now, and what would happen next. And some of them had caught glimpses of strange beings in futuristic armor, gray splashed with fluorescent colors, moving around inside the offices. Speculation ran rampant.

Meanwhile, Richard and Lyn sat in big leather chairs off to one side of the office—the only two chairs still intact, more or less. They were now merely interested observers, not deeply involved in this phase of the proceedings, which involved negotiating the final disposal of the being called Randall Nation and the withdrawal of the Circle fleet from Earth orbit.

The part Lyn and Richard were most interested in, of course, was the final disposal of Jameson himself—something Ultraa was pressing the case for, at that very moment.

"He's Mr. Cooperation now, isn't he?" chuckled Richard as he watched Jameson speaking earnestly with a huddle of people that included Ultraa and the leader of the Circle warriors.

Lyn simply shook her head.

"He must think he's going to get off."

"He probably will."

Lyn turned to Richard, a shocked expression on her face.

"What? How's that possible? We have him dead to rights! You got him to admit everything, right in front of me!"

Richard smiled.

"Yeah, I did, didn't I? I think I deserve an Emmy."

"Well, I played my part, too," Lyn pointed out.

"Absolutely. You made a fine rolled-up rug."

Lyn huffed.

"And the way you went about not saying anything," Richard added, "was awesome."

Lyn punched him.

Richard grinned at her.

"That's a far cry from what you did to me the last time we met," he said.

"Huh. You should just be glad you were sincere about making things up to me, when we met at the Starbucks." She grinned. "I was sure you were going to try something. I honestly never thought we'd end up sipping lattes and plotting to take down a government official."

"Yeah, well, he needs to go. And I'm done with his crap. No more missions for me. I wanted to do this, for my own sake as well as for Ultraa and you. But now I'm done." Richard rubbed his eyes tiredly. "Not that the jerk's necessarily going to get what he has coming."

"You do think he's going to get off? To get away with everything?"

"Not everything, no. But he'll still be here, still in power, when we leave today."

Lyn met his eyes, frowned, and leaned forward in her chair, rocking back and forth nervously.

"I hope you're wrong."

"I'm not. But you'll notice he's talking with Ultraa as more of an equal now—not pulling that business about 'you're not an official agent anymore' on him. That's a good sign, anyway."

Lyn watched as Jameson leaned in angrily toward Ultraa, barking sharp words at him. She gave Richard a dubious look.

"If you say so…"

And meanwhile, across the room:

"None of it was my fault! None of it was my doing!"

Jameson's face was red, either with outrage or embarrassment.

"You saw that this Nation character had me completely under his control. Most of us aren't fortunate enough to have superhuman powers to resist that kind of thing."

"It wasn't any superhuman power that let me resist him," Ultraa replied flatly. "But, in any case, I think it's disingenuous of you to blame him for *all* of it. We have no evidence that he controlled you during all of these operations you've been running."

The blond hero leaned in closer.

"In fact, I think he had very little to do with your operations. I think he's only been around here a short time, and most of this was *your* doing."

He rested his red-gloved hands on his hips as Jameson sputtered wordlessly.

"You didn't seem very 'controlled' when I confronted you about Damon," Ultraa went on. "And why would an alien mastermind want Esro's technology, for that matter?"

Ultraa shook his head. Then he drove his point home:

"No, I think this was all you, from the start."

Jameson took that in, and no one spoke for a moment. Then his eyes narrowed and he leaned back toward Ultraa.

"But you can't prove any of that," he shot back.

Ultraa got up in his face.

"You son of a—"

"Excuse me," said the seven-foot tall, armored alien, who had been ignored up till that point. He stepped between them. His helmet was off and tucked under one arm. His long, white hair trailed down his back, and his dark eyes shifted from one of the humans to the other. "I see that you two…gentlemen…have matters to work out between yourselves, but—"

"Yes, yes," Jameson said, dismissing and practically ignoring the powerful being who had nearly strangled him a short time earlier. He had determined the six warriors were merely field agents for the Circle. As such, he had no more use for them. "You want to take Nation with you. That's fine with me. We have no desire to keep him here, and you surely have much more secure ways of containing him."

"Indeed we do."

Ultraa nodded, saying, "Sure, that works for me, too."

"No one asked you," said Jameson curtly.

Ultraa shot Jameson a look that could curdle milk, then turned back to the warrior and studied the big, armored being closely for a moment.

"I'm not entirely sure I understand who you of the Circle are, or what your agenda is, but…" His mouth formed a grim line. "I don't want Nation anywhere on this planet any longer than necessary. If you're carrying him far away from here, then you people are welcome to him."

The alien commando looked from Ultraa to Jameson and back, as if sizing up exactly who was in charge here now. Then he seemed to shrug and turned, walking over to where his companions stood huddled in conversation.

Ultraa glared at Jameson.

"That brings me to the other thing," the blond man said. "I want full agent status for myself, Ms. Li, and Brachis restored

469

immediately." He paused for a second. "And Vanadium, too, once we figure out what's going on with him."

Jameson glared at him.

"Absolutely not."

Ultraa squared off against the government man, filled with anger.

"After everything you've done, everything you've been involved in, directly or indirectly…"

He took Jameson's measure and leaned in closer.

"We may not be able to prove everything—"

"Anything," Jameson interjected.

"—but we can surely make your professional and personal life miserable, from now till the cows come home. I will personally testify before Congress. I will go to the President. I will spread word of the dirty dealings going on in your department to the ends of the earth. And you know as well as I do—people will listen to me."

Ultraa crossed his arms, his jaw set.

"They might not throw you into prison, but you'll be curtailed, hemmed in, investigated…"

Jameson glared back at him. Long seconds ticked past, as the room became utterly silent. On one side of the wrecked office, Richard watched with interest while Lyn held her breath, telling herself not to attack the man if she didn't like his answer. On the other side, the six aliens looked on in bemused fascination.

Ultraa had not blinked. Jameson stared back at him, his face as red now as Ultraa's gloves and boots. Sweat trickled down Jameson's forehead and hit his eye. He blinked.

"Fine," he said then. "Fine. Full status is returned to you and the girl—and to Brachis, if you can ever find him."

Ultraa nodded grimly.

"As for Vanadium… We never authorized his inclusion on your team. I can't restore what he never had. That's another issue for another day."

Ultraa considered this, his eyes never wavering. Then, "All right. That's acceptable, for now." He paused. "And this Field Marshal?"

Jameson's face assumed a sour look.

"Yes, yes. I will revoke his status as primary agent. That's yours again."

"All clearances are gone from his group?"

"Well, I—"

Ultraa leaned in again.

"I did some research. Do you even know who half of them are? Who they really are?"

"What? Yes, of course, I—"

Ultraa eyed him.

"No. Actually, no. I took the Field Marshal's recommendations on some, and…"

Ultraa nodded.

"So they're gone. Done."

Reluctantly, Jameson nodded.

A couple of minutes later, Jameson had signed the appropriate forms and couriers had accepted them, carrying them to the appropriate departments of the vast building. Everything was official.

Jameson slumped in his half-wrecked chair, running a hand through his thinning hair.

"We're back," Lyn crowed.

For the first time all day, Ultraa smiled. But it was a grave, businesslike smile. He turned from the beaten Jameson to Lyn, his disposition warming by the moment.

"You ready?"

"Ready?"

"To go get your sister."

Lyn matched Ultraa's smile. She hopped up, rushing over to him.

"You bet!"

Then she hesitated.

"Wait…"

She looked back at Richard. He hadn't moved; he was leaning back in his chair, his feet resting on a piece of debris, watching everything unfold with an air of weariness.

She tapped Ultraa on the shoulder and pointed, whispering something in the blond man's ear.

Ultraa listened, then looked over with interest at the dark-headed man in the long coat.

"Heavyweight, right?"

"Yeah."

"I remember you."

Richard shrugged.

"I've already apologized to the girl, at length. I guess I should to you, too."

Ultraa made a dismissive gesture. Then he ran a finger over his chin, considering the options.

471

"You helped Pulsar with this—with all of this, right?"

Richard nodded.

"So you don't have much loyalty to Jameson, then."

"Much? None." He snorted. "If I ever did, it's shot now."

Ultraa nodded.

"Pulsar wants you to join us. I'm willing to consider it, at least for now. We could use the help."

Richard thought about this for a few seconds. Then he stood, brushing off his dark slacks.

"Why not? It's not like I have anything better to do."

He winked at Lyn.

"But we're even now, right?"

Lyn grinned at him.

"Yeah. Even."

Richard nodded. Then, looking back at Lyn, he couldn't help but return her smile.

Ultraa seemed satisfied.

"Okay, let's move," he said, striding through the splintered doorway and past the Marines who stood idly about in the corridor.

Lyn and Richard followed.

"You mean she's not the leader of this outfit?" Richard asked as they exited.

This time, even Ultraa laughed.

13

The Field Marshal reacted in shocked surprise as the alarm wailed to life.

"Vas—?"

Leaping up from his executive chair, there in the heart of his Digimacht Enterprises headquarters building in the heavily wooded suburbs outside of Washington, DC, he moved with remarkable nimbleness around his desk and across his office. He threw open the door just as his lieutenant, Blitzkrieg, appeared around the corner.

"What is happening?" the younger man asked, eyes wide.

"I do not know," the Field Marshal replied, "but I cannot imagine that anyone would dare to attack us here, in our—"

"We're under attack," shouted a voice from the other end of the hall. A tall, muscular, dark-skinned man was emerging from the gymnasium, wearing sweat pants and a tank top. As the other two turned and saw him coming, a thin black film spread out from one of his hands and quickly covered him over, thickening by the second. As he reached the Field Marshal and his lieutenant, the man called Douglas Williams was no more—now there was only the Fury, a melding of human flesh and alien, organic armor.

The alarm continued to wail. Now the door to the cafeteria opened and Wendy Li raced out, her shiny silver uniform in place, belled cuffs rustling as she ran. The young, Chinese-American girl was followed quickly by Angela Devereux, also known as Distraxion. The blonde woman wore a blood red bikini, with thigh-high boots and long gloves of the same color. A pair of pink sunglasses completed her skimpy ensemble.

"What's going on?" Wendy asked breathlessly.

"Someone is at the front door," the Field Marshal said, striding regally past the others. He gave Blitzkrieg a significant look. "Let us go and welcome them."

Reaching the far end of the twisted maze of corridors that made up the Digimacht building, the German reached a huge, reinforced metal door. He punched in a code on the keypad next to it, and the door slid silently up into the wall above.

And he found himself nose-to-nose with Ultraa.

"You!"

The blond man in white and red stood squarely in the Field Marshal's path. His hands were balled in fists, resting on his hips, elbows out wide. His feet rested firmly on the concrete that covered the area just outside the squat, sprawling headquarters building entrance. His eyes, blue and sparkling, met the German's and locked in on them with palpable force.

"Me," Ultraa replied.

The Field Marshal started to back up a step, then forced himself to stop and stand his ground. He could hear the others coming up behind him, and knew he had to maintain the sense of being in command—of having the upper hand.

"Und vat do you want here, *vigilante?*" he demanded, with special emphasis on the last word.

But Ultraa only smiled—a thin, tight smile that spread quickly across his face and then evaporated like the morning mist.

"That's not exactly right," the man said. "At least, not any longer. Or haven't you heard?"

473

The Field Marshal frowned slightly.

"Vas?"

Looking past Ultraa for the first time, he became aware of two others who stood a few feet behind the American. One was all too well known to him: the Li girl. The older one—the sister of Wendy. The other person, though, did not look familiar. Tall, with medium-length dark hair, and wearing a long coat over dark clothes—no, he did not know this person. And that concerned him.

"What do you want here?" the Field Marshal demanded. "State your business and be gone from this installation before you are all arrested for trespassing on federal property."

"Federal property?" Ultraa repeated. "Seriously?"

"Ja," the German replied, wary.

"I never asked the taxpayers to foot the bill for my place," the American replied, frowning.

Anger welled up within the Field Marshal. He summoned up all of his intense hostility, straightened to his full height, meager as it might be, and stepped forward.

"I do not care what you have done in the past, or who you might once have been. Your time has come and gone and now it is my time. *Our* time. Now leave, or we will arrest you all and take you into federal custody. You will spend the next few months living in a penitentiary—if you are fortunate!"

The man in the coat behind Ultraa was laughing now. The Li girl snickered. Ultraa himself only smiled evenly back at the Field Marshal.

"I think you're the ones who should be concerned about where you'll be living next," Ultraa said.

"Enough of your games," the Field Marshal bellowed. "What is the meaning of this?"

"Go ahead and tell him," the man in the coat said. "You've milked it for all it was worth."

Still smiling a beatific smile, Ultraa nodded slowly.

"Yeah, you're right."

He leaned in closer to the Field Marshal.

"Your license has been revoked."

The Field Marshal blinked. He hesitated a moment, trying to make sense of this expression.

"Vas? My license...?"

"Your government sanction. Your license to act as an agent of the US Government. It's gone. It's done. It's reverted back to me and my associates."

The Field Marshal took this in and considered it. He knew of only one way to reply to it.

"You lie!"

"I'm Ultraa," the other man replied with utter sincerity, shrugging. "I don't generally lie. Why would I?"

"But—I have received no such word from the government!"

"Did Jameson lie to us?" Lyn asked, growing upset. "Some kind of trick, or…"

"No, I don't think so," Ultraa replied, his voice level. "He knows better. He probably just didn't feel like actually making the call to these people, and breaking the news. He left that job to us."

"Typical," said the man in the gray coat.

The Field Marshal eyed Ultraa more closely.

"You are serious."

Ultraa nodded.

The Field Marshal frowned, rubbing at his chin.

"If this is true, the man Jameson is a fool. Of course, I saw that from the beginning. But he was a useful fool, at first. Now…"

Ultraa ignored all of this.

"We want the girl," he said. "She's going back home to her family. The rest of you—I really don't care what you do, as long as you understand the US Government is no longer covering for you, or paying for your ….. "

The Field Marshal's face slowly dissolved into a glare of frustrated rage.

"This is madness!"

Ultraa laughed.

"The only madness was the government recognizing your crowd as any kind of legitimate operatives to begin with."

He leaned in, almost bumping the Field Marshal's chest.

"You know as well as I do that you and your people are up to no good. You've been involved in criminal activities from the moment you arrived from—*wherever* you came from. Now hand over the Li girl and evacuate the premises immediately and maybe I won't start investigating *all* of your activities just yet."

The Field Marshal blustered and sputtered. He gathered up his wits and his stratagems and he started to open his mouth to give the American a clever and stinging rebuke, when suddenly a blast of greenish light flared out from behind him and struck at Ultraa.

Ultraa's reaction defied belief. He was in motion even as the beam flashed out, and when it struck him, he had assumed his invulnerable mode. The energy discharge still hurled him twenty yards back, sending him tumbling head over heels until he rolled to a stop on the hard concrete—but it didn't kill him.

"Hey!" shouted Pulsar, rushing forward and raising one hand between herself and the Field Marshal. The air around her sparkled and a crackling, golden force field sphere formed around herself and the man in the long coat, protecting them both. She glanced back and saw that Ultraa was getting up, apparently no worse for the wear, then turned back to the German, glaring at him.

"Give me my sister or I'll bring this whole place down around your ears!"

But the Field Marshal had turned as well, ignoring her, facing back into the building. He was shouting at someone.

Before anyone could react, a dark blur streaked out of the building and collided with Ultraa just as he had regained his feet.

The man in the long coat whirled and started toward Ultraa, only to collide with the inside of Pulsar's force field.

"What was that?" Pulsar asked, mostly to herself.

A humanoid figure of smooth, featureless jet black tumbled away from Ultraa, then quickly regained its footing and advanced on him again.

"Williams," the German shouted. "Nein!"

"I think it is too late for that," growled Blitzkrieg, emerging from the doorway as well. "Might as well see this thing through."

Before the older man could stop him, Blitzkrieg streaked into action. His super speed carried him rapidly past the others and he crashed into Ultraa from the back, just as he was squaring off against the first attacker. As Ultraa went down again, both Blitzkrieg and the dark shape leapt upon him.

Now Distraxion in her red swimsuit emerged from the building, taking in the scene in an instant. Zeroing in on Pulsar, she moved to the outer edge of the shimmering force bubble and caught the young woman's attention.

"You don't want to do that," Distraxion said, raising her sunglasses and allowing her mind control powers to reach out for the girl in gold.

"No," Lyn replied, "*you* don't want to do *that!*"

Instantly the force field vanished. Before the blonde woman could react, Pulsar lashed out with a destructive burst of energy from her fingertips. It struck the surprised Distraxion a glancing blow, but one still powerful enough to spin her to the ground and leave her unmoving.

"You don't want to do that," Distraxion said.

"Pulsar," Ultraa cried from behind her. "Control yourself! Don't hurt anybody!" He intended to say more, but then had to fend off attacks from both the younger German and the man in black.

Lyn glared down at the inert form of Distraxion where she lay on the ground, then up at the Field Marshal—who appeared at a loss, unable to affect the unfolding events in any way.

"Just give me my sister and this can end," she hissed at him.

"Your sister is with us of her own free—"

"You're a liar!"

Lyn stalked forward, stepping over Distraxion.

The blonde woman reached up, grabbed Lyn by a shiny golden ankle, and twisted her down. Lyn's head banged on the concrete as she fell, and her eyes fluttered madly as she nearly lost consciousness.

"Yes," the Field Marshal exulted, at last seeing the opportunity for success here. "Subdue her. Quickly!"

Distraxion held the dazed Pulsar down by the throat with one hand, while raising her sunglasses with the other.

"Look into my eyes, little girl," Distraxion purred softly. "Look and know who your mistress truly is. You live only to serve—"

And then Distraxion found herself eating the concrete.

"Mmmmffgghhh!"

Lyn blinked and sat up.

"Who—what—?"

Just in front of her, the slender woman in the red swimsuit lay immobile, her breathing ragged. No one had touched her, and yet something—some force—pressed down from above, crushing her to the ground.

"Wha—*ohhhh!*"

Lyn turned around and grinned. The man in the long coat—Heavyweight—stood there, one hand extended toward Distraxion. Lyn shifted ever so slightly into her "second sight" and could suddenly see the waves of gravity emanating from that hand, increasing the blonde woman's weight.

"Wow. I think it may be time for you to consider a diet," she quipped.

"Mmmmffgghhh!"

She winked at Heavyweight.

"Thanks."

"Not a problem," Richard replied, winking back. Turning his attention to the Field Marshall, he exerted only a tiny fraction of his power and sank the older man, scowling, slowly to one knee.

"Go see to your sister," he said.

Nodding once to him, Lyn raced through the doorway.

14

"You people are fascinating," the green warrior of the Circle told Jameson.

The other alien commandos were busy unpacking a big piece of machinery that nearly filled the wrecked Pentagon office. Their leader stood to one side, helmet under one arm, supervising, while Jameson sat glumly behind his shattered desk.

"Either it is a wonder your race survived this long," the commando continued, running a hand back through his thick, white hair, "or else the entire galaxy should quake at the prospect of you becoming involved in interstellar politics in the near future."

Jameson waved his hand dismissively.

"I have nothing further to say to you people. I want all of you Circle jerks out of here, and out of here now."

The Kur-Bai rebel commando stared down at Jameson through narrowed eyes.

"I had a mission to do here, and I have accomplished it," he said, the distaste in his voice dripping from every word. "I *gratefully* leave it to my superiors to continue dealing with you... should they prove so foolish."

With that, the rebel warrior spun on his heel and marched across to where the others had completed assembling their machine.

"All is in readiness," the trooper in blue reported.

Green nodded.

"Put him in."

Two of the others, now stripped of their combat armor and instead wearing matte black military uniforms, lifted the still-unconscious body of Randall Nation—Rnn'dul Nah-Shonn—and lowered him into the machine. A panel started to slide closed across the front. Green reached down and stopped it partway across, before it could close entirely.

Blue blinked and looked up at him, puzzled.

479

Frowning, the leader ran his hands along the surface of the panel, reaching inside it as if inspecting it carefully. Then, apparently satisfied, he allowed it to close the rest of the way.

"Take him aboard the shuttle."

He gestured to the others and signaled.

"The sooner we are away from this place, the better."

The Circle commandos filed out of the office, making their way in two columns to the shuttle that had landed some minutes earlier. The big rectangular case that contained Rnn'dul Nah-Shonn floated along between them, advanced technology holding it aloft.

The cargo door angled down and the troopers pushed the big case up into the spacecraft, following it inside. Last to climb aboard, the leader hesitated at the foot of the ramp, looking back at the Pentagon and the Virginia skyline beyond it.

"This would not be so repulsive a planet if it held more individuals like the man in white and red—Ultraa—and fewer of Jameson's variety." He scoffed. "But of course, for every Ultraa on every inhabited world in the galaxy, there are a billion Jamesons. It seems inevitable."

Striding up the ramp, he sealed the door behind him. Seconds later, the shuttle lofted up into the sky. Quickly it achieved orbit, and soon it had reached the lead ship of the Circle fleet. Passing through into the landing bay, it sealed itself against the airlock and the inner hatch slid open.

"Get him into cold storage," the commando leader barked as his men hustled Rnn'dul Nah-Shonn's containment box out of the shuttle. The others saluted and pushed the big crate down the corridor.

Just before the box rounded the first corner, a slight clicking sound came from it. No one noticed.

Green watched them go, then turned and strode to an observation port. He stared through the transparent oval at the blue-white gleam of the Earth. Moments later, the planet began to shrink as the Circle fleet kicked in their engines and headed out of the system.

Green watched the Earth dwindle in the vast distance, becoming a pale blue dot that quickly faded into the blackness.

"If I never see that world again, it will be too soon," he muttered.

He did not yet realize that he and his entire fleet would be back only a short time later.

15

On the broad, concrete-covered patio in front of the Digimacht Enterprises headquarters building, Ultraa found himself tackled from two directions by two very different adversaries. He wasted no words, instead devoting himself to taking them both down, the better to help Lyn and to take the Field Marshal into custody—something he was now determined to do.

One of his attackers was obviously German, based on the accent he exhibited as they fought, and it seemed a safe bet the man was probably an associate of the Field Marshal. He was big, with close-cropped blond hair, and wore a dark gray jumpsuit. He seemed to possess super speed, possibly greater even than Ultraa's, though he had not yet displayed any flying abilities.

The other...*person*...presented more of a mystery. Nearly as big as the German, this one had no face, no features whatsoever—simply a slick, jet black coating of some sort that covered his entire body. He had yet to speak a word, merely attacking and falling back, attacking and falling back. He seemed somewhat awkward in his movements, as if he had only recently learned how to walk or get around.

And maybe he did, Ultraa thought to himself. *Or, at least, only recently while covered in* that *thing—whatever it is.*

The man in black was strong—impressively so. Occasionally, as well, he would fire intense green bolts of energy from his hands at Ultraa.

Caught between these two formidable opponents, Ultraa sought to fall back, to regroup, to gain some sort of advantage. He had seen his two companions out of the corner of his eye a few seconds earlier and knew they were dealing with their own problems at the moment.

His foes allowed him no time at all. They were on him again in an instant, the man in black wrapping around his legs and tackling him down while the German unleashed a barrage of electrical blasts from his fingertips.

Summoning up all of his determination, Ultraa cracked the black-clad figure across the jaw with his red-gloved fist. Then he leapt at the German, bringing him down, delivering a series of rapid punches to the man's muscular midsection.

Before this assault could have any real effect, a shiny black hand grasped him from behind, by the throat, and dragged him off of Blitzkrieg.

Ultraa wrenched free and spun around, swinging wildly at what he had decided was the more dangerous opponent. Both of his punches missed, as the dark figure dodged with startling speed. Behind him, Blitzkrieg raised his hands to attack once more—

—and a wave of force swept over him, driving him down to the cold concrete.

Yes, Ultraa thought to himself. *That evens the odds a little.*

Ultraa saw Heavyweight moving in closer, clearly exerting a great deal of force in order to keep his opponent pinned down. He wanted to help, but then the dark man came at him again, relentlessly, and this time managed to grasp him in a tight hold, one arm around his neck, squeezing tighter and tighter.

A few feet away, he could see the German barking something at Richard—who replied sharply in return. They appeared to be bickering, though Ultraa couldn't really spare the concentration needed to figure it all out.

Then suddenly Heavyweight seemed to let up, and Blitzkrieg slowly rose to his feet again. The two exchanged more words, both nodded, and then—

Are they wrestling?

The two had rushed forward, locking hands over their heads, and now they appeared to be engaged in a contest of strength and wills. Neither of them was using his powers.

Ultraa watched in amazement.

I guess I really don't know that guy, he thought. *If he were on my team, I would never let him—*

Before he could follow the matter further, a cracking blow to the jaw from his own opponent brought him back to the present.

Head in the game, he told himself.

A series of martial arts moves freed him from the man in black's grasp, and another flurry of them sent the dark man stumbling back. Back—but not down. He was proving to be extremely tough and extremely dangerous.

Another glance back and he saw Heavyweight and his German foe had apparently switched to boxing. Richard had his coat off now, and the two of them were exchanging stinging blows.

A blast of green energy caught Ultraa across the side of the head, and he fell to one knee, dazed. His opponent rushed him, grasping him roughly, pinning him tightly with both hands wrapped around his throat. Its strength was awesome. And now that he was unable to move, Ultraa could feel his invulnerability—a power tied intimately to his super speed—slipping away.

Looking up at that blank, featureless face, he gasped, "Who— who are you? *Why*—?"

The dark form continued to press down on him, and stars swam in his vision. From the corner of his eye, he could see Blitzkrieg and Heavyweight still slugging it out, neither of them backing down.

A couple of tough sons of—

He choked, gasping for air. The fingers tightened. He returned his attention to the man-form above him.

"Who—"

"Fury!" came the reply, in a voice alien and bizarre. "Fury!"

"Sorry," Ultraa gasped, his consciousness receding rapidly. "Never—never heard of you."

The shape pressed, pressed—and eased off.

And then, slowly, like candle wax melting, the black coating thinned and slid downward to the neck, revealing the face of an African-American man in his mid-thirties. His face, at first contorted with rage and hatred, softened as reason and rationality returned.

The grip released entirely. The man in black hovered there over him for another couple of seconds, then rocked back on his heels, his face now portraying puzzlement and confusion.

Ultraa sat up quickly, trying to breathe.

The other man was staring at him now.

"I know you," he said softly. "Ultraa."

Ultraa nodded, remaining cautious but sensing that his opponent's entire personality had just changed.

The other man—Fury—was frowning deeply now. He gazed off into the distance, then looked back to Ultraa.

"Somebody messed with my mind," he stated flatly, matter-of-factly.

"Oh?"

"I think I know who, too," he added, rising to his feet. He studied the area for a second, then cursed.

"Looks like she's gone."

Ultraa stood as well and dusted his white uniform off. The other seemed wholly benign now, at least toward him, and he saw no reason to try to change that. So he waited, watching to see what the man would do next.

What he did next was turn back to face Ultraa, right hand extended.

"I'm sorry," the man said. "I'm very glad to meet you. I'm Doug Williams."

If the fact that this man had been trying to murder Ultraa mere moments earlier wasn't going to faze the guy, Ultraa saw no reason why he should let it bother him overmuch, either. Especially seeing as how it seemed to be over now.

He took the man's hand and shook it firmly.

"It's an honor," Williams went on, smiling.

"Thanks."

Ultraa was looking at the fighting match evolving between Heavyweight and his German opponent.

"If you'll excuse me," Ultraa began, "I think I ought to help my friend here."

Williams nodded, then raised a hand.

"Wait just a second," he said. "Those two look pretty serious about this. Maybe you shouldn't interfere."

Ultraa started to object, then thought better of it. Shrugging, he walked over to where the two big men were fighting, standing just beyond their perimeter, hands on hips.

"Heavyweight," he called out to his new ally, "you have things under control there?"

A sharp grunt was all the reply Richard offered. Then he and Blitzkrieg crashed to the hard concrete again, rolling over and over.

"Okay," Ultraa said, suppressing a laugh.

"You ask me," Williams was saying, "your real problem's over there."

He pointed to where the Field Marshal stood near the door leading into his headquarters, clearly contemplating his next move— one that had the look of desperate flight at the moment.

Ultraa nodded, then hesitated.

"But isn't that your boss? Isn't this your team?" he asked, meeting the man's brown eyes.

"I thought so, yeah," Williams replied. "But that was when I was convinced they were on the up and up."

Ultraa gave him a questioning look that said, *Seriously?*

Williams held out for only a second or two before he had to laugh.

"Okay, okay. At least *somewhat* on the up and up."

He looked away, thoughtful.

"But if the Field Marshal really has been kicked out of government service now…and the rest of us with him…"

He glanced at Ultraa, who nodded solemnly.

"…then I have no further business with them. Especially now that they're not clouding up my brain."

Ultraa took that in, thought about it, and nodded again.

"Makes sense to me."

Then a sharp, violent sound echoed across the area, from just behind them, followed by a laugh.

Ultraa and Williams turned quickly at the sound and saw Blitzkrieg lying prostrate on the ground, unconscious, with Heavyweight standing triumphant over him.

"I knew I could take him, if I had the chance to study his moves."

Ultraa grinned. He found himself coming to like the guy more and more, almost in spite of himself.

"You didn't make his arms or legs heavier while you fought, did you?"

"Would I do that?"

"I don't know. You worked for Jameson."

Richard shrugged.

"Can't argue with that one," he admitted, walking over to them. And then, "Hey—so did *you!*"

Ultraa winced.

"I was hoping you didn't know that."

Richard tapped the side of his head.

"I know lots of stuff. And it's all up here."

"…Right."

Off to the side, Williams was watching the two of them, his eyes moving from one to the other. Finally he shook his head.

"I was thinking about asking to join your team," he said. "But now, I'm thinking I can probably find a better use for my time than playing referee."

Richard and Ultraa exchanged looks, then grinned and laughed.

"But he's not on the team either," Ultraa said after a second, indicating Heavyweight.

"I don't want to be," Richard shot back.

"That's a good thing," Ultraa replied.

"Yeah," Williams muttered, watching them again. "Like I said…"

They laughed again, as much to relieve the stress of the whole encounter as anything. Then Richard pointed to the Field Marshal, who appeared to be sneaking back into his headquarters.

"I think we should hang onto that guy," he said. "Maybe ask him a few questions."

Ultraa nodded. In a flash, he had rocketed across the concrete strip and landed beside the German, grasping him firmly by the arm. The gray-headed man glared at him.

Richard came up to Ultraa and frowned suddenly.

"Did Pulsar not come back yet?"

Ultraa looked around, eyes widening. In the fighting and the confusion, he had actually forgotten her.

"I—I don't know."

He handed the Field Marshal over to Heavyweight and lofted up into the air a few dozen feet, turning slowly, his hand shielding his eyes from the sun.

"Pulsar!" he called. *"Lyn!"*

16

"Wendy!"

Pulsar raced down the long, twisting corridors of the Digimacht building, calling out her sister's name as she went. There was no reply. The place seemed utterly deserted.

"Wendy! Where are you?"

She ran past numerous doors, all closed, all locked. Finally, after running for what seemed nearly forever, she slowed as she entered a broad, central hub. The walls, mostly drab, gray-painted sheetrock, gave way to a star-shaped intersection running off in five directions.

She huffed.

"Where are you?"

Still no reply.

She looked all around, growing more and more concerned by the moment. In her frustration and anxiety, she slipped into her "second sight" mode again.

"Wow—"

486

The walls, the corridors, the sheetrock all went away. Instead she found herself standing at the center of a spiraling spider web—a maze of wireframe circles and lines. The ebb and flow of energy, mostly in the form of electricity and data transmission lines, surged all around her.

"I will never, ever get used to this," she whispered, surprised afterward to have heard herself in something like a normal voice.

And then she noticed another variety of energy mixed into the tableau around her. It was silvery-white, radiating out in pleasant waves. She followed the emanations with her second sight back in the direction from which they came. After a few seconds, she located the source: a concentration of energy a relatively short distance away, on the other side of a pair of walls.

She knew. Instinctively, she knew. As if reading a fingerprint or smelling a perfume, she knew.

Acting just as instinctively, without any premeditation whatsoever, she raised both hands in the direction of the nearest wall between her and that concentration of energy.

The wall evaporated.

She stepped forward through the gap, and repeated the action.

That wall, too, ceased to exist in solid form.

The shiny shape coalesced into a human form now, as she stared down at it. But she could not make out any details. It was merely a glowing, silver-white blob.

"Oh. *Oh...*"

She allowed the second sight to fall away. Her normal vision returned.

Wendy Li lay bound and gagged on a small sofa in front of her.

"Wendy. Wendy!"

Ecstatic, Lyn rushed forward, pulling the gag out of her little sister's mouth and pulling at the ropes. Extending the slightest fraction of her power in a very contained manner, she burned the thin ropes to the point that she could snap them and pull them away.

"Are you okay?" she asked once the restraints were removed.

She frowned at her sister's lack of reply.

"Wen?"

The younger girl, wearing her silver mesh costume with the broad cuffs at wrist and ankle, looked up at her vacantly.

Lyn knelt in front of her, frowning. She studied her sister's eyes—the pupils were dilated.

"They did something to you, didn't they?"

Lyn growled in the back of her throat.

"I'll bet it was that witch in the red bikini."

"I…"

Lyn leaned in closer.

"What?"

Wendy Li brought both hands up and a concussive blast of staggering proportions smashed into Lyn's torso. If not for her reflexive triggering of her force field power, she would have been killed. Instead, she merely had the breath knocked out of her, and wound up through the doorway and crashing into the wall on the opposite side of the hall.

Wendy strode out after her, hands still raised.

"No!"

Lyn was back on her feet and moving to meet her sister's advance. She quickly brought up another force bubble around herself, and this time the concussive blast seemed to be absorbed or nullified entirely.

"Interesting," the science nerd in Lyn muttered, even as Lyn the super-agent sprang into action, shooting into the air and over Wendy's head.

The younger girl, dazed and unable to react quickly, stumbled about for an instant, confused by the move.

Lyn surrounded her in a shimmering golden sphere.

Turning, Wendy slowly frowned, then reached out with one delicate hand and touched the interior surface of the bubble. It popped as if it were made of soap.

Lyn started, wide-eyed. Nothing like that had ever happened before.

"You're kidding," she gasped.

Wendy raised her hands again, silvery-white energy crackling around her. Lyn, now backed against the wall of the corridor, moved on instinct. She reached out and grasped her sister's hands, meaning to direct them away before the girl could fire again.

The second their bare hands touched, the energy halos around them both utterly vanished. It was as if a switch had been thrown, and both their generators had been cut off. Now only two young women—two suddenly very *ordinary* women—stood facing one another in the dim hallway, hands clasped with one another.

The Li girls had been accused of many things in their lives, but "ordinary" had never been one of those things.

Lyn stared at her hands, and at her sister's hands within her own. She looked from them to Wendy's eyes, and watched as the glassy look slowly faded, replaced by a sparkle of intelligence, of awareness, gradually building, growing, until…

The scream nearly deafened Lyn.

The hands slipped out of her grasp.

No longer touching her big sister's skin, Wendy's power flared around her again, and she streaked off down the hall, in the direction of the exit.

"I will *kill* her!"

"Wendy! Wait!"

The younger sibling paid no heed. Lyn started to grab for her, but at that moment she felt her own golden energies crackling around her once more, and she could not help but pause and relish the sensation for a second. Then, her wits restored, she raced off after her sister.

77

"This is entirely unacceptable, Devenn," growled the crimson-skinned woman. "Entirely unacceptable. And it falls to you to address the situation."

"And what would you have me do about it, Alatair?" asked the big man in dark blue, who was stretching his arms and legs a short distance away across the exercise room.

The woman turned and faced him squarely, her bobbed white hair bouncing.

"Knowing what to do is part of your job, Devenn," she replied coolly.

He huffed at that.

"I'm certain the Admiral would not have ordered us away from the Kilan System without reason. Without a very good reason."

"You have more faith in our leaders than the rest of us do, I am afraid," Alatair said under her breath. Juggling three curved swords simultaneously, she executed an acrobatic maneuver that involved her momentarily standing on her hands, then back upright again, without losing any of the swords in the process. Devenn would have been astounded had he not witnessed that same feat on a nearly daily basis for several years running now.

"We were promised a shot at the Circle's commandos when Admiral DeSkai took over this fleet."

Devenn shrugged.

"Plans change," he replied. "Targets change. Enemies change."

"Very true," Alatair said, pirouetting as she flung first one and then a second sword high up toward the ceiling of the ship's recreation area.

Surrounded by its gigantic support fleet, the big flagship of the Kur-Bai Empire currently warped its way through hyperspace and toward a small, rocky, blue-white world on the far side of the galaxy. Its shock troops—the Empire's finest warriors—had not been allowed to lift a finger during the last campaign, which had ended with the nuclear destruction of two rebel planets. Now tension among the Elites was running high.

"How long must we sit here aboard this ship and merely practice?" demanded the rapidly spinning Alatair, her face flushed both with her exertions and with anger. "How long before our talents and abilities are required once more?"

"Soon, I am certain," the leader of the Elites replied. Devenn, nearly seven feet tall and wearing a blue uniform trimmed in red, unfastened his ceremonial half-cape and folded it carefully. "In fact, I believe we may encounter as many as three different enemies— three entirely different sets of challenges—once we reach Earth."

"Three?"

Devenn nodded.

"One, of course, has been rumored throughout the fleet seemingly from the moment we departed the Kilan System."

"Agents of the Worldmind," Alatair said, nodding. "I doubt that seriously. The Worldmind has not moved against us in decades."

She paused in her gymnastic routine, her light blue tunic and loose pants fluttering around her, to give Devenn a dubious look.

"Far more likely that the command staff have chosen to use that excuse to justify some catastrophic mistake they have made elsewhere," she said.

"I think not," Devenn told her, and she shrugged.

"Who are the other two enemies?"

He considered his words.

"Perhaps the very foes you have been yearning to meet in battle all along, for one," he said.

She paused again.

"What?"

Devenn moved in closer, his voice a near-whisper now.

490

"Alatair, listen to me. The Circle's top commandos—they weren't on Kilan-2 or Kilan-3."

"How do you know that?"

Devenn smiled, his craggy red face appearing to split open horizontally to reveal smooth white teeth.

"That, also, is part of my job, as you so accurately put it a moment ago," he said.

She glared back at him for a long second, then nodded.

"Fine. Then where are the commandos? Will we ever get our shot at them?"

"From what I have heard," Devenn replied, his smile widening dangerously, "they may well be in the vicinity of Earth."

"Earth?"

Alatair puzzled over that word for a moment.

"That's the planet we're heading for now, isn't it?"

The grin broadened still further.

"Indeed."

Alatair's expression had changed remarkably in the few seconds it had taken for the two of them to have this conversation. Now, her eyes wide, she nodded slowly and began to smile as well.

"There's more," Devenn added.

"Yes?"

"Reports indicate the natives of Earth have produced a small number of paranormals."

He laughed.

"Elites of the Earth, if you like."

"Is that so?"

"Quite so, yes," he said. His smile faded slowly.

"We may be facing both the Circle criminals with their armored commandos...and the cream of the crop among the Earth people's fighters."

Alatair considered that. Then she spun around, tossing all three swords into the air again, beginning her remarkable juggling routine once more. As she did so, she laughed.

"Then perhaps this mission will not turn out to be a total loss."

12

Wendy Li erupted from the Digimacht headquarters doorway in a blaze of white light, roaring up into the sky. Her wrath was beautiful and terrible in its glorious fury.

Slowly descending, she looked first at Ultraa, who hovered nearby. Then she turned to Heavyweight, who held the Field Marshal clutched in one hand. Then she looked at Fury, and at the unconscious body of Blitzkrieg.

But of the one she was seeking, there was no sign at all.

"Where is she?"

Ultraa shook his head.

"Who?"

Pulsar soared through the doorway and caught up with her sister, stopping to float a few feet away.

"Distraxion," she answered for Wendy, who appeared too upset to speak rationally. "She wants to find Distraxion."

"She's not the only one," Williams called up to them. "But I think she got away in all the confusion."

Wendy's shriek of anger nearly deafened both Lyn and Ultraa. White light flared brightly from her silvery form.

"Look, sis," Lyn began after her ears quit ringing and the spots in her vision cleared a little. "We can help you—"

"I don't *want* any help," she cried. "I'll find her *myself. I'll find her!"*

And then, like lightning, Wendy was gone.

Lyn watched her go, shaking her head.

"She gets that way sometimes," she said to the others.

"I think it's justified in this case," Ultraa replied, as he and Lyn settled to the ground, beside Heavyweight and Fury. "But still, we should go after her—if only to make sure she doesn't get hurt."

Lyn nodded.

"Oh, you'd better believe we're going—"

A swirling light appeared in the air to Lyn's right, and her voice trailed off as she saw it. Circular in shape, it was roughly seven feet tall, with colorful clouds spinning inside it in a dance of green and red and gold.

The four waited, no one moving, to see what this new development might portend.

The clouds in the circle parted and a small shape stepped through.

Ultraa's mouth dropped open.

"You have got to be kidding me," he stated flatly. "This guy? Again?"

"Oh, no," Lyn breathed, recognizing him.

"Who is he?" asked both Richard and Williams at the same time.

"I am Francisco," the little man in the khaki jumpsuit and heavy tool belt replied in his halting, uncertain way. He sketched a quick bow. "I serve the one you call the Warlord." He seemed to laugh at that statement, then followed it with, "Or, *both* of them, I suppose. No, no, actually, neither of them. Yes, yes, that's it. *Neither.*"

Ultraa shook his head, not knowing what to make of all that. But one part of it did ring a bell for him.

"You killed the Warlord."

"Ah, yes, yes. You remember." He seemed to be laughing again. "You. Remember. Ah, that *is* humorous, yes."

Ultraa was not laughing.

"You did kill him. Pulsar and I saw you do it."

"Of course, yes, yes," Francisco replied, sobering now. "One of them, yes. No question."

"One of them?"

"My duty, though, of course. Yes."

"Your duty? To kill someone? To kill your—your master?"

"Just so. Precisely. Yes."

Ultraa was flabbergasted now. Behind him, the others looked on mutely, watching and listening.

"Why was it your duty to kill him?"

"The Grand Design, of course. He was the Warlord of the moment. I am Francisco. He had failed, and risked the integrity of the Design. My duty was to eliminate that version. Then the Wheel could turn, and a new Warlord could enter the multiverse."

"There are...*more* of them?"

"Always. But only one at a time," Francisco explained patiently, crossing his arms. "Always only one, anywhere in all the layers of the multiverse, yes. Only one."

He hesitated, then laughed again—but it was not a laugh of good humor, this time. It was a bitter laugh indeed.

"Except," he said, "for now. Now, there are two."

He tsked.

"Yes, yes, two. Two Warlords. Imagine that! And what is Francisco to do with *two* of them? Such a thing is unprecedented! It threatens not just the Grand Design, but the very fabric of the universe—the multiverse—itself!"

Ultraa was trying to keep up with all of this.

"There are two of them now," he said, his eyes locked on those of the little man.

"Yes."

"You killed one, and now there are *two*."

"Yes, yes."

Francisco fidgeted nervously as Ultraa sorted through this information.

"Then I'd advise against killing these two," he said after a second. "We'd soon be up to our armpits in Warlords."

A joke? From Ultraa? Surprised, Lyn snickered. Even Richard and Williams guffawed a bit. Francisco stared back blankly.

"No, no," the little man concluded testily after a few seconds of this. "You do not understand. Clearly, clearly, you fail to grasp the situation."

"Then explain," Ultraa said, growing serious once more. "After all, you came to us."

"Yes, I came here, yes—I need your help."

He shrugged.

"I have accidentally allowed two Warlords to exist at once. A threat to everything, they are."

He paused, considering his words carefully.

"And neither of them is what I would describe as…stable."

Ultraa took this in, then nodded slowly.

"And you want our help?"

Francisco grinned suddenly.

"Yes, yes, your help. Yes!"

Ultraa stepped forward, protectively, between Francisco and the others.

"You. Need. *Our.* Help."

"Yes," the little man agreed, nodding. "I believe you have the gist of it."

"Against two Warlords."

Francisco was still nodding and smiling.

Ultraa looked back at the others. Bemused, they were merely taking it all in. He turned back to the bizarre little man, who appeared to be dancing around in a circle now.

"Why should we help you?"

Francisco stopped and gazed up at Ultraa's stern features again.

"Because I have helped you once already," he said.

"By killing the Warlord? We didn't want—"

"No, no, not that, no."

He smiled broadly.

"Your friends. I have sent them back to you."

"Our friends?"

"Esro?"

Lyn had stepped forward and her eyes widened.

"You're talking about Esro?"

"The red woman, and the man in armor," Francisco stated.

"That's them!"

Lyn was grinning.

"Where are they?"

"They are not yet," Francisco answered, as if that explained everything.

Lyn's face twisted in confusion.

"They are whatsit?"

"Not yet. Not back in this when. Not yet. Probably in…" He glanced at a large watch with many readouts, covering part of his forearm. "…maybe two days. Maybe less." He shrugged. "I sent them back to when they were most needed." He shrugged again. "Hard to tell, sometimes." He chuckled to himself. "*Times*, yes, time is hard to tell."

Lyn glanced at Ultraa.

"I have no idea what he means."

"Yeah, me neither."

"But it sounds…promising," Lyn continued. "For Esro, anyway. Maybe."

"I suppose so…"

At that point, Richard stepped between them.

"Hang on a second. I don't know what you two are talking about, and frankly I don't much care—but didn't this guy just say the whole universe was in trouble?"

Ultraa and Pulsar both turned back to look at Francisco.

"The…the *multiverse*, actually," the little man answered sheepishly.

"I don't know what that is," Richard said. "Is that anything like the universe? Is the Earth in that?"

Francisco appeared to roll that question around in his head for a moment. Then, "Yes, yes—for our purposes—yes!" He bounced impatiently from one foot to the other. "Now will you all come on? I need your help. The multiv—the *universe* needs you."

Richard looked at the others.

"I don't understand much of this, but I do know one thing—no universe, no Earth. No Earth, no me!"

"I can't argue with that logic," Williams said, stepping forward. "Count me in."

"Hang on a minute," Ultraa interjected. "I don't know that we can trust this guy. It could be some kind of trap."

Francisco sighed theatrically and faced Ultraa, appearing to summon up heretofore-unknown stores of patience.

"If the Warlord wanted you dead right now..." He tsked some more. "...He would simply appear, yes, and catch you all by surprise. And you would be dead."

"I wouldn't count on that," Ultraa snapped.

Francisco ignored him and continued.

"On the other hand, if you help me now and eliminate the insane Warlord in Red, I will be able to steer the other Warlord away from you—from your world. He will owe me, and I will owe you, yes."

Ultraa considered this for a moment.

"That actually sort of makes sense to me," he said, finally.

"Yeah," Lyn added. "Maybe he's just confused me into believing him, but..."

Ultraa looked at her.

"So you're in?"

She appeared conflicted, chewing a fingernail nervously.

"All right, fine," she said after a few moments. "I want to go catch up with Wendy, but... Like Richard said—with no universe, the rest doesn't matter." She left unsaid her second reason for going: *I just got you back—I'm not letting you disappear on me again!*

Ultraa nodded.

"Okay."

He turned to Francisco.

"We're going to trust you on this. You'd better be telling the truth."

"Yes, yes." He sighed again. "No one ever believes Francisco. Always alone, yes, always on his own..."

"Somehow I doubt that's exactly true," Ultraa said to him. "But, in any case—lead on."

Without another word, the little man unfastened a small box from his tool belt and held it up in front of him. He activated it, generating another swirling circle filled with shimmering mists.

"This way," he said, gesturing toward the circle. "This way!"

The four glanced at one another nervously. Then Richard growled a curse and leapt through. Williams went next, the dark coating sweeping up to cover his face once more. Lyn followed close behind him, and then Ultraa started to step through. He paused before he could enter it, however, and pointed a red-gloved finger at the strange little man.

"We're trusting you," he said. "Why, I have no idea. But the others agree it sounds important enough to risk their lives for. I'm not so sure."

"But—but the multiverse—"

"Yeah, I get that. But I don't know that I believe you."

Francisco seemed to consider this, then shrugged.

"The others are already through to the other side. We must hurry."

Ultraa looked back at him for another long moment, then set his square jaw and stepped into the circle, disappearing into the mists.

Francisco nodded to himself, well pleased. Then he looked back over his shoulder. His voice rang out loudly.

"Come on, come on," he said. "We do not have much longer, no, no. Must hurry."

The Field Marshal emerged from his place of concealment behind a stack of crates and walked forward, slowly at first but with increasing speed, brushing off his gray uniform as he went. He stood gazing at the swirling colors of the portal for a few seconds. Then, nodding once to Francisco, he stepped through in the wake of Ultraa and his friends.

Satisfied that all had gone according to plan, Francisco clapped his hands happily, then followed the German through. The portal blinked closed behind him.

"Hey," came the voice of Karl Koenig—Blitzkrieg—some minutes later, as he pulled himself dizzily to his feet and looked around, puzzled. "Where did everybody go?"

19

Within the holding area of the lead Circle starship, currently warping away from Earth's star system and back toward Kur-Bai space, sat a big, rectangular box. The box's surfaces were dark gray, shaped of some ultra-strong alloy of alien manufacture. Rows of lights blinked on computerized control panels built into its surfaces. Thick cables ran from the box to jacks set into the bulkheads of the ship, pulling energy into the box's systems. The box drew a great deal of power from the ship's generators—power enough to keep the contents nearly frozen and in suspended animation, and to keep the brain of the occupant so dormant that even its dreaming, subconscious thoughts could not possibly affect anyone on board the ship.

Yes, Randall Nation was defeated, and his grave threat had been ended forever.

Or so the Kur-Bai aboard the ship believed.

A faint clicking sound came from within the box. Slowly, one by one, the dials and indicators on its surface changed colors—not green to red, not precisely, as aliens and not humans had built the box and the starship around it—but the colors served that same purpose.

Another clicking sound, slightly louder, echoed softly within the hold.

A Circle technician, the only one currently working in the room, frowned and turned from his console, peering through the dim lighting.

A third click sounded.

Frowning more deeply, he stood and walked across to the box. He stared down at it, seeing the lights changing across its face. His frown slowly melted into a look of stricken horror.

The top panel of the box slid open.

Whirling, the Circle tech raced back across the hold, lunging for his console, for the comm unit built into the wall beside it.

He almost made it. Perhaps a half-second more and he would have been able to give some sort of warning to his shipmates. Unfortunately for him, he had not quite closed his fingers over the comm unit when the figure in the box sat up and saw him.

Instantly, the tech emitted a rattling, choking sound from his throat.

Mental forces lashed out across the cargo hold, seizing him in an iron grasp.

"Sit."

The tech sat. His eyes stared out glassily, now essentially disconnected from his brain.

Rnn'dul Nah-Shonn studied the other Kur-Bai carefully for a few moments. Then he stood and climbed up out of the box.

"Sleep," he said, and the tech dropped over in his chair.

Nah-Shonn stood in the center of the hold for another second. Then he walked over to the sleeping tech and lowered the man gently to the deck. Within a very few moments he had stripped him of his uniform and donned it himself.

"Not a bad fit."

Seating himself in the chair, he typed at the controls, then studied the display. Repeating this a few more times, he rapidly familiarized himself with the layout and design of the ship.

"Armaments? Where are—"

Another typed command revealed the munitions stocks of this ship and of the other five vessels in the Circle fleet.

"Oh, excellent. Yes."

After two more minutes of typing and studying the readouts, Nah-Shonn nodded to himself and stood. He now felt well acquainted with this ship and its crew. He knew precisely what he had to do, and how he would go about doing it.

Then he hesitated. The thought came back to him unexpectedly—thoughts of what he had seen inside the mind of the human. The one called Ultraa. That one had been unlike any human he had ever encountered before. The years...the memories, so many of them lost...the dark, blank depths of nothing, of sheer void...

Nah-Shonn suppressed an involuntary shudder and breathed in and out several times in rapid succession.

The human—Ultraa—could not be allowed to live. He had humiliated Nah-Shonn deeply; had brought him down, to bitter defeat, for the first time in so many years...

Nah-Shonn smiled to himself.

Revenge would be sweet. Revenge upon Ultraa, and upon the entire misbegotten planet that had produced Ultraa.

Striding quickly to the hatch, Nah-Shonn exited the hold and made his way toward the command level. As he walked along, all who encountered him immediately fell under his sway. By the time he reached the level of the bridge, he had a veritable army at his back.

At that moment, he rounded a corner and nearly ran headlong into the commando leader—the Kur-Bai who had worn green-trimmed armor when he had assaulted the Pentagon on Earth. The Circle warrior who had come to capture him, and who had succeeded—through no effort of his own.

"Well, well," Nah-Shonn said, grinning.

The Circle commando stopped, looked at the other's face, blinked, looked at the crowd following behind him...and then the sudden, horrifying realization struck him full force. He whirled, starting to run, yet knowing there was nowhere he could go. He barely took two steps before freezing abruptly at a word from Nah-Shonn.

The renegade Kur-Bai strode arrogantly around to face the commando leader, who stood slack-jawed and glassy-eyed.

"No, no," Nah-Shonn said to him. "That won't do. I restore your faculties and your speaking ability—though not your other motor functions. Not just yet."

The man gasped, still standing like a statue in the corridor. His eyes met the other's and he glared.

"How—how can you be free? You were frozen—in complete suspended animation!"

"Don't be so modest," Nah-Shonn replied. "After all, you sabotaged the containment box yourself."

The commando opened and closed his mouth soundlessly. Then, in a low, gravelly tone: "What?"

Nah-Shonn smiled his creepy, wide-mouthed smile.

"Remember."

Blinking again, rapidly this time, the man reeled as images he had been ordered to suppress came unbidden to his consciousness. He saw himself inspecting the box as it was being sealed—saw himself reaching inside, sticking a micro-detonator against the main components of the box's mechanism, then allowing the lid to close.

"Oh, no," he said aloud.

"Oh, yes."

"But... why did I...?"

Nah-Shonn shrugged.

"I cannot take all the credit. Your helmet, with its psychic defensive systems, was damaged during the battle. I was able to reach into your mind, in all the confusion, and plant a subtle, undetectable order—an order for you to disable whatever container you brought down to put me in."

The commando took this in, closed his eyes, and exhaled slowly. His strength seemed to flow out of him, leaving him utterly hollow.

Hollow, yes, Nah-Shonn thought to himself. *Hollow, and ready for me to pour in my own agenda, my own plans, my own orders. Just like all the rest of them.*

"This way," Nah-Shonn said, indicating the doors to the bridge with one hand. "I believe you wish to escort me to my new station."

The renegade Kur-Bai followed the commando leader onto the bridge. All around, officers looked up, saw him, reacted with terror—and then with utter obedience, as his mental powers swept through the room.

"This is quite comfortable," Nah-Shonn said as he supplanted the limp and drooling captain in the center seat. Now the entire fleet was under his command. The Circle crewmembers watched him through glassy eyes, their jaws slack, hands dangling at their sides, waiting upon his every word, his every utterance.

"Set a new course," he barked at the mentally enslaved navigator and helmsman.

He leaned back in the seat, lacing his hands behind his head, and grinned.

"For Earth."

20

From his place of concealment across the street, the Blue Skull cackled with glee as the powerful metal form of Vanadium smashed his way into the military storehouse.

The big war machine hurled guards left and right like leaves blown in the wind. Bullets ricocheted from his nigh-invulnerable hide. Doors collapsed like tissue paper beneath his unstoppable onslaught.

"Yes," the villain whispered intensely, "yes!"

At the end of a column of destruction, Vanadium stood before a massive metal safe door.

"Take it down," the Skull hissed. "Rip it down!"

Vanadium swung a blue-silver fist and sent it crashing into the heavily reinforced door, which rang like a bell in response but did not give way.

"Again," the Skull growled. "Hit it again!"

Vanadium raised his fist once more, then hesitated. Instead, he gently laid one shiny hand on the vault door's face and stood immobile for a few seconds.

"What—what are you doing?" the Skull demanded, communicating over the cybernetic link he had implanted in his own head. "Open the safe!"

The big metal man stood there a few seconds longer, as tiny green lights flickered down his arm and onto the face of the safe. Then he grasped the huge handle and pulled.

The massive door groaned and fell from its hinges. All of the bolts that had held it in place had been burned away.

Vanadium stepped over the threshold and into the vault.

The Blue Skull watched this happen in awe. His eyes widened with surprise, and a grin slowly spread over his face. He rubbed his gloved hands together.

"Even better. Yes. Even better."

At that moment his cell phone rang.

"What? Who—?"

He pulled the phone out and looked down at it. Frowning, he flipped it open.

"How did you get this number?"

Angela Devereux—the Skull's teammate, better known as Distraxion—snapped back at him breathlessly.

"Not now," she said, sounding harried and upset. "You've missed out on some big happenings while you've been out disobeying the Field Marshal's orders and robbing things."

"I care not for that fool's orders," the Blue Skull replied sharply. Then, "What things have I 'missed out on,' as you say?"

"The government pulled our certification—our official status," she told him quickly. "Ultraa and his friends showed up and there was a big fight. I'm not sure how it ended—I got away from there as soon as I could."

The Blue Skull nodded. This was surprising to some degree, but not entirely unexpected, given the blatant incompetence of the Field Marshal and his idiotic lieutenant, Blitzkrieg.

"Yes. Go on."

"The Li girl—Wendy—she got free of my hypnotic suggestions and now she's after me. Big time."

The Blue Skull could not help laughing at that.

"So you are running in terror from a little girl?"

Distraxion's voice hardened.

"A little girl that could boil my blood in my veins," she barked back.

"True," the Skull replied, taking it all in.

Neither of them said anything for a couple of seconds. Finally, Distraxion spoke up again, her voice now sounding desperate.

"So—what should I do?"

The Blue Skull considered making a sarcastic remark, then changed his mind.

The Li girl could make a useful hostage, he thought. *Leverage over her sister, and over Ultraa, among others.*

"Meet me under the Key Bridge—DC side," the Skull replied. "Fifteen minutes."

"Fine," Distraxion replied. She hung up.

Still considering the possibilities, the Blue Skull barely noticed when Vanadium settled alongside him, a massive metal box held under each arm.

"We will store those in my hideaway," he told the big metal man, indicating the boxes. "And then we have an appointment at the Key Bridge."

Tiny red eyes staring out dully, Vanadium nodded once and lofted into the air, still carrying the boxes.

"And afterward, I believe I should return to Digimacht and retrieve my valuables there, before the government gets their hands on them—if they haven't already."

He smiled to himself.

"And after that? Perhaps then it will be time to allow Vanadium to expand his services into the realm of assassination."

The faintest hint of blue flame danced in his pale eyes.

"I've always wanted my own city. Or country. Or continent…"

27

The four people of Earth emerged from Francisco's transdimensional portal first, and they stood gawking at the scene before them.

They stood in a barren desert, the sands a dark tan in color. The sky overhead shimmered a deep violet. The stars radiated bright gold. Moons by the dozens spun past, reflective of the absolute chaos reigning over this dimension—and within the soul of its master.

And before them, within a deep, bowl-shaped depression in the desert floor, stood a massive golden ring, upright on its side, supported by a gray stone base. Huge cables trailed away from it, and workers were fitting the last of what appeared to be a series of antennae onto it.

In front of the ring, his back turned to them, stood an all-too-recognizable figure. Long crimson cloak blowing in the breeze, hood pulled up over his head, and heavy gauntlets covering his hands, the Warlord stood gazing up at his creation.

Not the Warlord, though, Ultraa realized, upon seeing him there. *The Warlord in Red.*

Francisco emerged from the portal next, followed by another man Ultraa had not expected.

"Wha—"

He whirled, peering down at Francisco, his brow furrowed.

"What is *he* doing here?"

Francisco grinned back at him and shrugged. The Field Marshal stood rigidly, stoically, merely gazing around at the bizarre surroundings.

The others looked on, wondering if this indeed signaled the start of some half-expected betrayal. Instead, the Field Marshal continued to ignore them.

"Stay out of the way," Ultraa growled at the older man.

The others turned their attention from Francisco and the Field Marshal to the Warlord in Red and his machine.

"That guy's going to notice us any second now," Richard noted, a touch of nervousness in his gruff voice.

"Yeah," Williams agreed, the black film drawing back far enough for his face to show through. "If we're going to do something…"

"The machine," Francisco said plaintively. "You must not let him activate the machine! It will create a self-sustaining wave that will shatter the multiverse! It will destroy everything, everywhere!"

Ultraa spared one more long, unhappy look at Francisco and the German. Then he nodded curtly and stepped to the front of the group.

"We hit him. We hit him hard. We don't let up."

He indicated Lyn.

"Pulsar and I have faced this guy—or somebody a lot like him—before. He's tough. Don't give him an opening. Don't hesitate. Take him down. Hard."

"Sounds like my kind of tussle," Williams said.

"Yeah, that works," Heavyweight agreed.

Lyn merely nodded.

"Alright," Ultraa said. "Let's do it."

Without another word being spoken, the four moved into action.

Ultraa rocketed into the air, his super speed and flight powers combining to carry him, missile-like, toward the villain. Williams, now the Fury again as the strange, black film covered him over completely again, streaked after him. A second later, Pulsar was airborne and soaring up overhead, a shimmering force field surrounding her as she prepared to unleash a blast.

"Well, jeez, guess who can't fly in this crowd," Heavyweight muttered as he rumbled across the sands, his gravitational abilities powering up inside him.

Ultraa struck first, smashing into the Warlord in Red's back. The Fury hit a millisecond later, green energy beams spearing out from his fists and nailing the villain even before he had hit the ground. Pulsar's blast—so great that its usual golden color was tinged with purple—struck the Warlord as he rolled over to get up. And finally, Heavyweight exponentially increased the gravitational force pulling at the man in red's body, holding him down on the sandy surface as though beneath a giant's foot.

All of this happened in a mere instant. At the same time, Francisco ran forward, his eyes fixed on the big, circular machine. The Field Marshal moved stealthily to one side, seeking cover.

Ultraa curved back around and lit into the villain with both fists, standing before him and smashing away as he sought to rise. A green blast struck from one side and a golden one from the other. Heavyweight redoubled his efforts, preventing the villain from getting off his knees.

Now three seconds had passed, and the success the heroes were experiencing defied all the odds. Francisco himself could scarcely believe it. He was now halfway across the open, bowl-shaped depression, and the machine lay just a few dozen yards away. He fully expected these Earth people to die, and to die very soon. But if they could just occupy his erstwhile master a few moments longer, he could sabotage the machine and perhaps even find a way to use it against the Warlord in Red himself.

Four seconds gone now, and Ultraa and his friends still held the upper hand. The blond man in white and red led the way, legs firmly set in the sandy ground, fists smashing away at the golden mask and red-clad torso of his foe. Williams had closed in as well, and brought both fists down hard on the adversary's back. Pulsar

505

unleashed her third blast, striking him in the gut. Richard held on, teeth gritted, sweat dripping down his face, keeping the man locked in place under the weight of many gravities.

Five, six, seven seconds, and Ultraa began to believe they could win. The villain clearly was reeling under the assault—the most vicious, intense, and single-minded attack Ultraa could remember participating in—and none of them appeared to be tiring yet. Meanwhile, Francisco had gotten to within a dozen yards of the machine, and his eyes gleamed as he reached to his belt for the tools he would need.

In the eighth second after the attack began, though, everything changed.

The Warlord in Red activated his personal force field, driving Ultraa and Williams back and cutting off the effects of Richard's gravitic assault as if the man were no longer present.

"Look out," Ultraa began. "He—"

In the ninth second, the Warlord in Red pointed a finger up at Pulsar, where she hovered in the violet sky just above. A beam of red light speared from that finger.

Seeing him aiming at her, Pulsar switched from attack to defensive mode, surrounding herself in a tight force bubble.

The beam nonetheless tore through the golden sphere around her and struck her in the stomach, sizzling as it burned at her golden mesh suit.

Crying out, Pulsar sought to dodge, spinning to one side in midair.

The Warlord in Red followed her with the beam of energy, and quickly he had zeroed in on her again. No matter what force field she erected between herself and the attacker, his powerful blasts shredded them and struck her viciously.

In the twelfth second, he struck the side of her head and she tumbled out of the sky, dazed.

Ultraa stumbled back as the adversary redirected his fire at Williams and at him.

Seven seconds, he thought. *For seven seconds, we were winning. But now...*

Another blast from the Warlord in Red struck out at Heavyweight, sending him diving for cover and forcing him to release the gravitational hold he had been attempting to reestablish.

...now we're getting slaughtered.

Meanwhile, at the eleven-second mark, Francisco had reached the machine. Relief nearly overcame him, and he resisted the urge to dance in a little circle. Instead he fumbled with his tools for a moment, then studied the open circuit boards before him, and reached out to adjust—or sabotage—them all.

A hand came from nowhere, grasping his wrist and stopping him.

"Oh! Oh!"

He looked around.

The Warlord—the *blue* Warlord—stood gazing down at him. He gawked.

"I—what—you!"

He followed this instantly with:

"How?"

Then he saw that this Warlord wore a thin suit of something resembling glass armor under his blue robes.

"You have performed marvelously, my friend," the Warlord said, his voice crackling over a small speaker set into his armor's chest. "You—or rather the lackeys you recruited—have distracted the abomination, as I had hoped. And now—"

He reached down and began to attach a series of small devices to the machine's circuit boards.

"What—what are you *doing*?" Francisco demanded. "This machine will destroy *everything*! You told me so yourself!"

To this the Warlord did not offer a response. Instead he touched a control on his forearm. The devices he had placed on the great machine all lit up with flashing green lights.

Francisco was nearly beside himself, hopping from foot to foot.

"What—*what*—?"

But the Warlord merely raised a blue-gloved finger to the mouth area of his mask.

"Shhhhhh."

Francisco's eyes flickered nervously from his megalomanaical former master to the vast machine that would bring about the end of everything, and then to the group of humans who had come to help, but were now being roundly defeated by the other Warlord.

All he could think to do was to curl into a ball and whimper. And so he did.

22

Huddling in the shadows beneath the Francis Scott Key Bridge, and wearing a long, gray coat over her skimpy, red costume, Angela Devereux cast her eyes this way and that, searching for the glint of silver that would reveal the presence of her pursuer.

The metallic flash that drove a screech from her lips and sent her scrambling away did not turn out to be the one she feared, however. As she cringed behind a metal support and peeked out, she realized the shining form standing stock-still in front of her belonged not to Wendy Li, but to Vanadium, the huge juggernaut under the control of her erstwhile teammate.

Then an eerie, hollow voice came to her from behind, startling her once more.

"How have you come to this?" he asked.

"Wh—what?"

The Blue Skull strode out from the shadows, his ghastly head wreathed in azure flames.

"I had only just begun to gain some form of respect for you," he continued, gazing out at her. "But this—this is laughable. You dominated the Li girl for weeks. Now you act as if—" he laughed. "As if *I* were out to kill you, instead of a mere teenager."

"She's not just any teenager," Devereux shot back, anger growing inside her. "You know that."

The Blue Skull appeared to consider this for a few moments, turning and striding away from her. He walked through great bars of shadow and sunlight, there beneath the mammoth bridge supports at the edge of the Potomac River, the flames surrounding his skull flickering madly. Then he wheeled about and approached her again.

"She's just a girl," the Skull growled.

"Yeah, we've been over that," Distraxion replied angrily. "A very upset girl. A girl who can barbecue me if she gets a mind to."

"No," the Skull said then. "She might think she wants to kill you, but she wouldn't actually do it."

"You think not?"

"I know not."

He grinned a leering grin at her, sending chills up her spine.

"I have studied her psychological makeup—and her sister's, as well. Neither of them is bloodthirsty."

"You're sure about that?"

"Yes. The Li girl thinks she wants to kill you with her bare hands. Given the opportunity, though—say that she landed here, now, without your seeing her—she would only attempt to restrain you and take you into custody."

"Oh, is that all?"

"For starters, yes," the Skull whispered, just loud enough for Devereux to hear him. "But then... but then you would be interrogated."

Distraxion scoffed.

"Let 'em try. I'd just hypnotize them and walk right out of there."

"Yes, perhaps," the Skull said. "But then again, Ultraa would have alerted the authorities to your particular gifts. Your... *charms*, shall we say. So they would be prepared. They would have ways of interrogating you that would leave you entirely helpless and open to their questioning."

Devereux snorted derisively at this, turning away from that awful, leering face. But the Skull pushed on with his scenario.

"And then...and then, my dear Distraxion, you would—how do they say it? Ah, yes. You would *spill your guts.*"

"I doubt that."

"I do not. And not only would you reveal all that you know about yourself and your own actions and plans, but..."

Distraxion slowly pulled herself out of her own internal thoughts and concerns and began to allow the Blue Skull's words to sink in. Their meaning hit her all at once. She whirled about, facing him— and faced a pistol pointed directly at her.

"I am sorry, my dear, but—"

She tried to summon up her hypnotic powers. Her eyes began to flash.

The gun fired once, twice, a third time. Angela Devereux fell to the pavement, lifeless, there in the shadows beneath the Francis Scott Key Bridge.

The Blue Skull stood over her, staring down, lost in thought. Nearly a full minute passed.

"Wen Li approaches," came the hollow, flat voice of Vanadium, still standing motionless behind him.

509

The Skull looked up and saw the shiny silver form of the Li girl soaring past the top of the bridge and curving around in this direction. Quickly he moved next to Vanadium.

"Conceal us," he barked.

Vanadium activated a dampening field that rendered them both nearly impossible to detect, there in the dark patches beneath the bridge.

Moments later, the girl landed. Seeing Distraxion's body, she ran over to it and knelt down. She checked the pulse and other vital signs as best she knew how, then looked up. Her mouth was a tight, flat line, and tears were welling in her eyes.

"As I said," the Blue Skull whispered to no one in particular. "She could not have killed you. How fortunate—how very, *very* fortunate—that I do not share that condition..."

23

Jameson stood to one side as construction workers passed him and moved through his shattered doorway, carrying pieces of wreckage and construction equipment. Placing his hands in his pockets, he looked around at the disaster that was his office and groaned softly.

At least things can't get any worse than this, he consoled himself. *The aliens invaded, all right—and we beat them. Okay, well, they didn't exactly "invade"—they only wanted to capture that Randall Nation guy. And, sure, Ultraa and his friends did most of the work. But I contributed my part. And it's not like aliens are going to invade twice in one day. So I think we're good, at least till tomorrow morning.*

Thoughts of Randall Nation disturbed Jameson, because he had no way of knowing just how long the mysterious alien had lurked in the Pentagon, subtly affecting American defense policy—or, far worse, Jameson's own private schemes!

Taking his mind off such matters, seeking something light and entertaining to distract him, Jameson flipped on the small television he'd had brought in to replace the big plasma model that had been destroyed during the battle. On the screen, a tall, silver, manlike shape stood on a grassy lawn, bullets deflecting harmlessly from its surface.

What's this—the Sci Fi Channel? I ordered this thing set to Fox News permanently!

The big robot moved forward slowly, unconcerned with the gunfire, stopping only when it reached a blank white wall.

Jameson frowned and leaned in closer, realizing that the Fox News logo and banner were indeed on the screen.

"What is this?"

The camera pulled back at that moment, revealing the setting in terrible clarity. The white surface was the Washington Monument.

"Oh—"

Soldiers were moving in, assaulting the robot with small arms fire. Ignoring them, the robot raised one arm, brought it back, then swung it forward, crashing it into the side of the monument. Again it did this, and again. Chunks of marble rained down, leaving an ugly gash in the side of the obelisk.

"Adcock!" bellowed Jameson. "What's going on?"

Leaping to his feet, Jameson scurried around to his doorway and looked out, noticing only then that the area was deserted. Whether this was due to the construction or to people rushing to televisions to see what was happening, Jameson did not know.

Fumbling in his pocket, he located his cell phone and flipped it open.

Why didn't anyone inform me? Am I already that far out of the loop?

Distractedly punching in numbers, Jameson stumbled down the debris-filled corridor. Behind him, the abandoned television played on. The big robot continued to demolish the Washington Monument, and the soldiers continued to fire at it, doing nearly as much harm to the landscape as the robot was doing.

And then, stepping into the frame, came another shape, identical to the first. Another giant robot.

That second Xorex took up station on the other side of the monument. Together, it and its lookalike continued the assault.

A third Xorex stepped into view and turned toward the U.S. Capitol building, striding steadily across the lawn.

A fourth appeared and followed.

A fifth…

A sixth…

24

Ultraa was on the ropes. The blasts the Warlord in Red fired at him had gone from mild irritant to serious problem as time ticked by and his own power reserves had been burned. Now he lay on the hot desert sands, his apprentice as well as his new colleagues down around him, as the tall figure in red and gold strode forward.

"How dare you interfere in my holy crusade?"

The adversary gazed down at Ultraa, the eyes behind that shiny, golden mask gleaming with righteous rage.

"The multiverse must be scourged! Wiped clean! Only in glorious entropy and utter destruction can there be a new start—a new beginning for the All!"

"You're insane," Ultraa choked out through bleeding lips. "I thought the other Warlord was crazy, but he didn't hold a candle to you."

"Bah!"

The crimson-clad villain stood directly over Ultraa now, studying his face more closely.

"I know you," he said after a few seconds. "I have reviewed the recordings of my predecessors."

He gestured toward Lyn.

"You and the girl were involved in bringing down the floating city. You led to the Design declaring that Warlord to be a failure, and to Francisco slaying him."

He peered down through his golden mask and smiled.

"I suppose I should thank you for that. Had you not done what you did, I would not be here."

Ultraa growled and sought to rise.

The Warlord in Red kicked out with a heavy crimson boot, smacking him in the jaw and sending him sprawling onto his back, the dusty sand billowing up around him.

"I do not know how the four of you came to be here, but you are too late."

He directed a pointed finger at Pulsar where she struggled to rise, sending a deep red killing beam her way. Only her own hastily erected force bubble deflected it, though the strain nearly rendered her unconscious.

"The machine is complete. My plans have come to fruition."

Fury sprang from the sandy ground and leapt. The Warlord in Red shrugged off his emerald-hued blasts, caught him by the throat and held him suspended in midair, then sent a barrage of high voltage currency through him. The black substance covering Doug Williams seemed to cry out in pain, and it slid down his body, uncovering his head and upper torso. The Warlord in Red tossed him casually aside, and he lay there, unmoving.

"I have but to activate the switch, and all will be ended," he said. "An end to all! Glorious oblivion!"

"No!"

As Ultraa fought his own dizziness and injuries to rise once more, the adversary ignored him and strode imperiously back over to the big, circular machine. He regarded the wide control panel at its base, then settled his gloved hands upon it like a concert pianist about to play.

Ultraa's elbows buckled and he slumped to the sand.

"No…Have to get up…Have to stop him…"

But he could not move. Exhausted, beaten down, he watched as the Warlord in Red began to activate the machine.

"No…"

Crackling, serpentine bands of energy, of every color of the rainbow, formed in midair around the great circle of metal, swirling in a spiral pattern.

"The waves will spread, feeding upon themselves, continuously redoubling their potency as they expand. The wave effect will reach out, smashing through dimensional barriers, disintegrating all matter and all other energy in their path. Soon, very soon, the multiverse itself will cease to exist."

Ultraa summoned up every iota of strength and resilience he possessed, and managed to get up onto his knees. Blood ran down the side of his face, and his bottom lip was swollen. He cast a quick glance at Lyn—she didn't look in much better shape, and was out. The same was true of Williams and Heavyweight.

"Have to stop him…"

But something appeared to be going wrong for the enemy, even as Ultraa slumped forward again, unable to move, able only to watch. Instead of reveling in the triumph of his scheme, the Warlord in Red seemed agitated, moving from one area of the control panel to another, pressing the touchscreens with an ever-increasing frenzy.

"A problem?" Ultraa croaked through cracked, sand-caked lips.

The adversary ignored him, continuing to type away at the controls, apparently to no avail.

The blazing swirls of multicolored fire continued to spin about the machine, but instead of spreading out in wave fashion, they were focusing themselves into a much more narrow column, reaching directly up into the violet sky.

"This—this is impossible," the Warlord in Red declared, the anger seething from his voice. "Impossible!"

"No, not exactly," came another voice, eerily similar but ever so slightly altered. "For—as you above all others should know—*nothing* is impossible to the Warlord."

The crimson-clad villain spun about as another figure strode around from behind the machine.

"You!"

"Quite so."

The blue Warlord bowed slightly. Behind his silver mask, he grinned maniacally.

"What have you done? And—how can you be here?"

"A true Warlord would know all such answers already—thus proving my case."

The crimson adversary glared at him, even as his weapons systems cycled up to full power once more.

"But I am of course magnanimous," the blue-clad villain added. "I will grant you some measure of explanation—before wiping your taint from the multiverse forever."

The crimson foe growled deeply but continued to listen, even as he eyed the power level indicators inside his mask, waiting to strike.

Meanwhile, Ultraa and a now-awake Pulsar looked on, not quite believing what they were seeing, and unsure of how to proceed. If they had been unable to harm only one of these beings, how could they ever seek to defeat *two* of them? And so they glanced at one another, exchanged silent signals, and waited.

"What is the barrier?" demanded the blue Warlord of his crimson opponent, as if he were a schoolmaster with an underperforming student.

The red figure stood, haughty in his defiance now, hands on hips, and replied, "Simple! It is that which separates the many positive-matter universes of the multiverse from the domains of pure energy that lie beyond—beyond the reach of anyone or anything on our side of the barrier."

"Precisely."

The blue figure pointed a gauntleted hand upwards.

"Now look overhead. You see the great rift forming in the sky, yes?"

Quickly the Warlord in Red gazed up at the chaotic, turbulent sky, then brought his eyes back down to his opposite.

"Yes."

And then, behind his golden mask, his eyes widened in shock.

"You—you have altered the function of my machine!"

The blue figure nodded slowly.

"Yes," he said. "You have it."

He patted the base of the great ring lovingly with one blue-clad hand.

"Now, instead of radiating out naught but destructive waves in all directions, this machine will channel all of its vast, destructive energies into a single point in space, ripping open the great barrier dividing us from the higher realm of pure, undiluted power."

"What?"

"Neither I nor any of my predecessors has been able to break through that barrier," the blue Warlord explained, feeling expansive in his looming victory. "But now, abomination, you have enabled me to achieve the great dream of all our kind. Through the tear in the walls of reality this machine will create, energies beyond any mortal ken will pour. And all of it will be channeled here."

He grinned once more.

"And I will be here at the focus, absorbing it all."

The blue Warlord cackled maniacally.

25

"Yes, Mr. President," Jameson said into his cell phone, as calmly as he could manage. "I do see them. Yes, sir—we have our best assets on their way now—the Defender units."

Across the desk from him, a young aide in a dark suit and tie nodded once.

The two men sat in a temporary facility in another wing of the Pentagon. Much of the building had been evacuated, but Jameson stubbornly refused to leave.

What's happened to Adcock? he wondered to himself as the president barked into his ear. *It's like he knew the perfect time to go missing...*

"What's that, sir?" he asked into the phone after the President spoke. "The new team? Well, actually..."

He ran his clammy hand over his sweating face, trying not to panic. He had indeed placed several calls to that same "new team" in the past twenty minutes, but neither the Field Marshal nor anyone else at Digimacht was answering.

Could Ultraa have gotten to them already?

Jameson seethed.

Yes. Probably. Very probably.

The President was saying something.

"Sir? Ultraa? Um... That's a problem, too, I'm afraid..."

The young agent frowned, and Jameson gave him a half-shrug.

"I can't reach him either, sir," he said into the phone. "I'm afraid the Defenders are the best we can do for the moment."

He listened again.

"Yes, sir, absolutely. I will keep trying to contact Ultraa. Of course. Yes, I do know him, yes—he definitely will show up if he can. Yes, sir."

Jameson suppressed the urge to throw up. He listened for a few seconds, nodding but saying nothing.

"Yes, sir," he finally managed. "I will put everything we have into it. You just get to a safe and undisclosed location and leave the rest to us."

The president clicked off. Jameson hung up the phone.

"What *are* those things?"

He stared at the television on the far side of his office, watching the small but growing army of silver robots apparently intent on dismantling the monuments and the Capitol.

"They haven't advanced on the White House yet," the agent— *Shelton*, he recalled now—said. "Any significance to that, you think?"

"How should I know?"

Jameson rubbed his eyes with both hands, then sat back in his chair and sighed.

"I've never seen them before. And if *I* haven't seen them, they shouldn't exist!"

Agent Shelton nodded.

Jameson stared at the screen a few moments longer. The other man waited, unsure of what to do. He had been temporarily assigned to help Jameson during the crisis, but was beginning to wish he had drawn some other assignment—something less stressful and unpleasant. *Maybe like hand to hand combat with those robots*, he thought ruefully, glancing over at his new boss.

"Hey," Jameson said suddenly, as much to himself as to Shelton. "Big silver guys. Yeah! I *do* have another resource. I nearly forgot."

"Sir?"

Jameson looked at Shelton as if seeing him for the first time.

"Um, never mind. I'll handle it myself."

He started to get up, then found himself staring at the television again—at the growing horde of big robots depicted on the screen.

"I'm positive there was only one of them when this started," Jameson went on. "That was, what, twenty minutes ago? Now there are at least six of them." He squinted at the TV. "Seven."

"More than that," Shelton replied. "They're multiplying more quickly."

Jameson banged a hand on his desk.

"Where the hell are the Defenders? Go make sure they're on the way."

Saying nothing, a relieved Shelton hurried silently out of the room, closing the door behind him.

Jameson rubbed his chin, squinting at the expanding ranks of featureless silver automatons systematically dismantling Washington, DC, around him.

Heck of a time to lose both my old and my new team of agents, he thought. *All but a couple, anyway,* he added, already working on the plan for how he would bring his other resources into the action.

His eyes continued to trace the lines of the giant robots, engaged as they were in near-mindless demolition.

If we survive this, he added to himself, *I need to get me some of those things...*

517

26

"No!"

Shocked, outraged and humiliated, the Warlord in Red rushed toward his blue-garbed enemy. He raised his gauntleted fist, energy pulsating about it, to strike.

His blue counterpart brought him up short with a raised hand.

"Allow me to explain," he said.

The Warlord in Red hesitated, his natural curiosity momentarily overcoming his rage.

"I must admit," the blue Warlord continued, "that I was shocked at first to discover that you apparently possess greater engineering knowledge than I do. But, studying your machine from afar, I saw that it could be made to do what my own attempts were never able to do—allow me to tap into an essentially limitless source of power! Power that will enable all my plans to come to fruition."

He grinned.

"And you have performed splendidly," he added. "As my pawn."

The Warlord in Red heard these words, took them in, considered them long and hard—and unleashed a wailing howl that brought chills to the skin of all the others present.

"Unthinkable! Unacceptable!"

The red figure stood stock-still, looking from the machine he had believed to be his to the rival who had bested him.

"This cannot be! It *cannot!* You are an older version! Obsolete! Your time has passed! You should no longer exist! You are the abomination, not me!"

He glared at his counterpart.

"How can you be here? How can we exist together like this? Why hasn't reality rended itself apart in protest?"

The blue Warlord merely laughed.

"That is all a matter of metaphysics and of interpretation, I suppose," he said. "But it matters not. My null-field armor includes a thin layer of stasis shielding. The multiverse cannot perceive that I am here, and so our close proximity to one another does not cause the cataclysm it normally would."

The Warlord in Red took this in.

"I see it now," he gasped, eyes widening behind his golden mask. "You manipulated events. You manipulated me! You wanted me to believe you were beaten, so that I would go on with my plans—*your* plans!"

He spun to the side as movement caught his eye. Francisco was emerging from behind the machine, and the red enemy pointed an accusing finger at him.

"You! All along, *you* were in league with this traitor!"

Francisco stopped, frightened, and shook his head negatively, but the adversary ignored him.

"A fool," the Warlord in Red was saying over and over. "I have been a fool. I have allowed myself to be used by an inferior version, and to be betrayed by my Francisco. I do not deserve to go on. The Grand Design surely has decreed my time is at an end."

Hearing this, Francisco hesitated, then walked slowly toward the man in red.

"Though yielding to this...this other me...sickens me to my soul," the adversary continued, "I suppose I must admit defeat."

Francisco approached him more quickly now, reaching into his jumpsuit as he came. He drew forth a long, shiny silver dagger.

Ultraa and Pulsar had seen this happen before, with the predecessor to both of these Warlords. They knew what was bound to happen next, and neither of them moved—though whether they were unable to move, or simply unwilling, they would have to consider for themselves in the days to come.

Francisco raised the dagger high, as the Warlord in Red closed his eyes and awaited the blow. Meanwhile, the blue Warlord looked on with glee, his eyes flashing from the dagger to the machine to the great swirling hurricane of blinding, blazing energies overhead, as the rift in the sky began to open.

"No!"

The Warlord in Red reached out suddenly and grasped Francisco's wrist hard, twisting it. The dagger slipped easily from his grasp and clattered off the stone base of the machine, to lie gleaming in the sand.

The crimson enemy's voice now shook with a strange madness.

"No. I will *not* yield so easily. I will not be played for a fool—not by this abomination. *I will not!*"

"Then allow me to do what Francisco could not," the other Warlord barked, leaping forward.

The two titanic figures collided there in the sand, before the great machine that tore at the very fabric of the cosmos above their heads.

As bolts of violet lightning began to crash all around, the two Warlords smashed away at one another, unleashing every element in each of their prodigious arsenals. They assailed one another with particle beams, disintegration rays, heat and fire and cold and antimatter. They sent bullets and bombs and nanomachines hurtling and sweeping toward one another, each repulsing the other's attacks in kind.

Through it all, a now-revived Heavyweight and Fury watched alongside Ultraa and Pulsar. None of them dared intervene. This was a war between near-gods, either of which could slay them all—and one of which nearly had. Reduced to mere spectators, they sat on the hot sands and took in the display, and hoped that somehow they could find a way to save at least the Earth before it was all done.

The struggle seemed to go on for hours, though in reality it consumed far less time. Each of the two adversaries fought with a determined, homicidal glee, holding nothing back in a single-minded effort to utterly erase the other from existence. Their arsenals slowly emptying, they resorted to hand to hand combat, smashing away at one another with all their might.

At last the blue Warlord delivered a staggering, earth-shattering blow that sent the Warlord in Red hurtling backwards, crashing hard into the stone base of the machine. He slumped and lay against its side, unmoving, blood pooling around him.

The blue Warlord raised his gauntleted fists in exultation and triumph. Far above him, energies had begun leaking through the now-breached universal barrier and were swirling down along the path of the beam, heading towards the machine. Wasting no time, he clambered up the base and scaled the curving side of the circular construct, at last standing alone atop it. He leaned back his head and stared up at the energies flooding down toward him.

"Yes!" he cried. "Yes! All the power of an entire universe— mine to command!"

Unable to stand, the Warlord in Red was choking on his own blood. His spasming hands reached out and one touched something hard and cold on the ground beside him. He recognized it instantly.

Francisco's dagger.

His fingers closed around the silvery weapon where it lay in the sand. With the last of his strength, he flung it upward. It flashed along its path, reflecting light from the bizarre, violet-tinged sky for just an instant—and then it struck home, squarely in the center of the blue Warlord's chest.

"Gakkh!"

520

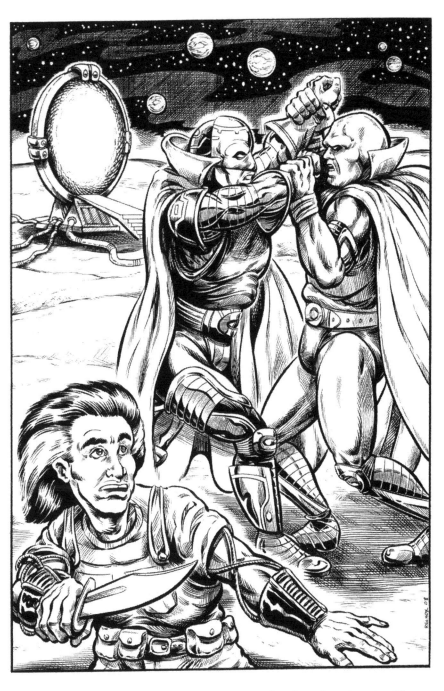

"I will not be played for a fool—not by this abomination!"

The blue Warlord's null-field armor cracked and split open. A greenish fluid poured out through the rent in the metal, followed by flames that exploded outward, hurling the man from atop the circle and sending him tumbling down to the rough sands.

The Warlord in Red cackled, even as the ground began to shake violently.

"Your armor is cracked," the red figure croaked hoarsely. "The multiverse knows you are here now! You are undone!"

Earthquakes already began to rumble as the fabric of reality heaved: two Warlords could never exist in the same place, at the same time. In all the levels of the multiverse, there could only, ever be one of them. Two at once created an increasingly violent effect that would surely tear all of reality asunder, at least within this localized area. The blue Warlord's stasis armor had prevented this from happening—up until now.

"Fool!"

The blue Warlord got to his feet, staring down in disbelief at his cracked armor and at his own blood now pouring out, mixing with the stasis liquid. Then his gaze moved to his abominable adversary and he started toward him, murder in his eyes.

"I am hardly beaten," he rumbled. "When the energies pass down the beam and reach here, it is I who will absorb them. All else will be swept away." He laughed. "You have scarcely altered the situation at all."

Hearing this, and taking in the entire situation, Francisco scampered across the sands to where Ultraa and his friends were slowly, painfully regaining their feet. He waved frantically for the blond man's attention. Ultraa bent down, and the little man whispered something frantically into his ear. Ultraa listened, stood up straight, looked down at Francisco questioningly.

The little man merely nodded.

Without another word spoken, Ultraa shot forward, summoning up all of his super speed. He plowed into the blue Warlord's back, knocking the villain to the ground, sending him tumbling through the sands.

As Francisco explained as quickly as he could what was happening, the other three humans moved into action. Fury ignored the agony racing down his left side from a series of hits he had taken earlier and launched himself into the air, striking the blue Warlord from the opposite side. Wrapping the villain in a bear hug, he squeezed his fingers into the long crack the dagger had opened in his armor, and with all his strength he pulled.

The stasis armor held together for a long second before giving way, tearing apart with a grinding shriek.

The ground shook harder, vast chasms opening up on either side of the area where they all stood. On regaining his footing, Ultraa perceived a wavy, hallucinogenic effect all around, as space-time warped and twisted.

Heavyweight exerted his power to keep the Warlord in Red from getting up. Pulsar smashed at the crimson-clad man with blast after blast from her airborne position. And then Ultraa grasped the blue Warlord by the scruff of the neck and dragged him in close.

"I have had more than enough of the both of you," he whispered roughly at the villain.

The Warlord said nothing in reply, but at the last instant his silver mask fell away, giving Ultraa a brief look at his true features.

A trick, Ultraa thought to himself, rattled to his core. *It's not true. Just another cheap trick.*

With all of his strength, he flung the blue Warlord bodily into the Warlord in Red. The two villains crashed together.

The universe spun madly about all of them. The world turned inside out and threatened to shake itself to death. The great machine the Warlord in Red had built and the blue Warlord had co-opted for his own use shimmered, vibrated, undulated like waves on a beach—and exploded. Giant chunks of flaming machinery flew out and rained down all around.

Frantically, Pulsar generated a force bubble over the entire area, shielding everyone from the tumbling shards of metal.

The two Warlords lay in a heap, limbs entangled, and then—and then—

"Whoa," Richard breathed, watching in awe.

"Yeah," Lyn agreed, from just above his head. In her second sight, she could see what was happening perhaps even clearer than the others.

The two Warlords twisted, blurred, blended together, melded—and melted—into one.

"Nooooooo," came a sound from the center of the swirl—an odd mixture of both their voices.

And then the two of them, together now in some horrific conglomeration, shrank smaller and smaller and smaller and...

BLOOP.

They blinked out.

Gone.

The universe had folded over, swallowed them up, and digested them.

The four Earth people and Francisco stood alone on the shimmering sands. The quakes subsided and the blazing eye in the heavens closed up, sealing itself instantly. Space-time reverted back to normal with an almost palpable sigh.

Several very long seconds passed, during which time nothing else happened that might herald the end of the world. Finally, the visitors from Earth began to relax, and then to realize they had actually won. They had saved the multiverse—and themselves—and defeated two unbeatable foes.

"We did it!" shouted Pulsar. *"We did it!"*

Ultraa grabbed Lyn in both arms and hugged her. Doug Williams and Richard clapped hands and pounded one another on the back warmly. Lyn broke loose from the others and hopped up and down excitedly, as Francisco looked on in bemusement.

"We really did do it," Williams said. "I'm not entirely clear on what *it* is, or was, but…yeah, we did it!"

Ultraa nodded.

"I think we did."

They stood there, gazing around at the now-empty desert.

"That," Richard said, after a few moments, "was very, very weird. If there was any doubt before, let me be perfectly clear—I do *not* want to join your team."

Ultraa grinned and hugged Richard in an embrace that nearly caused the other man's eyes to pop out, while the others laughed deeply.

Lyn turned to Francisco and bent down, meeting the little man's eyes.

"You can get us all back home now, right?"

"Yes, yes," Francisco replied, shuffling from one foot to another. "It is the least I can do, for all that you have done to help."

Lyn felt that the little guy was sincere, but yet something about his personality, his attitude, had subtly changed. Something in his expression, in his voice, concerned her.

He wanted them both defeated—or at least he acted like he did, she thought. *But what will he do now? What has he ever done, other than serve one or another of those crazy guys? Can we trust him on his own? Could we* stop *him now, if we wanted to?*

Ultraa was watching the two of them, and Lyn knew beyond a shadow of a doubt that he was thinking the same things. She would of course defer to his judgment, but she worried—worried that they might have to fight the little man, and worried about what might happen to him, or to them, if it came to that.

But Francisco merely smiled up at her and nodded. Then he paused, looked around, and called out in as loud a voice as Lyn had ever heard him use:

"Come out! I can send you home now!"

From behind a clump of rocks emerged the gray-uniformed Field Marshal. Cautiously at first, he strode up to the others, dusting off his jacket and trousers as he came.

"You!" Ultraa glared at him. "I forgot all about you. You've been here all along, and you did nothing!"

"And what would you have had me do?" the German demanded, summoning up whatever shreds of dignity he had left. "You and all your friends could scarcely stand against either of those two. I am a tactical leader. Tactics here would not help—you all saw that. Only blind luck saved you. That and the mutual animosity the two maniacs shared for one another."

Ultraa continued to glare at him for several seconds. Then he looked down at Francisco.

"You're going to send *him* home? Back to his own dimension?"

"Yes, yes. I brought him out of there, and I must send him back."

"*Vunderbar*," the Field Marshal stated firmly. "With my prospects in your world now in disarray, and your own restoration, I have no further interest in remaining there. I wish to return to the glorious Second German Reich."

"And there you will be going, yes," Francisco told him.

Raising one hand, the little man clicked a small device he clutched in his stubby fingers. The usual swirling portal opened.

The Field Marshal started to walk into it, then paused and looked at Pulsar.

"You should beware of your grandfather. You and your sister should look into his business—very closely."

Lyn gawked at him.

"What?"

Before anyone could stop him or ask what he was talking about, the German stepped into the portal. Just before the gateway closed, the others heard a chuckling, *"Auf wiedersehen!"*

Ultraa met Pulsar's eyes and shook his head.

"I'm glad to get rid of that guy, but somehow I feel like he got off too easy."

Lyn was chewing her bottom lip, deep in thought, and merely nodded once, curtly.

"And now, yes, now it is your turn," Francisco said to the rest of them.

"Thanks," Ultraa said, gathering the others around.

"My appreciation for what you have done is boundless," the little man was saying. "I only wish I were not sending you back to your deaths."

The portal snapped open, and each of them had taken one step towards it when his words sunk in.

"What?" Ultraa demanded. "Our *deaths?*"

"Yes, well, it cannot be helped, can it? No, no, not helped at all."

"What are you talking about?" Pulsar asked, her voice growing strident.

"The world-killers are presently devouring your planet. I sent your friend and his alien companion there, though you will probably arrive first, given the vagaries of space-time in the vicinity of—"

"Whoa, whoa, just a minute," Ultraa said, stopping him in mid-sentence. "The technicalities of it all don't really concern us. You said something is... *eating* the Earth?"

"Yes. Precisely. The planet-killers of the Worldmind."

The little man frowned, looking down, thinking for a second.

"You have encountered one of them previously. You called it a Xorex."

Ultraa heard that name and made the connection instantly.

"The big robot? The one we fought before?"

"One?"

Francisco repeated that word and laughed.

"No, no, not one. Not just *one*. Not any longer."

He laughed again.

"Now there are many more than just one. And they are hungry. Oh yes. Very, very hungry."

"More than one," Lyn repeated, he face twisting in surprise and concern. "How many more?"

Francisco shrugged.

"Thousands? Millions? I cannot say."

He smiled up at them, at their shocked and horrified expressions.

"But *you* will be able to say, and very soon. Oh yes. You will see for yourselves."

And with that, he swept the portal over them, and they tumbled in and down and through the swirling blackness.

27

The separation had gone badly.

A day earlier, the fiery energy-entity known as Kabaraak had forced itself back into two distinct forms, just as it had existed some months before. This time, however, the separation was intentional.

That made it no less painful.

For several hours, two fully-formed humanoid shapes had lain on the floor of a cave, high up in the mountains of western Virginia. Both of them burned with cosmic flames that never subsided and never consumed their bodies. Neither of them moved for a very long time.

Finally, one version of Kabaraak stirred. Rolling over, he sat up and looked around, his eyes seeing far into the infrared and ultraviolet. He saw the shape of his other self where he lay nearby.

"Do you hear me?"

Nothing.

Slowly, carefully, he managed to get to his feet. The bright flames crackled all over his luminous body. A horrible sense of disorientation—worse even than before—nearly overwhelmed him, and he hesitated, leaning against the cave wall, waiting for it to pass.

It did not exactly pass, but it receded enough, after a time, that he stood up straight again and looked upon his counterpart once more.

I know who I am—what I am, he thought to himself immediately. I am the more controlled, more peaceful half of our personality.

He considered that fact.

It is good that I recovered first, he concluded after a moment, looking down at his counterpart, who now embodied the angry, aggressive traits of Kabaraak. *Without the calming influences I exert, he would have abandoned the plan and followed his own agenda, as likely as not.*

His other, more ambitious half had been driven insane the first time they were separated. It had happened inadvertently, a thousand years in the past, during a battle with a squadron of Worldmind Enforcers. This time, however, they had *chosen* to separate. That scarcely made it any more agreeable of a condition.

Staring down at his counterpart, knowing he would awake soon, the calm and controlled half of Kabaraak made his decision.

I hope he will understand, in time.

Turning to face the sheer stone wall of the cave, he directed both of his arms outward, unleashing a torrent of blinding cosmic flame.

For two long minutes he continued this assault, molten rock and ash falling away as he did so.

Finally he ceased the bombardment and waited for the smoke to clear.

Where he had directed his awful energies, a deep gash had been cut deep into the stone wall of the cave. The surface of the cut was glassy, sparkling—he had transmuted it into an ultra-hard composite. More than ten feet high, it extended some twenty yards back into the mountain.

Reaching down, he scooped up his fiery counterpart and slung him over his shoulder, then carried him into the fissure he had made. Reaching the end of it, he set the other figure down, then turned and strode back out into the cave.

Just before he could act further, he heard a bellow and a scream. The other Kabaraak was awake, he was furious, and he was charging out of the cave.

Quickly the calm Kabaraak unleashed his power, blasting at the rock surface once more, attempting to bring the roof of the cave down.

He is disoriented, as I was, and will be clumsy. He will not escape before I can—

The fissure collapsed, closed. Kabaraak poured more of his power into it, until it shone like the interior surface had, transmuted into a nearly unbreakable composite substance, able to confine even power such as he—and his counterpart—possessed.

I must keep him here until the job is done. He must not be allowed to go free—to rampage across the world's surface.

He stood back, watching smoke curl away from the fused rock.

Given enough time, I can free him once more. But he will not be able to escape on his own.

Nodding to himself, the rational Kabaraak gazed at the glassy tomb one last time, then strode out into the night.

He could feel the beginnings of insanity creeping into the corners of his mind—insanity brought on by separation from his other half. And he could feel the gentle but insistent tug on all his limbs, on his luminous, burning flesh itself.

Dissolution. I am already beginning to unravel. So quickly, this time, he thought. *So quickly.*

Then he launched himself into the night sky.

It matters not. I have a job to do.

He flew on, streamers of fiery energy trailing in his wake.

And, if I am fortunate—and the inhabitants of the Earth are, as well—I have a world to save, too.

28

Within the bowels of Digimacht Enterprises, erstwhile headquarters of the Field Marshal and his now-dissolved team, a nondescript gray panel slid open soundlessly, revealing a dimly lit tunnel leading down beneath the building. Out of the darkness stepped a slender man in a gray jumpsuit. His black hair was cut short, and his pale eyes burned with a strange and eerie fire.

"Truly was I wise to have had this tunnel into the building installed," he hissed to himself, as he looked one way and then the other, making sure he was alone. "Now to secure my remaining possessions here, and—"

A beam of light stabbed out from somewhere ahead, blinding him. Cursing, he raised one hand over his face while fumbling with the other for his blue sunglasses.

Now the sound of marching feet came to him.

Instantly, Desmond Beaulieu began the bizarre metamorphosis that transformed him in mere seconds from mild-mannered lab technician to master criminal. The flesh of his head burst into flame and began to melt, along with his hair. In its place leered a horrifying skull, blue flames dancing at its crown.

"Theatrical, yeah—but it's not doing a whole lot for me, Beaulieu," said a voice from just ahead.

Caught completely off guard, the Blue Skull mentally activated the cybernetic controls he had implanted into his own head—controls that allowed him to direct all the actions of the powerful entity known as Vanadium. In response, the big, blue-silver juggernaut lumbered out of the tunnel behind him and stood at attention.

Before he could order Vanadium to act, however, the Blue Skull felt something small but sharp impact the left side of his chest. Less than a second later came two additional impacts, and he staggered back, wondering if he had simply been shot.

His gray gloved hand reached up and felt of the areas, finding some sort of darts that had pierced through his jumpsuit and into his flesh. Frantically he pulled them out, knowing all the while that he was too late—they had already delivered whatever payload they had contained, and directly into his bloodstream. Nearly overtaken by a sinking sensation, he stumbled backward, crashing into the immobile Vanadium, who made no move to catch him. Deflecting off the big body, he hit the floor and lay there a moment, stunned both physically and mentally.

"Well, well. You surely didn't waste any time getting back here," said the voice again.

A figure moved forward—the Blue Skull could see fancy dress shoes and expensive suit pants approaching, from his current vantage point.

"Who—?"

The man leaned forward, into the madly flickering blue light coming from the Skull's own cranial combustion.

"Ah. You."

"I appreciate your being so predictable," Jameson said, looking down at him impassively. "I honestly wasn't sure if you were ever going to use your tunnel or not."

The Blue Skull simply stared up, unbalanced and uncertain.

"I would have let you be, for the foreseeable future," Jameson continued, "since we've been gathering all sorts of interesting information on the various criminal organizations of this country simply by monitoring your communications. However…"

The Blue Skull sank back to the hard, cold floor, horrified by such news.

"…I find that I require your help immediately. Or, more precisely, I require the help of our big friend there."

Jameson pointed to Vanadium, standing stoically and silently behind the Skull.

"And since, with those cybernetic implants you gave yourself, only you can control him now…"

The government man shrugged.

"I have no choice but to bring our little charade to an end, and to, well…"

He considered his words for a moment.

"…To *draft* you, essentially. You and your friend there. Welcome to the Army!"

"That's ridiculous," the Blue Skull barked, summoning up the last of his rapidly evaporating bravado. "I was a federal agent already—until the word came down that the team was dissolved. Why should you want me now? And, more importantly, why should I go along with it?"

"Oh, let's not pretend," Jameson said. "We both know you never had any intention of serving as one of the Field Marshal's agents. You were just using that gig to its full advantage—free room and board, access to new technology and state of the art equipment, and the chance to subvert the big guy here."

He nodded toward Vanadium, whose tiny red pinprick eyes merely stared out impassively.

"As to why you'll work for me now…"

Jameson bent down and showed the Blue Skull the small pistol he held in one hand, before giving it to a uniformed agent who stepped forward and holstered it.

"You have enough micro-explosives in your bloodstream at the moment to turn you into a Leroy Nieman painting at the push of a button," he said. "Now, eventually they'll all dissolve. But until that time comes, consider yourself back in the service of your country." He grinned at Beaulieu, then hesitated. "This is your country, right?" He shrugged in answer to his own question. "Not that it matters."

The Blue Skull could only gawk back at Jameson. Things were not going at all the way he had intended.

"How," the criminal asked, his voice somehow comical as it now combined its usual deep and intimidating resonance with a spot of dazed confusion, "How do you know so much about my plans?"

Jameson smiled again.

"Do you think I would trust someone like the so-called Field Marshal—or *you*, with your reputation—with Uncle Sam's money, weapons, and technology—not to mention official government status—without taking extreme precautions? I have cameras and microphones in every room of this building."

"But I found them all," the Blue Skull protested weakly. "I found them easily, and disabled them."

"You found the ones I intended for you to find," Jameson replied. "Give me a little credit here. When it comes to deviousness…well, you may be an arch-villain, but I'm with the federal government."

The Blue Skull considered that point and concluded he had nothing to say in return. Wordlessly, he allowed Jameson's uniformed agents to lift him up and lead him away. The hulking form of the enslaved Vanadium followed after them, silent save for the resounding crash of his heavy metal feet upon the floor.

"What do you need me to do?" the Skull asked finally, as they passed through the building's front doorway.

Jameson grinned at him—a sight perfectly capable of chilling even the Skull's frigid blood.

"I need you to help me save the world, son," he said. "And then, once we know that world is secure…"

He shrugged.

"Then maybe we'll let you get back to robbing it."

29

Ultraa and his teammates—old and new—had emerged from Francisco's portal and now found themselves on the southern outskirts of Washington, D.C. Seeing great columns of smoke rising in the distance, they all headed for the center of the city as rapidly as they could manage.

The capitol lay sparkling like a jewel in the autumn sun as the white-and-red form of Ultraa swooped down over it. It was a sight he never grew tired of, though the reality of it today hit him with surprise and outright shock.

He spun about in midair and called back to the golden streak that followed him.

"Are you seeing this?"

The streak slowed and resolved itself into the shiny form of Pulsar, clad in her golden metallic outfit and surrounded in a nimbus of crackling energy. Hovering nearly motionless, she looked down and gawked.

"You have got to be kidding me," she breathed. "It's that same robot. But—"

Below them, at least half a dozen of the tall, silvery robots stood in various spots across the vast lawn of the National Mall.

"But—it—it—*spawned*, or something!"

"Yeah," Ultraa said, nodding. "Something like that."

"One was bad enough," Lyn groaned, her voice filled with distress.

Gunfire rattled out, coming from the line of soldiers who had dug in at various points surrounding the area the robots occupied. As they watched, several tanks and other pieces of heavy military equipment rolled across the Mall, taking up positions to aim at the bizarre interlopers, most of whom were busily engaged in dismantling the monuments.

"Surely they won't start shooting, right here in the middle of—"

Before Lyn could finish her sentence, the tanks opened fire. Shells struck two of the robots squarely, staggering them for a brief moment, but the shots deflected harmlessly away. A second volley an instant later ricocheted, and fragments struck the Washington Monument itself, just above where the robots had already been ripping loose chunks of the marble. The result was a ragged gap in the monument's base, about ten feet up. The thing looked nearly ready to topple over.

"Okay, I guess they will," Lyn observed.

Then they heard the screams.

"Look!"

Ultraa was pointing to the top of the Washington Monument. Lyn shot forward, and as she drew near she could see a number of people hanging halfway out of windows at the top of the tall marble obelisk, frantically waving their arms and yelling.

Before Lyn could reply, Ultraa had already crossed the remaining distance to the monument, swooping up towards the windows. Lyn wasn't sure exactly what he had in mind, but it was apparent to her that time was short. So she flew after him, angling down where he had gone up, hovering about forty feet in the air, to one side of the obelisk.

"Brace it, Pulsar," Ultraa called down.

"Um, yeah, no problem," Lyn muttered. Reaching out with both hands, she created a shimmering, golden force sphere just broad enough to completely encompass the shattered section of the monument. The tilting motion slowed, slowed, and halted.

"Yes!"

Then the structure groaned. Lyn tasted blood and realized she was biting her tongue. She wasn't exactly holding up the weight of the monument by herself, but she was keeping it balanced on its base, preventing it from toppling, which was bad enough. It was heavy—*so* heavy.

And then it lightened, the pressure upon her dropping to almost nothing. She looked around, seeking the source of the reprieve.

"I should have known."

Richard Hammond—Heavyweight—stood a few yards away, arms raised, pointing at the section of the monument.

"I had to get a lift from Doug," he said with a shrug.

Lyn looked up at the huge chunk of marble Heavyweight was keeping aloft above her.

"So you can go both ways," she noted, grinning.

He merely frowned at that.

"I mean, you can make things heavy *or* light."

"I could let go, you know," he growled after a second.

Giggling, Lyn rocketed up into the air again. Ultraa descended past her, moving quickly but much more slowly than usual, carrying two of the tourists along with him. No sooner had he set them down safely—with an intense *"Run! Go!"*—than he was rocketing back up to the top, picking up his next passengers.

But, Lyn realized with a sick feeling, there wouldn't be time to get them all. The monument had begun to tilt, the stone and metal framework cracking and crumbling above the section Heavyweight was holding.

"No!"

Gritting her teeth, Lyn formed another force bubble around the upper section, and poured out more power, and more, and still more. Gradually she was transforming the hollow bubble of force into a solid ball, completely encasing the upper section of the monument, holding it like a plaster cast. Sweat ran down her forehead, her cheeks. Some of the blood vessels in her eyes burst.

"Ultraa!" she gasped. *"Hurry!"*

He saw what she was doing, gawked at her for a split second, deeply impressed, and then redoubled his efforts. He gathered up the last of the stranded tourists and carried them away just as Lyn cried out in pain.

With a loud popping sound, Lyn's sparkling sphere vanished. The upper portion of the monument crumbled and fell down into the middle section being suspended by Heavyweight, knocking it free of his control. Tons of marble crashed to the grassy lawn of the National Mall, sending Richard and the civilians running for cover.

Lyn watched it fall, watched the impact as it hit the ground, and saw the debris flying everywhere.

"Tell me you got them all," she shouted hoarsely to Ultraa.

He gave her a smile and a thumbs-up.

Then all three of them looked at the ruins of the Washington Monument scattered across the lawn, and a deep sadness settled over them. Doug Williams—the Fury—had gone straight into combat against the big robots; seeing the collapse of the monument, though, he circled around and landed beside them, staring at the wreckage.

They might have remained that way for quite a while, but for the sounds of battle raging all around. Within seconds they had regained their wits and they flew back up into the sky, surveying the battlefield again.

"There," Ultraa said, pointing toward the largest concentration of Xorex robots.

Lyn, wiping blood from her chin, nodded.

Together, they rocketed back down into the fray.

30

The six starships of the Circle fleet dropped out of hyperspace and reduced speed drastically, closing in on the Earth at a slow but steady rate. Aboard the flagship, their new and self-appointed admiral relaxed in the center seat, enjoying the ride.

He was in no particular hurry.

After a time, the fleet reached the Earth and slid smoothly into high orbit. Officers and technicians, all laboring at Rnn'dul Nah-Shonn's command, worked quickly and efficiently, their only goal to please their new leader. They had no other choice—no free will remaining at all. Nah-Shonn's mental powers had ensnared them all.

As Nah-Shonn sipped at a drink brought to him by a particularly lovely ensign, one of the reconnaissance officers spoke up for the first time. A tall, slender Kur-Bai—Lt. Tanarian was her name, Nah-Shonn seemed to recall, not that he much cared—she turned and addressed him respectfully.

"Sir, sensors indicate an unknown energy pattern on the planet's surface."

Nah-Shonn yawned.

"An unknown energy pattern? So what? If it's something the humans are doing, how dangerous can it be?"

The lieutenant hesitated.

"Sir, it does not match any of our records for human mechanisms or power sources. I can find nothing like it in any of our current databases."

Nah-Shonn still wasn't interested.

"One moment," the lieutenant said then, frowning down at her board, studying the scrolling text and accompanying graphics. "I'm now registering the Worldmind Enforcer you mentioned before, sir—the unit calling itself Vanadium. I do see his energy signature."

She frowned at the readouts, studied them closer, and ran them again.

Nah-Shonn was still sipping at his drink and smiling at the pretty ensign when Lt. Tanarian gave a little shriek.

Nah-Shonn whirled, staring at her in surprise.

"Tanarian? What was that?"

"The two energy signatures, sir," she said, her voice trembling now. "The unknown one and that of the Worldmind Enforcer, Vanadium. They match, almost perfectly."

Nah-Shonn started to dismiss this information, but then something from his education of long ago nagged at him, and he paused, waiting.

"And the pattern, sir—it is replicating. Replicating wildly."

"Xorexes," Nah-Shonn breathed, his eyes widening. "The Worldmind's Planet-Killers."

Tanarian only nodded, her face betraying her profound fear.

"So they still exist."

He stood and walked over to the sensor displays, studying them for himself. Indeed he could see that the Xorexes were multiplying, and very rapidly. He remembered his Earth geography well, and could see that the entire East Coast of North America was infested with Xorexes—and they continued to spread as he watched.

He stared at the displays for several minutes, watching the unrelenting expansion of the infested area. Then, shaking his head in wonder, he returned to the center seat and dropped limply into it. Softly at first, he began to laugh.

"So. I come all the way back here, a starfleet at my disposal, in order to annihilate this wretched Earth—and I find that I can save all the effort. The job is already being done for me. And far more completely and efficiently than anything we could have done with mere weapons and ordnance."

He laughed more deeply.

"Astounding."

He stared at the forward display screen for a few moments, beginning to make out the areas of silver and the patches of excavated earth appearing through the cloud cover below. Then, still amazed by what he was seeing, he turned back to the pretty ensign and handed her his empty glass.

"Bring me another," he ordered. "And some for the rest of the bridge crew, as well."

He grinned; that eerie, too-wide mouth was enough to have frightened the ensign away if she were not under his complete telepathic control.

"I believe," he said, "we are about to have a most entertaining show to watch."

37

Ultraa was wasting no time. Continuing his flight path and increasing his already blazing speed, he zeroed in on the robot standing closest to the ruins of the Washington Monument. The big, silver figure seemed to sense him at the last moment, but even with its own remarkable speed, it could scarcely dodge the red and white streak that crashed into it.

Mysterious powers that even he didn't fully understand making him invulnerable during flight, Ultraa deflected off the robot's shiny surface and spun away. The robot, for its part, flew backwards upon the impact of the devastating blow, tumbling head over heels.

Scarcely a second later, that same robot regained its feet and shimmered, its surface changing from silver to white. Red details appeared in spots along its arms and legs.

Following Ultraa down, Lyn witnessed all of this, in the blink of an eye it took to happen.

"Wait—wait a minute," she cried out, as Ultraa recovered his composure and came around for another pass. "Remember, from before? It mimics our powers! It copies them when we get too close to it!"

Ultraa glanced at her as he went by, hearing her. He slowed down, considering what she was saying. In the split second this took, the robot he'd hit sprang forward, moving nearly as fast as Ultraa himself, and smashed into him, driving him down into the ground.

Lyn swooped around and hovered nearby, projecting a shimmering golden force field bubble around Ultraa as he struggled to his feet again. The robot that had attacked him started forward, met the field's surface, and staggered back, apparently startled.

Ultraa looked up at her, nodding his silent thanks. Then, "But what else can we do?" he asked. "Either we fight them or we don't."

Lyn frowned. She knew Ultraa possessed no distance weapons, and her own offensive capabilities did not extend very far—she'd never managed to create a force bubble more than about fifty feet away from herself, and that was pushing it.

Before she could reply, the Fury—or, as Lyn thought of him, the man in the glossy black bodysuit—shot past, hurling vivid green bolts of energy at the robot, causing it to spin around. Even as it did, part of its silvery torso darkened to black, and greenish forks of electricity danced over its arms.

"It copies powers," Lyn shouted to the man in black, remembering then that his name was Doug Williams. "If you get too close, or use your abilities on it, it can—"

Williams ignored her, landing in front of the robot and striking again and again with his bolts. The robot reeled backward at first, then recovered and hurled its own barrage of electricity back at him. Quite literally shocked, Williams dodged to one side, tripped, and went down roaring in pain as the lightning played over him. Lyn cringed as she heard his strangely distorted voice crying out through the layer of black material.

Ultraa swooped out of the sky and snatched up the Fury before the robot could deal him any additional damage. He carried the limp man a few dozen yards away and set him down on the grass.

"Ohh...Thanks," Williams said as he sat up, nodding to Ultraa. "I should have listened to your partner."

"That's a good idea," the blond man replied, "but only every now and then." He winked. "And we can't let her know that."

Williams laughed, then stood and lost any feelings of good humor instantly. The robots were duplicating again—now there appeared to be more than a hundred of them.

"What can we do?" he called to Ultraa. "We can't get too close. We can barely hurt them. And they're...reproducing!" His voice had grown tense, exasperated. "What do you suggest?"

"We keep fighting them," Heavyweight replied as he ran past. "We have no choice."

The Fury and Ultraa exchanged glances. Ultraa shrugged. Williams nodded. They hurled themselves back into the fray.

Meanwhile, Lyn circled overhead, equally uncertain of exactly what to do, her eyes widening as she saw the increasing number of robots—*Xorexes*, she remembered the alien woman calling them. Somehow they were reproducing themselves, as if by magic.

As she flew, Lyn noticed a silvery glint of light off to the southwest. Something shiny was approaching rapidly.

"Is that—yes!"

A broad grin burst across her face, and she propelled herself in the direction of the oncoming shape.

"Wendy! Hey!"

The girl in silver shot past her, then curved around and zoomed back.

Remarkably similar in appearance, the two sisters hovered there above the wreckage of the Washington Monument, facing one another. Lyn was a tad older and bigger, and wore shiny gold, while her sister was clad in a virtually identical suit of silver, though it sported belled cuffs with a feather motif at the wrists and ankles.

"Are you okay?" Lyn asked. "I wanted to come looking for you, but—"

Then she realized her little sister was crying.

"What's the matter? Did you not find that woman you were chasing?"

Wendy sobbed.

"I found her. I—I found—"

Lyn drifted closer and put one golden-sheathed arm around the girl.

"What?"

"I found her body! She was *dead!*"

Lyn started.

"What? Who—who could have—?"

"I don't know. *I don't know!* It wasn't me!"

Lyn shushed her gently.

"I know it wasn't you, sis. I *know* that. Nobody would think it was."

Wendy nodded.

"The police didn't think so—not at all. They asked me a few questions and let me go."

"Good," Lyn said, relieved her sister at least was not facing a murder charge. "So—how did she die?"

"I—I think somebody shot her. But there was nobody else around when I got there. Under that big bridge."

Lyn nodded.

"Look, Wen, she was a criminal, right? I'm sure she had lots of enemies. One of them just happened to get to her before you did. She would have been a lot better off just surrendering to you."

"Yeah," Wendy sniffed. "I would've only knocked a few of her teeth out, I guess."

Lyn chuckled, and then even Wendy managed a choked laugh herself.

The two huddled there for a minute or so, until Wendy regained her composure somewhat.

"Okay, sis," Lyn said finally, "I'm not thrilled about you being all involved in this stuff…but, given the circumstances… we need your help here. If we don't stop these…*things*…then nothing else really matters, y'know?"

Wendy looked down, as if seeing the robots for the first time. Her eyes widened, and she nodded.

"Okay, yeah. What should I do?"

Lyn pointed toward the red and white blur that was Ultraa, smashing into one robot after another, bludgeoning away at them with his indestructible body.

"Let's ask the man in charge," she said.

Together, she and her sister flew down toward the battlefield that was the Mall.

32

What looked to be a row of random human beings burst into flame as the long, silver staff waved in their direction.

"Humans burn easily enough, it would seem," said the Kur-Bai warrior. He was clad in silky, jewel-adorned red robes, and his long, lank, white hair spun about his narrow face as he leapt to the attack again, fire surging from his staff and engulfing his targets.

"Or at least your simulations do," answered Devenn. "But I believe the natives of this *Earth* will not be the primary targets of this operation. Nor even the secondary targets."

"We may still strike them if necessary, though, correct?"

Devenn eyed his teammate warily.

"*If necessary*, Yeist," he emphasized back at the man. "But I believe our main foes will be the Worldmind's agents, if they indeed exist. And of course the Circle criminals. The Admiral and the political leadership would prefer not to engage the humans—unless of course we find it necessary to annihilate their world entirely, from orbit."

"Then I am to restrain myself? I am not to seek combat with the Earth natives?"

"Again, only if necessary."

Devenn considered the words he had just spoken.

"And perhaps I should be the one to determine if such action is indeed necessary."

Yeist paused in his training and glared at Devenn.

"Why do we put up with the restrictions the Empire places upon us?" he growled, still playing the flame from his staff across the now-melted row of synthetic humanoid simulations. "Why do we not simply venture out on our own? With our talents and skills, surely we could—"

"Surely we could be labeled traitors and renegades and criminals by the Empire," Devenn angrily finished for him. "We could find ourselves in the same situation as the Circle. Forced to turn renegade in order to preserve our lifestyles—our lives!—and seeing the worlds upon which we dwelt blasted into radioactive rubble by this very Starfleet."

He faced the more slender man fully.

"Such is the life you would have for us?"

Yeist considered his words, stared down at the floor, and shook his head slowly.

"No. Of course not. It is just…"

He looked back up at his team's leader, frowning.

"None fight harder for the Kur-Bai Empire than do we. And yet—"

"—And we will continue to do so," Devenn said firmly, overriding him. "As we will for as long as we must."

Yeist didn't argue, but he did not look happy, either. Turning away again, he triggered his staff, the flames leaping up from each end. Across the chamber, the row of once-human shapes had melted down to an unrecognizable goop.

33

A big silver fist crashed into Wendy Li and sent her thudding to the ground. She lay there, moaning, stars bursting in her vision, as the battle raged on around her. After a minute of this, she shook her head and slowly attempted to get up.

Lyn was fighting nearby and hadn't noticed what had happened at first. Now, seeing Wendy on the ground, anger welled inside her and she shot downward, lightning flashing all around her. She landed by her sister, kneeling, and put one arm around her, steadying her.

"I'm—I'm okay," Wendy groaned, rubbing her eyes.

Lyn greeted this with a frown.

A battalion of the big robots approached. Hastily, Lyn erected a force field around the two of them, and the Xorexes shuffled past on each side.

Wendy made it to her feet.

"It's okay," she said. "I'm fine."

"No, wait," Lyn began, grasping her by the arm. "Are you sure you—"

"Let her get back in the fight," Ultraa said, hovering in place overhead. "We're all soldiers, now, and the world is depending on us—on *all* of us."

He met Lyn's angry look with a shrug.

"As much as I hate it," he said, "we can't stop to worry about every little injury."

"Every little—!"

She glared at the blond man angrily.

"She has no business being here! She's just a kid!"

"Hey," Wendy began to object, but the other two ignored her.

"I know she's a kid, and I know about the dangers of having someone so young involved in combat," Ultraa replied, giving Lyn a significant look. "And *you* know that better than anybody. But, right now, we don't have a choice."

Lyn looked from Ultraa to her sister, her mind running through her somewhat limited list of expletives, seeking the ones that best approximated how she felt at the moment. It didn't take her long to conclude that none of them came close.

"I need some more curse words," she growled as she let Wendy go. "I'll have to talk to Esro about that, if he gets back. *When* he gets back."

And he is coming back, she reassured herself for perhaps the thousandth time.

Ahead of her, Ultraa swooped down and smashed his invulnerable body into the nearest Xorex, shoving it forward into another one nearby. The three went down in a heap, tumbling across the smoking grass. Ultraa got to his feet before either of his adversaries and delivered a flurry of blows to each of them. Neither robot seemed particularly damaged by the attack.

None of this is accomplishing anything, he thought to himself miserably. *But...what else can we do? Dammit, we need Esro here, to think of some clever solution.*

He looked back at Lyn and Wendy, fighting valiantly but to no greater result than he was managing.

But instead of Esro, I have two kids to worry about. And the little sister—Wendy—wouldn't be here if I hadn't allowed Lyn to serve as an agent in the first place. What have I gotten myself into? What have I gotten them into?

As he wrestled with these dilemmas—not to mention two big robots that were trying to smash him to bits—he saw a flash of metal out of the corner of his eye. Zooming up to a safe distance, he turned in that direction and gasped.

What looked at first like another whole battalion of robots was descending on the Mall.

"Now what?"

They landed on pillars of flame: big, bulky, armored things about seven feet tall, with what had to be weapons systems attached to their arms and backs. Their faces were featureless curvatures of glass, or something like it.

As he looked closer, he recognized American flags emblazoned on the shoulders of the newcomers.

"Huh?"

Surging forward, the twenty-odd armored figures crashed into several of the nearest robots and opened fire on them with a wide array of firepower.

Lyn sailed down from above, pointing. "What are those things?"

"Oh, yeah," Ultraa said then, as much to himself as to his partner, recognizing them at last. "Esro showed me the plans once."

"Esro? Esro designed them?"

"Yep. He called them 'Defender' units."

543

Lyn wrinkled her nose in mock disdain.

"Then they'll need all the help they can get. Let's go!"

Following his young partner back toward the battle, Ultraa thought to himself, *In all honesty, I'm glad to see them here—glad to have some backup.*

And then, *But now that I think about it... Esro never produced any of them. He never even sold the plans.*

He frowned, even as he smashed a red-gloved fist into the cranium of the nearest robot.

Jameson. It has to be Jameson. Another thing he stole from Esro.

He grimaced at the mere thought of the government man who had once been his immediate superior in the Pentagon's chain of command.

So that's another one I owe you, once this is all over.

Ultraa and his teammates and new friends continued their assault on the robots, but very quickly Ultraa came to understand how utterly useless their actions really were. Pulsar and her sister were hurling bolts of golden and silvery lightning at the robots, who simply shrugged it all off. The Fury was zapping away, but he seemed to be receiving even worse than he was giving, as the Xorexes all appeared to have copied his powers by now. Only Heavyweight was doing much good, keeping a large group of the Xorexes pinned to the ground, squirming and struggling like insects beneath some massive boot. But he wasn't actually destroying any of them, and the moment he let up, the robots would be on the attack once more.

And all of that paled beside the fact that the number of Xorexes on the Mall had doubled and doubled again, just in the past few seconds—and now they had opened up huge craters in the Earth's crust, digging all around and tunneling down into the soil.

"There has to be a better way," he whispered to himself. "There has to be something we can do."

But nothing came to his mind, and all around him the robots continued to reproduce and to devour the very world on which they stood.

34

"This is not working," Ultraa growled to anyone nearby who might hear. "Not working at all. Somehow, it even seems like we're only making it all worse."

The National Mall was covered in battling figures. Mixed in amongst a veritable army of big, silver robots swarmed his ad-hoc team of paranormal-powered individuals, along with a battalion of armored Defenders. And for all the damage those two groups dealt out, the robots appeared to notice it scarcely at all.

Wide patches of the Mall's grassy lawn burned, flames licking at the shattered monuments. What was left of the Capitol dome remained upright by only the slenderest of supports, the building beneath it battered mostly to fragments. The landscape for miles in every direction revealed great gouges dug into the earth. And everywhere, *everywhere* roamed the inexplicably replicating Xorex robots, each of them momentarily taking on the physical characteristics of one or more of their adversaries long enough to unleash an attack using that person's particular powers. And every second, more and more of the robots appeared, seemingly budding out of the sides of the existing models.

Ultraa watched it all from on high, and cursed violently.

He surveyed the battlefield, his hand shielding his eyes from the afternoon sun, taking in the full tactical situation—which only angered him further, because he had yet to develop any sort of approach for dealing with it.

He looked down a few dozen yards to his left and saw Pulsar and her sister fighting a robot together. Lyn's incessant protective fussing over Wendy continued, but at least they appeared to be able to physically fight together as effectively as they verbally fought with each other.

He looked to his right and saw the glossy black shape of the Fury swooping in and out among the robots, smashing away at them. He was curious about the guy, but would wait until later, until a better opportunity arose, before investigating further—assuming there would *be* a later.

And just below him, Richard Hammond—Heavyweight—battled four of the monstrosities at once, alternating the pull of gravity on each to float it upward and then smash it down hard. Ultraa could see that this extended and excessive use of his power was taking its toll on the man—in fact, he was drenched in sweat and gasping for breath—but he dared not even suggest for Richard to ease up, as he was providing one of the few successes they'd experienced against the robots thus far.

I can give him a quick break, though, Ultraa thought.

In a flash he had swooped down, a human rocket smashing with outstretched fists into the nearest Xorex, sending that one crashing back into the two behind it. Spinning around, he punched the fourth, sending it sprawling back on top of the others.

Quickly Ultraa circled around again and landed beside Heavyweight, who was taking advantage of the free moment to catch his breath.

"Thanks, buddy," Richard said when he could breathe again. He flashed the man in white and red a smile. "It was getting tight there."

"Not a problem."

As he spoke, Ultraa's eyes followed the actions of the four Xorexes he'd just knocked down. Something occurred to him, which he quickly shared with Heavyweight.

"I think they're feeding on our powers," he said, gesturing at the cluster of robots they'd been fighting. "Not just copying them, but actually drawing on them—*siphoning* them—for energy, and to make their replicating abilities work."

Richard frowned and followed Ultraa's eyes. After a moment of watching the behavior of the robots, he shrugged.

"What makes you think so?"

Ultraa shook his head.

"I—I don't know it. But it seems reasonable." *It seems like something Esro would say,* he wanted to add. "They didn't start popping up everywhere like this until we showed up. And the more of us there are, the more of *them* there are."

The other man appeared to consider this.

"So what should we do, then? Leave? Give up?"

He mopped at his forehead.

"Because it looks to me like they are in the process of eating the freaking planet," he concluded, gesturing toward the vast, gaping pits the robots were opening and widening all around. Fires leapt up from the depths of some of them, lending a dim, hazy, hellish atmosphere to the area.

Ultraa shook his head.

"I don't know. I don't know. But I think what we have to do is to *contain* them. Bottle them up somehow. Sweep them into the ocean...or put them in a big box..."

"You have a box that big ready?"

Ultraa said nothing, merely staring out at the silver sea of robots. Then something caught his eye, and he actually took a step forward, excitement building inside him.

"Vanadium!"

The blue-silver form of Ultraa's erstwhile teammate soared over the Mall like a flying statue. He gave no indication of recognizing anyone—instead, he settled down into the midst of the big robots and began to smash away at them with virtually invulnerable fists.

Ultraa rushed over to him and called his name again, but the big metal man ignored him. The twin tiny, bright red lights set deep in Vanadium's dark eye sockets remained locked on the robots, not acknowledging Ultraa in the slightest.

Before Ultraa could do or say anything further, three Xorexes rushed towards them both, and Ultraa wheeled about to defend himself from the two that assaulted him. During the ensuing few seconds of battle, he managed to glimpse Vanadium off to his left, and realized that something very strange was happening there, between his former teammate and the other Xorex.

The two of them—twelve-foot-tall, silvery robot and seven-foot-tall, blue-silver enigma—had both stopped dead in their tracks.

Ultraa, puzzled, launched himself into the air and curved away from his own foes to move closer and see what was happening.

The two metallic adversaries stared at one another, unmoving, for several long seconds. Each moved its head in a series of jerky mechanical motions, as if seeking to view as much as possible of the other from every angle.

And then they both froze.

"Oh, no," Ultraa muttered, remembering what had happened to Vanadium the first time they had encountered a Xorex. "He's locking up again."

He swooped down, meaning to try to get Vanadium's attention—to wake him up, somehow, before something even worse happened. Before he could, however, something *did* happen—but not what Ultraa had expected.

Vanadium came to life, moving with catlike speed and agility, smashing his fist into the face of the big robot.

The Xorex reeled backwards, staggered two steps to the right, and faced Vanadium again, emitting a series of odd sounds. These were followed by what sounded like words in a wide variety of languages. Finally, the robot spoke in English.

"Why?" it said, very clearly. *"Why do you attack me, brother?"*

"Huh?" Ultraa exclaimed.

Vanadium appeared to hesitate, staring back at the big robot.

Ultraa swooped down instantly, landed, and rushed up to his former teammate.

"Vanadium! You in there, pal? *Hey!"*

He waved a red-gloved hand in front of the tiny red eyes, to no effect.

At that moment, he became aware of something he hadn't quite noticed before.

A series of small, nearly flat metal disks had been attached to Vanadium's head, all the way around, in roughly one-inch intervals, just above the level of his eyes. Multicolored lights on their surfaces blinked on and off.

"What in the world are those?"

Before Ultraa could put any more thought into it, the Xorex took a step toward them. Its lack of facial features only served to make the thing more disturbing. Leaning in, it raised its big, silver fist.

"Hey, buddy," Ultraa shouted at Vanadium. *"Wake up!"*

Still nothing.

Ultraa considered his options for perhaps a quarter of a second, then reared back and smacked Vanadium on the side of the head.

The Xorex halted its advance, as if puzzled.

Ultraa's blow sent Vanadium sprawling out on the grass, but the big man was back up and in a fighting stance so incredibly quickly that Ultraa could scarcely believe it. Involuntarily he took a step backward, readying himself for the possibility of being attacked from both directions.

As Vanadium advanced, Ultraa noticed that one of the small disks attached to his head, where Ultraa had hit it, was now dangling loose and emitting sparks.

With everything happening so fast and all at once, Ultraa hadn't quite put the very obvious clues together until that moment. It hadn't helped that Vanadium had been acting strange—strange for *him*— even before, when the first Xorex had shown up at the mansion. Now, seeing this, Ultraa became convinced that someone was controlling him via those little disks.

But—who?

A few possibilities came to mind immediately.

But that's not the most important thing right now, he knew. My immediate task is very clear.

He braced himself for his friend's assault, planning to get him into a clutch and work on removing those disks from close range. Indeed for an instant it did appear as if the big blue-silver man would attack him.

But then Vanadium stopped in his tracks, his blazing pinprick eyes flickering from Ultraa to the Xorexes nearby. He hesitated, appearing disoriented and confused, as if waging a fierce internal struggle of some sort.

"Hey, buddy," Ultraa began to say, "let me help you—"

Vanadium whirled and charged off in the opposite direction—directly into the thick of a whole crowd of Xorexes.

"Never mind," Ultraa finished. He shook his head in mixed confusion and disgust. "At least you're fighting the robots. I guess that'll do for now."

Within seconds, more than a dozen Xorexes had closed in around Vanadium, blocking him from Ultraa's view. Electricity danced off their silver hides, golden force fields popping on and off around them.

A blow to the back of his head sent Ultraa sprawling, stars swimming in his vision and serving as a reminder not to become distracted on the battlefield. A Xorex leapt on top of him, punching hard. Quickly Ultraa rolled to the side, regained his feet and punched the big robot away again, then looked back to where Vanadium was now fighting a veritable battalion of foes. They had him buried in a gigantic scrum. For a moment the blue-silver head appeared, and a matching fist swung out wildly. Instantly the horde of Xorexes smashed back down at him.

Ultraa looked on in shock.

Can even he stand up to that kind of punishment for long?

Silver fists rose and fell like jackhammers, electrical blasts rained down. Seconds later, Vanadium disappeared beneath the pile.

35

The Blue Skull watched with growing anger from his place of concealment on the National Mall.

He was angry because while Jameson was forcing him to use Vanadium in this battle, he had seen the opportunity to turn his metallic pawn against a more hated foe—Ultraa. But Vanadium had flatly refused the Skull's mental commands to attack the hero, and had instead dived into the fray with the Xorexes.

How could he have resisted? It shouldn't be possible.

Then again, the Skull realized he did not know everything about the blue-silver juggernaut's internal systems. They were of alien manufacture, after all. He felt relatively certain his control disks would keep the big war machine under control, but occasionally there was a slip, like this one. It was somehow...*disheartening* to the Skull.

It made him sad.

And, yes, angry.

Mostly angry.

Meanwhile the psychic feedback coming to him over his implanted cybernetic controls had become quite painful.

He did not pause to consider the irony of a man with a blazing skull on his shoulders complaining about a headache.

Is this some new tactic of Vanadium's, trying to resist me?

"Doubtful," he answered himself. "There can be no free will remaining to him."

Or is it a natural result of the experimental cybernetic system I devised? I had no way to test it before implanting it within myself...

He did not know, but he intended to keep it in place as long as it worked—pain be damned.

A hundred yards away, Vanadium smashed at the Xorexes, his fists becoming blue-silver blurs as he battered down the enemy. Yet for every one he crushed into the ground, two more seemed to leap to the attack.

"Must get him away from those robots," the Skull muttered, sending cybernetic orders with increasing desperation. "He must not waste his power on them!"

Such was his single-minded dedication to his criminal cause— and his hatred for Ultraa—that he scarcely considered the consequences, should the robots actually win.

Ultraa, on the other hand, had given that matter considerable thought, both in conversation with Lyn before their arrival, and now, as he fought the big robots in hand-to-hand combat.

Taking a break to check in with the military units on the scene, he learned more than he really wanted to know about the overall strategic situation. The Xorexes, in the relatively brief time since they began their assault on Washington, DC, had already dismantled most of the monuments, many of the federal buildings, and had even begun to excavate deep craters into the Earth's crust itself, both here and in several outlying areas. They appeared bent on taking the very world itself apart, piece by piece. And their numbers, which had been steadily increasing from the start, now appeared to be multiplying geometrically. And now they were turning up in other cities around the country—around the world.

Indeed, as Ultraa swooped back into combat, he could see little other than a sea of silver robots across the Mall, through the city, and all the way to the horizon. There could be little doubt now—the survival of the world itself was at stake. These robots—these Xorexes—had to be defeated, and soon. Yet the only people who knew anything about them were the alien Kur-Bai, and their whole contingent was now dead—save only, perhaps, the female who had gone off in pursuit of the first Xorex, taking Esro Brachis with her.

Esro, we need you here, buddy. And we need that lady, too— maybe even more.

Ultraa was not the only person thinking those thoughts. Less than a half mile away, Lyn Li swooped over the burning lawn of the National Mall, zapping away with shimmering beams of golden energy, tripping and smashing and battering the robot horde—to about as much real effect as anything anyone else was doing. And as she did so, she kept thinking, *Esro, get your sorry rear end back here, now. If you've ever going to make a dramatic entrance in your life, this would be a good time.*

Of course, no such thing happened.

"I don't understand what's going on," her little sister shouted to her as she swooped past. "I thought you always beat the bad guys! They're not supposed to win, are they?"

Lyn shook her head.

"I don't understand it anymore than you do, Wen. Just keep fighting. Slow them down as best you can. Maybe someone else will figure something out."

She spared a second's glance up on the hill. The Capitol was gone completely now—a horde of Xorexes had taken it apart, piece by piece, in less than a minute.

Anger flowed through her.

The Capitol! The dome! They dismantled the whole thing!

Lightning flickered all over her body, her golden mesh costume sparking and shimmering.

551

I'm gonna cook 'em, she thought. *I'm gonna pick out a few of them and just completely fry 'em!*

Choosing a cluster of five or six Xorexes below her, she reached out with both hands, even as she flew overhead, and created a shimmering sphere around them. It was, she would reflect later, probably the largest force sphere she had ever constructed. Strong emotions had always fueled her powers, and the combination of a seemingly hopeless situation, the disappearance of Esro, her frustration with Wendy, and now the destruction of the US Capitol all combined to push her over the edge. She squeezed the sphere around the Xorexes tighter. And tighter. And tighter.

"Aaaaaaahhhhh!"

Lyn's face, a mask of straining concentration, would have scared most anyone who knew and cared for her. Her mouth was twisted in a horrible grimace, her teeth clamped together, her eyes nearly closed as she scrunched herself up, pouring all of her reserves into this one act.

We may lose, but I'm taking some of these things with me before we go...

The golden sphere grew purple and contracted tighter, and tighter, and tighter. Now it was the size of a basketball. The pressure she exerted was enormous, and the force pushing back against her was equally so. Still she pressed, somehow now determined to crush the robots out of existence.

The sphere was now the size of a tennis ball, and blazing nearly as bright as a tiny sun. A ping pong ball. A marble.

Wendy swooped around, about thirty yards behind her, eyes wide. Realization of what was about to happen came to her first, but too late to prevent it.

"Lyn! *Wait!* Don't—"

The strain was too much. Lyn let go. The tiny sphere disappeared.

All that compressed pressure, along with the explosive force of the robots, released at once.

Lyn managed to avoid the worst of it, but the shockwave smashed into Wendy with full force, hurling her backwards, causing her to tumble like a rag doll, hurtling past her sister and off into the distance.

"Nooooo!" Lyn screamed, barely managing to erect a defensive shield in front of herself in time. The shockwave still hit her hard, too, though not nearly as hard as it had hit Wendy.

She moved, then, with all the speed at her disposal.

It was not enough. For all the speed she possessed, the blast had slowed her down long enough for Wendy to get too far away. She was about to hit the ground.

"No," she growled through clenched teeth. "Not again. *Not again!*"

Lyn knew she couldn't catch up to her sister, but she could at least try to catch her.

As she flew, the older of the Li women reached out with one golden arm and conjured up what she envisioned in her mind as a giant pillow, out beyond Wendy's trajectory.

This has to work. It has to. Come on!

Wendy fell, fell... and landed on a gigantic, shimmering, golden bubble that looked suspiciously like a throw pillow.

"Yes!"

As Lyn soared down under Wendy, the bubble vanished. Lyn caught her sister in her arms and lowered them both to the blackened earth.

"Wendy! Wen, are you okay?"

Wendy's eyes were closed. She mumbled something unintelligible, then her head lolled backwards and she slumped to the ground, limp.

Without another word, Lyn picked her up and rocketed off for the hospital. She only hoped she wouldn't find that it had been eaten, too.

36

Vanadium lay at the bottom of a crater. Crowding in all around him were the limbs of big, silver robots—robots that seemed so very strangely familiar to him.

Images danced in his head. Images provoked by these robots. From the moment the first one had appeared in Esro Brachis's yard, they had haunted him, bringing with them memories, unlocked from the depths of his damaged, heretofore inaccessible databanks.

In his mind he saw these robots, these Xorexes—armies of them, nearly limitless in number—soaring through space. Mixed in among them were units different from them—more like...like him.

Enforcers.

And behind them all, a...a *Worldmind*. A vast, planet-sized intelligence, directing all their actions, dictating their wills.

A Worldmind that was one of a small number of incredibly powerful cosmic entities.

Rivals. The Great Rivals.

He had no real idea what that meant, but somehow he knew it was true. It *felt* right. And it matched what he had remembered weeks earlier, when discussing with Ultraa the great force coming toward Earth.

It—the Worldmind—knew about Earth now, too. Its minions—the Xorexes—were here. Its lieutenants, the Enforcers...where were they?

Were they other copies of him—of Vanadium, himself? Was that truly *who*, truly *what*, he was?

The thought chilled him.

Maybe it is who I was, he thought. *Maybe once.*

But no longer.

At the moment, however, none of that mattered at all.

His usual state—that of determination to do good, tempered with a continuing sense of uncertainty and lingering amnesia—had given way to a much louder voice, echoing through his metallic mind. The voice was that of the Blue Skull, and try as he might, he could not resist it.

He knew all too well that the agents of the Skull's control over his mind were the small disks fastened to the exterior of his head. From the moment the Blue Skull had attached them, Vanadium had sought to remove them. Unfortunately, he had found that the single command with the most power over him—the one he had the least capacity to resist—was the imperative to leave the control disks in place. Try as he might, he simply could not make himself remove or disable them.

Growing self-knowledge, coupled with this mental domination, had driven him nearly into despair. Though his memories were far from intact, he instinctively knew somehow that this world could not fight back against the Xorexes. Soon it would be gone, dismantled by their rapacious appetite. Why go on?

Vanadium found, however, that as he fought the Xorexes, the level of control exerted by the Blue Skull had reduced a bit. Perhaps the villain was allowing him some range of self-control, in order to more efficiently fight the robots. And perhaps the Skull's technology was not quite as advanced as the villain had believed. Coupled with the disk Ultraa had damaged, Vanadium found he now

"This has to work. It has to. Come on!"

had more self-awareness than he had possessed in the time since the Skull had betrayed him. Not a lot, but *more.*

But how to put that to use?

At that very moment, a blow from one of the big robots crashed against his head, nearly sending his main databanks offline. But, as he recovered, he realized that another of the control disks had been damaged. The Blue Skull's influence over him had weakened still more.

Yes. Yes!

He moved. Pulling his legs under him, he surged upward, driving himself into the torsos of two Xorexes. The move scarcely damaged them, but another of the disks shorted out, and the mental domination lessened still further.

A Xorex smashed its fist towards him. Moving with blinding speed, he turned his head to take the brunt of the blow. The impact nearly knocked him out, the pain screaming through his banks of processors, but he could feel—*yes*—another disk gone.

As he continued to lead with his head, forcing the robots to strike him there, one question rattled around amidst the agony growing in his ringing, dented skull:

If this is the cure... can I survive it? Will I still be functional when the last of these infernal disks is gone?

He knew of no answer but to try.

Into the melee he plunged once more.

37

For several hours, the fiery energy-being known as Kabaraak had flown about the globe, searching for any signs of the Xorex robot, finding none.

During that time he had grown ever more insane.

The shock of separation, combined with the loss of half his intellect, was hurting him far more this time than it had after his previous division, a thousand years earlier, when his two parts had been forcibly separated during a battle with the Worldmind's Enforcers. Neither he nor his other half had truly appreciated just how debilitating the separation would be, this time.

Thus he had spent half his time searching for the Xorex, and the other half perched on one lonely mountaintop or another, here and there across the globe, his head cradled in his hands, wrestling with his own steadily-dissolving intellect.

Where can the Xorex be? He asked himself the question over and over. *Where is it?*

For quite some time, the Xorex had utterly disappeared from the Earth. And the longer the search took, the less able Kabaraak would be to deal with him—should he ever succeed in locating him again.

And so when the big robot turned up once more, Kabaraak had greeted this news with a mixture of relief, joy, and dread. Relief that the search was over; joy that he might soon be reunited with his other half, before his coherence completely broke down and he disintegrated into vapor; and dread that he might no longer retain enough power or enough mental acuity to challenge the Worldmind's foot soldier, the big Xorex robot.

And now, soaring over Washington, DC, a blazing trail of fire behind him in the sky, he looked down and saw not one but an *army* of Xorexes.

And he despaired.

No. No. I cannot defeat so many. Not in my current state. No.

Insanity clawed at his mind again, rending his thought processes, causing him to lose control and tumble down toward the ground, a fiery meteor streaking across the smoke-filled heavens.

Pulling himself together at the last instant, he rocketed back up through the haze, took in the tactical situation as best he could, and finally came to light on the roof of a round marble building situated next to the river. From there he watched the battle raging on, across the Mall, now spilling over into the city, and beyond.

I cannot. Too many, too many. No.

He raised his right hand up before his face and saw his blazing orange fingers beginning to fade, to disintegrate. His physical coherence, utterly disrupted by the separation from his other half, was nearly at an end.

So foolish, I was, he told himself, over and over. *It was my plan, my desire to help this world, these humans. And now I have doomed myself, and doomed my counterpart as well.*

The smallest finger on his right hand dissolved completely, changing to a bluish vapor that dispersed in the wind.

He stared at his reduced hand for long moments, then bent forward, burying his face in both fists, and groaned.

Doomed. I am doomed...as is this world...

And then an idea occurred to him. It seemed absurd to him at first—so absurd he hardly wanted to consider it.

But it nagged at him.

Could I—?

No.

No. No, I cannot. I cannot.

Yet the idea persisted.

He raised his head, looking out at the devastation surrounding him—at the planet itself being chewed up by the swarming army of robots.

No... No...I...

They were all about to die. The world was about to end. What difference would it make?

And yet...

The idea nagged at him, and would not leave him alone.

He pulled himself up to his feet and stood there, very shaky. Orange flames crackled across his body. He stumbled once, nearly fell, and regained his equilibrium. Barely.

He looked out at the battlefield once more.

Why not?

32

A veritable mountain of big, silver robots pressed down upon one spot in the center of the National Mall. Far, far beneath them lay Vanadium, slowly being crushed by their incredible weight.

That weight was simply enormous. Tons of metal pushed down on him. His seams, his internal support structures—his skeleton, if you will—all cried out in electronic agony. Warning signals from every portion of his body competed with one another for his conscious attention.

He was nearly done for.

Yet even as he felt his own strange mechanical form of life being extinguished, he realized the voice in his head—that of the Blue Skull—had receded to almost nothingness.

The disks are gone, he knew then.

Followed by, *Get these robots off of me, and I'm free.*

He said it to himself again, and felt the taste of it: *Free!*

Yet I will never be truly free, so long as I remain a prisoner of my amnesia—of my own lost past.

That could not be. If he survived the next few minutes, he would not allow himself to wallow in self-doubt and confusion any longer. It had to end. It *had* to.

No more worrying about the past, he resolved then. If I survive, I will simply be myself, whatever I am. I will simply be.

And I will be free.

Free!

Free!

The mountain of big, silver robots exploded.

From out of the depths roared Vanadium, his reactionless thrusters pushing him up, up, out of the crater he'd been buried in, and up, over the battlefield of the National Mall.

From his head dangled the last of the Blue Skull's metal disks, hopelessly smashed. He reached up and snatched it loose, throwing it away.

Swooping down low, he activated the full array of his sensors and scanned the area. Within seconds, he located his target, and roared down after it.

The Blue Skull, in his place of concealment, saw Vanadium coming. He gestured with one hand as he attempted over and over to access the cybernetic controls. They were all down, all dark.

"No!"

His eyes widened, and widened further as the blue-silver juggernaut bore down upon him. Crying out in fear, he leapt to his feet and raced away.

Vanadium caught him before he had traveled any distance at all. Settling to the ground and standing with both metal feet firmly planted in the earth, he grasped the villain and dangled him by his collar, his jackbooted feet kicking wildly a foot above the grass.

The Skull's blue flames flared out ferociously, swallowing up Vanadium in their burning embrace.

The big man shrugged them off—he who had flown through the deadly void of open interstellar space for centuries scarcely noticed something so petty. With a remarkable economy of motion, he simply flung the villain into the air. The Skull screamed once, flailing about, then hit the ground with a thud.

Vanadium strode across the scorched grass and stood over him. The Blue Skull did not move. He appeared to be lying in a position Vanadium had thought impossible for humans to achieve.

Perhaps I threw him too hard, he thought to himself.

He considered that possibility for a moment.

What a pity.

Turning away, Vanadium triggered his internal thrusters and rocketed into the sky again. Seeing Ultraa out of the corner of his eye, he sketched a salute—something he had seen Ultraa do in the past, as a sign of acknowledgement or respect.

Ultraa saw Vanadium up and moving around again. He saw the salute. Grinning, he returned it.

Looks like he's back, the blond man thought with some measure of relief. *Thank goodness.*

Then he looked at the grim tableau before him—mile upon mile of swarming robots that, having dismantled most every structure in the city, were now digging craters in the earth all around. He groaned.

But I think it's not enough, he thought. *Not enough. It's too little, too late.*

He sighed, then hurled himself into combat once more, knowing it was all futile now.

Too late...

39

Douglas Williams, clad in his jet-black suit of organic armor and calling himself the Fury, stood at the center of a circle of robots, slugging it out.

It was exhausting work, and yet, somehow, the suit around him didn't allow him to feel tired. It kept him going—seemed to encourage him to fight even harder. Part of him welcomed that feeling, but another part of him, he had to admit, found it somewhat disturbing.

Why are we even doing this? he asked himself. *It seems pointless. We've scarcely managed to disable a dozen of these things. But the way they keep reproducing...*

Yet, every time he considered stopping, just up and running away, he looked up and saw Ultraa battling on. The man was tireless—and he didn't wear any kind of armor that kept him going. Blood trailed from several wounds he'd received, but he fought on nonetheless. Doug had to admit that the man was, indeed, inspirational.

You're not the first to think that, he told himself. *He's been a national hero for years. And that's why. It's obvious now. The Field Marshal and the others were completely stupid to want to retire him, to take him out of action. This guy ought to be president, not unemployed!*

And so he fought on, and fought on, and...that was when he saw something truly remarkable, there on a field of unfathomable carnage.

Off to one side, in a space relatively free of robots, a shimmering doorway appeared in the air. It hovered there a moment, and through it stepped two figures.

"Huh?"

Doug shoved an attacking Xorex away from himself and looked again, puzzled.

The first figure through was a woman, though her skin was bright red and her hair was long and white. She wore a blue uniform of some kind, with golden bracelets around her wrists and ankles. The man next to her—a generic-looking white guy, with brown hair that looked like it hadn't been washed in weeks—wore gray and black armor, and carried a helmet in one hand.

The two were looking around, clearly shocked by what they were seeing.

Who could blame them? he thought to himself. *Then again, the way they just appeared here, I'm not sure I believe what I'm seeing, either.*

Despite the obvious exotic and alluring nature of the red-skinned woman, Williams found his attention drawn back to the guy—he kept thinking how familiar he looked.

Imagine normal clothes instead of that weird armor, and give him a shave, and...

"Esro Brachis?"

Williams ran toward them, even as Esro looked up, puzzled. As he neared them, he realized the woman was close to panic.

"Maker preserve us," she was crying. "The Xorex!"

Esro saw the man in glossy black armor coming their way.

"Who's this?"

"The Xorex is in its final stage," Mondrian was saying, oblivious to the approaching Williams. "This world is doomed. There can be no escape now."

She whirled and met Esro's eyes.

"The little man—he has killed us! He has sent us to a world near its end!"

Esro sought to calm Mondrian, even as he looked around again and felt grim panic gripping his heart.

Is she right? Is the world doomed? It surely looks that way...

"Aren't you Esro Brachis?"

The figure in glossy black had stopped a few feet away. Such was Esro's sense of dread that he had not even bothered to put on his helmet and take defensive measures.

"I'm Douglas Williams," the dark shape said. "Oh, sorry..."

The black coating melted away from his head, revealing a dark-skinned man somewhere in his thirties.

"I've always wanted to meet you," he said. Then he gestured around them. "Wish it didn't have to be under these circumstances."

Esro sort of half-nodded, one eye on the panicking Mondrian and one on Williams, then trained both of them on the battlefield that was Washington, DC.

"Just what in hell is going on here?" he asked.

"I wish I could tell you," Williams replied, shaking his head. "These things popped up a few hours ago. Ever since then, well..." he nodded toward the horde of robots digging vast pits into the earth all around, now that the buildings were mostly gone.

"Nobody's doing anything?" Esro asked, incredulous.

"Some are," Williams replied. "Ultraa and I have been doing what we could to—"

"Ultraa? Where is he?"

Williams shrugged.

"He flies by from time to time, then swoops down into one clump of them or another, and..."

"Esro, we must get offworld," Mondrian growled.

"We have to find Lyn and Ultraa first," he replied. "And Vanadium, too—though I have a feeling he's long gone, knowing him."

"No," Williams said. "If you mean the big metal guy, he's around, too."

He surveyed the battlefield quickly and then pointed.

"There he is."

Esro and Mondrian followed with their eyes.

Vanadium was in the process of smashing up out of a pile of robots. Wheeling around in midair, he crashed down into them with a force strong enough to shake the ground.

Mondrian saw him and screamed again.

Esro stared at her, shocked.

"What?"

But she didn't reply. She only continued to stare across the field.

Esro was near the end of his rope. He grasped Mondrian by the wrists and leaned in towards her.

"What is it? What's the matter? I mean, besides the end of the world."

"An Enforcer! It is too late! The Worldmind—he has sent all of his forces here. He may well be here himself now!"

"An Enforcer? That's just Vanadium. He's—I told you about him, right? He's one of our teammates."

"Actually, he was with *my* old team for a while," Williams said. "But I have a feeling he's back to himself now."

Esro shot him a puzzled glance, making a mental note to follow up on that strange comment, then turned back to Mondrian.

"That—that thing is no 'teammate,'" Mondrian was saying. "It is of the most elite class of warriors of the Worldmind—more powerful even than the Xorexes. We of the Kur-Bai served in the ranks that opposed the Worldmind and his hordes, ages ago, when he first came into our galaxy. Enforcers, Xorexes, and other nameless beings swept out of the depths of space, killing people, killing worlds. We lost many colonies to their advances. Many ships, many men and women."

She squared her jaw, her voice strengthening.

"But we drove them away. We enjoyed some critical outside help, of course. But we drove them away."

Before Esro could pursue this conversation further—and, frankly, he wasn't sure if it was even worth the effort, what with everything else going on—he became aware of a strange, silvery mist forming in the air around him.

"Hey, what in the—"

The mist hovered just in front of him. He waved a hand and it moved with him, swooshing through the air.

Frowning, puzzled, he stared at it. The others were ignoring him, staring out at the battle, not even aware of the mist.

Opening his right hand, he watched as the mist collected around his fingers. Closing his fist, the mist disappeared. Opening his hand again, the mist formed once more, almost like a thick glove.

He scratched his head—but with his left hand, while still staring at the right one.

"Okay, this is just bizarre…"

563

He motioned sharply with his right arm, as if trying to sling the mist away from himself. It shot out, directly away from his hand, forming a solid column of reflective silver about ten feet long. For as long as he held his arm in that pose, the column remained. As soon as he moved again, the column dissolved into mist and vanished once more.

Mondrian looked back at him, her eyes still showing fear.

"What were you saying, Esro?"

"I—I don't really know," he muttered, quickly closing his right fist. The mist vanished entirely.

"How can we get offworld? Quickly, you must think!"

Esro started to reply, then realized he was looking up at her. Way up.

"Mondy, do you know you're hovering two feet off the ground?"

40

Mondrian floated two feet above the charred grass of the National Mall. She opened her mouth, looked around, and closed it. She gasped.

Esro studied her closely.

"Your wristbands and anklets—they're sparkling."

It was true. The golden bands around her wrists and ankles shone like they had been polished to an impossible finish.

"I—yes, I can feel it. Some sort of power, flowing from them, into me. Through me."

It's like the mist, Esro thought then. And, his brilliant mind working in overtime, *Something happened to us, out there. Something—the giants. They did something to us. They—*

Fury turned and raced away from them. Esro looked up, watched as the man in black ran up to where Ultraa had appeared, out of a crowd of robots, stumbling to one knee. Williams bent down and helped Ultraa up, clasping hands with him.

"He seemed like a pretty decent guy," Esro mumbled. "Williams. I'll have to look him up later—assuming there is a later…"

Williams was pointing back toward Esro and Mondrian, and Ultraa saw them. His face lit up, and he rushed towards them. Esro ran forward, too, and they met in the charred grass, hugging one another fiercely.

"You're alive!" Ultraa shouted at him, grinning.

"I think so, yeah," Esro replied, laughing. "Mondy, too."

Ultraa let go of him with one last clap on the back, then looked beyond him to where Esro had been standing.

"Where?"

Esro looked back.

"She was just there a second ago. She—"

Mondrian swooped down, landing between them.

"I can fly," she said to no one in particular. "I can fly!"

"It's the end of the world," Esro replied testily, "but, yeah, I see that."

He ran a hand through his thick hair, exhaling slowly. He knew that part of his aggravation came from the fact that she had apparently already mastered her flying ability—and in like thirty seconds—while he was still trying to figure out why silvery fog came out of his fingers.

Ultraa grinned at her, clasping hands briefly and welcoming her back, then turned to Esro, having grown serious once more.

"I hope you can pull a rabbit out of your metal hat, here, my friend," he said. "Because, otherwise, we may all be finished."

Esro nodded. He took a quick glance at the tactical situation. The Xorexes had mostly abandoned this area of the Mall, with many of them now burrowing into the earth, digging vast craters as they continued to dismantle and demolish the world.

"I don't know," Esro groaned, rubbing his bleary eyes. "After everything we've been through, I can hardly think straight, as it is. Now all *this*…yeesh."

Ultraa appeared very disappointed, but only nodded. It had seemed like an insoluble problem to him, so he couldn't be upset with Esro for failing to come up with a miracle strategy or idea.

Esro thought for a moment. Then, "Say, where's Lyn?"

Ultraa blinked, looked around, started to point, then hesitated.

"She was with her sister, over there, a few minutes ago," he said. A deep worry crept into his voice. "But I don't see them now…"

"I'm sure she's okay," Esro replied quickly, knowing how upset Ultraa might get if something had happened to Lyn—and knowing that Ultraa would blame himself, no matter what.

"Besides," he added, "It looks like we're all gonna be toast soon."

Ultraa had a hand up to his brow, scanning the battlefield.

565

"When I left, there was only one of these things," Esro said, changing the subject. "What did you do?"

"You were chasing the thing," Ultraa replied. "Looks like you didn't catch it."

"Not quite. We got a little sidetracked."

He was studying the robots carefully, from the somewhat safe vantage point they enjoyed for the moment. All of the Xorexes still bore the red of Ultraa's gloves, the gold of Lyn's mesh suit, and the black of Fury's armor, along with a few other colors Esro didn't recognize.

"I guess they're still absorbing everyone's powers, huh?" he asked. "And it looks like, when one of them does it, they all do it. They all get the powers."

Ultraa nodded.

"Just makes it all worse."

He glanced back at Esro.

"In fact, I think that after they absorb our powers, they use them to fuel their reproduction—their duplicating ability."

He was still looking around for Lyn—and now clearly itching to fly away and conduct a more comprehensive search.

"Not a bad thought," Esro said. "It could explain why they have that power-absorbing ability in the first place, when they're already so blamed *tough*. It could just be a side effect."

Ultraa nodded slowly, distractedly. He had tuned Esro out. Lyn now consumed his thoughts.

Esro continued to think out loud.

"They all share what they absorb—yeah, that must be part of their duplicating system."

Now Mondrian was listening more closely, and she nodded.

"They share what they absorb equally," she explained. "That is why so many of them can appear in so short a time. It makes them far more dangerous than most any other foe my people have ever faced. If they are not stopped quickly, they can consume an entire world within mere hours. As you see now," she added.

Esro frowned.

"There has to be a way to turn that to our advantage. There has to be..."

"I'll be back, Esro," Ultraa said. He leapt into the sky and zoomed away.

Esro was chewing on his bottom lip.

"But what can we do with that...? Think, Esro. *Think!*"

"Look out!"

Mondrian spun around as a Xorex charged up the hill at them. Instinctively she pointed her right hand at it as she cried out to Esro.

A sparkling beam of energy lanced out, striking the robot dead center in the chest. It fell back, smoke billowing from a blackened spot in its silver plating.

Mondrian raised her hand and looked at it, aghast.

"Well, that's hardly fair," Esro muttered. "You got two powers out of the deal. All I got was this."

He gestured with one hand, and the silvery mist appeared again. He pointed at the robot as it started to rise again, and the mist shot out, forming a solid column of silver between his arm and the target. It struck hard, propelling the Xorex back into the burned grass.

"Weird, huh?"

He shook his hand and the column dissolved, the mist returning to his glove.

Mondrian stared at his hand. She started to say something, appeared to think better of it, and hesitated.

"What?" Esro demanded, exasperated.

"Nanomachines," she whispered.

"Say what?"

Esro looked down at his glove again, his eyes widening.

"Nano… little tiny machines," he said. "Yeah, I sort of get that…I guess…"

He looked up at Mondrian, frowning.

"In… In my armor? In *me?*"

He took an involuntary step back, stumbled, and fell over, throwing up.

47

"Pour me another," growled Gorann.

Devenn hefted the pitcher and filled the other man's glass, then his own.

Gorann quaffed the drink.

"I suppose if we cannot be smashing things into small pieces, this will do," he rumbled.

Devenn eyed his friend and teammate.

"Don't you suppose we should be practicing, like the others?" he asked, his face a mask of seriousness.

"Hah! The others *have* to practice. They set fire to things and blow air on them. How frightening."

He rubbed his massive hands together.

"We *break* things, you and I, Devenn. Very simple, very straightforward." He grinned. "I do not think we need concern ourselves with their *tactics* and *maneuvers*."

Gorann had said those last words with such dripping contempt that Devenn could only smile at his old friend and take another drink.

He had known Gorann for many years now; ever since their colony world, so distant from the heart of the Kur-Bai Empire, had fallen to the great Starfleet. They had been recruited into the regular Army forces together at first, and then had both quickly moved up through the ranks, at last achieving the status of Elites—with Devenn himself becoming the leader. Devenn knew Gorann better than he knew anyone else in the galaxy; knew his strengths—physical and mental—and his weaknesses. And he trusted him. In an Empire and a Starfleet filled to overflowing with hidden agendas and secret prejudices, having someone close to him that he could rely upon made Gorann invaluable.

Plus he's the only Kur-Bai in the fleet that can whip me in a fair fight, Devenn knew.

Indeed, the Kur-Bai warrior seated across the table from him was huge. Muscles bulged from every limb; his torso more closely resembled a vast tree trunk than a man's body. Green armor covered him in metallic bands, and a rugged helmet rested on the table in front of him.

"How much longer?" Gorann asked, tossing back another big mug full. "I'm sick of being shipbound." He popped his massive knuckles; one might have thought small-arms fire had broken out. "I am ready to pound someone severely, be they Circle, Worldmind, or—what did you call them?"

"Human," Devenn replied, finishing his glass.

Gorann shrugged. His shoulders looked like moving mountains.

"Whatever they are, I'm sure they will *break* well enough."

A wail vibrated through the bar—through the walls—through the entire flagship.

"That's it," Devenn said, setting down his glass and standing. "We will be dropping from hyperspace very soon."

Gorann nodded. He set his own big glass down on the table and wiped his face, then fumbled for his helmet.

"You okay?" Devenn asked, eyeing his teammate warily.

Gorann stopped what he was doing and glared at him.

"Who are you speaking to? Surely not to me!"

Devenn's mouth turned ever so slightly upward at one corner.

"Fine. Come on."

Fastening his small, ornamental red cape over his shoulders, Devenn moved quickly out of the bar. Gorann pulled his helmet down over his head and followed.

"Do you truly believe the Worldmind's creatures—the Xorexes, perhaps—will be there, at this...what did you call it? *Earth?*"

"It may be so," Devenn replied, not looking back. "Perhaps they have been marshalling their forces all this time, preparing for a major new campaign, here on the fringe, on the far side of the galaxy."

Gorann thought on this for a few steps as he followed his leader. He grunted noncommittally.

"And we think the Circle renegades are there?"

"Apparently the Admiral has received intelligence to that effect."

Gorann grunted again. They passed through a series of bulkheads and emerged into a long corridor leading toward their ready room.

"I hope the humans will present some sort of challenge themselves, at least," Gorann finally stated as they entered the room. Yeist and Alatair, already present, nodded courteously to them.

"Be careful what you wish for," Devenn observed as he gestured for the other three to form up in a formal procession and then moved to the front. "We know little about this *Earth*. We have encountered...*troublesome* low-tech worlds before, as you all will remember. We must take nothing for granted."

But the rumbling laugh that emerged from Gorann, along with the contemptuous snort from Yeist, told Devenn all he needed to know about his team's current level of confidence.

Or overconfidence, he reflected.

"Emblems in place?"

They all fastened small, golden, eight-pointed stars to their chests, to the left of center.

"Weapons check," Devenn barked. The others acknowledged the order but scarcely followed through on it.

The day is coming when we finally meet genuine competition, he knew. *The others do not want to admit such a thing—do not want to even allow for the possibility! But one day it will happen.*

Silently, hoping to himself that today would not be that day, he led the Elites out of the ready room and down the hallway towards the hangar bay.

42

The Xorex robots reigned over the battlefield, their victory nearly complete.

Thousands, perhaps millions of them now swarmed across the east coast of the United States, dealing out incalculable damage. While they had not yet crossed the Atlantic Ocean to Europe or Africa, they had expanded well up into Canada and down into Mexico and beyond.

Worse still, they were no longer concerned with moving laterally across the Earth's surface. They were now moving mostly *down*.

Down they dug, into the very bowels of the Earth. The matter they consumed simply vanished—shunted away, into a network of wormholes that carried it all to a central location, where other Xorexes would later use it as raw materials for constructing whatever the Worldmind ordered them to construct.

Rarely had the Xorexes been stopped, and never—*never*—this far into an operation. They were invincible, and they knew it. Their metal hides, impervious to most attacks, kept them safe. Their ability to absorb the energies and powers of anyone around them, automatically sharing that power, those abilities, with the rest of their collective, rendered them utterly unstoppable. And their numbers—their sheer, overwhelming numbers—guaranteed that, even if a few of them could be defeated, their overall mission would succeed.

The Earth would vanish, raw material for the Worldmind's designs.

And thus, secure in the knowledge of their complete invincibility, they scarcely took note at all of the planet's natives, as those fragile little beings continued their fruitless attempts to delay the inevitable.

So secure were they—so arrogant—that even when their sensors registered an energy source of very alien origin in their midst, they took no heed of it.

So arrogant were they that even when their sensors told them the alien energies belonged to that of one of the Worldmind's Great Rivals—or, more precisely, to one of that entity's elite agents—even then, they paid no attention.

And thus did the fiery form of Kabaraak come flying down from the heavens, his mind rent in half, his sanity all but gone, his energies ebbing, his physical coherence at its last stages before complete collapse.

And from miles away, Ultraa saw the blazing being swoop down, and he cried out.

Oh, no. Of all things—not this, not now. If they absorb that guy's powers, any chances we have left of stopping them will be gone!

Summoning up all his remaining reserves of strength, the blond hero moved with all the speed at his disposal to stop it—to stop Kabaraak from getting anywhere close to the Xorexes.

He raced through the air, moving more swiftly than he had ever moved before, his super-speed propelling him at many times the speed of sound. And he reached out for the fiery being, and he grasped for him—

—and he missed.

The blazing form of Kabaraak descended into the mass of Xorexes, flames roaring up around him.

The robots swarmed over him, mindless, hungry. They engulfed him.

Ultraa watched it happen, and utter despair gripped his heart.

"No…"

"YES! *YES!!*"

Ultraa looked up, shocked. Someone was happy about this?! Esro?!

Indeed, Brachis was flying towards him, his rocket boots roaring flame. Mondrian soared along beside him. And he sounded…*happy.*

"YAHOOO!" screamed Esro. "Go, you crazy matchstick, go!"

"No," Ultraa cried, stunned by his friend's words. "Don't you see? The Xorexes will copy his power!"

"Exactly!"

Ultraa gaped at his friend. Had the man lost his mind? Did he really think the clearly wounded being could do what none of the rest of them had been able to do—single-handedly defeat an army of Xorexes?

Or, more troubling still—what might Esro have gone through, wherever he had ended up, alongside this strange, alien woman? Did Esro really want the Earth to be destroyed even more quickly than was already happening?

Brachis came up beside him and hovered there, shaking a fist in apparent triumph.

Ultraa still stared at him, flabbergasted.

"Esro," he finally managed, "what—?"

Brachis flipped up his facemask—Ultraa hadn't known it could do that—and grinned.

"Just watch, buddy. Just watch!"

"But—"

And then...

POP.

POP POP.

Ultraa blinked, looked at Esro.

"What the—?!"

POP POP POP POP POP.

Esro was grinning even wider. Grinning a fierce, savage grin. A *victorious* grin.

POP POP POP POP POP POP POP POP POP POP POP POP.

Ultraa looked down at the hordes of Xorexes. They had stopped their dismantling and their fighting and were looking at one another, obviously startled and disoriented, obviously encountering something unexpected.

Something *disastrous*.

They were starting to disappear—to vanish like soap bubbles in a stiff breeze. Already their ranks had thinned appreciably.

POP POP POP POP POP POP POP POP POP POP POP POP POP POP POP POP POP POP POP POP POP POP POP POP POP POP POP POP POP POP POP.

"They absorbed Kabaraak's powers—*and his instability,*" Esro was shouting, to himself or to anyone still listening. "His cohesiveness—remember? When we met him before, he couldn't hold himself together! He was disintegrating!"

He pointed down at the robots.

"Those bastards absorbed *that*, along with everything else!"

Ultraa realized what his friend was saying then. Realized what had happened.

"Oooh," he said. Followed by, *"Wow."*

Now he found himself grinning, too.

POP POP POP POP POP POP POP POP POP POP POP POP
POP POP POP POP POP POP POP POP POP POP POP POP POP
POP POP POP POP POP POP POP POP POP POP POP POP POP
POP POP POP POP POP POP POP POP POP POP POP POP POP
POP POP POP POP POP POP POP POP POP POP POP POP POP
POP POP POP POP POP POP POP POP POP POP POP POP POP
POP POP POP POP POP POP POP POP POP POP POP POP POP
POP POP POP POP POP POP POP POP POP POP POP POP POP
POP POP POP POP POP POP POP POP POP POP POP POP POP
POP POP POP POP POP POP POP POP POP POP POP POP POP
POP POP POP POP POP POP POP POP POP POP POP POP POP
POP POP POP POP POP POP POP POP POP POP POP POP POP
POP POP POP POP POP POP POP POP POP POP POP POP POP
POP POP POP POP POP POP POP POP ...

43

"This is impossible," Rnn'dul Nah-Shonn growled, staring in unabashed shock at the big viewscreen on the bridge of the Circle flagship. *"Impossible."*

Around the bridge, technicians and other crew members studied readouts and scanner displays and chattered agitatedly among themselves.

Nah-Shonn stood, moving a few steps closer to the display, as if that would somehow cause it to make more sense. It did not.

"What exactly am I seeing?" he demanded after waiting several seconds as the consultations continued. "What is happening down there?"

The lead technician, Lt. Donaralian, shook her head slowly.

"I have never encountered anything like this before, sir," she said, her face reflecting her surprise and confusion. "None of us have. There is no record of it ever happening."

"What? *What* is happening?"

"Something—some unknown force—has disrupted the structural integrity of the Xorexes. And it's corrupted their shared system. They're passing it from one to the next."

She grinned at him.

"They're disintegrating. All of the Xorexes—they're *disintegrating!*"

The rest of the crew appeared to be just as happy at this news. They were Kur-Bai, after all, even if they were also renegades and members of a rebel sect, not to mention brainwashed by Nah-Shonn himself. They knew all too well the dangers creatures such as the Xorex posed to the universe, and they were quite happy to see them go.

Nah-Shonn was not so happy. He sat back in his chair, fuming, considering his options.

"So the Earth will survive, then," Lt. Donaralian said, as the technicians continued to marvel at the wholly unexpected development on the planet's surface below them.

"I wouldn't count on that," Nah-Shonn replied, sitting forward suddenly. "Arm all the thermonuclear warheads in the fleet," he barked. "And have the ships move into assault positions over the North American continent."

The other crew members looked around, surprised.

"Sir—are you certain you wish to—?"

Nah-Shonn glared at her, cast his gaze across the bridge at the assemblage of officers and techs, and instantly increased the level of telepathic control he was exerting over them all. A moment later, they had returned to docile compliance.

"All thermonuclear devices are armed, sir," Donaralian reported after a few seconds.

"How many?"

"Twenty-four."

Nah-Shonn nodded.

"Good enough."

He smiled his broad, eerie smile.

"Prepare to launch."

The six Circle ships, each holding orbit high above a different portion of North America, opened their launch tubes.

"Ready, sir."

Nation brought his hands down on his chair's arms and allowed his eerie smile to spread wider.

"Launch."

44

The Xorexes continued to disappear, dwindling rapidly to a scattered few still standing, dazed and mostly immobile, across the National Mall. Of the fiery form of Kabaraak there had been no further sign.

Ultraa and Esro and Mondrian all hugged one another, nearly delirious with happiness and relief. Heavyweight and the Fury rushed up and joined in the celebration, there on that devastated battlefield.

After a few more seconds of laughter and handshakes and back-slapping, Ultraa thought of Lyn again and pulled away, casting his gaze all around.

And he saw her.

A dazzling point of golden radiance, Pulsar shot overhead and then dropped down, electricity crackling around her.

"What happened?" Ultraa demanded, relief flooding through him. "Where have you been—and where's your sister?"

"I think she'll be okay," Lyn replied, the golden bubble crackling once more and then fading away as she stood on solid ground. "It looks like we can celebrate—"

And then she saw Brachis standing there, grinning at her.

"ESRO!!"

With a shriek of joy, she launched herself into him and carried them both over backward, falling to the scorched earth. Lyn clung to Esro with unashamed happiness, laughing maniacally.

"You big…stupid…*jerk!"*

"Um, yeah, I missed you, too, kid," he managed to get out in between her screeches and good-natured insults.

"Now I don't get to go into space, looking for you," she said after they had both been helped back up again and dusted the grass and soot off.

"Yeah—sorry about that," he replied. "But I don't know that you'd much care for it. At least, not the places Mondy and I have been for the last little while."

While a giddy Lyn continued to bounce up and down and Esro attempted to reintroduce Mondrian to the others, Ultraa stepped to the side and scanned the horizon again, his long years of battle experience reminding him to never think the battle over until it was definitely over. Sure enough, about a hundred yards away, he spotted his other formerly missing teammate, Vanadium. The big metal man did not look happy. His fists were balled up, his head tilted back, and his pinprick red eyes were staring straight up at the sky.

"Vanadium! Hey!"

Ultraa's call went unanswered. The big man ignored everything around him, continuing to stare upward.

Oh, no, he thought. *I was sure we had him back—back on our side, back in his right mind, more or less. But something is obviously still wrong—"*

In fact, Vanadium was terribly distracted at the moment.

From the beginning of the battle, he had been working through a million different permutations of the Xorex override codes, with the robots failing to acknowledge or accept any of them. *My codes are all far out of date,* he knew. *As am I.*

He had felt an odd desire to laugh, as he had seen the humans do. He suppressed it.

But the standard formula is simple enough, at least to another of their kind—assuming it has not been changed in the past thousand years...

At that moment another development had caused him to move the menace of the Xorexes over to one side of his brain, as with sudden and violent intensity his radiological sensors screamed bloody murder at him.

"Vanadium," Ultraa was calling again. "Come join us!"

Continuing to ignore his teammate, the metal man's tiny but incredibly powerful red eyes cycled from one wavelength to another, sweeping across the heavens, seeing thousands of miles up and in every direction.

"Vanadium! What's the matter with—"

Understanding with awful dread the nature of the situation in orbit, he returned his full attention to the Xorex code search. He had been close to cracking them—very close—and he needed them now. The *Earth* needed them.

Ultraa had walked over to him and was about to say something—something undoubtedly warm and friendly, if probably a bit concerned. But just as the blond man opened his mouth, the Xorex access codes fell into place, and the signal blasted out from Vanadium to all the remaining robots in the area.

"STOP!"

The single word, booming out from the blue-silver juggernaut with shocking force, nearly caused the humans and Mondrian to fall over. They gawked at him, stunned.

It had an additional affect, however. The last few remaining Xorexes heard it also, and they all received the broadcast code command that came along with it. Though he was alone—a single Enforcer, rather than the small battalions of his kind the Worldmind normally dispatched—he did now seem to possess their override protocols. His order was not the self-destruction command they were expecting from him, though. Instead he ordered them to shut down their duplicating and power-copying systems and abilities— something they had lacked the authority to do for themselves, according to the Worldmind's programming—and ordered them to stand by for further instructions.

Instantly, the POP POP POPping stopped.

Vanadium took a quick inventory across their network. Ten Xorexes remained.

He flashed out another order, by way of their overridden network:

"Form up on me."

Seconds later, Vanadium stood on a low hill, there on the National Mall, surrounded by the last few remaining Xorexes on Earth.

Ultraa stumbled back, taking this in with a deepening sense of dread. The Xorexes lined up behind Vanadium, looking for all the world like troops awaiting an officer's command.

Essentially, that's what they were.

"I thought he was back on our side," the blond man said to Esro. "I was sure…"

And then Vanadium launched himself into the air, accelerating upward at unbelievable speeds. The remaining Xorexes shot skyward after him.

"Where are they going?"

Ultraa shaded his eyes with a red-gloved hand and stared in awe—and fear—at the sight.

"Where's he taking them?"

Esro shrugged. He snapped his facemask back down and consulted the sensor array inside his helmet, then suddenly grabbed Ultraa by the arm.

"What is it?"

"We've got incoming," he replied, his eyes not moving from the radiological warning flashing brighter and faster on his heads-up display.

"What?"

Esro flipped his faceplate up again. His features were pale.

"It's out of the frying pan, into the nuclear fire, I think," he said.

"What are you talking about?"

Esro pointed up.

"I'm not entirely sure. But let's just hope that's where Vanadium's headed. Because otherwise, stopping the Xorexes won't have mattered much at all."

45

This planet defied the Xorexes. It defied the Worldmind itself! It deserves to bathe in nuclear fire.

So spoke the voice deep inside Vanadium's head—the voice of his most ancient programming, rising to the surface after so many years. He struggled to ignore it as he shot up out of the atmosphere and activated his sensors, searching for the warheads now plummeting towards the Earth.

You are an Enforcer—beloved of the Worldmind! The Xorexes will follow you. Let the bombs strike. Then go back down, cleanse the planet of any who survive, and consume its resources for the Worldmind. Do it!

Vanadium stifled the voice, driving it back down into the depths of his memories. He had heard whispers and echoes of such entreaties before, in the time since his revival on the Moon. But never so loudly, so insistently. It was excruciating.

I am Vanadium. Not a nameless, faceless Enforcer for the Worldmind. Vanadium! Friend to Ultraa and Pulsar and Esro Brachis of Earth. A protector of that world now.

The voice's reply—*Absurd!*—barked back at him so loudly he thought it actually would have been audible were he not in a vacuum at the moment.

Not at all, he told it. *I have found my purpose—a purpose for existence much greater and more important than merely following orders, than merely killing and destroying and helping the Xorexes to dismantle planets.*

The Worldmind created you. You are one of his elite officers!

My service to the Worldmind lies more than a thousand years in the past. I am something else now.

You are a fool. A self-deluded fool.

Perhaps that is true. Perhaps I am. But I have determined my course and I do not intend to stray from it again. Never.

His orders flashed out across the network to the Xorexes: Find the missiles. Disable or destroy them. Do not let them detonate.

Let them hit! Let these Circle idiots cleanse the surface of the planet—then you can call the Worldmind to bring all of his other lieutenants here and welcome the Earth to their dominion. To your dominion!

The Xorexes fanned out, each of them locking onto a different missile. Vanadium tracked their progress and directed their efforts as they attacked the first wave of warheads at his command, smashing them to bits as they fell. Two of the bombs exploded above the atmosphere, annihilating two Xorexes.

The second wave of bombs shot past, and the Xorexes closed in on them. Using powers stolen from Ultraa and Pulsar, they matched speeds and sent out force field bubble barrages, managing to deflect the courses of some of the missiles.

Two more warheads detonated prematurely, with their pursuers too close, annihilating two more Xorexes.

Then they added a bit of Heavyweight's abilities and disrupted the arcs of others. Finally, the powerful emerald blasts copied from the Fury detonated more of the warheads just above the atmosphere. The first wave was gone, and none of the bombs had gotten through.

Vanadium did a quick count and found six remaining Xorexes and eleven warheads still descending upon America.

You cannot stop them all, the voice screamed at him. *Let it happen!*

Silence!

Vanadium shot forward, closing in on a pair of missiles himself, even as he directed the surviving Xorexes after more targets.

Explosions registered on his sensors, but he did not spare the time or attention to see what had happened. He simply had to trust that they could get the job done. Instead he focused on the two he had chosen for himself—two already falling below the range of the position of the Xorexes—and increased his speed.

Now the friction of the atmosphere burned brutally on his metal hide. He was dropping at a speed far beyond anything that could be considered safe. Idly he wondered if he would even be able to pull out of his dive, assuming he did manage to catch the warheads.

Two targets lit up on his sensors just ahead.

There.

He chose the nearest and zoomed towards it.

Very little time remaining. Very little...

His blue-silver metal fingers reached out and grasped the big black cone as it shot through the atmosphere. Pulling himself close to it, he unleashed his devastating lasers from his red eyes, weakening the casing. Then he sunk his fingers into the surface and ripped, pulling away a portion of the bomb's carbon fiber covering. Turning loose the piece he had torn free, he jammed his hand down into the warhead's interior, releasing a swarm of nanites as he did so. Then he pushed away from the missile—*it is harmless now; the bugs will devour the nuclear material inside*—and poured all of his energy into stopping his descent, even as his sensors searched for the last one.

It was gone.

Panic gripped Vanadium. He diverted extra power to his radiological scanners but could find nothing beyond the residue from the warheads that had exploded earlier, in orbit.

Where is the last one? Where?

A nagging signal on a very low frequency caught his attention after a few seconds, and he moved his attention to it.

"—adium, old buddy, if you can hear me—this is Esro Brachis. We got the last one. I was able to track it and between Mondy and Lyn, they took care of it." He was laughing now, probably as much from giddy relief as anything. "Mondy has some nice tricks up her sleeves now, it looks like."

Vanadium allowed himself a microsecond's worth of relief as well—indeed, of happiness—and then he checked the Xorex frequencies.

All gone. All of them. Well. They might have been useful... But, then again, they were exceptionally dangerous. This is for the best.

He hovered there, halfway between the Earth's surface and the Circle fleet. Then he made up his mind what he had to do next.

It will be an interesting challenge for a Worldmind Enforcer, he thought as he rocketed upward, rapidly closing the distance between himself and the flagship.

And then he reconsidered his thoughts.

For an Enforcer, yes.   But what about for an Earth hero?

He redoubled his speed and brought his forward shielding up to maximum.

We shall see…

46

Rnn'dul Nah-Shonn watched in horror as the blue-silver war machine smashed into the forward hull of his flagship and began to tear into its armor plating.

It's coming for me!   That thing—it's coming for me!

The ship's lasers and particle beams had bombarded Vanadium to very minimal effect.   He had deflected some of the attacks with energy fields, avoided others due to his small size and great speed, and simply shrugged off the rest.   Now he was too close to fire upon—he was actually breaking through the hull and tearing his way into the ship.

Coming here!   Coming after me!   And I can't stop him!

His fingers brushed against the holster at his hip.

All I have besides my own powers is a pistol.   One little pistol. And a lot of good that will do against an Enforcer.

He grimaced, summoning up all the reserves of power at his disposal.

I must stop the thing now.   Now!

In his terror, Nah-Shonn lashed out at it with all of the awesome, freakish talent he possessed.   He fought with the fervor of one who is doomed and who sees that doom approaching, awesome and unstoppable.   And yet, for all his vaunted mental powers, he could do nothing against the alien, robotic mind of the Worldmind Enforcer, Vanadium.   In the past, on the one or two rare occasions when he'd encountered creatures of the Worldmind, he had managed to at least somewhat manipulate their thoughts, despite their largely non-organic nature.   But this one—this one seemed somehow different from the others.   His mental makeup had been changed, drastically altered from the norm.   Nah-Shonn understood then that in order to control this one, he would have to radically rethink his entire approach.

He simply didn't have that kind of time.

It was through the outer decks now, and coming, coming...

In his terror, and in his distracted efforts to assail the Enforcer Vanadium, Nah-Shonn allowed his grip on the crew of his ship to falter.

He stood before the main viewscreen, mouth slack, eyes wide, gaping at the images of the awesome being battering his inevitable, inexorable way toward him.

Thus he didn't notice Lt. Donaralian standing beside him. Lt. Donaralian, whose mind had now overthrown his weakened influence and whose outrage was vast and deep.

Lt. Donaralian, who grabbed Nah-Shonn's sidearm from its holster and shot him in the head.

47

The body floated out of the airlock but only registered as a tiny blip within Vanadium's mind until he noticed the message signal coming to him from the ship itself.

"He is dead," it screamed at him, once he started to pay attention to it. "Rnn'dul Nah-Shonn is dead! We have freed ourselves from his insidious control and executed him. We mean you no harm and wish only to depart! We give you his body as proof!"

Vanadium stopped his assault on the Circle ship long enough to scan the body with his sensors, even as it moved further and further away, beginning to curve down toward the atmosphere. It seemed to be him, but...

They may be telling the truth, he thought. *But I cannot trust them.*

Detaching himself from the flagship, he rocketed away in pursuit of the body. He closed the distance rapidly and grabbed onto it, angling back upward to avoid the heat of the atmosphere.

Yes, he realized after a few close-range scans at the genetic level. *It is him. They speak the truth.*

His pinprick red eyes flared bright as the sun. The body disintegrated.

There. Now it is done—it is over.

He gazed up at the six ships floating in the distance. Six ships belonging to a renegade faction of one of the most powerful star empires in known space.

But is it truly over?

He studied the spacecraft, scanning them, sensing their remaining armaments and defensive capabilities. Even without their nuclear arsenals, they were still formidable.

Do we let them go? Can I stop them? Does the Earth possess any capacity to fight them off, aside from myself and perhaps my companions?

He wrestled with these questions for several long seconds. Before he could arrive at any conclusions, however... *everything* changed.

The space just beyond the six Circle ships flared bright as day, space rippling all around. Just like that, the star-filled night was filled with ships. Big, capital ships. Wave after wave of ships.

Vanadium shielded his eyes, even as his sensors informed him of what was happening.

Before half of the fleet had dropped from hyperspace, the lead ships unleashed their weaponry in a hellish barrage. The six Circle ships evaporated like mist in the sun.

More ships arrived. And still more. A vast, awe-inspiring fleet filled the space above the Earth, blotting out the universe.

Targeting sensors locked onto him, directing vast and powerful weaponry at him from every angle. Weaponry enough to annihilate him a hundred times over. A thousand.

They know what I am—what they think I am. They will have no mercy.

He floated there above his adopted world, awaiting the end.

It did not come.

Instead, he noticed after a few seconds that the lead ship had opened a port in its hull, and four humanoid figures had emerged from it. They streaked towards him, arriving within moments. His tiny red eyes in their dark sockets flickered from one of them to the other, encountering strange and unexpected forms.

A massive one with thick, green armor plating... A tall and slender one in red and adorned with jewels, holding a long staff... A woman in light blue, holding what appeared to be two curved swords... And a man in dark blue with red trim, a sort of half-cape trailing behind him, his skin dark red, his eyes hard. And each of them wore a small, golden, eight-pointed star to one side of his or her chest.

583

These impressions struck him very quickly. Then he was grasped roughly by the four, and they bound up his arms in restraining braces.

A voice came to him, beamed over from one of the aliens.

"I trust you will not resist."

Vanadium considered his situation and simply nodded once.

"We are going to the planet's surface," the alien continued. "You will remain passive."

And before Vanadium could respond or even react, the four had dragged him aboard a shuttlecraft and sealed the hatch closed. Mere seconds later, they were rocketing down through the atmosphere, directly toward America's eastern coast.

42

"People of Earth," cried the alien leader clad in dark blue and red. "We are the Elites of the Kur-Bai Starfleet. We have been called to your world to address its infestation by agents of the Worldmind. You will not interfere with our operations."

Still standing on the wrecked National Mall, Ultraa had watched the four aliens—Vanadium apparently a prisoner among them—as they had descended from the heavens in an armored shuttle and landed nearby. Now he heard the booming voice of the man in blue and red—a voice whose tone brooked no argument, no bargaining, no choices.

"What do you make of this?" he asked the others.

Lyn and Richard looked at each other, shrugging expressively.

"I know who to ask," Esro replied. "Mondy?"

Mondrian was staring at the four aliens with what appeared to be reverential awe.

"Mondy! You with us?"

The Kur-Bai lieutenant blinked and looked back at Esro.

"Oh. Yes."

She gestured toward the four new arrivals where they stood regally on a scorched hilltop, gazing about with clear disdain.

"They are the Elites—the most powerful and feared warriors of my people. They have never been defeated in battle. They are as

close to—how do you say it here?—to *celebrities* as we possess."
She smiled wanly. "I have long desired to meet them."

Esro rolled his eyes.

"I tell ya what," he said. "We can save the autograph session for later. For now, howzabout getting them to let our buddy there loose."

Mondrian seemed to notice Vanadium among the Elites for the first time.

"Oh. Oh!"

She frowned.

"I seriously doubt they will release him."

Ultraa, Esro and Lyn all responded at once: *"What?"*

"He is of the Worldmind. They only destroy such as him."

Esro reddened.

"He's one of us, Mondy. *One of us!* I know you only see a *thing*—a cold killing machine of an alien race—a race alien to *both* of us. But he's not that anymore. He's our teammate. Our *friend*."

She looked at him dubiously; but not, he noted, with the utter skepticism that once would have met such a statement from Brachis.

"I...I suppose it is possible that it—that *he*—is different," she allowed after a moment.

"He is," Esro said. "And we have to get him back."

"We will," Ultraa stated firmly. He marched forward, directly toward the Elites.

"Excuse me," he called out to them as he approached.

They appeared to take no notice of him.

The others trailing along behind him, Ultraa walked right up to the Kur-Bai in blue and red. He got up in the big guy's face, allowing the man no choice but to acknowledge him.

"Hi," he said. "I'm Ultraa. This is my home, in case you weren't aware. And, as you can see—" He swept his arm around in a half-circle, indicating the ragged and burned Mall area. "—We have already taken care of that whole 'infestation' business."

The alien looked at him, seemingly perplexed.

"So, with that all being done, you folks can pack up and just head on to your next appointment, or whatever you do."

He gestured vaguely toward the sky.

"Out there. Somewhere else besides here."

The Elite in blue and red followed Ultraa's pointing finger, then returned his attention to the man himself, as if seeing him for the first time. He appeared to be sizing Ultraa up. Then he spoke, and his voice was deep and grave.

585

"You have fortitude, Human," he growled. "And courage. I respect that."

Ultraa nodded in acknowledgement of the compliment, but didn't budge.

"Allow me to introduce my team to you—to someone who obviously can appreciate their proficiencies. Something I am able to do all too rarely on these missions."

He gestured toward the woman in light blue who held two long, curved swords.

"This is Alatair. She is mistress of the wind and water."

The woman's eyes moved fleetingly toward Ultraa and away again. She did not otherwise budge.

"Gorann is our powerhouse," he said next, indicating the big muscular guy in green banded armor.

Gorann grunted sharply, his dark eyes flickering down to meet Ultraa's for a second and then returning to the horizon.

"Yeist commands the Staff of Fire," he said next, inclining his head towards the tall, slender man in red robes and jewels.

Yeist moved not a muscle, not a twitch. He leaned against his long, silver staff, low flames racing along its length, and kept his eyes focused on some random spot off to his right.

"And I am Devenn. I possess some few talents and skills, and am chief of the Empire's special forces."

He tapped the small, golden, eight-pointed star on his breast with obvious reverence.

"I have led the Elites for—" He worked the math out quickly. "—fifteen of your years now."

Ultraa nodded to each of them and offered a hand to Devenn, but it was not taken. He wondered if the slight was intentional or simply a cultural matter. Somehow he suspected the former.

"Welcome," he said, and introduced Lyn, Esro, Richard, Doug, and Mondrian—the last of whom barely even rated a notice from them, despite her being a Kur-Bai as well, and an officer of their fleet. Devenn, however, did give her golden wristbands and anklets a curious glance before returning his attention to Ultraa.

"Your world clearly has suffered a massive infestation—Xorexes, obviously," the big Kur-Bai said, his dark eyes now moving to the great excavations, and over the parts of Washington that still burned. "And Xorexes do not simply vanish. Probably they have burrowed underground, having sensed our coming. If we were to leave, well—" He shrugged. "They would surely re-emerge, and consume the rest of your planet in short order. The resources would be shunted back to the Worldmind, making it stronger. And the Xorexes would form back into a single unit once more, before plunging on into the galaxy in search of their next target."

He smiled a tiny half-smile at Ultraa.

"And that, obviously, we cannot allow. But we will interrogate this one—their lieutenant, the Enforcer—and see what he can tell us."

With that, the alien's eyes moved away from Ultraa, dismissing him as surely as if he had walked away.

"We destroyed them," Ultraa said. "They're gone."

Almost involuntarily, the big alien's eyes moved back to him.

"You what?"

He began to laugh.

The other three Elites had now taken notice of the conversation, and they moved around to either side. They, too, laughed.

"Not directly," Ultraa was saying, "but we fought them—fought them hard. And we engineered their destruction. More or less."

He nodded toward their prisoner, Vanadium, who stood to one side, bound by thick metal arm restraints.

"Along with our friend there. He had as much to do with it as anyone."

The laughter stopped.

The four Elites looked from Ultraa to Vanadium and back.

"This one—this Enforcer—is your *friend?*"

Ultraa nodded.

"I think you'll find he's not like the rest of his kind—the ones you're probably used to meeting. He's on our side now."

The others gaped.

"So there won't be any 'interrogations' of him. You will be handing him over to us before you leave."

Now even Devenn was staring in unabashed shock at Ultraa.

"Human," he said after a moment, "in all my travels around this galaxy, never have I encountered one as brash, as confident, as you—certainly not in the face of overwhelming power, unavoidable death."

He gestured with one blue-gloved hand toward the sky.

"Do you not know that our great fleet—one of the largest armadas ever assembled—awaits overhead? That we just arrived here from our last mission, which entailed the nuclear annihilation of not one but two inhabited worlds?"

He shook his head slowly, his hard, lined face directed straight at Ultraa.

"Truly you have courage—perhaps too much so! But you cannot stop us. It is comical to even consider such a thing. Instead," and he leaned in closer, "instead you should consider gathering up your friends—assuming they are as brave as you—and vacating this planet now."

He stroked his granite-like chin for a moment.

"I would even go so far as to vouch for you—your ship would not be fired upon."

He smiled more broadly than ever before at Ultraa, clearly pleased with his offer.

"So—do you find that satisfying?"

Ultraa's steely gaze did not flinch. He leaned in closer himself.

"I want Vanadium—the 'Enforcer' there—back. And then I want you and your people off my world. Now."

Devenn gaped at him for a long second. Then he seemed to quietly laugh.

"Perhaps I overestimated you," he said, with a touch of sadness. "Perhaps you are simply insane."

"Now listen," Ultraa began, and launched into a forceful defense of his teammates and his planet.

Meanwhile, as the others debated, Mondrian stood back and observed, deep in thought. She found it hard to imagine that a servant of the Worldmind—her people's oldest foe—could possibly have become an ally to these humans, much less a friend. And yet they seemed convinced of it. They had, according to Esro, associated with the big Enforcer for months, during which time he had assisted on numerous missions and proven himself loyal and dependable.

Her dark eyes moved from Vanadium to Esro, whose judgment she reluctantly had come to trust. Hard experience had taught her that while the erratic and eccentric human might be infuriating and annoying, Esro Brachis was a good person, an honest person, and indeed a hero.

If he vouched for the Enforcer—for Vanadium…

Steeling herself and breathing deeply in and out first, Mondrian moved closer to the one called Alatair, the woman in blue. Alatair held a long, curved sword with a golden pommel in each hand and, like a martial artist, was slowly moving through a variety of stances while she waited for Devenn to finish his parley.

"Excuse me," Mondrian said to the other Kur-Bai woman. "Perhaps I can add something to the deliberations here. I am a lieutenant in the Starfleet, and know something of these people. They—"

Alatair ignored her completely, continuing to practice gracefully with the swords, bringing them around with exquisite care, moving almost in slow motion.

Mondrian waited a moment for the woman to acknowledge her. "Excuse me."

Still nothing. It was as if Alatair could not perceive her.

Mondrian simply could not abide this. Celebrities or not, no one snubbed a Kur-Bai officer that way. She reached out and grabbed at Alatair's sleeve.

The woman reacted with shock, turning her burning eyes upon Mondrian at last.

"You dare lay hand on me?"

"Have no fear, Alatair," came a voice to Mondrian's right. "I have her."

The lieutenant looked around just in time to see the man in red sweeping towards her, his long staff raised and falling down, down, to smash her...

49

A blur, and then something stood between Mondrian and the Staff of Fire. She blinked, surprised.

"Esro?"

But she was wrong. It was not Esro who had defended her. He still stood a few yards away, unaware of what was happening so rapidly here.

She blinked again and saw that it was in fact Vanadium who had acted. He had moved with lightning speed, interposing himself between her and the tall Kur-Bai Elite. His arms, still bound in the metal casing restraints, were reaching up at what must have been a painful angle, blocking Yeist's downswing.

She opened her mouth to thank him, but before she could say anything, Yeist screamed in furious anger and spun away again. He moved rapidly through a series of motions, bright flames fluttering from the staff as he went. The action culminated with another strike, this one aimed at Vanadium's head. Again, the blue-steel behemoth managed to angle his body to deflect the blow.

"'Fear?'" cried Alatair to Yeist even as the fight ratcheted up. "I felt no fear—only insult!"

By this point, two or three seconds had passed, and Esro had taken notice of what was happening. He rushed to Mondrian's defense, getting between her and the two Elites.

"Everybody just stay cool," he said, flipping his facemask down and charging up his weapons systems.

"This impudent woman," Alatair barked, "this out-of-uniform *lieutenant*," and she spat that last word like a curse, "this likely *deserter*—she defends the Enforcer!"

"Humiliating," Yeist said. "Unacceptable."

He moved his Staff of Fire through another complex set of maneuvers, flames blazing behind it, before bringing it back behind his head, straight up with arms extended, and then down hard at Mondrian. The entire performance took less than two seconds. Before Esro could react—before he could even process what he was seeing—Vanadium moved his bound-up arms into the path of the blow again. This time flames gutted out on both sides of the impact, and the big metal man groaned, staggering backwards a step.

"This is intolerable," Alatair agreed. She swung both her scimitars out wide, spun them around in midair, then lurched forward, bringing them straight out from her with amazing speed.

Again, Vanadium was ready, having whirled around faster than she had moved. He raised those restrained arms again to block the attack. The swords crashed into the metal arm restraints with a resounding clang.

Alatair stumbled back, eyes wide, looking down at her swords, seeing with relief that they appeared unharmed.

Devenn, still locked in intense conversation with Ultraa, glanced back just long enough to get a sense of what was happening: *The pitiful humans are trying to get themselves killed by my team members. Fine.* Then he returned his attention to the conversation.

"See, now," Gorann growled at the other two Elites. "You two are wasting so much energy here. How hard can it be to restrain such as these?"

He brought up a tremendous fist, covered in green metal armor.

"I'll show you a way," he said. "A simple way."

The fist shot forward like a runaway train.

Vanadium brought up his arms.

Esro watched it all happening and laughed, not realizing it was the second time that day his big teammate had employed such tactics.

The huge fist impacted Vanadium's arms—and the restraining device attached to them. The resulting crash was deafening.

Everyone whirled around to see.

Vanadium wiped the soot from his armor. And he did so with hands—with arms—that were no longer bound. The restraints lay in smoking metal chunks on the ground.

Esro looked from the shattered device on the ground to Vanadium, who was starting forward.

"Now you've just gone and ticked him off," he told the Elites.

Alatair and Yeist glanced at one another warily, then stepped back and took up defensive stances, weapons raised, as Vanadium advanced on them.

"No, no," the huge, hulking Gorann rumbled, stepping in front of them. "I will handle this."

Cracking his tremendous knuckles, the Kur-Bai powerhouse in green banded armor moved to cut off Vanadium's advance, and the two behemoths squared off.

"I recognize you are a force for good, and I do not wish to fight you," Vanadium said in his hollow voice. *"I merely acted to protect Lt. Mondrian."*

Gorann frowned at this. He had fought Worldmind thralls before, but they had never really talked to him, much less attempted to reason with him. And the thought of them actually trying to protect someone—a Kur-Bai, of all people... It simply made no sense to him.

Shaking his head as if to clear it—as if he were hearing things—Gorann roared an unintelligible battle cry and rushed forward.

Vanadium stood his ground but made no move to defend himself.

The green-armored colossus got within ten feet of Vanadium before a crackling, golden sphere sprung up, as if from nowhere, around the blue-silver man. Gorann crashed into it and staggered back, surprised. An instant later, he crumpled to the ground, as though the Earth's gravity had increased just below where he stood. In fact, it had.

Vanadium turned around and saw what he had expected: Heavyweight and Pulsar stood there. Each had a hand extended, directing their powers against Gorann.

"No, my friends," Vanadium said, shaking his silvery head. *"Do not invoke their wrath against you, too."*

"Too late for that," Pulsar replied, her eyes narrowed with determination as she glared past him at the big Kur-Bai Elite. "You pick on one of us, you pick on all of us!"

"Um, yeah, what she said," Heavyweight agreed. He followed that with a quick aside to Lyn: "What have you gotten me into?"

"Into saving the world, I hope," she hissed back at him.

"Or ending it, maybe," he muttered, increasing the force as an obviously furious Gorann struggled to rise.

The other two Elites involved in the dispute rushed forward then. Alatair raised both her swords and as if in response the winds whirled about her, forming a mini-cyclone. She directed the swords ahead of her and the cyclone shot out, striking Pulsar and Heavyweight directly, tossing both of them through the air and sending them tumbling through the burned grass.

Meanwhile Yeist raised his staff above his head with one hand and the flames that licked along its surface sprang fully to life, roaring up in a blinding blaze. With a cry he pointed the staff toward Vanadium and sent a torrential blast of fire into the former Enforcer's chest. Vanadium made no sound as the fire wreathed all about him. In less than a second he was lost to the view of the others, completely overwhelmed in fire.

Yeist had no time to celebrate his apparent success. A shape all in jet black swooped down from above and collided violently with him, and both he and his attacker sprawled on the ground. The one in black—the Fury—was on his feet first. No sooner did Yeist, still lying back on the grass, raise his staff to fire once again, than the Fury blasted him with a bolt of emerald energy from his fist. The Staff of Fire tumbled from the Elite's grasp and bounced away.

Pulsar recovered quickly from Alatair's attack and shot skyward, circling behind the woman and directing both her golden-clad arms down at her. As Alatair generated another mini-cyclone about herself, Lyn erected a force sphere around her, completely enclosing the woman. In an instant the Elite realized what was happening, but she could not stop it. The cyclone, trapped with her inside the bubble, tore into her, sending her spinning around and hurling the swords from her hands. The two weapons bounced around dangerously inside the sphere, impacting Alatair twice. Seeing this, Pulsar released the force field and allowed both the Kur-Bai woman and her swords to fall to the ground, rattled but none the worse for the wear.

Alatair sat up, her light blue uniform torn in places and a little blood trickling down her side. She looked up at Lyn with what the human woman took to be an odd combination of anger and respect.

At that same moment, the flames surrounding Vanadium parted and the big metal man strode out unmarked. He took two steps toward Yeist, who had yet to recover the Staff of Fire. The red-clad Elite eyed him warily and raised one hand.

"I am unarmed," he said to Vanadium.

"Do you yield, then?"

"Yield?"

Yeist's expression conveyed a sense of confusion, as if such a concept had never occurred to him before—as indeed it had not.

"Of course he does not yield," Gorann roared, leaping forward—and astounding everyone in the area by actually causing his massive bulk to rise some four feet above the ground as he did so.

The impact when he landed shook the Earth. He raised both fists high, preparing to strike Vanadium a titanic blow.

Esro Brachis, who had surrounded himself with his own force field when the fighting had started, now dropped it and opened fire with both of his wrist blasters. The twin beams struck Gorann square in the face. The Kur-Bai behemoth cried out in pain and stumbled back, bringing both his massive hands up to block the attack.

"Human," the big Elite growled, "your pitiful armor will not save you! I will roll you into a thin foil, suitable for wrapping gifts for my nieces and nephews!"

"Gotta touch me first, big guy," Esro replied, firing again. He had briefly considered trying to use the new ability he seemed to have acquired, but frankly it horrified him to even think about it.

I'll have to do some research, some testing on that subject—as well as some very deep thinking—later, when there's time. And privacy.

Pulsar, again holding Alatair firmly within a force bubble, watched as the Fury and Heavyweight struck Gorann next, bringing him crashing down with the force of a minor avalanche. Heavyweight resumed his gravitic attack, holding the big man glued down to the soil.

Yeist scrambled for his staff, but the Fury swooped down and grabbed it up. The flames licked at his hands, but Williams's jet black covering seemed unaffected. He hovered just above the angry, red-clad Elite and held the Staff of Fire just out of reach.

"Lose something?"

All of this played out in a number of seconds. Ultraa and Devenn had turned and watched it all transpire. Both of them wore surprised expressions on their faces, though the causes differed; Ultraa was concerned for his friends' safety, while Devenn was simply shocked at how the conflict was going.

Neither of them said a word, simply looking on in amazement, until Ultraa finally turned to the Elites' leader and said, "Maybe we should stop them before someone gets seriously hurt."

Devenn started to reject this outright, then hesitated. After a moment, he nodded.

"Besides," Devenn growled as the fight came to its conclusion, with each of his three stunned comrades disarmed and restrained, "I would spare my teammates any further... *embarrassment.*"

Ultraa nodded.

"But I would point out," he said to Devenn, "that Vanadium has scarcely been fighting at all—yet—and *I* have not lifted a finger."

"Nor have I, Human," Devenn pointed out.

"True," Ultraa agreed.

The Kur-Bai commando leader eyed him warily, but with growing respect.

"Should you and I arm wrestle, then?" Ultraa suggested.

Devenn stared at the man in white and red for a moment, and then a smile slowly spread across his face.

"Not at this time," he replied. "There is no telling what other surprises you might have in store for me."

Ultraa smiled in return. Then he looked out at the others.

"That's enough," he shouted, his voice carrying across the battlefield. "Stand down, everyone."

"Yes," Devenn added, his deep voice booming. "He is right. *Enough.*"

"You sure about this, chief?" Esro asked.

Ultraa nodded.

"Let them go."

Reluctantly, Pulsar dropped the bubble from around Alatair. The woman moved quickly, grabbing up her swords and dusting off her soiled blue uniform, but she made no hostile moves. If anything, she appeared to be in shock.

Heavyweight released Gorann and the colossal Kur-Bai struggled to his feet, his big joints popping like firecrackers. He eyed both Richard and Esro warily but held his ground.

"So I should give this back, then?" Doug asked Ultraa, holding the Staff of Fire out in one hand.

Ultraa glanced at Devenn and the Elites' leader nodded once.

"Go ahead," Ultraa called back, and Williams tossed the staff to Yeist.

The Elites, looking over at Devenn questioningly, nonetheless backed off and moved into formation, standing at attention. Esro, Lyn, Richard and Doug were watching Ultraa closely, waiting to see what was happening. Vanadium stood impassively between the two groups, unscratched and unfazed, looking for all the world as if nothing had happened.

"I believe," Devenn said loudly to the assembled crowd then, "that the situation has changed somewhat."

"You got that right," Esro growled. Ultraa quickly waved him down.

"At this juncture," Devenn continued, "it would be prudent for us to consult our superiors in the fleet."

"That might be wise," Ultraa replied, nodding, his mouth a tight line, his eyes hard and locked on the Elites' leader.

Alatair nodded once to Devenn and withdrew a small communications headset from a pouch at her side.

A few yards away, Mondrian watched it all transpire with a growing sense of dread. And in those moments she came to understand that she faced a fateful and inescapable decision—one that could at the very least ruin her own life forever, and quite possibly bring about the end of the Earth, as well.

Yet I must choose, she thought. *I have no choice.*

And still she hesitated, as the fate of the Earth teetered in the balance around her.

50

Through it all, off to one side of the fray, Mondrian had witnessed the confrontation between Esro's team and the Kur-Bai Elites playing out with terrible, agonizing indecision. On the surface, her duty clearly lay with the Starfleet for which she served as a lieutenant. But she had grown very fond of these humans, and had come to be convinced her people were making a grievous error here.

The Admiral, the captains, the others of the fleet—they will not understand, she thought to herself. *They do not know these humans. Nor, she admitted at last, do they know Vanadium. They will not make the proper choice.*

She thought of what the fleet had done in previous, similar situations.

We call ourselves liberators, protectors of the galaxy, she thought, *but we have laid waste to nearly as many worlds as have the Worldmind's hordes. In order to save the galaxy, we destroy its inhabited worlds! Surely there must be another way—a better way! And perhaps these humans have found it—or at least a possibility of it. Perhaps they merely offer hope that some other way might exist.*

She stared down at her feet, her stomach in knots.

If so, dare we end that hope here, in its cradle? Should we not nurture it, and allow it to flower—to see what it might become, in time?

And then she looked at Alatair—proud, defiant Alatair, who had been defeated in battle.

Surely she is in denial now. She will refuse to accept this. As will the rest of the Starfleet, if we leave things this way.

Alatair had sheathed her blades and now wore the headset, seeking to contact the Starfleet.

They will not understand, Mondrian knew.

Silently she soared up into the air, the golden bands about her wrists and ankles sparkling as they propelled her aloft.

"Silence," called Alatair, holding up a hand.

The others remained at attention, waiting.

"I am receiving word from the fleet," she said.

She hesitated a second, then spoke more words in Kur-Bai into her headset. Hearing the reply, she frowned in puzzlement, then looked up at the others, who had frozen in mid-fight, awaiting the word.

"The Fleet Captain reports all planetary scans are complete. The Human spoke the truth. There is no more trace of the Worldmind infestation anywhere on this world—save only for the Enforcer here. Otherwise, they are all gone."

Devenn looked at her with open astonishment.

"This was merely the preliminary scan, yes?"

"No—they have completed the full battery of tests. There can be no deception—not that these *humans* have the capability of deceiving us to begin with. No, the infestation is gone."

Devenn looked from Alatair to Ultraa.

"How—*how* could you have—?"

Ultraa smiled flatly.

"We have our ways," he said. "Of course, Vanadium was a major part of it. We must have him back."

Devenn looked sidelong at Vanadium where he still stood impassively off to one side.

"No," he said, shaking his head. "No, that much is impossible. He—"

"He is different," Ultraa replied. "He is one of us now."

"No—"

Mondrian swooped down and grabbed the headset off of Alatair. The Elite woman whirled around, directing both hands at the erstwhile lieutenant, preparing to strike her with wind or water.

"Mondy—what are you doing?" cried Esro, swinging his faceplate back down again and powering up.

"Whatever I can," she called back to him. "But I need time!"

That was all Esro needed to hear. He opened fire with both blasters, knocking Alatair back off her feet before she could strike, and sending her tumbling through the blackened grass.

Gorann moved forward again, a huge paw flailing out for Esro, only to have the Fury zap him with a vibrant green beam, stunning him and causing him to stumble back. He cried out in pain and frustration.

Yeist brandished his staff, and Pulsar and Heavyweight squared off, ready to fight once more.

For the next four minutes, Ultraa and the others would battle these Elites—the finest warriors of the Kur-Bai Empire—to a complete standstill, in order to give Mondrian the time to do...whatever it was she was doing. All they could do was trust her, and hope it would be enough.

Two hundred feet above the fray, the Kur-Bai lieutenant in blue leveled off her ascent and pulled the headset on. She spoke hurriedly into it.

"Yes," she was saying, "this is Lt. Mondrian of the Seventy-Ninth Expeditionary Mission. I have been with the humans for some time now. I need to report to the Admiral, or to the Fleet Captain."

After a few seconds, both men came on the line.

"Lt. Mondrian, is it?" Admiral DeSkai asked. "How did you come to be on this world, Lieutenant?"

"I was stranded, Admiral," she replied. "But—as you have seen—the Earth has been freed of the Worldmind infestation. There is no further need for action here."

597

"There is still one, Lieutenant," the fleet captain said, breaking in. "There is danger from him—and danger that he might have spread some undetectable menace that will only appear after we have departed."

"No—with respect, Captain—no, sir."

"No?"

"The Enforcer who remains on the planet is no menace."

"Excuse me?" came the Admiral's surprised voice.

"Lieutenant," the Fleet Captain continued, "we can take you aboard shortly and accept a full report and debriefing at that time. Now please—"

Mondrian knew they were about to cut her off, and she searched her thoughts desperately for anything that would...

"Admiral! The ship I served on—the one that was destroyed here—it was captained by Turval DeSkai."

The Admiral had almost switched off. Now he hurriedly replied, "Turval? My nephew? Is he here?"

"No, Admiral," Mondrian said. In somber tones she related a quick sketch of what had befallen her ship—the ship of this man's nephew.

"He is dead, then," DeSkai whispered when she had finished.

"Yes, Admiral. But he was a fine officer—a fine man. I was very proud to have served under him."

"Lt. Mondrian, you said, yes?"

"Admiral," the captain broke in, "I can handle this from here, if you'd like to—"

The Admiral interrupted.

"No, no—now that she mentions Turval, I do recall him speaking of a Lt. Mondrian among his crew."

The Admiral's tone warmed.

"Yes. I remember now. He thought very highly of you, young lady."

"I respected him greatly, sir," she answered.

"Yes, yes...Well, clearly you are no Circle agent, left behind by that crowd. Good, good."

Grim satisfaction filled his voice.

"So a Circle agent was responsible for Turval's death. Well, we have more than paid them back for it."

"Yes, sir."

The Admiral seemed to be considering for a few moments.

"I will send down a shuttle to bring you aboard, Lieutenant."

"Thank you, Admiral. But, sir—"

"Yes?"

"This world—it is free of the infestation. The Enforcer here has indeed been altered—his programming has long been changed, somehow—and he represents no danger. You must believe me—I scarcely believed it myself for a long while, but I have seen the evidence. He fought alongside us—alongside me!—and has defended this planet from numerous threats. He wishes only to stay here and continue to protect this planet—and to protect his friends here."

Silence for several long seconds. Mondrian knew her claims must be leaving the fleet officers dumbfounded—*But will they believe me, or throw me in the brig after "sterilizing" half the planet?*

"By the stars," the admiral breathed at last. "Can such a thing be possible?"

"I have witnessed it, sir."

The Admiral took this in silently.

"And, Admiral," she went on after a moment, "imagine the usefulness of having a full-fledged Worldmind Enforcer at our disposal, here on this planet, to study from time to time?"

"To dissect?" asked the Fleet Captain.

"To debrief," Mondrian replied, aghast. "As needed."

"Ah," the Fleet Captain replied, sounding disappointed.

At the same time, however, she could almost hear a smile forming on the old Admiral's face.

"Yes," he was whispering. "Yes..."

Silence as the Admiral considered for a few more seconds, then:

"It would be unprecedented, but... Given that he is alone, and is apparently integrated into a group that can regulate his behavior, as I take it..."

"Yes, Admiral," she confirmed. "A very reliable, impressive group."

"So the Elites are reporting," the Fleet Captain noted with a tinge of unhappiness in his voice. "Quite formidable, indeed."

"They would need to be made auxiliaries of the Empire," the Admiral said. "Granted some sort of status..."

Mondrian's dark eyes flashed at that.

"I'm certain they would have no objection—they would surely be honored—"

"Yes...The possibilities here are very intriguing."

Then he paused.

"There is only one problem, Lieutenant. He would need supervising, day and night. He would require constant monitoring, to ensure he does not slide back into his original programming."

She grew puzzled.

"Yes, Admiral—and, as I have said, these people are—"

"These people are Earth people. Even granted a certain status within the Empire, they still would not be Kur-Bai. Their judgment would not be entirely trusted."

She frowned deeply now, worried that all of her arguments had gone for naught.

"But if we had someone here," he went on, "someone on permanent posting to this world..."

"Yes, Admiral," she replied quickly, hope growing again—and then the reality of what he must be thinking came to her, and her heart sank.

"You, in fact, Lieutenant," he said. "You speak their language. You have spent time among them, and know more about them than anyone else in the fleet. Yes. You will stay here—you will remain with the humans on their world. It will be your permanent posting."

Despite her hovering two hundred feet up in the air, Mondrian distinctly felt her feet going out from under her.

"From time to time you will report in, updating us on the planet, its activities and developments—and on the Enforcer, and his behavior."

She took this in mutely, resignedly.

"Do you agree, Lieutenant?"

Three long seconds passed—three seconds in which she thought of her homeworld, and all the things there that she would not be seeing and experiencing again for a very long time.

She had to answer. She had no choice. She had pressed for this very solution, and now it was offered, and she had no choice whatsoever.

What have I done? What have I done to myself?

"Yes, Admiral," she said softly. "I accept."

51

Ultraa stood on the low hilltop, Lyn and Esro beside him, the others arrayed behind them. Now Vanadium stood among them as well, as inscrutable as ever but somehow giving off an air of uncertainty. Heavyweight stood on one side of him and the Fury on the other.

Across from them were arrayed the Elites. The four alien champions stood in a line, facing back toward the humans. Alatair's hands rested on her hips, and her mouth was twisted into a frown. Gorann's massive arms were crossed over his chest, his expression blank. Yeist leaned tiredly upon his staff. Devenn, seeming more out of sorts than anyone else there, stroked his square-jawed chin idly and spoke in hushed tones with an officer from the flagship.

To the left of Ultraa was a delegation from the United States Government, including generals and senators. They waited there, muttering to one another idly, appearing extremely awkward, unsure of what to do or say.

To Ultraa's right had gathered a large group of Kur-Bai officers and soldiers in dress uniforms who had arrived minutes earlier aboard a small fleet of armed shuttles. In their midst stood Mondrian, who had not spoken to her Human friends since the end of the battle.

The Kur-Bai officer completed his conversation with Devenn, who gave the man a sort of bemused look, then laughed softly and nodded. He accepted a small wooden box from the officer and held it at his side.

At length Ultraa stepped forward and addressed the leader of the Elites.

"I'm getting the impression the situation has changed," Ultraa said, "though I'm not entirely sure how."

He gestured toward the gathered Kur-Bai military personnel and the parked shuttles and gunships.

"Are they here to demand our surrender, or what? Because we're a long way from—"

Devenn laughed long and hard at this.

"Oh, no," he replied. "You would have had to *lose* the battle to surrender, and you had not quite reached that point yet."

"We weren't gonna," Esro chimed in. "We had you guys on the ropes."

Devenn laughed again.

"Perhaps. Perhaps you did."

He squeezed Esro's armored shoulder in what looked to be a friendly fashion, and the Human tried not to cry out in pain as the big red paw dented his metal plating.

"I am glad we did not have to sterilize your planet," Devenn said good-naturedly to Ultraa, still smiling.

"Uh, yeah. Me too."

The big alien nodded.

"Your team fought well. Very well."

He looked from Ultraa to Esro to Lyn. Then his eyes moved back to Richard and Doug, before returning to Ultraa.

"I would welcome such as you into our ranks."

"We appreciate the compliment," Ultraa replied, "but just the same—"

"No," Devenn said, interrupting. "I do not think you understand."

He held out the wooden box and opened it.

"These are for you."

He took a small, golden, eight-pointed star from the box and handed it to Ultraa.

"What—?"

The blond man held it up and looked at it. Then he looked at Devenn, and saw that he wore one just like it. So did the other three Elites.

"What is it?"

"It is your new emblem of rank. We welcome you into our order."

He smiled broadly.

"You are the first non-Kur-Bai ever to be afforded this honor."

Ultraa's jaw dropped. He didn't know what to say.

The other three Elites stepped forward, offering their hands. Numbly he shook each of them.

"Hey, way to go, buddy," Esro said, beaming. He patted Ultraa on the back.

Ultraa looked at his friend, then back at Devenn.

"But—but what about—?"

The leader of the Elites smiled and produced another pin, handing it to Esro, who accepted it, dumbfounded.

"I'm not sure if you would have still qualified for that," Gorann rumbled, "if I had succeeded in rolling you into foil."

Esro laughed.

"I'm glad we won't have to find out."

Gorann seemed ambivalent about that, but nodded anyway.

Next Devenn handed a gold pin to Lyn, who reddened and nearly fell over with shock. And then he gave one to Richard and one to Doug, who offered effusive thanks.

"Are you believing this?" Williams whispered to Heavyweight.

"I'm just wondering if it'll get me a discount at any bars."

"Only on Venus," Doug replied with a grin.

"My luck, you're right," Richard growled.

The ceremony now apparently complete, Devenn closed the box.

"Hold on a second," Ultraa said.

Everyone froze.

"Pal," Esro hissed, "I'm thinking you should just let the nice aliens give us presents and then go on their merry way, y'know?"

Ultraa ignored him.

"That isn't all," he said to Devenn.

The big Kur-Bai looked at him askance.

"What?"

"You only gave the pins—and, I assume, the status—to part of my team."

"What do you mean?"

Then Devenn saw where Ultraa was looking, and he shook his head firmly.

"No. *No!* Never. He is the enemy. The *adversary*. His kind—"

"His *kind*," Ultraa shot back. "Not *him*. He is an individual. And he is one of us."

Devenn looked at Ultraa with naked amazement. The others all tensed. The situation had gone from relaxed to explosive again in a mere instant.

"Human, I have traveled from one side of the galaxy to the other, and encountered more strange and bizarre life forms than you can conceive exist. And never in all my journeys have I come across anyone so obstinate, so stubborn, so...so *determined* to get his planet blown to bits!"

Ultraa bunched up his red-gloved fists and leaned in, starting to say something. Then Lyn grabbed him by the arm and whispered in his ear. He listened, considered what she was saying, and smiled.

"Pulsar has made a great suggestion," he told Devenn.

The big alien studied the slight female for a moment.

"And what might that be? That you be taken at once to an asylum?"

"That we vote," Lyn said with a smile, even as she was affixing her pin to her uniform.

"That we—"

Devenn looked from the five humans, all now sporting their gold Elites pins, to the three Kur-Bai who stood behind him. Then he slowly ran his blue-gloved hand down his face, groaning.

Moments later, Vanadium had his pin.

"It looks so nice there," Lyn said, grinning.

The pin had magnetically adhered to Vanadium's chest, and he gazed down at it, then up at Lyn. She had the impression that if he could have smiled, he would have.

"I think you're off the most-wanted list now," she told him.

"It would appear so," he replied.

Nearby, Gorann turned to head for the shuttles, then paused and looked back at Esro.

"I do not think," he said, "that I care for you people very much."

He seemed to consider that thought for a moment.

"No," he said at length, "I do not. I do not care for you at all."

Then he reached out and took Esro's hand, shaking it with enough force to break the limb, were Brachis not wearing his armor.

"But welcome to our organization. Try not to embarrass us too much, Earth man."

"Your confidence is inspiring," Esro replied.

From among the gathered Kur-Bai officers, Mondrian stepped out of the crowd and approached Esro.

"There you are," he said.

He looked down at the grass between them, frowning, clearly saddened.

"We had some fun together, huh? But I guess this is it."

"Not at all," she replied.

His head snapped up.

"Huh?"

Quickly she told him what she had agreed to do.

He stared at her, amazed.

"You—you would do that—for *him?*"

"For him? For Vanadium?"

She thought about that, then shrugged.

"Not just for him. For many reasons. For the love you all clearly have for him, and for each other. For the sake of justice.

"I think you're off the Most-Wanted list now."

And," she admitted, "for me.   For the opportunity, for the experience."

Esro reached out and took her hand.

"And how about for *me?*   You think *I* might be one of those reasons?"

Mondrian pulled the hand back, but then met his brown eyes with her own nearly black ones, and allowed a small smile to play at her lips.

"Perhaps.   Perhaps you are a very small reason.   A very, very, very small—"

"Yeah, okay, I get it!"

But he laughed, and she laughed in return, and then he hugged her, and was gratified that she actually hugged him back.

"Oh! Wait a minute!"

He broke free of her and ran over to Ultraa.

"Mondy's staying! She's going to be one of us!"

"How's that?"

Esro ran through it.   Ultraa took it all in, getting a sense of the sacrifice she was making, and beginning to understand everything else that went with her decision.   He realized then that she had not only saved Vanadium, but might well have saved them all.

He whirled around and looked for the Elites. They were boarding a shuttle nearby.

"Devenn! Wait!"

The big alien looked back at him and groaned.

And then, one minute later, Mondrian had her pin as well.

"Is there *anyone else* on this planet," Devenn was growling, his eyes fixed firmly on Ultraa, "that you wish to induct into *my* order, Earth man? Because I may need to send back to the fleet for another box of pins."

Ultraa smiled beatifically.

"I think that should do it."

A small, brown dog ran past them. Devenn pointed to it.

"That creature. Would you wish it inducted as well?"

"No," Ultraa laughed, raising both hands in mock defense. "We're good now."

The big alien continued to glare at him for a long moment, then sighed. He reached out, grasped Ultraa's hand, and squeezed it—not hard enough to do any real damage.

"I believe I shall miss you, Human," he intoned deeply. "Perhaps fate will carry my group this way again in the future."

"I hope so," Ultraa said, nodding. "Of course, should that happen," Devenn continued, a gleam in his dark eye, "you would all have to consider yourselves drafted into the service—at least for the duration of the mission."

He eyed Esro.

"Or at least the ones we felt might actually be of use."

Esro stuck out his tongue.

"Understood," Ultraa replied, shaking the big hand.

"I've never been so glad to be considered a screw-up," Esro chuckled to Lyn.

52

"I...we...we survive..."

"..."

"Kabaraak-brother?"

"...Yes. I am here. We have successfully re-merged."

"..."

"..."

"...I did not believe we would survive, my brother. Had much more time elapsed..."

"...Yes. Indeed. In the cave, I felt it. I could sense our physical integrity failing. I...I feared..."

A pause.

"The Xorex. Is it...?"

"Destroyed. All of them are destroyed."

"All? It had spawned?"

"Oh, yes. Yes."

"And even still...?"

Laughter.

"For perhaps the first time, our coherence problems became an asset. Certainly they saved this planet, and both of us."

"...Ah."

"If not for you here, sealed in the cave, we would both now be gone, along with the robots."

"How so, my brother?"

"When the disintegration effect became strongest, the Xorexes, having absorbed it, had no defense against it, and no experience in handling it. They sublimated instantly. We, on the other hand…"

"We had one another's strength and power to draw upon. Yes, I see it."

"Even with one of us there, and the other trapped here in this cave."

"Yes. I felt it, too. It saved us."

"And now that we are reunited again, in one single body…"

"…Yes. I see it, now, through your eyes. I…yes, very good. You performed admirably, brother."

"Thank you."

Another pause, very long, this time. Then:

"And what of us now?"

"Now we prepare. For the future."

"How so?"

"The Worldmind's first overture has been turned back. The Xorexes have been stopped. And one of his own Enforcers has changed sides. I must admit, I did not expect this to happen—nor did I foresee the role we would play in their defeat."

"The Worldmind will not be pleased. He may engage in retaliation against our master."

"Unthinkable."

"Indeed. And yet, now, all too possible."

"It would mean a universal conflagration."

"Quite so. How many worlds would die if our master, Stellarax the Great, should engage the Worldmind in direct, open hostilities?"

"And now a third Rival has become involved."

"Yes. The Gray Man. Keeper of the cosmic anthill. The collector of all life."

"Three of them, three Great Rivals, all coming…*here*. To this tiny, fragile world. It is unprecedented. It is…"

"…Apocalyptic…"

"Yes. And yet…Despite overwhelming odds, this world did manage to survive its immediate danger. Perhaps something will save it yet again."

"Perhaps. But the master approaches. Soon enough…"

"Yes. Soon enough, he will arrive."

"Surely only a matter of months, at the most."

"I concur."

"And until then…"

"Yes. Until then."

"What will we do? Whose side will we take?"

"..."

"Brother?"

"I... I find I do not know."

"Yes. I feel the same."

"And so..."

"Yes. Much remains to be seen..."

53

Jameson sat in the ruins of his office, reduced to watching the dramatic events outside as they transpired on his television. Reduced to this—to being a mere observer, and not one of the major players, pulling the strings on everyone else—galled him tremendously. That, and the thought of how far he'd fallen, sickened him.

A number of different emotions surged within him, competing with one another for his attention. Part of him was angry--angry that his schemes had been exposed, at least to Ultraa and company. Another part was relieved that things had ended as positively for Jameson as they had, given the potential for disaster.

If anyone has to be privy to some of my secrets, Jameson thought resignedly, *I suppose I couldn't do much better than Ultraa. If he says he won't reveal anything without cause, I believe him. But that doesn't mean I have to like him knowing in the first place...*

He thought about the Circle, and actually laughed at how he had faced six deadly alien commandos and had stood up to them. Not bravely, necessarily, but he hadn't groveled at their feet, either. Certainly a large part of that had been sheer bluster. Jameson had been intimidating underlings probably since before those warriors were born--or hatched, or however they came into the world. But another part of it had been his own stubborn, dogged determination to force events to go his way, always. He'd had a deal with the Circle, and having their soldiers come smashing their way into the Pentagon was not the best way to maintain their relationship.

Oh, well, he thought, mulling over the remaining possibilities before him. *The Circle deal is dead. My power here will be severely curtailed in the days ahead--of that I have no doubt. And the people around me...*

609

He frowned suddenly, at that last thought.

"Where is Adcock?"

His longtime advisor and assistant, the mysterious Mr. Adcock, had not been seen around the Pentagon in days.

So of course at that precise moment, the hastily rebuilt door to his office opened and a slender man in a dark suit and sunglasses walked in.

"You!"

Jameson stood, glaring at the new arrival.

"Where on earth have you been?"

Adcock hesitated, standing just inside the doorway.

"I don't know if I would have phrased it *precisely* that way," he answered.

Jameson ignored that.

"You missed all the fun," he continued.

"So it would appear," Adcock replied. He stepped the rest of the way in and closed the ragged door behind him.

Jameson asked again where he had been.

"I was on detached assignment," Adcock responded.

"Not for me," Jameson growled. "Not at my order."

"No," Adcock said, a rare, thin smile playing about his lips. "A higher power."

Jameson considered responding to that, then thought better of it. *There's no telling what he means. Do I really want to know?* He pursed his lips. *Not really.*

"So," Adcock went on, pacing slowly and carefully through the piles of debris covering the floor, "judging by the state of things around here, I would venture to say our relationship with the Circle-- with the Kur-Bai--has fallen into a state of disrepair."

Jameson gave him a sour look.

"I think that's probably fair to say, yes," he replied sardonically.

Adcock nodded, continuing to pace. After several long, quiet seconds, he looked up at his boss again.

"I do know of another group, one that might be well worth our time to get to know. To perhaps set up a formal working partnership, in place of the Circle."

"Oh?" Jameson said, brightening. Then he thought for a moment and his face fell into a deep frown as he regarded his aide. "Wait, wait. This new group—are they aliens?"

"As a matter of fact," Adcock answered, "they hail from the Deneb IV star system of—"

Jameson cut him off with a quick, sharp slash of the hand.

"You're fired," he said.

54

On the drifting, shifting sands of a world in between dimensions of the multiverse sat Francisco, rocking slowly back and forth. He had sat there for days, waiting patiently for what he knew, sooner or later, must happen.

And, at last, it did.

A tiny point of light appeared just in front of him, floating over the gray sands. Slowly, slowly it grew, and as it grew, the light diminished and took on human form.

"Yes. Yes!"

The light faded entirely, and in its place stood a tall figure in robes and hood, wearing a metallic mask.

The robes were purple. The mask was black.

Francisco noted the changes in color and he sighed contentedly.

"Gone," he whispered happily. "Both of the others—gone now. This is a new one. At last."

The Warlord gazed down at Francisco and smiled benevolently.

"Hello," he said.

Francisco scrambled to his feet, then bowed deeply.

"Master," he said, clutching his stubby hands together. "I have waited patiently, and am so happy to see you again."

"Yes, yes," the tall figure replied airily. "Well, time for that sort of thing later. For now—we have much work to do."

Francisco nodded happily, preparing to open a portal to carry them both to the sanctum.

But the Warlord walked away from him and stood gazing at the wreckage of the machine his predecessor had constructed—and *that one's* predecessor had caused to be destroyed. He studied the shapes of the shattered pieces of equipment and the ruined remains of the control boards.

"They actually solved both of the questions," the Warlord whispered just loud enough for Francisco to overhear. "They discovered the means to either penetrate the great universal barrier— or to destroy all the levels of the multiverse." He nodded appreciatively. "Astounding. Simply astounding. I cannot understand why the Design would rule against either of them."

Oh no—oh, oh, no, not again, Francisco thought to himself, horror instantly growing and welling up inside him.

"They could not coexist, Master," he replied nervously, wondering why he should have to explain such a thing to the Warlord. "Plus, neither of those goals matched the plans of the Great Design."

"I disagree," the Warlord shot back at him. "I believe you ruled incorrectly, in both their cases. Of course they could not both exist at once. But both of them followed the Design as he saw it."

"But—but how can you say that?" Francisco demanded, omitting the word "Master," and doing it so very early in their relationship.

"I should think it obvious," the Warlord replied, striding across the sands, circling the machine, the little man scurrying along behind him. "Breaking through the barrier would have granted my blue predecessor vast powers—enough to accomplish any end. And utterly annihilating the multiverse—well, the Design calls for cosmic order, does it not? What greater, lasting order can there be, than the all-encompassing embrace of utter entropy? Of universal Armageddon?"

Francisco gawked up at his new master, dumbfounded.

"Yes," the Warlord continued, nodding to himself, "both of them exhibited laudable goals. Commendable vision and truly amazing accomplishments. Your own lack of imagination, I would argue, ultimately doomed them both."

"My—my *own* lack of—?"

"Because of this," the Warlord continued, "the Grand Design has deemed *you* to be the true threat to its ongoing agenda. And thus…"

His arm swept out of those rustling purple robes. His gauntleted hand brandished a long, silvery dagger. With nary a hesitation, he plunged it into Francisco's breast.

The little man's eyes widened with shock. He gagged, stumbled and fell, dead before he hit the ground.

The Warlord gazed down at him, hands clasped behind his back. Beneath his black mask, a single tear ran down his cheek.

"I am sorry, my old friend. Sorry it had to come to that. But the Design must always prevail—as none knows better than you did."

The body of the little man shimmered and vanished.

After a few moments of respectful silence, the Warlord cleared his throat, then slowly and dramatically raised his hand and gestured in the air before him. A portal appeared, multicolored lights swirling within its round face. Looking through it, he could see into his sanctum—and could see a tall, slender form standing there, waiting. Very obviously female, she wore a bright red jumpsuit and a black tool belt. Her long, blonde hair was tied back in a ponytail. She flashed a bright smile at him.

"Welcome home, my master," she said, her voice a soft purr.

The Warlord's eyes widened behind his mask.

"And you are?"

"Francesca," the woman replied. "I have only just arrived—as you must surely know."

The Warlord considered this. He stared at his new assistant—stared at her perhaps somewhat overlong. Then he nodded.

Perhaps, he thought, *I can put my multiverse-shattering plans on hold...if only for a little while.*

Francesca smiled again, dazzling white teeth nearly blinding him.

Yes, he thought. *For a little while.*

And then one last thought crossed his mind as he moved to step into the portal: *Sometimes the Grand Design exhibits a sense of humor I simply do not understand.*

His eyes took in the feminine form of his new assistant once more.

Not that I am complaining, of course.

Shrugging in resignation, he stepped through into his sanctum. The portal spiraled closed and vanished behind him, leaving only the faintest hint of laughter echoing gently across the barren desert.

EPILOGUE:
Three Days after the End of the World

It was all over.

The Kur-Bai fleet had departed. Washington was being rebuilt, along with the rest of the devastated eastern seaboard of North America. The vast, gaping holes that had reached deep into the Earth's crust were being filled in. The monuments were being reconstructed. Things were slowly, so slowly getting back to normal.

At the Georgetown University Hospital in downtown DC, Wendy Li rested comfortably, if somewhat anxiously. Her minor wounds having been tended to, her sister was now keeping an eye on her till their parents could arrive to pick her up.

Lyn sat in a chair at the side of the bed, holding her younger sister's hand. The girl had a big bandage on her forehead and smaller ones here and there on her neck and arms, but otherwise appeared to be in good shape.

And that's just what Ultraa told her when he entered and took up station next to Lyn.

"I forgot to demand a pin for you," he told her, after they had explained what had happened with the Kur-Bai and their Elites. "I'm sorry."

"Don't be," she said, smiling. "It sounds like you might have touched off an interstellar war or something, if you had."

"I nearly did anyway," Ultraa said with a laugh.

He patted Wendy on the shoulder.

"You did very well out there. You and your sister both. I'd be willing to make the same offer to you that I did to Lyn: training and official government agent status."

Wendy's eyes lit up.

"With you guys?"

"When you're old enough," Lyn interjected.

"Exactly," Ultraa agreed. "As in, not just yet. Soon, maybe."

Wendy pursed her lips, thinking about it, and nodded.

"Soon is good," she said. "I like school anyway. I'd like to stay anonymous there as long as I can."

Lyn nodded at that, wistfully thinking of how her own anonymity as just another student had been ended so abruptly.

No one spoke for several seconds, until after Lyn turned to Ultraa, giving him a puzzled look.

"What?" he asked, concerned about her expression.

"I—I don't know," she said. "Maybe..."

She chewed a fingernail for a second.

"I was almost sure you were going to break the team up now."

Ultraa's eyes widened.

"Break it up? Why?"

"Because Wendy got hurt... and because the world nearly got destroyed—what, three times, at least? And because—"

"The world *not* getting destroyed any of those times is a big argument for not breaking the team up," he replied. "And as for Wendy's injury..."

He gazed down at her, patting her on the shoulder, then looked back up at Lyn.

"She had no business being involved, but that wasn't her fault. She was manipulated."

"I know, I know," Lyn said, nodding. "But—"

"And proper training for her, once she's of age, will help with that."

He laughed at her visible surprise at what he was saying.

"You've convinced me that training and observation are better strategies than sending you back home, unsupervised, where your abilities will only get you into trouble."

"I wouldn't have gotten into trouble," Lyn replied in a hurt tone. "Not a whole lot, anyway..."

Ultraa raised one eyebrow at her.

"Yeah, okay, fine," she said, crossing her arms.

"Think how much better at properly using your abilities you are now," he said, "than you were when we first met."

Lyn laughed.

"That's true enough, yeah."

"So I think the team will stay together," he said. "It's growing, in fact."

"Huh."

Lyn laughed again, gazing at him in bemused wonder.

"What is it now?" he asked, exasperated.

"Oh, I had come up with a whole big argument for why we shouldn't be broken up."

"Oh yeah?"

Lyn sat up, her expression growing intense.

"Do you remember what you told me," she asked, "after Damon...after he died?"

Ultraa frowned.

"I suppose so," he said. "What—?"

"I'll never forget it. You said, 'In our line of work, people are sometimes hurt, or even die. But we can't give up, just because it seems too hard. Because the bad guys aren't giving up, either.'"

In spite of himself, he smiled.

"I said that?"

She nodded vigorously.

"Or something pretty close to it," she said. "I thought about stitching it on a pillow or something," she added sarcastically.

He snorted.

"Well, I couldn't quit, in any case," he said. "I can't. It's what I do. It's *all* I do."

"Well, neither can I," Lyn replied. "So—there we are."

"I'm not quitting either," came Esro's voice from the hall. "That is, if anyone cares."

"Get in here, you," Lyn called, grinning.

Brachis entered the room with Mondrian at his side. He had finally taken that long, hot bath he'd longed for, and now wore his customary jeans and Hawaiian shirt, his thick brown hair brushed back neatly for a change. Mondrian had somewhere acquired a smart business suit, which somehow looked appropriate on her, despite her bright red skin and flowing mane of white hair.

"Heck," Esro added, "I've even been out recruiting new members."

Ultraa looked from Esro to Mondrian.

"Of course," he said, shaking her hand. "You're very welcome among us."

"Thank you."

"She's got a sweet ride we can use, too," Esro said, grinning.

"I assume," Mondrian stated flatly, "that he is referring to the shuttle."

Esro nodded.

"The one the Xorex stole," he added. "The other one is long gone."

"That would be the same one you went off chasing to the other side of the galaxy, right?" asked Lyn, still not quite believing the stories Esro had brought back with him from that excursion.

"The very one," he agreed. "It turned up yesterday, abandoned in an Iowa cornfield."

"What do you make of that?" asked Ultraa, cocking an eye at him.

"I don't want to know," Esro replied. "But, anyway, Mondy got it repaired in no time flat. And we can use it."

"That's terrific," Ultraa said to her. "Thank you."

Smiling for the first time since they had arrived, she nodded back at him.

"I am with you as well," came a voice from the hall.

They all looked up.

"About time you showed up, big man," Esro said, smiling.

The crisp sound of Vanadium's metal feet on the tile floor echoed to them. As usual, he was employing the gravitic nullifiers housed in his feet to lighten himself to the point that he would not harm the floor. He nodded to the others, then to Wendy.

"I am pleased you are well," he told her.

She stared at him for a long second—nothing compared to the looks he had received from the hospital staff—then nodded.

"Thanks."

"And pleased to learn that Pulsar and I will not have to go in search of Esro, after all."

Lyn nodded.

Esro looked from Vanadium to Lyn. Then he turned to Ultraa.

"This was the search party you were putting together? *These two?"*

He brought his hands to his face in mock horror.

"And they hadn't even left yet?"

Ultraa shrugged.

"It's news to me. They must have been working that out on their own."

After another few moments, Wendy got their attention.

"You people do have a headquarters, right? I mean, you're not planning on having your team meetings in my hospital room all the time? Because I am so out of here as soon as the doc says I can go."

"Actually," came a new voice from the hallway, "the doctor just said you are good to go."

617

The others looked up and saw Heavyweight and the Fury—Richard Hammonds and Doug Williams—leaning in through the doorway.

"We just wanted to pay our respects," Richard said.

"Yeah—We'll give you guys some privacy," added Doug.

"Hey, you guys are part of the team now," Ultraa said firmly. "Get in here."

The two big men squeezed in among the others.

Wendy looked around at her tiny hospital room, now overflowing with super-beings, aliens and androids. She sighed.

"Yeah, you guys definitely need a headquarters."

"We have one," Esro growled, "and I pay the repair costs for it."

He gestured at the others.

"*Lots* of repair costs."

"And he loves every minute of it," Lyn added.

"Yeah," Esro admitted. "No doubt about it."

Mondrian laughed softly and discretely patted him on the back.

"Alright, let's clear out of here," Ultraa ordered. "Let the lady get dressed."

"You're gonna be fine, kid," Esro said to her, smiling, as the others filed out. "If Lyn's any example, you *Lis* are a tough bunch."

"Do you know what 'Li' means?" asked Wendy, sitting up and reaching for the clothes Lyn had brought her.

"I have a few ideas," Esro replied wryly, eyeing Lyn. "Maybe 'One Who Consumes Her Weight in Popcorn?' 'One Who Lives to Annoy Esro?'"

Lyn rolled her eyes, as usual. Wendy laughed.

"Actually, it means 'the course of life as it is intended to go.' Our grandma taught us that, years ago."

Esro's mouth opened and closed. He looked from Wendy to Lyn, who nodded.

"Yeah, that's pretty much it," she told him.

"So *this* is my life as it was intended to go? Are you kidding me?"

He rubbed his forehead.

"That—that's just depressing, somehow."

They all laughed.

"But," Lyn added, "Confucius once said something like, 'Your humble servant is not really qualified to understand Li.'"

Esro brightened at that.

"Not understand Li? That man sure did know what he was talking about." He put an arm around Lyn's shoulder and smiled sweetly at her. "Because—*Who can?!*"

She punched him in the stomach.

Mondrian took this all in, mystified, and chalked it up to more bizarre alien behavior. Which was pretty much correct.

A few seconds later, with the door closed so that Wendy could dress, the others stood around in the hallway, doctors and nurses and patients all openly gawking at them.

Esro took in the whole scene and nodded slowly.

"We *are* all one big team now, aren't we?"

"Looks that way," Ultraa replied.

"And I have a feeling we're going to be needed in the days ahead."

"Yeah," Ultraa said. "We've done a lot of good in the last few days—the Circle, the Xorexes, the Warlord, Randall Nation... A *lot* of good. But I think..."

"...It's not over yet," Lyn finished for him.

"It's never over," Ultraa agreed. "Not in this line of work. Not when the whole world depends on us."

"Yeah," Doug interjected, "So—what are the health benefits like, then?"

Ultraa laughed.

"I'm working on that," Esro answered him, grinning. "I think we all fall into the 'high risk' category, though."

Richard snorted.

"You can say that again."

"By the way," Esro whispered, leaning close in toward Williams, "that fancy suit you have—it looks awfully familiar to me."

Doug frowned, then nodded resignedly.

"Yeah," he replied. "I figured this was coming." He shook his head sadly. "We should probably talk."

Esro held up a hand.

"Don't jump to any conclusions," he told the other man. "From what I've seen and heard so far, you've been doing pretty well with it. As long as I'm able to get back to running some tests on it..."

He shrugged even as Williams's expression brightened.

"...Then I don't see why you shouldn't be the one to sort of field-test it in the meantime. If not beyond."

Doug took this in, flashed Esro a winning smile, and shook his hand firmly.

"I think this is what they call the beginning of a beautiful friendship," he said.

"Let's not get carried away," Esro replied with a wink.

Wendy emerged from the room, now wearing jeans and one of Lyn's gray Georgetown sweatshirts, and together they all moved down the hall toward the elevators.

"Speaking of *team*," Richard said as they waited for the doors to open, "what exactly is the name of this team?"

"Name?"

Ultraa frowned, looking from Lyn to Esro to Vanadium.

"Do we have a name?"

"The Misguided Idiots?" offered Esro. "The Suicidal Morons?"

Lyn punched him again. Mondrian watched her do so, then tried it for herself.

"Hey! Come on! Two against one!"

"I wished to see if it was as fun as it appeared," Mondrian told him, her expression serious.

"And?"

"Very much, yes."

Esro looked imploringly in the direction of the sky.

"Both of them? This just isn't fair!"

Lyn was twirling her black hair, thinking hard.

"The Avenging Defenders? The Justice Squad? The Fantastic…"

She did a quick headcount.

"…Seven?"

"The government has always called my teams 'Project Sentinel,'" Ultraa noted.

"Hey," Lyn chirped, brightening. "That's it! The Sentinels!"

The others all looked at her for a long moment, then shook their heads.

"No, no, no…"

Lyn sighed.

The elevator doors dinged open and the first few of them boarded.

"Keep trying," Esro said to Lyn as the doors closed in front of him. "I'm sure you'll think of something good eventually."

About the Author

Van Allen Plexico is a professor of political science and history and a freelance writer/editor. In addition to the *Sentinels* series, he is the author of the acclaimed SF/fantasy novel *Lucian: Dark God's Homecoming*, and he co-created and co-edited the adventures of retro-space hero Mars McCoy along with sword-and-sorcery hero Gideon Cain for Airship 27 Productions. His *Assembled!* books about Marvel's *Avengers* comics continue to garner praise and to raise money for charity. A member of the Pulp Factory, he also writes and edits for Airship 27 Productions, Swarm Press and other publishers. He has lived in Atlanta, Singapore, Alabama, and Washington, DC, and now resides in the St. Louis area along with his wife, two daughters and assorted river otters.

WHITE ROCKET BOOKS
www.whiterocketbooks.com

Van Allen Plexico's *Sentinels*
Super-hero action illustrated by Chris Kohler
  The Grand Design Trilogy
  Alternate Visions (Anthology)
  The Rivals Trilogy
  The Earth - Kur-Bai War Trilogy
…Sentinels: The Art of Chris Kohler

Van Allen Plexico's *The Shattering*
  Lucian: Dark God's Homecoming
  Baranak: Storming the Gates
…Karilyne: Heart Cold as Ice
  Hawk: Hand of the Machine
  Legion I: Lords of Fire
  Legion II: Sons of Terra
  Legion III: Kings of Oblivion

Anthologies
  Gideon Cain: Demon Hunter
  Blackthorn: Thunder on Mars

Other Great Novels
  Vegas Heist
    By Van Allen Plexico
..Blackthorn: Dynasty of Mars
..Blackthorn: Spires of Mars
    By Ian Watson
  My Brother's Keeper
..Marching as to War
    By David Wright

**All are available wherever books are sold
or visit**
www.whiterocketbooks.com

Made in the USA
Columbia, SC
04 June 2020